CENTURY RAIN

Ace Books by Alastair Reynolds

REVELATION SPACE

CHASM CITY

REDEMPTION ARK

ABSOLUTION GAP

DIAMOND DOGS, TURQUOISE DAYS

CENTURY RAIN

CENTURY RAIN

Alastair Reynolds

ACE BOOKS, NEW YORK

THE BERKLEY PUBLISHING GROUP
Published by the Penguin Group
Penguin Group (USA) Inc.
375 Hudson Street, New York, New York 10014, USA
Penguin Group (Canada), 10 Alcorn Avenue, Toronto, Ontario M4V 3B2, Canada
(a division of Pearson Penguin Canada Inc.)
Penguin Books Ltd., 80 Strand, London WC2R 0RL, England
Penguin Group Ireland, 25 St. Stephen's Green, Dublin 2, Ireland (a division of Penguin Books Ltd.)
Penguin Group (Australia), 250 Camberwell Road, Camberwell, Victoria 3124, Australia
(a division of Pearson Australia Group Pty. Ltd.)
Penguin Books India Pvt. Ltd., 11 Community Centre, Panchsheel Park, New Delhi—110 017, India
Penguin Group (NZ), Cnr. Airborne and Rosedale Roads, Albany, Auckland 1310, New Zealand
(a division of Pearson New Zealand Ltd.)
Penguin Books (South Africa) (Pty.) Ltd., 24 Sturdee Avenue, Rosebank, Johannesburg 2196,
South Africa

Penguin Books Ltd., Registered Offices: 80 Strand, London WC2R 0RL, England

First American edition: June 2005
Previously published in Great Britain in 2004 by Gollancz.

Library of Congress Cataloging-in-Publication Data

Reynolds, Alastair, 1966–
    Century rain / Alastair Reynolds.— 1st American ed.
        p. cm.
    ISBN 0-441-01290-6
        1. Women archaeologists—Fiction.   2. Time travel—Fiction.   I. Title.

PR6068.E95C44 2005
823'.92—dc22

                                                                                    2005040299

PRINTED IN THE UNITED STATES OF AMERICA

10   9   8   7   6   5   4   3   2   1

For Josette

ONE

The river flowing sluggishly under Pont de la Concorde was flat and grey, like worn-out linoleum. It was October and the authorities were having one of their periodic crackdowns on contraband. They had set up their customary lightning checkpoint at the far end of the bridge, backing traffic all the way across to the Right Bank.

'One thing I've never got straight,' Custine said. 'Are we musicians supplementing our income with a little detective work on the side, or is it the other way round?'

Floyd glanced into the rear-view mirror. 'Which way round would you like it to be?'

'I think I'd like it best if I had the kind of income that didn't need supplementing.'

'We were doing all right until recently.'

'Until recently we were a trio. Before that, a quartet. Perhaps it's just me, but I'm beginning to detect a trend.'

Floyd slipped the Mathis into gear and eased forward as the line advanced. 'All we have to do is hold the fort together until she returns.'

'That isn't going to happen,' Custine said. 'She left for good when she got on that train. You keeping a seat free for her in the front of the car isn't going to change things.'

'It's her seat.'

'She's gone.' Custine sighed. 'That's the trouble with recognising talent: sooner or later, someone else recognises it as well.' The big Frenchman rummaged in his jacket pocket. 'Here. Show the nice man my papers.'

Floyd took the yellowing documents and placed them next to his own on the dashboard. When they reached the checkpoint, the guard flicked through Floyd's papers and handed them back wordlessly. He thumbed through Custine's, then leaned down until he had a good view into the back of the Mathis.

'On business, monsieur?'

'I wish,' Custine said quietly.

'What's that supposed to mean?'

'It means we were looking for work,' Floyd said amiably. 'Unfortunately, we didn't find any.'

'What kind of work?'

'Music,' Floyd said, gesturing around the car. 'Hence the instruments.'

The guard jabbed the muzzle of his stamped-metal machine gun towards the soft fabric case of the double bass. 'You could get a lot of cigarettes into that. Pull your vehicle over to the inspection area.'

Floyd slipped the old Mathis back into gear and crunched it forward, steering into a bay where the guards performed more detailed searches. To one side was a striped wooden cabin where the guards amused themselves with cards and cheap pornography. A low stone wall overlooked a narrow, pebbled quay. An empty chair stood by the wall, next to a large trestle table covered with a cloth.

'Say as little as possible,' Floyd said to Custine.

As the guard with the machine gun returned to his post, another from the inspection area knocked on the roof of the car. 'Bring it out. Place it on the table.'

Floyd and Custine worked the case from the rear of the Mathis. It was cumbersome rather than heavy, and had already accumulated enough scuffs and scratches that a few more wouldn't matter.

'You want me to open it?' Custine asked.

'Of course,' the second guard said. 'And remove the instrument, please.'

Custine did as he was told, setting the double bass down gently. There was just enough room for it on the table next to the empty case. 'There,' he said. 'You're welcome to examine the case if you think I have the ingenuity to hide something in it other than the instrument.'

'It's not the case I'm concerned about,' the guard said. He motioned to one of his colleagues, who was sitting on a folding chair next to the striped cabin. The man put down his newspaper and picked up a wooden toolkit – an inspector of some kind, clearly. 'I've seen these two before,' the guard continued. 'They're back and forth across the river like it's going out of fashion. Makes you wonder, doesn't it?'

The inspector narrowed his eyes at Custine. 'I know this one,' he said. 'Used to be a policeman, didn't you? Some big cheese at Central Headquarters?'

'I felt a change of career would do me good.'

Floyd took a fresh toothpick from his shirt pocket, inserted into his mouth and bit down. The sharp end dug into his mouth, drawing blood.

'Quite a comedown, isn't it, from high-profile police work to this?' the inspector persisted, setting his toolkit down.

'If you say so,' Custine replied.

The inspector picked up the double bass, shaking it with a look of deep concentration on his face before returning it to the table. 'Nothing rattling around,' he said, reaching for his toolkit. 'Still, they might have taped something to the inside. We'll have to take this boy apart.'

Floyd saw Custine draw in a sharp breath and place his hands protectively on the double bass. 'You can't take it apart,' Custine said incredulously. 'It's an instrument. It doesn't *come* apart.'

'In my experience,' the inspector said, 'everything comes apart in the end.'

'Easy,' Floyd said. 'Let them have it. It's just a piece of wood.'

'Listen to your friend,' the guard suggested. 'He talks good sense, especially for an American.'

'Take your hands from the instrument, please,' the inspector said.

Custine wasn't going to do it. Floyd couldn't blame him, not really. The double bass was the most expensive item Floyd owned, including the Mathis Emyquatre. Short of another investigation dropping into their laps, it was also about the only thing standing between them and penury.

'Let go,' Floyd mouthed. 'Not worth it.'

The inspector and Custine began to struggle over the instrument. Drawn by the commotion, the guard with the machine gun who had stopped them originally left his post and began to saunter over to the action. The double bass was now off the table and the two men were yanking it backwards and forwards violently.

The guard with the gun slipped off its safety catch. The struggle intensified, Floyd fearing that the double bass was about to snap in two as the men wrestled with it. Then Custine's opponent gained the upper hand and pulled the instrument out of Custine's grasp. For a moment, the inspector froze, and then in a single fluid movement threw the double bass over the low wall on the other side of the examination table. Time dragged: it seemed an eternity before Floyd heard the awful splintering as the double bass hit the cobbled dock below. Custine sagged back into the chair next to the examination table.

Floyd spat out his toothpick, grinding it underfoot like a spent cigarette. He walked slowly to the wall and peered down to inspect the damage. It was ten, twelve metres to the cobbled quay. The bass's neck was broken in two, the body smashed into myriad jagged pieces radiating away from the point of impact.

A scuffing of booted feet drew Floyd's attention to his right. The second guard was on his way down to the quay, descending a stone staircase jutting out from the wall. Hearing a moaning sound to his left, Floyd glanced over to see Custine looking over the parapet. His eyes were wide and white as eggs, his pupils shrunken to shocked dots. Eventually his moaning formed into coherent sounds.

'No. No. No.'

'It's done,' Floyd said. 'And the sooner we get out of here, the better off we'll be.'

'You destroyed history!' Custine shouted at the inspector. 'That was Soudieux's double bass! Django Reinhardt touched that wood!'

Floyd clamped a hand over his friend's mouth. 'He's just a bit emotional,' he explained. 'You'll have to excuse him. He's been under a lot of pressure lately, due to some personal difficulties. He apologises unreservedly for the way he has behaved. Don't you, André?'

Custine said nothing. He just trembled, still fixated on the wreckage of the double bass. He wanted to reverse time, Floyd thought. He wanted to *unhappen* the last few minutes of his life and let them spool forward again. He would be obliging this time, answering the guards' questions civilly, and perhaps the damage that they would inevitably do to the double bass would not be irreparable.

'Say it,' Floyd whispered.

'I apologise,' Custine said.

'Unreservedly.'

'I apologise unreservedly.'

The inspector looked at him critically, then shrugged. 'What's done is done. In future you might take a leaf from your friend's book.'

'I'll do that,' Custine said numbly.

Down below, the guard kicked the remains of the double bass into the river. The bits of wood were soon lost amidst the oozing debris that hugged the banks.

Floyd's telephone was ringing when he let himself into his office on the third floor of an old building on rue du Dragon. He put down the mail he had just collected from his pigeonhole and snatched the receiver from its cradle.

'Floyd Investigations,' he said, raising his voice above the rumbling passage of a train and pulling the toothpick from his mouth. 'How may—'

'Monsieur Floyd? Where have you been?' The voice – it sounded as if it belonged to an elderly man – was curious rather than complaining. 'I've been calling all afternoon and was about to give up.'

'I'm sorry,' Floyd said. 'I've been out on investigative work.'

'You might consider investing in a receptionist,' the man said. 'Or, failing that, an answering machine. I gather they are very popular with the Orthodox Jews.'

'Receptionists?'

'Answering machines. They employ magnetic tapes. I saw a model for sale in rue des Rosiers only last week.'

'What a fascinating scientific world we live in.' Floyd pulled out his chair and lowered himself into it. 'Might I ask—'

'I'm sorry. I should have introduced myself. My name is Blanchard. I am calling from the thirteenth arrondissement. It's possible that I have a case for you.'

'Go ahead,' Floyd said, half-convinced that he must be dreaming. After everything that had happened lately – Greta walking out, the lack of work, the incident at the checkpoint – a case was the one thing he hadn't dared hope for.

'I should warn you that it is a serious matter. I do not believe it will be a quick or simple investigation.'

'That's . . . not a major problem.' Floyd poured brandy into a waiting shot glass. 'What kind of case are we talking about, monsieur?' Mentally, he flipped through the possibilities. Cheating spouses was always a lucrative line of work. Sometimes they had to be tailed for weeks on end. The same went for missing cats.

'It's murder,' Blanchard said.

Floyd allowed himself a bittersweet sip of the brandy. He felt his spirits plummet just as quickly as they'd risen. 'That's a real shame. We can't take on a murder case.'

'No?'

'Homicide's a job for the boys in the bowler hats. The boys from the Quai. They won't let me touch that kind of work.'

'Ah, but that is precisely the point. The police do not consider the incident to have been murder, or "homicide" as you call it.'

'They don't?'

'They say that it may have been suicide or misadventure, but in either case they are not interested. You know how it is these days – they are far more interested in pursuing their own investigations.'

'I think I get your drift.' An old habit already had him taking notes: *Blanchard, 13th arr., poss. homicide.* It might amount to nothing, but if the conversation was interrupted, he would do his best to contact the caller again. He scribbled the date next to his note and realised that it was six weeks since he had last made an entry on the pad. 'Supposing the police *are* wrong, what makes you think it wasn't suicide or an accident?'

'Because I knew the young lady involved.'

'And you don't think she was the type who might kill herself?'

'That I can't say. All I do know is that she did not care for heights – she told me so herself – and yet she fell from a fifth-floor balcony.'

Floyd closed his eyes, wincing. He thought of the smashed double bass, splintered on the cobbles. He hated fallers. He hated the idea of fallers, suicidal or otherwise. He sipped the brandy, willing the drink to blast away the image in his mind.

'Where's the body now?' he asked.

'Dead and buried – cremated, as it happens – as per her wishes. She died three weeks ago, on September the twentieth. There was a post-mortem, I gather, but nothing suspicious came to light.'

'Well, then.' Mentally, Floyd was already preparing to cross out his line of notes, convinced that the case was a non-starter. 'Maybe she was sleepwalking. Or maybe she was upset about something. Or maybe the railings on the balcony were loose. Did the police speak to the landlord?'

'They did. As it happens, I was her landlord. I assure you, the railings were perfectly secure.'

It's nothing, Floyd told himself. It might be worth a day or two of investigative time, but all they would end up doing was reaching the same conclusion as the police. It was better than no case at all, but it was not going to solve Floyd's deeper financial malaise.

He put down the fountain pen and picked up a letter knife instead. He slit open the first of several envelopes he had collected from his pigeonhole and spilled out a demand from *his* landlord.

'Monsieur Floyd – are you still there?'

'Just thinking,' Floyd said. 'It seems to me that it'd be difficult ever to rule out an accident. And without evidence of foul play, there's not much I can add to the official verdict.'

'Evidence of foul play, Monsieur Floyd, is precisely what I have. Of course, the unimaginative idiots at the Quai didn't want to know. I expect rather better of you.'

Floyd wadded the rent demand into a ball and flicked it into his wastepaper basket. 'Can you tell me about this evidence?'

'In person, yes. I would ask that you visit my apartment. Tonight. Does your schedule permit that?'

'I should be able to slot you in.' Floyd took down Blanchard's address and telephone number and agreed a time with the landlord. 'Just one thing, monsieur. I can understand the Quai not being interested in the woman's case. But why have you called me?'

'Are you implying that it was a mistake?'

'No, not at all. It's just that most of my cases come through personal recommendation. I don't get much work through people finding my name in the telephone book.'

The man at the other end of the line chuckled knowingly. The sound was like coal being stirred in a grate. 'I should think not. You are an American, after all. Who but a fool would seek the services of an American detective in Paris?'

'I'm French,' Floyd said, slicing open the second envelope.

'Let us not quibble over passports. Your French is impeccable, Monsieur Floyd – for a foreigner. But I will say no more than that. You were born in the United States, were you not?'

'You know a lot about me. How did you get my name?'

'I got it from the only reasonable policeman I spoke to during this whole affair – an Inspector Maillol. I gather you and he know each other.'

'Our paths have crossed. Maillol's a decent enough fellow. Can't he look into this supposed suicide?'

'Maillol says his hands are tied. When I mentioned that the woman was American, your name naturally popped into his head.'

'Where was she from?'

'Dakota, I believe. Or perhaps it was Minnesota. Somewhere to the north, at least.'

'I'm from Galveston,' Floyd said. 'That puts us a world apart.'

'None the less, you will take on the case?'

'We have an appointment, monsieur. We can discuss things then.'

'Very well, then. I shall expect you on the hour?'

Floyd shook the second letter from its envelope, which was postmarked from Nice. A single sheet of grey paper, folded in two, tipped out on to the desk. He flicked the paper open to reveal a handwritten message in watery ink that was only a shade darker than the paper on which it was written. He recognised the handwriting immediately. It was from Greta.

'Monsieur Floyd?'

Floyd dropped the letter as if it was stamped from hot metal. His fingers seemed to tingle. He hadn't expected to hear from Greta again – not in this life. It took him a few moments to adjust to her sudden intrusion back into his world. What could she possibly have to say to him?

'*Monsieur Floyd?* Are you still there?'

He tapped the mouthpiece. 'Just lost you for a moment there, monsieur. It's the rats in the basement, always at the telephone lines.'

'Evidently. Upon the hour, then? Are we agreed?'

'I'll be there,' Floyd said.

TWO

Verity Auger surveyed the underground scene from the safety of her environment suit, standing a dozen metres from the crippled wreckage of the crawler. The tarantula-like machine lay tilted to one side, two of its legs broken and another three jammed uselessly against the low ceiling of carved ice. The crawler was going nowhere – it couldn't even be dragged back to the surface; but at least its life-support bubble was still intact. Cassandra, the girl student, was still sitting inside the cabin, arms folded, watching the proceedings with a kind of haughty detachment. Sebastian, the boy, was lying about five metres from the crawler, his suit damaged but still capable of keeping him alive until the rescue squad arrived.

'Hang in there,' Auger told him on the suit-to-suit. 'They're breaking through. We'll be home and dry any moment now.'

The crackle and static accompanying the boy's response made him seem a million light-years away. 'I don't feel too good, miss.'

'What's wrong?'

'Headache.'

'Just stay still. Those suit seals will do their job if you don't move.'

Auger stepped back as rescue crawlers from the Antiquities Board emerged from above, forcing ice aside with piston-driven claws and picks.

'That you, Auger?' came a voice in her helmet.

'Of course it's me. What took you so long? Thought you guys were never coming.'

'We came as fast as we could.' She recognised the voice of Mancuso, one of the recovery people she had dealt with in the past. 'Had trouble getting a fix on you this far down. The clouds seemed to be having some kind of argument tonight, lots of electromagnetic crap to see through. What exactly were you doing this deep?'

'My job,' she said tersely.

'The kid hurt?'

'His suit took a hit.' On her own faceplate monitor she could still see the diagnostic summary for Sebastian's suit, hatched with pulsing red hazard indicators near the right elbow joint. 'But it's nothing serious. I told him to lie down and keep still until rescue arrived.'

The lead crawler was already disgorging two members of the rescue squad, clad in the faintly comical suits of the extreme-hazards section. They moved like sumo warriors, in squatting strides.

Auger moved to Sebastian, kneeling down next to him. 'They're here. All you have to do is keep still and you'll be safe and sound.'

Sebastian made an unintelligible gurgle in reply. Auger raised a hand, signalling the nearer of the two suits to approach her. 'This is the boy, Mancuso. I think you should deal with him first.'

'That's already the plan,' another voice squawked in her helmet. 'Stand back, Auger.'

'Careful with him,' she warned. 'He's got a bad rip near the right—'

Mancuso's suit towered over the little boy. 'Easy, son,' she heard. 'Gonna have you fixed up in no time. You all right in there?'

'Hurt,' she heard Sebastian gasp.

'Think we need to move fast on this one,' Mancuso said, beckoning the second rescuer to him with a flick of one overmuscled arm. 'Can't risk moving him, not with the particle density as high as it is.'

'Recover *in situ?*' the second rescuer asked.

'Let's do it.'

Mancuso pointed his left arm at the boy. A hatch slid open in the armour and a spray nozzle popped out. Silvery-white matter gushed from the nozzle, solidifying instantly on impact. In a matter of seconds, Sebastian became a human-shaped cocoon wrapped in hard spittlelike strands.

'Careful with him,' Auger repeated.

A second team then set to work, cutting into the block of ice immediately underneath Sebastian with lasers. Steam blasted into the air from the cutting point. They paused now and again, signalling each other with tiny hand gestures before resuming. The first team returned with a wheeled, stretcherlike harness, pushing it between them. Thin metal claws lowered from the cradle, slipping into the ice around Sebastian. The cradle slowly hoisted the entire cocooned mass – including its foundation of ice – away from the ground. Auger watched them wheel Sebastian away and load him into the first recovery machine.

'It was just a scratch,' Auger said, when Mancuso returned to check on her. 'You don't have to act as if it's an emergency, scaring the kid to death.'

'It'll be an experience for him.'

'He's already had enough experience for one day.'

'Well, can't be too careful. Down here all accidents are emergencies. Thought you'd have known that by now, Auger.'

'You should check on the girl,' she said, indicating the crawler.

'She hurt?'

'No.'

'Then she isn't a priority. Let's see what you risked these kids' lives for, shall we?'

Mancuso meant the newspaper.

'It's in the crawler's storage shelf,' Auger said, leading him over to the crippled machine. At the front of the crawler, tucked beneath sets of manipulator arms and tools, were a netting pouch and a hatch containing a compartmented storage tray. Auger released the manual catch and slid out the tray. 'Look,' she said, taking the newspaper out of its slot with great care.

'*Whew!*' Mancuso whistled, grudgingly impressed. 'Where'd you find it?'

She pointed to a sunken area just ahead of the wrecked machine. 'We found a car down there.'

'Anyone inside?'

'Empty. We smashed the sunroof and used the crawler's manipulators to extract the paper from the rear seat. We had to brace the crawler against the ceiling to prevent it from toppling over. Unfortunately, the ceiling wasn't structurally sound.'

'That's because this cavern hasn't been cleared for human operations yet,' Mancuso told her.

Auger chose her words carefully, mindful that anything she said now might be on the record. 'No harm was done. We lost a crawler, but the recovery of a newspaper easily outweighs that.'

'What happened to the boy?'

'He was helping me stabilise the crawler when he ripped his suit. I told him to lie still and wait for the cavalry.'

She put the newspaper back into the tray. The newsprint was still as sharp and legible as when she had retrieved it from the car. The act of picking up the paper – flexing it slightly – had even caused one of the animated adverts to come to life: a girl on a beach throwing a ball towards the camera.

'Pretty good, Auger. Looks like you lucked out this time.'

'Help me remove the tray,' she said, guessing that there was going to be no attempt to recover the entire crawler.

They extracted the sample tray, carried it to the nearest rescue crawler and slid it into a vacant slot.

'Now the film reels,' Mancuso said.

Auger walked around the leaning vehicle, throwing latches and sliding out the heavy black cartridges, clipping them together as she went for ease of transport. Once all twelve of them had been assembled, including those from the cabin monitors, she handed the bulky package to Mancuso. 'I want these shot straight to the lab,' she said.

'That's the lot?' he asked.

'That's the lot,' Auger replied. 'Now can we deal with Cassandra?'

But when she looked back into the glow of the cabin, she saw no sign of the girl. 'Cassandra?' she called, hoping that the channel to the crawler was still functioning.

'It's OK,' the girl said. 'I'm right behind you.'

Auger turned around to see Cassandra standing on the ice in the other child-sized environment suit.

'I told you to stay inside,' Auger said.

'It was time to leave,' Cassandra replied. She had, as far as Auger could tell, made an efficient and thorough job of donning her suit. Auger was impressed: it was difficult enough for an adult to put on an environment suit without assistance, let alone a child.

'Did you make sure—' Auger began.

'The suit is fine. I think it's time we were leaving, don't you? All this activity may have alerted the furies. We don't want to be here when they arrive.'

Mancuso touched Auger's shoulder with a power-amplified glove that could have crushed her in an eyeblink. 'Girl's right. Let's get the hell out of Paris. Place always gives me the jitters.'

Auger peered through the ceiling porthole of the rescue crawler, willing the red and green lights of the dropship to burn through the clouds and hoping that the clouds themselves would not become even more agitated. There *was* something wrong with the clouds tonight. Their talk was normally a slow and serene form of communication, revealed by changes in their shape, colour and texturing. Vast circuitlike structures of hard-edged blue-grey would take form over many minutes; these forms would gradually stabilise and then slowly fade. Tens of minutes later, new patterns would begin to emerge from the doughy grey of unstructured cloud. Such movements were merely the basic units of an exchange that might take hours or days to complete.

But right now the clouds were bickering. The patterns formed and decayed at an accelerated rate, with lightning a kind of emphatic punctuation to the dialogue. The clouds fissioned and merged, as if renegotiating age-old treaties and alliances.

'They do this sometimes,' Cassandra said.

'I know,' Auger replied, 'but not on my watch, and not right over the city I happen to be investigating.'

'Maybe it's not just happening over Paris,' Cassandra mused.

'I hoped so, too. Unfortunately, I checked. There's a major argument in the weather system centred right over northern France, and it started thickening up at about the time we arrived.'

'Coincidence.'

'Or not.'

Lightning illuminated the scene outside, picking out a linear obstacle course of blocks, ramps and deep, smooth-sided trenches, all cut from pale-blue ice with laser-precision. On either side of the Champs-Elysées, the collapsed forms of buildings were glazed with thin traceries of the same pastel ice, neatly stepped and edged where the Antiquities Board's remote-controlled excavators had halted when they sensed fragile masonry, steel and glass. Auger thought about the controllers who directed those machines from orbit and felt a growing desire to be up there with them, away from the hazards of the ground.

'Hurry up,' she said, *sotto voce*. 'This stopped being fun hours ago.'

'Was it really worth it, for a single newspaper?' Cassandra asked.

'Of course it was worth it. You know it was. Newspapers are amongst the most valuable Void Century artefacts we can ever hope to find. Especially late editions, updated in the last few hours before it all ended. You wouldn't believe how few of those survived.'

Cassandra pushed aside the curtain of black hair that had a habit of falling over her left eye. 'What does it matter if there are some details you still don't know, if you can still make out the bigger picture?'

Movement caught Auger's attention: through the ceiling porthole she saw a squadron of dropships lowering down through the clouds on spikes of thrust.

'It means we stand a chance of not making the same mistakes over again,' Auger said.

'Such as?' Cassandra asked.

'Screwing up the Earth, for instance. Thinking we can fix one technological mess by throwing yet more technology at it, when every attempt to do that already has just made things even worse.'

'Only a kind of superstitious fatalism would say that we shouldn't keep trying,' Cassandra said, folding her arms across her chest. 'Anyway, how could things possibly be any worse than they are now?'

'Use your imagination, kid,' Auger said. She felt the rescue crawler tremble as the thrust from the nearest dropship washed over it. Bright light played over the cabin, followed by a lurch as the recovery cradle grabbed hold of the rescue crawler. Then they were airborne, pulled into the sky as the dropship gained altitude. Through the side windows, Auger saw the Champs-Elysées fall away, the slumped buildings on either side soon hiding it from view. She made out the surrounding streets, unable to turn off the part of her brain that insisted on identifying them. Haussmann to the north, Marceau and Montaigne to the south.

'How could we make it worse?' Cassandra said. 'People can't live down there. Nothing can, not even bacteria. Surely that's as bad as it gets.'

'We scored today,' Auger said. 'We came back with a piece of the past – a window into history. But there's a lot more down there we haven't found yet. Gaps in our knowledge waiting to be filled. There's so much we forgot, so many things we'll never know unless we find the truth down there, preserved under the ice.'

'The Polity plans don't threaten any of that.'

'Not on paper, no, but we all know that the plans are only a prelude. Clean up the furies and stabilise the climate, then we can begin the real work: *terraforming*.' She said the last word with exquisite distaste.

As the clouds thickened around the rescue crawler, Auger caught a brief glimpse of the sinuous track of the Seine, a flawless ribbon of white ice dotted here and there with cordoned dig sites. Further away, picked out in darkling glints from hovering airships, she made out the lower two-thirds of the Eiffel Tower, bent to one side like a man struggling against a gale.

'Is it such a crime to want to make the Earth liveable again?' Cassandra asked.

'In my book it is, because we can't do it without erasing everything down there, severing every single thread back to the past. It's like whitewashing the *Mona Lisa* when there's a blank canvas next door.'

'So you advocate the terraforming of Venus instead?'

Auger felt close to tearing out her hair. 'No, I don't advocate *that*, either. It's just that if I'm forced into making a choice . . .' She shook her head. 'I don't know why I'm having this conversation with you, of all people!'

'Why wouldn't you?'

'Because you're one of us, Cassandra – a good little Thresher, a good little citizen of the USNE. You're even studying to work under Antiquities. I shouldn't have to explain any of this stuff to you.'

Cassandra gave a girlish little shrug, accompanied by a half-pout. 'I thought debate was supposed to be healthy,' she countered.

'It is,' Auger replied, 'so long as you don't disagree with me.'

*

Tanglewood wrapped the Earth in light, like a glimmering funeral wreath. The dropship moved cautiously, veering this way and that as it navigated between moving threads, each of which was an enormous chain of interconnected habitats. In every direction there were more and more loops, threads and knots of light receding into a faint, luminous scribble of headache-inducing complexity, each centre of mass following its own private orbit around Earth.

Hundreds of thousands of habitats, each a small city in its own right; hundreds of millions of people, Auger knew, all with lives as complex and problematic and hope-filled as her own. Traffic was constantly coming and going from different parts of Tanglewood, sparks of light slipping from one thread to another in all directions. The concatenated threads of linked habitats were in a constant process of severance and reunion, like DNA strands in some thriving Petri dish.

Her mood brightened when she felt the dropship braking for its final approach. Immediately ahead, strung together hub to hub, were the six counter-rotating wheels of the Antiquities Board. Already, she was certain, the news of her discovery would be filtering through the usual academic channels, and the pressure would soon be mounting for her to publish a preliminary summary of the newspaper's contents. She would be very lucky if she got any sleep in the next twenty-four hours. It would, however, be the kind of work she enjoyed – tiring but simultaneously exhilarating, leaving her in a state of exhausted euphoria at the end of it. And that would only be the beginning of the much longer process of detailed study, when she would see whether her initial hunches and guesses stood the test of time.

The squadron of dropships docked with the first wheel, coming to rest in a large low-gravity reception bay filled with ships and equipment. With a prickle of disquiet, Auger noticed that one of the parked spacecraft was a Slasher vessel. It was ostentatiously sleek: long and lean like a fast-swimming squid, with something of the same translucent elegance. Mechanisms and markings twinkled through the cobalt-blue lustre of its outer hull. Surrounded by the robust but clumsy artefacts of her own government, the Slasher craft looked insultingly futuristic. Which, in a way, it was.

Auger couldn't quite pinpoint the reason for her unease. It was unusual to see a Slasher ship in Tanglewood, especially with the heightened tension of recent months. But it did still happen now and then, and whenever there were diplomatic exchanges it was generally more efficient to use Slasher transport.

But in Antiquities? That, she had to admit, was a little unusual.

She pushed the unease from her mind, concentrating on the matter at hand. While various aggressive sterilisation procedures took place – the ships scrubbed for any latent traces of Parisian contamination – Auger scoured the rescue crawler until she found a pen and a pad of standard-issue Antiquities reporting paper and set about writing her statement regarding what had happened underground. As always, it was necessary to strike a balance between a cavalier disregard for the rules and a professional understanding that some rules were more flexible than others.

She had pretty much finished the report by the time the sterilisation procedures were completed. An airlock bridge was attached to the rescue craft and the lights around the outer door flicked to green, signalling that it was safe to disembark. The recovery crew were the first out, anxious to get off-shift to trade drinks and tall tales with their comrades.

'Come on,' she said, gesturing for Cassandra to exit ahead of her.

'After you,' the girl replied.

Something in her tone was still off, but Auger continued to put it down to her own nerves, amplified by the sighting of the Slasher vessel. She pulled herself to the airlock and, with well-rehearsed movements, drifted along the connecting umbilical.

At the far end, she was met by a pair of officials, both of whom wore pinstriped grey suits. She recognised one of the men as a high-level manager called August Da Silva. He was a small individual with a smooth, cherubic face and hair that was always impeccably combed and held in place with perfumed oils. Their paths had crossed before, over research budgets and minor procedural transgressions.

Da Silva made a show of separating Auger from the girl. 'This way for you,' he said.

'I need to look after Cassandra,' Auger said.

With a gentle push, Da Silva coaxed her into a small, windowless waiting room. The door was immediately closed and locked behind her, leaving her alone with only the padded walls for company. Auger thumped on the door, but no one came back or gave any explanation as to what was going on. Half an hour passed, then an hour. Auger began to stew in her own indignation, rehearsing the things she would say and the people she would lash out at when she was finally allowed to leave. Nothing like this had ever happened before; there were sometimes delays due to glitches in the sterilisation procedure, but the authorities were always careful to keep her informed in such circumstances.

After another half-hour, the door opened and Da Silva poked his perfumed head through the gap. 'Time to move, Auger. They're waiting for you.'

She managed a defiant sneer. 'Who the hell are *they*? Don't you realise

I've got work to do?'

'Your work will have to wait a while.'

Grumpily, she followed Da Silva out of the waiting room. He smelled of lavender and cinnamon. 'I need to collect the newspaper and the film reels so that I can begin documenting the discovery. This is major – there are thousands of people waiting to hear what that newspaper will tell us. They'll already be wondering why I haven't made a preliminary statement.'

'I'm afraid I can't let you have the film reels,' Da Silva said. 'They've already been sent away for secure processing.'

'What are you talking about? That's my damned data!'

'It isn't data anymore,' the man said. 'It's evidence in a criminal investigation. The boy died.'

The force of it hit her like a stomach punch. '*No!*' she breathed, as if denying it might make any difference.

'I'm afraid it's true.'

Her voice sounded ghostly and distant. 'What happened?'

'There was a rip in his suit. Furies got to him.'

Auger remembered Sebastian complaining of a headache. That would have been the tiny machines storming through his brain, replicating and demolishing as they went.

The thought made her sick.

'But we checked the fury count,' she said. 'It was zero.'

'Your detectors weren't sensitive to the latest microscopic strain. You'd have known that if you bothered to keep up with the technical bulletins. You should have allowed for that factor in deciding whether to go outside.'

'But he can't be dead.'

'He died during the ascent.' Da Silva looked back at her, perhaps wondering how much he was allowed to say. 'Complete brainstem death.'

'Oh, God.' She took a deep breath, trying not to lose it. 'Has anyone told—'

'His family? They've been informed that an incident took place. They're on their way over as we speak. The hope is that the boy can be brought back to some state of consciousness by the time they arrive.'

Da Silva was playing with her. 'You told me he died.'

'He did. Thankfully, they were able to bring him back.'

'With a head full of furies?'

'They pumped him full of UR, flushed out the furies with some of that magic Slasher medicine. Right now, the boy's still in a coma. He may have irreversible damage to major brain structures, but we won't know for a few days.'

'This can't be happening,' Auger said. She felt like a spectator to her own conversation. 'It was just a field trip. No one was supposed to die.'

'Easy to say now.' He leaned in closer, so that she could smell his breath. 'Do you honestly think we can keep a lid on this kind of thing? We've already got the Transgressions Board breathing down our necks. There've been a lot of screw-ups down on Earth lately, and word is they feel it's about time they made an example of someone, before something *really* stupid happens.'

'I'm sorry about the boy,' she said.

'Is that an admission of culpability, Auger? If so, it's going to make things a lot easier all round.'

'No,' she said, her voice faltering, 'it's not an admission of anything. I'm just saying that I'm sorry. Look, can I speak to the parents?'

'Right now, Auger, I'd think you are about the last person in the solar system they'll want to talk to.'

'I just want them to know I care.'

'The time to care,' Da Silva said, 'was before you risked everything for a single useless artefact.'

'The artefact isn't useless,' she snapped. 'No matter what happened down there, it was still a risk worth taking. You talk to anyone in Antiquities and they'll tell you the same thing.'

'Shall I show you the newspaper, Auger? Would you like that?'

Da Silva had it stuffed into his jacket. He pulled it out and handed it to her. She took it with trembling fingers, feeling all her hopes vanish in one instant of crushing disappointment. Like the boy, the newspaper had died as well. The newsprint had blurred, lines of text running into each other like icing patterns melting on a cake. It was already completely illegible. The illustrations and advertisements had become static, their colours bleeding together until they looked like splodges of abstract art. The tiny motor that supplied power to the smart paper must have been down to its last trickle of energy when she pulled it from the car.

She handed him back the useless, mocking thing.

'I'm in trouble, aren't I?'

THREE

Floyd swung the Mathis into a narrow street between tall-sided tenements. It was years since he had been on rue des Peupliers, and his memory was of broken cobbles, boarded-up premises and shabby pawnbrokers. The road was smoothly asphalted now and the parked autos were all gleaming nineteen-fifties models, low and muscular like crouched panthers. The posts of the electric street lamps gleamed with new paint. The street-level establishments were all discreet, high-class affairs: clockmakers, antiquarian booksellers, exclusive jewellers, a shop selling maps and globes, another specialising in fountain pens. As afternoon turned to evening, the storefronts threw welcoming rectangles of light on to the darkening sidewalk.

'There's number twenty-three,' Floyd said, easing the car into a space next to the apartment building Blanchard had given as his address. 'That's where she must have fallen,' he added, nodding towards a patch of sidewalk that showed every sign of having been recently scrubbed. 'Must have been from one of those balconies above us.'

Custine looked out of the side window. 'No sign of damaged railings on any of them. Doesn't look as though any of them have been replaced and repainted lately, either.'

Floyd reached back and Custine passed him his notebook and fedora. 'We'll see.'

As they got out of the car, a small girl wearing scuffed black shoes and a stained dress emerged from the building and walked out on to the street. Floyd was about to call out to her before she allowed the door to close, but the words stalled in his throat when he saw her face: even in the fading light, some suggestion of disfigurement or strangeness was apparent. He watched her skip down the street, finally disappearing into the shadows between the lights. Resignedly, Floyd tried the glass-fronted door that the girl had just come through and found it locked. Next to it was a panel of buzzers accompanied by the names of the tenants. He found Blanchard's and pressed it.

A voice crackled through the grille immediately. 'You are late, Monsieur Floyd.'

'Does that mean the appointment is off?'

In place of an answer there was a buzz from the door. Custine pushed it experimentally and the door opened a crack.

'Let's see how this plays out,' Floyd said. 'Usual drill: I'll do most of the talking; you sit and observe.'

That was the way they normally worked. Floyd had long ago found that his not-quite-perfect French lulled people into a false sense of security, often encouraging them to blurt out things that they might otherwise have held back.

The hallway led immediately to a carpeted flight of stairs which they took to the third-floor landing, both of them wheezing from the climb when they arrived. Three of the doors were shut, but the fourth was slightly ajar, a crack of electric light spilling on to the well-worn carpet. An eye loomed in the gap. 'This way, Monsieur Floyd. Please!'

The crack widened enough to admit Floyd and Custine into a living room, where the curtains had already been drawn against the advancing gloom of evening.

'This is my associate, André Custine,' Floyd said. 'This being a homicide investigation, I thought two pairs of eyes and ears might be better than one.'

Blanchard nodded courteously towards each of them. 'Would you care for some tea? The kettle is still warm.'

Custine started to say something, but Floyd was already thinking about how little time he had before his meeting with Greta and got in first. 'Very kind of you, monsieur, but we'd best be getting on with the investigation.' He removed his fedora and placed it on an empty chess table. 'Where do you want to begin?'

'I rather expected you to take the lead,' Blanchard said, moving to close the door behind them.

Floyd's mental image of the caller on the telephone had turned out to be reassuringly close to the mark. Blanchard was a thin, old gentleman in his seventies with a crook of a nose upon which balanced a pair of half-moon spectacles. He wore a kind of fez or nightcap that resisted precise identification; a quilted nightgown covered striped pyjamas, thick slippers his feet.

'Maybe you should go back to the beginning,' Floyd said. 'Tell me about the American girl. How much did you know about her?'

'She was a tenant, and she paid her rent on time.' For a moment Blanchard fussed with a fire iron, poking away at the ashes in the room's enormous Art Deco fireplace. On the mantelpiece, two bookend owls surveyed the proceedings with jewelled eyes. Floyd and Custine squeezed in next to each other on the sofa, shuffling awkwardly.

'That's all?' Floyd prompted.

Blanchard turned from the fireplace. 'She stayed here for three months, until her death. She kept the room two floors above this one. She would rather have had one a little lower – as I think I mentioned, she did not like heights – but none was available.'

'Did she complain to you about that?' Floyd asked. His eyes wandered over the walls, taking in an array of African masks and hunting trophies, none of which looked as if they had been dusted in recent memory. A portrait photograph hung next to the door, showing a handsome young couple in front of the Eiffel Tower. Their clothing and slightly stiff expressions suggested a picture taken at least fifty years earlier. Floyd studied the young man's face and measured it against the old gentleman who was their host.

'She complained to me, yes,' Blanchard said, easing himself into a chair. 'To her landlord, no.'

'I thought you were—' Floyd began.

'I was her landlord, yes, but she did not know that. None of the tenants are aware that I am anything more than another tenant. They pay their rent through an intermediary.'

'Odd arrangement,' Floyd observed.

'But a very useful one. I get to hear their official complaints and grievances and their unofficial ones as well, simply by chatting as we pass on the stairs. The woman in question never expressed her displeasure in writing, but she never failed to complain about the room whenever our paths crossed.'

Floyd flashed a glance at his partner, then looked back at Blanchard. 'The girl's name, monsieur?'

'The woman's name was Susan White.'

'Married?'

'She did not wear a ring, and never spoke of anyone else.'

Floyd noted down this information. 'Did she tell you how old she was?'

'I doubt that she was older than thirty-five. Maybe only thirty. It was not easy to tell. She did not wear as much make-up as the other young women, the other female tenants.'

Custine asked, 'Did she tell you what she had been doing before she came here?'

'Only that she had come from America, and that she had some skill as a typist. I should mention the typewriter—'

'Where in America?' Floyd interrupted, remembering that Blanchard had not been certain when they spoke on the telephone.

'It was Dakota. I remember that quite clearly now. It was in her accent, she said.'

'Then she spoke English to you?' Floyd asked.

'Now and then, when I asked her to. Otherwise, her French was much like yours.'

'Impeccable,' Floyd said, with a smile. 'For a foreigner, that is.'

'What was Mademoiselle White doing in Paris?' Custine asked.

'She never told me, and I never asked. Clearly, funds were not a problem. She may have had some work, but if that was the case then she kept very erratic hours.'

Floyd turned a page on his notepad, thumbing it down to blot the ink on the notes he had already made. 'Sounds like a tourist, spending a few months in Paris before moving on. You mind if I ask how you two got to know each other, and how far that relationship went?'

'It was an entirely harmless association. We happened to meet at Longchamp.'

'The races?'

'Yes. I see you've noticed the photograph of my late wife and me.'

Floyd nodded, a little ashamed that his scrutiny had been so obvious. 'She was very pretty.'

'The photograph doesn't begin to do her justice. Her name was Claudette. She died in nineteen fifty-four – only five years ago, but it feels as if I've spent half my life without her.'

'I'm sorry,' Floyd said.

'Claudette was a great fan of the races.' Blanchard got up again and poked around in the fire, to no visible effect. He sat down with a creak of ageing joints. 'After she died, there was a long time when I couldn't bring myself to leave this apartment, let alone go back to the races. But one day I persuaded myself to do just that, intending to put some money on a horse in her memory. I told myself that it was what she would have wanted, but all the same I couldn't help but feel a little guilty that I was there on my own.'

'You shouldn't have felt that way,' Floyd said.

Blanchard looked at him. 'Have you ever been married, Monsieur Floyd, or lost a loved one to a slow disease?'

Floyd looked down, chastened. 'No, monsieur.'

'Then – with all due respect – you can't really know what it is like. That feeling of betrayal . . . absurd as it was. Yet still I kept going, saving a little money each week, occasionally returning with a small win. And that was where I met Susan White.'

'Did the girl gamble?'

'Not seriously. She recognised me only as another tenant and asked if I might help her with a small wager. At first I was reluctant to have anything to do with her, since I almost felt as if Claudette was watching me, as silly as that seems.'

'But you did help her.'

'I decided that it would do no harm to show her how to study the form, and she placed a bet accordingly. Rather to her surprise, the horse triumphed. Thereafter she arranged to meet me at the races once or twice a week. Frankly, I think the horses fascinated her more than the money. I would catch her staring at them as they circled in the jockeys' enclosure. It was as if she had never seen horses before.'

'Maybe they don't have them in Dakota,' Custine said.

'And that was as far as it went?' Floyd asked. 'A meeting at the races, once or twice a week?'

'That was how it started,' Blanchard said, 'and perhaps that is how it should have ended, too. But I found that I enjoyed her company. In her I saw something of my late wife: the same zest for life, the same childlike delight in the simplest things. The truly surprising thing was that she appeared to enjoy my company as well.'

'So you started to meet up outside the racetrack?'

'Once or twice a week I would invite her into this room, and we would drink tea and coffee and perhaps eat a slice of cake. And we would talk about anything that crossed our minds. Or rather I would talk, since – most of the time, at least – she seemed content to sit and listen.' Blanchard smiled, wrinkles splitting his face. 'I would say, "Now it's your turn – I've been monopolising the conversation," and she would reply, "No, no, I really want to hear your stories." And the odd thing is, she seemed quite sincere. We'd talk about anything: the past, the movies, theatre—'

'And did you ever get a look inside her apartment?'

'Of course – I was her landlord. When she was out, it was a simple matter to use the duplicate key. It wasn't snooping,' he added a little defensively, leaning forward to make his point. 'I have a duty to my other tenants to make sure that the terms of the contract are being honoured.'

'I'm sure,' Floyd said. 'When you were in there not snooping around, did you notice anything?'

'Only that the place was always very neat and tidy, and that she collected a remarkable number of books, records, magazines and newspapers.'

'A proper little bookworm, in other words. Not a crime, though, is it?'

'Not unless they've changed the law.' Blanchard paused. 'There was one thing that struck me as rather unusual, though. Shall I mention it?'

'Couldn't hurt.'

'The books kept changing. They were the same from day to day, yes, but from week to week, they changed. So did the magazines and newspapers. It was as if she was collecting them, then moving them on elsewhere to make room for new ones.'

'Maybe she was,' Floyd said. 'If she was a rich tourist, then she might have been shipping goods back home on a regular basis.'

'I considered that possibility, yes.'

'And?' Floyd asked.

'One day I happened to see her in the street, a long way from the apartment. It was a coincidence. She was making her way down rue Monge, towards the Métro station at Cardinal Lemoine, in the fifth arrondissement. She was struggling with a suitcase, and the thought flashed through my mind that perhaps she had packed her belongings and left.'

'Skipping on her rent?'

'Except she had already paid in advance up to the end of the month. Guilty over my suspicions, I vowed to catch up with her and help her with the suitcase. But I am an elderly man and I could not make up the distance quickly enough. Ashamed that I could not be of assistance to her, I watched her vanish into the Métro station.' Blanchard picked up a carved pipe from a selection on a side table and began examining it absently. 'I thought that was the end of it, but no sooner had she vanished than she reappeared. No more than a minute or two had passed since she entered, and she still had the suitcase. This time, however, it looked much lighter than before. It was a windy day and now the suitcase kept bumping against her hip.'

'You told all this to the police?' Floyd asked.

'I did, but they dismissed it. They told me that I had imagined the whole incident, or imagined that the first suitcase was heavier than the second.'

Floyd made a careful note, certain – without quite being able to say why – that this was an important observation. 'And is this the "evidence" of foul play you mentioned on the telephone?'

'No,' Blanchard said. 'That is something else entirely. Two or three weeks before her death, Mademoiselle White's manner changed. She stopped coming to the races, stopped visiting these rooms, and spent more and more time away from her own apartment. On the few occasions when we passed each other on the stairs, she seemed distracted.'

'Did you check out her rooms?'

Blanchard hesitated a moment before nodding in answer to Floyd's question. 'She had stopped acquiring books and magazines. A great many remained in the apartment, but I saw no sign that they were being added to or relocated elsewhere.'

Floyd glanced at Custine. 'All right. Something must have been on her mind. I have a theory. You want to hear it?'

'Am I paying for this? We haven't discussed terms.'

'We'll come to that if we come to it. I think Mademoiselle White had a lover. She must have met someone in the last three weeks before she died.' Floyd observed Blanchard, wondering how much of this he really wanted to know. 'She'd been spending time with you – innocently, I know – but suddenly her new boyfriend wanted her all to himself. No more trips to the races, no more cosy chats up here.'

Blanchard seemed to weigh the matter. 'And the matter of the books?'

'Just a guess, but maybe she suddenly had other things to do than hang around bookstores and newsagents. She lost interest in stocking her library, so there was no need to keep on shipping trunks back to Dakota.'

'That's a lot of supposition,' Blanchard said, 'based on a rather striking absence of evidence.'

'I said it was a theory, not a watertight case.' Floyd took out a toothpick and started chewing on it. 'All I'm saying is, there might be less to this than meets the eye.'

'And the matter of her death?'

'The fall might still have been an accident.'

'I am convinced she was pushed.' Blanchard reached under his chair and produced a tin box printed all over with a scratched tartan pattern, a photograph of a Highland terrier on the lid. 'This, perhaps, will convince you.'

Floyd took the tin. 'I really need to watch my figure.'

'Open it, please.'

Floyd prised the lid off with his fingernails. Inside was a bundle of assorted documents and papers, held together with a single rubber band.

'You'd better explain the significance of this,' Floyd said, nonplussed.

'Less than a week before she died, Mademoiselle White knocked on my door. She died on the twentieth; this would have been around the fifteenth or sixteenth. I let her in. She was still flustered, still distracted, but now at least she was ready to talk to me. The first thing she did was apologise for her rudeness during the preceding fortnight, and tell me how much she missed the horses. She also gave me that box.'

Floyd slipped free the elastic band surrounding the papers and let them spill into his lap. 'What else did she tell you?'

'Only that she might have to leave Paris in a hurry, and that I was to look after the box if she did not return for it.'

Floyd glanced through the papers. There were travel documents, receipts, maps, newspaper clippings. There was a pencil sketch, carefully annotated, of something circular that he didn't recognise. There was a postcard: a sun-faded photograph of Notre Dame. Floyd flipped it over and saw that the card had been written and stamped, but never sent. The handwriting was neat and girlish, with exaggerated loops and curlicues. It was addressed to someone called Mr Caliskan, who lived in Tanglewood, Dakota.

'You mind if I read this?'

'Go ahead, Monsieur Floyd.'

The first part of the message talked about how the woman was planning to spend the afternoon shopping, looking for some silver jewellery, but that she might have to change her plans if the weather turned to rain. The words 'silver' and 'rain' had been neatly underlined. This struck Floyd momentarily as odd, before he remembered an elderly aunt who had been in the habit of underlining key words in the letters she sent him. The postcard was signed 'from Susan': Floyd speculated that it had been intended for an uncle or grandfather rather than a lover or close friend.

He opened one of the maps, spreading it wide. He had expected a tourist map of Paris, or at the very least of France, but this was a small-scale map of the whole of Western Europe, from Kaliningrad in the north to Bucharest in the south, from Paris in the west to Odessa in the east. A circle had been inked around Paris and another around Berlin, and the two circles were linked by a perfectly straight line in the same ink. Another circle enclosed Milan, which was in turn connected back to Paris by another line. The effect was the creation of an approximate 'L' shape, with Paris at the corner of the 'L' and Berlin at the end of the longest side. Marked in neat lettering above the lines were two figures: '875' above the Paris–Berlin axis and '625' along that between Paris and Milan. Floyd speculated that these were the distances between the cities, in kilometres rather than miles.

He scratched at the ink with his fingernail, satisfying himself that it was not part of the original printed design. He had no idea what the markings meant, but he speculated that Susan White might have been planning the next leg of her journey, and had been measuring the respective distances between Paris and the two other cities before deciding which to opt for. But what kind of tourist needed to know such distances so precisely? Trains and even aeroplanes did not follow straight-line routes, given the real and political geography of Europe. But perhaps that detail had escaped her.

Floyd folded the map, and then leafed through the rest of the paperwork.

There was a typed letter in German from someone called Altfeld, on thick letterhead paper printed with a company insignia for a heavy-manufacturing concern named Kaspar Metals. The address was somewhere in Berlin, and the letter appeared to be in reply to an earlier query Susan White had sent. Beyond that, Floyd's faltering German wasn't up to the task of translation.

'These don't look much like love letters,' Floyd said.

'She gave me one other instruction,' Blanchard said, 'in the event that she did not return. She said that her sister might come looking for her. If she did, I was to pass on the box to her.'

'She was worried about something,' Floyd said. 'That much we can agree on.'

'You're still not convinced that she might have been killed deliberately? Shouldn't you be keen to take on a murder case? I will pay you for your time. If you find no evidence that she was murdered, then I will accept your judgement.'

'I don't want to waste your money or my time,' Floyd said. Custine cast him a sidelong glance, as if questioning his sanity.

'I am authorising you to waste it.'

Floyd stuffed the documents back into the tin. 'Why don't you just hold on to this and see if the sister shows up?'

'Because every day that passes is a day longer since she died.'

'All due respect, monsieur, but this really isn't something you need concern yourself with.'

'I think it is very much my concern.'

'What did the police make of the box?' Custine asked.

'I showed it to them, but of course they weren't interested. As I said, entirely too unimaginative.'

'You think she might have been a spy,' Floyd guessed.

'The thought had crossed my mind. Please do not pretend it has not crossed yours.'

'I don't know what to make of any of this,' Floyd said. 'What I do know is that it never hurts to keep an open mind.'

'Then keep an open mind about the possibility that she was murdered. I owe it to the memory of that lovely young girl not to let her death go unpunished. I know in my heart that someone was responsible, Monsieur Floyd. I also know that Claudette is watching me now, and she would be very disappointed if I did not do my duty to Mademoiselle White.'

'That's very decent of you—' Floyd began.

'It's not just decency,' Blanchard interrupted sharply. 'There is a selfish component as well. Until her killer is found, there will always be doubts in my other tenants' minds that perhaps she did fall accidentally.'

'But the police have never made any such suggestion.'

'A suggestion does not have to be voiced,' Blanchard said. 'Please – take the box and see where *it* takes you. Talk to the other tenants – discreetly, of course. She may have spoken to some of them as well. What shall we say, in terms of a retainer?'

Floyd reached into his jacket and took out one of his dog-eared business cards. 'Those are my usual terms. Since this is a homicide investigation, my associate will also be assisting me. That means the rates are doubled.'

'I thought you wanted to save me money.'

'It's your call. But if we're going to investigate Mademoiselle White's death, there's no point in half-measures. Custine and I can cover twice as much ground in half the time it would take me on my own.'

Blanchard took the card and pocketed it without a glance. 'I accept your terms. For my money, however, I will expect a swift resolution.'

'You'll get it, one way or the other.'

'That suits me fine.'

'I need to know what she told you about her sister.'

'That's the funny thing. Until that last conversation, the one when she gave me the box, she never mentioned any family at all.'

'Did she give you a description of her sister?'

'Yes. Her name is Verity. She has blonde hair, not red – Mademoiselle White was particular about that detail – but she's otherwise about the same height and build.' Blanchard pushed himself to his feet. 'In that respect you are fortunate. I took a picture of her at Longchamp.' Blanchard pulled out a pair of photographs from beneath one of the owls on the mantelpiece. 'You may keep both of them.'

'Are these your only copies?'

'No. I had a number of duplicate prints made when I was expecting the police to take an interest in matters. I assumed they would want them for their inquiries.'

Floyd examined one of the pictures of Susan White. It was a full-length shot of her standing up against a backdrop of railings, with the elongated blur of a horse passing behind. She was holding on to her pillbox hat as if the wind had been about to snatch it away. She was laughing, startled and happy. She did not look like someone who would be dead in a few weeks.

'She was an attractive young woman,' Blanchard said, settling back into his seat. 'But I hardly need tell you that. She had the most beautiful red hair: it's a shame that you can't really see it, bundled up under that hat. She usually wore green. I always think redheads look good in green, don't you?'

'I wouldn't know,' Floyd said.

Custine examined the picture. 'Quite a looker. Are they all like that in America?'

'Not in Galveston,' Floyd replied.

Two further flights of stairs led up to the rooms that the American woman had occupied during her last three months of life. Blanchard informed Floyd that the apartment had not been occupied since her fall. 'It's barely been touched,' he added. 'The room has been aired out, but other than that it's exactly as she left it. Even the bed was made. She was a very tidy young woman, unlike some of my tenants.'

'I see what you mean about the books,' Floyd said, the floorboards creaking as he moved to examine the collection Susan White had accumulated. Books, magazines and newspapers occupied every horizontal surface, including a significant acreage of the floor space. But they were neatly stacked and segregated, hinting at a strictly methodical process of acquisition and storage prior to shipment. He remembered Blanchard's sighting of her making her way to the Métro station with a loaded suitcase, and guessed that she must have made dozens of such journeys every week, if the collection had been changed as often as Blanchard claimed.

'Perhaps you will see some rhyme or reason to it that escapes me,' Blanchard said, hesitating at the threshold.

Floyd bent down to get a better look at a stack of phonograph records. 'Were these part of the stuff she was collecting and shipping as well?'

'Yes. Examine them at your leisure.'

Floyd leafed through the mint-condition recordings, hoping for some insight into the woman's thought processes, but the records were as varied in content as the rest of the material. There were jazz recordings, some of which Floyd owned himself, and a handful of classical recordings, but the rest of the collection appeared to have been compiled at random, with no consideration for genre or intrinsic merit.

'So she liked music,' he commented.

'Except she never played any of those records,' Blanchard said.

Floyd looked at one of the records more closely, studying the sleeve and then the groove of the platter itself with a narrowed, critical eye. Lately, a great many low-quality bootlegs had begun to turn up on the record market. They sounded acceptable to the untrained ear, but to anyone who really cared about music, they were an insult. Rumour had it that the bootleggers were operating somewhere in the Paris area, stamping out the cheap copies in an underground pressing plant. Having been stung by one or two of these poor copies himself, Floyd had learned to sniff them out. It seemed likely that more than a few of the dead woman's records were bootlegs, but if she didn't even listen to them in the first place, she had only herself to blame.

Returning the record to its sleeve and standing up, Floyd noticed an old clockwork phonograph tucked away in one corner of the room, next to a more modern valve wireless. 'Was that phonograph hers?' he asked.

'No. It came with the room. It must have been there for thirty years.'

'And she never played any of these records on it?'

'I never heard her play any music at all. On the few occasions when I happened to be passing this room or visiting the one below it, I only heard noises from the radio.'

'What sort of noises?'

'I couldn't hear them properly. She always had the radio turned down very low.'

Floyd rubbed his finger through the dust on the top of the wireless. 'Have you used this thing since she died?'

'As I said, the room has been aired, but that is all.'

'You mind if I find out what she was listening to?'

'You are in my employment now, Monsieur Floyd. I authorise you to do as you see fit.'

'I'll check the balcony,' Custine said, 'see how easy it would have been to fall from it.'

Floyd knelt down next to the wireless set, having first smoothed out the scuffed and rucked-up carpet in front of it. It was a twenty-year-old Phillips set in a walnut-veneered cabinet; Floyd had owned one much like it during his first five years in Paris. He turned the wireless on, hearing the hum of warming valves and a crackle from the speaker grille. It still worked.

He felt a breeze on the back of his neck as Custine opened the double doors that led to the balcony. The distant sound of traffic pushed itself into the room, disturbing the silence like a disrespectful guest. Floyd's hand moved instinctively to the tuning dial, preparing to make the little arrow slide along the illuminated band displaying printed wavelengths and transmitting stations. He knew all the stations that still broadcast the kind of music he and Custine liked to listen to and play. There were fewer of them each year. Fewer each month, it seemed lately.

With the dial where Susan White had left it, Floyd turned up the volume. All he heard was static.

'It's off-station,' Floyd commented. 'Either that or whoever was sending on this wavelength isn't sending any more.' He took out his notebook, flipped to the first clean page and made a note of the position of the dial. Then he turned it, sliding the arrow from one end of the tuning band to the other. The wireless hissed and crackled, but at no point did Floyd tune in to a recognisable signal.

'Well?' Blanchard asked.

'There must be something wrong with the radio. I should have tuned into something by now.'

'The wireless set was working perfectly before Mademoiselle White occupied the room.'

'And maybe it was working when she was here as well. But it's dead now, unless every station in France has just gone off the air.' Floyd returned the dial to the approximate position it had been in when he entered the room, then switched off the wireless. 'It doesn't matter. I just thought there might be a clue to her state of mind, if we knew what she had been listening to.'

Custine came back in from the balcony, shutting the double doors behind him. 'It's secure,' he said. He touched his midriff. 'The railings come up to here. How tall was she, monsieur?'

'About your height.'

'Then I suppose she might have tripped and gone over, if she was unlucky,' Custine observed. 'But there's no way she could have fallen just by leaning against them.'

'Then discount that hypothesis,' the landlord said. 'Consider instead the possibility that she was pushed.'

'Or that she jumped,' Floyd said. He closed his notebook with a snap. 'All right, I think we have enough here for now. You'll keep this room as it is for the time being?'

'Until the matter is resolved,' Blanchard assured him.

Floyd patted Custine on the back. 'C'mon. Let's have a chat with the other tenants, see what they have to say.'

Custine leaned down and picked up the biscuit tin from where Floyd had left it, next to the wireless. 'The door to this apartment,' he said, addressing Blanchard. 'Was it locked when they found her?'

'No. It was open.'

'Then she could have been murdered,' Custine said.

'Or she could have left the door open because she had something else on her mind,' Floyd said. 'It doesn't prove anything. What about the front door – was that open as well?'

'No,' Blanchard said. 'It was locked. But it's a slam lock. When the murderer left, he would only have had to close it behind him: he didn't need a key for that.'

'And you haven't noticed anything missing from here?'

'I'd have mentioned it if I had.'

Custine patted the tin. 'Maybe they were looking for this but didn't find it because she'd already passed it on to Monsieur Blanchard.'

'Did anything in that box look like it was worth murdering someone for?' Floyd said.

'No,' Custine replied, 'but when I was at the Quai, I saw people murdered for a loaf of bread.'

Floyd turned to the landlord. 'I'll telephone you tomorrow if I have any news, otherwise I'll just continue my investigations until I have something worth reporting.'

'I would like to hear from you every day, irrespective of your findings.'

Floyd shrugged. 'If that's what you want.'

'You may call me in the evening. At the end of each week, I will expect a typewritten progress report, together with a breakdown of the running expenses.'

'You're serious about this, aren't you?'

'Something awful happened in this room,' Blanchard said. 'I can feel it, even if you can't. Mademoiselle White was frightened and a long way from home. Someone came and killed her, and that isn't right.'

'I understand,' Floyd said.

They had almost reached the door when Blanchard spoke again. 'There is something I forgot to mention. It might not mean anything, but Mademoiselle White kept an electric typewriter in her room.' He stood with his hand on a large wooden cabinet that was resting on a small bow-legged table. 'It was a German model – the name of the firm was Heimsoth and Reinke, I believe – very heavy. This was the box it came in.'

'An odd thing for a tourist to carry around with them,' Floyd said.

'I asked her about it, and all she would say was that she was practising her touch-typing, so that she wouldn't be out of form when she returned home.'

'You're right to mention it,' Floyd said. 'It's probably not important, but every bit helps.'

'Perhaps we should look at the typewriter,' Custine said.

'That's the point,' Blanchard replied. 'It doesn't exist any more. The typewriter was found smashed to pieces on the pavement, next to Mademoiselle White.'

FOUR

'Hello, Verity,' said Auger's ex-husband. 'Excuse me for dropping by, but our mutual friends were beginning to wonder if you were still alive.'

Peter Auger was tanned and muscular, like a man who had just returned from a long and relaxing holiday rather than a gruelling diplomatic tour of the Federation of Polities. He wore a very expensive olive-green suit, offset with a scarlet satin neckerchief and the tasteful gold pin of the diplomatic corps. His bright-green eyes glittered like cut emeralds, twinkling with permanent amused fascination at everything and everyone around him.

'Of course I'm still alive,' Auger said grumpily. 'It's called house arrest. It makes socialising something of a challenge.'

'You know what I mean. You haven't been answering the phone or p-mail.' To illustrate his point, Peter indicated the accumulating heap of message cylinders cluttering the inbound hopper of Auger's pneumatic tube.

'I've been getting my head together.'

'You can't go on like this. When they do come calling you need to be strong, not some gibbering wreck. I heard that the preliminary hearing was scheduled for later this morning.'

'You heard right.'

'You seem remarkably relaxed about it.'

'It's just a formality, a chance for both sides to stare each other out. It's the full disciplinary tribunal that's keeping me awake at night.'

Peter sat down, crossing one long leg over the other. For a moment, he studied the picture window, admiring the view of Earth and – superimposed on the brilliant white disc – a nearby precinct of Tanglewood. 'They change their plans,' he said. 'You need to be ready for surprises, especially now. They like to throw the odd curveball, especially when they're dealing with someone like you.'

'What's that supposed to mean?'

'Someone who's never gone out of their way to suck up to authority. To put it mildly. I hear you even managed to piss off Caliskan last year. Now that takes some doing.'

'All I did was refuse to put his name on a paper he played no part in preparing. If he had a problem with that, he could have taken it to tribunal.'

'Caliskan pays your salary.'

'He still needs to get his hands dirty if he expects academic credit.' Auger sat down with her back to the picture window, facing Peter across a rough-hewn wooden coffee table. It supported a lopsided black vase containing a dozen dead flowers. 'I didn't set out to aggravate him. I got on fine with DeForrest. It's not as if I have some automatic aversion to authority.'

'Maybe Caliskan's had other things on his plate,' Peter said in that quiet, knowing way of his that she had always found as maddening as it was appealing. Charm was what he excelled at. If anyone sensed his underlying shallowness, they usually mistook it for well-hidden great depth of character, like misinterpreting a radar bounce.

'How would you know, Peter?'

'I'm just saying that making enemies isn't the only way to get ahead in a career.'

'I don't make enemies,' she said. 'I just don't like people getting in the way of my research interests.'

'It was Paula's birthday last week.'

'I know, I'm sorry. It's just with all this—'

'Her birthday was a couple of days before any of that nastiness in Paris. "All this" had nothing to do with it.' Peter, as always, sounded calm and sympathetic even when he was rebuking her. 'Have you any idea how much that kind of thing means to a nine year old?'

'I'm sorry, all right? I'll send her a message, if that will make you happier.'

'It's not about making me happier. It's about your daughter.'

Suddenly she felt pathetic and shameful. 'I know. Fuck, I'm useless. She doesn't deserve me as a mother, just as you didn't deserve me as a wife.'

'Please – not the self-pity thing. I didn't come to tick you off about Paula. She's a kid, she'll get over it. I just thought a gentle reminder might be in order.'

Auger buried her face in her hands. From nowhere, after five days of stolid defiance, she had finally broken into tears. Was she sorry for her daughter, or for herself? She did not particularly care to know.

'Why did you come, then?' she mumbled through her hands.

'To see how you're holding up.'

She glared at him through sore, red eyes. 'Absolutely fucking splendidly, as you can see.'

There was a *whoosh* and a *pop* as another message tube slid into the hopper, clanging against those already languishing in it. Auger didn't even glance at it. Like all the others that had arrived in the last day, she was certain it was from an anonymous taunter. Why else send her maps of Paris, if not to rub her nose in what had happened?

'The other reason I've come,' Peter said, after a dignified pause, 'is to see if I can offer any help. I can arrange for strings to be pulled.'

'With your new friends in high places?'

'Political connections aren't something to be ashamed of,' Peter replied, with the assurance of a man who actually believed it.

Her own voice sounded frail and distant. 'How was it?'

'Quite a trip.'

'I'm almost envious.'

Peter's diplomatic work had often taken him into the Polity-controlled territories on the edge of the solar system. But his last mission had taken him much further: deep into the galaxy, via the hyperweb.

'You'd have enjoyed it,' Peter said. 'Of course, bits of it were absolutely terrifying . . . but worth it, I think.'

'I hope you showed appropriate awe and humility,' Auger said.

'It wasn't like that at all. They seemed genuinely delighted to have someone else to show all this stuff to.'

'Look,' she said, 'I could be less sceptical about all this if I thought our co-operation was what they were really interested in.'

'And you don't believe they are?'

'You know what the small print says. We get access to the hyperweb – on their very strict and limiting terms, I need hardly add – and in return they get access to Earth – also on *their* terms, funnily enough.'

'That's not quite how I read it. Why shouldn't they get something in return? They're offering us the entire galaxy, for pity's sake. Earth – a frozen, dangerous, uninhabitable Earth – seems a small price to pay for that. And it's not as if we're talking about handing them the entire planet on a plate.'

'Give them an inch, they'll take a mile.'

Peter kneaded his forehead, as if trying to make a headache go away. 'At least we'd have secured something for ourselves. One thing we need to understand – now more than ever – is that the Slashers don't constitute a single political bloc, however much it might suit our own ends to view them that way. It's certainly not the way *they* see the Federation. They view it as a loose, shifting alliance of various progressive interests, each with their own take on the best way to deal with Earth. It's no secret that there are

34

factions amongst the Polities that favour a more aggressive policy.'

A small chill shivered through Auger. 'Such as?'

'Use you imagination. They want Earth very badly, especially now that they can see a clear strategy for ousting the furies and initiating terraforming. All that's standing in the way, in all honesty, is us and our more moderate allies amongst the Slashers. The pragmatist in me says that we should do a deal with the moderates while a deal is still on the table.'

'For "pragmatist" read "cold-hearted cynic",' Auger said, and then immediately felt ashamed of it, because she knew it was unfair. 'Look, sorry. I know you mean well, Peter, and some of what you say probably makes a kind of twisted sense, but that doesn't mean I have to like any of it.'

'Like it or not, co-operation with the Polities is the only way forward.'

'Maybe,' Auger replied, 'but they'll set foot on Earth over my dead body.'

Peter gave her that infuriating smile. 'Look, I hate to be the bearer of bad news, but when that tribunal rolls around you're going to be facing an extremely competent prosecution witness. That's why I'm anxious to offer any help I can.'

'What do you mean? What prosecution witness?'

'The girl – Cassandra?'

Auger studied Peter intensely, through slitted eyes. 'What don't I know about her?'

'She's a Polity citizen. She may look like a girl, but she's a fully grown adult, with an adult's faculties and an adult's ruthlessness.'

Auger shook her head. 'No. Not possible.' But then she recalled the girl's odd reaction after the incident in Paris and the agile, prickly way she had defended collaboration with the Slashers. Then she remembered the sleek cobalt-blue form of the Slasher spacecraft docked inside Antiquities.

'It's true,' Peter said. He started picking through the dead flowers in the vase, frowning as he sought some final rearrangement of the shrivel-headed stems.

'Then how in hell did she slip through our security?'

'She didn't. Her presence on your field trip was officially sanctioned.'

'And no one thought to tell me?'

'Her presence was a very sensitive matter. If things hadn't gone so wrong, no one would have known about it.'

'And now they're going to blow it all out into the open in a tribunal?'

'They've decided that having Cassandra testify will be exactly the right gesture to consolidate ties with moderate Slashers. It will show that we trust them to play an active part in our judicial processes.'

'Even if that means hanging me out to dry?'

Peter spread his perfectly manicured hands. 'I said I'd do what I can.

Officially, I shouldn't even have mentioned Cassandra to you.'

'How did you find out?'

'Like I said, not all political contacts are necessarily a bad thing.' He pulled out two stems and placed them side by side on the table, like fallen soldiers. 'If Caliskan offered you a deal, would you take it?'

'A deal? What sort of deal?'

'Just a thought, that's all.' He pushed himself to his feet, smoothing out the creases in his suit. 'I'd best be going. It probably wasn't a good idea to come here in the first place.'

'I suppose I should say thanks.'

'Don't go breaking the habit of a lifetime.'

'I'm sorry about Paula's birthday. I'll make it up to her. Tell her that, won't you? And give my love to Andrew. Don't let them think I'm a bad mother.'

'You're not a bad mother,' Peter said. 'You're not even a bad person. It's just that you've let that planet . . . that city . . . *Paris* . . . take over your life, like some kind of possessive lover. You know, I think I could have handled things better if you'd actually had an affair.'

'If I don't look after Paris, no one else will.'

'Is that worth a marriage and the love of two children?' Peter held up his hand. 'No, don't answer that. Just think about it. It's too late for us.'

The flat certainty of this rather surprised her. 'You think so?'

'Of course. The fact that we're even able to have this conversation without throwing things around proves that.'

'I suppose you're right.'

'But do think about your children,' Peter said. 'Go into that tribunal prepared to be humble and to tell the truth, and say that you've made mistakes and you're sorry about them. Then I think you may have some hope of walking out of there.'

'And of keeping my job?'

'I didn't promise miracles.'

She stood up and took his hand, feeling it fit into her own with heartbreaking familiarity, as if they had been carved for each other.

'I'll do my best,' Auger said. 'There's too much work left for me to do. I'm not going to let those bastards screw me over just to make a political point.'

'That's the spirit,' Peter said. 'But remember what I said about humility?'

'I'll keep it in mind.'

She waited until he was gone before taking the vase and all its dead flowers into the kitchen, where she tipped the flowers into the waste.

*

'Verity Auger?'

'Yes.'

'Take the stand, please.'

The preliminary hearing took place in a high vaulted chamber in a part of Antiquities she had never visited before, but which had only involved a short escorted ride from her apartment. All around the room, vast photographic frescos cycled through scenes from pre-Nanocaust Earth.

'Let's begin,' said the chairwoman, addressing Auger from a raised podium backdropped by the flag of the USNE. 'It is the preliminary finding of this special disciplinary committee that your actions in Paris led to the death of the student Sebastian Nerval . . .'

Auger was the only one who did not turn to look at the boy, cradled in an upright recovery couch with a halo of delicate Slasher-manufactured machines still fussing around his skull, like so many attendant cherubim and seraphim.

'Objection,' said Auger's Antiquities defence attorney, rustling papers on his desk. 'The student is present in the room today.'

'Your point being?' the chairwoman asked.

'My point being that he can hardly be said to have "died" in any meaningful sense.'

'The law makes no distinction between permanent and temporary death,' the chairwoman replied, with the weary tone of someone who had already made this point on numerous occasions. 'The boy only survived by virtue of the fact that Polity medicine was on hand. Since this cannot normally be counted upon, it will play no mitigating role in the hearing.'

The defence attorney's round, molelike face was not in any way enhanced by the round, molelike spectacles he favoured. 'But the simple fact of the matter is that he *didn't* die.'

'Objection overruled,' the chairwoman said. 'And – if I might make a suggestion – you would be wise to familiarise yourself with the basic tenets of United States of Near Earth law before stepping into this room again.'

The attorney rummaged through his papers, as if searching for the one half-forgotten clause that would prove him correct. Auger watched as the papers slid from the desk into his lap, spilling to the floor. He leaned forward to collect them, knocking his spectacles against the side of the desk.

The chairwoman ignored him, turning instead to the woman sitting to Auger's right. 'Cassandra . . . that's the name you prefer to be known by, isn't it?'

'My preferred name is—' and she opened her mouth and emitted a complex, liquid trilling, a rapid sequence of notes and warbles. Genetic engineering had given all Polity citizens a sound-generating organ modelled on the avian syrinx, plus the necessary neural circuitry to generate and decode the sounds produced by that organ. Since it was now part of their genome, the Slashers would retain the capability for rapid communication even if they suffered another Forgetting or technological crash.

Cassandra smiled ruefully. 'But I think Cassandra will do for now.'

'Almost certainly,' the chairwoman said, echoing the smile. 'First of all, I'd like to thank you on behalf of Antiquities, and the wider authority of the USNE, for taking the time to return to Tanglewood, especially in these difficult circumstances.'

'It's no hardship,' Cassandra said.

Freed of any need to disguise herself, the woman was now unmistakably a citizen of the Federation of Polities. Her basic appearance was still the same: a small, unassuming girl with a lopsided fringe of dark hair and the pouting expression of someone accustomed to being told off. But now she was attended by a roving cloud of autonomous machines, their ceaseless movement blurring the territory of her body and mind. Like all Slashers, she was infested with countless droves of invisibly small machines: distant relatives of the microscopic furies that still ran amok on the surface of Earth. She wore plain white clothes of an austere cut, but the machines themselves formed a kind of shifting armour around her, a silver-tinged halo that glinted and sparkled at the edges. Doubtless, elements of her entourage had already detached themselves from the main cloud to improve her overview of the room and its occupants. It was entirely possible that some of those machines had even slipped into the bodies of those present, eavesdropping on thoughts.

'At the moment,' the chairwoman said, 'you are the only useful witness we have. Perhaps when the boy relearns language—'

'If,' Cassandra corrected. 'It's by no means guaranteed that our techniques will be able to reconstruct that kind of hard-wired neural function.'

'Well, we'll see,' the chairwoman said. 'In the meantime we have you, and we have the film spools recovered from the crawler.'

'And Verity's testimony,' Cassandra said, fixing Auger with an expressionless stare from within her aura of twinkling machines. 'You have that as well.'

'We do. Unfortunately, it rather contradicts your own.'

The girl blinked, then shrugged. 'That's a pity.'

'Yes,' the chairwoman agreed. 'Very much so. Auger argues that the Champs-Elysées site appeared to have been secured for human teams. Isn't that so?'

Auger said, 'I believe you've read my statement, your honour.'

The chairwoman glanced down at her notes. 'Analysis of the processed film reels shows that the excavated site had not been marked as safe for human visitors.'

'The markings are often too faint to read,' Auger said. 'The excavators mark them with dye because transponders don't last, but the dyes don't last long either.'

'Records confirm that the chamber had never been secured,' the chairwoman repeated.

'Records are often out of date.'

'That's hardly a good enough reason to go charging underground.'

'With all due respect, no one *charged* anywhere. It was a cautious investigation that unfortunately ran into trouble.'

'That's not what Cassandra says.'

'No?' Auger tried to read something in the Slasher's expression, but failed. It was still difficult to make the mental adjustment to the fact that Cassandra was not a girl but a child-shaped adult, at least as clever and ambitious as Auger and probably more so.

'Cassandra says that the risks were apparent from the word go,' the chairwoman said, 'and that you took a calculated decision to ignore them. The in-cabin tapes – what we've managed to get from them – seem to back her up. You went down that hole, Auger, even knowing that you had two vulnerable children in your care.'

'Begging your pardon, your honour: one child and one lying little shit. I should have been informed that we had a Slasher with us. The clouds knew, didn't they? They sniffed her out.'

'Watch your step,' the chairwoman warned. 'This may only be a preliminary hearing, but I can still find you in contempt.'

'Go ahead. It might save us all a bit of time.' Auger leaned forward in the stand, resting tight fists on the wooden railing. For a while she had really tried to play it the way Peter had suggested, with honesty and humility. She could see him now, behind the narrow glass screen of the observation gallery, shaking his head and turning away from the proceedings.

'I'll pretend – on this one occasion – that I didn't hear that,' the chairwoman said. 'However, can I take it as read that you have not changed your position since submitting your written statement?'

'You can take it as read,' Auger replied.

'Very well. We'll proceed with a full disciplinary hearing in five days from now. I need hardly remind you of the severity of this incident, Auger.'

'No, ma'am. You need hardly remind me.'

The chairwoman banged her gavel. 'Hearing adjourned.'

*

Auger folded the letter to her daughter, then popped the plastic seal on one of the in-bound cylinders. A paper map spilled out and flapped open. She slipped the letter into the empty cylinder, resealed it, then punched in the destination code for Peter's district of Tanglewood. The cylinder whisked away, speeding into the mind-boggling complexity of the pneumatic network. Depending on routing constraints, it stood a good chance of reaching Paula within a few hours. But when you were already more than week late with a birthday, Auger supposed, another few hours would make little practical difference, even to a nine year old.

Something caught her eye.

It was the map from the in-bound cylinder. She pressed it flat, puzzled by a missing detail. Where was the Périphérique? The ring-shaped motorway, with its elevated and underground sections, encircled Paris like a grey moat of prestressed concrete. Even with the city under ice, the Périphérique was still an important landmark. It was where Antiquities had established the high armoured barrier that served the dual purpose of holding back both ice and incursions by furies. Beyond the Périphérique, the mutant machines, in all their myriad forms, held absolute dominion. Field trips outside that boundary were even more hazardous than the one Auger had undertaken.

But there was no Périphérique on this map. At the time of the Nanocaust, the road had already been in place for more than a hundred years; rebuilt, realigned, widened and laid with guidance systems to cope with automated traffic, but still more or less recognisable, hemmed in by buildings and obstacles that prevented it from changing too radically. In the few physical maps that Auger had handled or examined, the Périphérique was always there: as much a part of the landscape of the city as the Seine or the many gardens and cemeteries.

So why wasn't it on this map?

With a mingled sense of curiosity and suspicion, she turned the map over and looked for details of when it had been printed. At the bottom of the map's card cover was a small copyright statement and the year 1959. The map had been printed more than a century before the end; even before the Périphérique had been finished. It was more than a little strange that there was no evidence at all of the motorway – not even any incomplete sections or ghostly indications of where they would be constructed – but perhaps the map had been out of date even when it was printed.

Why was someone sending her pointless facsimiles? If it was their intention to remind her of what had happened under the Champs-Elysées, she could think of less oblique ways of doing it.

Examining the map again, her eye picked out something else that wasn't quite right, another nagging detail that could not quite force itself into consciousness . . . but she refused to be drawn into someone else's tedious mind games. She folded the map and slipped it back into another tube, ready to be punched to a random destination.

'I don't need this,' she muttered.

There was a knock at the door. Peter? But the knock was too sharp and businesslike to be his. She thought about ignoring the caller, but if it was someone from Antiquities they would, sooner or later, find a way into her home regardless. And if they had news of the tribunal, she would rather hear it now.

She yanked open the door. 'What?'

There were two of them: a young man and a young woman. They were dressed in very dark, very formal business suits, offset with a flash of stiff white collar. They both had neat yellow hair gelled back in glistening rows, almost as if they were brother and sister. They gave off a taut energy, like a pair of highly compressed springs. They were dangerous and efficient and they wanted her to feel it.

'Verity Auger?' the woman asked.

'You know exactly who I am.'

The woman flashed a badge in Auger's face, bright with foils and holographic inlays. Beneath the stars and stripes of the USNE, a picture of the woman's head and upper body rotated through 360°. 'Securities Board. I'm Agent Ringsted. My colleague is Agent Molinella. You're to come with us.'

'I have another five days before the tribunal,' Auger said.

'You have another five minutes,' Ringsted said. 'Is that enough time for you to get ready?'

'Wait,' Auger said, standing her ground. 'My tribunal is a matter for Antiquities. I may have screwed up down there – that isn't an admission, by the way – but even if I did, there's no way it's an issue for Securities. I thought your remit was protecting the interests of the entire community. Haven't you got anything better to do than waste your time making my life even more difficult?'

'Have you heard that Transgressions is on your case?' Ringsted asked. 'Word is they want your head. They say procedures are getting too lax. People think they can just waltz around down on Earth as it suits them, without considering the consequences.'

Molinella nodded in agreement. 'Transgressions says that a criminal conviction and a robust punishment may be just the signal they need to send.'

'By "robust punishment", do you mean the kind that ends in the obituary columns?' Augur enquired caustically.

'You get the idea,' Ringsted said. 'The point being, at this juncture you may prefer to deal with Securities rather than Transgressions.'

'Aren't you supposed to be working for the same government?'

'Theoretically,' Ringsted allowed, as if it was a concept that had only just occurred to her.

'This is too surreal. What am I supposed to do?'

'You're supposed to come with us,' Ringsted said. 'We have a ship waiting.'

'One other thing,' Molinella said. 'Bring the maps.'

The ship was a blunt, unmarked shuttle of businesslike design. It powered away from the docking port nearest to Auger's home, cutting through local traffic on the kind of express trajectory that required high-level government authorisation. Soon they were moving through outlying precincts, skimming perilously close to the exclusion zone around Earth. They were obviously taking a short cut to the other side of Tanglewood, rather than going the longer, more fuel-efficient way around.

When Auger was alone – the agents sat up front with the crew, leaving her by herself in the passenger compartment – she took out the one map that she had brought along for the ride. She had stuffed it into her jacket, still rolled inside the tube she had put it in. Some contrary impulse had made her refuse to bring the others after being told to do so, but there was something about this particular map – the last to arrive in the hopper, and the only one that she had examined properly – that tugged at her curiosity. It had felt like a goad before, but now she began to wonder if it served some other function. She examined the map again, to make sure that she had not been mistaken the first time. But there it was: the same subdued colours, the same absence of the Périphérique, the same copyright date of 1959 and the same puzzling sense that something else was not as it should have been. She stared at the map, turning it this way and that, hoping that the thing that was troubling her would become apparent. In the calm of her study, she might have identified the detail after a few minutes' patient examination. But as the shuttle veered and surged, her thoughts kept being derailed. She was at least as anxious to know where she was being taken as she was to solve the mystery of the map.

Presently the shuttle began what she recognised as a braking and final-approach manoeuvre. Large Tanglewood structures loomed through the narrow little portholes. She saw spoked wheels, partial wheels, spheres and cylinders, all joined together like symbols in some weird alien language. While the basic architecture was not unusual by Tanglewood standards, this was not a district she recognised. The habitats were very dark and very old, crusted with the scar tissue of many layers of enlargement and reorganisation. Only a faint spray of tiny golden windows suggested any kind of human presence at all. Auger tensed: what the place most resembled was some kind of maximum-security prison or psychiatric complex.

In a particularly dark section of one of the spheres a little door clammed open, bracketed by red and white approach lights, and the shuttle aimed itself for this tiny aperture. Auger's hands were sweaty on the map, the ink beginning to smudge and stain her fingers. She folded it and pushed it back inside her jacket, trying to stop her hands from trembling.

The shuttle docked and the agents escorted her through the airlock into a labyrinth of sterile black corridors, twisting and turning as they wormed their way deeper into the sphere.

'Where are we?' she asked. 'What is this place?'

'You've heard of Securities,' Molinella said. 'Welcome to Contingencies – our older, rather more secretive and manipulative brother.'

'It doesn't exist.'

'That's precisely the idea.'

They led her through a series of security checks, one of which featured a large Slasher-manufactured snake robot marked with the crossed-out 'A' that meant it was most definitely not Asimov-compliant. Auger's neck tingled as the robot studied her.

Beyond the security area was a short corridor ending in a door that was open a few centimetres, spilling a fan of orange light across the grilled black decking of the floor. An armed and goggled guard standing in front of the door observed their progress down the corridor. Sounds came through the gap: high-pitched scratching and scraping noises that set her teeth on edge. There was a regularity and structure to the noises that Auger identified as music, although she could not say exactly which kind. She set her jaw against the unpleasant sound, determined not to let it unsettle her, as was undoubtedly the intention.

The guard stood aside, gesturing for her to step through the doorway. She noticed that he had earphones on beneath his helmet. Molinella and Ringsted stood back, letting her enter the room alone.

Auger pushed the door open, getting the full blast of the music, and stepped through. Inside was a windowless room about the size of her entire apartment, but furnished to a much higher degree of opulence. It looked, in fact, rather like a recreation of a drawing room from the eighteenth or nineteenth century, the kind that might have belonged to some ardent scholar of the natural sciences. Behind an enormous desk stood an elderly-looking man who was engaged with fierce concentration in the business of making the music. He had his back to her; he was wearing a purple satin smoking jacket, his silver-white hair combed back from his forehead and falling over the collar. His hands worked the instrument that he held clamped under his chin. The fingers of one hand pressed on the strings, while the other sawed away with a long wooden bow. The man's entire body moved in sympathy with the sounds he was making.

They were awful. Auger felt a faint but rising tide of nausea, but forced herself to stand her ground. The man reminded her of someone, someone she knew well, but in a completely different context.

Then he turned around, sensing her presence, and abandoned the music, letting the bow slide to a scraping halt.

It was Thomas Caliskan: the Musician. The head of Antiquities, and the man of whom she had recently made a personal enemy by denying him academic credit on one of her papers.

Caliskan placed his viola on the desk. 'Hello, Verity. How good of you to come.'

FIVE

At the entrance to the railway station, a bespectacled young man in a greatcoat tried to push a mimeographed pamphlet into Floyd's hands.

'Read this, monsieur,' he said, his French accent well educated. 'Read this, and if you agree with our aims, join us at the demonstration next weekend. There's still a chance to do something about Chatelier.'

The kid was eighteen or nineteen, the hairs on his chin as fine as peach fuzz. He might have been a medical student or a trainee lawyer. 'Why would I want to do something about Chatelier?' Floyd asked.

'You're a foreigner. I hear it in your accent.'

'The passport in my pocket says I'm French.'

'Very soon, that won't count for much.'

'Meaning I should watch my back?'

'All of us should,' the young man said. He forced the pamphlet into Floyd's hand. Floyd crumpled it and was about to throw it away when some moderating impulse made him push it into his pocket, safely out of sight.

'Thanks for the warning, chief,' he said to the boy.

'You don't believe me, do you?'

'Kid, when you've been around the block as many times as I have . . .' Floyd shook his head, knowing there was a gulf of understanding here that could never be explained, only experienced.

'It'll start with the usual hate figures,' the young man said. 'But it'll end with anyone they don't like the look of.'

'Enjoy it, kid. Enjoy feeling that you can make a difference.' Floyd flashed him a smile. 'It won't last for ever.'

'Monsieur . . .' the young man said, his voice trailing off as Floyd turned around and walked further into the station.

Gare de Lyon had begun the slow, drowsy decline into its nightly sleep.

According to the clattering indicator boards, a few trains had yet to arrive and depart, but the evening rush hour was clearly long over. There was a chill in the air, blowing down through broken panes in the latticed metal roof that spanned the station. For the first time in months, Floyd remembered what winter felt like. It was an unwelcome memory that he'd kept boxed away, and he shivered.

He reached into his pocket for Greta's letter, and came out instead with the political pamphlet the kid had given him. Floyd glanced back, but there was no sign of the young man. He balled the pamphlet and threw it into the nearest wastepaper bin. He found the letter he had been reaching for and re-read it carefully, satisfying himself that there had been no error, and that he was still on time.

'Late as usual, Wendell,' a woman said in heavily accented English.

Floyd snapped around at the instantly familiar voice behind him. 'Greta?' he began, as if it could be anyone else. 'I wasn't expecting—'

'I made an earlier connection. I've been waiting here for half an hour, foolishly imagining that you might actually arrive more than a minute ahead of schedule.'

'Then that's not your train pulling in over there?'

'Your detective skills obviously haven't failed you.' Greta posed elegantly in a black thigh-length fur coat, one hand resting against her hip and the other supporting a cigarette holder at face-level. She wore black shoes, black stockings, black gloves and a wide-brimmed black hat tipped to eyelevel. There was a black feather in the hatband and a black suitcase at her feet. She wore black lipstick and, today, black eyeliner.

Greta was fond of black. It had always made life easy for Floyd when it came to buying her presents.

'When exactly did my letter arrive?' she asked.

'I received it this afternoon.'

'I posted it from Antibes on Friday. You should have had it by Monday at the very latest.'

'Custine and I have been a little busy,' Floyd said.

'That heavy case load of yours?' Greta indicated her luggage. 'Help me with this, will you? Did you come by car? I need to get to my aunt's, and I'd rather not waste good money on a taxi.'

Floyd nodded towards the welcoming glow of *Le Train Bleu*, a café at the top of a short flight of iron-railinged stairs. 'Car's nearby, but I bet you haven't eaten anything all day, have you, stuck on that train?'

'I'd appreciate it if you would take me straight to my aunt.'

Floyd bent down to collect the suitcase, remembering what Greta had put in her letter. 'Does Marguerite still live in Montparnasse?'

Greta nodded warily. 'Yes.'

'In that case, we've time for a drink first. Traffic's murder across the river – we're better off waiting half an hour.'

'I'm sure you'd have an equally plausible excuse if I'd told you she had moved to this side of the river.'

Floyd smiled and began to lug the suitcase up the stairs. 'I'll take that as a yes. What have you got in here, by the way?'

'Bed sheets. Nobody's used my aunt's spare room in years, not since I moved out.'

'You could always stay at my apartment,' Floyd said.

Greta's heels clicked on the stone steps. 'Turf Custine out of his room, is that it? You treat that poor man like dirt.'

'I don't hear any complaints.'

Greta pushed open the double doors leading into the café, pausing a moment on the threshold as if having her photograph taken. Inside, it was all smoke and mirrors and opulently painted ceiling: a miniature Sistine Chapel. A waiter turned to them with a look of blank refusal on his face, shaking his head once.

Floyd helped himself to the nearest table. 'Two orange brandies, monsieur,' he said in French. 'And don't worry – we won't be staying long.'

The waiter muttered something and turned away. Greta sat down opposite Floyd and removed her hat and gloves, placing them next to her on the zinc-topped table. She flicked the end of her cigarette into an ashtray and closed her eyes in deep resignation or deep weariness. In the light of the café, he realised that she was not wearing eyeliner at all, but was simply very tired.

'I'm sorry, Floyd,' she said. 'I'm not in the best of moods, as you might have noticed.'

Floyd tapped the side of his nose. 'Detective instinct again. Never lets me down.'

'Not exactly made your fortune, though, has it?'

'Still waiting for the knock on the door.'

She must have heard something in his voice: some crack of hope or expectation. Studying him for a moment, she reached into her purse for another cigarette and slid it into the holder. 'I haven't come back for good, Floyd. When I said I was leaving Paris, I meant it.'

The waiter brought them their brandies, slamming down Floyd's like a bad chess player conceding defeat.

'I didn't seriously think anything had changed,' Floyd said. 'In your letter you said you were coming back to visit your aunt while she was unwell—'

'While she dies,' Greta corrected, lighting the cigarette.

The waiter was hovering. Floyd reached into his shirt pocket for a note, found what he thought was money and spilled it on to the table. It was the photograph of Susan White, taken at the horse races. It landed face-up, presenting itself to Greta.

Greta took a drag on her cigarette. 'Your new girlfriend, Floyd? She's quite beautiful, I'll give her that.'

Floyd returned the photograph to his pocket and paid the waiter. 'She's quite dead. You can give her that as well.'

'I'm sorry. What—'

'Our new investigation,' Floyd said. 'The woman in the picture threw herself off a fifth-floor balcony in the thirteenth. That was a few weeks ago. She was American, although that's pretty much all anyone knew about her.'

'Open and shut case, then.'

'Maybe,' Floyd replied, sipping at his brandy. 'There isn't one, incidentally.'

'Isn't one what?'

'A new girlfriend. I haven't been seeing anyone since you left. You can ask Custine. He'll vouch for me.'

'I told you I wasn't coming back. There was no need for you to become celibate on my account.'

'But you *are* back.'

'Not for long. This time next week, I doubt I'll be in Paris.'

Floyd looked through the café's steamed-up window, beyond the concourse to a platform where a train was inching out into the night. He thought of Greta on a similar train, returning to the south, the last time he'd ever see her unless he counted airbrushed photographs in the music weeklies.

Finishing their drinks in silence, they walked out of *Le Train Bleu* and back through the iron vault of the station. It was nearly empty now, save for a handful of stragglers waiting for one or other of the last trains. Floyd steered Greta back towards the street, via the entrance he had come in by. Nearing it, he became aware of a commotion: voices raised in anger or defiance.

'Floyd, what's wrong?' she asked.

'Wait here.'

But she followed him anyway. Rounding the corner, they were confronted by a tableau in light and shade, like a still photograph from a movie. Three hatless young men stood in aggressive postures beneath a streetlamp. They were all dressed in crisp black clothes, their trousers tucked into highly polished boots. Sitting on the ground, pinned in a circle of lamplight with his back against the base of the post, was the young man who had given Floyd the pamphlet earlier. His face was bloodied, his glasses mangled and shattered on the sidewalk.

He recognised Floyd, and for an instant there was something like hope in his face. 'Monsieur . . . please help me.'

One of the thugs laughed and kicked him in the chest. The youth bent double, letting out a single pained cough. One of the other thugs turned from the little scene, shadows sliding across his face. He had very sharp cheekbones, his short, fair hair oiled back from his brow and shaved close to his skull at the sides and back.

'Keep your nose out,' the thug said, something gleaming in his hand.

Greta squeezed Floyd's arm. 'We have to do something.'

'Too dangerous,' Floyd said, backing off.

'They'll kill him.'

'They're just giving him a warning. They could have killed him already, if they were serious about it.'

The pamphleteer started to say something, but his words were curtailed by another well-aimed boot to the chest. With a groan, his upper body slumped to the sidewalk. Floyd took a step towards the scene, wishing that he carried a weapon. The first thug waved his knife between them, and then shook his head very slowly. 'I said keep your nose out, fat man.'

Floyd turned away, feeling his cheeks tingle with shame. Quickly he led Greta away from the scene, back around to a different part of the station where he knew there was another exit. She squeezed his arm again, just as if they were promenading in the Tuileries Gardens on a Sunday afternoon. 'It's all right,' she said. 'You did the right thing.'

'I did nothing.'

'Nothing was the right thing. They'd have cut you up. I just hope they leave that man alone.'

'It was his fault,' Floyd said. 'Handing out stuff the way he did . . . he should have known better.'

'What exactly was he saying?'

'I don't know. I threw his pamphlet away.'

They reached the Mathis, hidden away in a backstreet. Another pamphlet had been tucked under the wiper. Floyd took it out and pressed it flat against the windshield, examining it under the stuttering glow of a dying sodium light. It was printed on better paper than the ones the young man had been distributing, with a photograph of Chatelier, smooth and handsome in military uniform. The text urged the president's friends and allies to continue their support of him, before digressing into a thinly veiled attack on various minorities, including Jews, blacks, homosexuals and gypsies.

Greta snatched the paper from him, scanning it quickly. Raised in Paris by a French aunt, she had little difficulty with the language.

'It's worse now than when I left,' she said. 'Back then they never dared to say anything like this so openly.'

'They have the police on their side now,' Floyd said. 'They can say what they like.'

'I'm not surprised Custine got out when he did. He was always too good for them.' Greta stamped her feet against the chill, gloves and hat back in place. 'Where is Custine anyway?'

Floyd took the paper from her, blew his nose in it then threw it into the gutter. 'Taking care of that little homicide investigation.'

'You were serious about that?'

'Did you think I was making it up?'

'I didn't think murder was quite your thing.'

'It is now.'

'But if she was murdered, shouldn't Custine's former associates be showing a little more interest? They can't all be too busy harassing dissidents.'

Floyd unlocked the car and put Greta's suitcase on to the back seat. 'If she had been French, they might have been more inclined to spend some time on the case. But she was just an American tourist, and that lets them off the hook. They say it's an open-and-shut case: either she jumped or she fell by accident. The railings weren't faulty, so there's no crime either way.' He held the door open for Greta while she settled herself in the front passenger seat and then moved around to the driver's side and got in.

'But you don't think it happened like that?'

'I haven't made up my mind.' Floyd waited for the car to cough itself into life. 'Given what we've learned so far, I wouldn't rule out accidental death or even suicide. But there are a couple of things that don't quite fit.'

'And who's paying for this independent investigation?'

'Her elderly landlord.' Floyd eased the car out into the street and began to navigate towards the river and the nearest crossing. A police car passed by in the opposite direction, toiling towards the station but in no obvious hurry to get there.

'What does her landlord have to do with it?'

'Took a shine to her, and thinks there was more to this business than meets the eye.' With one hand on the wheel, Floyd reached under his seat for the biscuit tin and passed it to Greta. 'See what you make of that little lot.'

Greta removed her gloves to lever off the tin lid. 'These things belonged to the dead woman?'

'If the landlord's on the level, she gave him that box for safekeeping just before she died. Now why would she do that if she didn't have some concerns for her safety?'

Greta leafed through the bundle of paperwork. 'Some of this is in German,' she noticed.

'That's why I asked you to take a look at it.'

She returned the paperwork to the tin, replaced the lid and put it on the back seat next to her suitcase. 'I can't look at it now. It's too dark in here and I get sick if I read in cars. Especially the way you drive.'

'That's all right,' Floyd said. 'Take the tin with you and look through it later, when you have a moment.'

'I came to look after my aunt, not to help you with your case.'

'It'll only take you a few minutes. And you don't have to look at any of it tonight. I'll swing by tomorrow, take you out for lunch. You can tell me all about it then.'

'You're good, Floyd. I'll give you that.'

He tried to sound casual, as if none of that had been planned. 'There's something in there that looks like a train ticket, and a business letter to do with some kind of factory in Berlin – a steelworks, maybe. I'm wondering why a nice young lady like Susan White had any business with a steel company.'

'How do you know she was a nice young lady?'

'Because they're all nice until proven otherwise,' he replied, smiling innocently.

Greta said nothing for another three blocks. She just stared out of the window, as if mesmerised by the rushing flow of head- and tail-lights. 'I'll look at this stuff, Floyd, but that's all I'm promising. It's not as if I don't have other things on my mind at the moment.'

'I'm sorry about your aunt,' Floyd said. He steered the car on to the end of the line of vehicles waiting to cross the river, relieved to see that his earlier story of the murderous traffic situation had not been completely fanciful. Ahead, a truck had broken down and some men were bashing away at the exposed cylinder head with spanners. Guards had gathered around the scene, the curved magazines of their cheap machine guns gleaming like scythes. They stamped their feet and passed around the glowing spark of a single cigarette.

Presently, Greta said, 'The doctors give her between two and eight weeks, depending on who you speak to. But then what do they ever know?'

'They do their best,' Floyd said. He still didn't know what was wrong with Greta's aunt, not that it was likely to make much difference.

'She won't go to hospital. She's clear about that. She watched my uncle die in hospital in thirty-nine. All she has left now are her home and a few weeks of life.' The inside of her window was beginning to steam up; he watched Greta scratch her fingernail down the glass, leaving a narrow line in the condensation. 'I don't even know for sure that she hasn't already died. It's been a week since I had any news of her. They disconnected her telephone when she couldn't pay the bill.'

'I hope you're in time,' Floyd said. 'If I'd known, I'd have tried to send you an airline ticket.'

She looked at him hopelessly. 'You'd have tried, Floyd, that's all.'

'What about the rest of the band – couldn't they have stumped up the cash to get you back to Paris?'

He had inched the car forward another three vehicle lengths before Greta answered. 'There is no rest of the band, Floyd. I walked out on them.'

Floyd tried his best to suppress any hint of triumph, any hint of 'I told you so', in his voice. 'I'm sorry,' he said. 'Why didn't it work out? They seemed decent enough fellows to me. Hopheads, but no worse than any other jazz men.'

'That's not much of a recommendation.'

'Well, you know what I mean.'

'There was nothing wrong with them. They treated me all right and the tour wasn't going too badly. We'd gone down well in Nice, and we had a couple of good engagements lined up in Cannes.'

'So why'd you walk?'

'Because none of it was going anywhere. One night, it hit me with the force of a revelation: they were not going to make it. If I stayed with them, I wasn't going to make it either.'

'Is that how you felt when you walked out on me and Custine?'

'Yes,' she answered, without a moment's hesitation.

Floyd eased the car past the broken-down lorry, touching a finger to the rim of his hat as the guards pointed the barrels of their guns in the vague direction of the Mathis. 'Well, at least you're honest.'

'I find it helps,' Greta replied.

They had their papers ready. Floyd watched the guard at the checkpoint grunt through his documents, then pass them back with a look of pursed disapproval, as if Floyd had committed an error of detail but was being let off with a caution. They were always like that, no matter how spick and span the paperwork. He supposed it was what got them through the day.

'Here,' Greta said, passing her documents over Floyd.

The guard took the papers, examining them under torchlight. He moved to hand them back, then hesitated, taking a closer look. He licked a finger and paged through Greta's passport, pausing here and there like someone examining a collection of rare stamps or moths.

'Been travelling a lot for a German girl,' he said in heavily accented French.

'That's what a passport's for,' Greta replied, her Parisian accent flawless.

Floyd felt ice run through his veins and reached for Greta's knee, squeezing it gently, willing her to silence.

'A mouth on you, too,' the guard said.

'It comes in handy. I'm a singer.'

'You should learn some manners, in that case.' The guard handed the papers back, making a show of giving them to Floyd rather than Greta. 'This passport expires next year,' he said. 'Under the new arrangements, not everyone will find it easy to obtain a replacement. Especially mouthy German girls. Perhaps you should reconsider your attitude.'

'I doubt it'll be a problem for me,' Greta said.

'We'll see.' The guard nodded at his colleague and slapped a hand on the window pillar. 'Move on, and learn your girlfriend some manners.'

Floyd did not breathe normally until they had crossed the Seine, putting the river between them and the checkpoint. 'That was . . . interesting,' he said.

'Buffoons.'

'Buffoons we have to live with,' Floyd snapped. Nervous, he crunched the gears. 'Anyway, what did you mean, that it won't be a problem for you?'

Greta shook her head. 'It meant nothing.'

'Sounded like it meant something to you.'

'Just drive, Floyd. I'm tired, all right? I'm tired and I'm not looking forward to any of this.'

Floyd aimed the car towards Montparnasse. It started raining, first a light drizzle that softened the city lights into pastel smudges and then a harder rain that had people scurrying for the shelter of restaurants and bars. Floyd tried finding something on the car wireless, sliding past a momentary burst of Gershwin, but when he reversed the dial and tried to find the station again all he heard was static.

Floyd helped Greta carry her things up the stairs, into the spare room next to the small kitchen on the first floor of her aunt's house. The entire place was cold and smelled faintly of mildew. The light fittings either emitted a feeble, stuttering glow, or failed to work at all. The telephone was dead, as Greta had claimed. The floorboards sagged beneath Floyd's feet, sodden with damp and beginning to rot. The broken skylight above the stairwell had been repaired with a piece of corrugated iron against which the rain drummed sharp-nailed, impatient fingers.

'Put my things on the bed,' Greta said, indicating the tiny bunk-sized cot squeezed into one corner of the room. 'I'll go and see how Aunt Marguerite's doing.'

'You want me to come along?'

'No,' she said, after thinking about it. 'No, but thanks anyway. From now on I think it's best if she only sees familiar faces.'

'I thought I counted as a familiar face.'

She looked at him, but said nothing.

'I'll see if I can scrape up something to eat,' Floyd said.

'You don't have to wait if you don't want to.'

Floyd placed her things on the bed, along with the tin box containing Susan White's papers. 'I'm not going anywhere. At least not until this weather clears up.'

They had been let into the house by a young woman who rented a small room on the third floor. She was a French girl called Sophie, a stenographer by profession, with prescription glasses and a nervous, braying laugh that culminated in a nasal snort. Floyd filed her under 'perpetual spinster', and then felt immediately guilty when Greta told him about the girl.

'She's been an angel,' Greta said, when Sophie was out of earshot. 'Buying food, cleaning, writing letters, generally taking care of my aunt's affairs . . . all the while still paying her rent. But she's been offered a job in Nancy, and she can't delay taking it up any longer. It's been good of her to stay this long.'

'And that's it? No other relatives but yourself?'

'No one who can be bothered,' Greta said.

While Greta was upstairs with Marguerite, Sophie showed Floyd around the enamelled metal cabinets in the kitchen. The place was spotlessly clean, but most of the shelves were bare. Abandoning any thoughts of eating, Floyd made himself tea and waited in the spare room, taking in the cracks in the plaster and the tears and stains in the fifty-year-old wallpaper. From somewhere else in the old building he heard very low voices, or rather one very low voice holding up one end of a conversation.

Sophie poked her head around the door and said she was going out to see a film with her boyfriend. Floyd wished her well and then listened to her footsteps descend the creaking old staircase, followed by the click as she closed the front door without slamming it.

As quietly as he dared, he left the spare room and climbed the stairs to the next floor. The door to Marguerite's bedroom was slightly ajar and he could hear Greta's voice more clearly now, reading aloud from the local pages of a newspaper, bringing Marguerite up to date on Paris life. Floyd edged closer to the door, freezing as he stepped on a creaking floorboard.

Greta paused in her monologue, then turned the page over before continuing.

Floyd reached the door. He looked through the gap and saw Greta sitting on a bedside chair, one leg hooked over the other, the paper spread across her lap. Behind her, he could just make out the bedridden form of her aunt. She was so frail, so drained of life, that at first glance the bed just looked as if it had yet to be made, the bunching of the blankets only accidentally suggestive of a human form. He couldn't see Marguerite's head from the doorway; it was hidden behind Greta's back. But he could see one of her arms, poking like a thin, dry stick from the sleeve of her nightgown. Greta held her aunt's hand in her own as she read from the newspaper, stroking the old woman's fingers with infinite kindness. It made something catch in Floyd's throat, and for the second time that evening he felt ashamed of himself.

He stepped back across the hallway, avoiding the bad floorboard, and returned to Greta's room. This couldn't be Marguerite: not the lively woman he had known only a handful of years ago. So little time couldn't have done so much harm to her.

She had been suspicious when he had first started dating her niece; even more suspicious when it turned out that he wanted her for his band. But by turns the two of them had come to a grudging state of mutual understanding, and that chill had thawed into an unlikely friendship. Oftentimes, when Greta had gone to bed, Floyd had stayed up playing chequers with Marguerite, or talking about the old films from the twenties and thirties that both of them loved so much. He had lost touch with her during the last couple of years, especially once Greta had moved into a flat of her own on the other side of town, and now he felt a wave of sadness pass through him like a sudden chemical change in his own blood.

Looking for a distraction, he opened the tin again and took out the postcard, noting once more the deliberate way in which the words 'silver' and 'rain' had been underlined. If 'silver rain' was indeed a message – and he had no real evidence that it was – what did it mean to the mysterious Caliskan, to whom the postcard was addressed?

He put the card aside as Greta came into the bedroom.

'I told you not to wait,' she said.

'It's still raining,' Floyd replied. 'Anyway, I was just going through this stuff again.' He looked into Greta's face, noticing that her eyes were wet with tears and fatigue. 'How is she?' he asked.

'She's still alive, which is something.'

Floyd smiled politely, although privately he wondered if the kindest thing would not have been for the woman to have died before Greta arrived. 'I made some tea,' he said. 'The kettle's still warm.'

Greta sat down next to him on the bed. 'Do you mind if I smoke instead?'

Floyd stuffed the postcard back into the tin. 'Go right ahead.'

Greta lit her cigarette and smoked it wordlessly for at least a minute before speaking again. 'The doctors call it a respiratory obstruction,' she said, then took another drag on the cigarette. 'They mean lung cancer, although they won't come out and say it. The doctors say there's nothing anyone can do for her. It's just a question of time.' She laughed hollowly. 'She says it's all the cigarettes she smoked. She told me I should stop. I told her I already had, for the sake of my singing voice.'

'I think we can allow you one or two white lies,' Floyd said.

'Anyway, maybe it wasn't the cigarettes. Twenty years ago they had her working on the armament production lines. A lot of women her age are unwell now, because of all the asbestos they had to work with.'

'I can believe it,' Floyd said.

'Sophie spoke to the doctor yesterday. They say a week now, maybe ten days.'

Floyd took her hand and squeezed it. 'I'm sorry. I can't imagine what this is like for you. If there was anything I could do—'

'There isn't anything anyone can do,' Greta said bitterly. 'That's the point.' She took another hit from the cigarette. 'Every morning the doctor comes around and gives her some morphine. That's all they can do.'

Floyd looked around the dismal little room. 'Are you going to be all right here? You don't sound as if you're in the best state of mind to be cooped up in here. If you've said goodnight to your aunt, she won't know if you leave and come back first thing in the—'

She cut him off. 'I'm staying here. It's where I told her I'd be.'

'It was just an offer.'

'I know.' Greta waved her cigarette distractedly. 'I didn't mean to sound ungrateful. But even if I hadn't promised to stay here, I don't need any more complications in my life at the moment.'

'And I count as a complication?'

'Right now, yes.'

Without wanting to sound confrontational, Floyd said, 'Greta, there must have been a reason for that letter. It wasn't just because you needed a ride to Montparnasse, surely?'

'No, it wasn't just that.'

'What, then? Something to do with the way you spoke to that jackass at the checkpoint?'

'You noticed?'

'I couldn't help it.'

Greta smiled thinly, perhaps remembering the way she had spoken: that small, meaningless instant of triumph. 'He said that mouthy German girls might have trouble with their passports in a year or two. Well, he's right – I'm sure of that. But it won't matter to me.'

'Why not?'

'Because I won't be here. I'm taking the flying boat to America as soon as I'm finished here with my aunt.'

'America?' Floyd echoed, as if he might have misheard her.

'I knew it wasn't happening with you and Custine. As I said, that's why I left Paris. But what I didn't count on was getting the same feeling with the other band.' Greta rubbed her eyes, perhaps to keep herself from sleeping. 'We were in Nice one evening. The show had gone well and we were sitting around in the bar afterwards, accepting drinks from the clientele.'

'Nice work if you can get it,' Floyd said. 'After Custine and I finish, we usually go out of our way to avoid the clientele.'

Greta shook her head. 'Always putting yourself down, Floyd. Always living in the past and clinging to your own cherished sense of inadequacy. Is it any wonder things don't work out for you?'

'About this meeting in the bar.'

'A man was there,' Greta said. 'An American: a fat man with a bad suit, a worse haircut and a very thick wallet.'

'There are always consolations. Who was he?'

'He didn't tell any of us at first, just said he was "in town" and that he'd parked his boat in the marina at Cannes. He told us he liked the band, although he made a few pointed remarks about how we needed to keep up with the times if we were ever going to "get ahead". He meant we were old-fashioned, but good at what we did.'

'I hear that a lot as well,' Floyd said.

'Well, the man kept us in drinks for the evening. But you know what those guys are like – after a few hours they barely knew what planet they were on, let alone what club they were in. With them taken care of, the man started concentrating on me. Said he was a television producer.'

'Television,' Floyd echoed, as if it was something he vaguely recalled someone mentioning once.

'It's bigger in America than it is here,' Greta said, 'and it's growing by the year. They say that if you can afford a new auto, you can afford a new television.'

'It'll never catch on.'

'Maybe it won't, but the point is that I have to try. I have to see for myself if I have what it takes. The man said they're crying out for new talent.' Greta reached into her jacket pocket and handed Floyd the business card that the television producer had given her. It was printed on good card stock, with the man's name and business address next to a pair of silhouetted palm trees.

Floyd scanned it for a second and gave it back to her. 'Why would they want a German girl?'

'I speak their language, Floyd. And the man said there'd be novelty value in it.'

'They'll use you up and burn you out.'

'And you'd know, would you?'

Floyd shrugged. 'I'm just being realistic.'

'Then let them use me up. I'll take that over a slow death in some dead-end jazz band, playing music that no one wants to hear any more.'

'You really know how to wound a fellow,' Floyd said.

'Look,' Greta said, 'the fact is that my mind's already made up. I've saved enough money to take the flying boat. I'll give them two years. If it hasn't happened for me by then, maybe I'll return to Europe.'

'It'll never be the same,' Floyd said.

'I know that, but I still have to try it. I don't want to be lying on my own deathbed fifty years from now, in some damp old house in Paris, wondering what would have happened if I'd taken the one chance life offered me.'

'I understand,' Floyd said. 'Believe me, I do. It's your life and it's none of my business what you do with it. But what I don't get is why you're telling me any of this. You still haven't answered my earlier question. Why did you send me the letter?'

'Because I'm offering you the chance to come with me. To America, Floyd. To Hollywood. The two of us.'

He supposed that on some level he had known this was coming, ever since she mentioned America. 'That's not a proposition to be taken lightly,' Floyd said.

'I'm serious about it,' Greta said.

'I know. I can tell. And I'm grateful that you asked.' Meekly, he added, 'I don't deserve a second chance.'

'Well, you're getting one. But I'm serious about leaving as soon as this whole horrible business is over with.'

What she meant was: when her aunt was dead.

Floyd didn't dare think about the implications yet, didn't dare allow himself to be seduced by the idea of joining her, with everything that it would mean for his life in Paris.

'How about this,' Floyd said. 'I can join you there soon, but I can't travel with you – not while we're still working on this homicide enquiry. And even if we solve the case, I'll still have a lot of business to deal with. I couldn't just up sticks from one week to the next.'

'I want you to go with me,' she said. 'I don't want some vague promise that you'll fly out when you've cobbled together enough money. Knowing you, that could take the better part of a decade.'

'I just need some leeway,' Floyd said.

'You always need leeway,' she said. 'That's your problem. If money is the issue, I have some spare. Not enough for a ticket, but enough if you sold that car and whatever else you could stand not to take with you.'

'How long afterwards? I mean, after she . . .' Floyd trailed off, unable to come out and say it. 'You mentioned a week to ten days.'

'I'd need a week or so afterwards to deal with the funeral. That gives you at least two weeks, maybe longer.'

'I'd worry about Custine.'

'Give him the business. God knows, he's worked hard enough to deserve it.'

She had, Floyd thought, obviously given the matter some consideration herself. He imagined her working out the details on the train as she journeyed up from the south, and he felt both flattered and irritated to have been the subject of so much undeserved attention.

'Why are you giving me this second chance?' he asked.

'Because there's still some part of me in love with you,' she said. 'In love with what you could be, if you stopped living in the past. You're a good man, Floyd. I know that. But you're going nowhere here, and if I stick with you here then I'm going nowhere either. And that's not good enough for me. But in America things could be different.'

'Is that true? That you still love me?'

'You wouldn't have come to the station if you didn't feel the same way about me. You could have ignored that letter, pretended it never arrived or that it arrived too late.'

'I could have,' Floyd admitted.

'Then why didn't you? For the same reason I wrote to you – because as much grief and heartache as we cause each other when we're together, it's worse when we're apart. I wanted to be over you, Floyd. I kidded myself that I was. But I wasn't strong enough.'

'You're not over me, but you'll leave me anyway if I don't agree to come to America with you?'

'It's the only way. It's either be together, or not be on the same continent.'

'I need some time to think about it,' Floyd said.

'Like I said, you have a couple of weeks. Shouldn't that be enough?'

'A week or a year, I don't think it'd make much difference.'

'Then don't agonise over it,' Greta said. She moved closer to him, holding his hand tightly and snuggling her head against his shoulder. 'I grew up in this room,' she said. 'It was the centre of my universe. I can't believe how small and dark it seems now, how terribly sad and adult it makes me feel.' Her grip on his hand tightened. 'I was happy here, Floyd, as happy as any girl in Paris, and now all it makes me feel is that I'm a good way through my life and there's a lot less of it ahead now than when I was last here.'

'It gets us all in the end,' Floyd said. 'Growing up, I mean.'

She slid closer to him, until he could smell her hair; not just the perfume from the last time she had washed it, but the accumulated smells of the arduous journey she had made today: the smoke and the grit and the odour of other people, and, buried in there somewhere, something of Paris.

'Oh, Floyd,' she breathed. 'I wish it wasn't happening like this. I wish there was some other way. But when she's gone, I don't want to spend a minute longer in this city than necessary. There'll be too many sad memories, too many ghosts, and I don't think I want to spend the rest of my life feeling haunted by them.'

'You shouldn't,' Floyd said. 'And you're right to make this move. Go to America. You'll knock them out.'

'Oh, I'm definitely going,' she said, 'but I won't be truly happy unless you come with me. Think about it, Floyd, will you? Think about it like you've never thought about anything in your life. It could be your chance as much as mine.'

'I'll think about it,' Floyd said. 'Just don't expect an answer before morning.'

He thought about making love to her – he had been thinking about it since the moment he opened her letter. He had little doubt that she would let him, if he tried. He also had little doubt that what she most wanted from him was to be held close, until, emotionally and physically drained, she fell into a shallow and uneasy sleep. She muttered things in German that he didn't understand, imprecations that sounded urgent but which might have meant nothing at all, and then gradually she fell silent.

At three in the morning, he eased her into the bed, pulled the covers over her and walked out into the rain, leaving her alone in the room where she had grown up.

SIX

Auger found it uncomfortable to be alone in the same room as Thomas Caliskan, as if she had wandered into an obscene and sticky trap. He was a very thin man with a neatly groomed sweep of collar-length silver hair brushed back from an aristocratic forehead. He favoured costumes of silk and crushed velvet with long-tailed jackets, elaborate and carefully anachronistic. He wore owlish spectacles of blue-tinted glass. He often closed his eyes while speaking, as if attending to some very distant, very quiet melody, and when he moved his body, his head seemed momentarily reluctant to follow, as if anchored to a particular point in space and time.

'Do you mind if I continue playing for a moment? I find a little finger exercise focuses the mind wonderfully.'

'They say the same thing about execution.'

'Have a seat, Verity.'

Auger sat down. The chair was a chaise longue upholstered in dimpled green velvet. She suspected it was exactly as authentic and valuable as it appeared.

In front of the chaise longue was a small coffee table, upon which rested a flat, square object with an elaborate printed design on it. While Caliskan resumed his playing, Auger picked up the object, recognising it as the cardboard – processed wood pulp – sleeve for a gramophone recording. There was something inside it. She tilted the sleeve, letting the recording slip into her fingers. It was a thin black disc made of a heavy plastic-like material, engraved on both sides with a complex spiral pattern.

The disc was typical of millions that had been manufactured between the ends of the nineteenth and twentieth centuries. It was pressed from shellac, which she recalled was some kind of insect-derived resin. The spiral grooves contained encoded sounds designed to be read by a diamond-tipped stylus as the disc was spun at a few dozen rotations per minute. The playback caused a steady deterioration in the quality of the recording, as the stylus wore away the grooves and embedded tiny particles of grit in the disc itself. Even the original recording had been captured by a chain of analogue processes, each of which introduced random structure into the sound.

But it was also a true analogue artefact, and therefore of immense historical value. A recording stored in the volatile memory array of a computer system could be erased or doctored in an eyeblink, and the evidence trail artfully concealed. A recording like the shellac disc could be destroyed, but it could not easily be altered. Forgery was equally difficult, due to the complex chemical make-up of the disc and its packaging. When such items survived to the present day, therefore, they were regarded as extremely reliable windows on the historical past, pre-Nanocaust, pre-Forgetting.

Auger examined the label, reading that the disc contained music by the composer Mahler: *Das Lied von der Erde*. Auger knew very little about composers in general, and even less about Mahler in particular. All that she remembered was that he had died well before the beginning of her period of interest.

Caliskan stopped playing and returned the viola and bow to their stand. He watched her studying the disc and asked, 'Intrigued?'

Auger put the delicate black disc back in its sleeve, and returned the sleeve to the table. 'Is that what you were playing?'

'No. That was a little Bach. The Sixth Brandenburg Concerto, for what it's worth. Unlike the Mahler, neither the score nor the original recording were ever lost.'

'This is an original recording,' Auger said, fingering the record sleeve. 'Isn't it?'

'Yes, but until very recently none were known to have survived. Now that we have that recording, someone somewhere is trying to reverse engineer Mahler's original score. A hopeless enterprise, of course. We've more chance of unearthing an intact one.'

She still had that prickly sense of being tested or led into a trap. 'Wait. I'm missing something. You're telling me that this piece of music was completely lost?'

'Yes.'

'And now you've found an intact recording?'

'Exactly so. It's a cause for great celebration. The record you just examined was recovered from Paris only a matter of weeks ago.'

'I don't see how that can be,' Auger said, careful not to accuse him outright of lying. 'Nothing bigger than a pinhead comes out of Paris without my knowing about it. I'd definitely have heard if something as significant as that had been unearthed. In fact, I'd probably be the one who found it.'

'This is something you missed. Shall I tell you something else very interesting?'

'Oh, why not.'

'This is the original, not a copy. This is the actual artefact, exactly as it was recovered. No restorative work has taken place.'

'That's also highly unlikely. The disc might have survived three or four hundred years with relatively little damage, but not the packaging.'

Caliskan had returned to his monstrously large desk. Sitting behind it, he looked like a little boy visiting his father's office. He steepled his fingers, peering over them owlishly. 'Go on. I'm listening.'

'Paper doesn't last, especially not the wood-pulp paper they were using in that era. Ironically, the cotton-pulp paper from much earlier lasts a lot better. Not as easy to bleach, but the alum they used in the wood-pulp process undergoes hydrolysis and produces sulphuric acid.'

'Not good.'

'That's not all. There are metal tannins in the inks that also lead to deterioration. Not to mention airborne contaminants. Then the glues dry up. The labels come off and the sleeve begins to come apart at the seams. The dyes fade. Lacquer on the card turns brown and cracks off.' Auger picked up the sleeve and examined it again, certain she must have missed something. 'With the right methods, you can correct a lot of that damage. But the resultant artefacts are still incredibly fragile – far too valuable to be handled like this. And this one definitely hasn't been restored.'

'As I just told you.'

'All right. Then it must have spent three-hundred-odd years in a vacuum chamber, or some other preserving agent. Someone must have taken deliberate steps to keep it intact.'

'No special measures were taken,' Caliskan insisted. 'As I said, it's exactly as we found it. Here's another question: if you suspected the recording was a fake, how would you prove it?'

'A recent fake?' Auger shrugged. 'There are a lot of things I could try. Chemical analysis of the shellac, for one thing, but of course I wouldn't want to touch it until we'd laser-scanned the grooves and got the whole thing on magnetic tape.'

'Very sound methodology. What else?'

'I'd run a radiocarbon analysis on the cellulose fibres in the paper.'

Caliskan rubbed his nose speculatively. 'Tricky, for an object suspected to be only three or four hundred years old.'

'But doable. We've made some refinements in the calibration curves lately. And I wouldn't be trying to date it exactly, just establish that it wasn't recent.'

'And your anticipated conclusions?'

'I try not to anticipate conclusions, but I'd put good money on that artefact being a clever hoax, no matter how watertight its provenance.'

'Well, you'd be right,' Caliskan said. 'If you ran the usual tests, you'd conclude that the artefact must have been manufactured very recently.'

Auger felt a curious sense of deflation, as if she had been excited about something without quite realising it. 'Is there a point to this, sir?'

'The point is, it still sounds like Mahler to me.'

'I wouldn't know about that,' Auger said.

'Do you miss music?'

'You can't miss what you've never known, sir.'

'You've never known rain, either. Not real rain, falling from a real sky.'

'That's different,' she said, needled that he knew so much about her. 'Sir, do you mind if I ask what this is all about? What are you doing here, so far from Antiquities? What business do you have dragging me halfway across Tanglewood?'

'Careful, Verity.'

'I have a right to know.'

'You have no right to know anything. However, since I'm feeling generous . . . I take it you were told about the Contingencies Board?'

'Yes. I also know there's no such thing.'

'There is,' Caliskan said. 'And I should know – I happen to run it.'

'No, sir,' she said. 'You run Antiquities.'

'That, too. But my sideways promotion into Antiquities was only ever a matter of expediency. Two years ago, something dropped into our laps. A find . . .' He paused before correcting himself. '*Two* finds, if you like – both of staggering strategic value. A pair of linked discoveries that have the potential to change our entire relationship with the Polities. Discoveries that could, in fact, alter our entire relationship with reality.'

'I don't like Slashers,' Auger said. 'Especially after what happened in Paris.'

'Don't you think we should let bygones be bygones?'

'Easy for you to say, sir. You weren't touched by *Amusica*. You didn't have that taken from you.'

'No,' Caliskan said. 'The *Amusica* virus didn't touch me, just as it didn't touch one person in a thousand. But I lost something rather dearer to me than the mere perception of music.'

'If you say so.'

'I lost a brother to Slashers,' he said, 'in the final stages of the Phobos offensive, when we were trying to retake the Moon. If anyone has a right to hate them, I do.'

She didn't know that Caliskan had even had a brother, let alone that he had died in the last war. 'Do you hate them, sir?'

'No. I treat them as what they are: a commodity to be exploited, as and when it suits us. But hatred? No.'

She decided it might be time to listen. 'And the connection with Antiquities?'

'A very profound one. As the nature of the second discovery became clear, we realised that we needed to work with Antiquities on a more fundamental level. The simplest solution was to replace DeForrest with myself, so that I had an absolute overview of all Earth-based activities.'

'I always said it was a political appointment.'

'But not in the way you meant it.' His tinted spectacles caught the light, like two little windows into clear blue sky. 'Now I want to ask you about the maps.'

She prickled, realising that she had been under surveillance all along. She should have known they would keep their eye on her. 'Were you responsible for sending them? Were the maps some pointless test, like the Mahler recording?'

This seemed to amuse him. 'They warned me about you.'

'And what did they say?'

'That you'd speak your mind. I already knew from personal experience that you have little respect for authority.' His tone softened. 'They also told me you have a good eye for detail. Now tell me what you made of the maps.'

A small inner voice told her that more depended on her answers than was immediately apparent. She felt her voice catching in her throat, her usual fluency deserting her. 'I only looked at one, and there was something about it that didn't make sense.'

'Continue,' Caliskan said.

'According to the copyright information, the map was printed over a century before the Nanocaust, yet it was in excellent condition – just like the Mahler recording.'

'Did the period of the map strike you as significant in any way?'

'No,' she said. 'Only in so far as it just about falls within my frame of interest.'

'Only just?'

Auger nodded. 'Yes. I'm pretty good on Paris in the Void Century, up to twenty seventy-seven. Things get a bit foggier if you go back to nineteen fifty-nine. It's not that I don't know anything about that period, just that I'm much less familiar with it than I am with the later decades.'

Caliskan pushed his glasses back up the bridge of his nose. 'Let's say I wanted to talk to someone who was an avowed expert on precisely that period. Given your network of academic contacts, who would you suggest?'

Auger thought for a moment. 'White,' she said. 'Susan White. I'm sure you're familiar with her work. She authored that report on the EuroDisney excavation last year.'

'Know her well, do you?'

'Not especially,' Auger said. 'We've exchanged a few messages and had the odd conversation at academic conferences. I may have refereed one of her papers; she may have refereed one of mine.'

'You consider her a rival, don't you?'

'We're both fighting for the same research budget. It doesn't mean I'd scratch her eyes out.' Sensing that her usefulness to Caliskan was coming to an end, she said, 'Look, I'm sure I could put you in touch with her.'

'Actually, we've already contacted her.'

Auger shrugged, her point made. 'Well, then, what do you need me for?'

'There's a problem with White. That's why we've come to you.'

'What kind of problem?'

'I can't tell you, I'm afraid.' He clapped his hands together and showed her the palms. 'That's a matter for the other candidate. Don't feel bad about it, Auger: you were always our second choice, but as a second choice you came very highly recommended.' Caliskan dipped his head towards his desk, picked up a massive black pen and began to make an entry of some kind in a journal, the nib scratching against high-quality paper.

'And that's it?'

He looked up momentarily from his writing. 'Were you expecting something else?'

'I thought . . .' Auger stopped.

'You thought what?'

'I failed, didn't I? I didn't get whatever it was you wanted me to get.'

Caliskan's pen halted its scratching. 'I'm sorry?'

'There was something in the map I was supposed to see.' Committed now, she felt a heady rush of certainty as the elusive detail she'd been missing clicked into place. 'Well, I did see it. I just didn't know what to make of it.'

Caliskan returned the pen to its inkwell. 'Continue.'

'The map doesn't make any sense, even for one printed in nineteen fifty-nine. It's more like a map of Paris from the twenties or thirties, masquerading as one from thirty years later.'

'In what way?'

'The street names. There's no Roosevelt; no Charles de Gaulle; no Churchill. It's as if the Second World War never took place.'

Caliskan closed his journal and slid it to one side. 'I'm very glad to hear you say that,' he said. 'I was beginning to think that perhaps you weren't the right woman for the job after all.'

'What job?' Auger asked.

From a desk drawer Caliskan produced a ticket, embossed with the Art Deco flying horse of Pegasus Intersolar. 'I need you to go to Mars for me,' he said. 'Some property has fallen into the wrong hands and we'd rather like to have it back.'

The name of the ship was the *Twentieth Century Limited*. Auger glimpsed bits of it – never the whole thing – as she was being processed aboard, led from one pressurised embarkation point to the next. It was a huge vessel by Thresher standards, six or seven hundred metres long, but the liner was making its run to Mars at much less than normal capacity. With the increase in tensions across the system, people had cut back on unnecessary travel. So far the hostilities had been confined to dissenting elements amongst the Slashers, but two USNE ships had already been caught in the crossfire, resulting in the loss of civilian lives. Inessential outposts had been mothballed and a number of intersolar transit concerns had declared bankruptcy.

When she had finished her drink in the observation lounge – watching Earth and Tanglewood recede – she checked the local time and made her way back to her cabin. She had opened the door and was moving to flick on the light when she realised that the light was already on and the cabin occupied. Auger flinched – for a moment she thought she had opened the wrong door – but then recognised her luggage and coat on the end of the bed.

It was her room, and the two people sitting on the edge of the bed were Ringsted and Molinella, the Securities Board agents she had already met in Tanglewood.

'Verity Auger?' Ringsted asked.

'Oh, for heaven's sake,' she said. 'Of course it's me.'

'Check her out,' Ringsted said.

Molinella stood up and pulled out something that looked like a pen. Before Auger could react, he had expertly pinned her against the door and was holding one of her eyes open and aiming the end of the pen into it. Intense blue-green light zapped her retina and sparked painfully across her brain.

'It's her,' Molinella confirmed, releasing his hold.

'You *know* it's me,' Auger said, shaking her head to clear her vision of afterimages. 'We've already met. Don't you remember?'

'Sit down,' Molinella ordered. 'We have a lot to get through.'

'Give me a break,' Auger snapped. 'We've only just left port. We have another five days until we get to Mars.'

'Five days would barely cover it even if we had the luxury of that much time.' Molinella fixed her with the blank expression of a tailor's dummy. As before, both agents wore suits, but this time the cut was not quite as formal. They could, Auger supposed, just about pass for a pair of slightly strait-laced Thresher newlyweds.

'But we don't have five days,' Ringsted said. 'For security reasons, we must complete your briefing today.'

'Are you not staying on this ship until we reach Mars?' Auger asked.

'Yes,' Ringsted said. 'As Caliskan doubtless explained, the Slashers will have this ship under observation, just as they monitor all long-range Thresher traffic. We couldn't get a person on or off the *Twentieth* in mid-voyage without attracting far too much attention, and attention is the one thing we don't want right now.'

'Well, then. What's the hurry?'

'Is that door shut?' Ringsted asked, looking over Auger's shoulder. 'Good. Now pull up a chair. We have a lot to discuss.'

'First of all, I need to show you something,' Molinella said. He reached into his jacket pocket – the same place he kept the pen – and removed a matt-black cylinder like a cigar holder. He unscrewed the top and slid out a hypodermic, dense with bright-green fluid.

'While you were waiting for the ship,' Ringsted said, 'you were fed and watered in Caliskan's section of Contigencies.'

'I know,' Auger said.

'What you don't know is that there were harmless chemical tracers in your food. They've worked their way into your body and tagged themselves on to every new memory you've laid down since you became Caliskan's guest.'

Molinella took up the narrative. 'The agent in this syringe reacts with those tagged neural structures, dismantling them. Again, the effects won't be fatal, but you'll remember nothing that Caliskan told you, and nothing that we're *about* to tell you. In fact, you won't retain a single memory from this entire period. Of course, we'll only use it on you if we absolutely have to.'

'So if I screw up, or even get on your nerves, I'll wake up with a large hole in my memory.'

'Which won't be much help on the eve of a tribunal,' Molinella added. 'But let's hope it doesn't come to that, shall we?'

'Let's,' Auger agreed, with exaggerated pleasantness. 'But you still haven't told me why I need to learn all this now.'

'The reason,' Molinella said patiently, 'is that a day from now there will only be one person on this ship who knows anything about the contents of this briefing. And no, that doesn't mean that Agent Ringsted and I are going anywhere.' He returned the syringe to its container and the container to his pocket, patting it gently. 'If you see us outside this room once this briefing is over, treat us like any other pair of passengers. There'll be no point in asking us further questions. We literally won't remember you.'

'We'll begin with the essentials,' Ringsted said. 'The lights, please, Agent Molinella.'

Molinella stood up and dimmed the cabin lights.

'This is very cosy,' Auger began, but she had barely opened her mouth when patterns of light appeared on one blank wall of the cabin. She traced the rays back to a ruby-stoned ring on Molinella's finger.

The patterns of light resolved into what she presumed was the seal of the Contingencies Board, accompanied by a warning that the ensuing information was covered by a level of security so chillingly high that Auger had never even heard of it.

'Aren't I supposed to have signed something by now?' she asked.

Ringsted and Molinella looked at each other and laughed. 'Just watch,' the woman said. 'And save your questions for later.'

The security seal vanished, replaced by a picture of what Auger assumed to be the Milky Way galaxy, seen from above.

And then a man appeared, superimposed over the image of the galaxy. He wore a mid-grey suit with red cuffs and looked very athletic, his muscles straining against the seams of the fabric. He was very handsome and self-assured and Auger recognised him with a jolt.

It was Peter.

'Hello, Verity,' he said, spreading his hands in a gesture of apology and mild embarrassment. 'I suspect this probably comes as something of a surprise. All I can do is apologise for the secrecy, and hope that you'll forgive me – all of us, in fact – for the necessary subterfuge.'

She opened her mouth to say something, but Peter raised one palm and flashed a knowing smile. 'No, don't say anything. You'll just have to listen to what I have to say and fill in the gaps yourself. I'll do my best not to leave out anything critical.'

'Peter,' she said, unable to stop herself. 'What are . . .'

Oblivious of her interruption, the recording continued. 'Let's get the obvious stuff out of the way, shall we? Everything you think you know about me is correct. I am in the diplomatic service, and I have just returned from an extended tour of the Polities, culminating with a trip into the hyperweb. That's the public story, and it's all true. But there's more to it than that. I was also functioning as an undercover agent, gathering intelligence while playing the role of a sweet-talking airhead diplomat.' He smiled again, anticipating his ex-wife's reaction to this news. 'At, I should add, considerable risk to both myself and my friends amongst the Slashers. Things are getting very serious out there now, and spies aren't looked upon too favourably. As it is, I've probably exhausted my usefulness. A pity, as I rather enjoyed being a spook.' Peter's measured, actorly voice seemed to come from somewhere in the cabin, rather than the projector ring.

'I suppose I should get to the point, though. And the point, rather predictably, is the hyperweb itself.' Peter turned around and spread a hand across the face of the Milky Way, like a farmer casting seed. A bright web of lines appeared, transecting the spiral, and then the entire ensemble rotated to reveal a three-dimensional structure. 'This is our best guess as to the extent of the hyperweb network as mapped by Slasher explorers,' he said. 'It's exceedingly difficult to come up with a rendering like this. When explorers pop out of the far end of a given portal, unless they've exited near some unique, immediately recognisable landmark, like a supernova remnant or a supermassive outgassing star, there's no way for them to calculate exactly where they are in the galaxy. All they can do is fix their position using reference points, for which purpose pulsars turn out to be rather more suitable than stars.'

'Who made it?' Auger muttered under her breath. 'That's all we really care about.'

Something twinkled in Peter's eye as he turned back to the camera. How well he knew her, she thought, even now. 'The one thing we don't know is who built it. Neither do our friends in the Polities. Of course, there's a great deal of guesswork, some of it rather compelling. The system is clearly of alien origin, but whoever built it – and presumably *used* it – doesn't seem to be around any more.' Peter, Auger could tell, was rather enjoying this. From airhead, vain diplomat to airhead, vain spy: it really wasn't much of a leap. Then she rebuked herself for her snideness, conjecturing that Peter would almost certainly have been executed (or something worse) had his duplicity become known to his Slasher hosts.

She felt a flicker of admiration: quite unlike her, and most especially so where her ex-husband was concerned.

'What we suspect is this,' Peter continued. 'The system is old. It's been here for hundreds of millions of years, at the very least. It may be nearly as old as the solar system. Most of the portals that the explorers have found are anchored to solid bodies: terrestrial planets, moons, large planetoids. The Sedna portal is a classic example, and as far as the Slashers know it's the only active portal in our system.'

Something made the hairs on the back of her neck tingle. It was the way he said 'as far as the Slashers know'.

Peter tuned back to the representation of the Milky Way, stroking his chin thoughtfully. 'We still have no idea how the damned thing functions. Even the Slashers are in the dark on that one, despite their best efforts to convince us otherwise. They have some theories about metric engineering – triple-bounded hypervacuum solutions to the Krasnikov equations, that kind of thing. But really, if we're all honest with ourselves, they're pissing in the wind.' He tapped a finger against his upper lip. 'But let's give them credit where it's due. They found a way to use it. They grafted some of their technology on to the portal mechanisms, found a way to manipulate the throat geometry so they could squeeze a ship through in more or less one piece. You have to admire them for that. Like it or not, they're way ahead of us.'

Peter laced his hands behind his back, standing with his legs spaced slightly apart. 'Now let's talk hard numbers. How far have they reached? What have they actually found out there?'

Auger sat forward, sensing that some kind of climax was imminent.

'We still don't know exactly when they found the Sedna portal,' Peter said. 'Our best guess is that it was somewhere around fifty years ago, between twenty-two ten and twenty-two fifteen. Since then they've surveyed – or at least visited – somewhere in the region of fifty to sixty thousand solar systems. Pretty impressive, by anyone's measure. There's just one nagging little problem: they haven't actually *found* anything to justify all this effort.'

Auger nodded to herself. She paid scant attention to rumours about the hyperweb, but even so, one thing kept shining through: the whole affair was a bitter disappointment.

'Or at least,' Peter continued, 'nothing they want us to know about. It's tricky for them, really. They want access to Earth, and the only thing they can really offer us – apart from a drip-feed of UR and other dangerous little toys – is permission to use the hyperweb as paying passengers. So they try to dress up the brutal truth of what they have found out there, which is an endless catalogue of dead, uninhabitable rocks and crushing cold giants.' Peter unlaced his hands from behind his back and leaned conspiratorially toward the camera. 'The funny thing is, though, that even if they *had* found something out there, they probably wouldn't tell us that either.'

'Please get on with it,' Auger said, as if it would make any difference.

'The illusion,' Peter said, 'that the hyperweb has turned up nothing of value is maintained even in Slasher circles, at surprisingly high levels of security. That's why it's been such a tough old nut to crack.'

Now the picture behind him changed again. It zoomed in on one specific arm of the galaxy, the scene behind him punctuated by stars. Something loomed out of the darkness between them: a blue-grey world of unnatural smoothness, one crescent picked out in orange-red by an off-stage sun or cluster of suns. The other limb was a frigid blue, like the colour of moonlight on snow. The view zoomed towards the sphere, until it was much larger than Peter. At this extreme magnification, it was possible to make out some detail on the surface of the sphere. It was nothing at all like the texturing and weathering of a planetary surface.

The sphere was made up of countless neatly interlocked platelets, arranged in a pattern of mind-numbing regularity. It looked less like a planet than some crystalline molecule or virus.

'Let's bring in some scale here,' Peter said.

A box surrounded the sphere. Numbers popped up on the axes, indicating that the diameter of the sphere was around nine or ten of whatever units of measurement were in force.

'What . . .' Auger began.

'These numbers are units of one light-second,' Peter said. 'The sphere is nearly ten light-seconds in diameter. To put that into context, you could fit the sun into that structure and still have plenty of elbow room. You couldn't fit in the Earth as well, since the Earth's orbit around the sun is eight light-minutes wide, or about fifty times too big to fit into the sphere. But if you put the Earth in the middle, you'd have more than enough room to include Earth's moon.'

'Excuse me,' Auger interrupted, 'but was it me, or did he just call that thing a structure?' The agents ignored her, and she grudgingly returned her attention to the recording.

'I suppose we shouldn't be too surprised that we've actually found something unambiguously alien,' Peter said. 'After all, we always knew they were out there somewhere. The hyperweb is all the evidence we need of that. But to find something this huge . . . well, I don't think anyone was expecting that. The first big question, of course, is what the hell is it? And the second big question, what can it do for us?'

The sphere shrank, receding to a dot and finally to nothing. Now the view of the galaxy returned, with the intricate ratlines of the hyperweb superimposed as glowing vectors. 'Now for surprise number two: the Slashers have found more than one of these things. In fact, they've found around twenty of them, spread throughout the galaxy.' Peter clicked his fingers and blue-grey spheres the size of golf balls dropped into place on the map. 'You can't see it on this scale, so you'll have to take my word for it that none of these objects show up in any significant location, other than always being within easy reach of a portal. The Slashers call them "ALS objects", ALS standing for "anomalous large structure". Just rolls off the tongue, doesn't it? And if they've found twenty in such a short period of time – and since we know that the hyperweb is much more extensive than the mapped connections would imply – we can be sure that there must be thousands, maybe tens of thousands of these things out there. Sitting between stars, brooding like eggs.' Peter waited a beat. 'Or time bombs.'

The image changed again, focusing once more on a single blue-grey ALS sphere. The view had a pared-down, schematic quality to it. The spherical shading faded, leaving only a ring of very thin material.

'This is the cross section,' Peter said. 'The Slashers mapped the interior using neutrino tomography. They put a fifty kilowatt neutrino laser on one ship and flew it to one side of the ALS. Another ship carried a corresponding neutrino detector – an array of ultra-stiff sapphire crystals primed to undergo lattice vibration on the arrival of a single neutrino. The transmitting ship varied the path of its beam through the ALS, while the receiver ship kept track along the predicted beam, measuring the rise and fall in neutrino flux as the beam passed through the ALS at different angles. What they found indicated a hard, thin shell of unknown composition about one kilometre thick. They also detected a significant concentration of mass at the core, forming an inner sphere a few thousand kilometres in radius. In other words planet-sized, and with exactly the density profile you'd expect for a typical large terrestrial like Venus or Earth. The rest of the sphere seems to be hard vacuum, to the limit of the neutrino sweeps.'

Auger turned to Ringsted and Molinella. 'This is amazing, no question. It scares me that you're even telling me this stuff. But I still don't understand what any of it has to do with me or my tribunal.'

'You'll see,' the woman said.

Peter was still speaking, oblivious of her interruption. 'Based on these clues, the Slashers concluded that the ALS objects were physical shells wrapped around planets. Sometimes the planets even seem to be enclosed complete with moons. It is evidence of a very advanced technology – comparable even with the hyperweb itself. But why *do* this? Why imprison an entire world inside a dark sphere, isolating it from the rest of the universe? Well, maybe they aren't dark inside. No one knows that for sure. And maybe they only look like prisons from the outside. The state of matter inside that shell could be something very odd indeed. Are these planets that

73

have been quarantined because of some awful crime or biological cataclysm? Are they antimatter worlds that have somehow drifted into our galaxy, and must be shielded from outside contact on their way through? Are they something *worse*? According to our intelligence, the Slashers have no idea in spite of all their research. Just a lot of guesswork.'

Peter stared into the camera, his eyes gleaming, and he permitted himself the tiniest of self-satisfied smiles, the merest crinkle lifting the corners of his mouth.

'Well, we think *we* know. You see, we've found a way into one of the spheres that the Slashers know nothing about. And you, Verity, are going to take a little trip inside.'

SEVEN

Floyd's telephone dredged him from sleep just after eight in the morning. It hadn't stopped raining since he had returned from Montparnasse. It lashed against the window in hard diagonal lines, the wind chivvying the glass in its loose-fitting metal frame. Somewhere else in the apartment he heard Custine whistling cheerily, pottering around with washing-up. Floyd grimaced. There were two things he hated early in the morning: telephone calls and excessively cheerful people.

Still half-dressed from the night before, he stumbled out of bed and picked up the telephone. 'Floyd,' he said, his voice thick from what little sleep he had managed. 'And how are you, Monsieur Blanchard?'

This seemed to impress his caller. 'How did you know it was me?'

'Call it a hunch.'

'It's not too early for you, is it?'

Floyd scraped grit from the corners of his eyes. 'Not at all, monsieur. Been up for hours, working on the case.'

'Is that so? Then perhaps you have something to tell me.'

'Early days, yet,' Floyd said. 'Still collating the information we gathered last night.' He stifled a yawn.

'Then I presume you have a few leads already?'

'One or two,' he said.

Custine bustled in, pushing a mug of black coffee into Floyd's free hand. 'Who is it?' Custine asked in a stage whisper.

'Guess,' Floyd mouthed back.

'And these leads?' persisted Blanchard.

'Bit too soon to say how they'll pan out.' Floyd hesitated, then decided to try his luck. 'Actually, I've already got a specialist working on the documents in the tin.'

'A specialist? You mean someone who can read German?'

'Yes,' Floyd admitted feebly. He sipped at the viciously strong coffee and willed Blanchard – and the world in general – to leave him alone until later in the day. Custine sat down on the edge of Floyd's fold-out bed, hands in his lap, his flowered apron still around his waist.

'Very well,' said Blanchard. 'I suppose it would be naïve to expect concrete progress so soon in the investigation.'

'Unwise, certainly,' Floyd said.

'I'll be in touch later, then. I shall be most interested to hear what your specialist has to say about Mademoiselle White's papers.'

'I'm waiting with bated breath myself.'

'Good day to you, then.'

Floyd heard the gratifying click as Blanchard terminated the connection. He looked at Custine. 'I hope you turned up something useful last night after I left.'

'Probably less than you're hoping for. How did it go with Greta?'

'Less well than I was hoping.'

Custine looked sympathetic. 'I guess from that conversation with Blanchard that you'll be seeing her again?'

'Later today.'

'At least one more chance, then.' Custine stood up and began untying his apron. 'I'm going downstairs to buy some bread. Smarten yourself up and we can discuss our respective experiences over breakfast.'

'I thought you said you hadn't turned anything up.'

'I'm not sure that I have. At least, nothing I'd stake money on. But there *was* something – an observation made by Mademoiselle White's neighbour.'

'What sort of observation?' Floyd asked.

'I'll tell you over breakfast. And you can tell me how you got on with Greta.'

Floyd leafed through the morning newspaper while Custine fetched the bread. He skimmed the headlines – something about a murder on the first page – until a familiar name jumped out at him on the third page. There was a reference to Maillol, the same inspector who had given Blanchard Floyd's name. Maillol was a good apple in an increasingly rotten barrel who had chosen to be sidelined rather than pursue the political agenda that Chatelier was forcing upon the police. Once a rising star of the Crime Squad – which was how Floyd had met him – Maillol's days of high-profile cases and headline arrests were long over. Now he was working scraps from the table, unglamorous assignments like anti-bootlegging operations. According to the article, Maillol had uncovered an illegal record-pressing scam in the Montrouge quartier. The article described the investigation as 'ongoing', with the police following up a number of additional leads concerning other criminal activities taking place in the same complex of abandoned buildings. The news depressed Floyd. As glad as he was that he might now be able to scour the record markets without worrying that some apparently priceless piece of jazz history – say, a Gennett recording of Louis Armstrong from 1923 – might actually have been pressed about a week ago, it was dispiriting to think of a good man like Maillol reduced to such meagre fare when suspicious deaths were going uninvestigated.

He went into the bathroom and showered in lukewarm water stained with rust from the apartment's ancient plumbing. There was a bad taste in his mouth and it wasn't the shower water or the memory of the orange brandy he had shared with Greta. Drying himself, he heard Custine coming back into the apartment. Floyd put on a vest and braces and a clean white shirt, leaving the choice of tie until he had to face the outside world. He padded into the tiny little kitchen in his socks. A warm-bread smell filled the room and Custine was already spreading butter and jelly on to a slice.

'Here,' the Frenchman said, 'eat this and stop looking so miserable.'

'I could do without him ringing us at eight in the morning.' Floyd scraped back a seat and slumped down opposite Custine. 'I'm in two minds about this whole business, André. I'm beginning to think we should call it off before it goes much further.'

Custine poured some more coffee for them both. His jacket was dark with rain, but otherwise he looked impeccably bright-eyed and well presented: cheeks and chin clean-shaven, his moustache neatly trimmed and oiled. 'There was a time yesterday when I would have agreed with you.'

'And now?'

'Now I have my suspicions that there might be something to this after all. It's what that neighbour told me. Something was going on, that's for sure.'

Floyd started on his bread. 'So what did the neighbour have to say?'

Custine tucked a napkin into his collar. 'I spoke to all the tenants who were present last night. Blanchard thought they would all be home, but two were absent, or had at least left the building by the time we began our investigations. We can catch up with them later; at the very least it'll give us another reason to drag things out.'

'The neighbour,' Floyd persisted.

'A young man, law student.' Custine bit into his jellied bread and dabbed delicately around his mouth with the napkin. 'Helpful enough chap. In fact they were all helpful once they realised that they weren't dealing with the Quai. And a murder – well . . .' He waved the bread for emphasis. 'You can't shut 'em up once they get it into their heads that they might be material witnesses in a murder case.'

'What did the law student have to say for himself?'

'He didn't really know her at all, said he kept very odd hours as well and that their paths didn't cross very often. Nodding acquaintances, that sort of thing.'

'Did he fancy her?'

'Fellow already has a fiancée, from what I gathered.'

'It sounds as if he barely knew Susan White. What did he have on her?'

'It's what he heard,' Custine said. 'You know what these buildings are like – walls like rice paper. He would always know if she was home: she couldn't move around without the floorboards creaking.'

'That's all?'

'No. He heard noises, strange sounds,' Custine said, 'like someone playing the same note very quietly on a flute or recorder, over and over again.'

Floyd scratched his scalp. 'Blanchard said he never heard her playing any music at all, not on the radio or on that old phonograph. But he did mention noises.'

'Agreed. And you think he'd have noticed if she kept an instrument in her room, wouldn't you?'

'So it wasn't an instrument. What else could it have been?' Floyd mused.

'Whatever it was must have been coming through the wireless. The way the student described it, the notes sounded rather like code. He heard long notes and short notes, and sometimes he was aware of repetition, as if a particular message was being repeated.'

For the first time that morning, Floyd felt the onset of something approaching alertness. 'Like Morse code, you mean?'

'Draw your own conclusions. Of course, the student didn't have the presence of mind actually to record any of these sounds as he heard them. It wasn't until she died that he thought anything of it, and even then he didn't attach any particular importance to it.'

'No?'

'He's been studying for three years, renting almost a dozen different rooms in the process. He says he'd be hard pressed to think of a single neighbour who didn't have at least one strange habit. After a while, he said, you learn to stop dwelling on such things. He admitted to me that he was fond of gargling mouthwash, and that at least one of his fellow tenants had commented that this was rather an odd thing to do at two in the morning.'

Floyd finished off his bread and coffee. 'We'll need to get back into her room, examine it thoroughly this time.'

'I'm sure Blanchard will be happy to oblige if he feels it's in the interests of the case.'

'Maybe.' Floyd stood up, scratching his chin and making a mental note to shave before leaving the building. 'But I'd prefer to keep a lid on this for now. I don't want him getting all excited over the possibility that she might have been a spy.'

Custine looked at him with a knowing twinkle in his eye. 'But you're considering it, aren't you? You're at least toying with the possibility?'

'Let's stick to concrete evidence, meaning eyewitnesses. What about the other tenants? Get anything from them?'

'Nothing useful. One fellow reported seeing an odd little girl hanging around the place on the day of the accident.'

'Odd in what way?'

'Said the child looked rather sickly.'

'Well, then,' Floyd said with a flourish of one hand, 'round up the usual sickly children. Case closed.' But nagging at the back of his mind was the memory of the girl who had been coming out of Blanchard's building when they had arrived the evening before. 'There couldn't really be a connection, could there?'

'The fellow was just trying to be helpful,' Custine said defensively. 'At least the tenants all have your card now, and everyone I spoke to promised to get in touch if anything jogs their memories. No one knew anything about a sister.' He set about buttering himself another slice of bread. 'Well, that's my news. Your turn.'

The Mathis slid through thick Thursday-morning traffic, ankle-deep water hissing around the wheels where the overloaded drains had backed up and overflowed on to the street. The rain had finally eased and the sun was glinting fitfully off wet stonework and the fluted iron columns of street lamps; gleaming off statues and the Art Nouveau signs guarding the entrances to the Métro. Floyd loved Paris like this. Through his blurred and slitted eyes the city looked like an oil painting that needed a few more days to dry.

'So about Greta,' Custine said, from the passenger seat. 'You can't put it off for ever, Floyd. We had a deal.'

'What deal?'

'That I'd tell you about my interviews, and you'd tell me about Greta.'

Floyd's knuckles tightened on the wheel. 'She isn't back for good. She won't be rejoining the band.'

'And there's no hope of talking her into it?'

'None at all.'

'Then why is she back, if it isn't to torment you with what might have been? She's cruel, our imperious little Fräulein, but she isn't *that* cruel.'

'Her aunt's dying,' Floyd said. 'She wants to be with her until the end. That's part of it, anyway.'

'And the rest?'

Floyd hesitated, on the verge of telling Custine to mind his own business. But Custine deserved better than that – his future was at stake here just as much as Floyd's. He just didn't realise it yet. 'She's not going back to the touring band either.'

'Fell out with them?'

'Seems not, just didn't feel they were going anywhere, and that she wouldn't be either if she stayed with them. So she got an idea into her head.'

'She's going solo?'

Floyd shook his head. 'More ambitious than that. Television.' He said the word like an obscenity. 'She wants to be part of it.'

'Can't blame the girl,' Custine replied, shrugging. 'She's got the talent, and she's definitely got the looks. Good for her, I say. Why aren't you cheering her on?'

Floyd steered the car past a hole in the road where some overall-clad workmen were swapping jokes but showing no other sign of activity. 'Because she's talking about television in America,' he said. 'In Los Angeles, of course.'

Custine said nothing for a few blocks. Floyd drove on in silence, half-imagining that he could hear the grinding of his partner's mental gears as he worked out the implications. Finally they slowed for a set of traffic lights.

'She's asked you to go with her, hasn't she?' Custine guessed.

'Not exactly asked,' Floyd said. 'More like delivered an ultimatum. If I go with her, there's a chance for us to be together. She said we could see how it works out. If I don't, she walks out of my life and I'll never hear from her again.'

They moved off again as the traffic light changed. 'That's quite an ultimatum,' Custine said. 'Understandable from her point of view, though – it would be useful to have a burly American boyfriend around to fend off the sharks.'

'I'm French.'

'You're French when it suits you. You pass as American just as easily when *that* suits you.'

'I can't go. I have a life here. I have a business. I have a business partner who depends on me for his livelihood.'

'You sound like someone trying very hard to convince himself of something. Would you care for my opinion?'

'Something tells me I'm going to get it anyway.'

'You should go with her. Take the boat or plane or whatever to America. Look after her in Hollywood, or wherever it is that these television people have their empire. Give it two years. If it hasn't worked out, Greta will still be able to make a good living back here.'

'And me?'

'If she makes a good living, maybe you won't have to worry about earning one.'

'I don't know, André.'

Custine thumped the dashboard in frustration. 'What have you got to lose? We may have a case at this moment, but most of the time we barely have two centimes to rub together. It's all excitement now, but if this murder investigation doesn't pan out, we'll be back exactly where we were this time yesterday: knocking on a lot of doors in the Marais. Except we won't have a double bass.'

'We'll always find detective work.'

'Undoubtedly. But if there's one thing I've learned in your employment, Floyd, it's that there's only so much money to be made from tracking down mistresses and missing cats.'

'What would you do?' Floyd asked.

'What I have always done,' Custine replied. 'Follow my instincts and my conscience.'

'I'll hand the business over to you, of course, if it comes to it.'

'Then you've at least thought things through that far. I'm glad, Floyd. It shows that you are thinking clearly, for once in your life.'

'I'm considering the options. That's all.' Floyd steered the car on to the street where Blanchard lived. 'Nothing will happen until we solve this case.'

'An unexpected breakthrough?' Blanchard asked when he opened the door to his rooms and let them inside. So little outside light made its way into the stairwells and corridors that the atmosphere of the building had barely changed from the previous evening. 'Clearly a lot can change in an hour.'

'I told you we had some leads,' Floyd corrected him. 'In the meantime, my partner and I need to have another look in Mademoiselle White's room.'

'Do you think you missed something significant the first time?'

'That was a glance, not an investigation.' Floyd nodded at the little briefcase Custine had brought with him. 'This time we're here to do a proper job.'

'I'll show you up to the room, in that case.'

They waited a moment for the landlord to button on a cardigan and fetch his keys. Politely, Floyd and Custine followed him as he ascended the stairs to Susan White's room on the fifth floor.

'Just to confirm – no one but you has touched this room until we saw it yesterday?' Floyd asked.

'No one at all.'

'Could anyone else have found their way in without you knowing about it?'

'They would need a key,' Blanchard said. 'I have Mademoiselle White's key. It was on her person when she died – the police returned it.'

'Could someone have copied that key?' Floyd persisted.

'Conceivably, but it's numbered for an apartment. No reputable locksmith would duplicate it without consent from a landlord.'

Blanchard let them into the room. In daylight it looked larger and dustier but otherwise was as Floyd remembered it from the evening before, crammed with books, newspapers, magazines and records. The balcony doors had been latched open an inch to air out the place, and the filmy white drapes drawn across them were moving in the breeze.

'We'll need some time alone up here,' Floyd said. 'Please don't take offence, but we tend to work best without an audience.'

Blanchard hovered at the door, and for a moment Floyd wondered if they were ever going to get rid of him.

'Very well, then,' Blanchard said eventually. 'I shall give you some privacy. Please, leave everything as you found it.'

'We'll do just that,' Custine assured him. He waited until the door had closed behind the landlord before asking, 'Floyd – what exactly *are* we looking for?'

'I want to know what she was listening to on the wireless. Go and check that the old man isn't still snooping around outside, will you?'

Custine went to the door, opened it a crack and checked the hallway. 'No, I can hear him moving down the stairs. You want me to check on the neighbours as well?'

'No need. They're probably at work.' Floyd knelt down and started fiddling with the huge old wireless set. He had brought his notebook and made sure that the dial was still tuned to the same wavelength as when they had last examined it. Once again, the tuning band's pale illumination glimmered to life as the valves heated up, and there was crackling as he turned the dial and slid the arrow along the band from station to station. But there was still no music, no voices, no codelike noises.

'Perhaps the neighbour was imagining it,' Custine said.

'Blanchard also mentioned hearing noises. I don't think the two of them were imagining the same thing independently.'

'There must be something wrong with the wireless, in that case.'

'Maybe there is. Look at this.'

Custine knelt down next to Floyd and followed his partner's gaze. 'It's a carpet, Floyd. They're a surprisingly common feature in houses.'

'I mean the scuff marks, you idiot,' Floyd said affectionately as he indicated two scratches in the carpet, spaced about the width of the wireless set. 'I don't know if they're recent or not. I noticed them when we here last night – the carpet was rucked up, as well – but I didn't put two and two together until now.'

'And now you're thinking . . . ?'

'I'd say they were caused by someone dragging the wireless away from the wall.'

'They must have been in a hurry to make such a messy job of it.'

'My thinking exactly.' Floyd patted Custine on the back. 'Let's have a look, shall we?'

'Can't hurt.'

'Make sure that door's bolted. I don't want the old man coming back in and seeing us fiddling with the wireless. That'll really put ideas into his head.'

'It's secure,' Custine said, after checking the door.

Between them they heaved the wireless set away from the wall, taking care not to add any more scuff marks to the carpet. It was a job for two people, and Floyd didn't doubt that he would have had a difficult time of it had Custine not been there. 'Look,' he said, when they had the wireless a clear half-metre from the wall. 'Three screws on the floor and some wood shavings, suggesting that they were ripped out of the back of the wireless, for some reason.'

Custine peered over his shoulder, holding a handkerchief to his face against the dust. 'Someone's fiddled with it,' he said.

'In a hurry, too.' Floyd pulled aside the thin wood backing of the wireless, which was hanging loose, attached by only one screw. 'It wouldn't have taken five minutes to unscrew the back, but whoever did this obviously didn't have time to find a screwdriver. They must have poked something into the gap and levered the backing away just enough to get at the innards.'

'Good thing I have a screwdriver, then,' Custine said and went to fetch his briefcase. Custine always kept a set of locksmith's tools handy, no matter what case they were working on.

'Now see if you can get that backing off,' Floyd said.

Custine removed the remaining screw and the plywood backing dropped free, revealing the guts of the wireless.

'That's . . . interesting,' Floyd said.

'Here,' Custine said. 'Let's turn it to the light. I need a better look.'

They angled the contraption until the open back was facing the balcony windows. A shaft of morning sunlight speared the room, crisscrossed by specks of dust, and fell upon the exposed heart of the wireless, gleaming back from a bird's-nest tangle of wire, glass valves and enamelled parts. Practically the entire volume of the wooden cabinet was crammed with electrical components arranged in a looping, knotted jumble of intestinal complexity.

'That's like no wireless I've ever seen,' Custine said. 'It looks more like some mad piece of modern art, something you'd waste good money to stand in front of, stroking your chin and looking thoughtful.'

'Maybe she was a spy after all,' Floyd replied.

'But what *is* this thing? What was she making?'

Floyd turned off the wireless, then gingerly pushed a finger into the mess of wires, being careful not to disturb anything. Some of the wires were loose, he noticed: their bare metal ends sparkled in the daylight, and he could see nubs of solder where they had been ripped free from the larger electrical parts.

'It looks insane to me,' he said. 'But you know more about these things than I do. Does any of this make sense to you?'

'That depends on what you mean by "make sense",' Custine replied. 'I recognise most of these parts, certainly. Smoothing condensers here . . . a pair of decoupling capacitors there . . . standard valve heaters over here . . . and this, I think, is a two-gang tuning condenser. It's all common stuff, frankly; the oddity is seeing so much of it in such a little space. But she wouldn't have needed access to any specialist supplies: a few dozen wireless sets and she would have had everything she needed.' He smiled. 'Apart, of course, from a degree in electrical engineering and a very steady hand with a soldering iron.'

'Maybe neither was a problem for her. After all, if you can train a spy to learn a code, you can train them to make things.'

'So you seriously think Susan White made this contraption?'

Floyd looked at his partner. 'Her or one of her associates. I see no alternative explanation.'

'But why did she need to make it at all? If she was a spy, couldn't she have brought her own wireless equipment with her?'

This question troubled Floyd as well, but he had no satisfactory answer. 'She must have been worried about being discovered,' he suggested. 'If she came into this country via official channels, she'd have had to go through customs.'

'But aren't spies supposed to have secret compartments in their luggage, that sort of thing?'

'Still too much risk of being discovered. Better to have some kind of coded shopping list of radio parts and instructions on how to put them together.'

'All right.' Custine stood up and leaned against the wall, one finger tapping his moustache. 'There are clearly still some things we don't understand. But let's at least consider what might have happened. Susan White arrives in Paris as a foreign spy and finds a room for herself. She now needs to keep in touch with her compatriots – whoever and wherever they might be.'

'Or else she needs to listen in on someone else's signals,' Floyd said.

Custine conceded Floyd's point by raising a finger. 'That's also a possibility. Whatever the reason, she assembles this receiver, starting with a simple wireless set. She might even have been using it when she was disturbed. The intruder killed her by throwing her over the balcony, just as Blanchard suspected. Then they noticed the wireless, or had already seen her using it. Clearly they wanted to destroy it, but they couldn't remove it from the room without drawing attention to themselves. And perhaps they – singular or plural – had very little time before they had to leave the room. After all, there was a dead body on the pavement.'

'And a smashed typewriter,' Floyd added.

'Yes,' Custine said, sounding less confident. 'I'm not quite sure where that fits in. Perhaps they used it to bludgeon her.'

'Let's just assume the killer was in a hurry for now,' Floyd said.

'Whoever it was had just enough time to pull the wireless away from the wall, jimmy open the back and get their hand inside. They did what damage they could, hoping to render the wireless inoperative. Doubtless if they'd had more time they would have done a more thorough job of it, but as it is, it looks as if they only wrenched a few wires loose and left it at that.'

Floyd pulled aside one knot of wires, wishing he had a torch. 'We need to make this thing work,' he said.

'What we need to do,' Custine said, 'is hand this whole matter over to the relevant authorities.'

'You think they'd take it any more seriously now that we have a broken wireless to show them? Face it, André: it's all still circumstantial.' Delicately, Floyd picked out one of the bare-ended wires and searched for its counterpart. 'If we could fix this . . .'

'We don't know whether the murderer took anything out of it.'

'Let's assume they were in too much of a hurry, and let's also assume they didn't want to be caught with anything on them that would link them to this room.'

'It's not like you to be so optimistic.' Custine frowned, moved to the door and placed his ear against it. 'Hang on – someone's coming up the stairs.'

'Let's get this thing back against the wall. Hurry!'

Floyd held the cover loosely in place while Custine secured it with a few turns of one screw; the others would have to wait. Behind them, the door rattled as someone tried the knob.

'It's Blanchard,' Custine hissed.

'Just a moment, monsieur,' Floyd called, while the two of them inched the cumbersome wireless set back into place, scraping and rucking up the carpet in the process.

The landlord knocked loudly on the door. 'Open, please!'

'Just a moment,' Floyd repeated.

Custine moved back to the door and unlocked it, while Floyd stood in front of the wireless, doing his best to smooth the carpet back into place with the heel of his shoe. 'We felt it best to lock the door,' Floyd said. 'Didn't want any of the neighbours poking their noses in.'

'And?' Blanchard asked, stepping into the room. 'Did you find anything?'

'We've only been here five minutes.' Floyd gestured at his surroundings, wishing that he had not chosen to stand so close to the wireless set. 'There's a lot to work through. She was a busy little beaver, Mademoiselle White.'

'Mmm.' Blanchard observed them both through narrowed eyes. 'The point is, Monsieur Floyd, that I had already deduced as much based on my own observations. It is fresh insights that I seek, not things I have already worked out for myself.'

Floyd moved away from the wireless. 'Actually, I need to ask you something. Did you ever see her up here with anyone else?'

'I never saw her with anyone else the whole time I knew her.'

'Never?' Floyd asked.

'Even when I followed her towards the Métro station, I did not see the exchange take place.'

Floyd remembered Blanchard telling them how he had shadowed Susan White while she struggled towards the station with a loaded case. Floyd had forgotten that detail until now: it was in his notebook, but not at the forefront of his mind. Now that he suspected that she had been in contact with fellow agents (unless, as Custine had said, she was using the wireless to intercept someone else's transmissions), he began to develop a vague idea of how she had worked. She was a foreign agent in an unfamiliar city, and for much of the time she was acting alone. Perhaps she received orders and intelligence through the modified wireless. But she could not be totally alone in Paris, or else the handover in the Métro station could never have taken place. So there must be other agents out there, from the same side as her: a small, loosely organised web of them spread across Paris, who kept in contact via coded radio transmissions. And unless the radio transmissions were originating from very far away, there must be someone in the area sending those orders.

Floyd felt a weird sense of vertigo: a combination of fear and thrill that he knew he would not be able to resist. It would pull him deeper, and it would do what it would with him, whether he liked it or not.

'You do think she was murdered, don't you?' Blanchard asked him.

'I'm coming around to the idea, but I'm still not sure whether we'll ever know exactly who did it.'

'Have you made any more progress with the documents?' Blanchard persisted.

Floyd had left a note with Greta the night before, saying that he would pay her a visit later today. 'There might be something in them,' he said. 'But look, Monsieur Blanchard, if she gave you those papers for safekeeping, then she must have felt that her life was in danger.'

'Which is exactly what I have been saying all along!'

'The point is, if the murder was premeditated, then it might also have been well executed. No loose ends, nothing to lead to the killer. Don't believe those dime-novel mysteries: the killer doesn't *always* make a mistake.'

'If you believe that sincerely, then we may as well conclude our contract now.'

'It's too early for that,' Floyd said. 'I'm just saying that at some point we might have to give up.'

'Give up, or retreat in the face of danger?'

Custine coughed before Floyd could say anything he might regret. 'We really shouldn't take any more of your time this morning, monsieur,' he said smoothly. 'We have a lot more to do in this room, not to mention the parallel lines of enquiry we should be pursuing.'

Blanchard considered this and nodded politely. 'Very well. Monsieur Floyd, at least your associate still appears to consider the case solvable.' For a moment, his attention seemed drawn to the disturbed area of carpet in front of the wireless, and a flicker of comprehension troubled his face. Then he turned and left them alone.

'I can't help liking the old coot,' Floyd said, 'but I do wish he'd get out of our faces.'

'It's his money. He just wants to make sure that it's being spent wisely.' Custine paused and dug into his toolkit again, before shaking his head. 'I was hoping I might have something in here I could use to splice those wires back together, but I don't. I'll need to return to the office.'

'You think you can fix it?'

'I can try. If we assume that nothing has been removed, then it's only a matter of reconnecting the broken wires.'

'They all looked the same to me,' Floyd said, peering through a narrow gap in the balcony curtain. Five storeys below, the mid-morning sun had turned the wet street into a sparkling mirror. He watched passers-by stepping between puddles, and then something caught his eye.

'Of course they do,' Custine said. 'Nevertheless, there should be a manageable number of permutations. If I haven't got anywhere by the end of this afternoon, I doubt that more time will make any difference.' Custine waited a moment. 'Floyd? Did you hear a word of what I just said?'

Floyd turned from the window. 'I'm sorry.'

'You're thinking about Greta again, aren't you?'

'Actually,' Floyd said, 'I was thinking about that little girl standing across the street.'

'I didn't notice any girl when we arrived.'

'That's because she wasn't there. But now it looks as if she's watching this room.'

He let the curtain slip back into the place. He'd had enough of a look at the little girl to make him doubt that she was the same one they had seen coming out of Blanchard's apartment the evening before. But there was still something about the way light fell on her face that made him want to look elsewhere.

'You don't seriously think a child has something to do with this murder, do you?' Custine asked.

'Of course not,' Floyd said.

They took the stairs down to the Mathis. By the time they reached the car, the watcher was gone.

EIGHT

Auger's shuttle hauled away from the *Twentieth Century Limited* and aimed itself in the general direction of Mars. She pressed her face against the glass of a porthole, feeling the vibration in her bones as the shuttle stammered its steering jets in rapid, chugging sequence. Though she had little idea of where she was being taken – or how her task fitted into the story Peter had told her – she was still glad to leave the clapped-out old space liner. After five days, its charms had worn perilously thin, with even a guided tour into the ship's bowels to view the last working antimatter engine in the solar system providing little more than an hour's mildly diverting (and frankly terrifying) entertainment. Mars at least was ripe was possibility, and she felt a tingling sense of anticipation as the planet's butterscotch face loomed larger. It wasn't just lack of funds that had kept her from visiting Mars before. She reckoned there was something ghoulish about the tourists who did make the trip; some morbid craving to revel in the horror of what had happened to the planet. But now that she had been sent here on someone else's orders, it was difficult not to want to see it for herself.

The Scoured Zone began south of the Hellas Planitia and reached as far north as Cydonia, encompassing all of the crater-pocked uplands of the Arabia Terra. Between the poles, the rest of Mars was dusted in shades of brittle blue-green: vast prairies of hardy, gene-tweaked vegetation laid down over a hundred years earlier. Canals, etched across the surface with laser precision, were twinkling back ribbons of reflected sunlight. At the hubs and junctions of the irrigation system, Auger made out the off-white sprawl of cities and townships, the tentative scratches of roads and the lines of tethered dirigibles. There were even a few wispy streaks of cloud and a handful of hexagonal lakes, clustered together like cells in a beehive.

But between Hellas Planitia and Cydonia nothing grew, nothing endured, nothing lived or moved. Even the mindless clouds exhibited a wary disregard for that whole area. It had been that way for twenty-three years, since the last days of the brief but bitter war that had erupted between the Slashers and the Threshers over rights of access to Earth.

Auger barely remembered the war. As a child, she had been cosseted from the worst of the news. But it really hadn't been all that long ago, and there was still a sense that certain scores had yet to be settled. She thought of Caliskan, losing a brother to the Slashers in the battle to reclaim Phobos. The war must have seemed like yesterday to him. How could he accept Slasher involvement in Earth so readily, after what they had taken from him? How could he be so cold, so political?

Another series of manoeuvres followed, smoother this time, and then – quite without warning – Auger found her view of the Scoured Zone obstructed by the illuminated, machine-lined walls of a docking bay sliding slowly past. Beyond the bay, glimpsed for an instant, was a curving, airless horizon of very dark rock.

She had been misinformed about Mars. It had never been her destination.

The welcoming party on the other side of the airlock consisted of eight men and women in USNE military uniform, accompanied by two snake robots.

'I'm Aveling,' said the tallest, thinnest man in the group, observing Auger with pale aluminium-grey eyes. He had a ruined voice: a slow, parched rasp that she had to strain to understand. 'You'll be taking orders and instructions from me for the duration of your mission. If that's a problem, get over it now.'

'And if I don't get over it?' she asked.

'We'll put you on the first ship back to Tanglewood and that unpleasant little tribunal you should be facing.'

'Only with half my memory missing,' she said.

'Correct.'

'If it's all right with you, I'll try the taking orders thing for now, see how that works out.'

'Fine,' Aveling said.

He had the look of a serious hard bastard, the kind who was even more intimidating because he appeared intelligent and cultured, while also giving off the unavoidable impression that he could kill anyone in the room before they'd taken their next breath. She had been told nothing about him, but she knew instantly that he was a veteran of the war and that he had probably killed more Slashers than she had met in her life, and that he had probably never missed a night's sleep because of it.

'I'd still really like someone to tell me what I'm doing on Phobos,' Auger said as Aveling's party led her away from the shuttle, with two snake robots slithering along behind.

'What do you know about Phobos?' Aveling asked. He sounded as if his voice box had been stitched back together from tatters, reconstructed like a shredded document.

'I know to keep away. Other than that, not much. Mars is basically civilian, but you military boys have the moons sewn up pretty tight.'

'The moons offer the perfect strategic platform for defending the planet against Slasher incursions. Given the existing security measures already in place, they're also a perfect venue for conducting any sensitive business that might come our way.'

'Do I count as sensitive business?'

'No, Auger. You count as a pain in the ass. If there's one thing I hate more than civilians, it's having to be nice to them.'

'You mean this is you being nice?'

They led Auger to a small, windowless chamber with a couple of closed doors leading away into other rooms. The room contained three seats, a low table and a flagon of water accompanied by two glasses. A grey cabinet occupied one wall, crammed with magnetic tapes in white plastic spools, with a p-mail hopper set next to it.

They left her alone. Auger poured herself a glass of water and sipped at it experimentally. She had finished half the glass when one of the other doors whisked open and a short, tough-looking woman entered. She had an efficient, low-maintenance bob of straw-coloured hair, framing a face that might have been pretty except for the scowl that seemed moulded into it. She wore coveralls with many pockets and loops, the top zipped low enough to reveal a grubby white T-shirt beneath. Quick, intelligent eyes appraised Auger. The woman took the stub of a cigarette from her lips and flicked it into one corner of the room.

'Verity, right?'

'Yes,' she said cautiously.

The woman leaned down, rubbed one hand against her thigh and then offered it to Auger. 'Maurya Skellsgard. Have those pricks been treating you all right?'

'Well . . .' Auger began, suddenly lost for words.

Skellsgard sat down on one of the other seats and helped herself to some water. 'What you have to understand about those people – and believe me, it took me a while to arrive at this conclusion – is that you're better with them than without them. Aveling is a cold-hearted son of a bitch, but he's *our* cold-hearted son of a bitch.'

'Are you military?' Auger asked.

Skellsgard downed her glass of water in one gulp, then poured another. 'Hell no – I'm just a snotty-nosed academic. Until a year ago I was happily minding my own business trying to come up with a mathematical treatment of pathological matter.' Anticipating Auger's question she continued, 'The normal mathematics of wormhole mechanics says you need something called exotic matter to enlarge and stabilise a wormhole throat. That's matter with negative energy density – already seriously weird stuff. But as soon as we got our hands on a few crumbs of intelligence about the hyperweb, it became clear that this wasn't really a wormhole in the classical sense. Pretty soon we realised we needed something several degrees weirder than exotic matter to make it hang together. Hence . . . pathological matter.' She shrugged. 'We're physicists. You have to allow us our little jokes, no matter how piss-poor they are.'

'It's all right,' Auger said. 'You should hear some of the jokes archaeologists think are funny.'

'I guess we're both in the same boat, then: a pair of pain-in-the-ass civilian experts Aveling has no choice but to work with.'

Auger smiled. 'That guy just loves civilians, doesn't he?'

'Oh yes, can't get enough of 'em.' Skellsgard emptied her glass a second time. Her knuckles were barked and grazed, dark crescents of grime caked under her very short fingernails. 'I heard about the tribunal. Sounds as if they've got you by the short and curlies.'

'I deserve it. I nearly killed a boy.'

Skellsgard waved that away. 'They'll fix him, if his family's as rich and influential as I heard they are.'

'Well, I hope they do fix him. He wasn't a bad kid.'

'What about you? I heard that you're married to Peter Auger.'

'*Was* married to him,' Auger corrected.

'Hmm. Please don't tell me Mr Perfect is really a pig behind closed doors. I don't think I could stand having my illusions shattered.'

'No,' Auger said, wearily. 'Peter's a decent enough man. Not perfect . . . but not bad, either. I was the problem, not him. I let my work take over.'

'I hope it was worth it. What else? Any kids?'

'A boy and a girl I love very much, but who I don't make enough time for.'

Skellsgard looked sympathetic. 'I guess that must have simplified things when it came to Caliskan's nice little offer.'

'They'd have thrown away the key,' Auger said, 'put me somewhere like Venus Deep. By the time I got to see my kids again they'd have barely recognised me. At least this way I have a chance of coming through this with my life at least vaguely intact.' She shifted in her seat, uneasy about discussing her private life. 'Of course, it might help if I knew what the hell it is I'm supposed to do.'

Skellsgard regarded her shrewdly. 'What have they told you so far?'

'They told me about the Slasher intelligence on the ALS objects,' Auger replied.

'Good. That's a start, at least.'

'They said they'd found a way into one. They also told me I was supposed to go inside. I guess Phobos has something to do with that.'

'More than a little. About two years ago, the USNE found an inactive portal right here, buried under a couple of kilometres of Phobos topsoil. That was when I was drafted on to the team. I'm the closest thing to an expert on hyperweb travel outside of the Polities. Which, I hasten to add, isn't saying much. But at least now we have a real one to play with.'

'And you've made it work?'

'As long as you don't mind a bumpy ride.'

'And the Slashers still know nothing about it? How come they didn't find it when they were running Phobos?'

'They didn't look deep enough. We only stumbled on it by accident, when we were excavating a new living chamber.'

Auger suddenly felt very awake and very alert. 'I want to see it.'

'Good. That was sort of the idea of bringing you here in the first place.' Skellsgard hitched up a frayed sleeve to glance at her watch. 'We'd better get a move on. There's an incoming transport due any minute.'

'I still don't know what Paris has to do with all this.'

'We'll come to that,' Skellsgard said.

The chamber was large and very nearly spherical, the in-curving walls gouged and blasted from coal-dark Phobos core material and then sprayed with some kind of plastic on to which platforms, lighting rigs and catwalks had been bolted or glued. Occupying much of the interior was a glass sphere about half as wide as the chamber, supported in a complex cradle of bee-striped struts and shock-absorbing pistons. Catwalks, caged ladders, pipes and conduits wrapped the sphere in a gristle of metal and plastic. White-clad technicians perched at various locations around the sphere, tapping equipment into open access ports. With their headphones, goggles and gloves they looked like safecrackers engaged in some spectacular heist.

'We're just in time,' Skellsgard said, consulting an instrument-crammed panel bolted to one bar of the viewing cage in which they stood. 'Transport hasn't come through yet, but we're already picking up bow-shock distortion ahead of it.' On the panel, the needles on numerous analogue dials were twitching into the red. 'Looks like it was a rough ride. Hope they packed their barf bags.'

The technicians had cleared out of the area around the recovery bubble. Machines moved into different positions. Auger even noticed three snake robots in defensive/offensive postures, poised like spitting cobras.

'They expecting something nasty?' she asked.

'Just a precaution,' Skellsgard said. 'Once that ship's in the pipe, we can't communicate with it or the remote portal at E2. That's a thirty-hour communications blackout. It makes us twitchy.'

'And why is that?'

'Theory says there's no way that the Slashers could tap into this leg of the hyperweb even if they knew it existed. But theory might be wrong. Also, we're defending against the possibility that the E2 portal might have been compromised by what the military boys are calling "indigenous E2 hostiles".'

The needles on the analogue dials jammed hard into the red. From somewhere beyond the bubble – shining through it with X-ray intensity – came a cruel blue light, brighter than the sun. Auger turned away, holding a hand over her eyes. She could make out the sketchy, anatomical shadows of her finger bones. As quickly as it had arrived the light was gone, leaving only a tracery of pink afterimages on her retinas. Through pained eyes, Auger squinted at the bubble just in time to see a blur of motion as the incoming transport arrived. The ship rammed into the cradle like a piston. The cradle lurched, cushioning the deceleration. This happened in absolute silence. Then the cradle reached the limit of its motion and the entire glass bubble bulged visibly, compressing its huge pneumatic supports with an enormous steely groan, followed by a slow, sighing relaxation back to its original position.

'You keep mentioning E2,' Auger said. 'Is that supposed to mean something to me?'

'Earth Two,' Skellsgard said, without batting an eyelid.

Somewhere, the vacuum integrity of the bubble had been breached. Air shrieked into it, the breeze already tugging at Auger's hair. Klaxons and warning lights went berserk. Auger renewed her grip on the cage's support railing. The white-suited technicians were already scurrying back to their posts.

'That looked rough,' Auger remarked.

'They'll live,' Skellsgard replied.

'Has anyone *not* lived?'

'Once, back when we were still ironing out glitches in the system. It wasn't pretty, but we've learned a few things since then.'

The transport began to descend, passing into some kind of enclosed structure nestling in the base of the bubble. Doors sealed it from view.

'C'mon,' Skellsgard said. 'Let's take a closer look.'

Auger followed her through a network of caged ladders down to the lower level. The glass bulb of the bubble loomed over them. It had been patched and sealed in many areas, with fresh star-shaped flaws marked and dated in luminous paint.

'All this was built in a year?'

'It's been two years since they found the portal,' Skellsgard said. 'Hey, give the military guys some credit – they did make some progress before I came on the team. Even if most of it consisted of poking the portal with a series of increasingly large sticks.'

'All the same . . . I'm still pretty impressed.'

'Well, don't be. We've been as clever as we can be, but we couldn't have achieved any of this without a healthy dose of Slasher know-how. And I don't just mean the kind of intelligence we got from Peter.'

'What other kind is there?'

'Technical assistance,' Skellsgard said. 'Contraband technology. Not just the obvious stuff like the robots, but control gear – cybernetics, nanotech, all the stuff we need to interface with the pathological-matter mechanisms of the original portal.'

'How did you steal that kind of thing?'

'We didn't. We asked nicely and we got it.'

Beneath the bubble, the newly arrived transport emerged from the airlock structure, lowering on a piston-driven platform. The cylindrical craft was shaped like an artillery shell, its skin a rococo crawl of complex pewter-coloured machinery. There was evidence of damage. Hinged banks of machinery packed around the cylinder were either mangled or missing entirely, sheared off leaving patches of bright metal. Various panels and ports had been ripped free, exposing scorched, frayed viscera of wiring and fuel lines. The whole thing still smelled faintly of burning oil.

'Told you it was a rough crossing,' Skellsgard said. 'But she should be good for another round-trip, once we get her patched up again.'

'How many trips did it take for her to get into that state?'

'One. But it's not *usually* that bad.'

The ship slid sideways on its platform. Two of the three snake robots slinked over to it, weapons and sensors popping out of their head spheres. A gang of white-clad technicians were already fussing over the transport, plugging bits of equipment into it and making cautious hand gestures to each other. One of them shone a torch into the dark patch that was one of the cabin windows. Meanwhile, one of four intact transports slid over from a storage rack, guided by other technicians. Auger watched as it moved up into the airlock, disappearing and then re-appearing inside the recovery bubble, with its nose aimed towards the far wall. The pressure leak had already been fixed and most of the klaxons had now fallen silent. Odd as it seemed, it all had the feeling of business as usual.

'What'll happen now?' Auger asked.

'They'll run some pre-flight checks, some tests on the ship and the weather conditions in the link. If everything behaves itself, we'll be looking at an insertion in about six hours.'

'Insertion,' Auger repeated thoughtfully, looking at the blunt machine and the narrowing shaft it was aimed at. 'It's all very phallic, isn't it?'

'I know,' Skellsgard said confidingly, 'but what can you do? The boys must have their toys.'

She opened a cabinet and pulled out two white smocks. She passed one to Auger and donned the other one, closing the Velcro seams tightly. 'Let's see how they're doing, shall we?'

With the snake robots still monitoring events, the technicians used a variety of heavy-duty tools to open the ship's airlock. It finally gave way with a gasp of equalising air pressure, then swung open and aside on complex hinges. Warm red light spilled from the interior of the transport. One of the technicians climbed aboard, then re-emerged a minute or two later accompanied by a cropped-haired woman dressed in what looked like the interior layer of an environment suit. The woman supported one arm with the other, as if she had fractured or broken a bone. A man emerged behind her, his face pale and drawn, etched with what looked like years of fatigue. Skellsgard pushed through the retinue of technicians and spoke briefly to the two passengers before giving them both a reassuring hug. A medical team had appeared from somewhere and began fussing over the two arrivals as soon as Skellsgard had finished with them.

'They had it pretty rough,' she told Auger. 'Hit some bad throat turbulence during the insertion at the other end. But they'll live, which is what matters.'

'I thought hyperweb travel was supposed to be routine.'

'It is – if you have the experience that the Slashers do. But we've only been doing this for a year. They can squeeze a liner through their portals and not touch the sides. For us, it's a major headache just to get one of these dinky little ships through in one piece.'

'What were you saying about Slasher technology just now? How can there be Slasher involvement with this if you say they don't even know about this place?'

'We have our share of sympathisers amongst moderate Slashers, people who think the aggressive expansionism needs a moderating influence.'

'Defectors and traitors,' Auger said scornfully.

'Defectors and traitors like me,' said a man's voice from behind them.

Auger turned to face a slender, sleekly muscled individual of uncertain age. He moved within a silver cloud of attendant machines, twinkling at the limit of vision. Auger stepped back, but the man raised a reassuring hand and closed his eyes. The cloud of machines diminished, sucked back into his pores like a time-lapse explosion in reverse.

Standing before her now, he looked almost human.

The latest generation of Slashers – as Auger had forgotten to her cost with Cassandra – were often indistinguishable from children. This neotenous trend was a matter of efficient resource utilisation: smaller people not only used fewer consumables but were also easier to move around – an important factor even given the near-limitless power of the Slasher bleed-drive. But this Slasher man looked fully adult, albeit youthful. Either he predated the neotenics (and their unstable prototypes, the war babies) or he belonged to one of the factions that retained some nostalgic bond with old-style humanity.

He had flawless, unlined skin the colour of honey, and liquid brown and slightly sad-looking eyes that none the less glittered with an easy enthusiasm. Despite the chamber being too cold for Auger's tastes, the man wore only a single layer of clothing: simple white trousers and a white shirt loosely cinched across his chest.

'This is Niagara,' said Skellsgard. 'As you might have gathered, he's a citizen of the Federation of Polities.'

'It's all right,' Niagara said. 'I won't be the least bit offended if you call me a Slasher. You probably regard the term as an insult.'

'Isn't it?' Auger asked, surprised.

'Only if you want it to be.' Niagara made a careful gesture, like some religious benediction: a diagonal slice across his chest and a stab to the heart. 'A slash and a dot,' he said. 'I doubt it means anything to you, but this was once the mark of an alliance of progressive thinkers linked together by one of the very first computer networks. The Federation of Polities can trace its existence right back to that fragile collective, in the early decades of the Void Century. It's less a stigma than a mark of community.'

'And do you care about that community?' Auger asked.

'In a broad sense, yes. But I'm not above betraying it if I think its longer term interests are best served that way. How much do you know about the current tensions in the Polities?'

'Enough.'

'Well, let me refresh your memory on the basics. There are now two opposing factions within the Federation: the aggressors and the moderates. Both parties broadly support the same goal of repairing the Earth. Where they differ is in their approach to the USNE. The moderates are happy to negotiate access to Earth via reciprocal deals: access to the hyperweb, licensed use of bleed-drive and UR technologies, that sort of thing.'

'Eve was only tempted by one apple,' Auger said. 'The USNE still remembers what your brilliant machines did to our planet.'

'None the less, the offer is on the table. As you'll have gathered from your dealings with Cassandra, the moderates are serious about this proposal.'

'And the aggressors?'

'The aggressors take the view that the USNE will never sign a deal with the moderates – that there are too many people who think like *you*, Verity. So why wait for something that will never happen? Why not just take Earth now, by force?'

'They wouldn't.'

'They can and they will. The only thing stopping them has been a certain trepidation: the fear that the Threshers would destroy Earth rather than let it fall into Slasher hands. A "scorched-earth" policy in the most literal sense. Tanglewood is more than just an orbital community. It's also a repository for enough targeted megatonnage to turn the Earth into a glowing cinder.'

'So what's changed?'

'Everything,' Nigara said. 'For one thing, the battle planners think they may be able to take Tanglewood quickly enough to prevent those warheads from being deployed en masse. Even if they can't, the new models for repairing the Earth suggest that the warhead strike could be . . . tolerated. We can brush radioactivity under the carpet using continental subduction zones. And when we restock the planet, the re-introduced organisms will be modified to tolerate an enhanced level of background radiation.'

Auger shuddered, imagining what that kind of tectonic reorganisation implied for her beloved cities. 'So an invasion is inevitable?'

'I'm saying it is rather more likely now than it was six months ago. That's why some of us – moderates – have long advocated a strengthening of the Thresher position. Call it a deterrent.'

'And it's that simple? You help us make this alien junk work just so that we will have a chance of standing up to your own people when the shit comes down?'

'Would it help if I made it sound more complicated than it really is?'

'Excuse me if I don't take you at your word, Niagara, but I've only met two Slashers in my life and one of them was a lying little shit.'

'If it's any consolation,' he said, 'Cassandra is one of the staunchest moderates in the entire movement. If you ever needed a friend in the Polities, she's it.'

Skellsgard interposed herself between Auger and the Slasher, holding up her hands as if blocking a fight. 'I know this comes as a shock,' she said to Auger, 'but they really aren't all villains who'd sooner see us wiped out of existence.'

'Believe me, I sympathise with your position,' Niagara said to Auger. 'I know that terraforming Earth would erase your life's work. I'm simply of the opinion that the end would justify the means.'

'Do you believe that, Niagara: that the end always justifies the means?' Auger asked.

'Mostly,' he said. 'And some would say that – judging by your own track record – you share something of the same philosophy.'

'Over your dead body.'

'Or the dead body of a boy?' He shook his head. 'Sorry. That was uncalled for. But the point remains: you've always had a certain unflinching instinct for what needs to be done to achieve a particular outcome. I admire that, Verity. I think you have every chance of completing this mission.'

'Now we're getting somewhere,' she said. 'How much do *you* know about all this?'

'I know that sensitive property has gone missing at the other end of that hyperweb connection, and that you are excellently equipped to recover it.'

'Why can't you recover it?'

'Because I don't know the territory like you do. Nor does Skellsgard, or Aveling, or anyone else in this organisation. The only person who did know it well enough was Susan White, and she's dead.'

'That's a detail Caliskan didn't quite get around to telling me.'

'Would it have made a difference to your decision?'

'It might.'

'Then he was right not to mention it. But there's more to my answer than you might be aware of. It's not just that I don't know the territory. I can't even enter it – I would die if I tried.'

'And me?'

'You won't find it a problem.' Niagara turned to face the transport that had just been loaded into the bubble. Technicians were still attending to various details around the outside, but everything about their actions suggested that all was going according to plan.

'You want me to get in that thing, don't you? Without a clue as to what's at the other end.'

'It's a thirty-hour journey,' Niagara said. 'There'll be plenty of time to catch up on the way.'

'Can I back out?'

'It's a little late for that now, don't you think?' Without waiting for an answer from Auger, he turned his attention to Skellsgard. 'Is she ready for her language lesson?'

'Aveling said to do it now. That way she'll have time for it to bed in before she reaches E2.'

'What language lesson?' Auger asked.

Niagara raised a hand. A mist of twinkling silver machines erupted from his palm and crossed the space to Auger's head. She felt the onset of a bright shining migraine, as if her skull was a fortress being stormed by an army in flashing chrome armour, and then she felt nothing at all.

She came round to a headache, a falling sensation and a voice in her ears speaking a language she should not be able to understand.

'*Wie heisst Du?*'

'*Ich heisse Auger . . . Verity Auger.*' The words slipped out of her mouth with ridiculous ease.

'Good' the voice continued, in English this time. 'Excellent, in fact. That's taken very nicely.' It was Maurya Skellsgard speaking, sitting to her left in the confined space of what she guessed must be the hyperweb transport. On Auger's other side, in the third of the three seats, was Aveling.

They were in free fall.

'What's happening?' Auger asked.

'What's happening,' Aveling said, 'is that you were speaking German. Niagara's little machines rewired your language centre.'

'You have French as well,' Skellsgard added.

'I already *had* French,' Auger replied huffily.

'You had an academic understanding of written French skewed to towards the later years of the Void Century,' Skellsgard corrected. 'But now you can really speak it.'

Auger's headache intensified, as if someone had just tapped a very small tuning fork against her skull and made it ring. 'I wouldn't have agreed to have this . . .' She wanted to say 'shit', but the word stalled somewhere between her brain and her voice box. 'This *horrid* stuff in me.' Where the hell had 'horrid' come from, she wondered?

'It was either have it or forfeit the mission,' Aveling said. 'In thirty hours you'll be in Paris, acting alone, with only your wits to help you. No weapons, no comms, no AI assistance. The only help we can give you is language.'

'I don't want machines in my head.'

'In which case,' Skellsgard said, 'it's your lucky day. They've already been flushed out, leaving only the neural structures they created. The downside is that those structures won't last for ever – two, maybe three days once you get to Paris. Then they'll start eroding.'

Curiosity got the better of Auger. 'Why not leave the machines in, if it makes so much difference?'

'Same reason Niagara can't come with us,' Skellsgard replied. 'The censor wouldn't let them through.'

'The censor?'

'You'll see it soon enough,' Aveling said, 'so don't worry your pretty little head about it. That's *our* job.'

Auger felt the buzzing, slightly brittle alertness that came with too much coffee and too much intense study. Once, about fifteen years earlier, she had studied mathematics so furiously that after an evening manipulating complex bracketed equations, simplifying forms and extracting common terms, her brain had actually started to apply the same rules to spoken language, as if a sentence could be bracketed and simplified like some quadratic formula for radioisotope decay. That was how she felt now. She only had to look at a colour or shape and her new language structures would gleefully shriek the corresponding word into her skull, in a mixed cacophony of German, French and English.

'I could get very angry about this—'

'Or you could just get over it and accept that it had to be done,' Skellsgard said bluntly. 'I promise you there'll be no side effects.'

Auger knew that it was senseless to protest any further. The machines had already come in and done their worst. The simple fact was that had this ever been presented to her as a rational choice, she would still have chosen it over the tribunal.

If that made her a hypocrite, ready to accept Slasher science when it suited her, so be it.

'I'm sorry if all this seems abrupt,' Skellsgard said sympathetically. 'It's just that we really didn't have time to sit around and debate things. We need that lost property back in safe hands as soon as possible.'

Auger forced a sort of calm upon herself. 'I take it we're on our way?'

'It was a successful insertion,' Aveling said.

They were sitting three abreast, surrounded by instruments, controls and fold-down panels. The technology was a curious mixture of the very robust and the very fragile-looking modern, including some equipment that had obviously come straight from Slasher sources. Holding things together were bolts, nylon tie-lines and spitlike swabs of heavy-duty epoxy. Aveling had one hand on a joystick mounted on a fold-down panel in front of him. Above the panel was a flat screen displaying a series of irregular concentric lines, like a drunkenly fashioned cobweb, with the lines slowly oozing out towards the edge of the screen. Some kind of navigation system, Auger guessed, representing their flight through the hyperweb. Of the outside view nothing could be seen, since the ship's armoured shutters were locked tight.

It was about as exciting as a ride in an elevator.

'Well, now that we're all in this together,' she said, 'I presume you can tell me what it's all about.'

'What we generally find,' Skellsgard said, 'is that it's easier if we show you. That way we skip the whole "you can't expect me to believe this shit" stage.'

'What if I promise not to doubt a word that you say? After all, I've already seen the artefacts in Caliskan's office. I'm pretty sure they weren't faked.'

'No, they were all real.'

'Which means they must have originated somewhere. Caliskan said they hadn't been preserved, and yet they appeared to come from somewhere around nineteen fifty-nine.'

'Which would tend to imply . . .' Skellsgard prompted.

'That you've found a way back to nineteen fifty-nine.' She paused, choosing her next words with care. 'Or at least something that looks a lot *like* nineteen fifty-nine, even if it isn't exactly right in all the details. Is that far from the mark?'

'No, it's pretty close, actually.'

'And this version of nineteen fifty-nine is inside the ALS object that Peter talked about. The one he said you'd found a way into.'

'They told us you were good,' Skellsgard said.

'So where does Paris come into it?'

'At the end of this hyperweb is something very like Paris. You'll enter it and make contact with an individual named Blanchard.'

Auger kept her voice calm, taking this one step at a time. 'Someone else from the team, like White?'

'No,' Skellsgard said, glancing at Aveling. 'Blanchard's E2 indigenous.'

'Meaning what?'

'Meaning he grew up inside it. Meaning he has no idea he isn't living in the real Paris, on the real Earth, in the real twentieth century.'

Something like ice passed through Auger. 'How many are there like him?'

'About three billion. But don't let that put you off.'

'All you have to do,' Aveling said, 'is find Blanchard and recover the item that Susan White passed to him for safekeeping. It won't be difficult. We'll give you an address, which will be within easy reach of your point of entry. Blanchard will be expecting you.'

'I thought you said—'

Aveling cut her off. 'You'll pose as Susan White's sister. She'll already have told him to hand over the goods to you if you show up. Aside from anything else, that's why we needed a woman.'

Auger thought for a moment, trying to assimilate all this new and puzzling information. Her mind was full of questions, but she quickly decided that as much as she wanted to know every detail of the task, she had best begin with the basics.

'And the nature of this lost property?'

'Just some papers in a tin,' Aveling said. 'They'll mean nothing to Blanchard, but everything to us. You persuade Blanchard to give you the tin. You make sure the papers are inside. Then you return to us – with the papers – and we put you on the first transport home.'

'You make it sound so simple.'

'It is.'

'Then why do I have the nagging suspicion that there must be a catch?'

'Because there is,' Skellsgard said. 'We don't know for sure what happened to Susan, but we do know that she felt threatened, and that she gave those papers to Blanchard for safekeeping. There's a chance she was murdered.'

Aveling withdrew his attention from the oozing lines of the navigational display and sent Skellsgard an irritated look. 'She didn't need to know it was murder,' he said. 'If it *was* murder.'

'I felt she did,' Skellsgard replied, shrugging.

'Well,' Auger said, 'was it murder or not?'

'She fell,' Aveling said. 'That's all we know.'

'Or was pushed,' Skellsgard said darkly.

'I'd really like to know which it was,' Auger insisted.

'It doesn't matter,' Aveling said. 'All you need to know is that E2 is hostile territory – which is something White forgot. She was careful to begin with: they always are. Then she exceeded the remit of her mission, took risks and ended up dead.'

'What kind of risks?'

Before Aveling could get a word in edgeways, Skellsgard said, 'Susan felt she was on to something – something big, something significant. Because she wouldn't return to the portal, all we got from her were cryptic messages, things scribbled on postcards. If she'd at least taken the time to build a radio sender, or return to the base station, she could have told us something more concrete. But she was too busy chasing leads, and in the end it got her killed.'

'Supposition,' Aveling said.

'If we don't think she was on to something,' Skellsgard said, 'why are we in such a hurry to get those papers back? It's because we think there might be something in them, isn't it?'

'It's because we can't risk cultural contamination,' Aveling corrected. 'Analysed with the right mindset, the papers might reveal White's origin. We don't know how indiscreet she was. Until we get the papers, we're in the dark.'

Skellsgard looked at Auger. 'I guess all I'm saying is . . . take care out there, OK? Just get in and do the job. We want you back in one piece.'

'Really?' Auger asked.

'Oh, sure. Can you imagine what the return trip would be like if I only had Aveling for company?'

NINE

It was the middle of the morning by the time Floyd returned Custine to Susan White's apartment, heavy toolkit in one hand. Custine's practicality never ceased to amaze him: the man could turn his hand to almost anything, whether it was repairing the Mathis, fixing the plumbing in their apartment or attempting to repair the jury-rigged receiving equipment of a dead spy. Floyd knew a little about fixing boats, but that was about his limit. He had questioned Custine once about where this practicality came from, but the only explanation Custine had offered was that a certain skill with electricity and metal was very useful for an interrogator in the Crime Squad.

That was as much as Floyd wanted to know.

He waited in the car while Custine was let in, then drummed his fingers on the steering wheel for another five minutes until Custine's form loomed in the fifth-floor window. Custine did not expect to get any results before the middle of the afternoon, but they had arranged to speak by telephone at two regardless.

Floyd pulled away from Blanchard's street and drove to Montparnasse, negotiating the smaller side streets until he found the house where he had left Greta the night before. In daylight the house seemed a little more cheerful – but only a little. Greta opened the door and escorted him up to the sparsely stocked kitchen that the tenant Sophie had shown him around the night before.

'I called the telephone company,' Floyd said. 'It should be working now.'

'So it is,' Greta said, surprised. 'Someone rang through on it only an hour ago, but I was so distracted that I didn't really think about it. How did you persuade the company to reconnect her? She still can't afford to pay them.'

'I told them to put the charges on my bill.'

'You did?' She cocked her head. 'That's awfully decent of you. You're not exactly rolling in money either.'

'Don't worry about it. It's not as if . . .' His voice trailed off.

'Not as if it'll be for ever?' she finished for him. 'No. You're right. It won't be.'

'I didn't mean to sound callous.'

'It's all right.' Now she sounded cross with herself. 'I'm taking it out on whoever's within firing range. You don't deserve this.'

'Don't worry about it. You're doing a pretty swell job from where I'm standing. How is Marguerite today?'

Greta spread honey on to a slice of buttered toast. 'About the same as yesterday, according to Sophie. The doctor's already given her a shot of morphine for the day. I don't know why they can't give it to her later, so that she could at least get a good night's sleep.'

'Maybe they're worried that she'd get too good a night's sleep,' Floyd said.

'That wouldn't be such a bad thing,' Greta said quietly. She was dressed all in white today, her black hair tied back in a white bow. The bow shone luminously, like something in a washing-powder commercial. Greta passed him the toast, then licked her fingers clean with girlish little pops of her lips. 'Thanks for staying with me last night, Wendell,' she said. 'It was kind.'

'You needed the company.' He bit into the toast, tilting it to avoid spilling honey on his shirt. 'About Marguerite. Would it be all right if I said hello to her? I know what you said last night, but I really would like her to know that I care.'

'She may not even remember you.'

'I'm ready for that.'

'Well, all right,' Greta said heavily. 'I suppose she's as sharp now as she'll ever be. But don't stay too long, will you? She gets tired very easily.'

'I'll keep it brief.'

She led him upstairs, Floyd finishing off the toast as he went. The floorboards creaked as he made his way across the landing. Greta eased open the bedroom door, slipped inside and spoke very softly to Marguerite. Floyd heard the old woman answer in French. She spoke nothing else, not even German. She had been born in the Alsace region, Greta had told him once, and had married a German cabinet-maker who had died in the mid-thirties. At home they had spoken only French.

When things became difficult for Greta's family in Germany – Greta was Jewish on her mother's side – they had dispatched her to live with Marguerite. She had arrived in Paris in the summer of 1939, when she was nine years old, and had lived in the city for most of the last twenty years. There had been a great deal of anti-German sentiment after the failed invasion of 1940, but Greta had weathered most of it, speaking French with a pronounced Parisian accent that revealed nothing of her true origins. On first meeting her, Floyd had never guessed that she was German. The disclosure of that secret to him had been the first of many intimacies, each of which had brought a small, stabbing thrill of mutual trust.

She called to him from inside the room. 'You can come in now, Floyd.'

The door opened wider to reveal Sophie, who was just leaving, carrying a tray with her. He stepped aside to let her pass, then walked into the shuttered quiet of the bedroom. There were subtle squares and oblongs on the walls where paintings, photographs and mirrors had been taken down. The bed had been made neatly around Marguerite, presumably in readiness for the doctor's visit, and the old lady was now sitting almost upright, supported by three or four plump pillows. She wore a high-collared, long-sleeved floral nightgown that seemed to belong to the nineteenth century. Her white hair had been combed back from her brow and her cheeks dabbed lightly with rouge. Floyd could just about make out Marguerite's face in the muted light, but what he saw was a thin, cursory sketch of the woman he had known. He thought it would have been easier if there had been no similarity at all, but she was recognisable, and that made it all the more difficult.

'This is Wendell,' Greta said gently. 'You remember Wendell, don't you, Aunt?'

Floyd presented himself, holding his fedora in both hands like an offering.

'Of course I remember him,' Marguerite said. Her eyes were surprisingly bright and clear. 'How are you, Floyd? We always called you Floyd rather than Wendell, didn't we?'

'I'm . . . doing swell,' he said, shuffling his feet. 'How are you feeling?'

'I am all right now.' Her voice was a rasp. He had to concentrate to make out her words. 'But the nights are difficult. I never imagined sleeping could take so much energy from me. I'm not sure how much I have left.'

'You're a strong lady,' he said. 'I'm sure you've got a lot more energy than you think.'

She placed one of her thin, birdlike hands atop the other and rested them on her stomach. The newspaper was spread across her lap like a shawl, open at the Parisian news pages. 'I wish I felt that were true.'

She knows, Floyd thought. She might have been frail and she might not always have quite this good a grip on what was happening around her, but she knew perfectly well that she was ill, and that her illness was never going to let her leave this room.

'What's it like outside, Floyd?' Marguerite asked. 'I listened to the rain all night.'

'It's clearing up a bit,' he said. 'The sun's coming out and . . .' His mouth suddenly felt dry. Why had he insisted on this visit? He had nothing to say to Marguerite that she must not already have heard a hundred times before, from similarly well-intentioned visitors. He realised, with a spasm of shame, that he hadn't come up here to make her feel better, but to make himself feel better instead. He was going to stand before her and never once allude to the fact that she was terminally ill, as if there was an elephant in the room that no one dared acknowledge. 'Well,' he said, fumbling for words, 'it's beautiful when the sun comes out. The whole city looks like a painting.'

'The colours must be beautiful. I've always loved the spring. It's nearly as breathtaking as the autumn.'

'I don't think there's a time of year when I don't love this city,' Floyd said. 'Except perhaps January.'

'Greta reads the paper to me,' Marguerite said, patting the pages spread before her. 'She only wants to read the light news, but I want to know it all – the bad as well as the good. I don't envy you young people.'

Floyd smiled, trying to remember the last time anyone had called him young. 'Things don't seem too bad to me,' he said.

'You weren't here in the thirties, were you?'

'No, I wasn't.'

'Then – with all due respect – you probably have no idea what it was really like.'

Greta glanced at him warningly, but Floyd shrugged good-naturedly. 'No. I have no idea.'

'It was good, in many ways,' Marguerite said. 'The Depression was over. We all had more money. There was more to eat. Nicer clothes. Music we could dance to. We could afford a car and a holiday in the country once a year. A wireless and a gramophone, even a refrigerator. But there was also a meanness to those times. There was always an undercurrent of hatred bubbling just beneath the surface.' She turned her head towards her niece. 'It was hatred that brought Greta to Paris.'

'The Fascists got what they deserved,' Floyd said.

'My husband lived long enough to see those monsters come to power. He saw through their lies and promises, but he also knew that they spoke to something nasty and squalid in the human spirit. Something in all of us. We want to hate those who are not like us. All we need is an excuse, a whisper in the ear.'

'Not all of us,' Floyd said.

'That's what a lot of good people said in the thirties,' Marguerite replied. 'That the message of hatred would only be heeded by the ignorant and those who were already filled with bile. But it wasn't like that. It took strength of mind not to let yourself be poisoned by those lies, and not everyone had that strength. Even fewer people had the courage to do something about it; to actually stand up to the hatemongers.'

'Was your husband one of those brave people?' Floyd asked.

'No,' she said. 'He wasn't. He was one of the millions who said and did nothing, and that's how he went to his grave.'

Floyd did not know what to say. He looked at the woman in the bed, feeling the force of history streaming through her like a current.

'All I'm saying,' she continued, 'is that the message is seductive. My husband said that unless those hatemongers were annihilated – wiped from the Earth, along with all their poison – they would always come back, like weeds.' She touched the newspaper on the bed. 'The weeds are returning, Floyd. We mowed the lawn in nineteen forty, but we didn't put down the weedkiller. Twenty years later, they're back.'

'I know there are a lot of people saying bad things,' Floyd said. 'But no one really takes them seriously.'

'No one took them seriously in the twenties,' she countered.

'There are laws now,' Floyd said. 'Anti-hate laws.'

'Which aren't enforced.' She tapped the paper with one sharp-nailed finger. 'Look at this story: a young man was beaten to death yesterday because he dared to speak up against the hatemongers.'

Floyd's voice suddenly sounded as weak as Marguerite's. 'A young man?'

'By the railway station. They found his body last night.'

'No!'

Greta slipped her hand around his sleeve. 'We should be going now, Floyd.'

He couldn't say anything.

Marguerite folded the paper and pushed it from the bed. 'I didn't mean to lecture you,' she said, with a kindness that cut him to the core. 'I just wanted to say how little I envy you now. There were storm clouds on the horizon twenty years ago, Floyd, and they're gathering again.' Almost as an afterthought, she said, 'Of course, it's not too late to do something about them, if enough people care. I wonder how many people walked past that poor young man last night, when he was in need of help?'

Greta edged him away from the bed. 'Floyd has to go now, Aunt Marguerite.'

She reached out and took his hand. 'It was nice of you to come up and see me. You'll come back, won't you?'

'Of course,' Floyd said, forcing a smile to disguise his discomfort.

'Bring me some strawberries, won't you? This room could do with brightening up.'

'I'll bring you some strawberries,' he promised.

Greta led him downstairs, still holding his arm. 'That's how it is with her,' she said, when they were safely out of earshot. 'She's sharp as a tack about the news, but she doesn't even know what time of year it is. You're lucky she remembered who you were. Let's just hope she doesn't remember asking for strawberries.'

'I'll find her something.'

'At this time of year? Don't worry about it, Floyd. She most likely won't remember a thing about it the next time you go up there.'

If she sounded cruel, Floyd thought, it was only because she loved Marguerite so much.

They sat down in the kitchen again. A pigeon was cooing on the windowsill. Greta picked up a piece of stale bread and threw it at the glass, scaring the bird away in a bustle of grey feathers.

'It might not be the same young man,' she said, guessing what was on Floyd's mind. 'Maybe you don't read the papers these days, but people are always getting beaten up.'

'We both know it was the same kid, so why pretend otherwise?'

'We went over this last night. If you'd tried to do anything, they'd have cut you up.'

'The old me might have tried.'

'The old you would have had more sense.'

'You're just trying to make me feel better about it.' Floyd looked up at the ceiling, picturing the bedroom he had just visited, the ordered placement of its furniture and the stillness of its occupant. 'She might not have much of a grip on the time of year, but she knows how things are going.'

'Maybe it's not as bad as she fears. Old people always think the world's going to ruin. It's their job.'

'Maybe they're right,' Floyd replied.

Greta bent down to pick up the bread she had just thrown at the pigeon. 'Perhaps they are. And maybe that's as good a reason as any to think about leaving Paris.'

'Nice segue.'

'I don't suppose you've given any more thought to what we talked about?'

'I mentioned it to Custine,' Floyd said.

'How did he take it?'

'He took it well. The same way he takes everything.'

'André's a good man,' Greta said. 'I'm sure he'd do a fine job of running the agency.'

'He'd probably have Paris eating out of his hand within the year.'

'So why not give him the chance?'

'I've been here twenty years,' Floyd said. 'If I leave now, am I saying that the last twenty years of my life were a mistake?'

'Only if you want to think of them that way.'

'I'm not sure there's any other way.'

'It's not the same city you arrived in,' Greta said. 'Things have changed, and not many of them for the better. It wouldn't be an admission of defeat. How old are you now, Floyd? Thirty-nine? Forty? It's not so old. Not if you don't want it to be.'

'Have you had a chance to look at the papers in that box?'

'Nice segue yourself,' she said, allowing him a tolerant smile. 'All right. We'll talk about it later. Yes, I have looked in the box.'

'Anything you can tell me?'

'Can we talk about it somewhere else?' Greta asked. 'This place is getting to me. Sophie's here for the rest of the morning. I could really use some fresh air.'

Floyd reached for his fedora. 'Then let's go for a stroll.'

Floyd found a place to park the Mathis on rue de Rivoli, near the Louvre. The rain had given up for now, although the clouds on the edge of the city had the inky look of thunder about them. But it was pleasant enough on the Right Bank, with the sun doing its utmost to dry the pavements and provide some late-season business for the ice-cream vendors. It was one of those autumn days that Floyd never took for granted, knowing that there might not be another like it before winter stole slyly in.

'Well,' he said, feeling his mood improve. 'What it's going to be: culture or a stroll in the Tuileries?'

'Culture? You wouldn't know culture if it bit you on the nose. Anyway, I said I wanted some fresh air. The paintings can wait. They've been there long enough.'

'Suits me. More than half an hour in any public institution and I start feeling like one of the exhibits.'

Greta took the biscuit tin with her, tucking it under one arm as they walked. The Tuileries Gardens ran between the museum and place de la Concorde, stretching in an elegant formal ribbon along the Right Bank. They had been part of the city since the time of Catherine de Medici, four hundred years earlier. It always amazed Floyd to think of these geometric green spaces enduring through all the changes that had overtaken Paris in that time. The gardens were one of Floyd's favourite places in the city, especially on a quiet morning in the middle of the week.

Deckchairs had been positioned around the large octagonal basin at the western end of the gardens. Greta and Floyd found themselves a pair of adjacent chairs and started scattering the scraps of stale bread she had rescued from the kitchen.

'I don't know what you want me to make of this,' Greta said, tapping the tin. 'I mean, if you go looking for something odd or unusual, you're almost bound to find it.'

'Tell me what you have. I'll worry about making sense of it.'

'What was the name of the woman again? Susan something? I have her Christian name on the postcard, that's all.'

'Susan White,' Floyd said. 'If that was her real name.'

'You're really convinced she was up to something?'

'More than I was yesterday. Custine's still trying to make sense of what she did to the wireless set in her room.'

'Well,' Greta said, 'I don't mind admitting that this is as good a way as any to take my mind off my aunt.'

'Whatever helps.' Floyd tore off a chunk of stale crust and tossed it to a gathering of anxious, squabbling male ducks. 'Come on, then, what have you got for me?'

'I can't help you with the maps and sketches, but I might be able to shed some light on this.' She fished in the tin until she found the letter printed on headed paper.

'That's the one from the steelworks in Berlin?' Floyd asked.

'Kaspar Metals, yes.'

'So what's it all about?'

'All I have to go on is this one letter,' Greta said, 'so there's necessarily some guesswork involved. But it looks to me as if Susan White got wind of a contract that Kaspar Metals was handling.'

'Not one she had a role in herself?'

'No. Definitely looks as if there's a third party involved. Judging from the letter, White must have already dug up some information about this contract, enough that she wouldn't look like a complete outsider.'

A small, formal party approached the duck pond. There were eight or nine suited men, all wearing trilbies, surrounding an elderly man in a wheelchair who was being pushed along by a sturdy nurse.

'Tell me about the contract,' Floyd said.

'Well, it doesn't go into any great detail – that must have been covered in an earlier letter – but it looks as if the firm was being asked to cast a big, solid chunk of aluminium. Three big chunks, actually – and the quote talks about additional costs for machining to the desired spherical shape.'

Floyd watched the old man in the wheelchair throw bread into the pond with trembling hands, drawing the ducks away. 'There was a diagram in the tin,' he said. 'Something round. Must have been part of the same caboodle.'

'You look disappointed,' she remarked.

'Only because I thought we might be on to something, that maybe the plan was for a bomb. But if the casting is solid . . .' He shrugged.

'There's some talk about the objects forming part of an artistic installation, but that could be a cover.'

'None of this makes any sense,' Floyd said. 'If she was an American spy, why would she have needed a German firm to make those things, no matter what they're meant for? There must be a hundred American firms that could have done the same work.'

'Look,' Greta said, 'just suppose for a minute that she was a spy. What do they do, apart from spying? They also keep tabs on the activities of other spies.'

'Agreed,' Floyd said. 'But—'

'What if she was put here to keep her eye on another operation? White finds out something about the Berlin contract. She doesn't necessarily know all the details, but she knows she has to find out more about it. So she writes to Kaspar Metals, posing as someone connected to the organisation that arranged the initial order.'

'Possible,' Floyd allowed.

Greta tossed some more bread into the duck pond. 'Actually, there is another thing I should mention.'

'Go on.'

'The letter also covers costs for transportation and delivery of the finished goods. Now, this is the interesting part: it was broken down into three separate billing items. Somewhere in Berlin, somewhere in Paris and somewhere in Milan.'

'I don't remember seeing addresses in that letter.'

'You didn't. The man who wrote the letter must have assumed that both parties already had that information.'

Floyd had been wondering where the Milan connection would come in. 'Except *we* don't have that information,' he said. 'All we have is a couple of lines on a map of Europe.' He remembered the L-shaped figure, with the neatly marked distances between the three cities. 'I still don't know what the markings on that map mean, but they obviously relate to the work being done by that factory in some way.'

'One last thing,' Greta said. 'That train ticket. It was for the overnight express to Berlin, and it hasn't been used.'

'Is there a date on the ticket?'

'Issued on September fifteenth for travel from Gare du Nord on the twenty-first. She'd reserved a sleeping compartment.'

'She died on the twentieth,' Floyd said, recalling the details in his notebook. 'Blanchard said that she gave him the tin on the fifteenth or sixteenth – he couldn't be sure which. She must just have booked the ticket and never used it.'

'I wonder why she didn't simply get on the first train to Berlin, rather than book passage on one that wasn't due to leave for four or five days?'

'Maybe she had other business she had to attend to first, or maybe she'd called ahead and made an arrangement to visit the factory on a particular day. Either way, she knew she wasn't getting on that train for a few days, but she also knew she was in danger and that the tin might fall into the wrong hands.'

'Has it occurred to you, Floyd, that if someone killed her because of what was in that tin, they might do it again?'

The party with the elderly man had retreated from the duck pond, the wheelchair crunching away across the gravelled promenade in the general direction of the Orangerie. Beyond the party, looming above the trees lining the Seine, the slick, wet roof of the Gare d'Orsay on the Left Bank shone in the sunlight. Despite its name, it was many years since the Gare d'Orsay had been a railway station. There had been vague plans to turn it into a museum, but in the end the city authorities had decided that the most effective use of the grand old building would be as a prison for high-profile political detainees. Seeing the prison, something tugged at this memory, some elusive connection waiting to be completed.

He dished out the remainder of the bread to the few ducks that had stayed loyal. 'I know there are risks. But I can't just drop the case because some people might not want me to succeed.'

Greta studied him carefully. 'How much does this dogged determination have to do with what Marguerite just told you?'

'Hey,' Floyd said defensively, 'this isn't about anything other than getting a job done for a client. A job that happens to pay pretty well, I might add.'

'So that's all it boils down to: money?'

'Money and curiosity,' he admitted.

'No amount of money will make up for a broken neck. Take what you have and go to the authorities. Give them all the evidence and let them piece things together.'

'Now you sound like Custine.'

'Maybe he has a point. Think about it, Floyd. Don't get in too deep. You're a big man, but you're not a strong swimmer.'

'I'll know when I'm in too deep,' he said.

Greta shook her head. 'I know you too well. You'll only realise you're in too deep when you start drowning. But what's the point of arguing? I'm hungry. Let's walk to the Champs-Elysées: there's a place there that does good pancakes. You can buy me an Esquimo ice cream along the way. Then you can take me back to Montparnasse.'

Floyd surrendered, offering her a hand. They set off in the direction of the avenue, Floyd watching as the wind whipped up in the distance and hoisted someone's umbrella into the sky.

'How's the band doing?' Greta asked.

'The band ceased to exist when you left,' Floyd said. 'Since then we've not exactly been snowed under with offers.'

'I was only ever one part of it.'

'You're a damned good singer and a damned good guitar player. You left a big hole.'

'You and Custine are both good musicians.'

'Good doesn't cut it.'

'Well, then you're better than good.'

'Custine, maybe.'

'It's not as if you're the worst bass player in the world, either. You always knew you could make it work if you only wanted it badly enough.'

'I make the moves. I can lay down a pretty steady beat.'

'You say that like it's a bad thing. There are a hundred bands in Nice who could use a bass player like you, Floyd.'

'But I can't do anything you haven't seen before. I can't make it new.'

'Not everyone wants it new.'

'But that's the point. All we ever do is play the same old swing numbers in the same old way. I'm tired of it. Custine can barely bring himself to take out his saxophone.'

'So do something different.'

'Custine keeps trying. You know how he was always trying to get us to play that fast eight-beat stuff, when all we ever wanted to do was stay in four-four?'

'Maybe Custine was on to something.'

'He heard a guy playing here a few years ago,' Floyd said. 'Some heroin fiend from Kansas City. Looked sixty, but he was really about my age. Called himself Yardhound or Yard-dog or something. He kept playing that crazy improvisational stuff, like it was the wave of the future. But no one wanted to know.'

'Except Custine.'

'Custine said it was the music he'd always had in his head.'

'So find a way to help him play it.'

'Too fast for me,' Floyd said. 'And anyway, even if it wasn't, no one *else* wants to hear it. It's not stuff you can dance to.'

'You shouldn't give up that easily,' Greta admonished.

'It's too late. They don't even want straight jazz anymore. Half the clubs we played last year are out of business now. Maybe it's different in the States, but—'

'Some people won't ever get it,' Greta said. 'They don't want to see black people and white people getting along, let alone playing the same music. Because there's always a danger that the world might actually become a better place because of it.'

Floyd smiled. 'Your point being?'

'Those of us who care shouldn't give up that easily. Maybe we need to stick our necks out from time to time.'

'I stick my neck out for no one.'

'Not even for the music you love?'

'Maybe there was a time when I used to think jazz could save the world,' Floyd said. 'But I'm older and wiser now.'

Walking the gravel path, they passed the party with the elderly man again and something in Floyd's head clicked like a key in a well-oiled lock. Maybe it was the conversation he'd had with Marguerite, or perhaps the juxtaposition of the man and the political prison across the river, but Floyd suddenly recognised him. The man lolled forward in the wheelchair, his jaw slack, a thin worm of drool curling down his chin. His skin was glued to his skull like a single layer of papier mâché. His hands trembled with some kind of palsy. Beneath his blanket, it was said that the doctors had hacked away more than they had left behind. Whatever trickled through his veins was now more chemical than blood. But he had survived the cancers, just as he had survived that assassination attempt in May 1940, when the advance into the Ardennes had come to an inglorious end. The shape of the face was still recognisable, along with the outdated, priggish little moustache and the vain swoop of thinning hair, white now where once it had been black. It was almost twenty years since his ambitions had crashed and burnt during that disastrous summer. In the carnival of monsters that the century had produced, he was only one amongst many. He'd talked hate back then – but who hadn't? Hate was how you made things happen in those years. It was the lever that moved things. It didn't necessarily mean he believed it, or that he would have been any worse for France than any of the men who had come after him. Who could begrudge him a morning in the Tuileries Gardens, after all the time he had served in the Gare d'Orsay? He was just a sad old man now, less a figure of revulsion than one of pity.

Let him feed the ducks.

'Floyd?'

'What?'

'You were miles away.'

'Years away,' he said. 'Not quite the same thing.'

She steered him towards an ice-cream stand. Floyd dug into his pocket for a few coins.

TEN

Auger awoke to the rapid metallic popping of thruster jets, like a rivet gun. Her first thought was that something must have gone wrong, but Aveling and Skellsgard both looked alert and focused rather than alarmed, as if this was something they had encountered before.

'What's happening?' she asked groggily.

'Go back to sleep,' Aveling said.

'I want to know.'

'We're just dealing with some tunnel irregularity,' Skellsgard said, using her free hand to point to the contoured display in front of her joystick panel. She was flying now, while Aveling took a rest. The moving lines on the display panel were bunched and crimped together. 'The walls are pretty smooth most of the way through, but every now and then we come across some structure or other, which we have to steer around.'

'Structures? *Inside* a wormhole?'

'It isn't a wormhole,' Skellsgard began. 'It's a—'

'I know: it's a quasi-pseudo-para-whatnot. What I mean is, how can there be any kind of structures inside this thing, whatever it is? Isn't it smooth space-time all the way through?'

'That's what you'd expect.'

'You're the theorist. You tell me.'

'Actually, there's a good measure of guesswork involved here. The Slashers didn't tell us everything, and they probably don't have all the answers themselves.'

'So give me your best guess.'

'OK. Theory one. You see these stress-energy readings? They relate to changes in the local tunnel geometry ahead of us.'

'What are you sensing them with? Radar?'

Skellsgard shook her head. 'No. Radar – or any EM-based sensor, for that matter – doesn't work too well in the hyperweb. Photons are absorbed into the walls or scattered chaotically by interaction with the pathological matter. And looking ahead is like trying to see sunspots with your naked eye. Neutrinos or gravity-wave sensors might work better, but there isn't enough room for them in the transport. All that's left is sonar.'

'Sound?' Auger asked. 'But we're moving through a near-perfect vacuum, aren't we?'

'As near as dammit, yes. But we can persuade a kind of acoustic signal to propagate through the lining of the walls. It's like the compression wave that the transport's surfing, only about a billion times faster. It propagates through a stiffer layer, a different phase of pathological matter with a much higher rigidity. It's how we send signals down the pipe, so that we can talk to the portal at the E2 end. Trouble is, it doesn't work when a ship is in the pipe: we act as a kind of mirror, bouncing any signals back the way they came. But we *can* send our own signals up the line. They're not strong enough to reach all the way to the far portal, but they do act as a kind of feeler, sounding out obstructions and irregularities in the walls.'

'That still doesn't tell me what causes those irregularities in the first place.'

'Here, take a look at this,' Skellsgard said, directing Auger's attention to a knot of very close contour lines oozing into view on the display. 'This is the computer's best guess at the shape of an approaching irregularity in the tunnel lining, based on the echoes from the sonar. If the contours were bunched together symmetrically, we'd be looking at a constriction, a narrowing in the tunnel ahead of us. But that isn't what's happening here. There are places where the tunnel lining looks as if it's been etched away, and places where it bulges inward. Theory one says that this is symptomatic of some kind of decay of the basic fabric of the link, either due to lack of maintenance or not enough ships using it.'

'Not *enough* ships?'

'It could be that the ships are meant to perform some repair function when they pass through. That's what we call the "pipe-cleaner hypothesis".'

'Fine. What about theory two?'

'This is where it starts to get seriously speculative,' Skellsgard warned. 'Some people studying the link have made records of these irregularities, accumulating data from many transits. Of course, the data is very noisy and subject to the interpretive vagaries of the navigation system. So then they take those records and feed them into maximum-entropy software to squeeze out any latent structure. Then they take the output from *that* process and feed it into another bunch of programs designed to sniff out latent language. One such procedure is called the Zipf test: it involves plotting the logarithmic frequencies of the occurrence of different patterns seen in the walls. Random data has a Zipf slope of zero, whereas the Zipf slope of the tunnel patterning is pretty close to minus one. It means that the signals in those walls are significantly more meaningful than – say – squirrel-monkey calls, which only get down to minus point six on a Zipf plot.'

'Not conclusive, though,' Auger said.

'But the researchers don't stop there. There's another statistical property known as Shannon entropy, which even tells you how rich the communications are. Human languages – English, say, or Russian – have Shannon entropies around the eighth or ninth order. That means if I say eight or nine words in one of those languages, you can have a pretty good stab at guessing what the tenth is going to be. Dolphin calls have Shannon entropies in the range of three to four, whereas the tunnel scrawls are up at seven or eight.'

'Less complex than human language, in that case.'

'Granted,' Skellsgard said, 'but their true complexity might be masked by the errors we introduce in decoding the sonar images. Or the messages themselves may be blurred by erosion or some other process we don't understand.'

'So theory two is that the patterns are deliberate messages.'

'Yes. They might be analogous to old highway signs: speed limits, temporary restrictions, that kind of thing.'

'You're not serious.'

'You haven't heard anything yet, Auger. Want to hear theory three?'

'Oh, why not?'

'This is definitely *not* accepted wisdom, I should warn you. Theory three says that the tunnel patterns are a kind of advertising.' Auger opened her mouth to say something, but Skellsgard kept on talking. 'No, wait. Hear me out. It makes a warped kind of sense when you think about it. Why wouldn't a galactic supercivilisation have advertising? It seems to be pretty much glued to our culture, after all.'

'But adverts . . .' Auger was finding it difficult to keep a straight face.

'Think about it. Anyone travelling along one of these links is the perfect captive audience. They're locked in, sucker bait. Got nowhere else to go, no other scenery to look at. What better place to put some advertising? Hell, I'd love to know what they're selling. Maybe it's planet-building services, or stellar renewal, or the option to trade in your old black hole for a new one.'

Auger smiled. 'A supernova can happen any time. Make sure your solar system is properly insured.'

'How about: tired of the Milky Way? Why not look at some of our great properties in the Large Magellanic Clouds. The best views in the local group – and it's still within commuting distance of the galactic core.'

Auger chuckled, getting into it. 'Expansionist primates infesting your stellar neighborhood? We have the pest-control solutions you need.'

'Your old God not up to the job? Upgrade your deity now by calling . . .' Skellsgard started giggling.

'You're right – it's almost believable, isn't it?'

'Almost,' Skellsgard said. 'And I definitely prefer it to theory four.'

'Which is?'

'That the walls are covered in graffiti.'

'Goodness.' *Goodness.* Had she really said 'goodness'? Auger shook her head, like someone about to sneeze. 'Are you telling me that somebody's actually been paid to come up with that?'

'Yes. It even makes sense based on the Shannon entropies, apparently. If you look at human graffiti—'

'Enough, Skellsgard. I'd rather not hear about graffiti, human or alien.'

'It's a bit depressing, isn't it?'

'More than a bit.'

'Well, don't worry about it,' Skellsgard said, waving a hand dismissively. 'Not many people take it very seriously. There's the small problem that the tunnel patterns have a habit of changing, depending on stability conditions. Of course, it might be very clever graffiti—'

'Is there a theory five?'

'Not yet. But I'm sure someone's working on one.'

Auger laughed. Everything she knew about academia told her how true that was. Skellsgard's composure cracked as well, and it was only when they finished laughing, sighing with exhaustion and their eyes wet with tears, that Aveling opened his eyes and stared at them, his face as impassive as ever.

'Civilians.'

In the twenty-ninth hour, something changed in the spiderweb crawl of Skellsgard's stress-energy display. The contours began to arrange themselves in a systematic and intricate pattern quite unlike the asymmetric bunching and stretching caused by the tunnel markings.

'You might want to look at this,' she said.

'Is something wrong?' Auger asked.

'No. We're just coming up on something a little unusual, that's all. We always hit it somewhere between the twenty-eighth and twenty-ninth hours, although it's never in quite the same place from trip to trip.'

'More graffiti or tunnel turbulence?'

'Nope. Much too stable for that.'

Auger leaned forward, relaxing her seat buckle. She kept her voice low. Aveling was asleep, snoring lightly, and she had no particular desire to wake him up. 'So what are we looking at?'

'We're approaching a widening in the fabric of the tunnel. It's like a bubble, somewhat elongated in the direction of travel.' Skellsgard made a few micro-adjustments to their flight path, signalled by a sequenced volley of steering jets. 'At first, we didn't know what to make of it.'

Auger tried to make some sense of the slowly moving contours, but she suspected it would need weeks of practice to untangle the information into anything approaching a three-dimensional image of their surroundings.

'And now?' she asked.

'We call it the "interchange cavern",' Skellsgard told her. 'As far as we know, the Slashers have never found anything like this in any of their travels. All the connections they've mapped have been simple point-to-point affairs. You might get multiple clusters of portals located close to each other in space, but you never get junctions in the hyperweb threads themselves.'

'Except for this?'

'Well, there's obviously something special about this link because it feeds into the heart of an ALS. We think the interchange cavern allows selective access to different points in the crust of the captive planet.' With one blunt fingernail she tapped particular features in the contour display. 'There are nineteen possible routes out of the cavern, as far as we can tell, not counting the one we just arrived by. Trouble is, our steering control is only sophisticated enough to allow us to change course in time to reach six of the exits. Of the remaining thirteen, we've managed to drop lightweight instrument packages into four of them, but we never heard anything back. They probably didn't even make it to the ends of their threads.'

'What about the six exits you can reach?'

'We always come out underground, within a few hundred metres of the surface. But five of the six exits are no use to us. Given time, we could tunnel our way to daylight, but it would take years, and every kilogram of rock we excavate would have to be brought back through the link.'

'I'm missing something here,' Auger said. 'What's so difficult about digging through rock, given that you've already excavated half of Phobos?'

'There's a catch: our tools don't work on E2. We'd have to dig our way out with our fingers.'

Auger asked the obvious question. 'Wait. If you can't reach the surface, how do you even know it's the same planet? What if the threads lead somewhere else entirely?'

'Gravity's the main clue. It's always within a per cent or two of the same value, no matter where we pop out. Geochemistry varies a little, too, but not enough to lead us to think we're inside a different planet each time. We can plot these data points against our knowledge of E1 and take a stab at figuring out where we are – at least to within a continent's accuracy – but only one exit lets us reach the surface.'

'Because it's closer?' Auger asked.

'No. Because there's another tunnel right next door. We only had to dig through a few dozen metres of actual rock before we hit a pre-existing shaft. If it wasn't for that . . .' Skellsgard's expression became philosophical. 'Well, Susan would still be alive, and you'd still be looking at a tribunal.'

'Thanks for the reminder.'

'Sorry.'

They passed through the interchange cavern without incident. Less than an hour later, Aveling's sensors began to pick up the reflections from the approaching throat: the faint echo from the same kind of bow shock wave that had signalled the arrival of the other transport in the Phobos cavern. He told Skellsgard and Auger to secure themselves for arrival, which meant additional seat restraints and webbing, tightened to the point of discomfort. Auger recalled the violent arrival of the ship in Phobos and prepared herself for the worst.

When it came, it was mercifully quick, and she had no sooner registered the fact that the ship was slowing than she felt the arrestor cradle clang into position around the hull. The ship surged forward, halted and then lurched back as pistons took up the recoil. And then suddenly all was very calm, with Aveling reaching above his head to flick switches, powering down vital systems.

Auger had weight now, an unwelcome burden after thirty hours in free fall. It was an effort to move her arms to undo the seat harness, and a struggle to lift herself from the seat. Her muscles protested for a few moments as she began to stretch, and then, sullenly, resigned themselves to the task.

Presently, someone knocked on the door.

'That'll be Barton,' Aveling said.

Barton turned out to be a younger version of Aveling, only with a slightly more enlightened attitude towards civilians. He ushered them out of the transport, through a connecting airlock and into a rock-walled spherical cavern that was recognisable as a much smaller counterpart to the one at the Phobos end. Much equipment surrounded the recovery bubble, but there was no means to swap the existing transport for a refurbished one. Despite the damage it had sustained on the trip (light, Aveling said), the ship would simply be rotated through 180 degrees and sent on its way again.

Auger was introduced to two other people in the chamber: a tough-looking female military specialist called Ariano and another civilian technician called Rasht, a small, feline man with a sallow complexion. Neither of them looked like Slashers, and both appeared to have been working double shifts for at least a week.

'Any news on the others?' Aveling asked Ariano.

'Nothing,' she said. 'We're still transmitting on the usual frequencies, but nobody's called home.'

Auger leaned against a red-painted handrail, unsteady on her feet. 'What others?'

'Our other deep-penetration agents,' Ariano said. 'There are eight of them out there, some as far away as the United States. We've been sending out orders for them to return here.'

'Because of what happened to White?'

'That's part of it. The link is also showing signs of instability, and we don't want anyone to end up marooned here.'

'This is the first I've heard about any instability,' Auger said uneasily.

'It'll hold long enough for you to complete your mission,' Skellsgard replied.

'We're also concerned about the political situation at home,' Ariano said. 'We know things are hotting up back there, and that some people are talking about a Slasher invasion. If they're right, there's a danger we'll lose Phobos. We can't afford to have anyone still here if that happens.'

'All the more incentive to get things done as quickly as possible,' Aveling said. He clicked his fingers at Ariano and Rasht. 'Get the ship prepped for the return leg. I take it you have cargo?'

Rasht was standing next to an incongruous-looking tower of cardboard boxes. The topmost box was crammed with books, magazines, newspapers and gramophone records. 'Five hundred kilograms' worth. A few more trips and we'll have sent home everything Susan delivered.'

'Good,' Aveling said. 'Get it loaded and secured. You can ship out as soon as you're ready.'

'Wait,' Auger said. 'Is that ship leaving without me?'

'There'll be another one back sixty hours after this one departs,' Aveling said, his voice unctuous with sarcastic sweetness. 'That gives you at least two and a half days to complete your mission. If you get back with the tin sooner than that, you can simply sit tight here and wait for the next transport.'

'I still don't like the idea—'

'This is the way it's going to happen, Auger, so deal with it,' Aveling said bluntly, terminating the conversation by turning away.

The three of them trooped off the catwalk, leaving Barton, Ariano and Rasht to load the transport for its return flight. They reached a circular deck surrounding the chamber. Prefabricated cubicles ringed the deck, along with equipment lockers and control consoles. In the deep pit below the bubble, powerful generators snored to themselves, umbilicals snaking across the floor like draped tentacles.

Everything she saw, she realised, must have come through the link – even the bubble itself. The first few journeys must have been interesting, if not fatal.

'Let's get you freshened up,' Skellsgard said, leading Auger to one of the cubicles. 'There's a shower and washroom in there, and a wardrobe full of indigenous clothes. Help yourself, but remember you need to be comfortable wearing what you choose.'

'I'm comfortable with what I'm wearing now.'

'And you'd stick out like a sore thumb as soon as you entered Paris. The idea is to be as inconspicuous as possible. Any hint of strangeness and Blanchard may get other ideas about handing over the goods.'

Auger showered, rinsing away the musty smell of the transport. She felt oddly alert. During the past thirty hours she had only slept intermittently, but the novelty of her situation served to hold tiredness at bay.

As Skellsgard had promised, the wardrobe was well equipped with clothes from the same time period as the E2 artefacts she had already examined. Trying them on in various permutations, she couldn't help but remember the ludicrous fancy-dress party she had attended on the *Twentieth Century Limited* in a desperate bid to ward off boredom. At least the garments here all originated from the same period, even if there was no guarantee that she was putting them on in anything resembling a sensible combination. It was trickier than she had expected. Lately, Tanglewood fashions had tended towards the utilitarian and consequently Auger was not used to things like dresses and skirts, stockings and heeled shoes. Even at the kind of academic functions where everyone else made an effort to dress up, she'd always been the one who made a point of showing up in work-stained coveralls. Now she was expected to pass as a woman from the mid-twentieth century, a time when even the wearing of trousers was uncommon.

It took half an hour, but eventually she settled on a mix that didn't strike her as glaringly off key, and which – equally importantly – she could still just about walk around in without looking drunk. She chose the shoes with the flattest heels amongst those on offer, which were still higher than she would have liked. She added black stockings and a knee-length skirt in navy blue with fine silver pinstripes that allowed her to walk without too much trouble, and paired these items with a pale-blue blouse and a jacket in the same fabric as the skirt. Rummaging in the back recesses of the wardrobe, she found a hat that completed the ensemble. She tugged here and shrugged there, settling the unfamiliar garments in place. She then stood in front of the mirror and toyed with the angle of the hat, trying to see herself as an anonymous woman rather than as Verity Auger in fancy dress. Only one thing mattered: if she saw herself in the background of some pre-Void Century photograph, would she merit a second glance?

She couldn't tell. She didn't think she looked disastrous, but neither was she certain that she was about to blend in with anything or anyone.

'You ready in there?' Skellsgard called from outside.

Auger shrugged and let herself out. Skellsgard, to her surprise, had also put on clothes from the same period. They seemed to suit her about as well as they suited Auger.

'Well?' Augur asked, self-consciously executing a little twirl.

'You'll do,' Skellsgard said, cocking her head as she appraised the outfit. 'Main thing is not to worry about it too much. Look confident, as if you know you belong, and no one will give you a second glance. You hungry?'

They'd eaten rations on the way over, but the weightlessness had done nothing for her appetite. 'A bit,' she decided.

'Barton's fixed us some food. While we're eating we can go over the rest of the stuff you need to know. Before that, though, we need to put you through the censor.'

'I was wondering when we'd get to that.'

ELEVEN

When they had finished eating, Floyd left Greta smoking a cigarette while he persuaded the waiter to let him use the telephone. Fishing out his notebook, he called Blanchard's number and waited for the landlord to answer.

'I need to speak to Monsieur Custine,' Floyd said, after they'd exchanged pleasantries. 'He should be waiting for my call.'

Without another word, Blanchard passed the receiver to Custine. 'Floyd,' he said excitedly, 'I'm glad you called.'

Floyd picked at his teeth with a fresh toothpick. 'You've got something?'

'Possibly.'

'Get rid of the old man. I don't want him listening in on your latest piece of speculation.' Floyd had his back to the bar, but a mirror offered an excellent view of the patrons. He watched them idly while he listened to Custine and Blanchard having an animated discussion at the other end of the line. Presently he heard the click as a door was closed.

'I'm alone now,' Custine said. 'He'll give me a minute, no more.'

'Let's make the most of it, then. Did you get the wireless to work?'

'Yes, rather to my surprise.'

'Mine as well. How did you manage that?'

'Trial and error, Floyd. I identified the severed wires and the contact points where they needed to be re-attached. It was then merely a question of some very delicate and methodical soldering, trying out the various permutations until something happened. We're lucky that whoever sabotaged that wireless was in a great hurry, or they could have done a much more thorough job.'

'All right,' Floyd said. 'I'm officially impressed. Consider yourself in line for a promotion the next time a vacancy appears.'

'Very droll, Floyd, considering that I am your only employee. I will confess that I was a little impressed with myself, if truth be told. But what is truly interesting is that the wireless still did not pick up any of the usual stations.'

'Then it's still broken.'

'Not quite. I tuned it to the wavelength you noted on our first visit, and then made careful adjustments around that position. Eventually I found a signal. It was weak, but it may be that the wireless has suffered some more permanent damage that I couldn't see. Then I moved the needle all the way up and down the dial, but that was all I found: just a single station.'

'And what were they transmitting?'

'Noises, Floyd, just as we were led to expect. Short tones and long tones, like Morse code.'

'I hope you made a note of them.'

'I did my best. I became aware that the pattern was repeating, with a minute or so of silence after each repetition. I attempted to scribble down the sequence of tones, but I couldn't record them all before the station stopped transmitting.'

'Then they went off the air for good?'

'So it would seem. It must have been sheer luck that I stumbled on the end of a sequence of transmissions.'

'All right. See what else you can get out of it, without making Blanchard too suspicious.'

'Do you think this is significant?'

'It might be,' Floyd said. 'Greta's turned up something interesting in that paperwork.' He checked his watch. 'How much longer do you think you need?'

'Give me until four. That should be sufficient.'

'All right. I'll meet you there – I want to ask the tenants a few follow-up questions. In the meantime, keep a lid on what you've discovered.'

Custine lowered his voice. 'We'll have to tell him at some point.'

'I know,' Floyd said, 'but let's make sure we have a clear idea of what she was up to first.'

Floyd put down the receiver, drawing a frosty glance from the waiter. He went back to the table where he had left Greta, then snapped at his fingers at another waiter and settled the bill, adding a modest tip. 'I'll drive you back to your aunt's place,' he said.

Greta gathered her gloves. 'What did Custine have to say for himself?'

'He might just have earned his Christmas bonus.'

They returned to the Mathis. Floyd ripped a political pamphlet from underneath a windshield wiper and drove Greta back to Montparnasse, stopping so that she could pick up some groceries along the way.

'Give my regards to Marguerite,' he said as Greta got out of the car.

'I will.'

'I'd like to see you again. How does this evening sound?'

She reached for the bag of groceries. 'Floyd, we can't keep dancing around the one subject you don't want to talk about.'

'Then we'll talk about it this evening.'

'Until you change the topic.'

'Humour me.'

She closed her eyes in weary resignation. 'Call me later. I'll see how things go with Marguerite.'

Floyd nodded: anything was better than a rejection. 'I'll call you this evening.'

'Floyd . . . take care, all right?'

'I will.'

She pulled an apple from the bag of groceries and threw it at him. Floyd caught it and slipped it into his pocket. He started up the Mathis again and drove back across town to rue des Peupliers. He got Blanchard to buzz him in, then walked up to the fifth floor and knocked on the door to Susan White's apartment.

'It's Floyd,' he announced.

Custine opened the door cautiously and then let him in. He had pushed the wireless set back against the wall, leaving no sign that it had been tampered with. Even his tools were packed away.

'Anything new?' Floyd asked.

'Nothing. Whoever was transmitting those signals is still off the air.' Custine made a tiny adjustment to the dial. He sat down cross-legged on a pillow in front of the wireless, his unlaced shoes placed neatly side by side next to him. 'I'll keep trying.'

'Good. In the meantime, I need to talk to whoever it was you said saw that child hanging around the place.'

'The little girl? Floyd, you don't seriously think—'

'I'm not ruling anything out.'

'Then speak to the gentleman on the second floor. The room next to the broom cupboard. But he'll only tell you what he told me.'

'Maybe I can jog his memory.' Floyd looked guiltily down at his friend. Custine had been in here working hard while Floyd had been promenading through the gardens and eating ice cream. 'You want anything? I can fetch you a coffee.'

'I'm all right, thanks.'

'You eaten?'

128

'Not since breakfast.'

Floyd reached into his pocket. 'Have an apple on me.'

Floyd took the stairs down to the chequered linoleum of the second-floor landing. He knocked on the door next to the broom cupboard, waited a few moments and then knocked again. He pressed his ear against the door and listened for signs of life, but there was no sound of anyone inside. He tried the handle, but the door was locked. Floyd shrugged: it was the middle of the day and therefore quite likely that the tenant was out earning a respectable wage. He'd been the only one to mention the odd child to Custine, but that didn't mean none of the others had seen something. Perhaps they just needed to be asked the right question.

Floyd flipped his notebook to a clean page and knocked on the door of the other apartment on the second floor. After a moment, he heard the shuffle of approaching slippers followed by a rattle of locks and chains. An elderly woman in a floral apron appeared at the door, opening it just enough to eye him with the instant suspicion Floyd normally reserved for salesmen.

'Excuse me for disturbing you, madame,' he said. 'My name is Floyd and I'm investigating the death of the young American woman three weeks ago. I believe my partner, Monsieur Custine, may already have paid you a visit.'

'Yes,' the woman said guardedly.

'There's nothing to be alarmed about. It's just that one of the other tenants made a remark that meant nothing at the time, but which might be significant now.'

She wasn't going to let him into her rooms. 'I told your partner everything I could about the American girl. I hardly knew her.'

Floyd didn't need to ask the old woman's name – Custine would have already made a note of it. 'This wasn't specifically about the American woman. All the same, did you ever speak to her?'

'Not a word. We passed on the stairs now and then. I didn't go out of my way *not* to speak to her, but at my age . . .' Something in her expression seemed to soften, some crack of trust opening up even though she still guarded the door like a fortress. 'I've lived in this building for a great many years, monsieur. There was a time when I made a point of getting to know everyone who lived here. But nowadays the young people come and go so quickly that it's barely worth learning their names.'

'I understand,' Floyd said sympathetically. 'I live in a building like this in the fifth. It's always the same – people coming and going.'

'Still, a young man like you – you would probably have known her name. She was very pretty.'

'From what I can gather,' Floyd said, 'she was a very nice young lady. That's why it's all the more important that we find out what happened to her.'

'The police say she fell.'

'There's no doubt about that. The question is, was she pushed?'

'They say she was just a tourist. Why would anyone want to harm someone like that?'

'That's what I'm hoping to find out.'

'Have you spoken to the widower on the next floor up?'

'Monsieur Blanchard? Yes, we've had a chat. He was very helpful.'

'He knew her better than any of us.' The woman leaned towards Floyd and lowered her voice. 'If you ask me, there's something not quite *right* about that.'

'I think it was all above board,' Floyd said. 'The American girl liked to put money on horses. Monsieur Blanchard helped her study the form.'

The woman pursed her lips, evidently not convinced by Floyd's defence of the landlord. 'I still think that a man of his age . . . well, never mind. Who am I to judge? Was there anything else, monsieur?'

'Just one thing: are there any children living in this building?'

'There was a young couple with a baby on the fourth floor, but they moved to Toulouse last year.'

'Since then?'

'No children.'

'Then you've never seen any other children in this building?'

'People visit now and then and bring their children with them.'

Floyd tapped his pencil against the notepad. 'But what about unaccompanied children?'

'Occasionally. Monsieur Charles, who lived on the sixth floor, used to have a daughter visit him on Sundays.'

'Lately?'

'Not since they buried him in D'Ivry.'

'And since then? Any other children?'

'Not to my knowledge, no.'

'Think carefully, madame. Have you ever seen a little girl in this building, especially in the last few weeks?'

'I think I would remember, monsieur, given how unusual it would have been.'

Floyd snapped shut the notepad without having written a word. 'Thanks for your time, madame.'

'I'm sorry I couldn't be more help.'

'You've been more than helpful.' Floyd touched a finger to the brim of his hat and stepped away from the door as she closed it. He heard the securing of multiple locks and chains.

There were no other rooms on this floor, so Floyd set off up the stairs towards the third-floor landing. He had reached the halfway point when he heard the urgent unlocking of the old woman's door as latches were thrown and chains undone. He halted with one hand on the banister and looked down.

'Madame?'

'I just remembered,' she said, her voice quavering. 'There was a child.'

'A little girl?'

'A very strange little girl. I passed her on the stairs late one evening, when I was returning to my rooms.'

'Where had you been, if you don't mind my asking?'

'Nowhere. I sleepwalk occasionally – it's a terrible thing to admit – and sometimes I let myself out of my rooms and wake up at the bottom of the stairs. It must have been three or four weeks ago when this happened. I glanced at her face, and . . .' She shuddered.

'Madame?'

'When I woke up the next morning, monsieur, I thought I must have dreamed about that little girl.'

'Maybe you did,' Floyd said.

'I hope so, monsieur, because when I looked at her face, I saw the face of evil itself, as if the Devil was in this building, in the form of a little girl. And the worst thing was that when she looked at me, I could see that she knew exactly what I was thinking.'

'Could you describe her?'

'About eight or nine. Maybe a little older. Her clothes were dirty, ragged. She was very thin. I saw her arm on the banister – it was like a skeleton's, all lean and bony. Her hair was too black, as if it had been dyed. But the worst thing was her face. Like the face of a witch, or something left out in the sun too long.'

'Let me put you at your ease,' Floyd said, smiling. 'You must have had a nightmare.'

'How can you be so sure?'

'Because that's not the little girl I was hoping you'd seen, who might possibly be a witness.'

'You're certain?'

'The girl I'm looking for had the face of an angel. Little pigtails and rosy cheeks.'

'Thank goodness,' the woman said, after a moment. 'Then I must have dreamed it after all. It's just that when you mentioned a little girl . . .'

'I quite understand. I had a very bad nightmare myself only the other night. When I woke up, it took me a while to realise it hadn't really happened. You mustn't feel bad about it, madame. She won't be back – you needn't worry about that. I'm just sorry I made you remember her in the first place.'

'It wasn't your fault.'

'Please, try not to dwell on it. I'm very grateful for your help.' Floyd reached into his pocket. 'Did my partner leave you with a card, just in case anything else occurs to you?'

'Yes, I have the card.'

'Please don't hesitate to call.'

She closed the door. Floyd hoped he had reassured her – the last thing he wanted to do was go around scaring old people out of their wits – but as he turned away he heard her securing at least twice as many locks and chains as the first time.

'We didn't build any of this shit,' Skellsgard said. 'We just inherited it. Unfortunately, it means we have to play by their rules, not ours. And their rules say nothing dangerous makes it into Paris.'

They stood next to a two-metre-high hinged, circular door set into the wall. The frame was peppered with bee stripes and warning decals, with padded handrails set around it. Whatever was beyond that door, the signs clearly indicated, was unlikely to be good for one's health.

'Nothing dangerous?' Auger asked. 'You mean like weapons, bombs, that kind of thing?'

'I mean like anything the E2 people shouldn't have. Almost nothing we can actually make gets through the censor. Not just the obviously dangerous stuff, but anything with the potential to screw up the world beyond the portal. Which means almost any technological artefact from E1.' Skellsgard pulled a lever, engaging a complicated mechanism that swung the armoured door away from the wall.

Auger wasn't sure what she had been expecting – another chamber, perhaps. Instead there was only a glowing membrane of electric yellow stretched drum-tight across the frame. The light it emitted wavered and wobbled, like the reflection from a swimming pool. It threw odd shadows and highlights across the room, making Auger feel faintly seasick. She could see nothing through it, yet the yellow conveyed a subtle impression of depth and peculiar perspective.

'This is the censor?' she asked nervously.

'Yes. And before you ask, we don't know how it works. All we know is that we can only push certain things through it. Other things . . . it either rejects or destroys, depending on what kind of mood it's in.'

Auger examined the edge of the frame, which was set into the rock. Clearly this was a human add-on, bolted on to whatever had been here before. The portal had presumably been installed at the same time as the hyperweb connection, long before Skellsgard's people had reopened it.

'What's on the other side?' she asked.

'The rest of the world. Another chamber, actually, but one that's connected directly into the tunnels under Paris.'

'Can't you just bypass the censor? Dig through the rock on either side?'

'Doesn't work,' Skellsgard said. 'Nothing we've tried gets us out of this chamber. We've tried blasting and cutting through on either side of the portal, but it's like chewing through diamond. The builders must have reinforced this chamber for exactly that reason, to make everyone use the portal.'

'But you've been through it. You can cross the censor.'

'*We* can,' Skellsgard said, 'you and I, but not someone like Niagara. His body's so full of machines that the censor would cook him alive. Nanotechnology's one of the big no-nos. No matter how well we try to hide it, the censor always detects it and *always* fries it.'

'Then no nanotech weapon can reach Paris. That's good, isn't it, if it means the Slashers can't get through?'

'Yes, but it doesn't stop with nanotech. Any complex manufactured object is blocked, no matter how innocuous its function. No guns. No comms gear. No watches or clocks. No cameras, sensors or medical equipment.'

'What does that actually leave?'

'Not much. Clothes. Paper. Simple tools, like spades and screwdrivers. Basically anything *it* deems safe. We actually managed to fool it, once, but in a very trivial way. It won't let a gun through, not even a replica of a twentieth-century weapon. But we were able to dismantle a weapon and smuggle through its component parts – that worked. But what was the point? It's easier to find a real gun on E2.'

Auger reached out towards the beguiling yellow surface. 'Can I touch it?'

'Hell, yes. You can put your hand through it. Going to have to put your whole body through it anyway, so there's no harm.'

Auger pushed her finger towards the eerie yellow membrane. It took longer than she had expected for her finger to encounter any surface. Then she felt a prickle of sensation in the very tip. She pushed harder, and the yellow surface began to visibly deform, puckering inwards from the point of contact. She was reminded of surface tension on water, the way it formed a skin that resisted gentle pressure. A rust-brown discoloration appeared in the yellow, radiating away from her finger in a concentric pattern.

'Are you absolutely sure this is safe?' she asked again.

'We've all been through it hundreds of times,' Skellsgard said. 'Bodies aren't a problem. It discriminates between complex biological processes and nanotech pretty well.'

'Pretty well?'

'Just push.'

Auger increased her pressure. There was a snapping sensation and suddenly her hand was engulfed in yellow up to the wrist. The surface had flattened itself again around her limb. There was no pain, merely a chill tingle. She wriggled her fingers. They all seemed present and correct. She withdrew her hand and checked by sight – still all there.

'See, simple,' Skellsgard said.

'I still don't like it.'

'You don't have to. I'll go on ahead and show you how safe it is. There's a trick to this, so watch me closely. When I'm through you can pass me your hat.'

Auger stood back. Skellsgard reached up and grasped the horizontal handrail above the censor firmly with both hands. With a gymnastic fluidity, she pulled herself up off her feet and swung her body towards the yellow surface. By the time she reached it she had gained sufficient momentum to push through in one movement. The surface puckered, then swallowed her with a snap. Auger's last glimpse was of the back of Skellsgard's head disappearing into the censor.

A moment later, a hand pushed through and snapped its fingers. Auger recognised the blunt fingernails. She removed her hat and offered it to the hand. Hand and hat vanished back through the censor.

Auger reached up and took hold of the handrail. She pulled herself from the ground, muscles screaming at the unaccustomed effort. She pulled her legs as high as they would go and swung herself into the yellow. It was almost certainly less elegant than Skellsgard's effort, but she supposed everyone had to begin somewhere.

The moment of transition, the passage through the yellow, was like an electric shock without the pain. She felt every atom of her body flooded with a sharp, inquisitional light. She felt herself being scrutinised, rummaged through, turned this way and that like a cut gem. It lasted an eternity and an instant.

Then it was over, and she was lying in an undignified heap with the hem of her skirt somewhere around her hips and one shoe off her heel. Someone had thoughtfully arranged a padded mat on the other side of the censor.

'Here's your hat,' Skellsgard said. 'Welcome to Paris.'

Auger picked herself up, straightened her clothes and placed the hat back on her head. The chamber in which they had arrived was much smaller than the last one, but it was crammed with a similarly bewildering assortment of machines and lockers. None of the contents looked quite as advanced, however: from what Auger could judge, almost everything here must have been sent through in tiny instalments and then reassembled (which naturally precluded anything really complicated) or – more likely – had been purloined from the outside world of E2 and then adapted to serve some new function. There was a lot of electrical equipment, ungainly humming things in grey or green metal cases, connected together with tangled rubberised cables; flickering monochrome screens, showing wave traces; black things like typewriters, but which clearly weren't. A generator chugged away in one corner.

'You feeling all right?' Skellsgard asked.

'More or less. Shouldn't I be?'

'There was a small risk that some of Niagara's machines might not have been flushed out before you came through. Didn't see any particular point in alarming you unnecessarily.'

'I see,' Auger said tersely.

'There's something else as well. Usually when we go through that thing, we don't feel anything. It only takes an instant and it's all over. But every now and then, something else happens. Maybe once in a hundred trips through the censor, it's different.'

'Different in what way? Different as in painful?'

'No – not like that. It's just that sometimes it seems to take longer. Much longer – as if you're in that yellow limbo for a lifetime. You learn and feel things you can barely articulate. When you come out of it, you almost remember what it was like. It's like waking from a beautiful dream, clutching at threads as they fade away. You sense something of the minds that made this place. You feel them looking through you, vast and ancient and long dead, but still somehow aware, and curious as to what *you* make of their creation.

'Have you . . .'

'Once,' Skellsgard said. 'And that was enough. It's why I don't go through that thing any more often than I need to.'

'Jesus,' Auger said, shaking her head. 'You might have told me this when I was on the other side. Now I have no choice but to go through it again.'

'I just wanted you to know that if it does happen . . . which it probably won't . . . you shouldn't be afraid. Nothing bad will happen, and you'll come out of it in one piece. It's just a bit more than some of us can take.'

'What were the minds like?' Auger asked, curiosity overcoming outrage, despite herself.

'Distant, huge and unchanging, like a range of mountains.' Skellsgard smiled self-consciously, then shook her own head, as if trying to break a mental spell. 'It never happened again. I got over it. We all have a job to do here. Talking of which, how do you like the set-up? This is effectively the nerve centre of E2 operations, the point from which we communicate with all the field agents.'

Barton looked up from a folding table set with food and coffee. 'Show her the Enigma.'

'Her mission profile says she doesn't need to know about that,' Skellsgard replied.

'Show her anyway.'

Skellsgard shrugged and led Auger to a skeletal shelf unit containing about a dozen of the black typewriters. 'You recognise these things?'

'Not really – they look like typewriters, but I'm sure they're something more sophisticated than that.'

'They're Enigma machines,' Skellsgard said. 'Commercial enciphering equipment.'

'Made locally?'

'Yes. The military use them, but anyone can buy an off-the-shelf model for their own purposes. We use them to send secure messages to our field agents.'

'Like Susan?'

'Exactly like Susan. Before she left here, we gave her one of these machines and instructions for converting a commercial wireless to intercept signals on our chosen frequency. Once she'd set up home, she used local tools and parts to modify the wireless. From our end, we encipher signals using an Enigma machine with the appropriate rotor settings for the given day of the month. Susan had a list of the settings so that she could set up her own Enigma accordingly. The enciphered messages came through the wireless in standard Morse code, but would have been completely unintelligible to anyone without an Enigma to decipher them back into plain text.'

'Wait,' Auger said, raising a hand. 'I remember a little about these machines now. Didn't they play a role in the Second World War? Something involving submarine warfare?'

'Yes,' Skellsgard said. 'Enigma was cracked, eventually. It required several cunning breakthroughs in cryptanalysis methods and electromechanical computing. In fact, the task of cracking Enigma pretty much kick-started the entire computer revolution in the first place. But none of that happened here. There *was* no Second World War on E2.'

'I figured as much from the map Caliskan sent me, but I didn't know what to make of it.'

'Make of it what you like. Fact is, the E2 timeline diverges significantly from our history. On E2, the war fizzled out in nineteen forty. There was a brief front in the Ardennes, and then it was all over. The German advance stalled. A *coup* took out the leadership – Stauffenberg and Rommel were part of that – and within two years the Nazi party had collapsed from within. People still talk about a Great War here, because there was never a second to rival it. No Second World War, no massive endeavour to crack Enigma. Computing here is still stuck at the same level as in the nineteen thirties, which – to all intents and purposes – is pretty much the same as the *eighteen* thirties. And that's both good and bad. On the downside, it means we can't go out and steal computing equipment or any kind of sophisticated electronic hardware. There are no transistors, no integrated circuits or microprocessors. But we can be sure that no one on E2 is capable of deciphering our Enigma traffic.'

'So you were using this thing to talk to Susan?'

'Yes,' Skellsgard said. 'But it was a strictly a one-way conversation. It's one thing to build a radio receiver. It's much more complicated to build a transmitter with the necessary range, and even more difficult to run it without drawing attention. Given time, she could have done it – we'd given her the instructions – but she was more interested in pursuing her own little investigation.'

'The one that got her killed.'

'I knew Susan. She wouldn't have allowed herself to get into something unless she felt the risks were worth it.'

'Meaning she was on to something? But according to Aveling . . .' Auger looked across to Barton, who had just raised his head, presumably on hearing Aveling's name. She lowered her voice. 'But according to Aveling, the only reason Caliskan wants those papers back is in case the locals get their hands on them.'

'Don't underestimate the danger of that,' Skellsgard said. 'It would only take one nudge in the right direction for them to realise they're inside an ALS. The illusion is good, but it isn't flawless.'

'Still, you don't think that's the only reason, do you? It seems as if everyone here had a good opinion of Susan. If she said she was on to something—'

'Then maybe she was. But we won't know what it was until we get those papers back. And then hope that there's enough of a clue in them.'

'There's still one thing I don't get,' Auger said, keeping her voice low.

'Why me? If you know the territory as well, couldn't you have posed as this long-lost sister instead of dragging me halfway across the galaxy instead?'

'There's a catch,' Skellsgard said.

'Another one? But of course there is. You know, I'm thinking I should start a collection.'

'For some reason, Susan wanted *you* to be the sister. We know this from the last postcard she sent us.'

Auger frowned. Up to this point, she had never had anything more than a distant professional relationship with Susan White. Academic rivalry aside, she neither liked nor disliked the woman, but she didn't really know her at all. 'I don't get it,' she said.

'We didn't get it either.'

'Couldn't one of you have just pretended to be the sister? A name's just a name, after all.'

'There's more to it than that. She might have primed Blanchard with a physical description of you. She knew you by sight, didn't she?'

'Yes,' Auger admitted, remembering the times they had bumped into each other at conferences. 'And we weren't so different in appearance, now that I think about it.'

'We can't take the risk of sending in someone who doesn't fit Blanchard's expectations. If he gets suspicious – thinks he's being set up – then we may never see those papers again. That's why we need you.'

'Then what Caliskan said was a lie. I was only ever the one candidate on his list.'

'Guess he needed to appeal to your vanity,' Skellsgard said.

'Guess it worked, too.'

TWELVE

Floyd continued his tour of the building in rue des Peupliers, knocking on doors and sometimes getting an answer. He worked methodically and patiently, turning on the charm when it was required. By the end of his enquiries, it was clear that at least two other tenants had seen the girl in the building, hanging around on the stairs. They couldn't be specific about dates, but the sightings had all occurred within the last three or four weeks: consistent with there being a link to the White case. Once observed, the girl was not usually seen again by the same witness. Another tenant might have seen an odd child in the street outside, but he was insistent that this child had been a boy rather than a girl. Floyd and Custine had seen a strange girl leaving the Blanchard building the evening before, and Floyd had noticed what he thought was a different girl watching White's window from outside earlier that day. Floyd still hadn't spoken to the witness on the second floor, the one who had mentioned a child to Custine the night before.

Floyd had no idea what to make of it all. Strange little children hadn't figured prominently in any of his previous investigations. Perhaps he was latching on to any anomaly in the hope that it might break open the case. Maybe if he visited any similar apartment building in the city and asked a similar set of questions he'd get a similar set of responses.

He was done by four. He walked back up to Susan White's room and knocked on the door. His shirt was sticky around the collar. All that trudging up and down the stairs was making him sweat.

'You get anywhere, chief?' he asked Custine when he opened the door.

Custine let Floyd inside and closed the door. 'No. There've been no further transmissions. I removed the back of the wireless again, thinking that one of my connections might have come loose, but all was well. The station is simply not on the air.'

'Maybe they've gone off the air for good.'

'Perhaps,' Custine said. 'All the same, I shall try again tomorrow. Perhaps the transmissions only take place at a certain time of day.'

'You can't spend the rest of your life up here.'

'One more day, that's all.'

Floyd knelt down next to Custine. 'Show me what you got before.'

'It's incomplete.'

'I'd like to see it anyway.'

Custine removed a sheet of paper from the top of the wireless set on which he'd marked a sequence of dots and dashes in neat pencil. 'You can see the pieces I missed,' he said. 'Of course, there's no guarantee that tomorrow's transmission will be the same as today's. But at least I'll be ready for it tomorrow. I should be able to make an accurate transcription.'

'If you haven't got anything by the middle of the day, we close this line of enquiry.'

'There is something going on here, whether you like it or not.'

'Maybe there is, but we can't waste Blanchard's money just sitting around waiting for a transmission that may never return. There are other leads that need to be followed up.'

'Generated by the material Greta examined?'

'That, and something else.' Quickly he told Custine about the paperwork in the tin and what Greta made of it. 'There's a Berlin connection: some kind of heavy-manufacturing contract and what looks like a sketch of a blueprint.'

'For what?'

'Haven't figured that out yet, but whatever it is, there are three of them.'

'I hope you got more detail than that.'

'Three large aluminium castings,' Floyd said. 'Big, solid spheres.'

'How big is big?'

'I might be misreading the sketch, but it looks to me as if these things are at least three metres in diameter.'

'Big,' Custine agreed.

'Looks like they're meant to be suspended from something, like a kind of gallows. One sphere gets shipped to Paris, another to Milan, while the third stays in Berlin.'

'Perplexing,' Custine said, stroking his moustache. 'What would this American girl have been doing involved with a contract like that?'

'Greta and I talked about that. We figured that maybe it wasn't her contract at all, but one that she was taking an interest in for some reason.'

'Back to the spy theory, in other words.'

'Sorry,' Floyd said, 'but all roads really do keep leading to Rome.'

'Where are you going to take things now? Did the box offer any other leads?'

'We have the address and telephone number of the metalworks in Berlin.'

'Have you called it yet?'

'No, but I plan on doing so as soon as I get back to the office.'

'Be careful, Floyd. If there is an espionage connection, poking your nose into things might not be your wisest move.'

'And what do you think you've been doing all afternoon?'

'That's different,' Custine said dismissively. 'All I'm doing is trying to intercept a wireless transmission.'

'And no one would be able to tell that you're doing that?'

'Of course not,' Custine answered, but not with complete confidence. 'Look, I'll spend one more morning on this. Then I'll put the wireless back exactly the way I found it and move on.'

'I'm just saying—'

'I know. And I understand. I think we've both convinced ourselves that there's more to this than meets the eye, haven't we?'

'I guess Blanchard was right all along,' Floyd said, standing and stretching his legs.

'Have you spoken to him again today?'

'Not yet, but I intend to. I figure I need to tell him that we're at least making a kind of progress.'

'You mentioned another lead.'

Floyd shuffled his feet awkwardly. 'Look, don't think me a fool, but I've noticed that strange little girls keep showing up in this case. There was that girl we saw—'

'I know,' Custine said, waving his hand. 'And the girl that the tenant on the second floor mentioned, and the girl you saw standing outside. Peripheral details, Floyd: no more than that.'

'How can you be certain?'

'I'm certain of nothing. But the one thing my years at the Quai taught me is that small children tend not to be prime suspects in murder cases.'

'Maybe this isn't your usual homicide case,' Floyd said.

'Are you seriously proposing that a *child* murdered Susan White?'

'If she was standing by the balcony rail,' Floyd said, 'it wouldn't have taken much of a shove to send her over. You don't need much strength for that.'

'If her position was that precarious to begin with, it's entirely possible that she just lost her balance.'

'André, you know as well as I do that she was pushed.'

'I'm merely playing devil's advocate, Floyd. Even if you can present a case to the Quai, the examining magistrate will still have to be convinced before the police will take matters further.' Custine took the paper upon which he had recorded the wireless transmissions and folded it twice before slipping it into his shirt pocket. 'And there's another problem with your child-as-murderer hypothesis.'

'Which is?'

'We know that whoever murdered Susan White sabotaged this wireless. Quite aside from the effort required to pull off the backing panel, they would also have needed the strength to drag the wireless away from the wall and then slide it back again.'

'You managed it on your own.'

'I had plenty of time,' Custine said. 'There's also the small detail that I am not a child. I can't judge exactly how much effort was required, but I doubt that it was within the ability of a little girl.'

'Then she had an adult accomplice.'

'In which case,' Custine said patiently, 'we may as well assume that the adult accomplice was the murderer.'

'I still think there's something significant about these children.'

'Floyd, you know I have the utmost respect for you, but another valuable lesson I took away from my time at the Quai – back when solving crimes was its chief activity, rather than harassing enemies of the state – is that it is just as important to ignore certain details in a case as it is to follow up on others.'

'You're saying I'm barking up the wrong tree?'

'The wrong tree, the wrong copse, perhaps even the wrong area of forestation entirely.'

'I'm reluctant to rule anything out.'

'Good: rule nothing out. But don't be distracted by ridiculous theories, Floyd. Not when we already have concrete leads.'

Floyd sighed, a moment of clarity intruding upon his thoughts. Custine was right, of course. Now and then, Floyd had a habit of pursuing blatantly unlikely lines of enquiry. Sometimes – even if all they were investigating was a minor case of spousal infidelity – they led to a critical breakthrough. More often than not, however, he needed a gentle reminder from Custine to return to the orthodox approach, and more often than not Custine's stolid, honed, scientific methods turned out to be exactly what the case required.

This, Floyd realised, was exactly one of those times.

'You're right,' he said. 'If only one of those strange kids had shown up, I guess I'd have thought nothing of it.'

'The central defect of the human mind,' Custine said, 'is its unfortunate habit of seeing patterns where none exist. Of course, that is also its chief asset.'

'But sometimes a very dangerous one.'

Custine stood up, wiping his palms on his trousers. 'Don't feel bad about it, Floyd. It happens to the best of us. And there's never any harm in asking questions.'

Custine gathered his tools, hat and coat and together they walked down two flights of stairs and knocked on Blanchard's door. Floyd delivered a sanitised version of events: yes, it seemed likely to him that Susan White had been murdered; it even seemed likely to him that she had been something other than an innocent American tourist.

'A spy?' Blanchard asked.

'Too soon to say,' Floyd answered. 'There are still leads we need to look into. But you'll hear from us as soon as we have something concrete.'

'I spoke to one of the other tenants. It seems you have been asking questions about a little girl.'

'Just ruling out any possible witnesses,' Floyd said.

'What could a little girl possibly have to do with this?'

'Probably nothing at all,' Custine interjected, before Floyd was tempted to expound his unlikely theories to Blanchard.

'Very well,' Blanchard said, eyeing the two of them. 'I must emphasize how important it is to me that you find Susan's killer. I feel that *she* will not sleep soundly until the matter is resolved.'

He said it as if he meant Susan White, but he was looking at the photograph of his dead wife.

They drove back through thick Thursday-afternoon traffic, taking avenue de Choisy north to place d'Italie and then cutting through a darkening rat's maze of side streets until they were on boulevard Raspail. Floyd turned the radio dial, searching for jazz, but all he got was traditional French accordion music. It was the new thing now. Traditional was in; jazz out. Chatelier himself had called jazz morally corrupting, as if the music itself was a kind of narcotic that had to be wiped from the streets.

Accordion music always made Floyd feel seasick. He turned off the wireless.

'There's something I need to ask,' Custine said.

'Say it.'

'There's a possibility we haven't really discussed. It concerns the old man.'

'Go on.'

'Do you think it's possible he killed her?'

Floyd thought about it for a moment, then shook his head. 'Makes no sense, André. If the police weren't interested, why would he risk re-opening that can of worms?'

'Human nature being what it is, anything's possible. What if he has a secret need to be discovered? Once the police abandoned their inquiry, he'd have had no choice but to call in private detectives.'

'All the evidence we've seen so far points away from Blanchard.'

'But we know he had access to her rooms. He's the one person who has keys for every room. What if she did have a lover, and Blanchard found out about it?'

'Explain the wireless, or the smashed typewriter, or the box of papers.'

'Perhaps he's playing some kind of double-bluff game with us, strewing our path with misleading clues while hoping we have the sense to see through them and—'

'Is this the way they teach you to think at the Quai?'

'I'm just saying that we shouldn't exclude the possibility. He seems like a nice enough old gentleman, but the worst ones generally do.'

'I think you've been sitting in that room for too long, André.'

'Perhaps,' Custine said. 'Still, a little suspicion never goes amiss in this line of work.'

Floyd turned the car on to boulevard Saint-Germain. 'I agree that we can't rule it out, all the other evidence notwithstanding. I'll even admit that the thought had crossed my mind.'

'Well, then.'

'But I still don't believe he killed her. That said, if you feel you need to explore the possibility . . . well, I'm sure you can nose around the problem without being too tactless. Ask him again about the police not taking up the case. Ask him if he knew of anyone who might have been jealous of the time he spent with the girl.'

'I'll be the very model of discretion,' Custine said.

'You'd better be. If he loses his temper and throws us off the case, we're going to have to start looking for new premises in a less salubrious part of town.'

'I didn't think there *was* a less salubrious part of town.'

'My point exactly,' Floyd replied.

He parked the Mathis. Nothing new in his pigeonhole; no bills or mysterious letters from long-lost girlfriends. That, he supposed, had to count as a kind of good luck.

But the elevator had broken down again, jammed somewhere up on the fourth floor. The engineer from the elevator company was sitting on the lowest flight of stairs, smoking a cigarette and studying the racing pages. He was a small, shrewlike man with pomaded hair who always smelled of carbolic soap. He nodded at Floyd and Custine as they tramped past.

'Busy, Maurice?' Floyd asked.

'Waiting for a new part from head office, Monsieur Floyd.' He shrugged expressively. 'With the traffic the way it is today, could be hours before they get here.'

'Don't break a sweat,' Floyd said.

Maurice saluted them and went back to his newspaper.

Entering their office, Custine put away his tools, washed his face and hands and changed his shirt and then set about making tea. Floyd sat at his desk, pulled the telephone across and called the Paris operator to request an international call to Berlin. He gave her the number of Kaspar Metals, reading from the letter in the tin, and waited for the connection to be made.

After a while, the operator's voice came back on again. 'I'm sorry, monsieur. That number must be wrong.'

Floyd gave her the number again, but there had been no mistake. 'You mean no one picks up the telephone?'

'No,' she said. 'The line is totally dead.'

Floyd thanked her and returned the receiver to its cradle. One more dead lead, then. He drummed his fingers and then dialled Marguerite's number in Montparnasse.

'Floyd,' Greta said, answering.

'How are things?'

'She's resting.'

'Can I see you this evening?'

'I suppose so.'

'Easy on the enthusiasm, kid.'

She sighed. 'I'm sorry, Floyd. It's just that I may not be in the best of moods.'

'Then you could use some cheering up.'

'And you're the man for the job, I take it?'

'Custine and I have been working hard on the case. I think we all need a treat tonight. How about I take the three of us out to dinner, and we finish off the evening in *Le Perroquet Pourpre*?'

'I suppose I can make it,' she said, not sounding at all sure of herself. 'Sophie's in tonight, studying, so I could ask her to look after Marguerite—'

'That's the spirit. I'll drive over in an hour. Spruce yourself up – we're hitting the bright lights tonight.'

'I'll do my best,' she said.

Custine and Floyd drank tea and discussed the case, making sure they'd shared all the essential observations, comparing notes on their interviews with the tenants. While they talked, a scratchy old Bluebird pressing of Sidney Bechet playing 'Blues in Thirds' spun on Floyd's phonograph.

'What we're left with,' Custine concluded, 'is an odd American woman who liked to mess around with wirelesses, assuming that *she* did that and not some previous tenant.'

'We're left with a bit more than that,' Floyd said. 'We know she had an odd interest in a manufacturing contract in Berlin. We know that when she died, her typewriter died with her. We know she had a habit of accumulating books and things.'

'Unusual observations collectively, but all perfectly explicable in and of themselves.'

'But taken together—'

'Not enough to make a convincing case that she was a spy.'

'What about the children?'

Custine gave Floyd a reproving look. 'I was rather hoping you wouldn't mention the children again.'

'I still never got to speak to the one tenant who had a really good look at the girl.'

'I'll visit him again tomorrow, if it will make you happy. In the meantime, might I suggest that we restrict ourselves to firm leads?'

Floyd thought for a moment, his mind adrift on the rise and fall of Bechet's saxophone. The disc was scratched and ancient, the music almost buried in a surf of hisses and clicks. He could have replaced it with a cheap bootleg tomorrow, and the sound would have been as clear and clean as a tin whistle. But it wouldn't have been the right kind of clarity. The knock-off might have fooled ninety-nine people out of a hundred, but there was something raw and truthful engraved into this damaged old shellac, something that cut through the noise and thirty years like a clarion.

'The Berlin connection's a dead end,' he said. 'And we don't know what she was doing with the books and magazines.'

'And records,' Custine reminded him. 'Except, of course, that we have Monsieur Blanchard's sighting of her entering Cardinal Lemoine Métro station with the loaded suitcase, and her subsequent reappearance with an empty one.'

'As if she'd exchanged the contents with another spy.'

'Precisely. But again, it's circumstantial. She could just as easily have handed the contents to a shipping agent.'

'This is the bit that doesn't make sense,' Floyd said. He anticipated the record sticking on a particular phrase, timing the stamp of his foot against the floorboards to coax the needle into the next groove. He did it so expertly that the jump was barely audible. 'Whether or not it would ever stand up in court, we have more than enough evidence that she was engaged in some kind of espionage activity. But what was she doing with the books and things? Where did *they* fit in?'

'Part of her cover story as a tourist?'

'Perhaps. But in that case, why not behave like a respectable tourist instead of some cultural magpie, filling steamer trunk after steamer trunk with all that stuff?'

'Unless there was something vital buried in all that material,' Custine said. 'It's a pity we don't know what was in the suitcase.'

'But we know what was left in her room, and there's every reason to believe she would have continued shipping it out if she hadn't been distracted.'

'And yet nothing we saw looked in any way to be worth the attention of a spy. Books, magazines, newspapers, records . . . all of which could have been obtained in the United States, with varying degrees of difficulty.'

'There was something about them that mattered to her,' Floyd said. 'Here's another thing: "silver rain".'

'Silver rain?'

'Mean anything to you?'

'I can't say it does.'

'Susan White made a point of underlining just those words on a postcard she never got round to sending.'

'Could mean anything. Could mean nothing at all,' Custine said, shrugging.

'Sounds like a codeword to me – a codeword for something unpleasant.'

'It would,' Custine said, smiling at Floyd. 'But that's because you've got spies on the brain.'

'There's still the matter of the typewriter.'

'Well, that's a funny thing. I've been thinking about the typewriter, and there may be more to it than meets the eye. Do you remember Blanchard showing us the box it came in?'

'He said it was a German model,' Floyd said.

'Yes. And when he showed us the box – and mentioned the name – it made me think of something. The trouble is, I can't quite work out how the two are related.'

'What did it make you think of?'

'A room in the Quai: a windowless cell in the section where the interrogations used to take place, lit by a single electric light. A cell with ceramic tiles on the walls – the kind you can clean easily. The problem is that I can't quite see why there'd be a typewriter in that sort of room.'

'To take down minutes?'

'What went on in those rooms, Floyd, was very much not the kind of thing that made it into minutes.'

'Then why the typewriter?'

'I don't know. Perhaps I'll remember later, when my mind's on something else.'

They said no more as the Bechet record played out, and then for a long while they sat listening to the hiss and scratch of the needle in the run-out groove, as if hoping for a message in the scuffing noise, some whisper of a clue that would crack open the case. Nothing came.

Floyd stood up and pulled the needle from the record. They left the office and walked down the stairs, stepping around the telephone engineer who was still sitting there with the racing pages, waiting for his replacement part to crawl across Paris. They drove to Montparnasse, Custine waiting in the Mathis while Floyd fetched Greta.

She stepped out into the twilight air, thin and angular in black, like a sketch in *Vogue*. She wore a black fur stole and a black pillbox hat with a spotted veil, and when she stood under the lamplight she looked like a million dollars, until she was near him, and then she looked tired and sad and on the edge of something she couldn't face.

'Let's go eat,' Floyd said gently. 'And then let's go hear some real music.'

They drove to a little Spanish restaurant Floyd knew on the quai Saint-Michel. He ordered a good bottle of champagne, a 1926 Veuve Clicquot, waving aside the others' objections that he couldn't possibly afford it. It was true, technically, but Custine had worked hard and Greta deserved a good night out, a chance to forget about Marguerite for a few hours. The food was as good as Floyd remembered, and even the roving guitarist, Greta had to admit, was not as atrocious as some she'd heard. While Floyd settled the bill, Greta and the guitarist talked about tunings and fingerings. The handsome young man in a black shirt offered Greta his guitar and she played a few tentative notes before shaking her head with an embarrassed smile. The guitarist said something kind in return as he shrugged the guitar strap back over his shoulder. Floyd smiled, too: Greta had been holding back, not wanting to blow the kid away. He must have been new in town.

After the meal they drove to *Le Perroquet Pourpre*, a club on rue Dauphine. Only a few years ago there had been six or seven like it a row, but most of its neighbours were gone now, boarded up or turned into cheap bars with jukeboxes and flickering altarlike television sets in the corner. *Le Perroquet* was still clinging to business, and was one of the few places still willing to let Floyd and Custine on to the bill without Greta. The walls were covered with photographs of jazz men, from Jelly Roll and Satchmo, through Duke and Beiderbecke, Coleman Hawkins and Django. Some of them had even played on rue Dauphine. The owner, an amiable, bearded Breton called Michel, spotted the three of them entering and waved them over to the bar. He asked Greta how her tour was going and listened as she told a white lie about leaving the band for a few days while her aunt was unwell. Floyd asked Michel if business was satisfactory, and Michel offered his usual pessimistic shrug, which hadn't changed much in nineteen years.

'The young people still have ears for good music,' he said. 'The trouble is they don't get a chance to hear it any more. Jazz is political music – always has been, always will be. That's why some people would rather see it dead.'

'Maybe they'll get their way,' Floyd said.

'Well, you're always welcome here. I just wish I could afford to have you play more often.'

'We take what we're given,' Floyd said.

'Are you available for the middle Saturday next month? We've just had a cancellation.'

'I think we can probably squeeze you in.'

'Greta?'

'No,' she said, lowering eyes already obscured behind the veil. 'I don't think I'll be able to make it.'

'Pity. But Floyd and Custine always put on a good show . . . although perhaps you might consider hiring a temporary piano player?'

'We'll think about it.' Floyd said.

'Just so long as you keep it nice and melodic, boys. And not so fast that the punters can't tap a toe.' He eyed Custine warningly. 'None of that difficult eight-beat stuff you keep sneaking in.'

'Maybe the young people want to hear something new for a change,' Custine said.

'They want something new, not something that sounds like a bull loose in a china shop.'

'We'll behave ourselves,' Floyd assured him, patting Custine consolingly on the arm.

Michel set them up with drinks: beer for Greta and Custine, wine for Floyd, who needed a clear head for the drive back to Montparnasse. Leaning on the bar, occasionally breaking off to serve another customer, Michel fed them all the latest news on the local music scene: who was in, who was out, who was hot, who was not, who was sleeping with who. Floyd feigned a polite interest in it all. Although he didn't much care for gossip, it was good to think about something other than the murder case and his own problems for a while. He noticed Custine and Greta starting to laugh more, which made him feel better, and before very long they were all enjoying the company and the music and Michel's habit of keeping their glasses topped up. At eleven the band came on and stumbled through a dozen swing numbers, big-band productions stripped down for a four-piece, and while it wasn't the worst thing Floyd had heard, it was a long way from being the best. It didn't matter. He was with his friends, it was snug and smoky down in *Le Perroquet*, the greats seemed to be looking on benevolently from their photographs on the walls, and for a couple of hours all was right with the world.

Skellsgard and Auger stooped along a dark, low-ceilinged tunnel of rough-hewn rock, doing their best not to get too filthy in the process. They had eaten and made some further refinements to their outfits. Auger's brand-new handbag bulged with maps and money, some of the latter counterfeit, some of it stolen. They had left the censor chamber via a heavily armoured metal door, accessing a dug-out passage that led off in either direction. Skellsgard had a torch, a fluted silver thing with a sliding switch, obviously manufactured in E2. Nervously she shone it up and down the shaft, as if half-expecting something, then set off to the right. She explained to Auger that excavation work in one direction had been abandoned as soon as the other end of the tunnel intersected an old works shaft put in by the Métro engineers.

'Did you tunnel all this out yourselves?' Auger asked.

'Most of it. It was easier after we hit the existing works shaft.'

'It must still have been back-breaking work.'

'It was, until we found we could get an air hose through the censor. We kept a compressor on our side, and then built a simple pneumatic drill that could be smuggled through as individual components. We reassembled it on this side and supplied it with air via the hose passing through the censor. That helped a bit, although the censor had a nasty habit of changing its mind now and then.'

'What about electricity? Can you run that through as well?'

'Yes,' Skellsgard said, 'but we never managed to make anything work. Even a torch turned out to be too difficult to break down into simple components. The censor wouldn't even let an incandescent bulb through in one piece. In the end we had to run gas through to light lamps, like nineteenth-century coal miners.'

'It must have been hell.'

'The only thing that kept us going was the rumble of the trains, which told us we were getting nearer to civilisation. None of the other exit points have any kind of artificial background noise. At least here we knew we only had a few dozen metres of earth to tunnel through before we hit the train tunnel.'

'I'm expected to dodge trains now?'

'Only in emergencies. We can trip the power by short-circuiting the electrified rails, but only for short periods. The station's closed now, so the trains aren't running.'

'Why? What time is it?'

'Four-thirty in the morning on a Friday in October.'

'I had no idea.'

'Don't worry about it. No one ever does.'

Soon they came to a blockage in the tunnel: a tight-fitting wooden door of obvious age. Skellsgard shone her torch around the perimeter of the door until she found a concealed handle. She pulled it, groaning with effort. Just when it seemed as though nothing was going to move, the door hinged slowly back towards them.

Beyond was another dark tunnel, but this time their voices echoed differently. It was a much larger space and it smelled of sewerage, metallic dust and hot oil. Skellsgard's torch gleamed off eight parallel lines of polished metal running along the floor, leading off to the left and right. There were two sets of parallel railway tracks, with two conductor rails for each running line.

Skellsgard set off to the right, keeping tight against the wall, with Auger following close behind.

'It's not far to Cardinal Lemoine. Normally you'd be able to see the station lights from here.'

'I'm scared,' Auger said. 'I'm not sure I can go through with this.'

'Scared is good. Scared is just the right attitude.'

The station was still dark when they climbed out of the tunnel on to its platform. Wherever Skellsgard's torchbeam fell, Auger saw clean ceramic tiles in pale greens and yellows, period signs and advertisements in blocky capitals. Oddly, it didn't feel particularly strange or unreal. She had already visited many buried Métro stations under the icebound Paris, and they had often survived more or less intact. It was easy to imagine that this was just another field trip into the city of ghosts.

Skellsgard showed her to a hiding place and crouched down beside her. 'I know you can do this, Auger. Susan must have known it, too, or she wouldn't have lined you up for it.'

'I suppose I should be grateful,' Auger said doubtfully. 'If it wasn't for her, I wouldn't be about to see any of this.'

'I hope you like it as much as she did. It was the horses Susan wanted to see.'

'Horses?'

'She'd always wanted to know what they were like – as living, breathing things, not some shambling, arthritic reconstruction.'

'Did she get her wish?'

'Yes,' Skellsgard said. 'I think she did.'

The morning rush hour began on cue. From their hiding place – tucked into a gap between two electrical equipment lockers at one end of the platform – Auger watched as the ceiling lights stammered on. She heard the humming of generators powering up and somewhere the melancholy whistle of a lone worker. She heard a jangle of keys and a slamming of doors. A lull of ten or fifteen minutes followed and then she watched the early birds begin to assemble on the platform. The electric lighting washed out the colours like a faded photograph, but even taking that into consideration, she was struck by the drabness of the people: the autumnal browns, greys and greens of their clothes and accessories. Most of the commuters were men. Their faces were sallow, unhealthy-looking. No one was smiling or laughing, and almost no one was talking to anyone else.

'They look like zombies,' she said quietly.

'Cut them some slack,' Skellsgard said. 'It's five in the morning.'

A train slid into the station with a tinny squeal of brakes. Doors opened and some of the passengers got on while others disembarked.

'Now?'

Skellsgard put a hand on her shoulder. 'Wait. The next train will have more people on it.'

'You've done this before, I take it?'

'I still get nervous.'

After a few minutes, another train arrived and Skellsgard eased them into the flow of exiting passengers. From being detached spectators, they were suddenly in the jostle of a human tide. The smell of the other people hit Auger: tobacco and cheap aftershave. It wasn't a bad smell, but it instantly made everything more real. In her daydreams, she had often fantasised about drifting through the old city like a ghost, watching but not participating. Her imagination had always neglected to fill in the smell of the city, as if she was viewing things through a sheet of impermeable glass. Now there could be no doubt that she was fully present in the moment, and the shock of it was visceral.

She looked at the people around her, measuring herself against them. The clothes she had chosen now felt too sharp and ostentatious. She could not seem to find a natural walking rhythm or work out what to do with her hands. She kept clutching and then letting go of her handbag.

'Auger,' Skellsgard hissed, 'stop fidgeting.'

'I'm sorry.'

'Just keep walking ahead and *stop worrying*. You'll do fine.'

The flow of commuters took them up to the street, through a dreary succession of tiled corridors. Auger surrendered her ticket to an uninterested official and stepped into the steely light of early morning. Skellsgard steered them away from the Métro exit, out of the way of the other commuters. At this time of day, the streets were still relatively empty. Cars and taxis rumbled by occasionally. A white municipal truck pottered slowly along the other side of the road, cleaning the kerbside with rotating brushes. On either side of the street, balconied buildings rose up three or four storeys. Lights had come on in some of the rooms and through the curtains and blinds, Auger made out the silhouettes of people preparing for the day.

'It all looks so real,' she observed.

'It *is* real. Get used to it. The moment you start thinking this is some kind of game, some kind of simulation, is the moment it'll give you a bloody nose.'

'What now?'

'We calm you down. There's a place around the corner that does all-night coffee. You want one?'

'I want to crawl into a corner and suck my thumb.'

'You'll get over it. Everyone does. Eventually.'

Skellsgard led her further from the Métro station. They walked down rue Monge and on to boulevard Saint-Germain. In the distance, overlapping neon signs formed a scribble of light. They passed a newspaper vendor: more newspapers than Auger had seen in her entire life were just sitting there, for the taking. They passed a narrow alley between two tenements in which a man was casually urinating, as if that was his job. A little further on, a heavily made-up woman stood, skirt hitched up to stockinged knee, in a shabby-looking hotel doorway. For an electric instant, the woman and Auger made eye-contact. Auger hesitated, some part of her wanting to reach out to the woman and interrogate her about how it felt to be a part of this living tableau. Skellsgard tugged her gently forwards, past a steamed-up basement window from which some kind of music, brassy and discordant, spilled out into the street.

'I know how you feel,' Skellsgard said. 'You want to speak to them. You want to test them, find their limits. To know how human they really are and how much they really know.'

'You can't blame me for being curious.'

'No, I can't. But the less interaction you have with these people, the easier this whole thing will be. In fact, the less you think of them as people, the better.'

'Back there you told me off for saying they looked like zombies.'

'All I'm saying is you need to find a way to maintain a modicum of detachment.'

'Is that how Susan White felt?'

'No,' Skellsgard said. 'Susan got too close. That was her big mistake.'

Skellsgard pushed open the doors of the all-night café. It stood in a row of crumbling Directoire-period buildings on boulevard Saint-Germain that hadn't survived the Void Century.

'Sit here,' Skellsgard said, directing her to a seat next to the window. 'I'll deal with the coffee. You want milk in it?'

Auger nodded, feeling a weird dizziness. She looked around the room, taking in the other customers, measuring them against herself. Monochrome photographs lined the wall: faint Parisian scenes annotated in neat, inked script. Behind the counter, the staff – hair neatly oiled, shirts and aprons crisply white – fussed with gleaming, gurgling apparatus. At the table next to her, two elderly men in flat caps were debating something in the back pages of a newspaper. Beyond them, a middle-aged woman worked on her fingernails while she waited for her coffee to cool. Her white gloves lay crossed on the table before her.

Skellsgard returned with their drinks. 'Getting any easier?'

'No.' But Auger took the coffee and cradled the hot metal mug in her hands. She kept her voice low, the two of them continuing to speak English. 'Skellsgard, I need to know something. How much of this is definitely real?'

'We've been over that.'

'No, we haven't. You talk as if it's all real. It feels real enough. But do we really know for sure?'

'What brought this on? The censor?'

'Yes,' Auger said. 'When we came through that screen, we lost any continuity with the real world. You treated it as if we were just passing through a curtain, but what if there was more to it than that? What if reality ended on the other side of the censor, and all this – everything we see around us – is exactly what you just assured me it isn't: a kind of simulation?'

'Why does it matter?' The question was not as glib as it seemed. Skellsgard was watching her very carefully.

'If this is a simulation, then nothing we do inside here can have any possible consequence for the outside world. This whole city – this whole world, for that matter – might only be a representation inside some alien computer.'

'Quite a computer, if that's the case.'

'But it would still mean that these people . . .' Auger lowered her voice even more. 'These people wouldn't *be* people. They'd just be interacting elements of some super-complex program. It wouldn't matter what happened to them, because they're just puppets.'

'Do you feel like a puppet?'

'How I feel is irrelevant. I've entered the program from the outside. What I don't see is how you can be so certain we're inside an ALS and not a computer-generated environment of some kind.'

'I told you we pushed a pneumatic air-hose through the censor.'

'That proves nothing. If the simulation is good, then it would have handled that detail as well.' Auger sipped at her coffee, flinching at the bitter taste of it before deciding that it wasn't the worst she'd ever drunk. 'All I'm asking is whether you've considered this possibility.'

Skellsgard stirred too much sugar into her coffee. 'Of course we've considered it. But the hard truth is that we can't know for sure. Not yet, and maybe not ever.'

'I don't follow. If this is a computer-generated environment, then it must have limitations.'

'You're thinking way too parochially, Auger. This environment doesn't have to have any limits at all.'

'What about physics?' Auger picked up one of the cardboard coasters that were strewn on the table and held it between thumb and forefinger. 'This feels real to me, but if I looked at it in a scanning tunnelling microscope or ran it through a mass spectrometer – what would I find?'

'Exactly what you'd expect, I guess. It would look just the way it should.'

'Because this environment is simulated right down to atomic granularity?'

'No,' Skellsgard said, 'not necessarily. But if the machine running the environment is sufficiently clever, it can make your microscope or your spectrometer show you whatever it thinks you expect. Remember: any tools you might bring to bear on the problem are themselves part of the problem.'

Auger sat back in her seat. 'I hadn't thought of that.'

'It's pretty much academic anyway. There aren't any scanning tunnelling microscopes just lying around here waiting to be picked up.'

'Then you've not performed such tests?'

'We've done what we can, given the very limited tools we've been able to put our hands on. And none of those tests have revealed anything other than the physics we'd expect.'

'But just because you can't get your hands on those tools doesn't mean they don't exist somewhere.'

'Break into physics laboratories, you mean?'

'No, nothing that drastic. Just monitor their publications. This is the twentieth century, Skellsgard. It's the century of Einstein and Heisenberg. Those men can't be sleeping on the job, surely.'

'Well, there's a problem with that. Fundamental science is nowhere near as advanced here as it was in our nineteen fifty-nine. Remember I told you there was no Second World War here, and therefore no computer revolution?'

'Yes.'

'Well, it had even greater effects than that. There was no Manhattan project, either. No one has the A-bomb here. Without the A-bomb, there's been no need to develop a ballistic-missile programme. Without a ballistic-missile programme, there's no space race. There *are* no huge government-funded science agencies.'

'But surely there's still some scientific research and development going on.'

'In dribs and drabs. But it's unfocused, underfunded, socially unpopular.'

Auger managed a half-smile. 'No change there, then.'

'What I mean is, it's almost as if . . .' But something made Skellsgard stop and shrug.

'Almost as if what?' Auger prompted.

'Well, I was going to say . . . it's almost as if someone's holding it back deliberately.'

'Who would stand to benefit from that?'

'Well,' Skellsgard said, 'at a guess, anyone who didn't want the people here to know what their world was really like.'

THIRTEEN

Floyd crunched the Mathis's tyres against the pavement outside Blanchard's building on rue des Peupliers. Floyd and Custine had made an early start after breakfast, and although Floyd's head was ringing like a cracked bell – too much wine, too much music – with it came a kind of fragile alertness. His throat was raw from talking over the noise in *Le Perroquet Pourpre* compounded by all the coffee he had pushed down it since waking.

'Go easy on Blanchard,' Floyd said as he let Custine out of the car, toolkit in hand. 'I don't want you even to hint that we suspect he may have done it.'

'I suspect nothing,' Custine said. 'I merely wish to close off that particular possibility.'

'Make sure you don't close off the case while you're at it.'

'Trust me, Floyd: when it comes to these matters, I have at least as much experience as you.'

'Have you remembered anything else about that typewriter in the Quai?'

'I can still see that cell. Beyond that, nothing. But I'm sure it will come to me.'

Floyd drove back to the office. The elevator was working, for now at least. He rode the grinding, groaning box to the third floor and let himself into his rooms. He poured a cup of tepid coffee, then picked up the telephone and made another attempt to call the number in Berlin. Same result: the line was still dead. The operator couldn't tell him whether the number was incorrect, or if the telephone at the other end had simply been disconnected. He fingered the letter from Kaspar Metals, unwilling to throw away what seemed like the strongest lead in the case.

While the telephone was still hot, he thumbed through his directory until he found the number of an old contact in porte d'Asnières. Formerly a skilled metalworker, he had been laid off from the Citroën factory after an industrial accident and now worked from home. Although not a musician himself, he made a modest living by repairing brass instruments.

The man picked up on the seventh ring. 'Basso.'

'It's Floyd. How are you doing?'

'Wendell. What a pleasant surprise. Do you have something for me to look at? A trombone someone sat on?'

'Not today,' Floyd said. 'Custine and I haven't been getting out enough to mistreat our instruments. I was hoping that you could answer a couple of questions for me.'

'About repairing instruments?'

'About metalworking. Something's come up in the case we're working at the moment and I don't know what to make of it.'

He heard Basso settle into his chair. 'Tell me.'

'I've got something that looks like a sketch made from a blueprint, and a letter related to a contract with a Berlin metalworks. What I can't figure out is what the contract is for.'

'Do you have anything to go on?'

'It looks like the main work was the casting of three big spheres of solid aluminium.'

'Big spheres,' Basso said ruminatively. 'How big, exactly?'

'Three, maybe three and a half metres across, if I'm reading the sketch properly.'

'Big indeed,' he concurred.

'You have any idea what they might be?'

'I'd need to look at the sketch, Wendell. Then I might be able to tell you something. Did you say solid aluminium?'

'I think so.'

'I wondered for a moment whether they might be bells. Can you bring the sketch over, Wendell? I might be more use to you in person.'

'This morning?'

'No time like the present.'

Floyd agreed and put down the telephone. Five minutes later, he was on his way to the seventeenth, with Custine's saxophone in the passenger seat next to him.

By the time Auger and Skellsgard left the café on Saint-Germain, the sky had brightened. There was more traffic about, more windows open, more pedestrians on the streets. The city was coming awake.

'Look at it this way,' Skellsgard said. 'We have no evidence to suspect that this is a simulation, at least while science here is still stuck in the nineteen thirties. But there's another angle.'

'And what's that?'

'We assume everything we see is real, made out of something more or less like normal matter. Maybe someone – some entity – created this place as a kind of snapshot, a backup copy of the real Earth. By intention or otherwise, the backup copy is running forward in time, progressing away from the instant when it was created. Therefore this is an actual planet, populated by real people. Physics works flawlessly. The only thing that isn't real is the sky.'

'Because we're inside an ALS sphere?'

'Exactly. And whatever other functions that sphere has to serve, the one thing it presumably *must* do is provide a convincing backdrop for the world it contains.'

The sun had begun to edge over the rooftops on the other side of the Seine.

'Then what's that?' Auger said.

'A fake sun. A source of light and heat, nothing more. We know there's no room for a real sun inside an ALS – not if you're going to squeeze a planet in there as well. So whatever *that* is, it must be painted on to the inner surface of the sphere.'

'It looks real to me.'

'Of course, but you're stuck on the surface of this planet with a fixed point of view – as is everyone else here.'

'What about the Moon? Is that real?'

'We don't know. It looks real enough, and the Slasher intelligence suggests that some of the worlds inside ALS objects have their own moons. But without being able to get out there and check, it could be made of green cheese for all we know. Whatever the case, something raises lunar tides, and something takes care of the solar component as well. They've certainly covered the obvious details.'

'They'd have to, to maintain the illusion.'

'Absolutely.'

'So what about the non-obvious ones?'

'That's where astronomy comes in. Thing is, Auger, given the inevitable limitations, it would be pretty difficult to maintain this illusion for ever. They can fake the Sun and the Moon, and the stars in the night sky. They can even fake parallactic movements of the stars, to make it seem as if the Earth is orbiting the Sun. They can fake eclipses and a whole lot more. But there has to be a limit. The shell might be able to withstand scrutiny from the kind of astronomy they have here. But there is no radio astronomy here, no space-based astronomy. If any of those technologies came along, I doubt that the illusion could be sustained for very long.'

'But we had radio astronomy by now.'

'Another by-product of the Second World War. We also had space-based astronomy – not to mention interplanetary space probes – within a decade or so. Any one of those things would be the clincher, Auger.'

'What would happen if the people living here discovered the illusion?'

'Anyone's guess. The news might cause society to unravel overnight. Or it might spur on a technological revolution, enabling them to develop the tools necessary to break through the sphere. If that were to happen, I doubt that it would take them more than a generation or two.'

'They might even overtake us,' Auger said.

'That, too. The point is, within a relatively short period of time they may have the means to test the accuracy of the ALS. If they find an error – some detail that doesn't make sense – then we'll know for sure that it isn't a simulation, because a simulation could be as perfect as its builders wished. We'll also know – finally – that this isn't the real past, the real nineteen fifty-nine.'

Auger looked at her companion. 'As if that was ever likely. The maps already tell us that this isn't any slice of history from our own past.'

'But we can't be absolutely sure of that,' Skellsgard said. 'You're making a judgement based on your own historical knowledge, and concluding that the maps don't fit into it.'

'I guess so,' Auger allowed.

'But your knowledge is a construct stitched together from the wreckage left behind by the Nanocaust. It's incomplete and quite possibly wrong in key details.'

'Innocent mistakes.'

'Maybe, but it could be more than that. It would have been the ideal time for someone to doctor the records, to change our view of the past to suit their own needs.'

'Which sounds suspiciously like paranoid conspiracy-mongering to me.'

'All I'm saying is that whenever we make any judgements about the nature of the nineteen-fifty-nine timeline here, we have to keep in mind that our own historical knowledge is incomplete and possibly flawed.'

'All the same . . . you don't seriously believe that you've actually opened a window into the past, do you?'

'It was an issue,' Skellsgard said. 'A serious one, too, because the one thing we didn't want to do was screw around with our own timeline. That was why we brought your predecessor on to the team.'

'Susan?'

'Her job was to sift the evidence, to roam around the environment, measuring it against our historical knowledge. In the end she found a number of instances where this version of Paris flatly contradicts what we have excavated on E1 – for instance, structures that had been demolished here but which still existed at the time of the Nanocaust. Susan's preliminary conclusion: whatever this place is, it isn't a window into our past.'

'I'm glad you sorted that out.'

'Susan was supposed to tie together all the evidence and make a definitive report. But then she got sidetracked—'

'And killed,' Auger said darkly.

'Yes.'

Auger slowed her footsteps. 'This boxful of papers I'm supposed to find – do you think it relates to what you've just been talking about?'

'Until we see what's in it, we won't know.'

'It seems to me,' Auger said, 'that Susan would have made her mind up pretty quickly about this timeline. It wouldn't have taken her long to figure out this wasn't *our* nineteen fifty-nine. So what else was she interested in?'

'Susan kept digging,' Skellsgard said. 'It wasn't enough for her just to hand in that report and not want to know more about what had happened here. She wanted answers to her questions. She wanted to know who made this place, and why. She wanted to discover the precise moment at which it diverged from our history, and she wanted to know why that happened as well. Was it a chaotic accumulation of small changes, a snowballing butterfly effect, or did some single, deliberate act of intervention change history? And if so, who was responsible for that? And if someone did that, are they still working behind the scenes, influencing things?'

'Which brings us back to your theory about arrested development.'

'The thing is, Auger, if someone *is* working behind the scenes – for whatever reason – they probably wouldn't have taken too kindly to Susan digging around the way she did.'

'She was an archaeologist,' Auger said. 'Digging is what we do.'

'Can't argue with that,' Skellsgard said.

They boarded a train at Saint-Germain-des-Prés and took the number four line to Montparnasse-Bienvenüe, then changed on to the elevated number six line, taking it west across the rooftops to Dupleix. The train was full of people on their way to work, strap-hanging in long grey raincoats, heads buried in the morning editions. Nobody paid much attention to the view through the windows, but it was all Auger could do to stop herself gasping in wonder at the panorama of the city sliding by outside, meticulous in every detail. It was both exactly as she had imagined it would be and nothing at all like she had expected. The old photographs could only convey so much. There was an entire human texture that simply hadn't registered, like the absence of colour in a monochrome print. Everywhere she looked in the angled, intersecting streets, she saw people going about their business, and it was both marvellous and chilling to think of them having their own lives, their own dreams and regrets, knowing nothing of what they really were. Auger felt a shaming, voyeuristic thrill, and snapped her attention away as soon as anyone was in danger of meeting her gaze.

At Dupleix they left the train, descending a latticed iron staircase to street level. They walked down de Lourmel until it intersected with Emile Zola, and then walked a short way along Zola until they reached a pale-stone five-storey establishment that identified itself as the Hôtel Royale.

'You're booked in here for three days,' Skellsgard said, as they walked into the carpet-lined lobby, 'but chances are you'll be out a lot sooner than that. If you need to stay longer, you have more than enough cash to cover your expenses.'

Behind the lobby counter, the concierge was busy signing in a couple who must have arrived on an overnight train. They were flustered, and appeared to be disputing some detail of their booking.

'Promise me one thing,' Auger said.

'I don't do promises, but let's hear it.'

'If this works out – if I get your precious box of papers back into safe hands – then let me have some time here alone.'

'I don't know about that.'

'I'm here already, Maurya. What harm can it do?'

'Aveling won't like it.'

'Aveling can shove it where the sun doesn't shine. The least he can give me is some time to play tourist.'

'He'll say the deal was no tribunal, nothing more.'

The couple moved away from the desk to the waiting elevator and the concierge beckoned Auger and Skellsgard forward. Auger shifted mental gears, forcing herself to speak French. The words emerged with surprising fluidity, as if some stiff part of her mind had suddenly been tuned and lubricated.

'My name is Auger,' she said. 'I have a reservation for the next three nights.'

'Certainly, madame.' The concierge glanced at Auger, then Skellsgard, then back to Auger. 'Your bags have already arrived. How was your journey?'

'Fine, thank you.'

He handed her the room key. 'Number twenty-seven. I will have your luggage sent up in a moment.'

'Is there a telephone in the room?'

'Of course, madame. We are a modern establishment.'

She took the key and turned back to Skellsgard. 'Guess I'm on my own now.'

'You have the telephone number of the safe house near the station. One of us will be there around the clock. Call to keep us updated on what happens over the next few days. We'll need to arrange downtime when you return to the tunnel.'

'Somehow, I think I'll remember.'

'And go easy with Blanchard. If he doesn't hand over the goods on the first try, don't turn up the pressure. We don't want him getting wind that they're more valuable than they appear, or he may do something rash.'

'I'll do my best.'

'I know you will, Auger.' Skellsgard leaned in and gave her a quick sisterly hug. 'Take care, all right?'

'Whatever happens,' Auger said, 'I'll be glad I've seen this much.'

'I'll see what I can swing with Aveling about getting you some tourist time. No promises, OK?'

'No promises.'

Behind Auger, the elevator chimed open.

The telephone was an antique, but she had handled examples like it in the museum section back home, lovingly restored and wired into a simple telephonic network. She entered the Paris number a digit at a time, waiting for the pleasant *whirr* as the clockwork dial spun sedately back around to its starting position. Slow, but calming. Even in the entering of a number, there was time for reflection. The task could be safely abandoned before completion. A well-bred Slasher, used to near-instantaneous communication, would have regarded the rotary telephone as not much of an improvement over semaphore. To a Thresher, by contrast, there was something deeply reassuring and trustworthy about any kind of electromechanical hardware. It couldn't lie, or distort the information it carried. It couldn't invade the mind or the flesh.

At the far end of the line, a similar telephone rang. Auger felt an impulse to hang up before Blanchard responded, convinced that she wasn't ready to go through with this. Her palm was slippery on the handset. But she forced herself to stay on the line, and after another few moments someone answered.

An old man's voice said, 'Blanchard.'

'Good morning, monsieur,' she replied in French. 'My name is Verity Auger. I'm not sure if you know my name, but—'

'Verity? As in the sister of Mademoiselle Susan White?'

'Yes,' she said. 'I'm calling about . . .'

Out of courtesy, or some misguided need to demonstrate his own skill, he shifted to English. His native French accent was obvious, but his speech was perfectly comprehensible. 'Miss Auger, I am not sure if you have heard the news. If not, then perhaps—'

'It's all right, sir,' she interrupted, also switching to English. 'I know what happened to my sister.' She heard an intake of breath: relief, perhaps, that he didn't have to break that particular piece of news to her.

'I am very, very sorry about what happened to her. I was fortunate to know your sister quite well. She was a very nice young woman.'

'Susan spoke well of you, sir. It's obvious that she thought of you as someone she could trust.'

'You speak of her belongings?'

'Yes,' Auger replied, glad that he had raised the subject without prodding. 'I understand that my sister left some items—'

'It's not much,' he said quickly, as if she might be expecting the crown jewels.

'I never expected it to be, sir. All the same, whatever she left still has value to us . . . to her family, I mean.'

'Of course. Might I ask where you are calling from, Miss Auger?'

'Paris, sir. A hotel in the fifteenth.'

'Then you are really not very far away. You can take the number six line to place d'Italie, and then walk the remaining distance. Shall we make an appointment?'

She knew she mustn't sound too surprised that he had agreed to hand over the box so easily. 'Any time you like, sir.'

'At the moment the box is not in my possession. I gave it to a private detective who is investigating the circumstances surrounding Susan's death.'

'Circumstances, sir?'

'The possibility that it may not have been accidental,' he elaborated.

Auger's hand tightened on the phone. At no point in her briefing had anyone mentioned a private detective snooping around. It had to be a new development, something Aveling and the others didn't know about.

Already she was off-script.

'It's really kind of you to take an interest, sir. This detective—'

'Oh, don't worry about him. I'm quite sure he's had time to examine Susan's things thoroughly by now.'

'Then when would be—'

'An associate of the detective is here now. I can speak to him and arrange for the items to be back in my possession by . . . shall we say by the end of the afternoon?'

'The end of the afternoon? *Today*, sir?'

'Is that a problem?'

'Not at all, sir. Not in the least.' Her heart was thudding in her chest.

'Let me have the name of your hotel and the telephone number. We shall say four o'clock in number twenty-three rue des Peupliers, unless you hear from me. If you press the buzzer by my name, I shall let you into the building. My rooms are on the third floor.'

'That's perfect, sir.'

'I very much look forward to making your acquaintance, Miss Auger.'

'And I look forward to meeting you, sir,' she replied.

Basso opened the door to his tiny flat in porte d'Asnières, sniffing the air like a bloodhound. 'Wendell,' he said. 'I didn't think you'd remember the way. Is that a patient you have with you?'

Floyd offered the saxophone case. 'She probably needs a little attention.'

'I thought you said you had nothing that needed repairing.'

'I did,' Floyd said. 'But I'm sure you can find something wrong with it.'

Basso took the case and placed it down on the table next to his umbrella stand. 'You're too kind. I am sure that the saxophone is in excellent health. But I never turn down a patient.' He peered over Floyd's shoulder. 'Are you still driving that old relic?'

'It's difficult to fit a double bass into anything smaller.'

Basso shook his head amusedly. 'You'll still be saying the same thing when that car's forty years old. Now come in and have some tea.'

Floyd removed his fedora. 'Actually, I could really use some coffee. As strong as you can manage.'

'Like that, is it?'

Basso ushered Floyd into his dark living room. An unfeasible number of clocks ticked and whirred to themselves, some mounted on the walls, others perched on shelves and on the long granite mantelpiece. Supporting himself with a stick, Basso shuffled to one of the clocks, swung open its case and made some tiny adjustment with a tool he carried in his pocket.

'I was thinking about what you said about the spheres,' Floyd said. 'Being bells, I mean.'

Basso wandered into his kitchen and raised his voice. 'What about them?'

'I don't see how they could be. I've never heard of a completely round bell. How would it chime?

'I didn't mean *that* kind of bell, you buffoon. I meant diving bells, the kind you climb into. The size seemed about right.'

'But they're solid.'

After a little while, Basso came back in with a single cup of coffee. It had

165

the stiff, black consistency of marine fuel oil: just the ticket, as far as Floyd was concerned.

'When you said solid, I didn't think you meant solid all the way through. I assumed you meant that the shells were to be formed from solid metal with no perforations or joints.'

'I'm pretty sure they're solid spheres.'

'Let me see the sketch.'

Floyd passed him the paper and sat quietly, ingesting the coffee, while Basso turned the paper this way and that, squinting and frowning. A few seconds before eleven, there came a series of near-simultaneous clicks and ratcheting sounds from the clocks, as of mechanisms gearing up, and precisely on the hour the assembled clocks emitted a cacophony of chimes that lasted the better part of a minute. During this time, Basso continued studying the sheet of paper as if nothing was happening.

When the clocks had settled down again, he lifted his face towards Floyd and said, 'Well, you're right. It *is* solid, and it does seem to be about the size you mentioned.' With a blunt forefinger he traced the other faint lines marked on the paper. 'This seems to be some kind of support arrangement, to suspend the sphere. Why the fine cables, I wonder?' His finger moved again. '*This* seems to be a kind of cross-section through a vat or tub. At a guess, I suspect that the sphere is supposed to be immersed in whatever goes into this tub.'

'Ring any bells? Other than the submarine kind, I mean.'

'I'm afraid I've never seen anything like this. Do you have any other information?'

Floyd offered him the letter from Berlin. 'Just this.'

'It clearly refers to the same contract,' Basso said, reading down the paper, his lips moving softly as he mouthed the German. 'Three spheres. Copper–aluminium alloy, with very high machining tolerances. Here's something about the support mechanism. Acoustic dampening, if I'm not misreading it.'

'What does that mean?'

'It's an arrangement designed to cut down on the transmission of vibrations.'

'And how would it work?'

'That would depend on the application. If the sphere was the source of the vibrations, like the engine in a submarine, then it might need to be cushioned so that those vibrations didn't escape out through the hull and into the surrounding water, where they could be picked up by enemy sonar.'

'It doesn't look like any kind of marine engine to me,' Floyd said.

'No . . . it doesn't. Which raises the other possibility, which is that the sphere is the thing that has to be protected from vibrations.'

'What sort of thing are you thinking of?'

'It could be almost anything,' Basso said. 'Any kind of sensitive scientific or commercial apparatus might benefit from that kind of protection.'

'Guess that narrows it down slightly,' Floyd said. 'For a while back there we wondered if it might be some kind of bomb.'

'No, I don't think that's what it is. The apparent solidity,' he mused, ticking off key points on his fingers, 'the very precise machining specifications, the need for dampening – they all point to it being some kind of measurement apparatus. What kind, I couldn't begin to imagine.' Basso returned the paper to Floyd. 'Of course, I could be completely wrong.'

'But you might be on the right track.' Floyd finished the thick, black coffee. It was like pouring hot asphalt down his throat. 'Thanks, Basso. You've been helpful.'

'Although it probably wasn't worth your driving all the way over here to see me.'

'That's all right,' Floyd said. 'I had to bring the patient with me, didn't I?'

Basso rubbed his hands. 'Let's have a look at her, shall we?'

Floyd stopped on the way home to pick up provisions and have a leisurely lunch at a café near the Trocadero. By two he was back at his desk, pulling out his notebook and thumbing through to Blanchard's number. It was much earlier than the time he had arranged to call Custine, but he was anxious to know if there had been any progress with the wireless set.

Floyd let the telephone ring for half a minute, hung up and then waited a minute or two before trying again, with no success. He concluded that Blanchard must have been elsewhere, perhaps upstairs in Susan White's room, if he hadn't left the building entirely. He tried once more five minutes later, but still there was no answer.

Floyd was placing the receiver back on its cradle when he noticed something that had been pushed beneath the squat, black pedestal of the telephone. It was a sheet of folded paper, and it had not been there that morning. He pulled it out and opened it up. He recognised a block of text in Custine's very neat, curlicued handwriting. The message read:

Dear Floyd

I hope and pray that you find this letter in good time. I could have placed it openly on your desk, or even in your pigeonhole, but for reasons that will shortly become apparent, I believe this would have been a very unwise course of action.

I have just returned by taxi from rue des Peupliers. I find myself in a great deal of trouble. I must not say too much, for the less you know about it, the less chance there will be of my friends from the Quai finding some way of connecting it to you. In any case, I am sure they will be in touch with you soon. In the meantime, I must make myself scarce. I do not think it is safe for me to remain in Paris for very much longer. I will try to make contact, but for both our sakes, I suggest you make no effort to find me.

Now destroy this message. And then take very good care of yourself.

Your friend and colleague AC

PS – I do not think Heimsoth and Reinke make typewriters.

Floyd sat, stunned. He re-read the message, hoping that he had been hallucinating, but nothing about the letter had changed. Something had happened and now Custine was on the run.

He felt as if he needed a drink. He picked up the bottle to pour himself a finger of brandy, but then returned it to the table unopened. What he really needed, some quiet, detached voice told him, was utter clarity of mind, and he needed it fast.

The case had been progressing smoothly. They were on to something big – he'd become increasingly sure of that – but nothing had prepared him for this sudden, savage turn of events. What could possibly have happened? He replayed the sequence of events in his mind, thinking about Custine's intentions for the day. Everything had been normal when he left Custine at Blanchard's building earlier that morning, complete with his tools. The big man had planned to have another listen to the wireless, to see if those Morse signals came through again. He'd also intended to quiz the missing tenant on the second floor, and to nibble around the delicate matter that Blanchard might have had something to do with the murder. There was scope for the old man to have taken offence if Custine had barged in with a tactless line of questioning, but that was the last thing Custine would have done. His experiences in the Quai had made him much better at that tact and diplomacy stuff than Floyd.

So what the hell had happened?

Floyd's hands were trembling. *Get a grip*, he told himself sternly. What Custine needed now was for Floyd to stay in control. The way to stop himself collapsing into a bundle of nerves was to act, to keep moving.

His first instinct was to drive to rue des Peupliers, but it hadn't been his plan to go there until later in the afternoon. The one thing he didn't want to do was anything that might suggest he'd received a communication from Custine. But there'd been no answer when he telephoned Blanchard. Perhaps that would have prompted him to fire up the Mathis and drive across town, even if he hadn't seen the letter on his desk . . . or perhaps it would never have crossed his mind that there was a problem.

Do something, he told himself.

He re-read the letter. No clue as to Custine's current whereabouts, so no need for Floyd to bluff about that if anyone asked him. Although he had a suspicion . . . He put it out of his mind – it would be safer for both of them if he didn't even speculate about where Custine might be holed up.

He read it again, forcing his hands to still themselves. The reference to the typewriter: what was *that* about? Had something finally jogged Custine's memory?

Do something.

Floyd went to a shelf and pulled down a commercial directory for the Paris area. He flipped through until he reached the 'H' section and then ran his finger down the page until he found the entry for the Paris office of Heimsoth and Reinke, more than a little surprised to discover that the firm even existed.

Quickly he dialled the number.

'Heimsoth and Reinke,' said an efficient female voice. 'May I help you?'

'I have an electric typewriter that needs repairing. Can you tell me if there is a location in the Paris area that deals with that sort of thing?'

'A typewriter?' she asked, sounding surprised, Floyd thought.

'It's a Heimsoth and Reinke model. I found it amongst the items I inherited when my aunt passed away. It doesn't seem to work, but it looked rather expensive and so I imagined it might be worth having it fixed to sell on.'

'There must be some mistake. This firm doesn't make typewriters, and it certainly doesn't repair them.'

'But the box the typewriter's in says—'

He could hear the woman's patience wearing thin. 'Heimsoth and Reinke make enciphering equipment, not typewriters. Our most popular model is the Enigma, which might conceivably be mistaken for a typewriter.' The tone of her voice told him that only the very ignorant could possibly have made this mistake.

Floyd asked, 'What would my aunt have been doing with an enciphering machine? I thought such things were meant for spies and soldiers.'

'That's a common misconception. Over the last thirty years we've sold many thousands of Enigma machines to various parties, including banks and businesses that wish to protect their commercial interests. Of course, the military models are more complicated, but there's no law that says an individual can't own an Enigma machine. Are you still interested in having it repaired, assuming that it is indeed broken?'

'I'll think about it,' Floyd said. 'In the meantime, thank you for your assistance.'

As Floyd placed the receiver back on its cradle there was a knock at the door. But the timbre of the sound was wrong, somehow, as if someone was already inside the apartment. Floyd had no sooner arrived at this conclusion when he observed three pairs of polished shoes approaching him across the floor of the adjoining room. He looked up, taking in two uniformed officers of the Quai and a third man, alarmingly young and sleek, who was dressed in the long raincoat and heavy serge suit of a plainclothesman. The uniformed officers retained their hats, but the plainclothes inspector had already removed his bowler.

'Can I help you—' Floyd started.

The plainclothesman spoke as the three of them entered the main office. 'I'm so very glad to find you at work, Monsieur Floyd. I heard you on the telephone – I hope we aren't interrupting anything important.'

FOURTEEN

'I have no idea what this is about,' Floyd said, 'but where I come from, it's customary to knock.'

'But we did,' the young inspector said pleasantly.

'I meant knock and then wait to be invited in. As a matter of fact, you might even try calling ahead to make an appointment. It's called common courtesy.'

The inspector smiled. 'But we did. Unfortunately, the line was busy whenever we tried. Of course, that convinced us that there was someone home now, otherwise we would have paid you a visit later this afternoon.'

'And the purpose of this visit is what?'

'My apologies,' the young plainclothesman said. 'I am Inspector Belliard of the Crime Squad.' He stopped in front of Floyd's desk and picked up a black china paperweight in the shape of a horse that had been holding a ream of typed and carbon-copied documentation in check. 'Nice antique,' Belliard said. 'It would make a wonderful blunt instrument.' He tossed the horse to one of his partners, who fumbled the catch and let it drop to the floor, where it shattered into a dozen jagged pieces.

Floyd fought to keep a lid on his temper – the one thing they clearly wanted him to do was lose it badly. 'That almost looked deliberate,' he said. 'Of course, we both know it was an accident.'

'I'll writ you a chit for it. You can claim compensation at the Quai.'

'Do they hand out chits for electrocution burns? I might need one of those as well.'

'What an odd question,' Belliard said, smiling thinly. He moved to the window, pulling back the blinds to examine the view. Floyd noticed that for a moment neither Belliard nor his men had their eyes on his desk. He used the instant to slip Custine's letter back under the telephone, hoping that none of the men would notice the sudden movement or the slight chime as the handset resettled on its cradle.

'I guess you're here to harass my partner,' Floyd said.

Belliard turned from the window, blowing a line of dust from his fingers. 'Harass your colleague, Monsieur Floyd? Why on Earth would we want to do that?'

'Because it's what you've always done?'

The young man scratched the tip of his nose. He had a very slender face, nearly hairless, like one of the dummies Floyd frequently saw in the windows of gentlemen's outfitters. Even his eyebrows appeared to have been pencilled in. 'Funny you should mention your partner,' the man said, 'because it's Custine we were hoping to have a chat with.'

'I know all about your "little chats",' Floyd said. 'They usually involve a quick trip to the bottom of the stairs.'

'You're much too cynical,' Belliard said, chidingly. 'It doesn't become you, Monsieur Floyd.'

'I've grown into it like an old shoe.'

'These are new times, a new Paris.'

Floyd picked up a pencil and rolled it between his fingers. 'I think I preferred the old one. It smelled better.'

'Then maybe you should air out the place a little,' Belliard said, opening the office window. A sudden stiff breeze blew through the room, sending papers flying on to the carpet and slamming shut the main and connecting doors. Belliard turned from the window and walked towards Floyd, making no effort to avoid the case notes and paperwork now littering the floor. 'There. Better already. It wasn't the city that had a bad smell about it, it was your office.'

'If you say so.'

'Let's stop playing games, shall we?' Belliard moved back to the side of the desk directly opposite Floyd and planted the heels of his hands on the edge of it. He was looking Floyd straight in the eye. 'There's been a murder in the Blanchard building.'

'I know,' Floyd said. 'I'm the poor sap investigating it.'

'Not that one. I mean the one that happened about three hours ago.'

'I don't follow.'

'Blanchard is dead. He was found on the pavement beneath his balcony, just like the unfortunate Mademoiselle White.' Belliard looked at one of his men. 'You know, perhaps there *was* something in that business after all.'

Genuinely shocked despite the forewarning in Custine's message, Floyd found it difficult to form the words he wanted to say. 'Blanchard's dead? Blanchard's actually been murdered?'

Belliard looked at him with pale, discriminating eyes, as if judging the exact degree by which Floyd was surprised. 'Yes,' he said, his thin, bloodless lips moving but the sound reaching Floyd delayed, as if travelling across a great divide. 'And the unfortunate thing is that the last person seen in his presence was your associate Custine. As a matter of fact, he was observed leaving the building in something of a rush.'

'Custine didn't do it,' Floyd said automatically.

'You sound astonishingly sure of that. How could you possibly know that, unless the man himself has offered you an explanation or an alibi?'

'Because I know Custine. I know he wouldn't do something like that.' Floyd's throat was suddenly dry. Without asking anyone's permission, he poured himself a sip of brandy and knocked it back.

'How can you be so certain? Do you have that much insight into his character?'

'I have all the insight I need,' Floyd snapped, 'and it wouldn't matter a damn whether I did or not, because it still wouldn't make any sense. Blanchard took us on to solve his homicide case – why would one of us murder our own client?'

'Maybe there was always an ulterior motive,' Belliard said. 'Or perhaps the murder was completely impulsive: an act of sudden, blinding rage, entirely without premeditation.'

'Not Custine,' Floyd said. His eyes drifted to the telephone, where the slip of white paper was still jutting out visibly from underneath the base, in spite of his attempt to hide it. Belliard couldn't see it from his present angle, and might not make anything of it if he could, but if he *did* notice it . . . Floyd felt nausea flood through him like water through the Hoover Dam.

'No matter what he may have told you, André Custine was a violent man,' Belliard said, almost sympathetically. 'A man died in custody under his questioning. You knew that, didn't you? An innocent man, as it happened; not that his innocence would have been much consolation while Custine was breaking every finger on one of his hands.'

'No!' Floyd said, aghast.

'I see from your expression that he didn't tell you. What a shame. All this might have been avoided, otherwise.'

Feeling detached from himself, as if bobbing above his body like an invisible balloon, Floyd said, 'What do you mean?'

'Simply that Blanchard might still be alive. Evidently, Custine lost it again.' Belliard pursed his lips disapprovingly, as if being forced to listen to an off-colour joke. 'There's no telling what might have set him off.'

'Don't you idiots get it?' Floyd said. 'There was one homicide connected with the Susan White case and now there's been another. Don't go trying to pin this on Custine just because of his past, just because you and he have some unfinished business. You'll be going after the wrong man while the right man gets away with it again.'

'A nice theory,' Belliard said, 'and I'd be tempted to give it the time of day if there wasn't one niggling little detail out of place.'

Floyd closed the telephone directory, trying to make the action seem as casual and automatic as possible. 'Which is?'

'If your man Custine is the innocent party here – just happened to be in the wrong place at the wrong time – then why was he in such a hurry to leave the scene of the crime?'

'I don't know,' Floyd said. 'You'll have to ask him that yourselves. No, actually, I *do* know: Custine was no fool. He'd have known exactly how you'd try to pin this on him, for old time's sake.'

'Then you allow that he may have fled the scene?'

'I allow nothing,' Floyd said.

'When was the last time you saw Custine?'

'This morning.' Floyd noticed that one of the other officers was writing notes in a spiral-bound notebook with a black marbled fountain pen. 'I dropped him at the Blanchard place while I went off to make some other enquiries.'

'"Some other enquiries",' Belliard repeated, a mocking note in his voice. 'That does sound so very professional, when you put it like that. What was Custine supposed to be doing?'

Floyd shrugged: at this point he saw no need to lie. 'There was something about the White case that bothered us. Custine needed to get a better look at the wireless set in her room.'

'And that was the last time you saw him or heard from him?'

'I tried calling the Blanchard apartment not long before you arrived. No one picked up.'

Belliard looked at Floyd with an amused glint in his eye. 'That doesn't quite answer my question.'

Floyd reminded himself that the last thing he should do was lose his temper with these Quai men, and forced himself to speak calmly and civilly, like a man with nothing to hide. 'That was the last contact I had with Custine.'

'Very well,' Belliard said. 'And was there any sign that Custine had been here in your absence? He's your associate, so I presume he has his own key to your premises.'

'There's no sign that he's been back.'

'Nothing disturbed, nothing missing, no messages?'

'Nothing like that,' Floyd said, as wearily as he dared.

Belliard motioned for the other officer to snap shut his notebook. 'We're done here, I think.' He reached into his jacket and pulled out a business card. 'Now it's my turn. We found one of your business cards on Blanchard's body, and another turned up with the witness who saw Custine fleeing the scene. By way of reciprocity, here's my card.'

Floyd took it. 'Any particular reason why I might need this?'

'Custine may try to contact you. It's not unusual, especially if someone's just gone on the run. He may need personal items, he may need funds. He may wish to put his side of the story to a friend.'

'You'll be the first person I call if that happens.'

'Make sure that I am.' Belliard reached for his hat, then stopped himself. 'I almost forgot: there's a small favour I need to ask of you.'

'I'm all ears.'

'I need to use your telephone. We have a team still sweeping the crime scene and I'd like to call them before I make my next move, just in case they've turned something up. There's a wireless in the car, but it's a long walk downstairs and I won't be able to call through to Blanchard's apartment directly.'

'Go right ahead,' Floyd said, feeling his blood temperature drop about ten degrees. 'I hope that counts as co-operating with your enquiries.'

Belliard lifted the receiver from its cradle and started dialling. 'Very much so. And don't let me walk out of here without signing you a chit for that horse.'

The edge of Custine's letter glared at Floyd, peeking out from underneath the telephone like a flag of surrender. If they found that note, Floyd thought, then he and Custine were both as good as dead. They would take Floyd down into the Quai and make life unpleasant for him until he gave them some lead that would bring them Custine. And if he died before they got it out of him, they'd simply make sure they had enough men on the job to cover all the possibilities. They had scented blood now: the chance to punish Custine for the way he had betrayed them all – in spirit if not in name – before his enforced retirement. It had been a long time coming, and they were not going to be in the most forgiving frame of mind.

Belliard started speaking, his French almost too rapid and clipped for Floyd to follow. It was French with a heavy seasoning of police jargon: almost another language in its own right. The inspector leaned against the table and began to drag the telephone towards him by fractions of an inch, gradually exposing more and more of the letter.

He's going to see it any second now, Floyd thought, *and he isn't going to be able to resist taking a look at it. It's what anyone would do, in the same circumstances.*

He heard someone try the outer door but find it locked. A voice called out in thick peasant French. Belliard motioned for one of the officers to open the door, while he continued speaking. Floyd picked up snatches of Belliard's side of the conversation: something about the wireless itself being smashed to pieces on the pavement, along with Blanchard. And it sounded as if it had been a violent death this time, with no attempt to make it look like anything other than murder.

The second officer reached the outer door and unlocked it. He opened it a crack and Floyd saw another officer standing there, a man who must have been waiting in the car downstairs. Floyd had a moment to register this scene and then the door was wrenched violently from the officer's hand as another gale suddenly tore through the apartment, snatching into the air the few papers that hadn't already found their way to the floor. In that squall of flying paper, Floyd saw the note from Custine flutter out from under the telephone, across the room and out through the open window, like a moth on the wing.

Belliard concluded his call and returned the telephone to Floyd's desk. 'Perhaps I shouldn't have opened that window after all,' he said, looking down at the carpet of dishevelled papers. 'It'll take you a month of Sundays to tidy up this lot.'

'That's all right,' Floyd said, wondering how obvious his relief was. 'It was about time they had a good sort.'

Belliard reached into his jacket and pulled out a book of chits. 'How much for the horse?'

'Don't worry about it,' Floyd said. 'I was going to throw it out anyway.'

After he had locked the door behind the Quai men, Floyd moved to the window, still open to the mid-afternoon city, and peeled aside the dusty slats of the blinds. He watched the black police sedan below grumble into life and move away. He looked up and down rue du Dragon, noting the positions and makes of the other vehicles parked there and paying particular attention to any that he did not recognise or that seemed out of place in the rundown backstreet, with its potholes and waterlogged drains. There, three shops up, was another dark sedan. He couldn't tell the model from the angle of his view, but it looked similar to the police car he had just seen depart – probably an unmarked police vehicle. Behind the oily gleam of the windshield, he saw a man sitting patiently with his hands folded in his lap.

Floyd had to give them credit. Less then four hours had passed since the murder, but the efficient boys from the Quai had already assigned a crack team from the Crime Squad to it. Admittedly, they hadn't had to look very far for a lead – not the way Floyd and Custine had helpfully distributed business cards around the premises. But they had still organised a tail, and maybe more than one. Floyd had an idea of the way the Quai worked: if you thought there was one man putting you under surveillance, then there was probably a second or a third you had no idea about.

Floyd let the blinds flick back into place. He felt drained, as if he had just staggered to his feet after receiving a stomach punch. Everything had changed since he had walked into the office, laden down with groceries and rather fewer problems than he imagined he had. Why was it never good news that put problems into perspective? Why did it always take another set of problems?

He sat back down at his desk and tried to compose his thoughts. The basic details of the investigation remained unchanged, but now it was a double-homicide case, and the police had belatedly decided to take an interest. Or – more probably – they had latched on to Blanchard's death as a pretext for punishing Custine. It still didn't look as though they had much interest in the first homicide.

But even though the letter was gone, Custine had still given him a vital clue. The typewriter hadn't been a typewriter at all, but a sophisticated piece of enciphering equipment. Several things suddenly made a lot more sense – and they all backed up the spy hypothesis.

Susan White had cooked her wireless to tune into coded transmissions. The dots and dashes had looked a lot like Morse, and maybe they were derived from it, but that was only the beginning of the encryption. Morse, as Floyd knew well from his days sailing out of Galveston, was just a way of sending the written word over the airwaves. Anyone with a Morse book could crack that kind of message even if they had no prior knowledge of the code, which was fine for parlour games, but nowhere near secure enough for spies. That was where the Enigma machine came in. The signals coming over the wireless set had already been scrambled by whoever sent them. White's smashed Enigma machine had been her means of unscrambling those messages back into something readable.

It meant that she was definitely a spy. No doubt about that now. It also meant there wasn't a hope in hell of ever learning what was in those Morse transmissions.

Floyd snapped out of his reverie and checked the time: three-thirty in the afternoon. Forcing himself into the role of a man who had had no contact with his partner, he decided that his most likely course of action would be to visit the scene of the crime and get the full story for himself. Floyd splashed some water down his throat, then grabbed his hat and coat. He was about to leave Susan White's tin of documents where it was on his desk when a thought flashed into his mind: whoever had murdered Blanchard had probably been after the tin. First Susan White had been murdered, and now the landlord. Presumably whoever had committed the second homicide must now know that the tin was elsewhere. And with all those business cards lying around, it wouldn't take them long to make the connection with Floyd.

He picked up the tin. From now on, wherever he went, the tin was coming with him.

Floyd turned the Mathis into rue des Peupliers, slowing as he noticed a trio of police cars gathered near number twenty-three. In his rear-view mirror he saw the dark sedan he had noticed on rue du Dragon glide past him towards the junction with rue de Tolbiac, slowing as the driver noted Floyd's location. The kid pursuing Floyd was an amateur, and Floyd had made no effort to elude him on the drive across town to Blanchard's street. There was almost certainly someone more experienced on the same surveillance detail.

Floyd parked halfway up the street, stopped the engine and observed the scene in silence for a few moments. Although the death had happened at least five hours earlier, and probably more like six, there was still a large crowd of onlookers gathered on the sidewalk beneath the balcony. Their shadows were beginning to lengthen in the afternoon light. For a morbid instant, Floyd wondered if the body was still there, crushed and disfigured by the fall. That seemed unlikely, though, and the more Floyd looked, the more obvious it became that the spectators were only gathered around the entrance to the building because they were hoping to snatch a titbit of forensic gossip from the Quai officials – police and scientists – who were presumably still coming and going from the crime scene.

Floyd smoothed his hair, slipped his hat on and left the car. He walked up to the gathering of onlookers, recognising none of them. Two uniformed officers were standing guard at the door, bantering with the crowd. Gently, Floyd pushed his way through the people until he was in plain sight of the policemen.

'Can I help you, monsieur?' asked the older of the two officers.

Floyd showed the man his identity papers and business card. 'I'm a private detective,' he said. 'Monsieur Blanchard – the late Monsieur Blanchard – happened to be my client.'

'Bit late then, aren't you?' the officer replied, to a chuckle of approval from his colleague.

Floyd tried to sound as breezily unconcerned as the police officer. 'Monsieur Blanchard had me investigating an earlier incident that occurred in this building. Now that something's happened to him, I can't help wondering if there's a connection.'

'Your client's dead,' the older officer said. He had bad breath and a shaving problem. 'Doesn't that mean no one's paying your wages?'

'He gave me a generous retainer,' Floyd said. 'Anyway, I still have a personal involvement with this case. My associate appears to be the prime suspect.'

'How would you know that?' the officer asked.

'I had a visit from Inspector Belliard. He filled me in.' Floyd lowered his voice. 'Have you talked to these people yet?'

'These aren't the residents. Interviews with the residents are taking place inside.'

'All the same, they might have seen something.'

'They didn't. They'd have said so otherwise.'

Floyd turned to the people around him; by now he was the focus of attention, rather than the ominous dark smear on the pavement. 'This is my case as much as theirs,' he said, addressing the gathering, making eye contact with as many of them as possible. 'A woman was murdered here three weeks ago and these bright young things from the Quai didn't bother taking it seriously. Now there's been another suspicious death.'

Floyd reached into his jacket and pulled out a sheaf of business cards. 'If any of you people care about preventing a third homicide, now's the chance to do something about it. Think back over the last few days, perhaps the last few weeks, if you like, and try to remember anything that struck you as unusual. Maybe it was someone hanging about that you didn't recognise. Maybe even a child. My guess is that whoever was responsible for the first killing had something to do with the second.'

A middle-aged woman in a droopy hat reached out and took one of the cards from his hand. 'I saw something,' she said. 'I tried to tell these men, but they weren't interested.'

'Call me and we'll talk about it,' Floyd said.

'I can tell you now. There was a big man, like a wrestler. Very well dressed, but all sweaty and out of breath. He came running out into the street and tried to flag down a taxi. There was an argument: someone else was already waiting for the cab and the big man didn't like it. They almost came to blows.'

'You saw this?' Floyd asked.

'I heard it.'

'When?'

The woman looked across the gathering to a male friend. 'What time was that commotion?'

'I looked at my watch,' the other bystander said, taking the burnt-down stub of a cigarette from between his lips. He wore a chequered flat cap and a pencil moustache. 'It happened at exactly—'

'I didn't ask you, I asked the lady.' Floyd turned back to the woman. 'Did you actually see this happen?'

'I said I *heard* it,' she repeated. 'A commotion in the street, cars honking their horns, voices raised.'

'But you didn't actually see the big man yourself?' he persisted.

'Not with my own eyes, no,' she said, as if this was only a subtle distinction. 'But he did' – she pointed at the man again – 'and what with the commotion I heard—'

'This is a street in the middle of Paris,' Floyd said. 'You'd be hard pressed to find a single half-hour when there wasn't some sort of commotion.'

'I know what I saw,' the spivvy man said, before pushing the exhausted stub of his cigarette back between his lips.

'That argument over the taxi,' Floyd asked him, 'did you notice anything else happening at the same time?'

The man looked around at his fellow watchers, wary of a trap. 'No,' he said, after due deliberation.

'Well, that's funny,' Floyd said, 'because by rights there should have been a body on the sidewalk.'

'Well, there was . . .' the middle-aged woman said, but on a falling note.

'Before the fight over the taxi? Or just afterwards? Think about it carefully, because rather a lot depends on it.' While he was speaking, Floyd noticed a younger woman looking at him from the back of the crowd. She kept opening her mouth, as if on the point of saying something, but other people kept interrupting.

A man in a butcher's apron raised his hand. 'Why did you ask about a child just now?'

'Just covering all the bases.'

'I did see a child. A little boy. A very nasty-looking one, hanging around here.'

Before Floyd could pursue that information, a new voice emerged from the doorway leading into Blanchard's apartment building. 'Send him inside. We need to talk to him.'

Floyd quickly handed out the rest of his business cards, urging the witnesses to contact him if they remembered anything else. He watched as someone passed a card to the woman at the back of the crowd. Then he slipped past the two policemen into the dark, mildewed hallway of the apartment building.

'Hello, Floyd. I notice you've been scattering cards around like confetti lately,' the newcomer said, still standing in the shadows.

'The last time I checked, there wasn't a law against it.'

'You're right to phrase it that way,' the man replied. 'These days, one can't be too careful about anything, including the law. Shut the door behind you.'

Floyd found himself doing as he was told. The man's voice was simultaneously both commanding and reassuring. It was also a voice Floyd had heard before.

'Inspector Maillol?'

'It's been a while, hasn't it? How long ago was the Monceau stabbing – five, six years?'

'At least.'

'An ugly business all round. I'm still not convinced we caught the right man.'

Floyd's involvement with the case had been tangential – one of his then clients had been linked to the victim – but it had still been enough to bring him into contact with the men from the Big House. Politely enough, Maillol had told him to stop treading on their steel-capped toes. Floyd had taken the hint.

'I assume you've already had a nice chat with my colleague Belliard?'

'He got his point across,' Floyd said.

'Belliard has his methods; I have mine.' Maillol looked every bit the evil interrogator: he had a thin, drum-tight face through which the bones of his skull seemed about to burst, a cruel little mouth and crueller little eyes behind rimless glasses. The last five or six years had done nothing to soften that countenance. He took off his homburg and scratched at the shaven egg of his scalp.

'I hope your methods are an improvement,' Floyd replied.

'Your friend is in a great deal of trouble,' Maillol said, without prevarication. 'All the more so now that Belliard has taken an interest in the case.'

'I got the impression I wasn't exactly off the hook either.'

'Belliard is one of the bright young things. The right suit, the right hat, the right car, the right wife. He even has the right political connections.'

'Chatelier?'

'Who else?'

Something in the man's tone of voice eased Floyd. 'I take it you're not exactly singing from the same hymn sheet.'

'Times are changing,' Maillol said. 'This is not the same city it was a few years ago.'

'Funny – that's exactly what Belliard said.'

'But he undoubtedly said it as if it was a good thing.' Maillol slipped his hat back on, pressing it down firmly. It made a scratching sound against the stiff stubble above his ears. 'I am serious about Belliard: he is not a man of whom you wish to make an enemy.'

'You're his superior.'

'In theory,' Maillol said. 'Sadly, I lack both his ambition and his connections. Do you read the papers, Floyd?'

'I keep up with the funny pages.'

'I shouldn't be working this case. Officially I'm not even here. I'm supposed to be working anti-bootlegging investigations in Montrouge.'

'I read about that. I also heard that you dropped my name when Blanchard was looking for a private eye.'

'You were the obvious choice. I was concerned about the death of the American girl: something about it didn't add up. But the director of prosecutions was satisfied with the accidental-death verdict, so there was nothing I could do.'

'But now the police must take both cases seriously, surely.'

'That depends on whether they want either of them solved or not.'

'Belliard seemed pretty keen to get results.'

'Ah, but what kind of results? He was wrong to ignore the earlier killing: he missed a perfect opportunity to blame her death on some handy minority. But now he has Custine in the frame, he will more than make up for that oversight.'

'He hates Custine that much?'

'They all do.'

'And you?' Floyd asked.

'I knew Custine. We worked together ten years ago, in the seventeenth.' Maillol reached inside his jacket and removed a slim metal cigarette case embossed with a mermaid. He offered a cigarette to Floyd, who declined, before lighting one for himself with a small lighter inlaid with ivory. 'He was a good detective. A hard man, but always one you could trust.'

'Then you'll know he isn't capable of this.'

'Why did he run, in that case?'

'He may have left the scene of the crime,' Floyd said, 'but only because he was smart enough not to hang around. He didn't push Blanchard off his balcony.'

'Someone must have done it,' Maillol said, tapping ash on to the floor. 'Your friend is the perfect suspect.'

'It seems that Custine was already in a taxi when the body hit the street.'

'Which still doesn't let him off the hook. We won't know until the coroner's report comes in, but it's still entirely possible that he killed Blanchard.'

'I don't see how.'

'He might have stabbed or shot the old man, without killing him instantly. He leaves Blanchard in a weakened condition, knowing he won't last long, and rushes downstairs to hail a taxi. Upstairs, meanwhile, Blanchard finds enough strength to stumble around, which unfortunately leads him to fall out of his window.' Before Floyd could frame an objection, Maillol raised a hand and said, 'Merely a scenario, of course. There are others. The point is simply that the observed sequence of events is not necessarily inconsistent with your friend having committed murder. Believe me, I've investigated far stranger cases.'

'Then maybe you've developed an overactive imagination,' Floyd said. 'How's this for an alternative scenario: Custine was up there with the old man, either in the same room or nearby. He had every right to be up there – after all, we'd been invited into the building to work the White case.'

'And the trifling matter of Blanchard's death?'

'Someone else did it. Custine witnessed it, or came in too late to do anything about it. Of course he fled. In his position, any sane man would have done the same thing.'

'The law will still take a dim view of it.'

'But you understand, surely,' Floyd said, 'knowing what you do about Custine, about his relationship with his former colleagues . . . what else could he have done?'

Maillol conceded the point with a downward stab of his cigarette. 'The fact that I know Custine's history or might have done the same thing in his shoes changes nothing.'

'He's innocent,' Floyd insisted.

'But you can't prove it.'

'What if I could?'

Behind his glasses, Maillol widened his cruel, pale eyes the merest fraction. 'You have something tangible?'

'Not yet. But I'm sure I can put together enough—'

'It will take more than circumstantial evidence to protect him from Belliard.'

'Then I'll find what it takes.'

'You're a reasonable man, Floyd.' Maillol took a lengthy drag on the cigarette before continuing. 'I realised as much when our paths crossed over the Monceau case. I told you to back off then and you did. I appreciated that. And I know you mean well by your partner. For what it's worth, I doubt that Custine did this. But the only thing that will get him off the hook is another suspect.'

'Then I'll find you another suspect.'

'Just like that?'

'Like I said, whatever it takes.'

'Do you have anyone in the frame? If you do, you should tell me immediately. Not doing so could constitute the withholding of evidence.'

'There's no one else in the frame,' Floyd said.

'I wish you were lying, for Custine's sake.' Maillol flicked his spent cigarette to the floor, where he crushed it underfoot. His shoes, Floyd observed, were very scuffed and old. 'Unfortunately, I rather suspect you are telling the truth.'

'I've only been on the case a couple of days.'

'But now there is no case,' Maillol said. 'The man who was employing you is dead.'

'What are you saying?'

'You care about Custine. You may even know where he is. But this is a battle neither of you can win. If Custine has a chance, now is the time for him to leave Paris. That's what I would do.'

'It's only men like Custine who are standing between this city and the wolves.'

'Then perhaps we should all give some thought to leaving,' Maillol replied.

FIFTEEN

The telephone was ringing when Floyd unlocked the door to his office on rue du Dragon. He picked it up with a tingle of trepidation, thinking it might be Custine, but hoping that his partner had more sense than to call him on a number that was more than likely being monitored by the Quai.

'Hello?' he said, sitting down behind his desk.

'Is that Floyd Investigations?' The voice on the other end of the line belonged to a woman speaking French, but with an accent he couldn't quite place. 'My name is Verity Auger. I'm calling about my sister.'

Floyd sat upright and tore a clean sheet from his pad, scraping the nib of his fountain pen against it until ink blurted out. 'Your sister?' he asked.

'Susan White. I believe you're investigating her murder.'

'I am indeed,' Floyd replied. 'You can speak English, too, if it's easier. Your French sounds pretty good to my ears, but if we're both Americans . . .'

'I had a good idea that you were American,' she said, switching to English, 'but it seemed a bit rude to assume too much.'

'How did you hear of me?'

'I was in the crowd on rue des Peupliers when you handed out those cards. By then I'd also spoken to some of the other tenants, and they'd mentioned that you were asking questions about Susan. I should have spoken to you then, but it's a delicate matter and I didn't want to bring it up in front of all those people.'

'And what delicate matter would that be?'

'I'm calling about my sister's belongings. I understand that poor Mister Blanchard gave them to you before he . . .'

'I have them,' Floyd said. 'It's just a box containing some papers, but you're welcome to them. You have my address on that card, right?'

'Rue du Dragon, yes.'

'Do you need directions?'

'No. I'm sure I'll find my way. I can be there within the hour. Will that be all right? Or we can make it later today if that suits you better.'

Floyd was about to agree to meet her in an hour, but something held him back. He was going to give her the box, no doubt about it, but he also wanted to find out what she did with it when she left his office. With Custine out of action, putting a tail on her was going to be complicated. Greta couldn't take care of it on her own, even if she could be dragged away from Montparnasse at such short notice.

Even as he hesitated, a plan began to assemble in his head, but it was not the sort of thing he could throw together in an hour or two. 'Look,' he said quickly, before she grew suspicious, 'today is a bit of a problem. I have to leave the office on another case.'

'You're a busy man, Mister Floyd.'

He couldn't tell if she was mocking him, or quietly impressed. 'It's nothing too exciting. It would just make things easier if we could make an appointment for first thing tomorrow morning.'

'That sounds perfectly acceptable.'

'Nine o'clock it is, then.'

'See you there, Mister Floyd.' She put down the telephone.

Floyd hung up at his end and stared down at the blotted sheet of paper, upon which he had written nothing at all. Then he paged through his telephone directory until he found the number for Maurice Didot, the elevator engineer.

'It's not broken down again, has it, Monsieur Floyd?'

'Not exactly,' Floyd said, 'but I'm hoping you might be able to arrange something for me.'

'I'm not sure I understand.'

'Can you be here at half-past eight tomorrow morning?'

'Half-past eight, on a Saturday?'

'I'll explain everything,' Floyd said. 'I'll also make it worth your while.'

An hour later, he found Greta in the kitchen in Montparnasse, leafing through a movie magazine while she finished a cigarette. On the cover was a publicity photograph from the latest gloomy *policier*. She looked up, her eyes tired and her make-up smudged.

'I wasn't expecting you so soon.'

Floyd closed the door behind him. 'There's been a development. A real serious development.'

'Sit down.' She closed the magazine and slid it across the table.

'It's Custine,' Floyd said.

'What about him?'

'He's on the run.'

'This had better not be some kind—'

'Do I sound as if I'm joking?' he said sharply. 'Monsieur Blanchard is dead.'

'Monsieur who?'

'The landlord of the building on rue des Peupliers – the man Susan White entrusted with that box of papers. The man who employed Custine and me to prove she was murdered. They found him dead on the sidewalk this morning.' Floyd pulled up a chair and sat across the table from her.

'No,' she said softly.

'Yes. And Custine happened to be in the building carrying out the investigation at the time.'

'Surely you don't think he had anything to do with it.'

Floyd buried his head in his hands. 'I want to believe he didn't. Everything I thought I knew about the man says he couldn't have done this.'

'Well, then.'

'But he was supposed to talk to the landlord about the possibility that he might have killed Susan White. Not by confronting him directly . . . but just nose around the question, to rule it out.'

'Did you seriously think—'

'We had to exclude the possibility. Just because he seemed like a kindly old man with a plausible story—'

'But you told me the police weren't even interested in investigating the girl's death. Why would the old man risk the finger of suspicion pointing his way?'

'Custine and I wondered if he really wanted to be found out. If he killed her for attention and didn't get it, of course he'd want to hire us.'

'You need nasty, suspicious minds in your line of work.'

'It was just a hypothesis,' Floyd said defensively. 'The point is that I authorised Custine to turn up the heat on Blanchard. And a few hours later they find Blanchard face down on the sidewalk.'

'You think Custine may have probed too deeply?'

'We're talking about a man who used to work interrogation duty at the Quai, a man who specialised in the application of fear and pain to get a result.'

'Someone's been putting doubts in your mind.'

Floyd gazed at her through his fingers. 'Today I heard something about Custine that I didn't know before.'

'Let me guess. One of Custine's former colleagues had a little word with you?'

'He said that an innocent man died in his custody, under questioning.'

'Do you believe that?'

'I have no reason not to believe it.'

'Custine's your *friend*, Floyd.'

'I know, and I feel lousy for even thinking that he might have had something to do with Blanchard's death. But I can't help the way my mind works.'

'Were there any witnesses?'

'People saw Custine fleeing the scene. That may or may not have been before the body hit the street. Someone else saw a strange little boy.'

'And that's supposed to mean something?'

'Strange little children keep turning up in this case like bad pennies.'

'You think a *child* might have done this?'

'I think a child might be involved, but I don't know how, I don't know why.'

Greta ground out the cigarette on her ashtray, then tapped the edge with coal-black fingernails. 'Forget the children for a moment. Have you had any contact with Custine?'

'Not in person, but he left a note in my office. He must have gone there straight away, as soon as he realised how much trouble he was in.' Floyd sat back in his chair and picked his shirt away from his chest. It was sodden with sweat, as if he had been running around on a hot summer day. Forcing some semblance of calm into his voice, he said, 'I'd only just had time to read the message when I got a visit from one of the boys from the Big House – lovely fellow by the name of Belliard – and two of his henchmen.'

'I've never heard of him.'

'Hope you never do. He's got a real bee in his bonnet about Custine, and I think he'd like to take me down at the same time.'

'What did he say?'

'He wanted to know if I'd had any contact with Custine. I lied, of course, but they know Custine's bound to get in touch with me sooner or later.'

She scrutinised him long and hard before framing her next question. 'And what does Custine want from you?'

'Nothing. He says he can take care of himself.'

'But he's your friend,' she said again. 'My friend, too. We have to help him.'

Floyd studied her face, trying to read her mood. 'How is Marguerite?'

'Do you really want to know, or are you just changing the subject?'

'I really want to know,' he said. 'Do you think the situation in Paris is getting as bad as she says?'

'It's clearly not getting any better.'

'Maillol said more or less the same thing when I ran into him at Blanchard's place. It's frightening that such a change could creep up on us unnoticed.'

'I'm sure people said the same thing twenty years ago.'

'You're thinking of Marguerite's comment about the weeds coming back?'

'Yes,' she said simply.

'Maybe she's right. Maybe it takes an old person's perspective to see things so clearly.'

'All the more reason to leave,' Greta said.

'Unless people do something about it here, now, before it's too late.'

'People like you, Floyd?' She had difficulty hiding her amusement.

'People like *us*,' he said.

'There's something else, isn't there?'

'Yes. I've heard from Susan White's sister. She telephoned the office just before I drove over.'

'It's quite the day for developments. What did she want?'

'The tin.'

'Are you going to let her have it?'

'I want her to have it. But I also want to tail her when she leaves the office. For that I'm going to need a little bit of help.'

'I see.'

'Will you do it? If not for me, then for Custine?'

'Don't push your luck, Floyd.'

'I mean it. Maillol said he could get Custine off the hook if I could come up with something tangible.'

'Like what?'

'Another suspect. I know it's a long shot, but the girl's my only lead. If I don't follow her, Custine's finished.'

Floyd and Greta pushed through the doors into *Le Perroquet Pourpre* and followed the line of framed jazz photographs that led downstairs into the basement. At eight on a Friday evening a few regulars had already arrived, but otherwise the place was quiet, with most of the tables still unoccupied. A young kid in a striped shirt was playing 'East St Louis Toodle-Oo' solo on the house piano, trying to match Duke's moves but not quite getting there. Michel nodded coolly at Floyd and Greta, served them drinks without saying a word and went back to polishing the zinc-topped bar. Every now and then he'd raise an eye to the door at the top of the stairs leading down into the room, as if expecting someone else.

Floyd and Greta sipped their drinks without speaking. Five minutes passed, then ten.

'You know why we're here,' Floyd said, eventually.

Michel stopped polishing and made a big show of putting aside his towel. 'You take the easy route getting here?'

'No one followed us,' Floyd assured him.

'You sure of that?'

'As sure as I can be.'

'That's not much of a guarantee.'

'It's the best I can give you. You know where he is, don't you?'

Michel took their empty glasses. 'Follow me.'

He raised the folding section of counter at the end of the bar and led them into a back room full of casks and empty wine bottles. Another door led into a meandering brick corridor lined with wooden beer crates. Halfway down this corridor, Michel stopped at an unmarked white door and fished out a set of keys. He opened the door and stepped into another storage room, also piled high with crates. They appeared to fill the room to the back wall, but when Floyd looked closely he saw that the crates had been arranged to conceal another door.

'Through there,' Michel said. 'Keep it quick, and keep it quiet. No offence, Floyd, but I'm taking a serious risk here.'

'And it's appreciated,' Floyd assured him.

The concealed door admitted them to a tiny room not much larger than a broom cupboard. The walls were covered with flaking plaster, which was coming off in scabs to reveal damp, cracked brickwork. A single electric light bulb provided illumination. A mattress on the floor was the only item of furniture. Half-lying on this mattress, his back propped against the wall with only a few thin pillows for comfort, was Custine. A bag of provisions sat by his side. He wore the same clothes he'd had on that morning, but now they were crumpled, sweat-stained and dishevelled, as if he'd had them on for a week.

Custine placed aside a scrap of newspaper he'd been reading. 'Don't mistake this for ingratitude,' he said, 'but how did you find me?'

'Lucky guess,' Floyd replied.

'Or rather, a process of deduction,' Greta said. 'How many friends do we have left in this city?'

'Not many,' Custine admitted.

'So it wasn't that difficult to draw up a short list. Michel was pretty near the top.'

'It's good of him to keep me here,' Custine said, 'but I can't stay for long. It's too dangerous for him, and too dangerous for me. I take it you weren't—'

'Followed? No,' Floyd said.

'I'm in a lot of trouble.'

190

'Then it's up to us to do what we can to get you out of it,' Greta said.

'But first we have to know what happened,' Floyd added. 'All of it, André, from the moment I dropped you off at rue des Peupliers this morning.'

'Did you get my note?'

'Of course.'

'Then you know about the typewriter.'

'The enciphering machine? Yes. What I don't quite understand is—'

'We used them at the Quai,' Custine said, 'for secure communications between different establishments when we were trying to crack major organised-crime operations. The kind of people who tap *our* telephone lines. When Blanchard showed us the typewriter case – at least, what he thought was a typewriter case – I knew I'd seen one like it before. It was just a question of remembering when and where.'

'I'm glad you did,' Floyd said. 'It cleared up a few things.'

'She was a spy.'

'I agree.'

'And she wasn't acting alone, either, not if someone else is still sending those coded transmissions. She almost certainly has associates in the area.'

'As a matter of fact,' Floyd said, 'one of them's due to walk into the office at nine tomorrow morning.'

Custine's eye widened. 'The sister?'

'She showed up, just like Blanchard said she would.'

'Be very, very careful how you play this,' Custine warned.

'I've got the matter in hand. Now I'd like to hear your side of the story. What the hell happened today?'

Custine rearranged himself on the mattress. 'I began my investigations on the second floor, with the tenant you didn't manage to speak to yesterday. He still wasn't in, so I proceeded to Mademoiselle White's room and once again set about trying to record those radio transmissions.'

'Did you get anything?'

'Yes – and this time I had the benefit of a Morse book. But as I transcribed the message it became clear that it was meaningless – just a random sequence of letters. I stared at them and stared at them until something about them began to seem oddly familiar. That was when I remembered the Enigma machine in the Quai. It hit me then: it was utterly pointless trying to extract any information from the message. Even if we managed to get our hands on an intact Enigma machine of the same kind that Susan White was using, we would still have no idea of the particular settings that would need to be applied to decipher the message.'

Floyd scratched his head. 'How long would it take us to work through all the possibilities?'

Custine shook his head dismissively. 'Years, Floyd. The encryption's not meant to be easily broken. That's the whole point.'

'So this whole wireless business was a wild-goose chase?'

'On the contrary. It told us rather a lot about Susan White, even if it didn't tell us what was in those messages. We also know that someone made a point of smashing her Enigma machine. Whoever did that knew exactly how important it was.'

'So she was killed by an enemy agent,' Floyd speculated.

'I think we can assume so,' Custine replied. 'And whoever did that must have destroyed the rotor settings for the machine as well. Nothing in the tin she entrusted to Blanchard resembles a list of such settings. They may have been written down elsewhere. She may even have committed them to memory.'

'Talking of Blanchard,' Floyd prompted.

'When the futility of intercepting those signals dawned on me, I put the wireless back as I'd found it the day before, complete with broken connections. I packed away my tools and set off down to Blanchard's rooms, where I intended to bring up the delicate matter we discussed yesterday.'

'And did you?'

'I never got a chance,' Custine said. 'When I knocked on the door to his rooms, I found it ajar. I pushed it open and called out to him. No one answered, but I heard . . . sounds.'

'What sort of sounds?'

'Scuffling, grunting. Furniture being shoved around. Naturally, I entered. That was when I saw the child: a little girl, perhaps the one we saw outside the apartment yesterday, perhaps another one.'

'What was the child doing?' asked Floyd, a sick feeling beginning to churn in his stomach.

'It was killing Monsieur Blanchard.' Custine said this with a perfect, detached calm, as if he had gone over the events in his head too many times to be shocked by them any more. 'Blanchard was on the floor, with his head pressed against the leg of a chair. The child was squatting over him, holding one hand over his mouth while it grasped a clawed fire iron in the other. It was smashing the fire iron against his skull.'

'How could a child overpower a man like that?' Floyd asked. 'He was elderly, but he wasn't particularly frail.'

'All I can report is what I saw,' Custine said. 'The child seemed to have enormous animal strength. It had stick-thin arms and legs, but was still hammering that fire iron down on him as if it had the strength of a blacksmith.'

'You keep calling the child "it",' Floyd observed.

'It looked at me,' Custine said. 'That was when I knew it wasn't any kind of child.'

Greta looked at Floyd, concern filling her eyes. Floyd reached out and touched her arm reassuringly. 'Go on,' he said to Custine.

'It was dressed like a little girl, but when it looked at me, I knew it was something else – something more like a demon than a child. Its face reminded me of a piece of shrivelled fruit. When it opened its mouth, I saw a dry, black tongue and a few rotten stubs of teeth. I *smelled* it.'

'He's frightening me,' Greta said, shuddering with revulsion under Floyd's hand. 'Is this supposed to be one of those children you say keep turning up?'

'Whatever they are, they aren't children,' Custine repeated. 'They're things that resemble children unless you look closely. That's all.'

'This isn't possible,' Greta insisted.

'We've both seen them,' Floyd said. 'So did some of the tenants in Blanchard's building.'

'But . . . *children*?'

'Somehow they fit into this,' Floyd said. 'One of them probably killed Susan White.'

'What happened next?' Greta asked, fascination gradually overcoming apprehension.

'The child looked at me,' Custine said. He reached into the little bag of provisions next to his mattress and took out a bottle of whiskey, helping himself to a nip. 'It looked at me and made a sound I will never forget. It opened its mouth – that was when I saw the tongue and teeth – and it . . . *sang*.' He said the word with distaste, washing it from his mouth with another slug of whiskey.

'What do you mean, it "sang"?' Floyd asked.

'Or wailed, or shrieked – I really can't describe it adequately. It was not a sound a child was ever meant to make, like a kind of monstrous yodel. Don't ask me how, but I knew what it was doing: it was calling out to others like itself. Summoning them.' Custine screwed the top back on the bottle and returned it to the bag. 'That was when I fled.'

'You knew that would look bad.'

'Nothing would have been as bad as staying in that room. I looked around for a weapon, but the child-thing already had the one item in the room capable of doing any damage. I just wanted to get as far away from there as possible.'

'You hailed a taxi?'

'Yes,' Custine said. 'I took it straight to rue du Dragon, where I left you the note. Then I came here.'

'The men from the Big House think you killed Blanchard,' Floyd said.

'Of course they do. It's what they want to believe. Have they spoken to you?'

'I had a real nice chat with an Inspector Belliard shortly after you fled the scene.'

'Belliard is poison. Protect yourself, Floyd. Have nothing more to do with the case. Have nothing more to do with *me*.'

'Bit late for that.'

'It's never too late for common sense.'

'Well, maybe this time it is. I spoke to our old friend Maillol. He was sceptical, but deep down I'm pretty sure he thinks you're innocent.'

Custine shook his head resignedly. 'One good man can't help any of us.'

'I told him I'd clear your name. He said he'd look at any evidence I was able to turn up.'

'I'm warning you, as a friend: leave this whole business alone. Do what I intend to do, which is to get out of Paris at the earliest opportunity.'

'There's nowhere for you to run,' Floyd said. 'I can hop on the flying boat and be in America two days later. You can't. Wherever you go in France, the men from the Quai will find you eventually. Our only hope is to clear your name.'

'Then you have set yourself an impossible task.'

'If I give Maillol one of those children, things might look a bit different.'

'No one will believe that a child was capable of those murders.'

'But if enough witnesses come forward – enough people who've seen one of these demons hanging around – that might change things.'

'Floyd,' Custine said, with sudden urgency, 'please use your head. Those things are out there, even as we speak. They are in the city. They move without attracting suspicion. Furthermore, they seem to be doing their utmost to kill anyone who had the slightest connection with Susan White – which now includes the three of us.'

'Then I guess that makes it personal,' Floyd said.

'Drop the case, my friend. Drop the case and go with Greta to America.'

'Not yet. Like I said, I've already got an interview lined up with the sister.'

'You are playing with fire.'

'No,' Floyd said, 'I'm playing with the only lead left in this whole case. And the only thing that's going to lead me to those children, and get you off the hook.'

Custine slumped back against the wall. 'I can't argue with you, can I?'

'It's no more than you'd do for me.'

'Which only goes to show that we both lack common sense.'

'It's overrated anyway,' Floyd replied, smiling.

'Be careful,' Custine said. 'Those children may be demons, but there's no guarantee that the sister isn't just as dangerous.'

At nine the next morning, Floyd watched Verity Auger walk into his office. The slatted light shining through the blinds caught her from one side, electric silver highlights dancing on every curve and curl. She wore a dark pinstriped business suit with low-heeled shoes, and if she had arrived with a hat she must have hung it up outside. Her neatly parted light hair fell in a straight line down to her shoulders and then flounced back up at the ends, as if it had changed its mind at the last moment. Her hair made Floyd think of the flukes of whales in old Dutch lithographs. She had very fine eyebrows, and her face seemed to shift from severe to serene and back again between heartbeats.

She had already helped herself to a seat before it occurred to Floyd that she really did not look very much like her sister.

'I'm sorry about the state of my office,' Floyd said, indicating the piles of barely sorted paperwork. 'Someone decided it needed rearranging.'

'You needn't apologise,' Auger said, resting a handbag on her lap. 'I'm just grateful that you've agreed to see me at such short notice.' She looked him squarely in the eye. 'I appreciate that this is all very unusual, Mister Floyd.'

'There's nothing "usual" where a homicide's concerned,' he said. 'And I don't imagine any of this has been easy on you.'

'I won't pretend it's been easy,' she said. 'On the other hand, I won't pretend that Susan and I were the closest of sisters, either.'

'Family trouble?'

'Nothing so dramatic. We were just never very close when we were growing up. We were half-sisters, for a start. Susan's father died before I was born. She was four years older than me, which might not sound much, but it's a world of difference when you're children. Susan may as well have been a grown-up for all that we had in common.'

'And later, when you were both older?'

'I suppose the age difference became less important, but by then Susan was spending less and less time at home. She was always running off with boys, bored out of her mind with our little town.'

'Tanglewood, Dakota,' Floyd said, nodding.

Her eyes widened in what was either mild surprise or mild disbelief. 'You know it?'

'I know *of* it, but only because of what I learned from the papers in your sister's tin. Funny thing is, I looked it up in a gazetteer and it doesn't seem to exist.'

'You mean it wasn't in the gazetteer. I assure you it exists, Mister Floyd. I would have a great deal of trouble explaining my childhood if it didn't. Do you have an ashtray?'

Floyd passed her one. 'It must be a real one-horse town.'

Auger shook her head as she lit a cigarette. 'It has wild ambitions of becoming a one-horse town.'

'Like that, is it? In which case, I understand why your sister felt she had to leave. A place like that can begin to feel like a prison.'

'Where are you from, if you don't mind my asking? I don't even know your first name.'

'I'm from Galveston, Texas.' Floyd said. 'My father was a merchant marine. I was a trawlerman by the time I was sixteen.'

'And you ended up in Paris?' Auger blew out a line of smoke. 'I hope you weren't the navigator.'

'I was the navigator, wireless operator and a lot of other things until the day I decided I liked making music more than catching fish. I'd just turned nineteen and I'd heard that Paris was the place to be if you wanted to make it as a musician. Especially if you were American. Bechet was here, Baker, Gershwin. So I caught a boat to Marseille and decided to try to make my name. I landed in nineteen thirty-nine, a year before the tanks rolled into the Ardennes.'

'And?'

'I'm still trying to make my name.' Floyd puffed out his cheeks and smiled. 'I gave up on my serious jazz ambitions after about six months. I still play as a hobby, and now and then I make more money out of it than I do from the detective business. But I'm afraid that's more of a sad reflection on the business than my luck as a musician.'

'How did you get into this line of work? It's something of a jump from trawlerman to private detective.'

'It didn't happen overnight,' Floyd replied, 'but I had an advantage before I even landed. My mother was French, and I had the paperwork to prove it. The French army was undermanned and unprepared for the German army lining up on the border. When they finally woke up and realised they were being invaded, they weren't too fussy about who they let into the country.'

'And did you man those guns?'

'I told them I'd think about it.'

'And?'

'I thought about it and decided there were things I'd rather be doing than waiting around for German Seventy-Sevens to pound the hell out of me.'

Auger abandoned her cigarette, barely smoked, stubbing it out in the ashtray. 'Didn't the authorities come after you?'

'There were no authorities. The government had already cut and run, leaving a city run by mobsters. For a while back there, it really looked as if the German invasion was going to succeed. It was only luck that those armoured divisions got bogged down in the Ardennes – bad weather working *for* us, for once. That and the fact that we realised they were in trouble in time to put some bombers over them.'

'A close thing, in other words. It almost makes you wonder what would have happened if that advance hadn't stalled.'

'Maybe it wouldn't have been so bad,' Floyd said. 'At least there'd have been some kind of order under the Germans. Still, it was the right outcome as far as I was concerned. There was a lot of dirty work to go around. A man who could speak American and French and pass as either was very valuable in those days.'

Auger nodded. 'I can imagine.'

Floyd waved a hand, compressing years of his life into a single dismissive gesture. 'I got a job as a bodyguard and chauffeur for a local gangster. That taught me more ropes than I ever knew existed. When the local gangster opposition wiped out my boss, I made a couple of sideways moves and found myself running a small, struggling detective agency.'

'Shouldn't there be another chapter – the one where you end up running a huge, successful detective agency, with branches all around the world?'

'Maybe next year,' he said, smiling ruefully.

'I like your attitude, Mister Floyd. You don't seem to feel that the world owes you a living.'

'It doesn't. I've played jazz with some of the best musicians alive. And I've seen them paid in bottles of medicinal alcohol, which they gladly sucked down until they went blind from it. While I still have a roof over my head, I can't feel too sorry for myself. This little operation won't make me or my partner Custine rich men, but somehow or other we stumble on from year to year.'

'Actually – and this is going to sound somewhat indelicate – it's your little operation I came to talk to you about. Or rather one particular investigation being conducted by your agency.'

'I wondered when the small talk was going to end. Pity – I was actually beginning to enjoy it. Shall we get to Susan's belongings?'

He could see the relief on her face. 'You have them, then. I was so worried when I heard about what happened to her landlord.'

'I have the box she gave him for safekeeping,' Floyd said. 'I don't have anything else, and it's only good luck that I have the box.'

'Why did Mister Blanchard give it to you?'

'He thought the contents might shed some light on why she was killed. The old man was pretty convinced she was murdered.'

Auger sighed. 'Well, I can understand why he might feel that way. But it wasn't murder.'

'You know that for a fact?'

'I knew my sister. Not well, as I've already told you, but well enough not to be surprised that this happened.'

Floyd opened the desk drawer and took out the biscuit tin. He placed it on the desk between himself and Auger, then removed the metal lid so that she could see the items inside. 'Go on,' he said.

'Susan had problems. Even when she was still living at home, she was always getting into trouble, always making up stories to suit whichever version of the truth she wanted people to believe at a particular moment.'

'Her and half the human race.'

'The trouble with Susan was that she didn't know where to stop. She was a fantasist, Mister Floyd, living in a dream world of her own making. And it only became worse as she got older. It was one of the reasons we drifted apart. I was on the receiving end of her fantasies one too many times.'

'I don't see what that has to do with her being killed.'

'What started as simple fantasising gradually took on a darker edge. I think she began to believe her own fairy tales. She started seeing enemies everywhere, imagining that people were whispering things behind her back, plotting against her.'

'In these times she might have had a point.'

'Not the way you mean it. She was a paranoid delusional, Mister Floyd. I have the medical files to prove it.' Auger reached into her handbag and produced a sheaf of papers. 'You're welcome to examine them. Susan received treatment for her delusional problems throughout her twenties, up to and including electroconvulsive therapy. Needless to say, none of it worked.'

Floyd took the papers and flicked through them. They looked convincing enough. He passed them back to Auger, noticing as she took them that she had no rings on her fingers. 'I'll take your word for it,' he said. 'But what I don't understand is how your sister ended up in Europe, if she was so unwell.'

'In hindsight it was a silly idea,' Auger said, stuffing the medical papers back into her handbag, 'but she'd had a promising few months and the doctors thought a change of scenery would do her even more good. She didn't have much money herself, but between us, the family was able to scrape together enough to put her on the boat and give her some pocket money to spend when she got here.'

'That must have been some pocket,' Floyd said, remembering the rate at which Susan White had bought magazines and books.

'I can't account for Susan's actions once she was here,' Auger said. 'She could be very persuasive, and it's possible she may have exploited the good trust of other people to get what she wanted.'

'That's possible,' Floyd allowed. 'Mind if I ask something that might sound a little indelicate?'

'I'm not easily offended.'

'How did you know she was dead, if she was so out of touch? From what we can tell, Susan had almost no contact with anyone else in Paris. The authorities didn't know who she was and didn't care, either. And yet you've arrived from Dakota just over three weeks after she died.'

'I didn't know she was dead until I reached the apartment building,' Auger said. Her face was an unreadable mask: she might have been incensed or indifferent, for all Floyd could tell. 'But I had a very good idea that something must have happened to her. Susan didn't keep in touch with me, but she did send regular postcards back to our uncle in Dakota. He'd heard from her about once or twice a week since she arrived in Paris.'

'So the postcards dried up?'

'Not just that. The last few she sent showed signs that she was going off at the deep end again.' Auger paused and lit another cigarette. Floyd wondered why she bothered: she had barely smoked the last one. 'She started going on about people being out to get her. The same old story, in other words: everything we hoped she'd put behind her. Well, clearly she hadn't. But it was worse this time, as if in Europe her fantasies had come to full bloom. Nobody is the same person on vacation as they are at home, Mister Floyd: we all change a little, sometimes for the better. With Susan it was very much for the worse.'

'What was in these postcards?'

'The usual stuff, only magnified. People shadowing her, people out to kill her. Conspiracies she saw all around her.'

'Was she in the habit of underlining things that mattered to her?'

He caught a moment of doubt cross her face. 'Now and then, I suppose. Why?'

'Nothing,' Floyd said, waving the question away. 'Passing thoughts.'

Auger looked at the tin sitting on the desk between them. 'She mentioned that box. She said she had accumulated a lot of evidence and given it to her landlord for safekeeping.'

'But if she was delusional, none of the papers in that box are worth anything.'

'I'm not saying that they are,' Auger answered. 'But Susan made a final request, in one of the last postcards we got from her. It said that if anything was to happen to her, she wanted me to come and collect that box. She said it was the most important thing any of us could do for her, and she would die happy if she knew that the box would eventually end up in safe hands.'

'And did you answer her?'

'I sent a telegram back to her saying I would collect the box should anything happen to her.'

'But you knew it was valueless. Are you seriously telling me that you came all the way across the Atlantic for a boxful of worthless papers?'

'They weren't worthless to Susan,' Auger said, with a bite in her voice. 'They were the most important things in her world. And I made a promise. I don't know about you, Mister Floyd, but I don't break promises, no matter how pointless or absurd they might be.'

Floyd reached out and pushed the tin across to Auger. 'Then it's yours. I can't see any reason not to give it to you, especially after what you've just told me.'

She touched the box guardedly, as if not quite believing her good luck. 'You'll just let me walk out of here with this, no questions asked?'

'Questions have been asked,' Floyd said, 'and you've answered them to my complete satisfaction. I'll be honest with you: I looked through everything in that box and saw nothing of value. If I'd found cash, or bearer's cheques, or the key to a safety deposit box, I might have wanted some more concrete proof that you are who you say you are. But a handful of old maps, some meaningless papers and an expired railway ticket? You're welcome to it, Miss Auger. I just hope it brings your sister some peace, now that the box is back in family hands.'

'I hope it does, too,' Auger replied. She picked up the box and slid it under her seat. 'There's just one more thing to deal with. You've been very reasonable, Mister Floyd, and I'm sorry to take your case away from you as well.'

'My case?' Floyd asked.

'Like I said, there was no murder. My sister may have killed herself deliberately – she attempted suicide once before – or she may have had an accident in her delusional state, imagining herself to be under attack. But the one thing I am absolutely certain of is that there was no murder, and therefore there is no murder case.'

'It's all right,' Floyd said. 'The case closed itself the moment Blanchard hit that sidewalk.'

'Right,' she said, nodding. 'You were his agent in the investigation?'

'Yes, and now that he's not around, there's no one to pay our expenses. Anyway, from what you say, there wasn't exactly a case to begin with.'

'Do you think Blanchard's death had anything to do with Susan's?'

'It's crossed my mind,' Floyd said. 'One shouldn't speak ill of the dead, of course . . . especially of someone who's only been a dead a matter of hours. But it occurs to me that maybe Blanchard had an idea of what had really happened all along. Maybe he felt he could have done more to help her, and that guilt began to weigh on his mind. In the end, it was too much for him to bear.'

'Then Blanchard killed himself because Susan died? Is that what you're saying?'

'The two deaths can't be unrelated. Suggesting that the landlord killed himself as a result of some vague sense of responsibility might not satisfy a jury, but it's a lot neater than blaming some mysterious third party.'

'Look,' Auger said, 'I'm sorry about the way this has happened. You've been the piggy in the middle of something that didn't concern you.' She reached into her handbag and pulled out a plain manila envelope. She slid it across the table towards Floyd, who left it sitting there like a ticking bomb. 'It's not much, but I do appreciate your efforts – you looked after the box, after all – and I feel you deserve some kind of termination fee now that the case is closed.'

Floyd put his hand on the envelope, feeling its seductive plumpness. There were easily several hundred francs in it, maybe more. 'There's no need for this,' he said. 'My contract was with Blanchard, not you.'

'It's common human decency, Mister Floyd. Please accept it. I talked to some of the people at the apartment building and I know you've not been having an easy couple of days. Please accept this as recompense.'

'If you insist.' Floyd took the envelope and dropped it into the same desk drawer that had held the biscuit tin. 'And I do appreciate the gesture.'

'Then we're done, I think,' Auger said, standing up. She slipped her bag over her shoulder and tucked the tin under one arm.

'Guess so,' he replied, also standing.

She smiled. It was the first time he had seen any recognisable expression on her face. 'Somehow I expected there would be more to it than this. Papers to sign, legal people to argue with . . . I didn't think I'd walk out of here with the tin without putting up a fight.'

'Like I said, it's just a tin with some papers in it. And I wouldn't want to make your life any more difficult than I have to. Losing a sister like that . . .'

She reached across and took his hand. 'You've been very kind, Mister Floyd.'

'Just doing my job.'

'I hope things work out for you and your partner. You deserve some good luck.'

Floyd shrugged. 'Me and everyone else on the planet.'

She turned around, looking back at him over her shoulder. Her hair framed her face in a nimbus of shining white, like the sun behind a thundercloud. 'Thank you again. I can see myself out.'

'It's been a pleasure doing business.'

She paused at the door. 'Mister Floyd? You never did tell me your Christian name.'

'Does it matter?'

'I'd like to know. You've been so kind, after all.'

'The name's Wendell.'

'Don't you like it?'

'It's always sounded like a sucker's name to me. That's why my friends call me Floyd.'

'As a matter of fact,' she said, 'I rather like it. Wendell seems such an honest sort of name – to me, at least.'

'Then to you I'm Wendell.'

'In which case . . . goodbye, Wendell.'

'Goodbye, Miss Auger.'

'Verity, please,' she said, correcting him, then walked out of the office, closing the door behind her.

Floyd waited a moment and then slipped his hand into his pocket, reassuring himself that the postcard was still there.

He liked her. She had the looks and seemed to be a nice enough lady. But he couldn't help wondering how she would have reacted if he'd mentioned 'silver rain'.

SIXTEEN

Auger shut the door behind her, clutching her handbag and the biscuit tin to her chest as if they might be snatched away at any moment. On the landing outside the detective's premises, a heavily made-up old woman studied her with sly, knowing eyes while enveloping herself in a haze of silver-blue cigarette smoke. She said nothing, but the look on her face conveyed both accusation and bored indifference, as if she had witnessed every possible sin in the world and had long since ceased to be shocked by any of them. Her attention flicked momentarily to the tin Auger was holding so protectively, then her eyes lost focus and whatever gleam of malice had been there a moment before. Auger was about to take the stairs down to the next landing when she noticed that another woman – this one young, with very black hair held back from her face with a spotted red headscarf – was on her hands and knees, waxing and polishing the lower steps.

The woman looked up as Auger was about to descend. 'Please,' she said, nodding towards the black iron framework of the elevator shaft that rose up the centre of the stairwell.

Grateful that the elevator car was ready and waiting, Auger stepped inside and slid shut the trellised gate, then pressed the button for the ground floor. With a thud and a whine, the elevator began its inching descent, creeping past the cleaning girl. The elevator descended another floor and then came to an abrupt, rattling halt, exactly between landings. Auger swore and pressed the button again, but the elevator refused to budge. She tried forcing open the sliding gate, but it had locked itself tight.

'Hey,' she called out. 'Can someone help me? I'm stuck in this thing.'

She heard the cleaning girl say something, but it sounded more sympathetic than useful. Auger tried the elevator button again, but with no more effect than before. Feeling suddenly dejected, it began to dawn on her that she might be stuck inside it for hours while some overworked engineer made his grumbling way across the city on a Saturday. Assuming anyone had the presence of mind to call for assistance, which might be one assumption too many. She called out again – if the cleaning girl didn't answer or understand her, then perhaps she might be able to rouse Floyd – but this time she heard nothing at all in reply.

A minute passed with no further sign of movement. All she could hear was the sound of her own breathing and the occasional metallic rattle as her movements caused the elevator car to chafe against its restraints. The building sounded utterly deserted.

She heard a door shut somewhere above her, followed by a rapid succession of descending footsteps. The footsteps quickened in pace and then became thuds, as if someone was skipping two or three steps at a time. Auger peered through the meshwork screen that constituted the elevator car's roof and saw a dark figure circle the landing immediately above her. Before she could call out, the figure had bounded down the steps surrounding the part of the shaft in which she was stuck in a series of flighty jumps and was on the landing below, continuing towards street level. Auger had only seen the figure in full view for an instant, and that blurred by motion, but she had not been able to make out any facial details. The figure was wearing a high-collared coat, a fedora jammed low on his head with the brim turned down. For an absurd moment she wondered if it might have been Floyd, but even as the idea occurred to her, she dismissed it as stupid.

A moment later, the elevator buzzed back into life and resumed its descent. It came to a halt on the next landing and, not wanting to take any further chances, Auger opened the gate and made the rest of her journey on foot. With the box still in her possession, it was a relief to reach daylight. Somehow she felt safer outdoors, illogical as that may have been.

She looked up and down rue du Dragon, but there was no sign of the running man, or of anything else obviously out of place. The street was as quiet and sleepy as it had been when she had arrived, but there were some pedestrians walking along it, and if anyone was to try anything against her, she knew she could count on one or two witnesses from the equine butcher's shop on the ground floor of Floyd's building.

A little further down the street, Auger stepped into the doorway of a boarded-up hosier's shop, long out of business, and snapped the lid from the tin. Inside, as Floyd had shown her in his office, was a thick rubber-banded bundle of paperwork and documents. She took this bundle and stuffed it into her handbag. Having no further use for the tin, she pushed it into a pile of cardboard boxes and other debris that had built up in one corner of the shop doorway.

She stepped back into the street and walked to the south end of rue du Dragon, crossing rue de Sèvres on to the much wider thoroughfare of rue de Rennes. As she reached the corner, she heard the rumble of a car starting somewhere behind her, and as she walked north on rue de Rennes, she risked a glance over her shoulder and saw the grilled nose of the vehicle emerging on to the same street. The car rolled forward until the cab was in full view, but the sunlight flaring from the windscreen prevented her from making out the driver. Auger quickened her pace, and when she allowed herself another glance back, there was no sign of the car. But there were many similar cars parked along the roadside, and it would not have been difficult for the driver to lose his amongst them.

Auger continued along rue de Rennes, stopping every now and then to try to flag down a taxi. But either it was the wrong time of day, or there was some Parisian knack she hadn't yet grasped, for the taxis sped on in an indifferent blur of black metal and chrome, leaving her muttering under her breath. Auger glanced back once more and thought she saw the same car again, inching along at walking pace, but no sooner had her suspicions begun to build than the car swerved away down a side street.

Auger told herself sternly that she was being just as paranoid as Susan White's fictitious persona. The trick was to see things from Floyd's point of view, not hers. The detective could have no possible idea of the significance of the paperwork in the box. Her story was entirely reasonable, and Floyd should have no grounds to doubt her word. Susan White had even mentioned that her sister would be coming for her belongings.

Still nervous, but forcing herself to act a little more calmly, Auger realised that she had arrived at the entrance to the Métro station at Saint-Germain-des-Prés. She would have preferred the speed and safety of a taxi ride, but the train was the next best thing. She fished money from her purse, still not completely familiar with the coinage, and bought a one-way ticket. A train was grinding into the underground station as she cleared the turnstile.

Auger got aboard, moving along the compartment as the doors closed themselves and the train lurched away. She found a seat next to two young women who had their faces buried in fashion magazines. The train burrowed its way south, slowing into Saint-Sulpice, the station's walls plastered with faded sepia-tinted advertisements for perfume, stockings and tobacco. As people moved on and off the train, Auger checked them out in her peripheral vision, searching for anyone who looked like Floyd or the figure she had seen descending the stairs. But she recognised no one, and as the train pulled away into the darkness of the next tunnel, she allowed herself to relax a notch. After a minute or so, the train slowed into the next station on the line, Saint-Placide, and Auger once again kept an eye on the passengers coming and going. This time, however, it was with less apprehension and more a guarded interest in the private lives of these unwitting prisoners. It was then that Auger noticed a woman stepping out of the train two carriages ahead of the one she was in. The woman had a pretty face framed by very black hair, and it took Auger a moment to place her as the girl who had been cleaning the stairs in rue du Dragon. She had removed her headscarf and apron, but her features were unmistakable. Rather than heading for the exit, the woman walked alongside the train until she reached carriage next to Auger's, reboarding just as the doors hissed shut and the train hurtled back into darkness.

Auger clutched the handbag tightly against her stomach, resisting the urge to open it to make sure that the paperwork was still safe and sound. Presently, the train began to slow into Montparnasse. Auger made sure she was standing right next to the door as the train pulled to a stop, and was relieved when a surge of people followed her from the train, enveloping and jostling her towards the tiled corridors and stairs that led to the number six line. She pushed ahead of them, all the while clutching her handbag against her like a living thing that needed protection. Climbing stairs, she glanced back and saw the black-haired woman behind her, but almost lost amongst the faces and hats of the other passengers. The number six line ran on an elevated section of track, and when Auger reached daylight she was relieved to see that a train was already in the station, on the point of departure. She ran for it, nearly tripping in her painfully tight shoes, and just managed to get aboard as the doors slid shut. As the train pulled away and Auger caught her breath, she saw the black-haired woman still waiting on the platform.

Auger checked her watch. It was just before ten. Barely an hour had passed since she had walked into the detective's office.

Floyd picked up the telephone on the first ring. 'Greta?'

'It's me,' she confirmed, sounding a little out of breath.

'I lost her,' Floyd said. He was sitting in the sad, shuttered spare room in Montparnasse. Sophie was upstairs with Marguerite, and the house had a peculiar kind of Sunday-morning calm about it, even though it was only Saturday. 'I expected her to get into a taxi as soon as she left the office. But she was on foot, and there was no way I could keep up with her in the car without her getting suspicious. I don't think she recognised me, but I wasn't going to take any chances. Better to lose her this time and hope we can pick her up again near Blanchard's apartment.'

'You think she'll go back there?'

'She might have unfinished business, especially when she gets a look at what's inside the box.'

'Maybe she will. In any case, we haven't lost her yet. I know where she's staying.'

Floyd brightened. Now and then a piece of unexpected good fortune dropped into his hands like an early Christmas present. 'You managed to keep up with her?'

'Not exactly,' Greta said. 'I followed her on foot until she reached the station at Saint-Germain. I skulked in the shadows while she bought a ticket, then bought one for myself while she headed for the train. I got on the same train as she did, but made sure I wasn't in the same carriage. I moved up the train in Saint-Placide, then followed her as she changed on to the number six line at Montparnasse. Luckily, I know that station pretty well: I spent most of my childhood changing trains there. I saw the direction she was taking, but she managed to get on to a train before I reached the platform.'

'Then you lost her.'

'Only for a couple of minutes. I caught the next train out of Montparnasse. We were on the elevated line, moving west, and you have a good view of the street from those elevated stations, so I kept my eyes peeled. It paid off. I saw her walking away from the station at Dupleix, just as we were slowing down. I got off the train, hared down the steps and followed her all the way home, always hanging a block behind her.'

'I'm impressed,' Floyd said. 'Did she look as though she thought she was being followed?'

'I'm not a mind-reader, Floyd, but she seemed a lot less twitchy than before. My guess is she thought the change of trains had thrown anyone following her off her scent.'

'I'll make a detective out of you one of these days, just you watch.' Floyd reached for his notebook and pen. 'Tell me where she's staying.'

Greta gave him the address of a hotel on avenue Emile Zola, a short walk from Dupleix Métro station. She was calling from a brasserie frequented by change-of-shift car workers from the nearby Citroën factory. 'I can't tell you her room number, or how she likes her toast done. And I can't stay here all day, either.'

'You don't have to. I can be there within the hour.'

'There's no way you can get here sooner?'

'I'll have someone on my tail as well, remember,' Floyd said.

'Another of those horrible children?' she asked, nervousness creeping into her voice.

'No, just Belliard's goons. They followed me to Montparnasse. I think I can lose them if I cross the river twice, but that will take time. I don't want them thinking I'm taking an interest in Verity Auger. If they do, awkward questions might be asked.'

'What do you mean, "awkward questions"?'

'The kind that will involve a heavy dental bill.'

'Be here as soon as you can. This is as far into this as I want to go, Floyd. I never had aspirations to play the girl detective, and I'm not on your payroll.'

'You did a good job,' Floyd said as she hung up. He set his receiver down and began to plot his route across Paris, incorporating as many sudden turns and reversals as he dared.

Auger turned the key, locking the door from inside, and crashed on to the bed, suddenly overwhelmed by relief and exhaustion.

She closed her eyes for a few minutes, then hauled herself to the pea-green washbasin and splashed some cold water on to her face. 'Stay sharp,' she said aloud. 'The hard part might be over, but you still need to make it back to the portal. Don't get too complacent, Auger. And don't talk to yourself, either. It's the first sign of madness.'

She removed her horrid, tight Parisian shoes and dialled down to the front desk for a pot of coffee. Then she called down to the lobby again and asked to be connected to an external number.

'Just a moment, madame.'

Someone picked up on the third ring, answering in poorly enunciated French. 'To whom am I speaking?'

'This is Auger,' she said.

'Good,' Aveling answered, slipping immediately back into English. 'Do you have—'

'Yes, I have the items. Can you get a message through to Caliskan?'

'Not possible, I'm afraid.' He was speaking from the safe house, a rented room a minute's walk from Cardinal Lemoine. No direct telephone connection existed between the surface of Paris and the concealed chambers underground. 'We're having some technical difficulties with the link.'

'Tell me it isn't serious.'

'It's being worked on. It's not the first time the link has become unstable, and it'll most likely sort itself out within a few hours. It's probably not related.'

'Not related to what?'

'Anything you need worry about.'

'Tell me, you patronising . . .' She tried to insult him, dredging her repertoire for something suitably nasty, but it was as if a mental roadblock had been installed between her brain and her mouth.

'There's political trouble back home,' Aveling interjected before she could continue. 'That Slasher offensive everyone was expecting? It's begun. But don't you fret. Just bring the box and let us worry about the bigger picture. We're all very happy with the way you've handled things so far. It would be a shame to spoil things now, wouldn't it?'

'I could just burn the papers,' Auger said. 'Or throw them away somewhere where no one will ever find them. What's the problem with that?'

'We'd rather you returned them to us. That way we can make sure nothing has gone astray.'

'I can make it to the portal,' she said, 'but I'm not certain that's such a great idea at the moment. I'm pretty sure someone followed me here, from the detective's office.'

'What kind of someone?'

'Someone working for him, I think. He seemed very willing to hand over the box. With hindsight, it looks as though he always intended to have someone tail me.'

'And he's just a local detective?'

'Yes, the one I told you about after I spoke to Blanchard.'

'He's probably just curious. Do your best to shake him off your tail, but don't worry about him.'

'There's more going on here than you've told me,' she said.

'Listen carefully,' Aveling said. 'It's exactly ten-forty now. Check your watch and synchronise.'

'Done.'

'At exactly noon we will arrange for a two-minute power interruption on the Métro line running through Cardinal Lemoine. I'll be waiting for you inside the tunnel, at the door, and for obvious reasons, it would not be good to be late. No excuses, Auger – we're all counting on you. I'll see you in eighty minutes, with the paperwork.'

She said nothing.

'Will you be there?' Aveling asked.

'Yes,' she said. 'Of course I'll be there.'

Room service arrived with a knock on the door. She hung up on Aveling and opened the door as far as the security chain allowed before letting the boy enter and place her coffee service on the bedside table. She tipped him generously and then locked and chained the door from the inside. The coffee was on the lukewarm side of hot, but it was considerably better than nothing. She spooned cream and sugar into it and had drunk half a cup before she began to feel calm again.

She was definitely not being told everything. Auger supposed that this suspicion had always been lurking at the back of her mind, but now she was certain of it. And there was something else, something even more troubling that had been nagging at her quietly since she had first learned of Susan White's involvement in this whole business.

Why had White made such a point of involving Auger when they were little more than professional acquaintances? Auger could understand White being concerned about her own safety and wanting to make sure that the papers didn't fall into the wrong hands. She could understand the requirement for someone from the other side of the portal to come and retrieve them. But why Auger, specifically? Sure, she had the necessary background on Paris, the deep knowledge of the city, but there had to be more to it than that. At first glance, it looked as if White was playing a posthumous trick on Auger, setting her up for a hazardous job out of professional spite. But they'd been cool rivals rather than enemies, with no mutual animosity that Auger was aware of. In truth, they were rather alike.

So it had to have been something else. White was clever and calculating – she'd have done nothing without an excellent reason. And the only explanation Auger could come up with – the only one that seemed plausible to her, given what she knew of the woman – was that it was a matter of trust.

Auger was an outsider. She had ties to Caliskan – that was unavoidable for anyone with an Antiquities background – but they weren't exactly thick as thieves. More important was the fact that she was not part of Aveling's operation. A little more than a week ago, she'd had no knowledge of E2 whatsoever. Which meant, presumably, that Susan White had decided that she couldn't trust Aveling or his people.

All of them? Auger wondered. Or did she just suspect that somewhere in the organisation there was someone who couldn't be trusted?

Auger preferred the second hypothesis. It made more sense to her than the idea that the entire organisation, from Phobos to E2, was compromised. If that was the case, then they would surely have found a way to avoid bringing in an outsider, no matter how much it inconvenienced their plans.

Auger thought about what she had already learned for herself. Everyone agreed that there was something important about those papers. Susan White had gone to the trouble of passing them on for safekeeping and making arrangements for their return to the other side of the portal. Caliskan, Aveling and all the others involved in the Phobos operation seemed to agree on the significance of the documents, or else Auger would never have been co-opted to retrieve them. And there was someone else who considered them to be significant: whoever had killed White and now

Blanchard. Whoever that was, they seemed less than keen to see those papers return to Phobos. Which implied – unless Auger's imagination was running away with itself – that the person or persons who had committed those two murders were in some way linked to the contents of the papers.

Which brought her to the papers themselves. What did *they* have to say on the subject?

Auger took the bundle of documents from her handbag and began to arrange them on the maroon bedspread, eventually covering it completely. She laid each item out neatly, but imposed no sorting methodology on the papers other than the order in which they emerged from the bundle.

She stepped back from the bed and looked at the dead woman's legacy.

'Talk to me, Susan,' she said. 'Give me a hint as to what all this is about.'

Auger poured herself another cup of coffee, added cream and sugar and set about rearranging the material on the bed, hunting for some meaningful combination. But no permutation of the papers looked any more or less significant than the last. Unless she was missing something subtle, the message must be in the content of the documents rather than any pattern they formed. None of these papers would have had any particular significance to a local. They might have struck someone as rather an eccentric collection of documents, especially if they had been traced to a young American tourist, but there was no smoking gun, no one document that shrieked of an otherworldly origin. There was, in fact, nothing in the collection that could not have been acquired by an ordinary person with access to the usual libraries and bookshops. There were no top-secret blueprints or duplicated documents from E1; nothing even remotely hinting that Susan White was an explorer who had arrived in Paris through a quasi-wormhole link from some unguessably distant part of the Milky Way.

Auger scrutinised the papers once more to make sure she was not missing something, but barring the use of invisible inks, microdots or some other such subterfuge, there was nothing intrinsically destabilising about any of the items Susan White had acquired. There was, in short, nothing that would have caused any obvious difficulties had it fallen into local hands. In all likelihood, the documents would have been thrown out and the biscuit tin kept instead.

But Caliskan and his organisation had staged a high-risk operation to recover these documents. And the emphasis had indeed been on 'recovering' them: there had been no talk of simply discarding or destroying them. No: Caliskan wanted them back, and that meant that the documents were themselves suspected of being important.

They knew that Susan White had been on to something. They just hadn't wanted to tell Auger, knowing that it might have scared her off. She had been foolish not to ask more questions about the significance of the lost property before she agreed to recover it. But Caliskan and his people had counted on her clutching at any straw to avoid the disciplinary tribunal, and they must have known that she would not think too deeply beyond the immediate objective. The fact that they had been right, that she had played so willingly into their scheme, only made her feel more foolish.

'Verity,' she chided herself. 'You silly, silly girl.'

Shaking her head, Auger returned her attention to the papers.

'You knew what this was about,' she said, addressing Susan White's imagined presence, which she pictured brooding like herself over the tableau of harmless documents. 'You knew what this was about and you knew that it was worth someone murdering you for.'

Auger reached out and examined the largest of the maps. It was the first time she had paid proper attention to it. Why had it ended up in the woman's collection of papers, when others like it could be bought cheaply at almost any stationery shop? A similar map was almost certainly amongst the items White had already passed through the portal.

Auger opened the map fully, laying it gently over the other documents without disturbing them. Covering half the bedspread was a political and geographical map of Europe, with lines marked on it in a dark-blue ink. Auger scratched gently at the lines with her fingernail, as Floyd had done, satisfying herself that they were not part of the original design. They formed a tilted 'L' shape, with one arm reaching from Paris to Berlin and the other from Paris to Milan. Inked circles surrounded the three cities, and neat digits above the lines indicated – Auger was certain – the distances between them in kilometres. But beyond this observation, the meaning of the markings eluded her. What was so critical about the distances between these cities that this map had to be smuggled out of E2 at all costs, when that information was readily available in the archives back home?

Auger folded the map, taking pains not to damage the thin paper upon which it was printed. As she returned it to its place amongst the other documents, her attention was drawn to a railway ticket. It was for an overnight sleeper train to Berlin, purchased not long before Susan White died, but dated for travel just after her death.

Auger scanned the other documents looking for a German or Italian connection. It did not take her long to find an official-looking letter from a heavy-engineering concern located in a suburb of Berlin. The letter was printed on very good paper, with an impressive letterhead in scarlet ink. Her newly installed German crunched through the text with machinelike efficiency.

The letter was in response to an earlier query – evidently part of some longer chain of correspondence – concerning the manufacture of a number of specialised items. From what Auger could gather, this contract involved the forging and machining of three large metal spheres at the Berlin works of Kaspar Metals. The letter also referred to the transportation and installation of these aluminium spheres in Berlin, Paris and Milan, together with a number of associated parts. The fact that the spheres were large and heavy was obvious from the attention that the letter placed on their delivery. They would require specialised arrangements and were much too heavy to be flown, even given the distances involved. The letter went on to stress the difficulty of delivering the objects without damage, according to the instructions of the 'artist', and that this would incur additional costs.

Metal spheres. What, she wondered, was that all about?

Auger searched through the other documents and pieces of paper, looking now for anything related to the German contract. Almost immediately she found a carefully executed sketch of a sphere hanging from a heavy-duty gantry or support cradle, attached to it by many delicate springs or wires. The sphere was marked as being more than three metres in diameter.

Auger wished that she had access to the historical archives back in E1. Although they were not exhaustive, they would have given her some guidance as to whether the spherical objects were also part of the E1 historical timeline. Perhaps some ambitious artist had indeed commissioned the forging of such aluminium spheres, and Susan White had simply got the wrong end of an innocent stick. Auger couldn't count on it, but a detail like that might just have survived the Forgetting.

But even if that was the case, Auger reminded herself, this was E2, where the timeline had already swerved twenty years away from E1 chronology. The chances of an artist pursuing the same project in two very different histories were small indeed. The same thinking applied even if the spheres were part of some clandestine military or scientific project being conducted by the E2 locals. Even if it had a traceable analogue in E1, it was very unlikely that a similar initiative would have been undertaken in the altered Europe of E2. But not, she had to admit, unthinkable: if there was a good enough strategic reason for something, then it might crop up in both the E1 and E2 chronologies, despite the altered political landscape. What seemed less likely was that something would be developed in E2 and not E1, especially if that something depended on a scientific underpinning. The scientific worldview of E2 had barely advanced since 1939.

There was, Auger realised, a more troubling possibility: the project Susan White had uncovered might not have anything to do with the locals at all.

In which case, who was running it? And what were they planning to do? She didn't have an answer yet, or even the beginnings of one, but she did have the sense that she was on the right track. She could almost feel Susan White's ghost nodding in frustrated encouragement, desperately willing her to make the next – and incredibly obvious – deductive leap.

But Auger couldn't do that; not yet.

She looked at her watch. It was nearly eleven, which gave her just over an hour to make it to the Métro tunnel before the juice was cut.

Hastily, but with care, she gathered the documents, wrapped them in a sheet of writing paper from the desk and returned them to her handbag. She would have liked the time to look at all the other things in detail, but she didn't have that luxury. And with Aveling's warnings about the unreliability of the link, Auger was more than anxious to make a safe return to the other side. As much as this living memory of Paris entranced her, as much as she longed for all the time in the world to explore it, she did not want to become its prisoner.

Auger pulled aside the filmy net curtains covering the window. Since she had returned to the hotel, it had started raining: a soft October rain that muffled the city's sounds to a muted hiss of late-morning traffic. She stood there for a moment and watched the pedestrians below, scurrying along under dark umbrellas and glossy raincoats. It was impossible not to see them as living beings, with their own interior lives. Yet their very existence was still a kind of sham.

Skellsgard had spoken of this world being like a photographic exposure, a snapshot of a moment in time that had, for reasons unclear, continued to evolve forward in time from that instant, while preserved in the armoured shell of the ALS. There was no guessing the means by which that snapshot had been taken, or whether anyone alive on the real Earth had felt the slightest hint that it was happening . . . the smallest interruption in their thoughts, the merest instant of collective *déjà vu*. Perhaps the event had gone completely unnoticed.

But thereafter the two histories had diverged. The real counterparts of the people moving around in E2 had gone on to live out genuine flesh-and-blood lives in the historical timeline of the real E1. The snapshot could not have been taken later than May 1940, nor could it have been taken very much earlier than that, for events in E2 leading up to the Ardennes advance seemed more or less to follow the E1 timeline. The real world, E1, had shortly thereafter been plunged into a catastrophic war. Many of those who had been alive at the instant the snapshot was taken would certainly have died during that war, or during the miserable conflict-filled decades that followed. Even if they had somehow slipped through the historical cracks

214

and avoided death by war, or famine, or political oppression, then many of them would have lived lives blighted and lessened by the brutal circumstances of those years.

And yet, as grim as those lives might have been, as squalid and miserable and tragic, they had been played out according to the right script. It was the lives of their counterparts on E2 that had followed a deviant path. And almost everyone born on E2 since the timelines diverged would either not have existed at all on E1, or would have been very different people. In every sense they were living on borrowed time. And not just 'on' it, but 'in' it.

For a moment, a repugnant idea flashed through Auger's mind. How much simpler would it be, how much neater, if these lives had never happened? If the snapshot had preserved only Paris and the rest of the world, but not the people in it. If it had been like one of those nineteenth-century photographs of the city, the exposure necessarily so long that the people blurred themselves out of existence, leaving only spectral traces.

The thought made her shiver, but she could not quite erase it from her mind.

Glancing at her watch, she gathered her coat and left the hotel room. As she teetered out through the lobby, still not quite steady on her heels, the concierge raised an eyebrow. But the telephone on his desk chose that moment to ring, and by the time he answered it he had forgotten all about the awkward American woman, and the hurry she seemed to be in.

SEVENTEEN

At the Métro station on rue Cardinal Lemoine, Auger bought a one-way ticket and entered the midday crush of passengers. People took lunch seriously in Paris, and thought nothing of crossing half the city to meet with a colleague, partner or lover in some well-regarded brasserie or restaurant. Auger could not be certain whether or not she had been tailed from the hotel on Emile Zola, but she took every advantage of the flood of travellers to make herself difficult to follow, jostling her way through the crowds and racing up and down stairs and escalators in an effort to shake off any pursuer. Even so, when she reached the underground platform, she slowed her progress and let the waiting train whisk away without her. The platform was not quite deserted once the train had left, but that would be too much to hope for. There were always people who seemed to have nothing better to do than loiter in Métro stations, oblivious to the passage of the trains and the urgent schedules of the other commuters. A young man in a checked jacket and flat cap was reading the racing news, a cigarette balanced on the edge of his lower lip. A plump but pretty young woman was attending to her make-up with the aid of a little brass mirror, her expression a pout of absolute concentration.

Auger looked at her watch again, anxious to get the next part over with. But it was still a couple of minutes to noon, and the electricity in the rails would not yet have been turned off. She pressed her handbag closer to her, observing the slow drift of new passengers on to the platform. She had moved to the very limit of the platform, where the rails disappeared into the darkness of the tunnel. At one minute to noon, she saw the lights of another train pick out the rails snaking out of the tunnel at the other end of the platform, and then the train arrived in a commotion of brakes and wheels. She looked at her watch again, willing the train to depart. The last thing she needed was for the train to get stuck in the tunnel between the station and her entry point.

The train moved off. It was very nearly noon. A few more people arrived on the platform, and then the hand on her watch said it was time to go. There was no visible change in the condition of the rails, but she had no intention of touching them to test Aveling's attentiveness. She would know soon enough if he had done his job.

Auger made her move as quickly as she dared. In one fluid movement, she knelt on the edge of the platform, swung her legs over and then lowered herself on to the grimy concrete upon which the rails were laid. Her hands were already filthy with soot and oil, and doubtless her rump was covered in the same black dirt. It didn't matter: if all went according to plan, she would never emerge from this tunnel again, and there would be no one to wonder why a smartly dressed young woman had allowed herself to get into such a state.

Someone cried out. She looked back in time to see the man with the racing paper raise a hand towards her, the cigarette dropping from his lip, while the plump girl lowered her mirror to see what all the fuss was about. But by then Auger had slipped into the concealing darkness of the tunnel, keeping the wall to her left and the closest rail to her right. Once she had gone more than a few metres into the tunnel, she knew that no one would be able to see her. Unfortunately, she could also see very little ahead of her, and this time she didn't have the brightness of the station to guide her. Moving as quickly as she could, Auger kept her back to the wall for support and walked crab-fashion into the blackness, trying not to think about the mice and rats that were undoubtedly scurrying near her feet, or the lethal voltage that might still be coursing through the rails. She had about a hundred metres to cover, and rather less than two minutes in which to do it.

Something shone in the darkness ahead of her: a blood-red light, very dim, but moving. For a horrifying moment, she thought it was a train approaching her through the tunnel, even though any trains should have arrived from behind, not ahead of her. Then her sense of perspective shifted and she realised that the light was a torch being shone in her direction by someone further down the tunnel.

'Hurry, Auger,' she heard a voice call out. 'The juice has to come on again in thirty seconds, and the trains will be moving not long after that!'

'Aveling?'

'Keep moving,' he said in reply. 'We really don't have much time.'

'I think a man saw me go into the tunnel.'

'Don't worry about him.'

As she moved forward, the red light gradually grew brighter. Very faintly, she began to make out the dark outline of a figure crouched close to the wall. It seemed much further away than she had been expecting: voices carried very well down the tunnel.

'Move, Auger,' he hissed.

'I'm doing my best.'

'Good. Don't trip now, because the rails are electrified.'

'You didn't have to tell me that. If anything it's even more likely to make me trip.'

'You have the goods?'

'Yes,' she said, clenching her teeth. 'I have the goods.'

As she picked her way forward, the figure with the torch gradually became clearer and, now that her eyes were becoming better adapted to the dark, she could make out a gap in the wall immediately next to him.

'Hurry now. We're picking up a current draw on the line.'

'Meaning what?'

'That trains are already running again. They won't waste much time after an intermittent fault, not during the midday rush.'

At last, Auger could see the outline of Aveling's features. She sped up for the final dozen metres, grasping for the sanctuary of that dark gap in the wall.

'I think I see a train entering Cardinal Lemoine,' Aveling warned.

'I'm nearly there.'

'Train's moving again. Hurry up, Auger. I'm not standing here for much longer.'

With little attempt to preserve her dignity, he pushed Auger through the crack in the wall, into the darkness beyond. The squeal of the approaching train grew louder, reverberating off the tunnel walls. 'Help me with this door,' Aveling said. 'We have to get it back into place.'

He guided her hands on to the old wooden door and she felt it shift under the pressure they were applying. The door crunched back into place at the last moment, with the lights of the train shining through the narrowing gap.

'That was close,' Aveling said.

'Do you think anyone on the train saw us?'

'No.'

'What about the man on the platform?' She described him briefly.

'Like I said, don't worry about him. He's a confidence trickster, spends all his days on that station snooping for victims. He won't be reporting anything to the authorities.' He turned off the red torch, then immediately switched on a much brighter white one. Auger squinted against the sudden glare, recognising the cramped and filthy gullet of the access tunnel.

'I repeat: you have the goods?'

'Yes,' she said, wearily. 'Like I already told you.'

'Good. I was beginning to worry that you weren't going to complete your mission. I'm glad to see you've decided to act sensibly. Give me the papers.'

'They're safe with me.'

'I said give them to me, Auger.' Before she could argue, he snatched her bag and flashed the torch on the bundle of documents within. 'It doesn't look like much, does it? Not for all the trouble you've gone to.' He pulled the papers out and returned the bag to her.

She thought about Susan White's likely suspicion that there was someone on the team who couldn't be trusted. Maybe it was Aveling, maybe it wasn't, but as long as Auger kept the papers in sight, she reckoned that no immediate harm could come to them. All she had to do was ensure that they made it back to Caliskan.

'I don't know what any of this is about, Aveling. Right now I'm not even sure I want to know. Can we just get this over with?'

'You won't be able to return just yet,' he said. 'We're still having some difficulties with the link.'

Another train rumbled through the nearby tunnel, the vibration of its passage dislodging dust from the ceiling of the access shaft.

'Due to the temporary problem you said would be fixed by now?'

'It's proving to be a little less temporary than we were hoping.' Aveling stopped and shone the torch ahead of them, aiming the beam along the gentle curve of the shaft.

Auger saw his frown. 'What's wrong?' she asked.

'Nothing. I just thought I heard something.'

'Probably one of your own people at the portal end,' Auger suggested.

Aveling unzipped his jacket and slid the papers snugly inside. 'Come on. Let's move on.'

Auger couldn't help noticing that he had slipped an automatic out of his jacket at the same time as he hid the papers. The locally made weapon gleamed an oily blue in the torchlight.

'I saw something move,' Auger said suddenly, dropping her voice to a whisper.

The torch beam skittered ahead of them like a nervous animal. 'Where?'

'Down the tunnel. Looked like a person, crouching against the wall.' She caught her breath, then added, 'It almost looked like a child.'

'A child? Don't be silly.'

'A child could easily have found their way down here.'

Aveling shook his head, but she could see that he was rattled. She didn't blame him. She had not enjoyed her previous journey along this tunnel, and she certainly wasn't enjoying this one.

'Is anyone there?' Aveling called. 'Anyone from the portal? Barton – is that you?'

'It wasn't Barton,' Auger said. 'Or Skellsgard, either.'

Aveling fired off a warning shot. The muzzle of the automatic spat orange flame into darkness, the bullet crunching through rock a dozen metres ahead of them. After the report of the gun had faded, echoes marching up and down the shaft for a few tense moments, there was only silence and their own breathing.

'Damn,' Aveling said.

'You saw something?'

'I *think* I saw something. But maybe it was just you planting the suggestion in my head.'

'You heard something before I saw the child,' Auger pointed out.

'I thought I saw something as well,' Aveling said, sounding a good deal less sure of himself.

'Something like a child?'

'It wasn't a child. If it *was* a child, then there was something badly . . .' But he left the remark uncompleted.

'Something's not right here,' Auger said. She pressed him against the wall, silencing him with a hiss. 'You know it.'

'We're just seeing shadows.'

'Or something's gone wrong. I know what I saw. I wasn't imagining it, even if you think you were.'

He answered her with a hiss of his own, all the while aiming the muzzle of the automatic along the shaft. She noticed that his hand was shaking badly.

'So what are you saying?' he snapped.

'I'm saying we should get out of here before we walk any further into trouble.'

'Look,' Aveling said as the torchlight suddenly came to rest on something on the floor, ten or twelve metres further down the tunnel. 'That's a body.'

It was too big to be a child. 'I think that might be Barton,' Auger said, with a kind of hopeless inevitability. 'I think that might be Barton, and I think he might be dead.'

'Not possible,' Aveling said.

He pulled free from her grip and moved further ahead, taking the torch with him. The light bobbed down the tunnel until Aveling reached the body. He knelt and inspected the dead man, the gun still shaking in his grip.

'This is bad,' he muttered.

Auger forced herself to join him by the body. Up close, there was no doubt that it was Barton. Aveling played the torch over the corpse, lingering over a cluster of bullet holes in the man's chest. There must have been twenty individual wounds, overlapping like lunar craters. They were tightly spaced, as if they had been fired in rapid succession at close range. His fingers were still curled lightly around the grip of another automatic. Auger pulled the gun free. Barton's hand was still warm.

'Now let's get out of here,' she said.

Aveling's arm jerked as he squeezed off another two shots into the darkness. In the muzzle flash, Auger thought she saw something as well: a small doll-like figure scurrying along close to the rough-hewn tunnel wall. The child-sized figure wore a red dress, but the face she had seen in the instant of the flash had not been that of a child at all, but something wizened and feral: half-hag, half-ghoul, with a vile grin full of sharp, blackened teeth. The automatic felt heavy in her hands as she pointed it into the darkness and tried to aim at the spot where she thought the scurrying figure would be by now. She clicked the trigger, but nothing happened. Cursing her stupidity, she fumbled for the safety catch and tried again, but Barton must have already emptied the clip.

'We're in a lot of trouble,' Aveling said. He stood up, keeping his knees bent in a crouch, and began to back away from the body.

'I definitely saw something that time,' Auger said, still holding the gun. 'It looked like a child . . . but when I saw the face—'

'It wasn't a child,' Aveling said.

'You were expecting something, weren't you?'

'Go to the top of the class.'

Useless as it was, she couldn't help but press the muzzle of the empty automatic against him. 'Start talking to me, you pig.' That was not the word she'd had in mind, but 'pig' was the worst she could bring herself to utter, even under these stressful circumstances. 'The child's from E1, isn't she?'

'What makes you say that?'

'Because whatever it is doesn't belong *here*. Now tell me what you know.'

'It's an NI infiltration unit,' Aveling said heavily. He danced the torch beam around the walls, but there was no sign of the child.

'A what?'

'Oh, come on, Auger. Surely you remember that nasty little war we don't like to talk about nowadays? Against our friends in the Federation of Polities?'

'What about it?'

'They sent their children against us. The Neotenic Infantry: genetically engineered, cloned, psychologically programmed killing machines, packaged to look like children.'

Despite herself, she couldn't help but be moved by the horror she heard in his voice. Anything that left that kind of a scar on a man like Aveling, she thought, had to be bad news.

'Did you fight against them?' she asked.

'I engaged them. It's not always the same thing. Those vicious little creatures could crawl into spaces we thought were secure and hide for weeks, somehow surviving on zero rations . . . silent, waiting like coiled snakes, almost in a coma . . . until they emerged.' His breathing was becoming ragged as he slipped deeper into memories. 'They were difficult to kill. Fast, strong, wound-tolerant . . . pain threshold off the scale. Highly attuned sense of self-preservation . . . and yet perfectly willing to die to serve a mission objective. And even when we knew what they were, even when we had a clear line of sight . . . it was almost impossible to turn our weapons on them. They looked like children. We were fighting four billion years of evolution telling us we shouldn't squeeze that trigger.'

'War babies,' Auger said. 'That was what we called them, wasn't it?'

'So you *do* remember your history.' His mocking tone did nothing to disguise his fear.

She thought back to Cassandra, the Slasher representative who had passed as an adolescent on the mission that had got her into this mess in the first place. The Neotenic Infantry had been a step towards the emergence of entire factions of child-sized Slashers. But it had also been a step that no one liked to talk about now, least of all the Slashers.

'I remember that they were a genetic dead end. They didn't work out well. They were mentally unstable and they wore out fast.'

'They were weapons,' Aveling said, 'designed with a specific shelf life.'

'But no one's seen any war babies for twenty, thirty years, Aveling. Please tell me what one is doing in a tunnel under Paris in E2.'

'Figure it out for yourself, Auger. The Slashers are here. They already have a presence in E2.'

Suddenly she felt very cold and very scared, and very far from home. 'We have to get back to the surface.'

'No,' Aveling said, regaining some of his nerve. 'We must get to the portal. The portal absolutely cannot be compromised.'

'It must already be compromised if they're here. How else did they arrive?'

Aveling started to say something, but seemed to have trouble getting his words out. He made a phlegmy choking sound and fell heavily against Auger, torch and gun dropping to the floor. Auger drew breath in to scream:

222

it was a natural human reaction, given that the person next to her had just been killed. But somehow she held it in. Shaking, concentrating on acting rather than thinking, she reached for the torch and replaced Barton's useless automatic with the one Aveling had been carrying.

Keeping low, she shone the torch down the shaft and by some accident managed to pin the child to the wall with the fat circle of the beam. The light paralysed the child for a moment. It looked at her with its horrid, shrivelled travesty of a face, wrinkled and bloodless lips framing a devilish, broken-toothed grin.

They wore out fast.

A dry, black tongue moved between the lips. In its tiny claw of a hand it held what she assumed was a gun, which it raised towards Auger. She fired first, aiming the automatic in the general direction of the child. The weapon kicked violently back against her palm as it discharged. Auger let out a small, anguished yelp of pain and surprise as the child creased in the middle and fell out of the spotlight cast by the torch. Its weapon clattered to the ground and the child let out a vile, draining shriek, like steam escaping from a boiling kettle.

Every instinct told Auger to run back the way she had come, back to daylight. She knew that there might be more of these creatures in the tunnel. But she had to see what she had killed or maimed.

She walked up to it, the gun still heavy in her hand, trusting that there was at least one more bullet in the magazine but preferring not to know for sure. The child's shrieking was dying away, becoming a faint, almost rhythmic moan.

She kicked the child's weapon away and knelt down next to the body. The mop of black hair on top of the creature's head had slipped to one side, exposing a wrinkled, age-spotted skull, pale and hairless. Up close, in the unforgiving light of the torch, the child's face was all sagging folds and bruised welts. It looked like perished rubber beneath a cracking layer of smudged make-up. The eyes were a rheumy shade of yellow. The teeth were rotten black stubs behind which the swollen black mass of a diseased tongue moved like some imprisoned monster, attempting to form coherent sounds between each wheezing moan. The child had a disgusting smell about it, like the recesses of an institutional kitchen.

'What are you doing here?' Auger asked.

In rasps, the child answered, 'You don't need to know.'

'I know what you are. You're a military abomination, something that should have been wiped out decades ago. The question is, why weren't you?'

Mouthfuls of fluid spilled through the broken portcullis of the child's teeth. 'We got lucky,' the child said, gurgling with what was either a slow choking death or mocking laughter.

'You call this lucky?' Auger asked, nodding towards the wound she had put in the child's stomach.

'I've done what I was put here to do,' the child said. 'I call that lucky.'

Then it died, its head lolling back suddenly and its eyes freezing in their sockets. Auger reached out in the darkness, feeling here and there until her hand closed around the weapon that the child had carried. She was expecting another automatic – another E2 artefact, at the very least – but the shape of the thing felt unfamiliar and alien. Standing up, she slipped the child's gun into her handbag and stepped away from the corpse.

She heard sounds behind her: frantic scraping and rustling noises. She whipped the torch around, expecting to see rats. Instead, she picked out a boy and a girl crouched near Aveling's body. They were rummaging in his clothes. As the light fell on them, they looked at her and hissed in anger.

'Get away from him,' she said, pointing the automatic. 'I've already killed one of you and I'll kill the rest of you if I have to.'

The boy flashed his teeth at her, pulling the wad of papers from Aveling's jacket. He was completely bald, like a miniaturised version of an old man. 'Thank you,' he said nastily. 'We can't have this falling into the wrong hands, can we?'

'Drop the papers,' Auger ordered.

The girl snarled something at the boy. She had something in one hand as well, glinting silver. She pointed it in Auger's direction, but Auger fired first, the automatic dancing in her hand as she discharged three rounds. The boy hissed and dropped the papers. The girl made another angry sound and snatched the papers from the ground, but as the torchlight played over her, Auger saw that she had hit the girl as well – more by luck than skill, certainly.

'Drop the papers,' she said again.

The girl pulled away from the circle of torchlight. The boy moaned, pawing at a star-shaped wound in his thigh. There was something horrible and doglike about his movements, as if he did not quite grasp the significance of his injury. He tried to stand, but his injured leg buckled under him in a way legs were never meant to buckle. The boy let out a high-pitched shriek of anger and pain. He reached into his little schoolboy blazer and began to pull out something metallic. Auger shot him again, this time putting a bullet through his chest.

He stopped moving.

She waved the torchlight down the tunnel, but there was no sign of the girl. Shocked and breathless, Auger stumbled after her until she saw something fluttering on the ground. She picked it up, recognising one of the documents she had just given to Aveling. There was no sign that the girl had dropped anything else. Auger jammed the paper inside her own coat, making a mental note to examine it later – if she survived that long. She returned to the boy, made sure that he was dead and then did the same for Aveling, shining the torch into his face until she was certain that there would be no reaction.

She heard movement further down the shaft: a dragging sound. Crouching low, she held the automatic at arm's length and tried to locate the source of the sound with the torch.

'Auger?' The female voice was weak and hoarse.

'Who is it?'

'Skellsgard. Thank God you're still alive.'

A short figure emerged from the darkness, using the wall of the tunnel for support. One leg was a stiff, bloodied mass, flesh the texture of raw hamburger visible through the ribbons of her trousers. Seeing the state Skellsgard was in, Auger caught her breath. She lowered the muzzle of the automatic, but didn't put it away.

'You're in a bad way,' Auger said.

'I'm lucky,' Skellsgard said, with a defiant scowl. 'They thought I was dead. If they'd had any doubts, they'd have finished the job properly.'

'Stay where you are. We have to get you back to the portal.'

'Portal isn't safe.'

'It's got to be safer than this tunnel.' Auger pushed herself to her full height, then quickly covered the distance to the injured woman. 'Oh gosh, look at you,' she said.

'Like I said, I'm the lucky one.' Her voice was like two pieces of sandpaper rubbing against each other. She had ripped one of her sleeves off and used it as a makeshift tourniquet around her upper thigh, just below the groin. 'I was bleeding badly, but I don't think they hit anything vital.'

'You need help – and not the kind you're going to get on E2.' Auger looked around, suddenly disorientated. 'Do you think they've all gone?'

'There were three of them.'

'I killed two. The third must have got away.' Auger thumbed the automatic's safety catch on and slipped the gun into her waistband. It jabbed painfully into her side, but she wanted it where she could get hold of it quickly if she needed to. 'Here, lean against me. How far is it to the censor?'

'About fifty metres back that way.' She gestured vaguely behind her with a toss of her head.

'Can you make it?'

Skellsgard transferred her weight to Auger. 'I can try.'

'Tell me what happened. I need to know everything.'

'I can only tell you what I know.'

'That'll do for now.'

'What did you get from Aveling?'

'Not very much,' Auger said. They were making slow progress, with Skellsgard's movements restricted to small, agonised hops. Auger didn't want to think about the pain she must be experiencing from her shredded leg. 'Aveling knew more than I did, obviously. I got the distinct impression that he knew there were Slasher elements already here. What I don't know is whether or not he knew *how* they'd got here.'

'We had suspicions,' Skellsgard said, 'but this is the first clear look we've had at them.'

'You want to hazard a guess as to how they got here?'

'There's only one way into E2,' Skellsgard said. 'We're sure of that. It's our portal, and it's been under our absolute control since we opened it. Anything foreign in E2 has to have come through the portal, and it has to have passed through the censor.'

'So I was told,' Auger said, 'but that didn't stop these . . . *things*.'

'War babies are biotechnological weapons, sure, but there's nothing mechanical about them – nothing that the censor should have rejected. I can believe they got through, somehow or other.'

'Recently?'

'No,' Skellsgard said. 'There's no way those children came through while we've been running the portal. Slasher agents might have penetrated our security, might even have passed themselves off as Threshers. But children? I think we'd have noticed.'

'They got here somehow. If the portal's the only way in, that's how they must have arrived.'

'Then there's only one explanation,' Skellsgard said. 'Do you mind if I stop for a moment? I need to rest.'

'Be my guest.'

Skellsgard paused for a minute before speaking again, keeping her eyes closed for much of that time. 'They can't have come through the portal while we've been running it. Which leaves only one possibility: they must have come through before that.' She screwed up her face, her eyes watering. Auger guessed that shock must be setting in.

'Do you have any idea when?' she asked gently.

'Mars has been under our control for around twenty-three years, ever since the armistice. We didn't discover the portal until two years ago, but that doesn't mean anyone else could have been secretly using it during all those years. We'd have noticed something going on. Just the power drain required to keep the portal open—'

'But clearly someone did use it.'

'In which case it must have happened more than twenty-three years ago. Just before the armistice, there was a period when Mars and its moons were under Slasher authority. It didn't last very long – about eighteen months, give or take.'

'You're saying those war babies have been in Paris for twenty-three years?'

'It's the only explanation I can think of. Any Slasher agents on E2 would have been stranded here once Mars was handed back to us. Actually, that would explain a lot. War babies were infertile, and they were never meant to grow old.'

'Aveling said something about a shelf life.'

'They were supposed to be "decommissioned" before senescence set in. Gotta love those Slasher euphemisms. But these war babies have been left to grow old on their own. That's why they look the way they do.'

'So what have they been doing all this time?'

'That's a very good question.'

'Can you move again?' Auger asked. 'I think we need to be on our way.'

Skellsgard grunted in agreement and resumed her hopping progress. 'We lost control of Susan White,' she said, between ragged breaths. 'One explanation is that she was working for the enemy. Having known Susan, I don't think that's very likely.'

'I don't think it's very likely either.'

'I'm more inclined to believe that she figured out part of what was going on here – that there was already a Slasher presence on E2.'

'Did she report this back to Caliskan?'

Skellsgard shook her head. 'No. I think she must have been worried about blowing her own cover. She may not have been working for the enemy, but she might have had her doubts about someone else on the team.'

'I sort of arrived at the same conclusion,' Auger said cautiously.

'Really?'

'Yes,' Auger said. 'Why bring me into the operation, unless she was unwilling to trust an insider to get the job done?'

'I think you could be right.'

'It means I have to make a decision about who to trust. With Aveling and Barton it's not exactly an issue any more. That leaves you, Maurya.'

'And?'

'I don't know what Susan thought about you. For better or for worse, I don't think I have much choice but to trust you.'

'Well, that's a resounding vote of confidence.'

'Sorry – I meant it to sound a bit more positive than that. Not that it makes much difference now that the papers are gone.'

'But you looked at them, right?'

'Glanced through them,' Auger said.

'Better than nothing. At least you have some idea about what was worth killing for. If we can get that news back to Caliskan, maybe he can put the pieces together.'

'And if Caliskan is the problem?'

'All Susan's letters were addressed to him,' Skellsgard said. 'Right until the end. That suggests she still trusted him, even if she had her doubts about everyone else.'

'Maybe.'

'We have to start somewhere.'

'Agreed, I suppose. But can we get a message through to him? Aveling told me there were problems with the link.'

'There are always problems,' Skellsgard replied. 'It's just got a lot worse since you arrived. Did you hear about the shitstorm brewing back home?'

'Aveling said that the Polities are stirring up trouble.'

'It's worse than that. We've got a full-scale civil war in Polity space, between the moderates and the aggressors. No one's putting any money on who's going to win that particular catfight. Meanwhile, the aggressors are moving their assets deep into the inner system, into USNE space.'

'Doesn't that constitute a declaration of war?'

'It would if the USNE wasn't so afraid of fighting back. At the moment, our politicians are just making a lot of exasperated noises and hoping the moderates will rein in the aggressors.'

'And?'

'Be nice if it happens.'

'I'm worried about my kids, Maurya. I need to be back there, taking care of them. If the aggressors move on Tanglewood—'

'It's all right. We heard from your ex just before the link went tits-up. He wanted you to know that he'll make sure your kids are safe.'

'He'd better,' Auger replied.

'Jesus, kid, he's only trying to reassure you. Cut the guy some slack.'

Auger ignored her. 'Tell me about the link. What, exactly, is the problem?'

'Problem is our friends from the Polities are a little too close to Mars for comfort. They know about link technology, of course. They already have the sensors to detect and localise active portals. If they even have a whisper of intelligence about there being a link around Mars, they'll be looking for it. Consequently we're having to run the link as quietly as we can, and that's why it keeps going down.'

'They must know about it already. How else could the children have got here?'

'But when we took Phobos off them, there was no sign that they'd ever discovered the portal.'

'Maybe,' Auger said, 'that was just what they wanted you to think.'

They had reached the heavy iron door that led to the censor chamber. It was ajar, a bright, septic yellow light spilling through from beyond.

'It's as I left it,' Skellsgard observed.

'Best not to take anything for granted, all the same. Wait here a moment.' Auger propped Skellsgard up against the wall and pulled the automatic from her waistband, praying that there was still at least one bullet inside it. She stepped over the metal lip of the door, squeezing through the gap into the room beyond, and whipped the gun from corner to corner as fast as she could.

No children: at least, none that she could see.

She helped Skellsgard into the room, then heaved shut the iron door. Together they spun the heavy-duty lock. The door could only be unlocked from the inside.

'How are you doing?' Auger asked.

'Not too good. I think I need to loosen this tourniquet.'

'Let's get you through the censor first.'

The bright-yellow barrier of the censor was the only source of light in the room. It flickered in Auger's peripheral vision, but when she looked at it directly, it remained completely unwavering. Fused into the rock around it, the framework machinery looked intact, as thoroughly ancient and alien as the last time she had seen it.

'I'm going to go ahead first and check,' Auger said. 'I'll be back in a few seconds.'

'Or not,' Skellsgard said.

'If I don't come back – if there's something waiting for me on the other side – then you'll have to take your chances on E2.'

Skellsgard shivered. 'I'd sooner take my chances in the Stone Age.'

'They're not that bad. They do have anaesthetic, plus some rudimentary knowledge of sterilisation. If you can get yourself taken to a hospital, you'll have a pretty good chance of being looked after.'

'And then? When they start asking awkward questions?'

'Then you're on your own,' Auger said.

'I'd rather risk the censor. Let me go first, will you? I'm already hurt, and there's no point two of us taking an unnecessary risk. If things are OK, I'll poke my head back through to let you know.'

'Take this,' Auger said, offering her the automatic.

'You fired this thing?'

'Yes, and I can't promise that there are any bullets left in it.'

She helped Skellsgard to the censor, then stood back as the injured woman supported her weight from the overhead rail and – with a grunt of effort and discomfort – succeeded in picking up sufficient momentum to swing herself over the threshold. The bright-yellow surface puckered inward, darkening to a bruised shade of golden brown, then swallowed her completely before twanging back to its intact state.

Auger waited, delving into her handbag for the weapon she had taken from the war baby. It was designed for a smaller hand than hers, but she could still grip it, even if it felt uncomfortable. It was made of metal and was very light compared with the automatic. But it was still a gun. There was a trigger and a trigger guard, and a sliding button that she figured was the safety catch. There was a perforated barrel with a hole in the end and a complex hinged loading mechanism that swung out from one side. The gun was machined from curved, sleekly interlocking parts, and she suspected that it could also be reconfigured for throwing or stabbing if circumstances demanded. It didn't look like something she would have expected to find in an E2 gunsmith's workshop, but neither was it twenty-third-century condensed-energy technology from the Slasher armament works in E1 space. As foreign as it looked, it was something that could conceivably have been made in E2 Paris, using local technology.

Something was pushing through the yellow surface: Skellsgard's face emerged with a pop of breaking surface tension. 'It's safe,' she said.

Auger disabled the weapon's safety catch and followed the other woman through the tingling barrier of the censor. Just before it swallowed her, she had time to remember Skellsgard's story of the endless yellow limbo she had once experienced during the passage through the censor; that sense of being scrutinised by minds as ancient and huge as mountains. Auger braced herself, some part of her wanting that experience, another fearing it with every atom of her existence. But the moment of transition was as brief as the first time. As before, she felt a mild elastic resistance that suddenly abated, as if she had burst through the skin of a drum. There had been no audience with God, or whatever godlike entities had created the censor and the duplicate Earth. Nor had any part of her been refused passage. Her clothes and the gun she carried were still with her when she entered the portal chamber. The censor's implacable logic had decided to allow those simple things through. Or perhaps it was much less concerned with artefacts escaping E2 than entering it.

'No one's come through,' Skellsgard said. She was leaning against a console, her face a pallid mask of exhaustion and shock.

'No sign of any children?'

'I don't think they made it this far. Fucking lucky that they didn't, or they might have done something irreversible to the link, or turned the far end into a temporary white hole. *Adios*, Phobos, and anything near it.'

'Let's take a look at your leg.'

'I've adjusted the tourniquet. It'll be OK for a while.'

Auger snapped a first-aid kit from its wall mounting. She fumbled the plastic catches open and rummaged through the contents until she found a morphine jab. 'Can you do this yourself?' she asked, passing the syringe to Skellsgard. 'I'm not too good with needles.'

'I'll manage.' Skellsgard bit the sterile wrapper from the syringe, then jammed the needle into her thigh, just above the wound but below the tourniquet. 'I don't know if this is the right thing to do,' she said. 'Guess I'll find out sooner or later.'

'We have to get the link up and running,' Auger said. 'Can we do it together?'

'Give me a moment.' She nodded at one of the desks down on the machine floor. 'In the meantime, go down to that console and throw all the switches on the top bank to their red settings. Then see if any of the dials stay in the green.'

'It's that simple?'

'One step at a time, sister. We're not cooking with gas here. We're dealing with major alterations to the local space-time metric.'

'My will's already up to date,' Auger said. She removed her shoes and made her way down the spiral access ladder as quickly as she could. She had never been down to the machine floor before, and the scale of the equipment looming around and over her was dauntingly impressive. Fortunately, it all looked intact. The transit craft was suspended overhead in the vacuum-filled recovery bubble, clutched in the bee-striped cradle, its blunt, stress-battered nose still aimed away from the mirror-lined shaft of the portal tunnel.

Once they'd turned it around, all they needed was a moment of stability from the link.

She made her way to the console Skellsgard had indicated and flipped the heavy-duty toggle switches one by one. The dials quivered, but although one or two needles continued to hover in the red for a few moments, they eventually sank back into the green.

'We're looking good,' Auger said.

Skellsgard had dragged herself to the railed edge of the upper catwalk and was looking down on Auger. 'All right. That's better than I expected. Now see that second bank of switches, under the hinged plastic hood?'

'Got it.'

'Lift the hood and start flipping them as well, and keep an eye on the dials. If more than two of them twitch into the red and stay there, stop flipping.'

'Why do I have the impression that this is the tricky bit?'

'It's all tricky,' Skellsgard said.

Auger began to flip the second set of toggles: slower this time, letting the dial above each switch twitch and settle before advancing to the next. Around her, with each switch that she threw, the machinery notched up its humming presence. Red and green status lights began to blink on items of equipment halfway across the floor, and even in the recovery bubble itself.

'I'm halfway there,' Auger said. 'So far so good. Will the ship fly itself?'

'One step at a time. We'll prep the ship once we've established throat curvature. Getting goose pimples yet?'

'Not yet.'

'You should be.'

Auger threw another switch. 'Whoah, wait,' she said. 'We're holding in the red on the fifth dial.'

'That's what I was worried about. All right. Reverse the last switch you flicked, see if that helps.'

Auger did as she was told. 'Back in the green,' she said after a few seconds.

'Try it again.'

'Still in the red. Reversing and trying again.' Auger waited, biting her tongue. 'Sorry. No joy. What does that mean?'

'It means we have a problem. All right. Leave that be and move to the second console, the one with the toolkit next to it.'

'Got it.'

'Throw the red switch on the right-hand side of the monitor and tell me what kind of numbers come up in the third column of the read-out.'

Auger scraped dust from the glass. 'Fifteen point one seven three, thirteen point zero four—'

'Roughly, Auger. I don't need decimal precision here.'

'They're all between ten and twenty.'

'Shit. That's not good. Stability's still compromised.'

'Can we get home?'

'Not easily.'

Auger turned from the console and looked up at Skellsgard. 'What if we wait? Will things get better?'

'They might do. Then again, they might get worse. And there's no telling how long this instability will last. Could be hours. Could be tens of hours or even days.'

'We can't wait that long, not when more of those kids might show up at any moment. When you say "not easily", what does that mean? That there *is* a way?'

'There's a way,' Skellsgard said. 'For one of us.'

'I don't follow.'

'We'll need to stabilise the throat geometry at this end, and that's going to cost us more power than we can supply in the long term.'

Auger shrugged. 'Doesn't matter. I don't care if the link folds once we're out of here.'

Skellsgard shook her head. 'Not that simple. Look, I don't want to give you a lecture on hypervacuum theory—'

'Suits me fine.'

Skellsgard smiled. 'The essential point is that the local throat has to stay open until we reach the far end. Things will get messy if it snaps shut, and they'll get really, *really* messy if it snaps shut violently. We'll run the risk of losing the link, for a start. And while the closure might be a relatively low-energy event as seen from the Paris end, all the energy released by the tunnel collapse will find its way to the Phobos end. It's like stretching a big elastic band between your hands and then letting go of one end – you get the picture? And even if the collapse isn't violent enough to bring down the link, we'd still be surfing a major stress wave in the transport. We'd have a soliton chasing us all the way home.'

'What's a soliton?'

'Like a ruck in a carpet, only with a seriously pissed-off attitude.'

'That's all I need to know. Now tell me what we can do about it. Can we stop the throat snapping shut?'

'Yes,' Skellsgard said. 'Once the ship's cleared the throat, the power can be ramped down to a level the generators can sustain until the ship gets home.'

'Doesn't sound too complicated to me.'

'It isn't. The problem is that it isn't a procedure we ever got around to automating. It was always assumed that we'd have a team here, or that we could hang around indefinitely until stability improved.'

'I see,' Auger said quietly. 'Well, you'd better show me what to do.'

'No way,' Skellsgard said. 'No disrespect, Auger, but this isn't exactly the kind of thing they teach you in history school. You're getting in the ship. I'll handle the throat.'

'What about the children?'

'They didn't get in here before. I'm pretty sure I'll be safe until a rescue party gets through.'

'But that will take days,' Auger said.

'About sixty hours if they can do an immediate turnaround on the ship, and if stability conditions are optimal. Longer if they're not.'

'I'm not leaving you here.'

'I can hold out,' Skellsgard said. 'You're the one with the critical information, not me.'

'I lost almost all that information in the tunnel.'

'But you saw it. That has to be worth something.'

Auger left the console and sprinted back up the ladder to Skellsgard. 'What exactly is involved in controlling the throat?'

'It's a very technically demanding procedure.'

'It can't be that technically demanding or you'd already have automated it. Talk to me, Skellsgard.'

She blinked. 'It's a question of waiting thirty, forty seconds after departure, then dropping power levels to about ten per cent.'

'Using those switches you've already shown me?'

'More or less.'

'I think even a lowly history grunt can handle that. All right: let's start prepping the ship. You can tell me the rest while we do it.'

'That is *not* the way we're doing this,' Skellsgard said.

'Listen to me: if you don't get medical attention for that leg, you're going to lose it.'

'So they'll grow me a new one. I always fancied a ride out to one of those Polity hospitals.'

'You want to take that chance? I don't think I would, especially with all hell breaking loose back home.'

'I can't let you do this,' Skellsgard insisted.

Auger took out the war baby's weapon and flashed it at Skellsgard. 'You want me to start pointing this at you? Because believe me, I will. Now let's prep the ship, sister.'

EIGHTEEN

At two in the afternoon, Floyd looked up as the brasserie door swung open. He had already looked up several dozen times since ordering his last coffee, as patrons came and went, and there were another three empty coffee cups on his table, along with a froth-lined beer glass and the stale crumbs of a nondescript sandwich. It was still raining outside, water sluicing down across the doorframe from a broken gutter above it. The patrons got a soaking when they left or arrived, but no one seemed to complain. Even Greta, when she arrived, seemed more relieved to find him still there than annoyed at the weather.

'I thought you'd have gone already,' she said, shaking her umbrella. Her clothes were dark with rain, her hair frizzy and tipped with tiny dewdrops.

'I figured it was best to keep with the original rendezvous,' Floyd said. He removed his coat from the seat opposite, where he had placed it to prevent anyone else from joining him at the table. He had wanted a clear view of the window, and of the hotel opposite, in the hope that he might see Verity Auger coming or going. 'I must admit, though, that I was beginning to worry I'd got the wrong brasserie. What happened?'

'She left,' Greta said, sitting down with visible relief. 'Almost as soon as I'd put down the telephone, I saw her leaving the hotel.'

'You want a drink?'

'I'd kill for one.'

Floyd signalled the waiter to their table and ordered another coffee for Greta. 'So tell me what happened. You followed her, obviously. Did she look like she was checking out of the hotel?'

'No – she didn't have anything with her other than a handbag. For all I knew she was going to be back in five minutes. But I couldn't take that chance.'

'You were right not to. Did you keep up with her?'

'I think I've got a bit better at this tailing business since this morning. I kept my distance and tried to change my appearance every block or so: folding up my umbrella, putting on my hat, sunglasses, that sort of thing. I don't think she saw me.' Greta spooned sugar into the coffee and gulped it down in almost one mouthful.

'Where did she go?'

'I followed her all the way to Cardinal Lemoine. That's where I lost her.'

'Lost her how?'

'That's the funny thing,' Greta said. 'I was with her all the way into the Métro station. I followed her to the platform and kept my distance. I hid behind some chocolate-vending machines. A train came in and then another. She didn't get on either of them, but they were all going in the same direction.'

'Weird,' Floyd said.

'Not as weird as what happened after that. Between one moment and the next she disappeared completely. She simply wasn't on the platform.'

'And no other train had come and gone?'

Greta lowered her voice, as if aware of how absurd her account sounded. 'I'm certain of it. I also know that there is no other exit she could have taken, not without walking right past my hiding place.'

Floyd sipped at his own coffee. By the fourth cup he had ceased tasting it, the drink purely a mechanical aid to his alertness. 'She can't just have vanished into thin air.'

'I never said she did. It looked that way, but there were a few other people waiting on the platform and I decided to brazen it out and ask them if they'd seen anything. At that point I figured I didn't have a lot to lose.'

'You were probably right,' Floyd said. 'What did you get?'

'At least one of the witnesses was certain he'd seen Auger jump down on to the tracks and disappear into the tunnel at the end of the platform.'

Floyd digested this while he drained his coffee cup. 'There's something about Cardinal Lemoine,' he said. 'Blanchard said he'd seen Susan White behaving very oddly near that station. He saw her enter the station with a heavy suitcase and come out a few moments later with an empty one. It can't be a coincidence.'

'But why would a woman disappear into a Métro tunnel?'

'For the same reason anyone else would: there's something in it that matters to them.'

'Or else they were both mad,' Greta said.

'I can't discount that possibility, either. Did you see her come out again?'

'I waited forty-five minutes. There was some kind of interruption in the service for a couple of minutes, but then the trains started running normally again. Several dozen trains went through. No one came back out of the tunnel.'

'And no one thought to report any of this to the station staff, or the police?'

'Not the man I was talking to,' Greta said. 'He wasn't the sort you'd catch doing anything so responsible.'

Floyd called for the bill. 'All right. The way I see it, we have two choices if we want to find Auger again. We can cover the hotel in case she goes back there, or we can cover Cardinal Lemoine and hope she comes out of the tunnel or goes back in again, if somehow we missed her coming out.'

'What about the next station up the line? What if she walked all the way through?'

'I'm hoping she didn't. Anyway, that would make even less sense than going into the tunnel in the first place. I can only assume that she must have arranged to drop off or collect something from inside the tunnel.'

'You talk about "covering" as if we have limitless manpower,' Greta said. 'Whereas in fact we have two people, and one of them needs to be looking after her aunt.'

'I know,' Floyd said. 'And I won't ask anything else of you. What you've done already has been a great help.'

'But I lost her,' Greta said.

'No. You established that there's something going on with Verity Auger that doesn't fit with her story. Until now there was still a faint chance that she might have been telling the truth about being Susan White's long-lost sister.'

'And now?'

Floyd wiped his upper lip clean of the moustache of coffee froth that had gathered there. 'Now? Now I'd put good money on both of them being spies.'

'You're in much too deep,' Greta said. 'If Custine was here he'd tell you exactly the same thing: take what you have and hand it over to the right people, Floyd. They have no axe to grind with you.'

'I have to get Custine off the hook, Greta. And the only way I'm going to do that is by following this woman.'

'You liked her, didn't you?'

Floyd reached for his coat. 'She wasn't my type.'

'Maybe so, but you liked her all the same.'

Floyd shook his head, laughing at the thought of it. But he couldn't look Greta in the eye.

*

In the armoured glass bulb of the recovery bubble, the status lights of the transit ship blinked on and off with hypnotic regularity. 'Rotating,' Skellsgard said, leaning against one of the high-level consoles. 'You sure about this, Auger?'

'Just tell me what to do. I'll take care of the rest.'

The bee-striped holding cradle began to swivel, turning the ship through 180 degrees. Unlike the gleaming machinery surrounding it, the transit ship looked like some impossibly battered relic from a museum of space history: the kind of capsule that would have been flown back from space by seat-of-the-pants jockeys relying on grit and slide-rule calculations to get themselves home. Auger had to remind herself that the ship had accrued all this damage during a single passage between portals, and that it would be approximately twice as battered by the time it emerged on Phobos, about thirty hours from now.

'Ship looks healthy enough,' Skellsgard said, tapping through monitor options. 'Which is a good thing – we have enough problems with the throat without having to worry about the ship as well.'

'You think you can last all the way home?'

Skellsgard nodded. 'I'll make it. It's not as if I have much of a choice, is it?'

'This is the way it has to happen,' Auger said. 'But that doesn't mean I don't want a rescue party launched the instant you get through.'

'They'll be on their way as soon as is humanly possible. You have my word on that.'

'All right. Let's get you strapped in.'

Auger helped Skellsgard along the high-level catwalk that led to the airlock set into the side of the recovery bubble. Skellsgard was getting weaker, Auger noticed: even with the attention she had received from the first-aid kit, she was clearly sliding towards unconsciousness. Auger just hoped she could get the woman underway before that happened. She was still hoping for another run-through of the commands required to keep the throat from sphinctering tight.

The airlock clammed open on heavy-duty piston-driven hinges. Auger barely remembered dragging herself out of the ship, it seemed so long ago. Gently, she assisted Skellsgard through the lock and into the pressurised connecting bridge that crossed to the waiting ship. 'I think maybe I should splint that leg before I zip you in,' Auger said.

'No time. I don't want to delay your rescue by one second more than is necessary. Anyway, they might have shredded me pretty good but I don't think anything's broken. Stop worrying on my account, all right? You've already helped me enough.'

Inside the ship was the arrangement of three acceleration couches Auger had come to know so well on the way over. Blotting out the woman's moans of discomfort, she laid Skellsgard on the right-hand couch, buckled the restraints securely around her and then folded down the navigation and communications panel. Auger reached for the loose tangle of the in-flight catheter system, assuming Skellsgard would not have the strength to crawl back to the tiny toilet. 'You want me to plug you in before you fly?'

'I'll manage,' Skellsgard said, grimacing. 'And if I don't, I think my dignity will take it. You have any thoughts about what I should tell Caliskan when I get back?'

Auger reached into her jacket and took out the one piece of paper she had been able to salvage from the attack. 'Can you hold out a minute? I need to write something down.'

'Just in case I fall into a coma?'

'That's one consideration, but I also need to write something down for myself.'

Auger left the ship and returned to one of the high-level consoles, where she had seen a notepad and pen. She ripped out a clean sheet of paper and wrote down everything she thought she had gleaned from Susan White's paperwork. Then she unfolded the piece of paper she had retrieved from the tunnel – the letter from the manufacturing works in Berlin. She flattened the letter on the desk and on another sheet of paper took down the particulars of the plant, including the address and the name of the man who had written to White. Then she jogged back to the ship, relieved to find Skellsgard still conscious.

'This is the only piece of documentation the war baby didn't make off with in the tunnel,' she said, slipping the letter into Skellsgard's chest pocket. 'Don't forget it's there.'

'I won't.'

Auger then folded the sheet containing her observations and placed it with the letter. 'This is everything I've figured out so far. It's not much, but maybe Caliskan can work out what's going on. Anyway, I might know a bit more when I get back from Berlin.'

'Who said anything about Berlin?'

'I'm following one of the leads Susan White never got around to herself.'

Skellsgard shook her head warningly. 'That's extremely dangerous. In Paris you're never more than an hour away from the portal if anything goes wrong. How long will it take you to get back from Berlin?'

'It doesn't matter: the portal's no use to me until the ship returns. I'm pretty sure I can make it to Berlin and back in plenty of time.'

'You mean you don't know for certain?'

'I haven't had time to plan this to the last detail,' Auger said. 'All I know is that there's a lead in Berlin and Susan would have followed it up if she hadn't been killed. I owe it to her to do what I can. There's an overnight train leaving tonight and I plan to be on it. I'll be in Berlin by tomorrow morning, and with any luck I'll be on my way back by the evening.'

'With any luck,' Skellsgard echoed.

'Look, don't worry about me. Just get yourself home and make sure Caliskan sees those pieces of paper. I have a feeling the letter is more important than any of us realise.'

Skellsgard squeezed Auger's hand. 'You really don't have to send me back instead of you.'

'I know.'

'But I do appreciate it. It's a brave thing you're doing.'

Auger squeezed the other woman's hand in return. 'Listen, it's no big hardship. It gives me a chance to see a bit more of this world before they pull me out of it for good.'

'You almost sound convincing.'

'I mean it. As much as part of me would love to be riding that ship back with you, there's another part that just wants to soak up as much of E2 as I can. I've barely scratched the surface, Skellsgard. That's all any of us has done.'

'Take good care of yourself, Auger.'

'I will.' Auger stood back from the cabin. 'All right. Let's close you up and get this show on the road.'

'You're clear on those throat adjustments?'

'If the ride gets bumpy, you'll know why.'

'Reassuring as ever.'

Auger pushed the door until it was nearly closed, then stepped away as servo-motors completed the job. Only a few inches of armoured metal now separated her from Skellsgard, but she suddenly felt vastly more alone. She walked back through the airlock, then ran through the sequence of umbilical disconnection commands, ending with the retraction of the connecting bridge. Through the scuffed and scratched window in the side of the ship, Skellsgard gave her a final thumbs up. Auger walked back to the main ring of consoles and tried to blank everything from her mind except the procedure necessary for dispatching the ship.

None of the individual steps were particularly difficult. Initial throat stabilisation and launch were handled by a pre-programmed routine that worked exactly as advertised. In the translucent bronze structures of the alien machinery, the suspended sparks and filaments of amber light quickened their movements almost imperceptibly. The surrounding clots and plaques of human machinery throbbed and flickered with red and green status lights and indicator numerals. On the console before her, analogue dials lurched hard into the red, but she had been told to expect this and kept her nerve. The grilled catwalk beneath her feet began to vibrate. She increased the power to the throat machines and a metal toolkit slid off a console halfway across the room, spilling spanners and torque wrenches to the ground and making her jump.

On the panel, a sequence of lights changed one by one to orange: throat aperture was now wide enough to accept the ship. The geodesic stress indices were low enough not to rip it to shreds, provided it plunged straight down the middle without grazing the sides.

Auger found a pair of protective goggles and bent the stalk of a microphone to her lips. 'You getting all this, Skellsgard?'

Her reply buzzed from a grilled speaker in the console. It sounded thin and distant, as if she was hundreds of kilometres away. 'Everything looks OK from in here. Let's get this over with.'

Auger checked that the orange lights were holding steady. 'Injecting in five seconds.'

'Spare me the countdown. Just do it.'

'Here goes, then.'

The movement was more violent than Auger had been expecting. The cradle suddenly lurched forward, propelling the ship faster and faster. In an eyeblink, cradle and ship had exited the main globe of the recovery bubble, the entire structure creaking in response to the sudden transfer of momentum. From her vantage point, Auger watched the ship haring down the mirror-lined injection tunnel, picking up speed like a torpedo. Two or three seconds later, the cradle reached the limit of its guidance rail and slammed to a halt, lobbing the ship ahead of it on the lazy arc of a ballistic trajectory. The throat of the wormhole – exposed now that the iris had opened – was a vortex of blue and violet static discharge just ahead of the ship, gaping like the mouth of a starfish. Spring-loaded arms whipped out from the ship's sides and glanced against the incurving wall, spitting coils of light and molten metal. An instant later they sheared away, warped into toffeelike shapes. But they'd done the work they were designed for, nudging the transport out of harm's way. With a final shower of golden sparks, the ship picked up yet more speed at an impossible rate, diminishing to a dot of light in a heartbeat.

All round her, emergency klaxons and warning strobes had come on. A recorded voice began to repeat a message about unsustainable power levels. Above the din she heard a distant voice: 'Auger . . . you reading this?'

Auger leaned closer to the microphone, checking her watch at the same time. 'Guess you're on your way. How was it?'

'Interesting.' Skellsgard's voice was already breaking up, becoming thready. Routing communications through the link was difficult enough when there was no ship en route, but it was almost impossible otherwise.

'Skellsgard – I don't know if you can hear me now, but I'm going to start controlled constriction of the throat in about fifteen seconds.'

The microphone crackled in reply, but it was nothing Auger could understand. It made no difference now, in any case. The die was cast.

She descended the spiral staircase to the lower console, checked her watch and began to drop the stabilising power as Skellsgard had instructed her. When she had notched it down sufficiently, the klaxons, strobes and recorded warnings turned themselves off, leaving her with only the warm hum of the surrounding machinery. The amber sparks and filaments had quietened themselves. She returned to the higher level and peered down the injection shaft, but there was no sign of the departed ship. Instead, the cradle was returning to the recovery bubble, while a circular sweeper mechanism was clearing the tube of any lingering debris from the mangled guidance arms.

'Skellsgard? Maurya?' she said into the microphone.

But there was no answer.

Auger checked her watch and counted ahead sixty hours. Someone might route a signal down the link once Skellsgard was home, but in all likelihood Auger would not know whether she had been successful until a new ship dropped into the bubble.

She did not want to be in Berlin when that happened.

Auger's third passage through the censor was as uneventful as the first two. She shivered and picked herself up, then set about gathering the things she would need for the rest of her mission. She found a torch that worked, then stuffed clean clothes and bundles of local currency into a red suitcase. She had retrieved the automatic from Skellsgard and found a fresh clip of ammunition on one of the storage racks in the censor chamber. Now the automatic nestled in her handbag, next to the war-baby weapon. It was good to feel armed as she started the slow and filthy walk back to the station. After ten minutes she had reached the Métro tunnel, the torch picking out the lethal gleam of the electrified rails.

Her breath caught in her throat.

She had forgotten all about the electricity.

With Aveling and the others gone, there was no one to short-circuit the supply while she got clear of the tunnel. It would be nearly a dozen hours before the trains stopped running for the night, and then she would have the additional problem of escaping from a locked Métro station. If she couldn't get out until the station was opened again the next morning – assuming no one arrested her for suspicious behaviour in the meantime – she would have wasted almost a day's worth of the sixty hours available before the ship returned. She could probably find a way to short-circuit the track, but not to restore the power once she was free of the tunnel. And if it wasn't restored, there would be too much danger of Métro engineers poking around in the tunnel, with the risk of them finding the entrance to the tunnel leading to the portal.

Auger waited in the sanctuary of the secondary tunnel until a train passed by. The brightly lit carriages slammed past only inches from her face, Auger squinting against the warm slap of disturbed air. Another train roared through a couple of minutes later, its compartments empty except for a few commuters. The midday rush was over now, but the trains continued to run on the same schedule. She cursed the Métro system for its mindless dedication to efficiency.

There was no alternative: she would just have to make a run for it. She guessed that she would have a minute and a half to reach Cardinal Lemoine, two if she was lucky, and could only hope that she would not trip or find herself caught in the tunnel if a train arrived sooner than expected.

Just get it over with, Auger told herself.

She would make a dash for it as soon as the next train had passed through. She readied herself, anxious not to waste a second. But after a minute no train came, and then another minute passed, and then another. She waited in the tunnel for five minutes until she heard the approach of another train as it squealed and clattered towards her. In that five-minute interval she could easily have reached safety, but the next two trains arrived in rapid succession, almost nose to tail.

She would just have to take her chances.

Even as the red lights of the most recent train were disappearing into the tunnel, she was on her way.

She kept her back to the wall, her coat snagging on the tangled pipes and electrical conduits that ran along the tunnel. She held the suitcase as high as her strength allowed, trailing it behind her. It thumped and scraped against the wall as she moved. She had not tripped before, she told herself, and she had managed to make the distance in the time Aveling had given her. Nothing had changed, except that the punishment for even the slightest slip would be rather more severe. She could not afford to make a single mistake; one misplaced footstep and it was all over.

How long had it been now?

Down the tunnel, just around a shallow curve, she could make out the cold glow of Cardinal Lemoine station. It still seemed very far away, further than she could possibly cover in the minute or so that must be remaining. Auger panicked. Had she got turned around somehow? Was she in fact heading deeper into the tunnel, lured by the impossibly distant light of the next station down the line? The panic brought a lump to her throat and an appalling desire to turn around and head in the other direction.

No, she ordered herself sternly, *just keep moving*. The passing trains had confirmed that she was moving in the right direction. And even if this was the wrong direction, she was committed now. She had no better chance of making it to safety in the other direction than if she continued to press on the way she was going. And as she edged closer to the light, placing each foot with tense deliberation, she began to feel as if she was making slow but steady progress. The light was now much brighter, glancing off the courses of enamel tiles lining the mouth of the tunnel. She could make out people standing on the platform, none of whom had noticed her yet. The suitcase bumped against the wall behind her, dislodging a loose chip of tunnel cladding.

Then the people began to move, drifting to the edge of the platform as if by a collective decision. Almost as soon as she had noticed this, the brilliant headlights of a train hove into view. It came to a stop at the platform, paused for what seemed only a handful of seconds and then began moving in her direction.

She wasn't going to make it.

As the train entered her stretch of tunnel, arcs danced between the electrified rails and the undercarriage of the train. The arcs were a cruel violet-blue, the colour of the wormhole mouth she had glimpsed earlier. The train lurched and swayed as it approached, seeming to fill the entire width of the tunnel. Auger wished she had paid more attention on the way in, checking the wall for nooks and crannies in which she might have taken shelter. Now all she could do was stand still and press herself against the wall as hard possible. Pipes and conduits dug into her spine like the torments of some apparatus of medieval justice. She pressed harder, trying to become part of the fabric of the wall, willing herself to melt into it like some camouflaged reptile. The train roared closer, rats scampering and garbage fluttering away in the air draught pushed before it. Surely, she thought, the driver must see her now. But the train kept coming, its steely roar filling her universe like a proclamation.

Auger closed her eyes. No sense in keeping them open until the last moment. The roar reached a crescendo, oil and dust hitting her lungs. She felt a violent jolt run through her left arm, as if the train had wrenched it from her shoulder. The roar continued, and then began to abate.

Reverberations chased the train along the tunnel, and then all was quiet again.

Auger opened her eyes and dared to breathe. She was all right. Her arm was still attached, and it didn't even feel dislocated. But the suitcase was lying half-open a dozen paces further back down the tunnel. The clean clothes she had packed for herself were draped over the nearest pair of rails, already crusted with filth. Two packets of counterfeit money lay between the tracks, while a third had ended up much further along the tunnel, at the limit of her torch's beam.

Auger grabbed the nearest bundle of money, but some instinct told her to abandon everything else and get out of the tunnel as quickly as possible. She doubted the money would be there when she returned to the portal, but there was plenty more where it had come from. Someone – most probably a poorly paid Métro engineer – would be enjoying a generous bonus.

She reached the end of the tunnel just as the next train was slowing into Cardinal Lemoine. She lingered in the darkness until the train came to a stop and the passengers on the platform began to jostle for the best positions around the sliding doors. The driver picked up a newspaper from the top of his control panel and turned idly to the back page, taking a pencil from behind his ear to scribble something down.

Auger used his moment of inattention to spring up on to the platform. Most of the disembarking passengers had already left the train and were spilling in ragged lines towards the exit. If she could only mingle with them, she thought she had a good chance of reaching daylight without anyone noticing that she had not in fact come off the train. But there was a wide expanse of open platform to cross before she reached the small crowd, and there were at least four seated bystanders she would have to pass by unnoticed.

The doors hissed shut and the train started moving. Auger walked as nonchalantly as she could along the platform, fixated on reaching the safety of the scurrying crowd. Once she was above ground she would be safe: just another woman fallen on hard times, someone to be actively ignored.

'Mademoiselle. This way please.' The Frenchman's voice was calm but authoritative.

She looked around for the source and saw one of the seated individuals rising and moving towards her with a determined look in his eyes. He had been reading a newspaper but had left it on the bench, now revealing himself to be wearing the dark-blue uniform of a Métro official. He was jamming his hat on as he spoke.

'I'm sorry?' Auger replied, answering him in French.

'Mademoiselle, you must come with me. I am afraid we must ask some questions of you.'

'I don't understand. What have I done?'

'That is to be determined.' He pointed to a nearby door marked with a 'no entry' sign. 'If you would step into our office, please. It would be best for all concerned if you do not make a scene.'

She did not move. The official was a short middle-aged man with a greying moustache and a pink nose marked by complex tributaries of broken veins. He most definitely did not want a scene, Auger thought.

'I still don't quite—'

'We had reports of a young woman entering the tunnel an hour or two ago,' he said in a low voice. 'We were inclined to dismiss them, but there were at least two witnesses. As a matter of precaution, I decided to keep watch on the tunnel myself in case anyone emerged.'

'But you didn't see anyone emerge,' Auger insisted. 'Not me, certainly. I just got off that train.'

'I know what I saw.'

'Then you must be mistaken.'

He shifted uncomfortably, doubtless wondering if he should use force to persuade her into the room, or call for assistance from another official. 'Please, do not make this difficult for me,' he said. 'We have every right to call in the police. If there is a simple explanation, however, that may not be necessary.'

'Is there a problem here?' asked another voice, differently accented.

Auger looked around. Another passenger was walking towards them, hands in the pockets of his long, grey raincoat. He wore a fedora with the brim tipped low over his face, but she recognised him immediately.

'Wendell,' she said.

'What's going on, Verity?'

She had no idea what was going on, but Floyd seemed to expect her to fall into a role, one for which only he had seen the script. Stumbling over her words, she said, 'I'm not sure, Floyd, but this man wants to take me into that room and ask me some questions.'

Floyd examined the man with a look of patient concern. 'Why on Earth would you want to do that?'

'Do you know this woman, sir?'

'Know her? I should think so. She's my wife.'

'Then perhaps you could kindly explain what she was doing crawling around in the tunnel.'

'I have no idea what you're talking about,' Floyd said. He took off his hat, smoothing down his hair.

The man scratched his veined bulb of a nose. 'I know what I saw. Perhaps it would be best for us to continue this discussion in my office.'

'As you wish,' Floyd said, 'but I assure you that you're making a very serious mistake.'

Auger sighed. 'Come on, Wendell. Let's get this over with, and then perhaps this silly little man will leave us alone.'

The man let them walk ahead of him, then used a key on a chain to unlock the faded green door into a bare, spartan private office. A single unshaded bulb hung from the ceiling like the lure of an angler fish.

'Sit here,' the man said, indicating a warped wooden table and a couple of pull-up chairs that had seen better days.

'I'll stand, if you don't mind,' Floyd said. 'Now, let me explain. Thirty minutes ago, I received a telephone call from my wife. She works in a haberdasher's on Gay-Lussac. All sorts of people visit the shop and occasionally the staff let customers use the upstairs washroom. Unfortunately, someone left the tap running. Why don't you tell him the rest, Verity?'

'The sink overflowed,' Auger said, watching for the minutest nod of encouragement from Floyd. 'The water built up and made the ceiling cave in. Everyone working below was either drenched or covered in dust and debris from the collapsing floor – that's why I look like this. All our stock was ruined. I called my husband and told him we were all being sent home early from work, and he came to the station to meet me – I don't want to wander the streets alone in this state.'

'Neither of you is French,' the man said, as if imparting grave news.

'There's no law against it,' Floyd replied. 'Anyway, you're welcome to look at my identification papers.' He showed the man his identity card and one of the false business cards he kept handy for occasions just like this. 'As you can see, my work as a literary translator means I spend most of the day in my own home. Go on, Verity – show the good man your papers as well.'

'Here,' she said, holding them out after rummaging in her handbag.

He looked at her documents, which were grubby with her fingerprints. 'Verity Auger,' he read. 'I shall remember that name. I shall also remember that neither of you is wearing a wedding ring.'

Beyond the closed door, another train arrived in the station. Auger was tempted to make a dash for it, but she feared that the official would be able to stop the train from departing. 'Look,' she said, 'I'm telling the truth, and so is my husband. What business would I have crawling around in a railway tunnel? It was bad enough taking the train looking like this, with everyone staring at me as if I was some kind of tramp.'

'I assure you, everything's above board,' Floyd said, smiling winningly.

'As my wife says, she'd hardly be likely to crawl around in a Métro tunnel.'

'Someone was crawling around in it,' the man insisted.

'That may be the case,' Floyd said, his tone conciliatory, 'but surely you can't suspect every woman who steps off a train with a bit of dust on their clothes.'

'I saw her . . .' the man began, but his voice lacked conviction. 'I saw *someone* come out of that tunnel.'

'And in the rush of passengers coming and going you must have lost track of the right person and ended up confusing them with my wife.' Floyd sounded very understanding. 'Look, I don't want to make things difficult for you, but my wife really needs to be getting home where she can have a hot shower and change her clothes.' He took Auger's hand. His fingers were rough, but gentle. 'Don't you, dear?'

'I'm worried about whether there'll be a job for me to go back to tomorrow,' Auger said. 'The damage to the stock looked very bad.'

'We'll cross that bridge when we come to it.' Floyd returned his attention to the official. 'Here. You've been very understanding. Will you accept this as a token of my thanks?' He had taken a ten-franc note from inside his coat, folded it discreetly in two and slipped it into the man's top pocket, almost without blinking.

'Your thanks? For what? I've done nothing.'

'My wife is still a bit embarrassed about her appearance,' Floyd said, lowering his voice as if the two men were sharing a confidence. 'She'd be grateful if you'd let us leave the station by the staff exit.'

'I couldn't possibly . . .'

Floyd slipped the man another ten-franc note. 'It's highly irregular, I know, but we really would appreciate it. Treat yourself to a drink on me.'

The man pursed his lips, weighing possibilities. He reached a conclusion very quickly. 'Stock damage, did you say?'

'We'd just moved everything in from the warehouse,' Auger said.

'I hope very much that your job will be safe, madame.' He opened the wooden door and ushered them back out on to the platform. 'This way,' he said, leading them in the opposite direction from the public exit.

'You're a very good man,' Floyd said. 'I won't forget you in a hurry.'

'You can be sure that I won't forget you in a hurry either, Monsieur Floyd.'

NINETEEN

It was still raining when they reached street level, but it was the last dregs of mid-afternoon drizzle, and the grey blanket of the sky was punctured by odd-shaped splashes of pastel blue. After all that happened underground, the mundane continuation of city life – the constant welter of pedestrians and vehicles – felt to Auger like a peculiar kind of insult. She waited until the official had returned to his subterranean world, locking a gate behind him, before speaking to Floyd.

'I don't know where to begin,' she said, addressing him in English now.

'You can begin by thanking me. I got you out of a fix down there.'

'That fix wasn't any of your business. What were you doing, following me like that?'

'I wasn't following you,' Floyd said. 'I just happened to see you in trouble.'

'You just happened to see me. Of all the Métro stations in the city, you just happened to be passing the time of day in Cardinal Lemoine?'

Floyd shrugged. 'Well, not exactly.'

Auger started walking away from him, raising her hand in the probably vain hope of catching a taxi. In her state, they were more likely to speed up than slow down.

'Where are you going?' Floyd asked, his tone reasonable.

'Anywhere but here. Anywhere I think there's a chance I won't be followed by a nosy man in a shabby raincoat.'

'Is that how they teach you to show gratitude in Dakota?'

She swung around, teetering a little on her heels. The pavement beneath her was slick and slate-coloured with rain. 'I'm not ungrateful,' she said, glaring at him, 'but my gratitude ends here. Now please walk away, or I'll have to call the police.'

'In your state? I'd like to see you try.'

A taxi sped by, making a special point of sluicing her with dirty brown rainwater. 'Just get away from me,' she said, screwing up her face as the water seeped into her shoes. 'We concluded our business this morning. Or don't you remember the nice termination fee I gave you?'

'Some of that termination fee just bailed you out of trouble,' Floyd replied.

'I wasn't worried about him. I was handling things perfectly well until you barged in.'

'He was right, though, wasn't he?' Floyd looked at her with an amused expression. He had very deep wrinkles around his eyes. He was a man who either laughed a lot or cried a lot.

'Right about what?'

'You did go into that tunnel. There's no point denying it – I had a tail on you from the moment you left my offices.'

'I noticed her,' Auger said. 'I hate to break the bad news, but she isn't very good.'

'She's cheap. The point is that she saw you duck into that tunnel, the one our friend claimed you just came out of.'

'I thought you said you weren't following me.'

'And I wasn't. Not personally. But given what I'd learned, I wondered if it might be . . . informative to sit and wait in Cardinal Lemoine.'

Gradually, she felt some of her anger abating, or perhaps being put away for later use. In a softer voice she said, 'Why exactly did you help me? You had nothing to lose by letting that man hand me over to the authorities, which is most likely exactly what he would have done.'

'Nothing to lose,' Floyd said, 'except that they'd never have got to the bottom of whatever it is you're up to.'

'And you think you have a better chance of that?'

'I'm halfway there,' he said.

'Well, that makes two of us,' she said, *sotto voce*.

'I'm sorry?'

She shook her head. 'I don't think you're a bad man, Wendell, but I do know that this isn't something you want to get involved in.'

He narrowed one eye. 'Now that's hardly the kind of thing you should say if you want me off your case.'

Another taxi made a concerted effort to drench her. She stepped away from the kerb, closer to Floyd. 'But why are you on my case? I told you who I am. I explained all about my sister.'

Floyd took out a narrow sliver of wood and placed it between his teeth. He bit down on it, making a dry cracking sound. 'You did, and it sounded mighty plausible. For about thirty seconds.'

'Then why did you let me walk out of your office with the tin?'

Floyd winked at her. 'Have a guess. And while you're at it, why don't I drive you somewhere you can get warm and dry and put some colour back into your cheeks?'

'Thanks, but I'll take my chances with the taxis. Failing that I'll walk, or construct some sort of raft.'

'My car's just around this corner. I can take you to your hotel or to my office. Either option would offer you a change of clothes and some warm water.'

'No,' she said, turning away from him again.

Just at that moment, a heavy truck roared past pushing a tidal wave of toffee-coloured water along the road ahead of it. Auger let out a little shriek of exasperation as a filthy spray enveloped her from head to foot. As the truck veered past, the driver offered a consolatory wave of his hand, as if everything that had just happened was an act of divine fate far beyond his own control.

'Take me to the hotel,' she said. 'Please.'

'At your service,' Floyd replied.

From Cardinal Lemoine, Floyd took Saint-Germain and Saint-Michel boulevards, until he reached the nexus of intersecting streets around Montparnasse. The few patches of clear sky that had emerged a little while ago had shrivelled away again, as if deciding that the effort simply wasn't worth it. The rain had stopped, but the entire city huddled under a swollen mass of ominous clouds that seethed and circulated overhead like so many prowling wolves.

'You have to understand things from my point of view,' Floyd said, glancing at his passenger in the rear-view mirror. He seemed to be taking his chauffeur duties very seriously and had insisted that she ride in the back, where there was more room. 'I was taken on to solve a case. It doesn't matter to me that the man who hired me is now dead. Until the case is closed, I have a duty to find out what happened. All the more so now that my partner is under suspicion of murder.'

'But I already told you—' she began.

'You already told me a pack of lies designed to get me to hand over the box,' Floyd said. 'Let's start at the beginning, shall we?'

'I'd keep your eyes on the road if I were you.'

He ignored the remark. 'Take this business about you and your sister coming from Dakota.'

'What of it?'

'You might have fooled Blanchard, but your accent isn't anything I recognise. I'm not even sure you're American.'

'You obviously don't know your own country very well.' Auger shifted in her seat, rearranging the damp folds of her coat. 'By your own admission, you've been in Paris for twenty years. That's easily long enough to have become out of touch.'

'If you're from Dakota, then I'm far more out of touch than I thought.'

'I can hardly be blamed for your ignorance. Tanglewood is a very small community and we have our own way of doing things. Have you ever met Mennonites, or Amish, or Pennsylvania Dutch?'

Floyd steered the car on to boulevard Edgar Quinet, skirting the huge cemetery at Montparnasse. 'Not lately,' he said.

'Well, then,' Auger said, as if this settled the matter conclusively.

The play of cloud-filtered light across the cemetery illuminated a huddle of mourners taking turns to cast flowers into the open pit of a grave. Their umbrellas merged into a single black canopy, like a private thundercloud.

'Well what?'

'If you'd met any of those people, I'm sure you'd find their accents and manners just as out of the ordinary as my own. Small communities breed their own ways.'

'Tanglewood must be very small indeed. Did I tell you I couldn't find it in the gazetteer?'

'I don't recall.'

'Anyway,' Floyd said, 'I can't begin to imagine what business a girl from a small town in Dakota would have in a Paris Métro tunnel. Or her sister, for that matter.' He met her eyes in the mirror. 'The thing is, Susan White also had a thing about Cardinal Lemoine. She was observed entering the station with a heavy suitcase and leaving with a light one.'

'If there's a significance to that, I'm afraid it quite escapes me.'

'According to the late Mister Blanchard, and judging by what I saw when he let me into her room, your sister had a mania for collecting things. Her room was a holding area for huge numbers of books, magazines and newspapers, maps and telephone directories. It looked as if she collected just about anything she could get her hands on.' Floyd waited a beat. 'Pretty odd behaviour for a tourist.'

'She liked souvenirs.'

'By the ton?'

Auger leaned forward. He smelled her perfume: it made him think of roses and spring. 'What exactly are you saying, Mister Floyd? Let's get it out into the open, shall we?'

He turned the car on to boulevard Pasteur, slowing down behind a bus carrying an advertisement for Kronenbourg beer. 'Your sister's actions simply don't add up.'

'I already told you she had mental problems.'

'But Blanchard got to know her pretty well, and he never suspected that there was anything wrong with her head.'

'Paranoiacs can be very manipulative.'

'What if she wasn't paranoid at all? What if all that was just a story you tried to sell me to throw me off the scent?'

'You're saying that my sister's actions might have had some rational explanation?'

'Miss Auger.' They were off first-name terms now. No more Verity, no more Wendell. 'I just watched you crawl out of a Métro tunnel. Right now I'm about ready to believe anything, up to and including the possibility that the two of you were not sisters at all, but fellow spies.'

'So now we're getting to it,' she said, rolling her eyes in disbelief.

'Let's look at the facts, shall we?' Floyd continued, unperturbed. 'Susan White obviously wasn't acting alone. She must have had an accomplice whom she met with in Cardinal Lemoine. The accomplice made the suitcase switch, or emptied the one White was carrying and took the contents away. My guess is that the accomplice then made their way into that self-same tunnel you just came out of. There's obviously something in there that means a great deal to you.'

'Go on,' she said, her tone mocking. 'Let's hear the rest of your preposterous little theory.'

'It isn't a whole theory yet, just the start of one.'

'I still want to hear what you think you've got.'

'My partner found something odd in Susan White's room. The wireless set had been altered, probably by Susan herself. It looks as if she was using it to receive instructions, or perhaps to tap into communications between rival spies.'

'Ah. So now we've got two groups of spies? It gets better, it really does.'

'Custine never did crack the code. Turns out his attempts were futile anyway: Susan was using an Enigma machine.'

'I'm quite sure that means something to you, but—'

'It's a sophisticated enciphering machine. Which makes me think she was a spy. So what does that make you?'

'You're being totally absurd.'

'Except I'm not the one who just crawled out of a Métro tunnel.'

For a long while, Auger said nothing at all. Floyd took boulevard Garibaldi as far as place Cambronne and then steered on to Emile Zola, heading towards Auger's hotel.

'Look,' she said, 'I can't expect you to understand any of this, but everything I told you about my sister was the truth. However, it's also true that she had some kind of fixation with Cardinal Lemoine station. I told you she believed forces were moving against her, didn't I?'

'Maybe you did,' he allowed.

'I can't explain the wireless, or that machine you mentioned . . . except to say that if you listen to the radio these days, there are a lot of odd transmissions. And who knows where she found that machine? I take it this is something you can buy, if you want one badly enough?'

'Get to your point, Miss Auger.'

'My point,' she continued, 'is that it's more than likely that my sister picked up one of these odd radio channels and absorbed it into her private conspiracy. As for the tunnel . . . well, I can't deny that she thought there was something down there. She mentioned it more than once in her postcards. She also mentioned that she had hidden something valuable in there. Whether she had or not, I couldn't say, but I knew I wouldn't be able to leave Paris without finding out for myself.'

'And this didn't strike you as being just the slightest bit dangerous?'

'Of course I knew it was dangerous. And of course I couldn't very well tell the man in the station what I was doing.'

Floyd's hands tightened on the steering wheel. 'So that's all it was? Just tidying up some of your sister's unfinished business?'

'Yes,' she said emphatically.

'It still doesn't explain why there have been two deaths. Got a neat explanation for that as well, have you?'

'As you already said yourself, Blanchard probably felt guilty about what had happened to Susan. Perhaps her death was an accident after all. Those low railings look unsafe to me.'

Floyd slowed the car to a crawl as they neared the hotel, looking for a suitable parking spot. The bad weather had brought everyone out in their cars, with only a few brave souls chancing the sidewalks.

'You know what?' he said. 'I'm half-tempted to believe you. I'd like nothing more than to close this case with a clear conscience. Maybe you are exactly who you say you are, and all the suspicious circumstances I keep seeing are just red herrings left behind by your sister.'

'Now you're beginning to talk sense,' Auger said.

'There's a woman in my life who wants to leave France,' Floyd said. 'She wants me to pack my bags and leave with her. A large part of me wants to go with her.'

'Maybe you should listen to that large part.'

'I'm listening,' Floyd said, 'and right now the only thing that's keeping me here is the thought that I might be turning my back on something big. That and the fact that my partner is in a lot of trouble with the police, and will be until this case is closed.'

'Don't get sucked into Susan's games,' Auger said. Making an obvious effort to sound uninterested, she asked, 'So who is this woman, anyway?'

'You've met her.' Floyd had spotted a parking space. He crunched the Mathis into reverse and prepared to ease the massive car into an available space, thinking of the car as a coal barge and the space as a vacant berth. 'She's the woman who followed you from my office.'

'The cleaning girl?'

'The cleaning girl, yeah. Except she isn't a cleaning girl. Her name's Greta and she's a jazz musician. Good at her job, too.'

'She's pretty. You should go with her.'

'Easy as that, is it?'

'There's nothing to keep you in Paris, Wendell.'

He looked at her. 'We're back on Wendell now, are we?'

'I've seen the state of your office – business isn't exactly booming. I'm sorry about your partner, but I assure you, there really isn't a case to be investigated here.'

The Mathis's rear fender kissed the front fender of a dented Citroën behind them. Floyd slipped the car into first gear and was inching it forward when Auger suddenly lunged hard across the back seat, away from the side nearest the hotel. 'Drive,' she said.

Floyd looked back at her. 'What?'

'Get out of here. Fast.'

'I can't. I have to pick up Greta.'

'Wendell – *just drive.*'

Something in her voice made him obey her without further question. He lurched the Mathis out of the parking space, not minding that he scraped the car in front of him in the process. He just had time to glance towards the lobby of the hotel and see the small child standing on the steps immediately in front of the door, playing with a yo-yo. The child was male, wearing shorts and a T-shirt and shiny buckled shoes over white socks. But there was nothing boyish about the child's face. Floyd would never have given the boy a moment's attention had Auger not been so obviously alarmed, but now that he looked more closely, he saw that his face was wrinkled and cadaverous: a withered parody of a child's.

The boy looked towards them and smiled.

'The boy?'

'Just get us out of here,' Auger said.

Across the street, the glass door to a brasserie swung open. Greta rushed out with her coat bundled over one arm, a waiter following her with a tray in his hand and a bewildered look on his face. Greta turned around without stopping and threw some money towards him.

Floyd hit the brakes.

'What are we waiting for?' Auger asked, her alarm increasing. She leaned forward anxiously and grasped the back of Floyd's seat, trying to see what was holding them up.

Floyd leaned over and popped the front passenger-side door. 'Make that "who", not "what". I had Greta watching the Royale in case I didn't pick you up in Cardinal Lemoine.'

Floyd's attention darted back to the boy. He had reeled in his yo-yo and was taking slow, thoughtful steps towards the car. Behind the Mathis, a queue of vehicles was already making its impatience known.

'We can't wait any longer,' Auger said, her knuckles white on the seat back.

Floyd signalled to Greta to move faster. She slipped behind the Mathis and slid in through the passenger-side door, pushing wet strands of black hair from her brow. Even before she had pulled the door shut, Floyd had the car moving again, picking up speed towards the Mirabeau bridge. At the intersection with the quayside road, he swung the car back north, towards the Eiffel Tower. The low clouds had snipped off the top of the structure, as if it had never been completed.

'Would someone mind telling me what's going on?' Greta asked, pushing her coat over the back of the seat.

'I found Miss Auger.'

Greta looked at the woman in the back of the car. 'So I gathered. But why the sudden excitement?'

'She told me to drive,' Floyd said. 'She sounded as if she meant it.'

'And you just do whatever she says?'

Floyd caught Auger's eye in the rear-view mirror. 'Is it safe now?'

'Just keep driving,' she said. 'Since you made a point of not crossing the river, I presume you're taking us back to your office?'

'Unless you have a better idea,' he replied. 'What happened back there? What made it unsafe for us to hang around?'

Auger shook her head once. 'It doesn't matter. Just drive.'

'It was the boy with the yo-yo,' Floyd said. 'Wasn't it?'

'Don't be ridiculous.'

He turned to Greta. 'You kept a good watch on the hotel since I left?'

'No, Floyd. I painted my fingernails and browsed fashion magazines. What do you think I was doing?'

'Did you see the boy?'

'Yes,' Greta said, after a moment's consideration. 'I did. And I didn't like the look of him either.'

From the back seat of the car, Auger watched Floyd check the mirrors as he turned the car into rue du Dragon. It was now late afternoon and the street had already taken on something of the gloom of evening. Auger found it difficult to believe that only seven hours had passed since she had paid a visit to the detective's office. It might as well have been weeks ago, for all she had in common with the determined and confident version of herself who had walked out of the building, prize in hand. She had thought that the mission was all but finished, barring the trivial business of returning to the portal. *You poor, pitiable fool*, Auger thought. Had she stood face to face with her former self, she would have slapped her cheek and laughed in spite.

'I don't see any nasty-looking children,' Floyd said.

'What about the tail from the Quai?' asked the woman in the front passenger seat, whose accent was distinctly German. Floyd had told Auger her name, but she had forgotten it as soon as she saw the boy waiting outside the hotel.

'I don't see anyone,' Floyd said. 'But you can bet someone's still got their eye on me.'

Auger leaned forward. 'Someone's following you as well?'

'I'm a popular guy.' Floyd parked the car outside the horsemeat butcher Auger remembered from her visit that morning. The shop front was covered in a mosaic of red, white and black tiles, with the figure of a red prancing horse picked out in a Romanesque style beneath the words '*Achat de Chevaux*'.

'Floyd,' said the German woman, 'this is all happening a little too quickly for me.'

'It's happening a little too quickly for me as well, if that's any consolation,' Floyd replied. 'That's why we're all going up to my office to have a nice little chat, and maybe we can sort some of this out.'

The German woman looked at Auger with a sneer of disapproval. 'Is she seriously going to walk along the street looking like that?'

'We'll take her upstairs, let her get clean and dry,' Floyd said. 'Then I'm sure you won't mind if she borrows some of the clothes you left behind.'

'She's welcome to any that will fit her,' the woman replied, looking Auger up and down with a less than complimentary eye.

'Thank you,' Auger said, with an exaggerated smile.

'Ladies, if you're going to start scratching each other's eyes out, could you at least wait until I've had a shot of whiskey? I can't stand violence on an empty stomach.'

'Shut up, Floyd,' the German woman said.

Floyd got out of the car and went around to the passenger side to open the door for Greta. Auger was already out of the car, looking around for anything she didn't like, or that seemed out of place. But the street was as quiet and sleepy as she remembered it, and even a loitering child would have stood out.

'He wants to talk to you,' the German woman said, tapping Floyd's arm and pointing to the shop with the horse sign. Behind the glass, the proprietor was gesturing at Floyd, waving him inside.

'Monsieur Gosset will have to wait,' Floyd said. 'He only ever grumbles about the rent, or the noise from his upstairs neighbours.'

The three of them entered Floyd's building. The elevator that had stalled Auger's exit earlier was waiting for them like an iron trap. They all got in and Floyd pushed one of the brass buttons. With a buzz and a lurch, the car began its climb to the detective's floor.

'I'm still waiting for an explanation, Floyd,' the German woman said.

'Maybe I should begin by introducing the two of you properly,' Floyd said, putting on a veneer of civility. 'Verity Auger, Greta Auerbach. I'm sure the two of you will get along like a house on fire.'

'Or something,' Auger muttered.

The elevator came to a stop. Floyd opened the gate and led them on to the landing. Gesturing for them to hang back, he walked to the pebbled-glass door that led into his office and examined the gap between the door and the frame, just above the lock. He turned back to them with a finger pressed against his lips.

'Something's wrong,' he whispered. 'I put a hair across this gap before I left this morning. It's not there any more.'

'You think someone's been in there?' Auger asked. Involuntarily, she touched her hip, feeling for the reassuring presence of the automatic. As tempted as she was to draw the gun now, she didn't want the hole she was in to get any deeper.

'Wait,' Floyd said. Very gently, he tried to turn the doorknob. Auger heard it click against resistance. The door was still locked.

'Maybe the hair blew away,' Greta suggested.

'Or maybe someone found their way inside with a skeleton key,' Floyd replied.

A door a little further down the landing opened a crack, a bar of watery daylight cutting across the carpet. An elderly woman pushed her powdered face into the hall and said, in French, 'Monsieur Floyd? You had better come inside, I think.'

'Not now, Madame Parmentiere,' Floyd replied.

'I really think you better had,' she said. Then she stepped back, the door creaking open another few inches. Looming behind her, a fire iron in his hand, was a large man dressed in a vest and braces.

'Custine!' Floyd said.

'You'd better listen to the lady,' the man said, lowering the fire iron. 'I don't think it's safe for us to go into the office. The boys from the Big House have this building under heavy surveillance, and every once in a while they send someone inside to see if you're home.'

'Come in, please,' Madame Parmentiere insisted.

Floyd shrugged and led the way into the woman's apartment.

The layout of the rooms was completely different from the offices occupied by the detective, and even to Auger the décor and ambience suggested that they had stepped back fifty or sixty years, into a Paris at the turn of the century. There were no concessions to the modern era: not a wireless set or telephone to be seen, and certainly no television. Even the clockwork phonograph that sat beneath the window looked as if it would have suffered a fit rather than play anything more modern than Debussy. The furniture was upholstered with a maroon velvet plush, the sweeping wooden legs and armrests covered in gold leaf. The interior doorways were framed by pairs of peacock's feathers, tilted like ceremonial scimitars. A brass bird's cage was suspended from the ceiling, but there was no evidence that a bird had ever occupied it. Stationed around the room were at least a dozen antique oil lamps, their tinted glasses throwing shades of blue, green and turquoise on to the immaculate white walls even though none of them were lit. The room faced south and was drinking in what little remained of the day's light.

Madame Parmentiere closed the door behind them. 'You cannot stay here long,' she said.

'I know,' said the man Floyd had referred to as Custine, 'and we won't inconvenience you for a moment longer than is necessary. But may we sit down for the time being?'

'Very well,' the old lady said. 'I suppose I had better make some tea, in that case.'

They all found seats, while Madame Parmentiere pushed her way through a curtain of gleaming glass beads into what Auger presumed was an adjoining kitchen.

'So who wants to start?' Floyd asked, sticking with French. 'Right now I don't know where to begin.'

'Who's she?' Custine asked, nodding in Auger's direction.

'The sister,' Floyd replied.

'Not much of a redhead, is she?'

'We were half-sisters,' Auger said.

Floyd spread his hands in a gesture of defeat. 'What can I say? She's got an answer for everything, André. Every damn question you can throw at her, she's worked it all out. She even had me half-believing that a well-bred girl might take to snooping around the tunnels of the Paris Métro.'

'I told you . . .' Auger began, but abruptly changed tack, addressing Custine. 'Anyway, who are you? I've got as much of a right to ask that question of you, as you have of me.'

'This is André Custine,' Floyd said. 'My associate and friend.'

'And equally hopeless case,' Greta added.

Auger looked around at them. 'I can't tell whether you like each other, or hate each other.'

'We've been having a trying few days,' Floyd replied, before suddenly lowering his voice. 'Is it me or is there a bad smell in this place?' he whispered.

'It's me,' Custine said cheerfully. 'Or rather the shirt I just removed. How else do you think I got into the building without being picked up?'

'Monsieur Gosset,' Greta said, her face lighting up with understanding. 'You smell like horsemeat!'

Floyd buried his head in his hands. 'It just gets better and better.'

Of the four of them, Custine was the only one who seemed completely calm and unfazed, as if this was exactly the kind of thing that happened most afternoons. 'I'd had enough of Michel's hospitality at *Le Perroquet*. He means well, but there's only so long a person can stay sane in that kind of room. Thankfully, he was able to use his contacts to find me temporary lodgings elsewhere, but I needed to return here first, having been in something of a hurry when I dropped by yesterday. But how to enter the building unobserved?' He smiled, clearly enjoying the chance to be the centre of attention. 'That was when it hit me: I could kill two birds with one stone. I knew that Gosset received a daily consignment of horsemeat from somewhere north of the city. I remembered the name of the delivery firm and that Gosset owed the agency a favour. A couple of telephone calls later and I'd secured myself a snug little hideaway in the back of the delivery lorry.'

'You won't be able to pull tricks like that for much longer,' Floyd observed. 'Sooner or later they'll be searching every truck in Paris, head to toe.'

'By then, I hope such subterfuge won't be necessary.' Custine reached up and took a cup and saucer from the tray that Madame Parmentiere had just brought into the room. In his huge hands, the delicate chinaware looked like fragile props from a doll's house. 'Anyway, here I am, although I don't intend to stick around for more than a few hours.'

'Given any thought as to how you'll get out of the building?' Floyd asked.

'I'll cross that bridge when it becomes a necessity,' Custine said, sipping at the very weak tea. 'Chances are they'll be expecting me to arrive, not leave, so they may be off their guard.'

'I like a man who thinks ahead.'

Custine aimed one little finger towards Auger. 'I only got half the story. You claim to be Susan White's sister, or half-sister, or whatever?'

'There's no "claim" about it,' Auger said. 'I am who I said I am. If you and Monsieur Floyd don't like it, that's entirely your problem.'

'This, incidentally,' Floyd said, 'is what passes for gratitude in Mademoiselle Auger's scheme of things. I was treated to it when I got her out of trouble in the Métro station and again when we were near the hotel.'

Custine studied Auger. 'What happened near the hotel?'

'Auger saw something she didn't like,' Floyd said. 'Now she's refusing to talk about it.'

Auger sipped at her own tea. The whole setting, with the four of them – not to mention their host – sitting down in these very genteel surroundings, felt ludicrously inappropriate. Less than an hour ago, she had been managing the controlled contraction of a wormhole throat, after dispatching a ship back to the real Mars in another part of the galaxy. Now she was balancing chinaware on her knee while sitting primly upright on an old-fashioned upholstered armchair, in a room where even the thought of violence seemed incongruous.

'I panicked,' she said. 'That's all.'

'Only when you saw that strange child,' Floyd said.

Custine made a low growling sound before speaking. 'What kind of child?'

'A nasty-looking little boy,' Floyd replied. 'Like something from a Bosch painting. Ring any bells, André?'

'Funnily enough—'

'Nasty little children have been popping up all over this case,' Floyd elaborated. 'A girl here . . . a boy there . . . maybe more than one of each. We've been trying to discount their significance, but Mademoiselle Auger was spooked by the boy she spotted long before she'd had a good look at him.'

'Meaning what?' Custine asked.

'Meaning she was looking out for a child, or something like one,' Floyd replied, fixing Auger with a determined gaze.

'I told you,' Auger said, 'I simply panicked—'

'Who are those children?' Floyd demanded. 'What do they have to do with the killings? Who are they working for? More to the point, who are *you* working for?'

'Excuse me.' Auger put down her cup and saucer and stood up from the armchair. 'This is all very nice, but . . .' She fumbled for the automatic, sliding it from her waistband. There was a collective intake of breath, even from Custine, as her hand reappeared with the gun. 'Just for the record,' she said, working off the safety catch, 'I know how to use this. In fact, I've already killed with it today.'

Floyd sounded calmer than he looked. 'So can we dispense with the cover story, at long last? Nice girls don't carry guns. Especially not automatics.'

'That's fine, then, because I'm really not a very nice girl.' Auger pointed the gun at Floyd. 'I don't want to hurt you.'

'That's good to know.'

'But understand this: I will if I have to.'

'She sounds as if she means it,' Custine said. The low rumble of his voice reminded Auger of a passing train.

Floyd stood slowly from his seat, putting down his own tea. 'What do you want?'

'A change of clothes. That's all.'

Floyd glanced at Greta. 'Clothes won't be a problem.'

'Good. Open your office. One of you has a key.'

Custine was the first to reach slowly into his pocket and tossed a key through the air. Auger grabbed it with her free hand and tossed it to Floyd. 'The rest of you stay here,' she ordered. 'If anyone moves, I'll shoot Wendell. Got that?'

'No one's going anywhere,' Custine said.

'Move very slowly,' Auger instructed Floyd as she started backing out of the apartment, keeping the gun trained on him. She risked a glance over her shoulder before entering the hallway, but everything was as they had left it, with the elevator still waiting. She backed herself against the wall next to the pebbled-glass door.

'Go inside,' she said. 'And if you've got a gun in there, don't think of using it.'

Floyd answered in English. When they were alone, it made more sense than French. 'Detectives only have guns in the movies.'

'You said Greta had left some clothes that would fit me. Find a suitcase and throw the clothes into it.'

Floyd unlocked the pebbled-glass door. 'What sort of clothes?'

'Don't get cute. Just throw in a selection and let me worry about it later.'

'Give me a minute.'

'You've got thirty seconds.'

Floyd disappeared into the warren of rooms. Auger heard doors being opened and closed in haste, things being thrown around and rummaged through. His voice echoing, he called back, 'Why don't you tell me what all this is about, now that we're on such excellent terms?'

'The less you know the better.'

'I've heard that too many times in my life to find it satisfying.'

'Get used to it. This is one time when it definitely applies. What's holding you up?'

'I'm looking for a suitcase.'

'A bag will do. Anything. I'm getting impatient here, Wendell. Don't make me impatient.'

'What colour stockings do you like?'

'Wendell . . .'

'It doesn't matter anyway. You'll just have to make do with what you're given.' More doors were opened and shut. She heard things scraping on wood. Floyd raised his voice again. 'So what's next, Auger? Back to the States, mission accomplished? Or are you not really from the States after all?'

'All you need to know is that I'm on your side,' she said.

'That's something, I guess.'

'And that I'm here to help you. Not just you, but you and everyone you know.'

'And those children? And whoever killed Susan White and Blanchard?'

'I'm not with them. Hurry up.'

'You could at least tell me who you're working for. Like it or not, I've helped you now. I didn't have to bail you out in the station.'

'And I said thanks. For what it's worth, you did the right thing, and if you could see the big picture you'd agree with me.'

'So describe the big picture to me.'

She tapped the barrel of the automatic against the doorframe. 'Don't push your luck. Have you found a bag?'

'Just filling it now.'

Auger felt something in her relent. In some small, grudging way she couldn't help but recognise a kindred spark of stubbornness in Wendell that she knew all too well.

'Listen,' she said, 'I'd tell you everything if I knew all of it myself. Well, maybe I wouldn't tell you *all* of it, but I'd tell you enough to satisfy your curiosity, if that was what you wanted. But the fact is that I haven't got it all figured out yet.'

'How much did Susan White have figured out?'

'Not everything, but more than I have, I think.'

'Let's hope that isn't why she ended up dead.'

'Susan knew she was on to something big, something worth killing for. I think she was scared by the scale of it.'

'Were the two of you both working for the same government?'

'Yes,' Auger said carefully. 'And it is the United States.'

Floyd returned carrying a double-handled canvas bag of dubious condition. It was brimming with clothes, almost all of them black or shades of purple and blue so close to black as to make no practical difference.

'But you were never sisters, were you?'

'Just colleagues,' Auger said. 'Now stay put and kick the bag in my direction.' He complied. 'That's good.' She picked it up, taking both handles in one hand. 'Thank your girlfriend for this. I know she wasn't crazy about lending me her clothes, but it'll all be worth it in the end.' She kept the gun pointing at Floyd. 'I'm sorry it had to happen this way. I hope things work out for all of you.'

'Why can't you just tell me everything you know and let me be the judge?' Floyd asked.

'Because I'm not that cruel.' Auger started backing towards the elevator. 'All right, here's the deal: I'm leaving now, and I don't want anyone following me. Is that understood?'

'Understood,' Floyd said.

Auger stepped into the elevator car, dropped the bag by her side and slid shut the trelliswork gate. 'No funny tricks on the way down this time, all right?'

'No funny tricks.'

'Good.' She pressed the lowest of the brass buttons. 'I said it before, but I'll say it again: it's been a pleasure doing business.'

The car began to descend.

'Wait,' Floyd called, his voice almost drowned out by the whining racket of the elevator. 'What did you mean by "not that cruel"?'

'I meant exactly what I said,' Auger replied. 'Goodbye, Wendell. I hope you have a long and fulfilling life.'

TWENTY

Auger hailed a taxi on boulevard Saint-Germain. By then she had exchanged her ripped and soot-smeared coat for a hip-length black jacket, with a matching hat tilted low to disguise her grubby face and hair. She would not bear up to close inspection, but in the twilight of late afternoon the transformation was adequate.

'Gare du Nord,' she told the driver, before showing him the paperwork she would need to cross the river. 'As quick as you can, please.'

The driver grumbled something about not being a miracle worker, but before very long they had crossed the river and were haring through the narrow backstreets of the Marais, dodging the thickening flows of Saturday traffic. Auger felt an absolute exhaustion looming over her like a crumbling precipice, ready to fall and crush her at any moment. She leaned her cheek against the rattling window of the taxi and through blurred eyes she watched the lights of shops, neon signs and cars slide by in hyphens of red, white, frigid blue and gold. The city looked as untouchable and unreal as a hologram; as fragile as the glass she was resting against. She was very tempted to think of it that way. None of it mattered, she told herself: nothing that happened here could have any consequence for *her* life, back in Tanglewood. There was no need to continue with the investigation Susan White had started, for nothing that came out of that investigation could possibly affect Auger's existence back home. Even if something terrible did happen here (and she could not quite shake the feeling that something terrible was indeed going to occur), then it would be no more tragic than the burning of a book or, in the worst case, a library of books. E2 might be lost, but a month ago she had not even known of its existence. Everything and everyone she really knew would continue unaffected, and within a few months the ordinary grind of her life, with its ebb and flow of routine pressures and crises, would have reduced these memories to a thin, dreamlike paste. And it was not as if everything from E2 would be lost for ever if something bad happened, for much had undoubtedly already been learned from the documents that had been smuggled back to Antiquities. And though she would feel some sympathy for the people trapped in E2, the trick was to remember that they were not really people at all, but the discarded shadows of lives that had already been lived 300 years ago. Feeling sorry for them would be like feeling sorry for the images in a burning photograph.

Auger felt her resolve collapsing by the minute. She did not want to get on the overnight train to Berlin, not when there was the much simpler option of staying in Paris and waiting for the ship to return. She had been sent here to do a job, and she had done it to the best of her ability. No one could possibly blame her if she stopped now, and thought only of her own preservation.

The taxi slowed and pulled up in the station forecourt, its engine still running while the driver waited for payment. For a moment, Auger could not move, frozen in a lull of indecision. She thought about asking the driver to turn around and take her to another hotel somewhere else in the city, where Floyd and the others would not think to look for her. Or she could follow through with her plan, go into the station and catch the train to Berlin, thereby heading deeper into Europe and deeper into E2. Just the thought of taking the train made a lump rise in her throat, as if she was being asked to step close to the edge of something high up that made her dizzy. She had not been trained for such a mission. Caliskan had primed her – barely – to recover the paperwork, but not to go deeper into E2. Surely there were other people who were bound to be better qualified for it than her . . .

The thought that this might be true stung her like a lash.

'You can do this,' she said to herself, repeating it like a prayer.

The driver turned around in his seat to face her, the hairs on his neck bristling against the collar of his shirt. He didn't care how long she took. The meter was still running.

'Here,' Auger said, thrusting some notes at him. 'Keep the change.'

A minute later she was inside the iron and glass vault of the station, looking for the ticket office. The platform swarmed with travellers, jostling and orbiting each other like a mass of grey bees, each knowing their mission and utterly oblivious to anyone else. Beyond, the trains waited with snorting impatience, pushing quills of white steam up towards the roof. Even as she watched, a sleeper drew out, headed for Munich or Vienna or some other city even further into the European night. Its red tail light spilled blood on to the polished surfaces of the rails.

First things first. Auger found the ticket office and was relieved to see that the line for international connections was much shorter than the others. She had already vowed that if there was no accommodation left on the night train, then she would simply board it and argue her case later. Bribery was always an option, as was theft. But there were still couchettes available on the seven o'clock service – later than she would have liked, but better than nothing.

She handed over the money, the ticket clerk barely batting an eyelid at her blackened hands and dirt-encrusted fingernails. She imagined that the clerks had learned not to bat their eyelids at many things.

'What platform?' she asked. The clerk told her, also warning her that the train would not be ready for boarding until thirty minutes before departure.

That gave her nearly an hour before she could get on the train. She used the first twenty minutes of that period finding a ladies' washroom and attending as best she could to the dirt and damage she had sustained in the tunnel. By the time she was done, she had turned the bar of carbolic soap black and the basin looked as if it had been used by a party of miners after a shift down the pit. But she looked and felt human again, and by the time she had changed into more of Greta's clothes, stuffing her own soiled and ripped garments back into the bag, she had also begun to feel that she was less likely to be recognised. With over an hour remaining before the train was due to depart, Auger was tempted to leave the station entirely to seek the comparative anonymity of a local bistro or brasserie. She had not eaten since breakfast, and her hunger was beginning to catch up with her. But she knew that if she left Gare du Nord, she might not have the courage to return, no matter how much money she had spent on the couchette. Instead, she settled on a restaurant inside the station, and within its mirrored labyrinth of an interior she found a secluded booth where she could watch whoever came and went without being the object of attention herself. She ordered a sandwich and a glass of wine, and willed the hands on the restaurant clock to whirl around to half-past six.

Through the glass doors of the restaurant, far across the concourse, she saw a man in a grey raincoat and hat pause at a newspaper concession. As he fiddled in a pocket for change, he looked around, like a tourist taking in the station for the first time. After making his purchase, he turned from the concession stand, pushing owlish glasses back up his nose. He flicked open the paper and started reading. It wasn't Floyd.

Auger's food arrived. She sniffed the wine, drank half the glass down in short order and for the first time since waking that day permitted a temporary calm to flow through her. In a little while she would be on the overnight train, safe in her berth. It was no more dangerous than staying in Paris – less so, perhaps, since she would be putting increasing distance between herself and the war babies. Once in Berlin, she would follow up on the address for the Berlin manufacturing firm and see where that led. At no point would she put herself in harm's way, or do anything that she felt might expose her true identity. Even if all she came back with was a description of the firm's premises, she would have achieved something useful. Caliskan would undoubtedly rebuke her for exceeding the terms of her mission, while expressing private gratitude for what she had done. And even as she followed up Susan White's aborted line of enquiry, Auger would be observing more of this world than she ever could if she stayed locked up in a Paris hotel room, cowering from every shadow.

Another man in a raincoat pushed open the doors to the restaurant. He was hatless, but for a moment – as the steam from the coffee machine blocked her view – it could also have been Floyd. But the man had no sooner stepped inside than a slender woman in a body-hugging emerald dress stood up from her table, and the two of them kissed like the illicit lovers Auger was sure they were. The man had a gift for the woman, which she opened with a gasp of nervous delight. It was some kind of jewellery. He ordered a drink and the two of them sat there holding hands for ten minutes, whereupon the man kissed her goodbye and vanished back into the bustle of the station. A minute later, Auger heard the whistle of a departing train, and knew with absolute certainty that the man was on it, heading back to his provincial house and his provincial family, that ten-minute assignation as much a routine as brushing his teeth and kissing his wife goodbye each morning. For a dizzying instant, the people around her suddenly felt as real as anyone she had ever known, and it was only by a supreme effort of will that she was able to reduce their lives once again to something more manageable, like an echo or afterimage.

Auger checked her watch. In a few minutes she would be able to board the train and find her couchette. An hour from now she would be halfway to the French border, and by the time she awoke she would, for better or worse, have arrived in Berlin. She signalled for her bill, then began gathering her things. Perhaps it was the wine, but now she felt a steely resolve to complete the investigation Susan White had begun.

A waiter in a white cummerbund brought the bill. Auger dug through her coinage, satisfied when she found enough to include a reasonable tip. Smiling, she slid the money towards the waiter and made ready to leave, deciding she would be better off not finishing the wine.

It was then that she saw the children.

There were two of them, standing quite still next to each other in the middle of the concourse. The boy held the lank thread of a yo-yo, while the girl carried a toy animal that looked as if it had been rescued from a dustbin. The boy wore a red T-shirt and shorts, with white socks and buckled black shoes, the girl a dirty yellow dress and the same kind of shoes. It was only when one really *looked* at them that it became clear that they were not really children at all, but ghouls in the rough shape of children. The rain had distorted their make-up, making it sag and run. Travellers pushed around them, but gave the children a certain distance, perhaps without realising it.

Auger lost sight of the diminutive figures as a group of people blocked her view. She swallowed and tried to keep her nerve. Her imagination might be running ahead of her. They might just have been street urchins, after all.

When the group dispersed, the two children were gone.

She closed her eyes in relief, then quickly finished what remained of the wine. She told herself to get up and leave the restaurant, while the train was still waiting. There was no point reacting in horror every time a child walked by. Paris was full of strange little boys and girls, and they were not all out to kill her.

A couple of businessmen moved away from the front of the restaurant. There were the children again: standing perfectly still, but now much closer to the door. They were not looking at her, but they *were* regarding something or someone with the unblinking attention of snakes. Another group of passers-by obstructed her view, and when they had moved away, the children were even closer, their attention clearly directed at the restaurant itself. A moment ago she might have stood a chance of leaving without them noticing her, but now she was trapped.

Auger looked down at the remains of her sandwich, then pretended to read the menu again. The last thing she wanted to be seen to be doing was taking an unusual interest in what was going on outside. The children might not necessarily know exactly what she looked like any more, after all.

When she risked another glance towards the door, only the little girl was standing outside. The boy was now inside the restaurant, waiting by the illuminated counter where freshly made cakes were laid out for inspection. A pair of flies hovered near the boy, seemingly more interested in him than in the sugary delicacies.

Auger sank down into the booth. She had a clear line of sight to the boy, but he did not appear to have noticed her yet. Staying rooted to the same spot of floor, his head was rotating in a slow and level arc, like a tracking surveillance camera. She was tempted to move behind the cover of another of the mirrored screens separating the booths, but knew that the boy would probably notice. His eyes blinked but rarely, as if he had to remind himself each time. In a few seconds he would be looking directly at her unless she moved. Belatedly, she remembered that she was carrying two weapons: the automatic and the sleek gun that she had taken from the war baby in the tunnel. The knowledge gave her a flicker of confidence, but she soon dismissed any thought of using the guns. The children were probably armed themselves, and there might be more of them than the two she had noticed. Besides, even if she dealt with the children, she would stand little chance of leaving this busy station without being apprehended and arrested.

The boy's gaze had almost speared her. Frozen, she knew that her only hope lay in his failing to recognise her. Perhaps he would not, given her state of dishevelment and the fact that she was wearing someone else's clothes. She had no sooner clutched at this straw than she forced herself to dismiss it, for the boy was obviously looking for *her* specifically, and would not be fooled by a few superficial changes.

Auger's hand reached under the table for the automatic. Perhaps she would have to use it after all, regardless of the consequences.

The boy looked at – or more exactly through – her. She felt as if a searchlight beam had swept over her. The smooth rotation of his head continued, taking his attention beyond her. His head had turned through nearly ninety degrees from the starting position of its arc and showed every indication of continuing, impossible though such a movement would be for a human child. Auger wondered how long it would be before someone else spotted the peculiar little boy, but as far as she could tell the other people in the restaurant had noticed nothing out of the ordinary.

Then the child's head stopped and reversed, until the boy was looking towards her again. This time she felt the focus of his attention: he wasn't just looking in her direction, but was concentrating on the booth in which she was sitting. A barely recognisable change came across the powdered and smudged mask of his face, the tiniest widening of his mouth suggesting a smile of triumph or gluttony.

The boy's head snapped back towards the restaurant door and he opened his mouth to emit a single shriek. To any casual bystander, it would have sounded like a meaningless, yodel-like exclamation – evidence, perhaps, of idiocy on the child's part. But Auger knew that the shriek was crammed with sonic information, and that the other child was fully capable of deciphering it.

Stiff-kneed, like a puppet that wasn't being worked properly, the boy began to walk towards Auger's booth. She tried not to react in any way, keeping her own attention on the clock, hoping that the boy would have second thoughts before he reached her. He had pocketed the yo-yo and now something gleamed in his hand, mirror-bright and sharp as glass.

A hand touched the boy's shoulder. The boy yanked his head towards the adult in fury and incomprehension, his face twisted into a scowl that served only to crack and dislodge the remaining scabs of make-up covering up his true appearance. The hand emerged from the dark sleeve of a suit belonging to one of the waiters. The man was large even amongst adults, and towered over the boy. Still trying not to look directly at what was happening, Auger saw the man crease himself down the middle to bring his moustached, fat-necked head into proximity with the boy. The man started to say something, his lips working silently across the room, and then there was a quick flash of silver and the waiter stepped back from the boy with a look of mild surprise on his face, as if the child had sworn at him in an ingenious and adult way.

The man crashed back into the display of cakes, sprawling across the zinc-topped surface. In the pure white of his cummerbund was a little spreading star of red, where he had been stabbed. The man dabbed at the wound with his fingers and lifted their reddened tips to his face. He started to say something, the words jamming in his throat. Around him, some of the other diners dropped their cutlery and started talking in alarmed voices. A man shouted something and a woman screamed. A glass went crashing to the floor.

The boy had gone.

Within a few seconds, complete pandemonium had erupted around the stabbed waiter. Auger could see only the backs of do-gooders crowding around him. Another waiter yelled into the restaurant telephone, while a third jogged across the concourse to fetch help. The scene had already begun to attract the attention of onlookers outside, waiting for trains. Some kind of railway official – a remarkably similar-looking individual to the man Floyd had bribed that afternoon – began to stroll towards the door and, seeing the size of the commotion, broke into a wheezing, heavy-bellied lope. Someone blew three sharp blasts on a whistle.

Auger stood up, gathering her things. Were the children still out there, waiting for her? There was no way of telling. What she did know was that she did not want to be here when – as seemed certain – the police arrived and began taking the names and addresses of witnesses. She could not afford to miss that Berlin train, and she certainly could not afford to fall into the machinery of the law. What if the station official at Cardinal Lemoine had decided to talk to his superiors after all?

She wiped crumbs from her lips and judged her moment, excusing herself past the concerned onlookers crowding around the wounded man. She might as well have been made of smoke for all the attention anyone paid her. Pausing at the door, she looked left and right along the concourse, but there was no sign of the two children. All she could hope was that they had decided to leave the station before too many witnesses described a vicious little boy with a knife. As quickly as she could without attracting unwanted attention, Auger made her way to the departures board and double-checked the platform for the overnight train to Berlin. It was waiting now: a long chain of dark-green carriages, with a black steam engine simmering at the far end. Along the length of the train, the station staff were still preparing it: there were trolleys loaded with linen, food and drink, and men in uniforms were coming and going through the open doors, barking to each other in heavily accented French. A station official shook his head at Auger as she tried to step on to the platform, tapping his watch with a finger.

'Please, monsieur,' Auger said. In the distance she heard the scraping whine of police sirens, nearing the railway station. 'I need to be on that train.'

It might have been the worst thing she could have said, if the man got it into his head that she was running from the authorities. 'Mademoiselle,' he said apologetically, 'Five more minutes, then you can board.'

Auger dropped her bags and dug into what was left of her money. 'Take this,' she said, offering him ten francs. 'It's a bribe.'

The man pursed his lips, looking her over. The sirens sounded very near now. Out of the corner of her eye, she saw people still cramming around the entrance to the restaurant.

'Twenty,' he said. 'Then you can find your couchette.'

'For twenty you can help me find it,' Auger replied archly.

The man seemed to find this an acceptable compromise, pocketing the additional ten-franc note and leading her down the length of two carriages until he found one that corresponded to the number on her ticket. Inside, everything was clean, bright and narrow. The man found her compartment and pushed open the door. There was a key on the inside of the door, which he removed and gave to Auger.

'Thank you,' she said.

The man inclined his head, then left her alone. There were two bunks in the sleeping compartment, but she had paid to have the entire cabin to herself. There was a neat aluminised basin and tap in one corner, plus a tiny cupboard and a small fold-down writing desk and stool. The walls were varnished wood with recessed electric lights. There was a communication cord and pull-down fabric blind, and a faded monochrome photograph of some cathedral she didn't recognise.

Auger slid the window down, letting in the noises of the station. Amidst the clatter of slamming doors, arriving and departing trains and announcements over the Tannoy, it was difficult to be sure, but she did not think she could hear the sirens now. Did that mean the police had passed the station by entirely, on some other errand? She looked at her watch again, willing the hands to slide around to departure time.

From somewhere nearby, outside the train, she heard a heated exchange of voices. Slowly, Auger inched her head out of the window so that she could look back along the length of the train. There was the man she had bribed, gesticulating and arguing with a pair of uniformed policemen. Angrily, they pushed past the man and began strolling along the line of carriages. They were walking very slowly, stopping at each compartment window. One of the men had a ribbed-metal flashlight, which he was shining into each compartment, tapping on the glass at the same time. The station official trailed behind them, muttering under his breath.

Auger forced herself to breathe again. Slowly, slowly, she moved her head back inside and slid the window up to its closed position. There was time to get out of the compartment, but what if another policeman was moving along the inside of the train, covering that line of escape?

The voices of the two officers came closer. She heard them tapping on the glass two or three compartments down from hers. It was much louder now. There was barely time to move her things out of sight, and certainly no time to think of hiding herself. All she could do was act as naturally as possible. Auger dragged the blind down halfway and sat, waiting.

There was a knock on the interior door. She held her breath, silently willing whoever it was to go away.

The person knocked again. A low, urgent voice whispered, 'Auger?'

It was Floyd. It was Floyd and she really did not need this.

Keeping her own voice low, she pressed her lips to the door. 'Go away. I said I didn't want to see you again.'

'And I think we have unfinished business.'

'In your imagination, perhaps.'

'Let me in. There's something I have to tell you. Something I think might make you change your mind.'

'Nothing you could say or do, Wendell . . .' But she silenced herself. The officers outside were now very close to her compartment.

'I kept something back,' Floyd said.

'What do you mean?' she hissed.

'From that box of papers. Figured it might be useful to have some bargaining strength.'

'I got everything I needed from those papers already, Floyd.'

'Is that why you're on your way to Germany? Because you already have all the answers?'

'Don't overestimate yourself,' Auger said.

'What happened back at the restaurant?'

She saw no harm in telling him. 'One of those child-things. It stabbed a waiter.'

'The kid was looking for you?'

What was the point of lying now? 'Give yourself a pat on the back. Now quit while you're ahead and leave me alone.'

'The policemen outside think you might have had something to do with it. You fled the scene, after all. Innocent witnesses don't do that. Ask Custine. He'll tell you all about it.'

'I'm sorry about Custine,' she said. 'I'm sorry he got involved in all of this and I hope you can find a way to help him. But it isn't my problem. Your entire little world isn't my problem.'

'You know what really hurts? The way you almost sound as if you mean that.'

'I *do* mean it,' she said fiercely. 'Now go away.'

'Those policemen aren't going to let you ride this train anywhere.'

She heard the whistle and snort of a departing train. But it wasn't the one she was sitting in. 'I'll deal with them.'

'Like you dealt with me this afternoon? You weren't going to use that gun, Verity. I could see it in your eyes.'

'Then you're an exceptionally poor judge of character. I would have used it, if necessary.'

'But you wouldn't have enjoyed it.'

There was a hard knock on the glass. A voice with a Parisian accent said sharply, 'Open the window.'

She slid the blind up and pulled on the leather strap that lowered the glass. 'Do you want to see my ticket?'

'Just your identification,' said one of the officers standing outside.

'Here.' Auger slid the papers through the gap in the window. 'Is something the matter? I wasn't expecting to have my papers examined until later.'

'Is there anyone else in that compartment with you?'

'I think I'd have noticed.'

'I heard you talking.'

With a casualness that surprised her, Auger said, 'I was reciting a list of the things I have to do in Berlin.'

The man made an equivocal noise. 'You're on the train alone, before anyone else. Why were you in such a hurry to get aboard?'

'Because I'm tired and I don't want to have to squabble with anyone else over who has the ticket for this compartment.'

The man reflected on this, before saying, 'We're looking for a child. Have you seen any unsupervised children hanging around?'

Just then another voice distracted the man. It was Floyd, outside now. He spoke in soft, urgent French too fast for her to follow, what with all the background noise of the station, but she recognised 'child' and a few other significant words. The other man responded with further questions, sceptical in tone at first, but with increasing urgency. He and Floyd exchanged a few more heated words and then she heard footsteps heading with some haste away from the carriage; a few seconds later, she heard the shrill, repeated warble of a police whistle.

Moments passed, then Floyd knocked on the door to her compartment again. 'Let me in. I just got those goons off your back.'

'And you have my undying gratitude, but you still have to get off this train.'

'Why are you so interested in Berlin? Why are you so interested in the Kaspar contract?'

'The less you ask me, Floyd, the easier time of it we'll both have.'

'The contract is for something unpleasant, isn't it? Something you want to stop happening.'

'Why do you assume I'm not actually trying to help it happen?'

'Because you have a nice face. Because the moment you walked into my office, I decided I liked you.'

'Well, like I said: you're not necessarily the best judge of character.'

'I have a ticket for Berlin,' he said. 'I also know a good hotel on the Kurfurstendamm.'

'Well, isn't that convenient?'

'You have nothing to lose by taking me along for the ride.'

'And nothing to gain.'

'Silver rain,' Floyd said.

It was said in such an offhand way that at first she thought she had simply misheard him. That was the only logical explanation. He couldn't possibly have said what she thought he had . . . could he?

She dropped her voice even lower. '*What?*'

'I said "silver rain". I was wondering if it meant anything to you.'

She flicked her eyes to the ceiling and opened the door to the corridor. Floyd was standing there, hat in his hand, looking at her with puppy-dog eyes.

'What you just said—' she began.

'It means something to you, doesn't it?' he persisted.

'Shut the door behind you.'

A whistle sounded and a moment later the train lurched as it began to crawl out of the station.

Floyd took out the postcard he had kept back. He passed it to Auger and let her examine it. She switched on the reading light and held it up for closer inspection. The train rattled and bounced, gathering speed as it negotiated the maze of interconnecting tracks beyond the ends of the platforms.

'It's significant, isn't it?' he prompted.

The postcard was a message from Susan White to Caliskan. Clearly, it had never been sent. Equally clearly, it had something to do with Silver Rain. But Silver Rain was a weapon from the past, a thing of wonder and terror, like a biblical plague. Silver Rain was the worst thing that could happen to a world. More than that: it was quite possibly the *last* thing that would ever happen to a world.

TWENTY-ONE

The train slipped through monotonous moonlit lowlands, somewhere east of the German border. Every now and then, the lit oasis of a farmhouse or a cosy little hamlet slid by in the night, but for long stretches of time they passed through endless dark fields, as lifeless and unwelcoming as the space between stars. Occasionally Auger glimpsed a fox, frozen in midstep, or the swooping passage of an owl skimming low across a field on some solitary vigil. The animals were drained of colour by the moonlight, pale as ghosts. These little pockets of life – welcome as they were – served only to emphasise the vast lifelessness of the territory itself. Yet the rhythmic sound of the train's wheels, the gentle rocking motion of the carriage, the distant, muted roar of the engine, the warmth of a good meal and a welcome drink inside her – all these things lulled Auger into a kind of ease, one that she knew was transient and not especially justifiable, but for which she was none the less grateful.

'So tell me,' Floyd said, 'how are we going to play the sleeping arrangements?'

'What would you suggest?'

'I can sleep on the seat I booked.' Floyd's expenses hadn't stretched to a couchette ticket.

'You can use the lower bunk,' she said magnanimously, dabbing a napkin at the corner of her mouth. 'It doesn't mean we're married. Or even particularly good friends.'

'You sure know how to make a guy feel appreciated.'

'I mean, Wendell, that this is purely business. Which doesn't mean that I'm not glad to have you in the vicinity, in case they show up again.'

'The children?'

She nodded meekly. 'I'm worried they'll have followed us.'

'Not on this train,' Floyd said. 'They'd be too conspicuous, even more so than in the city.'

'I hope you're right. Anyway, it isn't just the children.'

They had just finished dining in the restaurant car in the company of a dozen other travellers, most of them better dressed. Almost all of the other diners had now retired to the adjoining bar car or their individual cabins, leaving Auger and Floyd nearly alone. A youngish German couple were arguing over wedding plans in one corner, while a pair of plump Belgian businessmen swapped tales of financial impropriety over fat cigars and cognac in another. Neither of these parties was the least bit interested in a low, intimate conversation between a couple of English-speaking foreigners.

'What else, then?' Floyd asked.

'What you said . . . what you showed me on that postcard?'

'Yes.'

'Well, it dashes any hopes I might have had that I was actually imagining all this.'

'You weren't imagining those children.'

'I know,' Auger said. She sipped at the remains of her drink, knowing that she was a bit drunk and not caring. Right now, a little fogginess of mind was exactly what the doctor ordered. 'But the reference on that postcard to Silver Rain – well, it means that things are about ten times as bad as I thought they were.'

'Maybe it would help if you told me what this Silver Rain is all about,' Floyd suggested.

'I can't tell you that.'

'But it's bad, isn't it? When I dropped those two little words into your lap you looked as if someone had walked over your grave.'

'I was hoping that my reaction hadn't been so obvious.'

'It was written in sky-high neon. Those two words were the last thing you wanted to hear.'

'Or expected to hear,' she said.

'Coming from my lips?'

'From anyone's lips. You shouldn't have held back that postcard, Wendell. It was thoroughly dishonest.'

'And you pretending to be Susan White's sister – that's what you call setting an appropriate example, is it?'

'That's different. It was a necessary deception.'

'So was mine, Verity.'

'Then I suppose we're even. Can we leave it at that?'

'Not until I know what those two little words mean.'

'As I said, I can't tell you.'

'If I had to put money on it,' Floyd said, 'I'd say it was the codename for a secret weapon. Question is: who's on the trigger? The people behind you and White, or the people who killed White and Blanchard, and sent those children to stalk you?'

'It isn't our weapon,' she said fiercely. 'Why do you think Susan White was murdered in the first place?'

'So it's their weapon, not yours?'

'That's enough, Wendell.'

'I'll take that as a "yes".'

'Take it any way you like, it doesn't make any difference to me.'

'Let me join the dots here,' Floyd said. 'Susan White stumbles on to a conspiracy. The Kaspar contract in Berlin is part of it. So is Silver Rain, whatever *that* is. I guess all these things are connected somehow, although right now I don't see how those metal spheres can be any part of a weapon.'

'The spheres aren't the weapon,' she said icily. 'I don't know what they are, except that they must be involved in all this somehow. And if I knew that, I wouldn't be sitting on this train being pestered by you.'

'But you do know what Silver Rain is, don't you?'

'Yes,' she said. 'I know exactly what it is. I saw what it can do with my own eyes only a few days ago.'

'Where was that?'

'Looking down on Mars, from a spaceship. Where else?'

'Cute. How about the real answer?'

'The real answer is that it's a weapon. It can kill a lot of people in one go. More than you would want to believe possible.'

'Thousands?'

'Try again.'

'Hundreds of thousands?'

'Better.'

'Millions?'

'Warm. Start thinking entire planetary populations, and you're getting close.'

'Then it's some kind of bomb, like the big firecracker the Americans say they'll build one of these days.'

'An atom bomb?' She almost laughed at the quaintness of it, but checked herself in time. In the mid-twentieth century of her own timeline there had been nothing quaint about it, any more than siege towers and boiling oil had been quaint in the thirteenth. 'No, it's not an atom bomb. An atom bomb would be . . . bad, I grant you that. But whether you drop it from a plane or load it inside a missile, a bomb's a weapon with a specific focus of attack: a city or a town. Bad news if you're there when it drops . . . equally bad news if you live in the fallout zone. But for everyone else? Business carries on more or less as usual.'

Floyd stared at her with a kind of horrified fascination. 'And Silver Rain?'

'Silver Rain is much worse. Silver Rain touches everyone. There's no escape, nowhere to run, no way to protect yourself even if you know it's coming. There's no way to negotiate with it, or buy your way out.' She paused, knowing that she had to tell him enough to satisfy his curiosity, but must not even hint at the truth. Already she regretted the little 'Mars' wisecrack she had made earlier: things like that could get her into serious trouble. 'It's like a plague, spreading through the air. You breathe it in, and you feel fine. It doesn't hurt you. And then one day you just die of it. Horribly, but quickly.'

'Like some kind of mustard gas?'

'Yes,' she said. 'Just like that.'

'You said it can kill millions of people.'

'Yes.'

'Who would use such a weapon? Wouldn't they be just as likely to die at the same time?'

'If they didn't take the necessary precautions,' she said, 'then yes, they might.'

'And these precautions?'

'Too many questions, Wendell.'

'I'm just getting started.' He changed tack. 'The Kaspar contract: could those spheres be a cover for something else?'

'Such as?'

'This Silver Rain you won't talk about. Could the factory in Berlin be making this stuff?'

'No,' she said, shaking her head. 'Silver Rain isn't like that. It isn't something you make with foundries and lathes.'

'A chemical, then? If there's a foundry, there's probably a chemical works nearby.'

'It isn't something you make in a chemical plant, either.' A small, quiet voice at the back of her head whispered 'careful', but she pressed on regardless. 'Silver Rain is a special kind of weapon. It requires a very specialised manufacturing capability, one that just doesn't exist in Germany or France.' Or anywhere else on this planet, she added to herself.

Floyd swirled around the remains of his drink. 'So who is making this stuff?'

'That's the point: I don't know.'

'But you seem so familiar with it.'

'It can be made,' she said. 'Just not locally. Which means you'd need to import it, and then find a means of deploying it.' She thought of the censor, with its automatic blockading of all forms of nanotechnology. Unless there was some as yet undiscovered means of bypassing the censor, there was no way to bring something like Silver Rain into E2. The trick Skellsgard had pulled with the pneumatic drill – dismantling it into simple, solid components and smuggling it through in pieces – wouldn't work either. The only way to break nanotechnology down into smaller pieces and put it back together again later was with more nanotechnology.

The rhythm of the train, the wheels clicking across the joints in the rails, seemed to goad her thoughts onward, like a whip.

While it was true that the indigenous technology on E2 was nowhere near advanced enough to manufacture something like Silver Rain – and wouldn't be for at least a century – there was always the possibility that Slasher agents had established a covert research and development programme somewhere. Auger thought about this for a moment and then dismissed it. No amount of advanced knowledge could compensate for an industrial technology still stuck in the steam age. Silver Rain was incredibly complex even in terms of the nanotechnology available in Auger's timeline. But you couldn't even make the simplest item of nanotechnology here on E2. You couldn't even use the available tools to construct the specialised equipment necessary for manufacturing even the least sophisticated nanotechnological components. Given time, the necessary technical base could have been achieved – but not without some or all of that magical technology leaking into the world and thereby changing it. The Kaspar contract, on the other hand, looked more like the kind of covert programme that might actually work. Whatever function those spheres served, they had been manufactured using indigenous technology and know-how.

Which made the reference to Silver Rain all the more anomalous. Someone planned to use it: that was clear. But they couldn't make it within E2 and they couldn't smuggle it through the censor.

So they must have found another way of delivering it. If you couldn't enter the house by the front door, she mused, you found another way in.

You broke a window.

Another portal? Perhaps such a thing existed, but there was a high probability that it would also come with its own censor.

Which left the one possibility so horrifically obvious that she'd overlooked it completely. If they could find their way to the outside of the ALS, and if they had a means of cracking that shell, then they could simply deliver the Silver Rain directly, spraying it into the atmosphere from space.

But that couldn't be possible, surely. No one knew where the ALS was situated. The duration of the hyperweb transits was only weakly correlated with distance in actual light-years . . . and there was no indicator of direction at all. Auger's thoughts returned to the house analogy. The hyperweb was like a vast, meandering underground tunnel system that emerged here and there in the basements of isolated old mansions. But there were many, many mansions strewn across the landscape and no way of telling from the inside which one a particular tunnel had emerged in. The windows were bricked up, the doors barred and the skylights boarded over. If only you could rip away some of those barriers, then perhaps you might get a glimpse of the surrounding landscape, and have some chance of identifying the house into which the tunnel led.

Could the shell be cracked from the inside somehow?

'Verity,' Floyd said gently. 'Is there something you'd like to share with me?'

'I've shared more than enough.'

'Not from where I'm sitting.' He leaned back into the plush upholstery of his seat, studying her in a way that made her feel both uncomfortable and perhaps a little flattered. He wasn't a bad-looking man, really: a bit crumpled around the edges, perhaps, and in need of a wash and a comb, but she'd known worse.

'I'm sorry, Wendell, but I've told you all I can.'

'You don't even have all the answers yet, do you?'

'No,' she said, glad to be able to say something in complete honesty for once. 'All I have are the pieces of the jigsaw puzzle Susan White left me, which may or may not be sufficient to reconstruct the answer. If they are, I'm just too stupid to see it.'

'Or maybe the answer isn't that obvious.'

'That's what I keep wondering. All I know is that she must have been closer to the truth than I am right now.'

'And look what good it did her,' Floyd said.

'Yes,' Auger replied, saluting Susan's memory with a lift of her glass. 'But at least she died trying.'

Auger found herself alone on the Champs-Elysées, moving along one broad, tree-lined pavement amidst the surging flow of the crowd. She remembered being on the train with Floyd, but that particular investigation had led nowhere. When they had arrived in Berlin, they had found it covered with ice, inhabited only by bickering tribes of feral machines. The trip had been a waste of time: how could she ever have forgotten that crucial detail? Now she was back in Paris, alone and a little sad despite the vivacious mood of the other pedestrians. It was the middle of the morning and everyone was already overloaded with shopping and groceries and bright bouquets of flowers. Everywhere she looked there was riotous colour, from the clothes and belongings of the Parisians to the overflowing shop-window displays and the trees, which were hung with gemlike fruits. Cars and buses sped by in blurs of gleaming chrome and gold. Even the horses shone, as if suffused with some soft inner light. Above the bobbing heads of the pedestrians, the Arc de Triomphe rose over everything, pennanted in a thousand pastel colours. Auger had no idea why she was walking towards it, or what she would do when she arrived. It was simply enough to be swept along by the other walkers, carried on their tide. All around her, couples and gatherings of friends laughed and made plans for later in the day. She felt their gaiety begin to elevate her mood.

Behind her, she heard a steady rhythmic sound. She looked over her shoulder, through gaps between the people immediately behind her, and saw a child, a small boy, walking a dozen or so paces to her rear. The boy was the only other solitary person on the street, and as he walked – with a methodical, clockwork slowness – the other people made room for him, moving aside as if by some kind of magnetic repulsion. The little boy was wearing a red T-shirt and shorts, with white socks and buckled black shoes, and she knew that she had seen him somewhere before, not long ago. He had carried a yo-yo then, she remembered, but now a toy drum hung around his neck, upon which he was rapping out the insistent rhythm that had first drawn her attention. The tattoo he beat out was like a complicated heartbeat. It never varied, never slowed or quickened.

The little boy unnerved her, so she pushed forward with the flow of pedestrians. Gradually the drumming sound faded away. When she could hear it no more, she risked a glance behind her and saw only a thick mass of shoppers and promenaders, with no sign of the little drummer boy. She kept walking briskly, and when she looked back again a little later, there was still no sign of him.

But the mood of the avenue had changed. It wasn't the boy – she was certain that none of the other Parisians were properly aware of him – but the weather. The colours on the street were suddenly muted and drab and the flags on the Arc de Triomphe fluttered like old grey rags. The sky, an untrammelled blue a moment earlier, now seethed with coal-black rainclouds. Sensing the imminent downpour, people dashed for the shelter of shop awnings and Métro entrances. Up and down the Champs-Elysées, umbrellas formed a choppy sea of bobbing black.

It started raining, in dribs and drabs at first, darkening the pavement with a mottled pattern, but quickening until it was sluicing down in hard lines like drawn glass, spraying off the umbrellas, gushing from drainpipes. People who were still outside renewed their efforts to find shelter. But there were too many of them and not enough places to run to. Cars and buses threw showers of water on to the scurrying crowds. People dropped their belongings, abandoning them to the elements as they continued their frantic search for cover. The wind picked up and flipped their umbrellas over, lifting them into the sky. Auger, who had stopped, looked around at their expressions, watching the rain chisel fury into their faces. But she felt none of it. The rain was warm and sweet and it had the fragrance of expensive perfume. She lifted her face to the sky and let it anoint her, drinking it in. It was delicious: warm where it touched her skin, exquisitely cool as it slid down her throat. Around her, the people kept running, slipping and sliding on the wet paving stones. Why couldn't they just stop and savour the rain? she wondered. What was wrong with them?

Then the texture of the rain changed. It began to prickle her skin and eyes. It began to sting her throat. She closed her mouth, still holding her face to the sky but no longer gulping it down. The prickling intensified. The rain, gin-clear a moment ago, was now steely and opaque, coming down in chromed lines. Rivers of mercury poured from the drains and flooded the gutters, turning the pavements into mirrors. No one could stand up now, only Auger. Everyone else was flailing around, thrashing on the ground as they tried to struggle to their feet again. The rain flowed across their faces, puddling in their eyes and mouths as if trying to find its way inside. A horse, separated from its delivery cart, thrashed ineffectually in the street, struggling to stand until its legs snapped like sticks. At last even Auger turned her face from the sky. She held out a hand and watched the reflective shafts ram through the gaps between her fingers.

The clouds began to disperse. The downpour abated and blue sky began to push through again. The rain gradually slowed to a trickle and then stopped. The mirrored pavements began to dry as the sun crept out again. Cautiously, the fallen people picked themselves up. Even the horse somehow regained its footing.

'It's over,' she heard people say, relieved, all around her, as they resumed their progress along the avenue. No one seemed concerned that they had lost their belongings, only that the Silver Rain had ended. The street bloomed with colours once again.

'It's not over!' Auger shouted, the only person standing still as the pedestrians surged around her. 'It's not over!'

But no one paid her any attention, even when she cupped her hands and cried out even louder, 'It isn't over! This is only the beginning!'

The people walked past her, oblivious. She reached out and grabbed a young couple, but they wrestled free of her, laughing in her face. With a dreadful sense of inevitability, she watched them continue their progress towards the Arc de Triomphe. After a dozen steps, they faltered and stopped in mid-stride. At exactly the same instant, so did everyone else on the street.

For a moment, the Champs-Elysées was perfectly still, thousands of people suddenly completely motionless, some in the most ludicrous of postures. Then, very slowly, as one they lost their balance and toppled to the ground. Their perfectly immobile bodies littered the sides of the avenue as far as the eye could see. Even beyond the Champs-Elysées, a palpable stillness had descended over the entire city. Nothing moved, nothing breathed. The bodies had become silvery-grey, drained of colour.

All was quiet. It was, in a way, quite beautiful: a city finally freed of its human burden.

Then a breeze picked up, blowing along the length of the avenue. Where it touched the bodies, it lifted coils of shining dust from them, twining them through the air like long glittering scarves. As the dust peeled away from the bodies, it removed first their clothes and then their flesh, revealing chrome bones and steel-grey armatures of nerve and sinew. The breeze strengthened, abrading even the bones, smoothing the bodies into odd, abstract curves, like a landscape of intertwined sand dunes. Coils of dust snaked between Auger's lips, peppery and metallic.

She was screaming now, but it was pointless: the Silver Rain had come and no one had heeded her warnings. If only they had listened . . . but what good, she wondered, would it have done them anyway?

She heard, distantly, a rhythmic sound. Far off in the sea of blurred skeletal remains, a single figure remained standing. The little drummer boy was still drumming, still walking very slowly towards her, picking his way between the bones.

'Verity,' Floyd said softly. 'Wake up. You're having a nightmare.'

It took her several seconds to surface through the dream, even with Floyd shaking her gently. He stood next to her bunk, his head level with hers as she opened her eyes to the dimly lit railway cabin.

'I thought I was back in Paris,' she said. 'I thought the rain had begun.'

'You were screaming your head off.'

'They wouldn't listen to me. They thought it was over . . . they thought they were safe.' She was cold, drenched with her own sweat.

'It's all right now,' he said. 'You're safe. It was just a nightmare . . . just a bad dream.'

Through the gap in the curtain she could see the moonlit landscape slipping by outside. They were still on their way to Berlin, still on their way to that icebound, machine-stalked city, as dangerous in its way as the excavated bowl of Paris. For a moment she panicked, wanting to tell Floyd that they had to turn around, that this was a futile journey. But gradually her thoughts rearranged themselves as the dream began to fade a little. They were headed to a different Berlin, one that had never known a Nanocaust or any of the other horrors of the Void Century. That brightly lit, rain-soaked Paris had been a dream.

'They wouldn't listen,' she said softly.

'It was just a nightmare,' Floyd repeated. 'You're safe now.'

'No,' she said, still feeling as if the dream might reclaim her at any moment, still seeing the drummer boy stepping towards her through the maze of bones, as if that part of the dream was still playing somewhere in her skull, moving with clockwork deliberation towards an inevitable conclusion.

'You're safe.'

'I'm not,' she said. 'Nor are you. Nor is anyone. We have to stop it from happening, Wendell. We have to stop the rain.'

His hand closed around hers. Gradually she stopped shaking and lay there numbly, and for a little while she let him hold her hand, until she fell back into an uneasy sleep, drifting bodiless through the dust-strewn streets of an empty city, like the last ghost in town.

They arrived in Berlin by mid-morning on Sunday. All around the city, party banners and flags were on display again. Now that Rommel and von Stauffenberg were both safely in the ground, the bright young things had decided that it was time to give National Socialism another crack of the whip. The advertising men had come up with some careful changes: the old hard-edged swastika was gone, replaced by a rounded, softer successor. The party big shots still gave rallies in the Zeppelin Field, but they saved their best performances for the tiny, flickering window of television. Now there was a little slice of Nuremberg in every well-appointed living room, every beer hall and railway-station cafeteria. There was talk of parole for the big fish languishing in the Gare d'Orsay; perhaps even some kind of triumphant return to the Reichstag in the evening of his chemically sustained days.

'It shouldn't be like this,' Auger said quietly.

'Amen to that,' Floyd replied under his breath.

It was a short taxi ride to the Hotel Am Zoo, a good place at the fashionable end of the Kurfurstendamm decked out with high-class marble and chrome so clean and polished that you could eat your dinner off it. At least the hotel hadn't changed much. Floyd knew it well enough, since he and Greta had stayed there on two or three occasions in the early fifties. Given that familiarity, it had seemed like the obvious place to head for. But once Floyd had checked in and carried their very few belongings up to the single room they'd just paid for, he began to feel the onset of an annoying but familiar sense of guilt. It was as if he was consciously cheating on Greta, visiting this old romantic haunt of theirs with another woman. But that was absurd on two counts, he told himself. Greta and he were no longer an item – even if the door to them being an item again in the future hadn't been completely closed. And Auger and him – well, that was just ridiculous. Why had the thought even entered his mind? They were here to work on an investigative matter. Strictly business.

So what if he liked her? She was nice looking and clever and quick-witted and interesting (how could a lady spy be anything *but* interesting? he thought) but any other man would have said the same thing. Liking her did not take great strength of character. You didn't have to see past superficial flaws: there weren't any – except maybe the way she kept treating him like somebody who not only didn't need to hear the truth, but who couldn't *handle* the truth. That part he didn't like. But it only made her more fascinating to him: a puzzle that had to be unravelled. Or unwrapped, perhaps, depending on the circumstances. When she had finally fallen back to sleep after her nightmare, Floyd had lain awake on the lower bunk, listening to her breathing, thinking of her under the sheets and wondering what she was dreaming about now. He wasn't crazy about her. But she was the kind of girl he could very easily allow himself to become crazy about, if he wanted to.

But none of that meant anything. She must have walked through life with men like him falling at her feet, squashing them underfoot like autumn leaves. It probably happened so often that all she noticed was that nice crunching sound. What would a girl like Verity Auger want with a washed-up Joe like him? He was Wendell Floyd. A jazz musician who didn't play. A detective who didn't detect.

If he hadn't kept back that postcard, she wouldn't even have let him join her on the train.

In which case, maybe he wasn't so dumb after all.

'Wendell?' she said.

'What?'

'You seem preoccupied.'

He realised that he had been standing at the window, moping there for at least five minutes. Across the Kurfurstendamm, a group of workers were bolting together a tall pressed-steel monument to the first ascent of Everest. The young Russian airman was depicted standing astride the summit, raising his gloved fist in what was either a cheery salute to an overflying aircraft or impish defiance at a vanquished and obsolete God.

'Just thinking about old times,' he said.

Auger was sitting on the bed, leafing through a telephone directory. She had her shoes off, stockinged legs crossed over each other. 'When you were here before?'

'Guess so.'

'I'm sorry if I've made things awkward between you and . . .' She paused to jot down a telephone number, using a pad letterheaded with the name of the hotel.

'Greta,' he said, before she had a chance to say the name. 'And no, you haven't. I'm sure she knows the score.'

Auger looked up, her finger poised halfway down one page. She was sucking on a strand of hair, as if it helped her to concentrate. 'Which is?'

'That you and I are here on business. That you didn't even want me along for the ride. That there's nothing more to it than that.'

'She's not jealous, is she?'

'Jealous? Why should she be?'

'Exactly. No reason in the world.'

'We're just two adults with some mutual interests in Berlin—'

'Saving money by sharing a single room.'

'Precisely.' Floyd smiled. 'Now that we've got *that* out of the way . . .'

'Yes. What a relief.' She looked down at the telephone directory again, wetting a finger to turn one of the tissue-thin business pages.

'I should have found a different hotel,' Floyd said.

'What?'

'Nothing.' He turned back to the bed, his attention lingering on the shape of Auger's calves under those stockings. They weren't the longest legs he'd seen on a woman, or the shapeliest, but they were some way from being the worst.

'Floyd?' She'd noticed him staring, and he snapped his gaze up to her face, a little embarrassed by the direction his thoughts had been taking.

'Did you get anywhere with that telephone number?' he asked. She had used the telephone several times while he had been looking out of the window, but he hadn't been paying attention to the outcome. A certain amount of talking had been involved whenever she placed a call, since they all had to be relayed through the hotel switchboard, but his rudimentary German made listening in a pointless exercise.

'No luck so far,' she said. 'I already tried this number from Paris, but figured there might be a problem with the international connections.'

'I tried it as well,' Floyd said. 'It didn't work for me either. The operator said it was as if the line had been cut off. How could a big firm like that not have paid their bill, or not have anyone to answer their telephone? Haven't they heard of answering machines?'

Auger called through again. She spoke very good German each time, or at least what sounded like very good German to his ears. 'Nope,' she said. 'Line's totally dead. It isn't even ringing at the other end.' She smoothed a hand over the letter from Kaspar Metals, uncreasing it. 'Maybe this number's wrong.'

'Why would they print the wrong number on the letterhead?'

'I don't know,' Auger said. 'Maybe they changed the number but still had a lot of the old paper lying around. Maybe the man who sent this used old stock he'd had lying in his desk for years.'

'Sloppy,' Floyd said.

'But not a crime.'

'Did you check the directory as well?'

'It lists the same number,' she said. 'But the directory looks old. I don't know where to go from here. We have an address on the letter, but it's just a generic post-office-box address for correspondence to the whole steelworks. It's not specific enough to be useful. It doesn't even tell us exactly where the factory is.'

'Wait,' Floyd said. 'Maybe we can bypass Kaspar Metals entirely – just get in touch with the man who sent that letter, and see what he has to say.'

'Herr G. Altfeld,' Auger said, reading from the paper. 'But Altfeld could live anywhere. He might not even be in the telephone directory.'

'But maybe he is. Why don't we check?'

Auger found the Berlin area private-number directory and passed the heavy, dog-eared book to Floyd.

'Here we are,' Floyd said, leafing through it. 'Altfeld, Altfeld, Altfeld . . . a lot of Altfelds. There's got to be at least thirty of them. But not many with the first initial "G".'

'We don't know for sure whether that "G" refers to his first name,' she observed.

'It'll do for now. If we don't hit the jackpot, we'll move on to all the other Altfelds.'

'That'll take for ever.'

'It's elementary drudgework, the kind that puts a roof over my head. Pass me a pen, will you? I'll start making a list of the likely candidates. And see if you can rustle up some coffee. I think it's going to be a long morning.'

TWENTY-TWO

Auger knew it was the right number as soon as the man answered the telephone. His authoritative, slightly schoolmasterly tone only confirmed her suspicions.

'Herr Altfeld.'

'Excuse the interruption, mein Herr, and excuse my very poor German, but I am trying to trace the Herr Altfeld who is an employee of Kaspar Metals—'

The call was terminated before Auger could say another word.

'What happened?' Floyd asked.

'I think I struck gold. He rang off a little too enthusiastically.'

'Try again. In my experience, people always answer the telephone sooner or later.'

She dialled through to the hotel switchboard again and waited while her call was connected. 'Herr Altfeld, once again I must—'

The line crashed dead again. Auger tried once more, but this time the telephone rang and rang without being picked up. Auger imagined the sound echoing around a well-appointed hallway, where the phone rested on a little table under a print of a familiar oil painting – a Pissaro or a Manet, perhaps. She persisted, allowing the phone to keep ringing. Eventually, her patience was rewarded by the receiver being picked up.

'Herr Altfeld? Please let me speak.'

'I have nothing to say to you.'

'Mein Herr, I know you talked to Susan White. My name is Auger . . . Verity Auger. I'm Susan's sister.'

There was a pause, during which it seemed quite likely that the man would hang up the telephone again. 'Fräulein White did not have the good grace to keep her appointment,' Altfeld eventually replied.

'That's because someone murdered her.'

'Murdered her?' he repeated, incredulously.

'That's why you never saw her. I'm here in Berlin with a private detective.' Floyd's advice: tell the truth wherever possible. It could open a surprising number of doors. 'We think Susan was killed for a reason, and that it had something to do with the work being done at Kaspar Metals.'

'As I said, I have nothing to tell you.'

'You were good enough to offer to speak to my sister, mein Herr. Will you at least do us the same favour? We won't take up much of your time, and then I promise you won't hear from us again.'

'Things have changed. It was a mistake to talk to Fräulein White, and it would be an even bigger mistake to talk to you.'

'Why – is someone putting pressure on you?'

'Pressure,' the man said, laughing hollowly. 'No, I have no pressure at all now. A generous retirement settlement saw to that.'

'Then you don't work at Kaspar Metals any more?'

'Nobody works there any more. The factory burnt down.'

'Look, mein Herr, I think it would really help if we could talk. It can be anywhere of your choosing. Even if it's just for five minutes—'

'I am sorry,' Altfeld said, and hung up again.

'Pity,' Auger said, rubbing her forehead. 'I thought I was getting somewhere that time. But he really doesn't want to talk to us.'

'We're not giving up,' Floyd said.

'Shall I try to ring through again?'

'He probably won't talk to you. But it doesn't matter – we know where he lives now.'

The black Duesenberg taxi growled to a halt at one end of a leafy suburban street in the suburb of Wedding, five kilometres from the heart of the city. Long lines of cheaply built dwellings housed the many workers and bureaucrats who toiled in the nearby factories. The Borsig Locomotive Works was the largest employer in the area, but the Siemens factory was not far away and there was a string of other industrial concerns in the neighbourhood, including Kaspar Metals, they presumed.

'That's the house,' Auger said. 'The one on the corner. What shall I tell the driver?'

'Tell him to pull over a couple of houses beyond it.'

She said something in German. The taxi purred forward, then pulled to the side of the road and slid in between two parked cars.

'Now what?' Auger asked.

'Tell him to keep the meter running while we check out the house.'

Auger had another brief exchange with the driver. 'He says if we pay now he'll wait another ten minutes.'

'Then pay the man.'

Auger had already changed some of her funds into Deutschmarks. She passed a couple of notes to the taxi driver and repeated her instruction for him to wait. The driver turned off the engine and they got out.

'I'm impressed with your German,' Floyd commented as they opened the garden gate and walked up the little gravel path to the front door. 'Is that what they teach all the nice young spies?'

'They thought it might come in handy,' Auger said.

Floyd rang the bell. Presently, a shape loomed behind the frosted glass and the door creaked open. The man standing in the hallway was in his fifties or sixties, dressed in shirt and braces, with small metal-rimmed spectacles and a neatly trimmed moustache. He was shorter and thinner than Floyd. His features were delicate, and in his very fine hands he held a duster and an item of pottery.

'Herr Altfeld?' Auger said, followed by something in German that included the word 'telephone'. That was as far as she got before the man closed the door.

'Shall I try again?' she asked.

'He won't open it. He doesn't want to speak to us.'

Auger leaned in and rang the bell, but the man did not reappear. 'That was him, though, don't you think?'

'I guess so. This is the address that goes with the number you called.'

'I wonder what's got him so scared.'

'I can think of a thing or two,' Floyd said.

They walked back down the garden path and closed the gate behind them.

'Short of breaking in and tying him to a chair,' Auger said, 'how would you suggest we proceed now?'

'We wait in the taxi. If you can keep the driver copacetic, we'll just sit tight here until Altfeld makes a move.'

'You think he will?'

'Once he's sure we've left the neighbourhood, he'll want to get out of that house so he doesn't have to put up with us ringing the doorbell or calling him on the telephone.'

'This is all familiar territory to you, I guess, Wendell?'

'Yes,' he said. 'But usually the worst thing I have to worry about is a slug on the chin.'

'And this time?'

'A slug on the chin sounds just dandy.'

Auger persuaded the taxi driver to take them once around the block, so that they would appear to be leaving the scene if Altfeld happened to be watching them from behind his curtains. Once they had returned to Altfeld's road, the taxi driver parked the car in a different space further up the road than before, but still within sight of the house on the corner.

'Tell the driver he may be in for a long wait,' Floyd said, 'but that we'll pay him more than he'd earn taking other rides.'

'He still doesn't like it,' Auger said, after passing on Floyd's instructions. 'He says it's his job to take fares, not play private detective.'

'Feed him another note.'

She opened her purse again and spoke to the driver, who shrugged and took the proffered money.

'What does he say now?' Floyd asked.

'He says he could get used to his new profession.'

They waited and waited. The driver thumbed through the *Berliner Morgenpost* from front to back. Just when Floyd was beginning to doubt himself, the front door of Altfeld's house opened and a man emerged wearing a raincoat and carrying a small greaseproof-paper bag. Altfeld closed the garden gate behind him and set off down the street, stopping next to one of the parked cars and getting inside. The vehicle – a black nineteen-fifties Bugatti with white-wall tyres – grumbled into life and bounced away down the road.

'Tell the driver to follow that car,' Floyd said, 'and remind him to keep a nice distance.'

Contrary to Floyd's expectations, the taxi driver turned out to be reasonably proficient at tailing the other car, with Floyd only having to urge him to hold back once or twice. Two or three times, the driver swerved confidently down a side road and re-emerged after some twists and turns just a few cars behind the one they were following.

The pursuit took them back into town along more or less the same route they'd followed to reach Wedding. Soon they had crossed the Spree and were skirting the edge of the Tiergarten, Berlin's vast green lung. Near the western end – not far from the Hotel Am Zoo – the Bugatti slowed and veered into a parking place. The taxi cruised past, only stopping when they had turned a corner. Auger paid off the driver while Floyd walked to the corner and eyed Altfeld's car. He was just in time to observe the man emerge from the car, still carrying the paper bag. They followed him all the way to the Elephant Gate of the *Zoologischer Garten*, watching from a distance as he paid his entrance fee and strolled inside. Floyd knew the zoo very well. Greta and he had visited it on almost every one of their trips to Berlin, strolling around on carefree afternoons until the sky turned dark and the shimmering neon lights of the city beckoned.

Overhead, the sky threatened rain but never quite delivered it, like a yapping dog with no bite. Early on a Sunday afternoon, the zoo was beginning to fill up with families accompanied by fractious children who had a habit of bursting into tears at the slightest provocation. Floyd and Auger bought tickets and kept a decent distance between themselves and Altfeld. The crowds were just thick enough to provide cover, while still allowing frequent glimpses of the man in the raincoat.

They followed Altfeld to the penguin enclosure. Ringed by a spiked iron fence, it was a sunken concrete landscape of artificial rocks and shelves surrounding a shallow, squalid-looking lake. It was feeding time. A young man in shorts flung fish at the anxious, pressing mob of penguins. Altfeld stood by the railings, at the front of the small gathering of onlookers. There was no sign that he knew he was being followed. Soon the zookeeper picked up his empty bucket and moved elsewhere, and Altfeld took that as his cue to dig into his little paper bag and hurl silvery titbits to the birds.

Across the bowl of the penguin enclosure, someone caught Floyd's eye. It was Auger: she had made her way to the other side and had somehow managed to get to the front of the crowd of spectators, and was now pressed hard against the railings. Rather than paying attention to Altfeld, she was staring in obvious transfixed fascination at the bustling congregation of penguins, with their neat black morning suits, silly little flippers and expressions of utmost dignity, even as they belly-flopped into the water or fell over backwards. It was as if she had never seen penguins before.

Floyd guessed they didn't have many zoos in Dakota.

The onlookers began to disperse, leaving only a few people behind, amongst them Altfeld. As he flung the birds the last few scraps from his bag, he watched the penguins with the resigned detachment of a general overseeing some appalling military defeat.

Floyd and Auger approached the old man.

'Herr Altfeld?' Auger asked.

He looked around sharply, dropping the paper bag, and replied in English, 'I don't know who you people are, but you should not have followed me.'

'We only need you to answer a few questions,' Floyd said.

'If I had anything to say, I would have already said it.'

Auger stepped closer. 'I'm Verity,' she said. 'Susan was my sister. She was murdered three weeks ago. I know you corresponded with her about the Kaspar contract. I think her murder had something to with whatever that contract was for.'

'There is nothing I can tell you about that contract.'

'But you know the contract we mean,' Floyd said. 'You know it was out of the ordinary.'

He kept his voice low. 'An artistic commission. Nothing special about that.'

'You don't believe that, as comforting as it might seem,' Auger said.

'All we need to know,' Floyd said, 'is where the objects were sent. Just one address will do.'

'Even if I was prepared to tell you – which I am not – that information no longer exists.'

'You don't keep your paperwork filed away somewhere for reference?' Auger asked, raising an eyebrow in surprise.

'The documentation was . . . disposed of.'

Floyd blocked Altfeld's view of the birds. 'But you must remember something.'

'I never committed those details to memory.'

'Because someone told you not to?' Auger asked. 'Was that what happened, Mr Altfeld? Did someone put pressure on you not to pay too much attention?'

'It was a complicated contract. Of course I paid attention.'

'Give us something,' Floyd said. 'Anything. Just the approximate district in Paris to which one of the spheres was shipped would be better than nothing.'

'I don't remember.'

'Was the function of the spheres ever discussed?' Floyd persisted.

'As I said, it was an artistic commission.' Altfeld's voice had become tense, and his composure seemed ready to snap at any moment. 'Kaspar Metals was engaged in many other metallurgical contracts during the same period. Provided the specifications were followed, there was no need for us to question the subsequent use to which the items would be put.'

'But you must have been curious,' Floyd said.

'No. I had no curiosity whatsoever.'

'We think the spheres might be part of a weapon,' Auger said. 'At the very least, components of something with a military application. The same thought must have occurred to you. Didn't that give you pause for thought?'

'The purpose of the objects was a matter for the export bureau, not me.'

'Nice get-out,' Floyd said.

Altfeld looked up at him. 'If questions had been raised, export of the objects would have been blocked. They were delivered, so the matter is closed.'

'And that lets you off the hook, does it?' Floyd asked.

'My conscience is clear. If this troubles you, I apologise. May I be permitted to watch the penguins in peace now?'

'That contract was part of something evil,' Auger said. 'You can't wash your hands of it that easily.'

'What I do with my hands,' Altfeld said, 'is entirely my business.'

'Tell us what you know,' Floyd insisted.

'What I know is that you should stop asking questions and leave this matter alone. Leave Berlin now and return to wherever it is you came from.' He regarded Auger. 'I can't place your accent. I am normally very good, even with English speakers.'

'She's from Dakota,' Floyd said, 'but you don't need to worry about that. What you do need to worry about is telling me who has put the fear of God into you.'

'Don't be ridiculous.'

By now, they were the only people anywhere near the penguin enclosure. Floyd saw his moment, knowing he'd regret his actions immediately, but also well aware that there was no other means of getting anything useful out of Altfeld. He lunged and grabbed Altfeld by the collar of his raincoat and shoved him hard against the railings with his back to the enclosure, knocking the wind out of him.

'Now listen *sehr gut*,' Floyd said. 'I'm not an impatient man. I'm not a man who normally does this kind of thing. Matter of fact, I'm usually an easy-going sort of fellow.' Altfeld wriggled, trying ineffectually to escape Floyd's grasp. 'But the problem is that a friend of mine is in a lot of trouble.'

'I know nothing about any friend of yours,' Altfeld wheezed.

'I never said you did. But this little contract of yours – the one you don't want to talk about – is connected to the trouble my friend is in. It's also connected to the murder of Miss Auger's sister. That makes two of us who'd like to get closer to the truth, and only one of you standing in our way.'

'Let go of me,' Altfeld said. 'Then perhaps we can have a reasonable conversation.'

'Don't hurt him, Wendell,' Auger said.

Floyd looked around: no other spectators just yet. He kept the man pinned against the railings. 'This is as reasonable as it gets. Now why don't you tell me about the people who wanted these spheres made?'

'I will tell you nothing except that you are better off having as little to do with them as possible.'

'Ah,' Floyd said. 'Progress – of a sort.' He rewarded Altfeld with a slight reduction of pressure, allowing him to stand fully on his feet again. 'The question is – if they're so bad, why did you deal with them in the first place? Surely Kaspar Metals didn't need the work that badly?'

Altfeld looked around, doubtless hoping for assistance to wander by. 'Work was always welcome. We were not in the business of turning contracts away.'

'Not even contracts as technically demanding as this one?' Auger asked.

He glared at her, as if she should be ashamed to have an opinion on the matter. 'There was nothing unusual about it at first. The contract appeared relatively simple, as these things go. We were happy to take it on. But as the work progressed, so did the demands for the quality of the finished product. The specification became tighter, the tolerances smaller. The copper–aluminium alloy was difficult to cast and machine. At first we didn't even have measuring instruments capable of calibrating the objects' shape to the necessary degree of accuracy. And then there was the whole business of the cryogenic suspension—'

'Cryogenic what?' Auger interjected, alarm bells ringing in her head.

'I've said too much.'

Floyd took a renewed grip on Altfeld's raincoat and lifted him higher, until the back of his collar snagged on the spiked points of the iron railings. Floyd let him dangle. 'You've only just whetted my appetite.'

Altfeld's breath caught in his throat. 'Late in the contract, the client revealed that the spheres would have to withstand immersion in liquid helium, at a temperature only a whisker above absolute zero. This in turn created numerous difficulties. Now leave me alone!'

'It sounds as if you were being asked to do the impossible,' Floyd said. 'Why didn't you just back out of the contract, if the details kept changing?'

'We tried,' Altfeld said. 'And that is when I learned of our clients' capacity for ruthlessness. There was to be no backing out, they said.'

'I take it you called their bluff.'

'Yes. And then one of my senior managers – the man who had conducted the last round of negotiations with my clients – was found dead in his home.'

'Murdered?' Floyd asked.

'He had been bludgeoned to death in his conservatory. Yet this had happened on a sunny afternoon, when his home was in full view of many witnesses. No one was seen to come and go. At least, no one who could possibly have committed the crime.'

'Except maybe a child,' Floyd said.

Altfeld nodded gravely, and suddenly all the fight drained out of him, as if he had just been told something he desperately wished not to be true. Floyd sensed the change in his mood, as if on some level Altfeld was glad to be able to talk to someone at last, no matter how fearful the consequences.

'During the final stages of the contract, when the spheres were being evaluated and shipped, I saw children all over the place. They followed me wherever I went. They were always around, visible just out of the corner of my eye. I haven't seen any since the factory burnt down. I hope I go to my grave still able to say that.'

'They frightened you?' Auger asked.

'Once, I was close enough to one to look it in the face. It is an experience I hope never to repeat.'

Auger leaned closer to him. 'I can understand you being afraid of those children, Mister Altfeld. You were right to be afraid. They are very dangerous and they will kill to protect their interests. But we're not working with them. In fact, we're doing all in our power to stop them.'

'Then you are even more foolish than I suspected. If you had any sense you would leave this matter well alone.'

'We just need an address,' Floyd said. 'A lead. That's all we're asking for. Then you won't hear from us again.'

'But I will hear from them.'

'If you help us, then maybe we can stop them before they reach you,' Auger said.

Altfeld let out a small, henlike clucking sound, as if this was the least convincing reassurance he'd ever heard.

'At least tell us where the production took place,' Floyd said.

'I will tell you nothing. If you have found your way to me, I am sure you are capable of continuing your investigation without my assistance.'

Floyd found some strength he didn't know he had and hauled Altfeld even higher, lifting his collar free of the railing. He moved his grip down the buttons of his raincoat until he had the man by the waist and then levered him higher, until his head and upper body were leaning back over the railings and the sheer drop into the enclosure.

Altfeld let out a gasp of fright as his centre of gravity began to shift backwards.

'Tell me,' Floyd hissed, 'tell me or I'll push you over.'

Auger tried to pull Floyd away from Altfeld, but Floyd had had enough of lies and evasions. He didn't care how scared this man was; how innocent a part he had played in some larger conspiracy. All he cared about was Custine and whatever it was that had made Auger wake up screaming.

'Give me an address, you bastard. Give me an address or I'll feed you to the birds.'

Altfeld wheezed, as if suffering some kind of seizure. Between ragged breaths he gasped out, 'Fifteen . . . building fifteen.'

Floyd lowered him to the ground, leaving him sagging against the railings.

'That's a good start.'

By the time they returned to the hotel, it was too late to consider driving out to the industrial district where Kaspar Metals had been located. 'We'll take a cab out there first thing tomorrow,' Floyd said. 'Even if we don't find anyone around to talk to, there might be something left behind after the fire that we can use.'

'Altfeld was keeping something back,' Auger said. 'What, I don't know, but he wasn't telling us the whole story.'

'Do you think he knew anything about Silver Rain?'

'No, I'm pretty sure he didn't. Like I said, there simply isn't the manufacturing base available here to put it together. The metal spheres are part of something different.'

'But probably related,' Floyd said. 'Maybe we should pay Altfeld another visit, see if we can squeeze something else out of him.'

'We should leave him alone,' Auger said. 'He just seemed like a scared old man.'

'They always do.'

'Perhaps there's nothing else of use he could have told us,' she said, hoping to steer Floyd away from the idea of tormenting Altfeld further.

'Maybe there isn't, but someone has to know more. Altfeld might have handled the contracts, but whoever was doing the actual machining – the factory-floor work – must have had a better idea of what those spheres were for, if they were ever going to calibrate them correctly.'

'I don't know about that.'

'We'll go to the site of the factory first thing tomorrow and see what we can find out. If that opens up new lines of enquiry, we'll follow them. You said there was enough money to keep us in this hotel for a while?'

'Yes,' she said, 'but we can't stay here for ever. Or at least I can't. I need to be back in Paris by Tuesday. That means catching the overnight train tomorrow evening.'

'Why the hurry? We only arrived here this morning.'

'I just need to be back in Paris. Can we leave it at that?'

They went out to eat at seven, riding the S-bahn to Friedrichstrasse and then walking back along the banks of the Spree until they found a cluster of restaurants near the newly refurbished Reichstag. They ate a good curryworst, followed by chocolate cake, and listened to an old Bavarian couple trying to remember the names of all nineteen of their great-grandchildren.

Afterwards, Floyd and Auger walked the streets until Floyd heard live music coming from the window of a basement bar: guitar-based gypsy jazz of the kind he didn't hear enough of in Paris these days. He suggested to Auger that they spend half an hour in the bar before returning to the hotel. So down they went into the smoke and light of the music room, the sound suddenly much louder than it had been from the street. Floyd bought Auger a glass of white wine and a shot of brandy for himself. He sipped at his drink, appraising the band as fairly as he could. It was a quintet, with tenor saxophone, piano, double bass, drums and guitar. They were playing 'A Night in Tunisia'. The guitarist was good – an earnest young man with thick glasses and a surgeon's fingers – but the rest of them needed some work. At least they had a band, Floyd thought dolefully.

'Your sort of music?' he asked Auger.

'Not really,' she said, with a shy expression.

'They're all right. Guitarist has it down, but he shouldn't stick with these guys. They're going nowhere.'

'I'll take your word for it.'

'So you don't like jazz, or at least not this sort of jazz. That's all right. Takes all sorts to make a world.'

'Yes,' Auger said, nodding as if he had said something profound. 'It does, doesn't it?'

'So what do you like?'

'I have trouble with music,' she said.

'All music?'

'All music,' she affirmed. 'I'm tone-deaf. It just doesn't do anything for me.'

Floyd finished the brandy and ordered himself another. The band was now torturing 'Someone to Watch Over Me'. Cigarette smoke hung in the air in frozen coils, like a crazy, cloudy sunset in monochrome. 'Susan White was the same,' he said.

'The same as what?'

'Blanchard said he never caught her listening to music.'

'It's not a crime,' Auger replied. 'And how did he know what she got up to in her spare time? He can't have followed her everywhere.'

'She had a wireless in her room, and a phonograph,' Floyd said, 'but no one ever heard her listening to music on either of them.'

'Don't make a big deal out of it,' Auger said. 'All I said was that *I'm* tone-deaf. I don't know everything about Susan White.'

'Let's get out of here,' said Floyd, slamming down his empty glass. 'The smoke's making my eyes water and I wouldn't want anyone to think that the music or the company had anything to do with it.'

They took the train back to the hotel and said a polite goodnight. Floyd took the couch, lying down in his shirt and trousers with a spare blanket for warmth. He couldn't sleep. The plumbing played a metallic symphony until three in the morning. Through a gap in the curtains he watched neon numerals flicker on and off at the base of the Everest statue and thought of Auger asleep, and how little he knew about her, and how much more he wanted to know.

TWENTY-THREE

The car plodded along pot-holed roads, jinking across buckled railway tracks and passing under spindly overhead structures supporting conveyor belts and pipes for chemicals.

'Ask him to slow down,' Floyd said, tapping the taxi driver on the shoulder. 'I think that's a sign over there.'

Auger relayed the request, then peered at the tilted wooden board Floyd had indicated, which was almost lost behind a screen of tall grass. 'Magnolia Strasse. How appropriate.'

'This is Kaspar Metal's address?'

'What's left of it should be here,' she confirmed.

Beyond a broken-down wooden fence, a steam-driven demolition crane attended to the destruction of a low red-brick factory building with a wrecking ball, swinging it through the one remaining wall in a series of gentle arcs. Although there were still a few buildings standing, the spaces between them were littered with piles of brick, shattered concrete and twisted metal.

'If there was a steelworks here,' Floyd said, 'then someone's doing a swell job of hiding it.'

The taxi driver kept the engine ticking over while they got out and stood on the only patch of dry ground amidst an obstacle course of mud and puddles. It was bitterly cold, a persistent chemical dampness permeating the air. Auger wore black trousers and a narrow-waisted black leather coat that fell to her knees. The night before, in the hotel room, she had tried to snap the heels from her shoes, but without success.

'See if you can sweet-talk the driver into waiting for fifteen minutes,' Floyd said. 'We still need to check whether anybody left anything useful behind.'

Auger leaned into the driver's window and opened her mouth to talk. She got her message across, but the words didn't come with the expected fluency. Where yesterday there had been a gleaming linguistic machine, spitting out elegant, syntactically rich sentences, now there was a rusting contraption that creaked and groaned with the effort of every word. This worried her: if her German was crumbling now, what was going to be next?

'He'll stay,' she said, when the driver finally acquiesced.

'He took some persuading.'

'My German's a bit rusty this morning. That didn't help.'

They picked their way over dry, weed-infested ground to a gap in the fence. Two planks had fallen away, leaving a hole just wide enough for them to pass through. Floyd went first, holding back the high grass on the other side until Auger joined him.

'This is awful,' Auger said. 'There's so much damage that it's difficult to imagine a factory ever being here. The only proof we have that there was is that letter Susan White received.'

'When was the letter sent?'

'Remember the train ticket she booked but didn't use? She was just about to come here when she was murdered. The letter was sent only a month or so before that.'

'Look at the ground here,' Floyd said. 'No weeds anywhere – they haven't had time to break through the concrete yet.'

'Arson?'

'Difficult to know for sure, but I'm guessing so. The timing's too convenient otherwise.'

In the middle distance, the steam-driven crane they had seen earlier was plodding over to another condemned building, its demolition ball swinging as it crunched across rubble and concrete. A pair of green bulldozers had joined it, belching acrid smoke from their diesel engines. The operators were masked and goggled, sunk down in oilskins.

Auger looked around for a place to start searching for clues. 'Let's check out those buildings, see if we can find number fifteen,' Auger said.

'We don't have much time,' Floyd warned.

They crossed the ruins of the factory complex until they reached the remaining cluster of buildings. The shells of the buildings looked threatening and skulllike, their roofs and upper ceilings already removed so that the iron-grey sky was visible through the gaps and cracks in the fire-damaged structures. Auger had never much enjoyed trespassing, even when such things had been part of childhood initiation rites and carried little risk of serious punishment. She enjoyed it even less now.

'Number fifteen,' Floyd said, pointing to a barely readable metal plaque hanging at an angle on one wall. 'Looks like the threat of the penguins did the trick. I must remember that the next time I have to put the squeeze on someone.'

They found an open door nearby. Inside the building it was dark, since most of the ceiling was still in place above the ground-floor entrance.

'Watch your step, Verity.'

'I'm watching it,' Auger said. 'Here, take this.' She handed Floyd the automatic.

'If there's only one gun between us, I think you should keep it,' Floyd said. 'They make me nervous. I cling to the irrational idea that if I don't carry a gun, I won't find myself in a position where I need one.'

'You're in that position now. Take the automatic.'

'What about you?'

Auger reached into her handbag and pulled out the weapon that she had taken from the war baby in the tunnel at Cardinal Lemoine. 'I have this gun,' she said.

'I meant a real one,' Floyd said, regarding the strange lines of the weapon dubiously. But he didn't push the point: by now he had realised that Auger wasn't playing a game.

'Be careful, Floyd. These people are willing to kill.'

'That much I do know.'

'And if you see a child?'

Floyd looked back at her, the whites of his eyes bright in the darkness. 'You want me to start shooting children now?'

'It won't be a child.'

'I'll shoot to wound. Beyond that, I'm not making any promises.'

Auger looked back just before she followed Floyd inside. The demolition machines were making short work of a nondescript brick building, taking turns to rip at its carcass like hunger-crazed wolves. As the bulldozers reversed and then rolled forward again to attack, their engines raged with a dim mechanical fury. The goggled operators seemed to be holding them back rather than driving them.

'Let's make this quick, Floyd. Those things seem to be getting closer.'

Auger stepped further into the building and spun around to cover the entrance, but there was no sign of anyone or anything following them. Once inside, she pressed a sleeve against her mouth and nose to screen the dust from entering her lungs. It took half a minute for her eyes to adjust to the gloom. Along two main walls, and forming an aisle down the middle, were three rows of heavy equipment clearly too bulky or too damaged to be worth removing. There were lathes and drills and several dozen objects Auger didn't recognise, but which appeared to be related to the same

304

business of metal finishing.

'At least this looks like the right place,' she said.

'Watch the flooring here,' Floyd said. 'I can see right through to the basement.'

Auger followed him, placing her feet exactly where Floyd had placed his. With each step, the floor creaked, dislodging dust and debris. A crow flew away from a window sill in a silent flurry of black. She watched it flap away into the sky, until it looked like a piece of burnt paper blowing in the wind.

'There's nothing here,' Auger said. 'No papers, no documentation. We're wasting our time.'

'We've still got ten minutes. You never know what we might find.' Floyd had reached the far end of the workshop, where the rectangle of a door was just visible against the blackened plaster of the walls. 'Let's see what's through here.'

'Careful, Floyd.' Her hand tightened on the war baby's weapon, its child-sized grip chafing against her palm.

Floyd had already pushed open the door and stepped through. She heard him cough. 'There are stairs here,' he said, 'going up and down. Want to toss a coin?'

She heard the muffled collapse of another building; the howl of racing diesel engines. The demolition equipment sounded even closer.

'Let's stay on this floor.'

'I don't think we'll find much above us,' Floyd speculated. 'The fire damage will probably be worse the higher up we go. But something might have survived downstairs.'

'We're not going downstairs.'

'You got that torch?' Floyd asked.

She followed him into the adjoining room. One set of concrete stairs rose up, leading to another dark, enclosed space, while a second set descended down into even more profound darkness.

Floyd took the torch from her and shone it down into the gloom.

'This is a very bad idea,' Auger said.

'That's great coming from a woman who likes to spend her time dodging trains in tunnels.'

'That was an act of necessity. This isn't.'

'Let's see what we find. Just a couple of minutes, all right? I didn't come all this way to turn around now.'

'I did.'

Floyd started descending, Auger close behind him. He played the torchlight ahead of him, the beam glancing off cracking walls. The stairs twisted through ninety degrees, then another ninety.

'There's another door here,' Floyd said, trying the handle. 'It feels as if it's locked.'

'That's it, then.' She sighed, disappointed and relieved in equal measure. 'We have to turn around.'

'Let me see if I can force it first. Hold the torch for a moment.'

She took it from him, wondering – for a fleeting instant – if she ought to use the gun to persuade Floyd to return to ground level.

'Make it quick,' Auger said. 'I'm really getting worried about those machines.'

The door budged with an iron scrape that made her wince. Floyd could not get it open fully, but soon there was a gap wide enough for them to squeeze through. The torchlight fell on his face. 'You want to stay here while I check it out? I'll be as quick as I can.'

'No,' she said. 'I'm sure I'll regret saying this, but I want to see whatever's in there for myself.'

Fans and spears of blue-grey light rammed through gaps in the ceiling above them. It was still difficult to see anything outside the torch beam, but the room seemed to be empty.

'See anything?' Auger asked. 'No? Good. Let's go.'

'There's a railing here,' Floyd said. 'It looks as if it runs right around the room.' He directed the torch beam towards the floor beyond the railing, revealing it to be much lower than Auger had been expecting. They had emerged on to a balcony that ran around the upper level of a two-storey chamber. Picked out in random splashes of light entering through the ceiling, something huge and black and roughly spherical squatted in the middle of the floor.

'Voilà,' Floyd said. 'One metal sphere, for the use of.'

'Let me see.'

She took the torch and shone it on to the sphere. Behind her, she was vaguely aware of Floyd shoving the door closed again, but ignored the distraction. The sphere was surrounded by many other pieces of metal and machinery, including a kind of frame or harness from which it appeared to be suspended.

'Is that what your dear departed sister was interested in?' Floyd asked, with heavy sarcasm, stepping up behind her again.

'Yes,' Auger said, ignoring his tone. 'What I don't understand is what it's doing here. The three spheres were supposed to be shipped out to three different addresses.'

'I thought one of them was in Berlin.'

'It was,' Auger said. 'But it still had to be moved from the factory to somewhere else in the city.'

Gently, Floyd took the torch back. 'Now at least you know the things exist.'

'Hey – where are you going?'

'There's a ladder down to the floor. I want to take a closer look at that thing.'

'We should be getting back to the taxi.' But even as she spoke, she found herself drawn to follow him down to the floor of the underground room.

Close up, the sphere – which was indeed nearly three metres wide, she judged – conveyed a sense of massive solidity even though it could just as easily have been hollow. The surface was smooth in places, irregular in others, and there was a visible crack running from one pole to the other. It hung from the cradle on a single cable, attached to a metal eye welded at the top of the sphere. Coating the upper surface of the sphere was a talcum of grey dust, like icing sugar on a pudding. In another corner of the room – hidden until they descended from the balcony – was a large upright cylinder of the kind used to hold pressurised gases, while in another was a high-sided drum-shaped enclosure about three metres across, like an armoured paddling pool. Like the sphere, both items were covered with ash and dust.

Auger touched the metal sphere. It was cold and rough beneath her fingers and, despite its apparent mass, the sphere moved slightly under the pressure from her hand.

'So what do you suppose this was?' Floyd asked.

'The letter said it was for an artistic installation,' Auger said. 'Obviously, that was a cover story – the specification was too exact for that. My guess is that the company was being asked to manufacture very precise components for a bigger machine.'

'A secret weapon?'

'Something like that.'

'But what kind of secret weapon can you make out of a gigantic metal ball?'

'Three gigantic metal balls, remember,' Auger said, 'separated by hundreds of kilometres. There has to be a reason for that, as well.'

'Three secret weapons, then.' He walked away from the sphere and started rummaging through the debris-covered heaps of equipment on the nearest set of workbenches, throwing things to the floor with the casual ease of a burglar. Metal crashed and glass shattered. After a moment, Auger swore under her breath and joined in the reckless process, looking for anything, no matter how insubstantial, that might offer a lead.

'Or just one secret weapon,' she said, 'but so huge that it spreads across half of Europe.'

'It doesn't make any sense.'

'No,' she said, shaking her head. 'It doesn't. But this is it, Floyd. This is what it was worth killing people to protect. Not just the ones we know about, but all the other people who've probably had to die while all this has been planned, financed and put together.'

'Why did they leave it here, then?'

She pushed a battered old toolkit to the floor. It clattered thrillingly, spilling shiny spanners and wrenches from its innards. 'I don't think this sphere is the real thing.'

'It looks real enough to me.'

'I mean, I don't think this was ever intended to be delivered to the client. It's too crudely finished, and something obviously went wrong during the casting process. I'm not even sure this is aluminium or that aluminium–copper alloy Altfeld mentioned. It could just as easily be cast iron.'

'You're thinking this was a dry run?'

'Yes. A try-out for the final set, so they could practise the casting and machining, and work out how to move it around afterwards.' She shrugged. 'Or maybe it's one that went wrong and had to be abandoned during the finishing process. It doesn't really matter. What does is that it got left behind.'

'So whoever torched this factory, or arranged for its demolition . . .'

Even as he said the word, Auger heard the machines take apart another wall or floor, the roar of their engines sounding even closer and even more bestial.

'I don't think they had any idea this basement existed. They knew that the three main castings had been finished and delivered. My guess is that they burnt down the factory afterwards to hide any evidence of what had been made. But they never thought there might be a fourth sphere, still here.'

'Then we need to search the place really thoroughly,' Floyd said. 'If they missed this, there's no telling what else they left behind.'

'You're right,' Auger said. She felt her heart beating faster. She knew that she was much closer to an answer now than she had ever been. She could almost feel it, lurking at the back of her mind like a gift-wrapped present. 'You're right, and it would make sense to search this room with a fine-tooth comb. But we're not going to. We're leaving now, while we still can.'

'Just five minutes more,' Floyd said. 'Somewhere in here there might be a record of the shipping addresses for the finished spheres.'

'Long shot, Wendell.'

'They were careless, or in a hurry, or they'd never have left this down here in the first place.'

'Because they thought someone was on to them?'

'Who are we dealing with, Verity? Are you ready to tell me yet?'

'We're dealing with very bad people,' she said. 'Isn't that enough for you?'

'That depends on who's defining "bad".' Floyd tapped the barrel of the automatic against the metal sphere. It made a dull clank. 'Well, I guess Basso was right after all. It definitely wasn't meant to be a bell.'

'Basso?'

'A metalworker contact of mine. I showed him the sketch of the blueprint from Susan's things. He said it might be a plan for a bell. He meant diving bell. I thought he meant the kind you ring.'

Auger heard the roar of the demolition machines again, the crunch of stone and brick beneath their caterpillar treads.

'I don't think either kind of bell would be something people had to die to protect,' she said. 'Besides – it's broken.'

Floyd tapped the gun against the sphere again, narrowing his eyes as he listened for reverberations. He moved around the object and struck it again.

'You mean if it wasn't broken, it might sound prettier?' he said.

'Do it again.'

'Do what again?'

'Knock the metal, the way you just did.'

'I was only trying to see if it was really solid. I still like my idea that it might be an atomic bomb.'

'It's not an atomic bomb. Knock it again.'

Floyd tapped the automatic against the sphere, moving from spot to spot. 'It rings,' he said, 'but the sound is all off, like a cracked bell.'

'That's because it *is* cracked. But if it wasn't, it'd ring with a much purer note, don't you think?'

Floyd lowered the gun. 'I guess so. If it matters.'

'I think it matters a lot. I think ringing is exactly what these spheres are meant to do. I think you were right and Basso was wrong.'

TWENTY-FOUR

Floyd looked at her with half a smile. 'Ringing?'

'Ringing.'

'And that's worth at least two murders, and maybe a lot more than that? If you're going to build a bell, build a goddamned bell.'

'They're not goddamned bells,' she said.

Floyd pointed the butt of the automatic in her direction. 'For a nice girl from Dakota, you've sure developed a foul mouth all of a sudden.'

'You think this is foul,' Auger said, 'you should stick around a while.'

'You know, you can knock that enigmatic act off any time you like. I've about had it up to here.'

He had just finished speaking when there was a crash of collapsing masonry, shaking the entire room. Fist-sized shards of cement dropped from the ceiling, filling the air with powdery grey dust. Auger coughed, shielding her eyes and mouth with her hand.

'That sounded close,' she said. 'Maybe they're already demolishing part of building fifteen. We've got more than we expected: let's get out before we're buried alive.'

'For once I couldn't agree more.'

They climbed the ladder back to the balcony level, Floyd leading. The building shook again, more of the ceiling coming loose. A gap as wide as a man had appeared in it, revealing severed wood and concrete, pipes and electrical wires. Motors roared overhead, revving and ebbing as the bulldozers surged back and forth. The cast-metal plinth of a lathe or a drill leaned precariously over the hole.

'Move,' Auger hissed.

They ran around the balcony until they reached the door into the stairwell. Floyd pushed on it, trying to coax it open. When it refused to yield, he leaned his entire bulk against it and pushed until his face was a mask of effort, but the door showed no sign of moving.

'It's stuck,' he said, gasping for breath.

'It can't be stuck,' Auger said. 'We just came through it.'

'It was stiff, though. The whole frame must have subsided. I can't get it open.'

'Why did you ever close it?'

'I wanted to hear if anyone came after us. I figured they wouldn't be able to get the door open without making a sound.'

'I bet you're regretting that particular bright idea now, aren't you?'

Floyd gave the door one last shove, but it was obvious that even their combined efforts would not be enough to get it open. 'I can see you're the kind of person who likes to say "I told you so",' he said.

'Only when people deserve it. Now what are we going to do?'

'Find another way out of this building, that's what.'

'There isn't one.'

'Down the ladder again,' Floyd said. 'Our only hope is that there may be doors at the other end of the room.'

She looked at him dubiously. 'And if there are, do you think we stand any more chance of getting them open?'

'Until we've tried, we won't know.'

They hurried down to the floor, skirting around the sphere and the gas tank to reach the far end of the room. There were indeed doors there, twice as high as Floyd and wide enough to drive a truck through. The doors were obviously meant to slide back into the walls on either side, but when Floyd tried to part them, they remained as resolutely fixed as the door to the stairwell. Again he screwed up his face in determination and again the doors stayed put.

'I think they must be locked from the other side,' he said, between heavy, panting breaths.

'Then we're really up shit creek without a paddle, aren't we?'

Floyd looked at her, somewhat stunned by her choice of words despite the desperateness of their situation. 'Did you really just say that?'

'I'm a little tense,' she said defensively.

'Well,' Floyd said, 'now that you mention it, a paddle would actually be quite useful. Or better still a crowbar.'

'What?'

'I think I can see a gap between these doors. If we could wedge something into it, we might be able to prise them open enough to squeeze through.'

'Into another underground room?'

'No – I think I can see daylight. Look around. There's got to be something we can use.'

There was another violent crash. With a drawn-out groan, the plinth and lathe finally slid through the hole in the ceiling, dragging several tons of masonry and metal with them. The mass of twisted metal hung above them, suspended by a few pipes and wires that had become wrapped around it.

It was directly over the sphere.

'That thing's not going to stay up there much longer,' Auger said.

'So let's get out of here before it falls. You check the left side, I'll check the right. Any piece of metal will do.'

Auger started searching her side of the room, rummaging through the mess they had already created.

'And be quick!' Floyd shouted.

Auger's hands fell on a piece of perforated metal framing. It was broken at one end, tapered to just the right shape to fit between the doors. 'Wendell! I've got something.' She held the makeshift tool up for inspection.

'Attagirl. That'll do nicely.'

She jogged back to Floyd as fast as her heels would allow and passed the piece of metal to him. He hefted it, like a hunter evaluating a new spear.

'Hurry,' Auger said.

He slipped the sharp end into the fine crack between the two doors and started levering, applying his full weight to the task. The huge doors creaked and groaned. Simultaneously, the room shook and the hanging lathe slipped down a good half-metre before jerking to a halt again, suspended even more improbably.

'It's working,' Floyd said. 'I think it's going—'

Something gave a metallic crack and the doors sprang apart by a thumb's width. A fan of dreary daylight sliced the room in two.

'That's a good start,' Auger said. 'Now the rest.'

'I'm working on it.' Floyd renewed his struggle, adjusting the position of his feet to optimise his bracing position. 'But I'm not sure how long this thing is going to last. See if you can't rustle up another one, in case this one buckles.'

She stood rooted to the spot, desperate to slip through the crack.

'Verity! Get searching!'

Stumbling on her heels, she began to search the other side of the room. She felt her trousers rip against sharp metal and something cut into her knee. Tripping, she fell forward, her hand reaching out for support. Miraculously it closed around an iron bar.

Picking herself up, barely registering the pain in her leg, she hefted the new prize. 'Got something!'

'Bring it here. I think this boy's about to—'

The fan of light widened. The gap in the door was now big enough to push a face through.

Auger started making her way back to the double doors just as the room shook again, more violently than ever before. She halted in her tracks and looked up with a horrid sense of inevitability. The plinth and lathe eased through their flimsy restraints with a final squeal of freedom. Untethered, the equipment dropped through the air and landed on the upper surface of the sphere's support harness, before sliding off and falling to one side with a deafening chime of metal on metal.

The sphere rocked, but for a moment nothing more happened. Auger forced herself to move again, gripping the iron bar.

Then she stopped and looked at the sphere again. There was a whisking, whipping sound as the guy line's many constituent threads began to break, one by one. She only had an instant to register this before the entire line snapped, whiplashing against the harness with appalling force.

The sphere dropped.

It hit the floor and cracked wide open along its casting flaw like a piece of ripe fruit. Distorted now, not even approximately spherical, it still managed to roll, picking up momentum with each rotation.

Auger followed its trajectory with horror: it was rolling towards the double doors, and Floyd. She opened her mouth to scream something – some useless warning, as if Floyd could possibly not have seen what was happening – but by then it was far, far too late. The mangled sphere trundled into the double doors, forcing them open and wedging itself in the gap. The metal emitted a horrible noise as it buckled. It almost sounded like a human scream, cut off with sickening swiftness.

'No . . .' Auger breathed.

Everything was suddenly very quiet. Even the demolition machines had stopped. She let go of the bar and heard it clatter to the ground in some distant corner of the universe. Auger slowed as she neared the doors, trying not to think about what she was going to find.

Floyd was flat on the ground, lying perfectly still. His face was turned away from her, bright blood matting his scalp. His hat had rolled away into a corner.

'No,' Auger said. 'Don't be dead. *Please* don't be dead. You had no business being here. You didn't have to get involved.'

His body had fallen inside the doors, to one side of the sphere's path, and it didn't look as if it had rolled over any part of him. She took his head in her hands, very gently, and turned it so that she could see his eyes. They were closed, as if he had fallen asleep. His mouth was slightly open and his chest was rising and falling, but with a worrying irregularity, as if each breath was a struggle.

'Stay with me,' Auger said. 'Don't go dying on me, not now that we've come this far. Now that we've actually started to get somewhere. Now that I've actually started to *like* you.' She squeezed his head, her hands wet with his blood. 'Are you listening to me, Wendell? Wake up, you sad excuse for a detective. Wake the fuck up and talk to me!'

Laying his head gently on the floor, she stood, appraising the gap that the sphere had made in the doors. She could squeeze through it without difficulty, but there was no way she was going to leave Floyd to be buried alive. Sitting back on her haunches, she put an arm around his shoulders and slid another beneath his back and, groaning with the effort, she managed to arrange Floyd into a sitting position, balanced against the right-hand sliding door. His head lolled on to his chest, his eyes still closed.

Leaving Floyd where he was, with his back to the door, she scrambled over the sphere and through the gap it had made as it wedged itself between the doors, catching an elbow on the edge of the door as she went through. Beyond, just as Floyd had predicted, was a sloping ramp leading up to ground level. The air swirled with the dust of collapsed buildings.

She turned back to Floyd, reaching through the gap and grabbing him under the armpits. 'Come on,' she said.

Gritting her teeth with the effort, she managed to drag Floyd off the floor, so that he was halfway between a standing and a sitting position, but she could not lift him high enough to pull him through the gap. Exhausted, her arms feeling as if they were about to pop from their sockets, she fell back down on to the concrete of the ramp. Every instinct told her to get away now, before the machines caused the entire structure to cave in.

She found some last gasp of strength. This time she managed to get his head and shoulders to the level of the gap. His shirt ripped on the edge of the ruined door as she felt his weight shifting towards her, and then suddenly he was falling through the gap, on to the concrete ramp. He landed in an undignified sprawl, arms and legs tangled, face squashed against the ground, his mouth open like a drunkard's.

Carefully rolling him over, she knelt beside him and took his face in her hands, gently smoothing his hair back from his cheeks and forehead.

Floyd groaned and opened his eyes. He took a deep breath and wiped his tongue across his lips. 'What did I do to deserve this?'

'Thank God. You're all right.'

'All right? I've got a headache you could park the Hindenburg in.'

314

'For a moment back there I thought you were dead.'

'No such luck.'

'Don't say that, Wendell. I really meant it. I was worried sick.'

He touched the back of his head and came away with a wet palm. 'I guess I took a hit in there. Was it worth it?'

Still cradling his head, she drew his face towards hers and lowered her own to meet his, and kissed him. He tasted of dust and dirt. But she held the kiss, and when she moved to pull away, Floyd gently stopped her.

'It was worth it,' she said.

'I guess it must have been.'

She pulled away now, suddenly feeling awkward and silly. Floyd hadn't rejected her, but she felt as if she had made a terrible misjudgement. She looked down and willed the ground to open up.

'I'm sorry,' she said. 'I don't know—'

Floyd raised a hand, tangling his fingers in her hair, and pulled her in again. 'Don't apologise,' he said.

'I've made a fool of myself.'

'No,' he said. 'You haven't. I think you're wonderful. The only thing I can't understand is what a nice girl like you would ever see in a crumpled old has-been like me.'

'You're not a has-been, Wendell. Crumpled, maybe. And you could lose a bit of weight. But you're a good man who believes in finishing a job once you've started it. And you care enough about your friends to put your own life in danger trying to help them. This may come as a shock, but there aren't that many people like you around.'

'OK, but what about my good points?'

'Don't push your luck, soldier.' She eased back from him. 'You think you can stand? We need to leave here before we get into any more trouble. I'm still worried about your head.'

'I'll survive,' Floyd said. 'I'm a private detective. If I don't get clouted on the head at least once a week, I'm not doing my job properly.'

He got to his feet, wobbling a little, but able to make his way unassisted.

'We'll still need to get you checked out,' Auger said.

'I'll last until we're back in Paris,' Floyd replied. He touched the back of his head again, but the bleeding had slowed. 'Verity – there's one thing I need to say.'

'Go ahead, Wendell.'

'Now that we've broken the ice a bit . . .'

'Yes?'

'From now on I'd really like it if you just called me Floyd.'

'I will,' she said. 'On one strict condition.'

'Which is?'

'You call me Auger. Back home, only my ex-husband calls me Verity.'

'You sure about that, Auger?'

'Damn sure, Floyd.' She helped Floyd up the gentle slope of the ramp, towards level ground. 'You start seeing double, or feeling nauseous – I want to hear about it, all right?'

'You'll be the first to get the news. In the meantime, do you want to tell me what it is you figured out down there?'

'I didn't figure out anything.'

'But when I rang the bell, it . . . rang a bell for you, didn't it?'

'I don't know,' she said, shaking her head. 'I thought for a minute . . .'

'Thought what?' he prompted, as her voice trailed off.

'The spheres are designed to ring. I'm pretty sure of that. The shape, and the specified accuracy of the machining, and the way they are meant to be suspended . . . everything points to the same conclusion. But they're not intended to be rung like a bell. Nothing strikes them.'

'Then what makes them ring?'

'In my work,' Auger told him, 'in the job I did before I got involved in this mess, we worked with a lot of sensitive equipment. I'm actually an archaeologist, for what it's worth.'

'Aren't archaeologists supposed to be greying spinsters with half-moon glasses who never get to see daylight?'

'Not the kind I hang out with,' Auger said. 'We get our hands dirty.'

'With this sensitive equipment?'

'Thing is, in order to make it sensitive, we have to run a lot of it at very cold temperatures. We cool it down, *really* cold, so that it can work better.'

'And when Altfeld mentioned cooling requirements—'

'I started wondering if the spheres were part of some kind of detection apparatus, yes.' Auger bit her lip, focusing her thoughts. 'And now I think I know what it is.'

'So tell me,' Floyd said.

'The spheres form a single machine, as wide as Europe, one part of it in Paris, one part somewhere in Berlin, another somewhere in Milan. But they're really all part of the same instrument. It simply has to be that big for it to work.'

'And this instrument is what, exactly?'

'An antenna,' she said, 'just like the one on a wireless. Only it isn't radio waves it's set up to detect. It's gravity.'

'And you figured all that out just by looking at that sphere?'

'No. I'm good, but I'm not that good. We use tools for measuring gravity in my work as well. Sophisticated tools for peering through the ground, picking up the density changes caused by buried structures. Needless to say, we had to study the theory of how these things work when we were being schooled up, and that meant going right back to the early history of gravity-wave detection.'

'Maybe I don't read the right newspapers,' Floyd said, 'but I didn't know there was a history of gravity-wave detection.'

'There's definitely a history,' Auger said, 'but it isn't your fault that you don't know about it.'

They had reached ground level. The ramp emerged in a narrow canyon formed by two long rows of partially demolished buildings, still standing to their first or second storeys. Pipes, conveyors, conduits and catwalks threaded the space over their heads.

'Tell me what I need to know.'

'This isn't going to be easy for you to follow, Floyd.'

'It'll take my mind off my headache.'

'Then I have to tell you about space-time. You ready for this?'

'Hit me,' he said.

'There's an old saying amongst students of gravity: matter tells space-time how to bend; space-time tells matter how to move.'

'It's suddenly a *lot* clearer.'

'The point is that everything we see is embedded in space-time. You can think of it as a kind of rubbery fluid, like half-set jelly. And since everything has a mass of some kind, everything distorts that fluid to one degree or another, stretching and compressing it. That distortion is what we experience as gravity. The Earth's mass pulls space-time in around it, and the distortion in space-time around the Earth makes things fall towards the planet, or orbit around it if they have the right speed.'

'Like Newton's apple?'

'You're hanging in there, Floyd. That's good. Now let's move up a notch. The Sun pulls its own blanket of space-time around it, and that tells the Earth and all the other planets how to move around the Sun.'

'And the Sun?'

'Follows a path in space-time dictated by the gravitational distortion of the entire galaxy.'

'And the galaxy? No, don't answer that. I get the picture.'

'You get *half* the picture,' Auger said. 'What we've talked about so far is a permanent bending of space-time around a massive object. But there are other ways to bend space-time. Imagine two stars swinging around each other, like waltzers. You got that?'

'Sure. I'm admiring the view as we speak.'

'Make those stars super-massive and super-dense. Make them whip around each other like dervishes, spiralling in towards an eventual collision. Now you've got yourself a pretty fierce source of gravity waves. They're sending out a ripple, like a steady note from a musical instrument.'

'I thought you didn't like music.'

'I don't,' she said, 'but I can recognise a useful analogy when it comes along.'

'OK – so two stars circling around each other will give you a gravity wave.'

'There are other mechanisms for producing such a wave, but the point is that there are a lot of binary stars out there: a lot of potential gravity-wave sources dotted around the sky. And they all have a unique note, a unique signature.'

'So if I pick up a tone—'

'You can work out exactly where it originated.'

'Like knowing the flash pattern of a lighthouse?'

'Exactly that,' Auger said. 'But now comes the hard part. Somehow you have to measure those waves. Gravity is already the weakest force in the universe, even before you start worrying about measuring microscopic changes in its strength. It's like trying to hear someone whispering on the other side of the ocean.'

'So how can you do it?'

She was about to tell him when movement from above caught her eye: a glint of polished metal against the low grey sky. There was just enough time to register the small figure crouched on one of the overhead pipes, and the nasty little weapon it clutched in one clawlike hand.

'Floyd . . .' she started to say.

The gun fired, making a rapid, high-pitched laughing sound. Auger felt a sudden warm pain in her right shoulder, and then she was on the ground and the pain became worse. She was still looking up. The child stood balanced on the pipe, seemingly unfazed by vertigo. It held the gun aloft, releasing a sleek sickle-shaped clip from the grip and inserting another.

Floyd took out the automatic she'd given him. He thumbed off the safety catch and took a two-handed stance, squinting against the sky.

'Shoot the fucker,' Auger said, grimacing against the pain.

Floyd fired. The gun jerked in his hand, the bullet winging off the underside of the pipe. The child began to lower its own weapon, taking careful aim.

Floyd emptied another two slugs into the air. This time they didn't hit the pipe.

The war baby toppled from its perch, shrieking as it dropped to the ground. Its thin little arms and legs wheeled as it fell. It hit the ground, bouncing once, and then lay quite still.

It was a boy.

Floyd spun around, scanning the buildings for evidence of more children. Auger pushed herself up on her good elbow, and then touched the wound in her shoulder. She pulled her fingers away. There was blood on the tips, but not as much as she had expected. It still felt as if someone was twisting a hot iron poker around in her shoulder. She reached around the back and felt more wetness under her shoulder blade.

'I think that was the only one,' Floyd said, crouching over her.

'Is it dead?'

'Dying.'

'I need to talk to it,' she said.

'Hold it right there,' Floyd said softly. 'You've just been shot, kid. There are other priorities just now.'

'There's an exit wound,' she said. 'The bullet went through me.'

'You don't know how many went in, or whether they fragmented. You need help, and you need it fast.'

She pushed herself up and then struggled to her feet, using her good arm for leverage. The war baby lay where it had fallen, quietly gurgling in a pool of its own blood, its head twisted towards them. The eyes were still open, looking their way.

'It's the same boy,' she said. 'The one that stabbed the waiter in Gare du Nord.'

'Maybe.'

'I got a good look at its face,' she said. 'I know it's the same one. It must have followed us here.'

She hobbled over to the boy and kicked its gun away. The head moved, swivelling around to keep her in view. The mouth lolled open in a stupefied grin and blood drooled from the smoke-grey lips. The black tongue moved, as if trying to form words.

Auger pressed her foot down on the war baby's neck. She was glad she hadn't managed to snap the heels off her shoes now.

'Talk to me,' she said. 'Talk to me and tell me what the *fuck* you are doing building a resonant gravitational wave antenna in nineteen fifty-nine, and what it has to do with Silver Rain.'

The black tongue oozed and wriggled like a captive maggot. The child made a liquid gurgling noise.

'Maybe if you took your shoe off its neck,' Floyd suggested.

Auger reached down and picked up the war baby's weapon. She reminded herself that it had a full clip and that the baby had been ready to use it just before it had fallen from the pipe.

'I want answers, you shrivelled-up piece of shit. I want to know why Susan and the others had to die. I want to know what you fuckers intend to do with Silver Rain.'

'It's too late,' the child said, forcing the words out between gurgles of blood and bile. 'Much too late.'

'Yeah? Then why are you in such a hurry to stop anyone getting too close to this shit?'

'It's the right thing to do, Verity. You know it in your heart.' The child coughed, spitting blood in her face. 'These people shouldn't exist. They're just three billion dots in a photograph. Dots, Verity. That's all they are. Pull away and they blur into one amorphous mass.'

She thought of her dream, of the Silver Rain falling on to the Champs-Elysées. Of the beautiful people picking themselves up and thinking that life was about to go on, and being so terribly wrong. She remembered trying to warn them. She remembered the little drummer boy stepping through the bones.

Dizziness washed over her. She suddenly felt very cold and very weak.

Auger squeezed the trigger and did something abominable to the war baby.

Then she slumped to her knees and was sick.

Floyd gently drew her to her feet and steered her away from the bloody mess she had made.

'It wasn't a child,' she said. 'It was a thing, a weapon.'

'You don't have to convince me. Now let's get out of here before those shots attract the wrong kind of attention. We need to get you to a hospital.'

'No,' she said. 'You need to get me to Paris. That's all that matters.'

TWENTY-FIVE

Floyd stood in a public telephone kiosk just outside Gare du Nord. It was Tuesday morning and his head didn't feel any better. With both of them injured, but not wanting to have to deal with helpful or inquisitive strangers, the train journey back from Berlin had been a long and wearying one. There had been tense moments while their documents were inspected, neither of them daring to say a word until the officials had moved on. Floyd doubted that his own injuries were any cause for concern, but he was extremely worried about Auger. He'd left her in the waiting room, bandaged and drowsy, but still adamant that she didn't want to be taken to hospital.

'Maillol,' a man said on the other end of the line.

'Inspector? It's Wendell Floyd. Can we talk?'

'Of course we can,' Maillol said. 'As a matter of fact, you're just the man I wanted to speak to. Where have you been, Floyd? No one seemed to know where you'd gone.'

'Germany, monsieur. I'm back in Paris now. But I don't have much money and I'm calling from a public telephone.'

'Why not use the telephone in your office?'

'I figured it might not be safe.'

'Sensible boy,' Maillol said approvingly. 'Well, shall I start? I'll be quick about it. You're aware of my anti-bootlegging operation in Montrouge, aren't you? As it happens, we've turned up something interesting: a floater.'

'A floater, monsieur?'

'A body, Floyd, floating face-down in a flooded basement in the same warehouse complex where we found the illegal pressing plant. Identification revealed the individual to be a Monsieur Rivaud. Forensics say he can't have been in the water for more than three or four days.'

'It's early, monsieur, and I haven't had much sleep, but I don't think I know that name.'

'That's odd, Floyd, because you seem to have met the gentleman. He had one of your business cards on him.'

'Still doesn't mean I know him.'

'He also had a key that we traced back to Monsieur Blanchard's building on rue des Peupliers. Rivaud was one of his tenants.'

'Wait,' Floyd said. 'He wouldn't be one of the tenants on the second floor, would he?'

'So you do remember him.'

'I never met him. Custine interviewed him: that's how he came by the business card. When I went round to make follow-up enquiries, no one was home.'

'Probably because the young man was dead.'

Floyd closed his eyes. Just what the case needed: another death, no matter how peripheral it might be. 'Cause of death?'

'Drowning. It could be accidental: he might have stumbled and fallen into the flooded basement. On the other hand, Forensics turned up some curious abrasions on the man's neck. They look like finger marks, as if someone had held his head underwater.'

'Open and shut, in that case – homicide by drowning.'

'Except,' Maillol said, 'the finger marks were very small.'

'Let me guess: they were the right size for a child.'

'A child with long fingernails, yes. Which of course doesn't make any sense—'

'Except I already told you there are some bad children associated with this case.'

'And we have that stabbing in Gare du Nord, of course. We still haven't turned up the boy the witnesses saw.'

'You probably won't,' Floyd said.

'Do you know something about that incident?'

Floyd pulled a fresh toothpick from his shirt pocket and slipped it into his mouth. 'Of course not, monsieur,' he said. 'I just meant to say . . . the child's probably well away by now.'

Maillol said nothing for ten or twenty seconds. Floyd heard his breathing above the muted background chatter of typewriters and barked orders.

'I'm sure you're right,' Maillol said. 'But you see the problem from my point of view. I had no interest in the rue des Peupliers case beyond my desire to do what I could for Custine. But there was no connection between those two deaths and the goings-on in Montrouge.'

'And now?'

'Now I have a connection, and it doesn't make any sense. What was your man Rivaud doing nosing around in Montrouge?'

'I have no idea,' Floyd said.

'This is a loose end,' Maillol said. 'I don't like loose ends.'

'I don't like them either, monsieur, but I still have no idea what Rivaud was doing there. As I said, I never even spoke to the man.'

'Then perhaps if I had a word with Custine?'

'Actually,' Floyd said, 'Custine's the reason I'm calling.'

'Has he been in touch again?'

'Of course we've been in touch. What else would you expect? He's my friend and I know he's innocent.'

'Very good, Floyd. I'd be disappointed if you said anything different.'

'I can't tell you where to reach Custine. You understand that, don't you?'

'Of course.'

'But I think I'm close to finding your suspect. You're just not going to like it very much when I hand one of them over.'

'One of them?'

Floyd pushed coinage into the iron belly of the payphone. 'Custine didn't kill Blanchard. One of those children did. You spoke to the witnesses in Gare du Nord. You know how they described that boy.'

'Including one witness who spoke French with a pronounced American accent.'

'The child was real, monsieur. There are several of them, boys and girls, but up close they don't look like children at all. If I can deliver one of these monsters to you, I'll have kept my end of the deal, won't I?'

'We didn't *have* a deal, Floyd.'

'Don't let me down, monsieur. I'm trying to retain some lingering shred of respect for the authority in thin city.'

'I can't keep Belliard off your case indefinitely,' Maillol said. 'He's already following every lead that stands a chance of throwing up Custine. That bar you frequent? *Le Perroquet Pourpre?*'

'Yes?' Floyd asked, worriedly.

'There's a nice burnt-out shell where it used to be.'

'Michel, the owner – is he all right?'

'There were no deaths, but witnesses saw a couple of men in greatcoats with petrol cans fleeing the scene in a black Citroën. They were last seen heading in the general direction of the Quai des Orfèvres.' Maillol paused to let that sink in, then added, 'If Custine was hiding there, then you can be sure Belliard is closing on him.'

'Custine can take care of himself.'

'Perhaps, Floyd. The question is: can you? Belliard won't stop at one fish.'

'I just need more time,' Floyd said.

'If – and I repeat *if* – you hand one of these mock children over to me, alive and in a state amenable to interrogation . . . then I might, conceivably, be able to do something. Though how I'll explain matters to the examining magistrate, I don't know. Paris terrorised by a gang of feral children? He'll laugh me out of the Palais de Justice.'

'Show him the child, sir, and I don't think he'll be laughing for long.'

'I'll do what I can.'

'I'm glad to know we still have some common ground,' Floyd said.

'Common ground that is dwindling by the moment, *mon ami*. In return, I'll want your assistance to close off the Rivaud connection.'

'Understood,' Floyd said. He put down the receiver, then dug into his pockets for another coin for the next call.

The car slowed down, pulled out of the flow of traffic and scraped its right wheels against the kerb with a hiss of rubber. The rear passenger-side door was flung open and a hand – belonging to a large man lost in shadow in the front passenger seat – directed them into the back of the car. Auger climbed in first, then Floyd. He slammed the rear door shut just as the driver gunned the engine and pulled back on to rue La Fayette, his abrupt entry into the procession of vehicles greeted by a symphony of angry horns.

Custine turned around in the front passenger seat, while the driver – who turned out to be Michel – nosed the car on to rue Magenta.

'It's good to see you back, Floyd,' Custine said warmly. 'We were beginning to worry.'

'Nice to know I'm appreciated.'

Custine touched the brim of his hat in Auger's direction. 'You too, mademoiselle. Are you all right?'

'She's been shot,' Floyd said. 'I'd say that makes her pretty far from all right. Only problem is, she won't let me take her to a hospital.'

'I not needing hospital,' Auger said. 'I only needing station of the train.'

Custine looked at Floyd. 'Is it me, or did she speak perfect French the last time I saw her?'

'She had a bump on the head.'

'Must have been a bad one.'

'That's nothing. You should hear what's happened to her English.'

'What happened to you, Floyd?' Custine asked, noticing Floyd's bandaged head for the first time. Floyd's hat, which had rolled off his head in the basement of the Kaspar Metals building when Auger pulled him to safety, had never been retrieved.

'Never mind me. How are you? How is Greta? Is Marguerite still . . . ?'

'I spoke to Greta yesterday. She was – naturally enough – more than a little agitated at your sudden departure.'

'I didn't have time for a debate. You were there. You know what it was like.'

'Well, I'm sure she'll forgive you – given time. As for Marguerite . . . well, she's still holding on.' Custine slid his hat over one side of his face, masking himself as a police car droned past in the opposite direction. He waited until the car had turned on to a different street before allowing himself to relax again. 'I don't think anyone has much hope of her lasting the week, though.'

'Poor Greta,' Floyd said. 'She must be going through hell.'

'All this isn't exactly helping.' Custine looked uncomfortably at Auger, perhaps wondering how much had taken place between them while they were in Berlin. 'She's still expecting an answer from you,' he said delicately. 'That little dilemma hasn't gone away in your absence.'

'I know,' Floyd said heavily.

'You have to make a decision sooner or later. It's only fair.'

'I can't think straight until we get out of this mess,' Floyd said. 'And that means clearing your name. Not much point in handing over the investigation business to you if you're going to be running it from prison, is there?'

Custine shook his head. 'Leave it, Floyd. They will always find a way to take me down. I can be out of Paris by the middle of the week. I have friends in Toulouse . . . a man who can create a new identity for me.'

'I just spoke to Maillol again. He still thinks he can get you off the hook if I turn up another suspect.'

'Put it like that, it almost sounds easy.'

'It won't be. But before I can help you, I have to help Mademoiselle Auger.'

'Then take her to a hospital, irrespective of her wishes.'

'She made it pretty clear, Custine – there's something down in that station that can help her. That's why we're going to Cardinal Lemoine.'

'When was she shot?'

'Yesterday – nearly twenty-four hours ago.'

'Then she is more than likely delirious. In this instance, Floyd, the patient is very much not to be trusted.'

'I trust her. She's been saying the same thing since she was shot. She knows what's best for her.'

'Who *is* she?'

'I don't know,' Floyd said. 'But after all I've seen, I'm beginning to have my doubts about the Dakota story.'

*

Custine and Michel dropped them at the entrance to Cardinal Lemoine, then sped away into the traffic. It was nine in the morning, in the thick of the rush-hour, and no one paid much heed to either Floyd or Auger. Floyd's injury was obvious to anyone, even more so now that he had lost his hat. But a man with a bandaged head only attracted so much attention. An argument in a bar, an altercation with a lover or rival . . . there were infinite possibilities, and an equally infinite number of reasons not to ask. As for Auger, Floyd had cleaned, sterilised and dressed her wounds before they left Berlin, using pieces of cloth torn from his jacket as bandages, and once again before the train arrived in Paris. With a few layers of clothes on, the makeshift dressing wasn't obvious, and the only thing that marked her out as unwell was a stiffness on her right side and a paleness about her face. Floyd tucked her good arm around his and guided her into the tiled depths of the station, moving with the flow of the other commuters.

If the bullet or bullets had done serious harm, she would be dead by now. Internal bleeding killed you a lot sooner than this. But sepsis was a different matter. He wasn't sure exactly know how long it took to set in, but he knew it could be a slow and unpleasant way to go.

'I hope you're right about this,' he said, pressing his mouth to her ear and speaking English.

'I am right. Trust me, OK?'

'I take it there are other people down there who can help you?'

'Yes.'

'And that you'd rather trust yourself to them than to a hospital?'

'Yes.'

'I need some proof,' Floyd insisted. 'I can't just let you stroll into the tunnel and hope for the best.'

'I'm sorry, but that's exactly what you've got to do.'

He stopped on the stairs, letting the other passengers find their way past them.

'You'll let me know where I can find you later, won't you? I have to see you again, to know you're going to be OK.'

'I'll be fine, Floyd.'

'I still want to see you.'

'Just to know I'm well?'

'More than that. You know how I feel. Maybe I'm wrong, but I think I know how you feel as well.'

'It couldn't ever work out between us,' she said.

'We could at least try.'

'No,' she said firmly. 'Because that would only put off the inevitable. It won't work. It couldn't ever work.'

326

'But if you wanted it to—'

'Floyd, listen to me. I like you a lot. I meant everything I said in Berlin. Maybe I even love you. But that doesn't change the fact that we can't ever be together.'

'Why? We're not so very different.'

'We're more different than you realise. By now you've probably figured out a thing or two about me. Believe me, whatever it is you think you know isn't even close to the truth.'

'Then tell me the truth.'

'I can't. All I can tell you is that no matter what feelings we might have for each other, we can't be together.'

'Is there someone else back home?'

'No,' she said, a little quietly. 'As a matter of fact, there isn't. There used to be, but I liked my work too much and I slowly squeezed him out of my life. But there is someone else in your life, Floyd.'

'You mean Greta? Sorry, but it's over between us.'

'She's beautiful and clever, Floyd. If she's giving you a chance to start over again, I'd take it.'

'Her chance means leaving behind everything and everyone I know in this city.'

'Still sounds like a good offer to me.'

'You're just trying to get me to walk away, with no regrets.'

'Is that so wrong of me?'

'I can't help the way I feel about you. Greta's the one who left. I can see that she's beautiful and clever, but she just isn't a part of my life any more.'

'Then more fool you.'

Auger slipped free of him and resumed her progress down the stairs, towards the bustling underground platform. Floyd caught up with her a moment later, slipping his arm through hers again.

'You never really answered my question,' he said. 'Will I see you again, when they've fixed you up?'

'No,' she said. 'You won't see me again.'

'I'll stake out every station in Paris. I'll always find you.'

'I'm sorry. I wish there was some other way of ending this, but I don't want to give you false hopes. I think you deserve better than that.'

A train slid into the station as they reached the platform. 'Auger,' Floyd said. 'You can't hide in that tunnel for ever. I'll always be waiting for you.'

'Don't, Floyd,' she said. 'Don't waste the rest of your life on me. I'm not worth it.'

'No,' he said. 'You're wrong. You'd always be worth it.'

A hand suddenly grasped her sleeve, turning her away from Floyd. Floyd looked up, startled, as he felt another hand grab his arm. The man restraining Auger wore a bowler hat and a long raincoat over a heavy serge suit. Another plainclothesman detained Floyd.

'Inspector Belliard,' Floyd said.

'Glad to see that I made an impression,' said the young policeman holding Auger's arm. 'Did you ever get reimbursed for that damaged ornament?'

'I decided I could live without it. Who tipped you off? Maillol?'

Behind him, another voice rumbled, 'Actually, Floyd, I did everything in my power to help you. Unfortunately, I didn't count on being bugged by my own department. As soon as you called from Gare du Nord, they put a squad on to you.'

Belliard glared at Maillol. 'I warned you not to follow us here. I also warned you against taking an interest in the Blanchard case.'

'Floyd is a peripheral witness in my own investigation,' Maillol said sweetly. 'I had every right to question him.'

'You know he is withholding information about the whereabouts of André Custine.'

'I'm only interested in the Montrouge affair. Custine is no business of mine, as you've made abundantly clear.'

Belliard barked an order at his own man, then snarled at Maillol, 'We'll continue this discussion at the Quai, where you can explain why you attempted to sabotage a Crime Squad investigation. In the meantime, let's find somewhere discreet to deal with these two.'

That was when Auger made her move, slipping free of Belliard's grasp and darting into the swarm of passengers still milling around on the platform. Floyd lost sight of her just before the carriage doors hissed shut. Belliard pulled out his gun and badge and barged towards the train, shouting at people to get out of his way. He arrived at the side of the train just in time to hammer his gun against a window. But the train was already moving, picking up speed until the last carriage hurtled into the tunnel.

Belliard turned back to his man. 'I want every station on this line sealed off. She isn't getting out of the Métro.'

'I'll make sure she doesn't get far,' the man said, letting go of Floyd and walking quickly towards a puzzled-looking Métro official.

'You don't even know who she is,' Floyd said.

'She seemed unwilling to talk to us,' Belliard answered. 'That's reason enough for suspicion.'

'And me?'

'How does harbouring a fugitive sound?'

Maillol leaned in and spoke urgently. 'Floyd – you can't win this one.

They'll find the American girl, and they'll find Custine. Don't make it any worse for yourself than it already is.'

Floyd looked at the other plainclothesman, who was still engaged in discussion with the Métro official. It was now or never. He ducked away from Belliard and Maillol, losing himself as quickly as possible amongst the assembled commuters. Belliard shouted something and started coming after him: Floyd could see his bobbing bowler hat two or three heads behind him. Floyd lowered his own head and ploughed on, oblivious to the disgruntled shouts of the people around him.

'Floyd!' he heard Maillol cry out. 'Don't do anything stupid!'

Another train rattled into the station, spilling more passengers on to the platform. The surging, barging mass was exactly what Floyd needed. A gap was opening up between him and Belliard, giving him just enough time to fumble the automatic out of his jacket pocket. He had no idea what he was going to do with it, but he felt better with it in his hand.

He reached the limit of the platform and risked a glance back over his shoulder. Belliard's bobbing hat was still worryingly close. Worse than that, the policeman still had his own gun drawn, held at head-height with the barrel pointed towards the ceiling.

The rushing passengers formed a temporary screen, most of them unaware of the drama that was playing out. The distraction gave Floyd time to position himself at the edge of the platform just as the train accelerated past him, exiting the station. With a steely roar, the last carriage plunged into the tunnel. He watched its rear red light dwindle and wondered if he had the courage to follow it.

'Stop!' Belliard shouted.

Floyd turned around, raising his own weapon and pointing the muzzle straight at the policeman. Maillol was a few paces behind Belliard, shaking his head in dismay. By now the spectacle had begun to register with the commuters, who had cleared a space around the three men.

'Get back,' Floyd said. 'Get back and keep walking.'

'You won't get anywhere,' Belliard said. 'In a few minutes I'll have men covering every possible exit from the entire Métro system.'

'In which case, you might as well have a little fun catching me.'

'Drop the gun,' Maillol said, his tone pleading.

'I said walk away. That goes for you too, monsieur.' Floyd aimed a little high and squeezed off a single round, just to make his point. 'I will use this, so don't make me.'

'You're a dead man,' Belliard said. But he was walking backwards, his hands raised and his own gun dangling from a single finger.

'Then I'll see you in the bone yard,' Floyd replied.

He moved quickly, lowering himself to the level of the rails and slipping into the darkness of the tunnel. Behind, on the platform, he heard excited voices shouting. He heard someone blowing sharp blasts on a whistle. A train arrived in the station, slowing to a halt with its cab just beyond the mouth of the tunnel. Men were already assembling on the platform near the front of the train, some of them in uniform. One of them dropped to his knees and shone the beam of a torch into the maw of the tunnel, swinging it around. Floyd pressed himself against the brickwork, mere centimetres beyond the limit of the beam.

After a moment, the headlamps of the train dimmed to burnt-out embers.

They'd cut the power.

Floyd ran into a thickening, congealing darkness, stone chippings crunching beneath his feet. He kept his left hand against the wall, feeling his way forwards with his right hand in front of him. With every step he had to fight the fear that he was about to step over the edge of a precipice. Somewhere ahead there was another discharge of gunfire. Behind him, moving silhouettes were already clotting his view of the station. Multiple torch beams sliced the air, scissoring the darkness like anti-aircraft searchlights.

He heard Maillol shout, 'Floyd! Give yourself up while you still can!'

Floyd plunged deeper into the tunnel. He dared not shout out Auger's name while Belliard still thought she'd made her escape on the train.

He heard a single gunshot and a single inhuman shriek. The sound had come from deeper in the tunnel.

He could no longer resist calling her name. 'Auger!'

He might have been imagining it, but he thought he heard someone call his in return. His right hand tightened on the automatic and he forced himself to walk towards the sound, even though every muscle in his body wanted to turn back to the light, back into the safety of custody. Maybe they wouldn't hurt him, especially if he threw away the gun. In his present state, with his head bandaged, they might even treat him with kindness and understanding. He had just become a little confused, that was all. A bang on the head, a bit of disorientation: they'd sympathise, wouldn't they? Now that he was feeling sharper, he knew he had no business down in this tunnel, and all he could do was offer his embarrassed apologies. As reasonable men, they'd see things his way, wouldn't they?

'Floyd?' a voice hissed. 'Floyd – is that you?'

Her voice sounded pitifully weak. It was difficult even to guess how far away she was, especially with the commotion behind him.

'Auger?'

'They're here, Floyd. They're in the tunnel.'

He knew she wasn't referring to the police. He quickened his pace until his toe scuffed against something soft. Despite himself, he gasped in surprise. He knelt down, one heel touching a rail. He reached out and explored the form, finding an arm, then a neck, and finally a face.

'I'm tired,' she said, leaning into him. 'I don't think I can make it on my own.'

'I heard a shot.'

'There were several of them. I think I got them all.' She coughed. 'You shouldn't have followed me. I didn't want you to come down here.'

'I was never one for goodbyes.'

'Feel around and see if you can find my torch. I dropped it when they attacked. It can't be far away.'

Floyd fumbled in the darkness, finding the rails. He worked his hand between them, praying that the electricity wouldn't suddenly surge through them. His fingers closed around the ribbed shaft of the torch. He held it up, shook it, found the sliding switch. The torch flickered, then came back to life.

He turned it off. 'Got it. Now what?'

'Help me up. It isn't far.'

The men couldn't have been more than fifteen to twenty metres behind them. They were taking their time, their voices low and cautious, as if they now sensed something of the danger that might lie in ambush down here.

'How far exactly?' Floyd asked, still unwilling to move her.

'A couple of dozen metres. There's a wooden door in the wall. You'll feel it. Get me through the door. Then close it and get the hell out of here. I'll take care of myself after that.'

He helped her move along the wall. The voices and torches behind them moved closer, picking up the pace with a renewed urgency. Floyd's eyes were beginning to adapt to the low light, picking out vague, floating shapes in the darkness. He risked turning on the torch briefly, using his own body to shield it from the men. The beam flickered on and then off again.

'There,' Auger said. 'A gap in the wall. You see it?'

'Yes.' Floyd looked back. The voices sounded no more than nine or ten metres behind them.

'Force it open. Get me through. Then save your skin.'

Floyd clamped the torch between his teeth. Leaning Auger against the wall, he jammed his shoulder against the old wooden door and pushed as hard as he could. The door swung open. He started helping Auger into the cavity beyond, trusting that she knew exactly what she was doing and almost believing it. Then something wrenched him away from the side of the tunnel, sending him sprawling across the tracks. He felt his spine crack against the rails. The torch dropped from his mouth, clattering against steel with a crunch of shattering glass.

The automatic fell from his hand.

Floyd forced a breath into his lungs. They hadn't turned the juice back on. He thrashed his arms wide, trying to push himself off the rails. Barely distinguishable from the darkness that surrounded him, a child loomed over him. It planted a shoed foot on his arm, preventing him from reaching the automatic. He had just enough vision to make out the ghoulish curve of its smile, its sunken cheeks and the dead, recessed hollows of its eye sockets. Torchlight from the advancing party fell upon the child, freezing it like a statue. It was looking right at the men. It hissed like a snake, and something gleamed in its right hand.

The child's arm moved, directing the muzzle of its little gun back along the tunnel, in the direction of the search party. The weapon discharged, spitting out rounds in a single brief burst.

He heard one of the men cry out in pain, and then a volley of return fire scythed overhead. None of the bullets hit the child, who aimed the gun again and delivered another burst of rapid fire, scything the gun from side to side. Floyd heard more anguished shouts and screams. Torches fell to the ground and died.

With a groan of effort, he managed to slip his arm free of the child's foot. His fingers brushed the grip of the automatic, groped for a purchase and managed to drag the gun a little closer. His hand closed around the butt. He brought the gun around, supporting his wrist with his other arm. The child looked down, and for an instant its smug expression changed to one of bewilderment.

Floyd squeezed the trigger. The gun clicked in his hand. Nothing happened.

The child's smile returned. It lowered the muzzle of its gun towards Floyd, its fingers coiled around the grip like pale eels.

There was another high-pitched volley of bullets.

The child shook like a doll, suspended in the air as rounds tore through it. Auger kept firing, squeezing the trigger until the gun fell silent, its muzzle aglow. The remains of the child, shredded clothes and lacerated flesh melded into an inseparable mass, flopped to the tunnel floor like a butcher's offcut.

Floyd stumbled to his feet and followed Auger through the gap in the wall.

'Floyd, you can't come any further.'

'You think I want to take my chances out there? They'll assume I was the one shooting at them.'

'Trust me: you're still better off trying to reason with them.'

'They'll shoot first,' Floyd said.

She growled in frustration. 'You follow me, you're getting into very deep water.'

'I'll take that chance.'

'Then close the door, before those men get here.'

He did as he was told. 'You think they saw us come in here?'

'I don't know,' she replied, her voice still weak and her breathing ragged and irregular. 'But they'll want to know what happened to us. They'll comb every inch of the tunnel now. They're sure to find that door.'

'I hope you have another way out of here, in that case.'

'So do I.'

They were in a much narrower tunnel, with no rails on the floor. No train could have fitted inside it. It was too low for Floyd to stand up in, and even though he ducked, he kept barking the top of his head against the rough-hewn ceiling. Auger led him onward, pausing now and then to gather her strength.

'We were lucky,' she said. 'The children don't see very well in the dark now. As they get older, their vision deteriorates.'

'How old are they?'

'They've been here for at least twenty-three years, maybe more, getting more decrepit every day.'

'Something tells me you're ready to talk now.'

'In a moment, Floyd, you're going to have all the answers I always said you didn't want.'

TWENTY-SIX

Floyd made out a softening of the darkness ahead, like the first suggestion of day in the final hour before dawn. The voices of the search party did not sound far away, as if they were close to the other side of the door. Auger was right: it wouldn't take them long to find their way through, especially if they thought they were going after killers.

'So who sent these children? Who are they working for?'

'I don't know for sure. I wasn't briefed on that part. My people sent me here to do a simple job, which was to recover Susan White's box of papers. They didn't tell me there'd be complications.'

'But they knew there would be?'

'My bosses? Yeah. I'd say there's a pretty good chance they knew more than they told me.'

'Sounds as if you were sold down the river, Auger.'

'That's more or less my conclusion.'

'You ready to tell me who you are yet, and who your bosses are? They weren't straight with you, after all, so you don't owe them anything.'

'If they'd been straight with me, I'd never have come here.'

They reached the source of the light. There was a heavy door set into one wall of the shaft, huge and thick and circular, like the door to a safe or one of the armoured hatches on a tank. The pale light spilled through the crack where the door had not been fully closed. It had a wavering quality, like reflections from a swimming pool.

'This isn't good,' Auger said. 'That door should be closed by now.'

'What's happened to those friends of yours?'

'I was expecting them to be here by now – a few reinforcements, at the very least. Until last Friday we had a whole team here.'

'What happened on Friday?'

'The children penetrated the shaft, broke in via a tunnel of their own. Killed Barton and Aveling, two of my colleagues. Skellsgard took a hit, but she was all right. I got her out of here, told her to send help back for me. I had to leave the door open when I left since there was no one left on the other side to lock it.'

'When were you expecting this help to arrive?'

'It should have taken sixty hours, minimum. The earliest the cavalry could have arrived was sometime around midnight last night, but there may have been a delay at the other end before anyone could set out on the return journey. They would have arrived on the other side of that door, able to shut it properly.'

'Maybe if we go through that door, we'll have a better idea of what's happened.'

'You're not going to like what's through that door,' Auger warned.

'I'm in for the rest of the game. Let's do it.'

They nudged the door open wide enough to squeeze through. Floyd helped Auger up on to the metal lip, into the raised area beyond. He followed her, squinting against the strange, shifting light that filled the chamber.

'Now help me close the door,' she said.

They worked the door into its seal, then Floyd turned the hefty wheel that locked it from the inside.

'That'll keep them out for a good few hours,' Auger said. 'They'll need to bring cutting gear down into the tunnel, and there's no telling how long it will take them to break through even when it arrives.'

'But they'll get through eventually.'

'Yes, but you only have to hold out down here for three days or so. By that time, we'll have sent people through to help you get back to safety. You'll find provisions and water in the next room.'

'What next room?'

The chamber they were in was the size of a one-car garage, its walls gouged from dark, glistening rock. The floor was scratched metal. Several cabinets and work benches were arranged around the perimeter, set with what Floyd recognised as wireless transmitting equipment. There was a lot of it, and it was wired together in surprising ways, but there was nothing that looked like super-secret spy gear of the kind he had expected. The only odd thing in the room – and it was, admittedly, more than a little odd – was the peculiar plaque or mirror hanging against – or rather set into – the rear wall. It was the source of the light: a perfectly blank, flat surface as tall as a man that none the less conveyed a subtle, queasy sense of depth and shifting perspective. The surface was framed by a heavy construction that merged seamlessly into the walls of the cave. The frame was moulded from a translucent material like dark honey, twinkling with a suggestion of shimmering machinery buried deep within it.

It looked like nothing he had ever seen in his life.

'This is the censor chamber,' Auger said, peeling away the sticky wad of Floyd's jacket that was serving as a bandage, rearranging the fabric and then pressing it hard against her wound. 'There's first-aid gear here, but we'll have more to choose from on the other side of the censor.'

'The what?'

'That thing,' she said, pointing to the source of the wavering light. 'We call it the censor. It's like a checkpoint. It lets certain things through, and stops other things. I think we'll both be safer on the other side of it.'

'Keep talking,' he said, transfixed by the shifting, resonating surface.

'We don't know exactly what rules it applies,' Auger said, a remark that did nothing to reassure him. 'It's pretty strict about what it lets into Paris. But it doesn't seem to be so picky about the things it allows through the other way.'

'You're talking as if you don't even know how that thing works.'

'We don't,' she said simply. 'We don't even know who made it, or how long ago.'

'This is getting way too strange for me,' Floyd said.

'Then turn back and face those men.' Auger nodded at the censor. 'I'm not even sure it will let you through anyway.'

'Will it let you through?'

'Yes,' she said. 'I've been through it three times already, no harm done. But we're not the same. What applies to me won't necessarily apply to you.'

'How different can we be?'

'More than you know. But there's only way to find out. I'll go through first and wait for you on the other side. If you haven't come through after a minute or two, I'll . . .' But Auger could not finish whatever it was she meant to say.

'What is it?' Floyd asked.

'It isn't that easy. We've never seen the censor refuse a living thing. I don't know what it will do if it decides not to let you through.' Auger swallowed. 'It might not be pretty. When we tried to bring machines through from the other side – weapons, communications gear, that kind of thing – it usually didn't allow it. That's why we call it the censor.'

Floyd began to feel as if he had walked into a parlour game with only a vague idea of the rules. 'It blocked them somehow?'

'Destroyed them,' Auger said. 'Turned them into useless lumps of metal slag. Randomised them on the atomic level, erasing even any microscopic structures. Nothing worked any more. The only things it let us bring through were simple tools. Digging equipment. Knives. Clothes. Paper money. That's why there's nothing fancy in this room. Everything you see had to be found in Paris, smuggled in here and then cobbled together to serve our needs.'

Floyd stared at the flickering surface, hypnotised by it. He had been pushing Auger for answers since he had met her, always with a certain preconception in his mind, and now that he was getting the truth – in measured, drip-fed doses, admittedly – it was nothing like what he had imagined. It was the kind of truth that made him want to shrivel up and hide under a stone. The worst part was that there was a weary conviction in her voice that told him that none of this was a hoax. She was being straight with him now, or at least as straight as she dared.

There was something under Paris that had no right to exist, and Auger wanted him to step through it.

'Will I like what's on the other side of that thing, if it allows me through?'

'No,' she said. 'You won't. I'm pretty damn sure of that. But you'll be safer there than here. Even if those men make it into this room, they'll need some persuading to step through the censor. I think you can hold out until I return with help.'

'Then let's get it over with. You go first. I'll see you on the other side.'

'You're ready for this?'

'As ready as I'll ever be.'

'I've got to go, Floyd. I hope you make it through.'

'I'll be fine,' he said. 'Now off you go.'

She pushed herself through the censor, awkwardly swinging by her good arm from a rail positioned above it to give her momentum. The glowing membrane stretched at first like a sheet of rubber, resisting her progress. Then it snapped around her until she appeared embedded in it, only the back of her head and one elbow and heel showing. Bruiselike ripples surrounded her form. Then she was gone completely, the membrane flexing and rebounding like a trampoline, and Floyd was alone.

He pushed a finger experimentally against the drumlike surface and felt the faintest electrical tingling. He pushed harder. The tingling intensified. He stopped, removed his finger and pulled a toothpick from his pocket. Holding the toothpick by one end, he pushed the other tip into the surface until he felt that tingling again. He pulled out the toothpick and held it up for inspection. It appeared unharmed in any way, and when he slipped it into his mouth it tasted like all the others he'd ever chewed. Something still made him throw it away.

He pushed his finger in again, up to the quick at the base of his fingernail, and ignored the tingling as it sank into the surface as if into wet clay. The layer flexed back, until he had pushed a depression into it as deep as his forearm. Suddenly fearful, he released the pressure before the membrane could snap around him.

'Just do it,' he said, and threw himself at the surface.

Floyd came through. He fell in a crashing sprawl on the other side, smashing his bandaged head against cold metal flooring. All he could do, for at least a minute, was lie perfectly still as multiple pain signals hit his brain, where they were filed into pigeonholes, like letters in a sorting office. There was pain from his head, where he had hit the floor. His mouth hurt like hell – he must have bitten his tongue or the inside of his cheek, or something. There was pain from his knees and one elbow, and from the bruises on his back where he had fallen against the rails. His arm hurt where the child had pressed its shoe, holding him to the ground. But there was no shrill agony of amputation. He might have lost a finger or two, perhaps: he could believe that. But when he flexed his hands, even his fingers seemed to be more or less intact. Bruised and raw, certainly, but he could still play *something*, even if it had to be the maracas from now on.

He eased his head from the floor, then peeled the rest of his body into a sitting position. He looked around and found Auger sitting in a chair, slumped into it with exhaustion, but still awake.

'Floyd?' she asked. 'Are you all right?'

'Copacetic,' he said, rubbing his head.

'When you went through that thing . . . how was it?'

Floyd spat out a bloodied tooth before answering. 'It's funny. I'm sitting here now and it seems like it was only a couple of seconds ago that we were on the other side. But to another part of me, it feels as if I haven't seen you for half a lifetime.'

'So it happened to you,' Auger said. 'The thing that never happened to me. You got it, on your first trip through.' She sounded impressed and envious at the same time.

'All I remember,' Floyd said, 'is that I felt as if I was made of glass, and there was light shining through me. It was as though I was hanging in that shaft of light for the whole of eternity. I wondered if it was ever going to end. Another part of me didn't want it to end, ever. I saw . . . colours, colours like I'd never imagined before. And then it was all over, and I was lying here with a pain in my mouth. You know, if you could bottle that sensation . . .' He managed a self-deprecating shrug. 'Guess the damned thing isn't so picky after all.'

'Did you feel a mind? More than one mind?'

'I felt very small and very delicate, like something being looked at through a microscope.'

'It was an experiment,' Auger said flatly. 'No one like you has ever come through before. It was something no one had ever tried. I just didn't expect you to have that experience on your first trip.'

'Lady, one trip through that thing is enough for me.' He looked around, taking in the complexities of the room in which he had landed. Unlike the last chamber, this one at least looked something like the underground spy lair he had been imagining. It was very large, filled with machines and equipment that he could not begin to identify. 'Please tell me this is some kind of film set,' he said, steadying himself against the edge of a desk.

'It's all real,' Auger said, struggling to her feet. 'The only problem is that my friends aren't here yet. But there's good news, too.'

'There is?'

'The ship's back. I just don't understand why no one else came with it. They'd only have had to keep one seat vacant.'

Floyd dug into his mouth, extracting the last few chips of his ruined tooth. Somehow, dentistry was the least of his worries. 'Did you just say "ship"?'

'That thing,' Auger said. She pointed to the central feature of the room, the thing you couldn't miss. It was a giant glass bulb, as wide across as a house, suspended at eyelevel over a kind of pit filled with more machinery, equipment and desks. The bulb was encased in an arrangement of curving metal struts, bracing it to the walls of the chamber. On the other side from where they were standing, the bulb's surface extended out, forming a cylindrical shaft that pushed through the wall. Where the shaft met the wall, there was a thick, intricate crusting of the same weird substance Floyd had already seen framing the censor. As he looked more closely, he realised that the crusting covered the interior walls of the chamber completely with a dense, twinkling plaque. Portions of it had been sheeted over with metal panels, but large areas were still exposed.

There was something inside the bubble. It was a dented and battered object about the size of a truck, seemingly formed from sheets of metal that had been hammered into shape by enthusiastic cavemen. It was cylindrical, with a bullet-shaped nose. It had windows and was covered with odd projections – most of them bent and mangled – and unfamiliar symbols in faded and scorched paint, and the whole thing was encased in a kind of harness, like the cradles used to load bombs into aircraft.

'It's taken a beating getting here,' Auger commented.

'That's a ship?' Floyd asked.

'Yes,' she said. 'And don't sound so disappointed. It happens to be my ticket out of here.'

'It looks as though it's been around the block a few times.'

'Well, things must be getting pretty hairy for it to have accrued that much damage in one trip. I just hope it can cope with the return leg.'

'Where will it take you?' Floyd asked. 'America? Russia? Somewhere I haven't even heard of?'

'It'll take me a long way from Paris,' Auger said evasively. 'Right now that's all you need worry about. I'll be back in just over sixty hours, or if not me, then someone else you can trust. Whoever it is will have reinforcements – enough help to get you back to the surface in one piece.'

'Is that a promise?'

'It's the best I can do. Right now, I don't even know if that thing is going to hold together long enough to get me home.'

'Is there an alternative?'

'No. That ship is my only way out of here.'

'Then we'd better hope Lady Luck's on your side.'

Floyd looked around the rest of the room, his attention skating from one unfamiliar object to the next. The many desks were all inlaid with arrays of typewriter keys, but grouped densely together, with many more keys than seemed necessary. They had cryptic codes marked on them – arrangements of letters, numbers and childish scribbles. There were many switches and controls of a kind he didn't recognise, made of some sort of smoky, translucent material. There were flat, upright sheets of tinted glass arranged on the desks like sunshades, upon which text and illustrations – charts and diagrams – had been printed in bright, luminous inks. There were grilles and lights and slots, and racks holding oblong things that might have fitted into the slots. There were microphones on stalks – those at least he recognised – and clipboards, left strewn across some of the desks. He picked up the nearest clipboard and leafed through sheets of silky paper marked with rows and rows of gibberish, but gibberish clearly laid out according to some careful scheme, interspersed with elegant, sloping cascades of brackets and other typographic symbols. Another clipboard held pages and pages of labyrinthine, gridlike diagrams, like the street map of some insane metropolis.

'Who exactly are you?' he asked

'I'm a woman from the year twenty-two sixty-six,' Auger said.

'You know, what really worries me is that you sound as if you believe it.'

But Auger wasn't listening. She had moved to the side of what was perhaps the strangest thing in the room, other than the ship and the censor. It was a kind of sculpture composed of many dozens of shiny metallic spheres organised into a pyramidal spiral that reached almost to shoulder height. In the lobby of a company building, it wouldn't have merited a second glance. But here, amidst so much equipment that was obviously designed for a specific technical function, it was bizarrely out of place, like a Christmas tree in an engine room.

Auger touched the topmost sphere. She mouthed a 'What . . . ?' and the thing moved, partially uncoiling until Floyd saw that it had the form of a snake made from many linked spheres. Auger took a nervous step backwards as the snake rose up, curving its body into a high, threatening arc.

Floyd pointed his automatic and clicked off the safety catch.

'Easy,' Auger said, raising a hand in his direction. 'It's just a robot. They must have sent it over in the ship.'

Guardedly, Floyd let the automatic drop. '*Just* a robot?'

'A Slasher robot,' she said, as if this made a difference. 'But I don't think it means us any harm. If it did, we'd be dead by now.'

'You're talking about robots as if they're something you see every day.'

'Not every day,' Auger said. 'But often enough to know when I should be afraid, and when I don't need to be.'

The robot spoke in a rapid, piping voice. 'I recognise you as Verity Auger. Please confirm this identification.'

'I'm Auger,' she said.

'You appear to be injured. Is this the case?' While it spoke, the snake swayed the blank sphere of its head from side to side, like a charmed cobra.

'I'm injured, yes.'

'I am detecting a foreign metallic object lodged near your shoulder.' The robot's voice sounded the way Floyd imagined Disney might make a talking kettle sound. 'Do you authorise immediate medical intervention? I am programmed with the necessary routines to perform an operation.'

'I thought the bullet went through you,' Floyd said.

'Maybe there was more than one,' Auger answered.

'Do you authorise medical intervention?' the robot repeated.

'Yes,' Auger said, and almost immediately the snake moved, its spheres scraping against the floor. 'No,' she said sharply. 'Wait. There isn't time for a full operation. I want you to stabilise me, make sure I can last until we get back to E1. Is that possible?'

The snake paused, appearing to weigh the options. 'I can stabilise you,' it said thoughtfully. 'But my recommendation is that you allow an immediate operation. Otherwise there is a significant risk of death unless you consent to UR therapy.'

'I'll consent if it gets me out of here,' Auger said. Then she turned to Floyd. 'I've just had an idea, now that they've sent the robot.'

'I'm listening,' Floyd said.

She snapped her attention back to the snake. 'Are you Asimov-compliant?'

'No,' the robot said, with a sting of indignation.

'Thank God, because you may actually have to hurt some people. Recognise this man as Wendell Floyd. Got that?'

The robot's blank round head swung towards him. He felt a weird interrogatory chill, as if he had been stared at by a sphinx.

'Yes,' the robot confirmed.

'I'm authorising you to protect Wendell Floyd. People may enter this chamber via the censor and attempt to harm or abduct him. You are to defend him, using minimum necessary force. Do you have nonlethal weapons?'

'I have weapons that may be deployed in both nonlethal *and* lethal modes,' the robot said proudly.

'Good. I want you to use whatever force is necessary to keep Floyd alive, but keep the body count down. No killing, unless you have to.'

'It understood all that?' Floyd said.

'I hope so, for their sakes.' She addressed the robot again. 'Eventually – somewhere around sixty or seventy hours from now – someone will return in the ship. They will assist Floyd in returning to the surface. You are not to obstruct them. Understood?'

'Understood,' the robot said.

'Good. Were you given any special orders? Who put you aboard?'

'I was given special instructions by Maurya Skellsgard.'

'Skellsgard made it?' Auger clenched her fist in obvious relief. 'Thank God. At least something went right, for once. Can I talk to her? Is the communications link working?'

'The communications link is active, but unreliable.'

'Can you patch me through to Skellsgard, if she's on shift?'

'One moment.'

Elsewhere in the room, movement caught Floyd's eye. Across all the desks, the text-filled shades became clear as the luminous letters and diagrams vanished. Symbols jumped across the panels, followed by a jumble of numbers and diagrams that flickered past too fast to make out. Then the picture cleared to reveal multiple images of the same woman, looking at him from different angles around the room.

'Auger?' the face said. 'You there, sister?'

The snake robot was already attending to Auger's injury. It had curled part of itself around her, forming a kind of couch upon which she was gently supported. The larger spheres, Floyd noted, were capable of bulging and softening to form cushions. Other spheres, clustered near the head, had opened little doors in what had appeared to be seamless metal. Many jointed arms had emerged through these doors, tipped with all manner of sharp, glinting devices.

'I'm here,' Auger said. 'I'm glad you made it back safely.'

'All thanks to you,' Skellsgard replied. 'I owe you one, and I wish I was there to help. But the link's become too unstable since I made it back to E1. There was no guarantee we'd be able to get a ship back to you, let alone return.'

'I noticed that the ship took a hammering,' Auger said. The robot was nibbling away layers of her clothing, doing so with an astonishing gentleness. It reminded Floyd of a mantis chewing away at a leaf.

'It'll probably be even rougher on the way back. I wanted to come for you, but Caliskan refused to risk any more lives. That's why we sent the robot. Hope you weren't too surprised.'

'I take it the Slasher conflict has become more extensive?'

'You could say that. Look, no point in beating around the bush. The news at this end isn't good: you're coming back to a war zone. The aggressive parties have finally made their move. Moderate Slashers are doing their best to contain them, but it's not clear how long they can last. We're not sure how long we can hold Mars, let alone Earth.'

Auger glanced awkwardly in Floyd's direction. 'There's a complication at my end as well. I've brought someone into the chamber.'

'I hope whoever you're bringing back is already in the loop.'

'I think it's fair to say he's pretty fucking out of the loop. Remember that detective I mentioned?'

Skellsgard grimaced and closed her eyes, like someone waiting for a balloon to pop. 'I'm not hearing this, Auger.'

'I couldn't shake him. He's what you'd call tenacious.'

'You can't do this, Auger. The censor—'

'The censor let him through,' Auger said. 'He's already seen the ship, and the robot. The damage is done.'

'You have to send him back.'

'I'm planning on it. But we're in a siege situation here. Floyd can't get back to the surface, and more than likely people are already trying to break through into the outer chamber. I'm not sure whether they'll try to get through the censor, but I've tasked the robot to protect Floyd until we can send back a ship with reinforcements.'

Skellsgard's image broke up, then reassembled. Her voice sounded thin, like someone speaking through a comb. 'Caliskan won't OK it.'

'I'll deal with him. I'll come back myself if I have to. I'd send the damned robot out to take Floyd all the way to the surface if the censor would let it through.'

'May I say something?' Floyd asked.

'Go ahead,' Skellsgard replied.

'Auger isn't giving you the whole picture. Fact of the matter is, she's pretty badly hurt.'

'He telling the truth?' Skellsgard said, turning her perceptive gaze on Auger.

'It's nothing serious,' Auger said, then immediately winced as the robot began to examine the wound. Even Floyd had to look away: he had never been very good with injuries, and it had been as much as he could do to clean and bandage the wound for her earlier.

'That doesn't look like "nothing serious" to me,' Skellsgard said.

'I'll keep until I'm home. At least this way I can stay conscious for some of the trip. The robot's patching me up. Can the ship take care of itself?'

'No,' Skellsgard said. 'Ordinarily it could, but not with the way the link is now. The existing routines aren't designed to cope with the changing geometry. We uploaded patches before we sent it out, but the robot had to do a certain amount of hands-on piloting to get the ship to you in one piece.'

'No problem, then. Just get the robot to do the same thing on the return leg.'

'There won't be a robot,' Skellsgard said, wondering whether pain and blood-loss were affecting Auger's short-term memory. 'Even if you hadn't volunteered it to protect your detective, we'd need it to stay behind at the E2 end to stabilise the throat and ramp down the power after insertion. You remember how tricky it was to send me back without the throat collapsing catastrophically?'

'Yes,' Auger said.

'Well, it'll be twenty times more difficult now, and there isn't anyone warm to stay behind to manage the throat contraction. That's what we need the robot for.'

'Damn,' Auger said.

'If we could have squeezed two robots in, we'd have sent two. I was kind of hoping you'd be sharp enough to fly her back.'

'I think I'm going to be a little woozy,' Auger said. 'The robot talked about pumping me full of UR.'

'If the robot says you need UR, I'd trust the robot.'

'Absolutely, but I might not be conscious the whole way back.'

'In that case,' Skellsgard said, 'we have ourselves a problem.'

'Not necessarily,' Floyd said.

Auger looked at him. The faces on the screens looked at him, in perfect unison. Even the robot glanced at him, its blank sphere of a head somehow managing to evince polite scepticism.

'You got something to contribute?' Skellsgard said.

'If Auger can't fly the ship, then I'll have to.'

'You have no idea what's involved. Even if you did . . . shit, man, you don't know a wormhole from your butthole.'

'No, but I can learn.' Floyd directed his attention at the nearest floating image.

'Fine,' Skellsgard said. 'You can begin by telling me what you already know about matter/exotic matter coupling parities, and we'll go from there. I take it you do have some passing familiarity with the basic principles of pseudo-wormhole engineering? Or am I going to fast for you?'

'I can change a spark plug,' Floyd said.

Auger let out a small, pained yelp.

'I am going to administer a local anaesthetic,' the robot said. 'There may be some temporary loss of mental clarity.'

'Bring it on,' she said.

TWENTY-SEVEN

When the snake robot had patched her up, it carried Auger into the passenger compartment of the battered ship. Floyd was already inside, strapped into the rightmost of the three chairs, carrying on his conversation with Skellsgard. Inside, the ship did at least look new, despite its external appearance. The seats were heavy affairs of padded black material, with enormous cross-webbed buckles and head restraints. In front of each seat, folded aside until the occupant was in place, was a complicated arrangement of controls and screens, markedly more bulky and robust than anything Floyd had seen so far. There were very small windows surrounded by yet more banks of controls, lights and screens. Behind the padded seats was a very narrow companionway leading – as far as Floyd could tell – to a set of storage lockers adjacent to a washroom about the size of a small kennel, with an even smaller kitchen/medical cubicle next to it. He knew it was a medical cubicle because of the Red Cross symbol on one of the white equipment boxes bolted to the wall. The rest of the ship was not accessible from the passenger compartment, and must have been taken up with machinery and fuel, or whatever else it needed to function. Pumps and generators chugged and hummed, and occasionally there was a thump or whine from some hidden mechanism.

'How much has Auger told you?' Skellsgard said.

'Damn little.'

'Where did she tell you this ship was going to take her?'

'She didn't,' Floyd said.

'Huh.' This seemed to amuse the other woman no end. 'So what's your best guess?'

'My best guess is that we're going to take a trip down some kind of underground tunnel. Maybe we'll come out in the Atlantic and make the rest of the trip by submarine. Or maybe we'll be met by a squadron of flying pigs.'

'Something tells me you have doubts.'

'Call me a stickler for detail,' Floyd said, 'but I couldn't help noticing you mention something about Earth and Mars back there.'

'Those were codewords, you silly boy.'

'They'd have to be,' Floyd said.

'All right. Listen up, and listen good. This is what you absolutely need to know, if Auger can't make herself useful. You're going to be in this thing for thirty hours, give or take. It's going to be rough. How rough will depend on luck and the robot getting you off to a good start. But if I were you, I wouldn't take too many trips to the head.'

'I have a weak bladder.'

'Tell Floyd about the manual controls,' Auger said as the robot eased her into the left-hand couch, contorting its body to reach inside the ship.

'Floyd,' Skellsgard said, 'I want you to fold down the console panel in front of your seat, so that it's across your lap. Then latch it in place.'

'Done,' Floyd said.

'Get your hand around the joystick. Squeeze it. The display to your right should show a green-on-red stress-energy grid. Got that?'

Floyd did as he was told. 'I'm seeing a grid,' he said. 'I'm also seeing a lot more than that.'

'That's fine. Now, do you see the blue diamond-shaped marker, between the two yellow brackets?'

'I'm seeing several diamonds.'

'Move the joystick laterally. The icon that moves is the one you need to worry about. Ignore the fixed markers for now, and don't worry about all them teeny little numbers.'

'The grid is changing. It's like it's drawn on hot toffee, and I'm dragging a spoon through it.'

'That's the idea. Now flip up the red cover on the back of the joystick and get your thumb on the right pressure pad. The right, not the left. Squeeze it gently and tell me what happens to the grid.'

'The grid's moving. Everything's moving, drifting to the left.'

'That's expected. What you're seeing is a visual representation of the tunnel geometry ahead of the ship, approximately a light-microsecond downstream from the throat. The system is showing you a prediction of your drift based on that geometry.' Floyd opened his mouth to speak, but Skellsgard was ahead of him. 'Don't worry your pretty little head about the details. The key thing is that the geometry isn't stable, and if we let the ship fly itself, it'll keep nosing to one side of the tunnel or the other. You don't want that to happen, since the tidal stresses become exponentially stronger the closer to the sides you get. Now, the ship's guidance spines can absorb glancing impacts with the tunnel walls, but the telemetry I'm seeing at this end tells me that those spines took quite a pounding on the way over. Hull armour looks pretty crumpled as well.'

'The telemetry's right,' Auger said. 'I'm not sure the ship will hold together, even without additional stresses.'

'We'll have our fingers crossed at this end. In fact, we'll have everything crossed.' Resigned to the inevitable, perhaps, Skellsgard's voice suddenly became hushed and businesslike. 'The important thing is that the uploaded software patches should do a pretty good job even with the changing geometry, so you won't have to fly the ship all the way home.'

'That sounds good,' Floyd said. 'I don't think I could manage to do it for thirty hours straight.'

'But you'll still have to override the autopilot now and then. The simulations we've run at this end show that the guidance system doesn't cope well with abrupt changes in tunnel geometry, especially when the shear angles exceed seven hundred and twenty degrees.'

'Doesn't cope well?' Floyd asked.

'It crashes.'

'The ship crashes?'

'The software.'

'The *what*ware?'

Auger interrupted. 'She means the guidance system will stop working without any warning.'

'Can I start it again?'

'Yes,' Skellsgard said. 'You'll need to implement an immediate reboot. That's the easy bit – Auger can show you how to do that. The difficult bit is that you'll need to get the ship back on course before you scrape the sides of the tunnel.'

'Scraping sounds painful. And what kind of angle exceeds seven hundred and twenty degrees, anyway?'

'The kind you'll get a headache thinking about, so don't.'

Floyd moved the joystick again, getting the feel of it. 'How long will I have to get us back on track before we scrape?'

'Depends. Ten, maybe fifteen seconds. That should be enough time for you to override and correct your trajectory. There'll be an audible alarm when the guidance system crashes, telling you you're about to become an interesting smear on the inside of the tunnel.'

'Anything else I need to know?'

'Only about a lifetime's worth, but that's the way it is. Just keep an eye on the grid and try to anticipate the drift gradients before they sneak up on you. You should see bunching of the grid lines. The ship's response time is slow, so make sure you keep your control inputs small and discrete, giving the ship time to answer the helm before you make another correction.'

'Now you're talking a language I almost understand.'

'Have you ever flown transatmospherics?'

'I don't think so,' Floyd said.

'He used to be a trawlerman,' Auger said. 'Before that I think he drove barges of some kind. They're a kind of boat,' she added.

'Did those barges turn on a dime?' Skellsgard said.

'No,' Floyd said. 'Matter of fact, they took about a nautical mile to slow down. And you had to anticipate every bend in the river long before you saw it.'

'Or else you'd scrape the banks,' Skellsgard said, nodding approvingly. 'Well, all you need to do is think of this ship as a big old barge with some unusual characteristics, and the tunnel walls as banks you really, really don't want to scrape. Can you get your head around that?'

'I can try,' Floyd said.

'Then maybe you can bring this baby home in one piece after all.'

Floyd shrugged, letting the joystick return to its central position. Skellsgard was making a big effort to sound optimistic, but her cheerfulness was paper-thin. 'Say,' he began, 'if you're talking to us now, why can't you talk us all the way home? You know, the way the guys in the tower talk down planes in the movies when the pilot's had a heart attack and some poor Joe is at the controls?'

'We lose this link as soon as we shoot a ship into the tunnel,' Auger said. 'She'll be off-air until we arrive at the other end.'

'But I'll be waiting for you,' Skellsgard said. 'I can still monitor the condition of the link, even if I can't talk to you. I don't think any of us is going to get much sleep in the next thirty hours.'

'Don't worry about us,' Auger said. 'We'll get home safe and dry. Just make sure you're bright-eyed when we pop out the other end. I'll need another ship prepped and ready to make an immediate return trip, and a robot ready to fly it.'

'I thought you said you needed medical attention.'

'I'm not talking about myself. Floyd can't stay with us on the other side. We still have to get him back into Paris.'

Skellsgard nodded. 'Yeah, let's try to contain the damage, shall we?'

'I'm all for damage containment,' Auger agreed.

'Me, too,' Floyd said. 'But why do I feel as if I'm the damage?'

'Skellsgard,' Auger said. 'Listen to me. I think I know why Susan had to die. The stuff they were building in Germany? I think they were parts for a resonant gravity-wave antenna.'

'Mmm,' she said, frowning. 'Tell me more.'

'Three spheres dotted around Europe, cooled down close to absolute zero and rigged to vibrate if gravity waves pass through them.'

'You say there are three of these things?'

'One in Berlin, one in Milan, one in Paris. I think they're using three as a means of screening out background noise: any signal registered by all three of them must be significant.'

'Three would also give you a handle on direction, if you had accurate enough clocks at all three sites.'

'Maybe they have that, too.'

'It's still tricky, Auger. You'd need to hang these things in vacuum and hook up some pretty sensitive acoustic amplifiers before you had a hope in hell of getting anything useful out of them.'

'But it's all at least feasible using E2 technology, with a few refinements. A lot easier than building something like a laser interferometer or an orbital test mass, when no one's invented the laser or the artificial satellite yet.'

'You have a point there. You know about Weber? Guy from around the same time period as E2. He built a room-temperature bar detector using a chunk of solid aluminium. Same basic principle.'

'Did it work?'

'Not really. It wasn't sensitive enough. But the principle was sound, and it paved the way for the cooled-down resonant detectors that did work, about fifty years later.'

'Someone's jumped the gun here,' Auger said. 'They've built one, maybe even operated it.'

'Who do you think is behind it?'

'Slashers. The same ones who must have come through during the Phobos occupation. At the very least, they're a part of it.'

'Why, though? What's the point? We can do all the gravity astronomy we need from the vicinity of the real Earth.'

'It isn't about astronomy,' Auger said. 'I think it's about triangulation.'

'You're losing me, Auger.'

'Think about it. No kind of electromagnetic radiation can get through the shell of the ALS, which means that there's no way of determining the real location of E2 in the galaxy. But gravity's different. It seeps through. Now, so do neutrinos, but building a directional neutrino detector is at least as difficult as building a directional gravity-wave antenna, and a lot trickier to keep out of the public eye.'

'But why . . . oh, wait. *Now* I see. You rig up this thing and start looking for known gravity-wave sources. Bright high-period derivative binaries: double degenerates on the death spiral, that kind of thing.'

'Yes,' Auger said. 'You pick up their resonant frequencies – which are as unique as fingerprints. You measure how strong they are and with three spheres you can calculate which direction they're coming from. You put the pieces together, crunch some data, and you have—'

'The physical co-ordinates of the ALS,' breathed Skellsgard.

'They may already have them by now,' Auger said.

'But why? Why would anyone go to all that trouble?'

'Because they want to find it very badly,' Auger said. 'From the outside.'

'Jesus,' Skellsgard said. 'What are they actually thinking of doing with that information?'

'That's the bit that worries me. Look, maybe it's nothing, but for some reason Susan wrote "Silver Rain" in one of the letters she intended to send to Caliskan.'

Skellsgard said nothing for several seconds. 'Jesus squared. Are you sure?'

'I think they might be trying to inject it into the ALS. It's a nano-weapon, so it can't come through the censor. That only leaves them one option: find the ALS and drill a hole in it.'

Skellsgard blew air out through pursed lips. She had no more expletives, no more profanities. 'Who do you want me to tell? You reckoned Susan had some doubts about who she could trust.'

'I think she was right to. I'm taking a risk even talking to you, of course. Now I'm going to take another risk and suggest you get this information to Caliskan as soon as possible.'

'I'll do what I can. Like I said, it's not exactly business as usual at this end of the pipe.'

'I hear you – just do your best. In the meantime, see if you can check the feasibility of my little theory. Maybe there's a snag; maybe it can't be a gravity-wave antenna at all.'

'I'm on the case,' Skellsgard said. 'Gives me something to take my mind off the bad news, at least.'

'Glad to be of service.'

'You take care of yourself, Auger. I still owe you one.'

Thirty minutes later, they had the ship prepped – as Auger put it – and ready for departure. The cradle had rotated the entire craft through 180 degrees, so that the view through the forward-looking cabin windows showed the glassy shaft that ran from the main bubble into the wall of the chamber. Beyond the shaft, the walls became mirrored, converging not to infinity but to a kind of iris. The robot had disembarked, slinking away with maggotlike undulations of its pearl-necklace body. Floyd could not see it at all now, but Auger assured him that it would be attending to the details of their departure, managing several desks at once.

'Skellsgard?' Auger said, from her chair on the left side of the cabin. 'You still on the line?'

'Still here . . .' Momentarily, her voice broke up into staccato shards, as if they were hearing pieces of her message out of sequence. '. . . but you might want to cast off sooner rather than later. Conditions are getting seriously sub-optimal.'

'Shouldn't we wait things out?' Auger asked.

'You'll be relatively safe once you clear the throat.'

'Why does she not fill me with confidence?' Floyd asked.

'Never mind,' Auger said. 'Robot: you got that injection sequence ready?'

The piping voice of the machine assured her that all was ready. 'Throat stability is locally optimal,' it said, whatever that meant.

'You buckled in, Floyd?'

'I'm ready.'

'There'll be quite a kick. Be prepared.' Then she raised her voice. 'OK, robot, inject us whenever you want.'

'Injection in five seconds,' the machine said.

Ahead, the iris cranked open. Floyd narrowed his eyes against the intense, roiling glare that spilled between the opening blades. The light flowed in strange, sicklelike patterns down the mirrored shaft. From somewhere behind the ship, the mechanical sounds intensified, and he heard a sequence of thuds and clunks like some enormous clock gearing itself up to chime.

'Three seconds,' the robot said. 'Two. One. Injecting.'

Floyd's bruised spine yelled a protestation into his brain. He felt as if a family of gorillas was practising xylophone exercises on his vertebrae. He started to say something, some useless moan of animal discomfort, and then found that he did not have the strength to speak; even his lungs felt as if they were being squeezed like bellows. His head and neck mashed back into the seat restraints and he felt a mouthful of drool spill down his chin. His vision darkened around a central core of brightness.

They were moving.

They were moving so quickly that they were not even in the chamber any more. They had already traversed the glass shaft and the mirror-lined part of the tunnel and were speeding through the heart of the opening iris, into the unimaginable fury of the light beyond.

That was when it got really bumpy.

The pressure forcing him into the back of the seat had abated and in its place was a dreamy lightness-of-stomach feeling, as if they were falling, but the ship was now lurching from side to side, each violent movement accompanied by a tooth-grinding rattle of ravaged metal. This, Floyd thought, was how it felt to grind past an iceberg in an ocean liner. He imagined scabs of the ship's hull breaking off into the bright inferno of whatever it was they were flying through.

He didn't think it very likely that it was a tunnel under Paris any more. Or even a tunnel under the Atlantic Ocean.

'I'm closing the shields now,' Auger said. 'The view doesn't help much. Especially not after ten hours of it.'

She touched a control above her head, using her good arm, and iron eyelids *snicked* down over the windows. Interior lights came on, bathing everything in a low-key glow. Floyd watched the grid pattern, his hand ready to close around the joystick.

'I'll look after it for now,' Auger said, taking hold of a similar control on her side of the cabin. 'You can watch and learn.'

'There are a couple of questions I really need to ask,' Floyd said.

'OK,' Auger said. 'I guess you've earned them.'

'Where is this tunnel taking us?'

'It's taking us to Mars,' Auger said. 'Specifically to Phobos, one of Mars's two natural moons.'

'So it wasn't a codeword after all.'

'No,' she said.

'I figured that part out, for what it's worth. I also decided that I don't think you're a Martian.'

'No, I'm not.'

'But you're not from Dakota, either.'

'No, Dakota was a lie. But I am from the United States.' She offered him a nervous smile. 'Just not the one you were thinking of, although I suppose you could call them distant political relatives.'

'And your name?'

'That bit was true. My name's Verity Auger, and I am a citizen of the United States of Near Earth. I'm a researcher for the Antiquities Board. I was born in the orbital community of Tanglewood in the year twenty-two thirty-one. I'm thirty-five and divorced, with two kids I don't see as often as I should.'

'The odd thing is,' Floyd said, 'I don't doubt you for a moment. I mean, what other explanation could there be?'

'You seem very relaxed about it,' she said.

'Given all that I've seen, the only possible explanation is that you're a time traveller.'

'Ah,' Auger said. 'That's the problem, you see. I mean, time travel is definitely involved here, but not in quite the way you're thinking.'

'It isn't?'

'No. But you're half-right. You see, one of the two people in this ship is a time traveller. And it isn't me. Do you want me to carry on?'

'I thought I had you figured out for a moment,' Floyd said.

'One step at a time,' Auger told him. Then there was a shriek from some part of the instrument panel and a dozen red lights started flashing in synchronisation. Auger bit her lip and pushed her joystick to one side. Floyd felt the ship veer: a sickening feeling like a car hitting ice.

'Was that a . . . what did she call it? Smash?'

'That was a software crash, yes,' Auger said. She flipped a bank of switches, then threw back a glass cover to press a large red button. 'And this is the reboot sequence, so pay attention.'

'We've only just left.'

'I know,' she said. 'We've got thirty more hours of this to get through. I think the ride home is going to be a lot more interesting than I was hoping.'

TWENTY-EIGHT

They had been under way for six hours. The guidance system had failed two or three times an hour initially, but lately the ride had become lullingly smooth, with only the occasional stomach-churning veer or swerve. They had eaten a light snack of pre-packed rations (the food was tucked into unmarked foil pouches that, to Floyd's obvious delight and fascination, warmed the food automatically when they were opened) and Floyd had explored the tiny, intimate microcosm of the toilet, with its daunting methods of collecting bodily waste under weightless conditions. Auger had asked him if he felt any motion sickness, and he had replied truthfully that he felt none.

'Good,' she said, popping a dark pill into her mouth. 'It must be all that time you spent at sea. Good practice for a trip down a wormhole, even though you probably didn't realise it at the time.'

'Are you feeling ill?' he asked.

'Apart from the fact that I've got a bullet lodged in my body that the robot thinks might kill me? No. I've never felt better.'

'I meant the pill.'

'It's UR,' she answered, as if that explained everything. When Floyd just stared at her, she said, 'Universal restorative. General-purpose medicine. It will heal anything, cure any ill. It'll even keep you alive for ever.'

'Then you're immortal?' he said.

'No, of course not,' Auger said, as if the very idea embarrassed her. 'If I took one of these every day – or every week, or however often it is you have to take them – then I might be, I suppose. At least until the supply ran out, or I got some disease so fascinatingly exotic that even the UR couldn't fix it. But there isn't enough UR in the whole system for me to take it all the time, and in any case, my people don't agree with it.'

'You don't agree with medicine that makes you immortal?' he asked, a little surprised by her statement.

'There's more to it than that. My side – the USNE, the Threshers, call us what you will – doesn't have the means to make UR. What UR we do have access to is supplied in very small, expensive and controlled quantities by our moderate allies in the Polities.'

'Haven't you tried making it yourselves?'

She popped another pill from the cylindrical dispenser and held it up for Floyd's inspection. It looked no more impressive than a discarded button, or a nub of dark clay. 'We couldn't make it even if we knew the recipe. The technology embedded in this pill is one that we've chosen to reject.' With particular care, she returned the pill to its canister. 'Except, of course, when we really need it, which tends to be on high-risk operations like this. So call us screaming hypocrites, and see if we care.'

'What's so dangerous about a technology used to make pills?'

'The technology is a lot broader in its applications,' Auger said. 'That isn't really a pill. It's a solid mass composed of billions of tiny machines, smaller than the eye can see. You wouldn't even see them under a microscope. But they're real, and they're the most dangerous thing in the world.'

'And yet they can heal you?'

'They swim into your body after you've swallowed the pill. They're smart enough to identify what's wrong with you, and adept enough to put it right. The bodies of the Slashers are already swarming with tiny immortal machines. They don't even need UR, since nothing ever goes wrong with them.'

'Can't you be like that?'

'We could, if we wanted to. But a long time ago something bad happened that convinced us that the Slashers were wrong, or at least foolhardy, to embrace that technology so wholeheartedly. It wasn't just . . .' and then she said something that sounded worryingly close to 'banana technology', but which Floyd assumed – hoped, for the sake of his sanity – he'd misheard.

'Not just that,' she continued. 'But virtual reality, radical genetic engineering, neural reshaping and the digital manipulation of data. We rejected all that. We even established a high-level quasi-governmental organisation – the Threshold Committee – to keep us back from the brink of ever developing any of those lethal toys by accident. We wanted to stay on the cusp, the threshold, but never quite cross it. The Slashers call us Threshers. It's intended as an insult, but we're quite happy to apply it to ourselves.'

'This bad thing that happened,' Floyd said. 'What was it?'

'We destroyed the Earth,' Auger said.

'That'll do it.'

'The thing is, Floyd, it didn't have to happen the way it did. If we allowed your world to run forward in time from the present, maybe we'd never end up with what happened in twenty seventy-seven . . . and everything would be different now. Not necessarily better, but different.'

'I'm not following you.'

'You and I don't share the same history, Floyd. After nineteen forty, there's nothing in common between our two worlds.'

'What's the significance of nineteen forty?'

'That's the year when Germany attempted to invade France. In your timeline, the invading forces ground to a halt in the Ardennes, becoming sitting ducks waiting for the Allied planes to bomb them into the mud. The war was over by the end of the year.'

'And in your timeline?'

'The invasion was a staggering success. By the end of nineteen forty, there were very few places in Europe and North Africa that the German army hadn't occupied. By the end of nineteen forty-one, the Japanese had joined forces with the Nazis. They launched a surprise attack on America, turning the whole thing into a global conflict. It was mechanized warfare on a scale the world had never seen before. It's what we call the Second World War.'

'You don't say.'

'It lasted until nineteen forty-five. The allies won, but the cost was considerable. By the time the war was over, the world was a completely different place. We'd let too many genies out of too many bottles.'

'Such as?'

'I don't even know where to begin,' Auger said. 'The Germans developed high-altitude rockets to bomb London. Within a couple of decades, the same technology would put people on the Moon. The Americans developed atomic bombs that were used to flatten Japanese cities in a single strike. Within a couple of decades, those bombs had become powerful enough to wipe out humanity many times over, in less time than it takes you to make breakfast. Then there were the computers. You've seen the Enigma machines. They played a significant role in wartime cryptography. But the allies built bigger, faster machines to crack the Enigma messages. Those machines filled entire rooms and drank enough power to light up an office block. But they became smaller and faster: *much* smaller and *much* faster. They shrank down to the point where you could barely see them. Valves became transistors, transistors became integrated circuits, integrated circuits became microprocessors and microprocessors became quantum optic processors . . . and still it snowballed. Within a few decades, there was no aspect of living that hadn't been touched by computers. They were everywhere, so ubiquitous that you almost didn't notice them any more. They were in our homes, in our animals, in our money, even in our bodies. And even that was just the beginning. Because by the beginning of the new century, some people were not content with just having very small machines that could process a lot of data very quickly. They wanted very small machines that could process matter itself: move it around, organise and reorganise it on a microscopic scale.'

'Why do I have the impression that this wasn't necessarily a good thing?' Floyd asked.

'Because it wasn't. Oh, the idea was sound, and the tiny machines did a lot of good in many areas of human life. UR was on the good side of the equation. The trouble is, when you're dealing with what is in essence a new form of life, there simply isn't room to make too many mistakes.'

'And human nature being what it is . . .' Floyd said.

'It was late July twenty seventy-seven,' Auger said. 'For the last couple of years, we'd been busy releasing tiny machines into the environment in an attempt to fix the climate. The planet had been heating up for more than a century, as we spewed crap into the atmosphere. The oceans were screwed up. Sea levels were rising, flooding coastal town and cities. There were freak storms. Some places got colder. Some places got hotter. Some places just got . . . *strange*. Really strange. And that was when some coalition of dickheads had the idea that we ought to try squirting some intelligence into the weather system. "Smart weather", they called it.'

'Smart weather,' Floyd echoed, shaking his head incredulously.

'"Big dumb idea" would have been closer to the truth. It was going to solve all our problems. Weather we could turn on and off, weather we could boss around. We seeded the oceans and the upper atmosphere with tiny floating machines: invisible to the eye, harmless to people. Unthinkable numbers of them, self-replicating, self-redesigning, self-coordinating. They reflected radiation here; absorbed it there. Cooled down this place, warmed up that place. Made clouds bloom and disperse in geometric patterns, like something from a Dali painting. Made deep-ocean currents bend through right angles and flow through each other, like rush-hour traffic. They even made money out of it, painting thousand-kilometre-wide corporate logos across the Pacific Ocean in phytoplankton. They could arrange a local enhancement in the colours of the sunset, as viewed from your private island. A little more green tonight, sir? No problem at all. And you know, for a while, it actually worked. The climate stabilised and began to creep back to pre-twenty fifty conditions. The icecaps began to grow again. The deserts began to retreat. The hotspots began to cool down. People began to move back to cities they'd abandoned twenty years earlier.'

'Call me a fatalist,' Floyd said, 'but I sense a "but" coming along.'

'It was never going to work. Late in twenty seventy-six there were rumours – unconfirmed reports – of some weather patterns refusing to follow orders. Ocean circulation events no one could turn off. Clouds that wouldn't disperse, no matter what you did to them. A persistent obscene symbol off the Bay of Biscay that had to be airbrushed out of every satellite image. It was clear – even though no one was admitting it – that some of the machines had evolved a little too far. They were more interested in their own self-preservation than obeying sequenced shutdown-and-disassemble commands. So you know what the coalition of dickheads did, for an encore?'

'I'm sure you're about to tell me.'

'They came up with some even cleverer, slyer machines and said they'd sort out the first wave. And so they were given authorisation to inject these into the environment as well. Trouble is, they only made things worse. Teething problems, they said. Meanwhile, the out-of-control weather events were getting more freakish by the hour, far worse than anything we'd had to deal with before. Now it was mechanized weather. By mid-twenty seventy-seven, they'd thrown eight layers of technology into the fray, and things hadn't improved. But then there was a hopeful sign: in early July of that year, the obscene symbol dissipated. Everyone got very excited, saying that the tide was turning and the machines had begun to return to human control. They all breathed one vast collective sigh of relief.'

'Which, I take it, was premature.'

'The phytoplankton bloom making up the obscene symbol had vanished for a reason: the machines had eaten the plankton. They'd started using living organisms to fuel themselves. It was against the most fundamental structures built into their programming – they weren't supposed to harm living things – but still they did it. And it got much worse, really fast. After the plankton, they worked their way up the marine food chain pretty damn quickly. By mid-July there wasn't much left alive in the entire Atlantic Ocean, apart from the machines. By the twentieth of that month, the machines had begun to attack land-based organisms. For a few days, the whiz kids still thought they could keep a lid on things. They had some small successes, but not enough to make a difference. On the twenty-seventh, the machines digested humanity. It happened very quickly. So quickly it was almost funny. It was like the Black Death directed by Buster Keaton. By the twenty-eighth, with the exception of a few extremophile organisms buried deep underground, there were no living things left alive on Earth.'

'But someone must have survived,' Floyd said, 'or else you wouldn't be here to tell me any of this.'

'Some people made it through,' Auger said. 'They were the ones who'd already left the surface of the Earth, moving into space habitats and colonies. Primitive, ramshackle affairs, barely self-sufficient, but enough to keep them alive while they coped with the loss of the Earth, and the numbing psychic trauma of what had happened. It was about then that we split into two political groupings. My people, the Threshers, said that nothing like this could ever be allowed to happen again, which is why we rejected the nanotechnology that had led to the development of the machines – and so much more – in the first place. The Slashers, on the other hand, thought that the damage was done and that there was no point in limiting themselves out of some misguided sense of penitence.'

Floyd was silent for a few moments, as he attempted to get his brain around everything Auger had told him. 'But you told me you're from twenty-two-whatever-it-was,' he said eventually. 'If all this happened in the middle of the twenty-first century, there's still quite a lot of history you haven't told me about yet, surely.'

'Two hundred years of it,' Auger said, 'but I'll spare you the details. Really, not much has happened. The same political groupings still exist. We control access to Earth, and the Slashers control access to the rest of the galaxy. Most of the time, it's been reasonably peaceable.'

'Most of the time?'

'We had a couple of small . . . disagreements. The Slashers keep trying to repair the Earth, with or without our consent. So far, they've only made things worse. There's a whole ecology of machines down there now. The last time they tried – twenty-three years ago – we ended up having a small war over access rights. It turned messy – really messy – but we patched things up afterwards. It's just a shame about what happened to Mars.'

'Nice to see wars haven't gone out of fashion,' Floyd said.

Auger nodded sadly. 'But in the last few months, things have turned sour again. That's why I wasn't exactly thrilled to discover a Slasher presence in your Paris. It tells me that they're up to something, and that makes me worried. I can't help but think it has to be bad news.'

'Wait,' Floyd said. 'There's something I need to get straight here. A few hours ago you told me you were not a time-traveller.'

'That's right,' Auger said, tight-lipped.

'But you keep on telling me you're from the future,' he said, 'born in the year twenty-two-whatever. You've even given me a history lesson about some of the events that have occurred between my time and yours. Mad weather . . . mad machines . . . people living in space . . .'

'Yes,' Auger said helpfully, raising an eyebrow.

'Then you must have travelled back to the present. Why pretend otherwise? This ship must be your time machine, or whatever you want to call it. Are you taking me back to the future?'

She looked at him hard. 'What year is it, Floyd?'

'It's nineteen fifty-nine,' he said.

'No,' she said. 'It isn't. It's twenty-two sixty-six – more than three hundred years into what you think of as the future.'

'You mean it *will* be when we come out of the other end of this thing. Or have we somehow already entered the future?'

'No,' she said, with an infinite and alarming patience. 'It isn't nineteen fifty-nine now. It wasn't nineteen fifty-nine yesterday and it wasn't nineteen fifty-nine when we met last week.'

'Now you're making even less sense than usual.'

'I'm saying that your whole existence is . . .' She grasped for words that would make sense to him. 'Something other than what you think it is. On one level, it's not even true to say that you are Wendell Floyd.'

'Maybe the robot should have put you under after all. You're starting to sound feverish.'

'I wish it was a fever. That would make life a lot easier for all concerned.'

'Not least for me.' Floyd scratched at his bandage, wondering if the delusional one was himself. His arm floated free, light as a balloon. It was as if they were falling, as if in a dream. He was going to wake up back in his room in rue du Dragon and laugh all this off with Custine over bad coffee and burnt toast. One bump on the head too many, that was his problem.

But he kept on not waking up.

'So let's start with me,' he said. 'Start with this poor sap named Wendell Floyd. Explain how it is that I might not even be who I think I am.'

'Wendell Floyd is dead,' Auger said. 'He died hundreds of years ago.'

That was when an alarm started buzzing somewhere in the cabin. Floyd's hand reached for the joystick, ready to nudge the ship back on course. But Auger shook her head, holding up three fingers in warning. 'This is different,' she said. 'The guidance system is still on-line.'

'Then what's the problem?'

'I'm not sure. They only gave me the idiot's guide to flying this thing.' Auger threw banks of switches, making the screens light up with different numbers and diagrams. Nothing she did made the audible alarm turn off.

'Any clues?' Floyd asked.

'I don't think there's anything wrong with the ship,' she said. 'Everything looks good – or at least acceptable – on all boards. And it doesn't look as though it has anything to do with the tunnel geometry ahead of us.'

'What, then?'

She threw more toggles, tapping the nail of an index finger against one of the screens and frowning at the avalanche of tiny digits and letters. 'Not good,' she said. 'Not good at all.'

'Just tell me,' Floyd said, frustration beginning to well up in his voice.

'Something's coming up behind us. That's what this alarm is telling us. The proximity system is picking up some kind of rearward echo. I can't read the numbers well enough to work out what it is, but it could be another ship.'

'How could there be another ship?'

'I don't know,' she said. 'Believe me, I wish I did. The tunnel is vacuum-sealed at the Paris end. Even if it was somehow possible to get two ships into it at the same time – and I'm not even sure the mathematics allows that – then it still can't have happened. There is no other ship in the E2 recovery bubble. We should be the only rat in this drainpipe.'

'Something else then? Another machine, but not necessarily a ship?'

'I don't know. Maybe it's some debris we dropped behind us. It was a bumpy insertion, and some stuff probably got knocked off the ship. It might be following us, sucked along in our wake. If we have a wake.'

'But why would we not have seen it until now, in that case?'

'That's a damned good question,' she said under her breath, as if he was the last person in the world she wanted to know it.

TWENTY-NINE

Presently, Auger found a way to turn off the audible alarm. Floyd breathed a sigh of relief when the din ended and they were left with the usual churn of cabin background sounds. There was something soothingly maritime about those noises. They made him think of engine rooms: the distant, reassuring throb of diesel power.

'I wish they'd told me how to interpret this junk,' Auger said, lines of concentration furrowing her forehead as she stared at the streaming numbers. 'It's almost as if the damned echo is getting closer. But that can't be the case, can it?'

'I'll take your word for it,' Floyd said, shrugging helplessly.

'If it was debris, it wouldn't be getting any nearer. We should have lost most of it when we slid through the interchange cavern. And given all the uncontrolled collisions it would be experiencing against the tunnel walls, it should be losing ground on us, not gaining it. There also shouldn't be a lot left of it by now.'

'So scratch the debris theory. Maybe you're misreading those numbers,' Floyd offered. 'Or maybe there's something wrong with the ship, making it imagine there's something behind it when there isn't.'

'I'd really like to believe that,' she said.

'You might be getting worked up over nothing. Fact is, from the little that you've told me, there isn't a whole lot we can do except sit back and enjoy the ride. That's more or less the case, isn't it?'

'Somehow, that doesn't make it any easier to live with.'

'Then I'll try to take your mind off things until you can make some more sense of those numbers. We were talking about me, I think: specifically about how I didn't actually happen to exist.'

'Maybe we shouldn't go there, Floyd.' Auger could not snap her attention from the puzzling barrage of numbers. She kept staring at them with a poised alertness, like someone expecting a flash of gold in a mountain stream. 'It was a mistake to tell you what I did.'

'Sorry, kid, but you already opened that particular can of worms. It kind of gives a fellow the creeps to hear someone talking as if he died years ago. Are you going to elaborate, or do I have to turn on the charm?'

'Not the charm, Floyd. I'm not sure I could take it.'

'Then tell me about these rumours of my death. When, exactly, did they nail me into a box?'

'I don't know,' she said. 'And I don't even know for sure that you rated a box. I'm afraid Wendell Floyd simply didn't make enough of a dent in history for that detail to have survived. Remind me how old you are, Floyd – forty, forty-one?'

'Thirty-nine. You really know how to flatter a guy.'

'So you were born – when? Some time around nineteen twenty?'

'Spot on,' Floyd said.

'Which would have made Floyd eighty by the end of the century. But chances are he didn't get to see the year two thousand. He might well have died during the Second World War, or perhaps he lived a happy and peaceful life into old age and passed on surrounded by loving family members. Or maybe he ended his days as some crabby, antisocial bastard everyone couldn't wait to see the back of.'

'I've always had a sneaking regard for crabby, antisocial bastards,' Floyd said.

'Whatever happened,' Auger said, 'it was a human life. He was born, he lived, he died. He probably made some people happy and other people unhappy. He was probably remembered for a few decades after he died. After that, he'd just have been a face in old photographs – the kind that come out when you spring-clean, and you can't quite remember where they came from or who's who. And that was it. Wendell Floyd. He lived. He died. It was a life. End of story.'

'Why do I have the feeling that someone just walked over my grave?'

'Because someone probably did,' Auger said. 'Or they would have, if your grave wasn't buried under a few hundred metres of ice.'

'Where did the ice come into it?'

'I told you the Earth got screwed up. But never mind the ice. What matters is that at some point during the late nineteen thirties, something happened to Wendell Floyd.'

'A lot of things happened in the late nineteen thirties,' Floyd said.

'But the main event is one that you won't remember at all. No one does. But the funny thing is that it happened to everyone at the same instant, and it was the most important thing that ever happened to them in their whole lives. And yet it went utterly unremarked.'

'It happened to everyone?'

'To everyone who was alive whenever exactly it happened. Every *thing* that was alive. Every animal and plant on the planet. And every inanimate thing as well – every grain of sand on every beach, every blade of grass, every drop of water in every ocean, every molecule of oxygen in the atmosphere, every atom in every rock, all the way to the Earth's core.'

'So what was this incredible thing that happened?'

'It was like a photograph,' she said. 'Like the instant when the flash goes off and the image is burnt on to the plate. Except it wasn't a simple picture. It was a three-dimensional one, an image of astonishing, mind-blowing complexity. A photograph of the entire planet, down to the quantum horizon of information capture. Maybe even beyond Heisenberg . . . who knows? Our physics doesn't even hint at how they did it. We call it a quantum snapshot, but that doesn't mean we have clue one about what was involved in producing it. That's just a name we give it to hide our ignorance.'

'But no one could have done such a thing,' Floyd said. 'We'd have heard about it. It would have been all over the headlines.'

'It wasn't done by any agency on Earth. The snapshot was taken by an external power. Beings from another planet, or another dimension, or another time. We have no idea what they were like or what motivated them to do this. Only that it happened.'

'Martians, again?'

'Not Martians. Probably not even anything we'd recognise as an intelligent entity. They must have been far ahead of us, Floyd. About as far ahead of us as we're ahead of sponges, or beetles. Godlike, in every sense.'

'And they came along and took this photograph—'

'The snapshot. Like I said, we don't know how. Maybe they built a structure around the entire planet, in a matter of hours. A clever, subtle structure, which was somehow able to make the recording in an eyeblink without anyone noticing – and, more importantly, without significantly affecting the planet itself in any way. Or maybe they just kissed something against the planet, another object that became entangled with the quantum identity of the Earth, encoding all that information into itself, ready to be deciphered again in the future. We could speculate about the "how" for ever and never get close to the truth. What we can guess at more successfully, perhaps, is the "why". We think their motives were fundamentally benign. They were interested in preservation, in creating a record of the Earth that could be used to recreate the planet in the event of a future catastrophe. We call that the "backup copy" theory. According to that view, the entities that did this are like cosmic archivists, or system administrators. They go around the galaxy, visiting worlds that are at a sensitive stage of evolution, and they make copies using the quantum-snapshot process.'

'And what happens to these "copies"?' Floyd asked.

'That's the big question. Our best guess – and there is some intelligence to support this – is that the copies are dispersed throughout the galaxy, preserved in a kind of storage media. Think of these storage media as safety-deposit boxes, each of which contains a single photograph. One might be the image of Earth at a particular moment in the late nineteen thirties. Another might contain a snapshot of Earth from sixty-five million years ago, or the ancient history of another planet entirely. We think we've found some of these boxes. We call them anomalous large structures, or ALS spheres. They're stellar-sized objects of obvious alien origin: huge armoured spheres vast enough to contain entire planets and a sizeable volume of space around them.'

'Have you looked inside any of these boxes?'

'The best anyone has been able to do was take a fuzzy image of the contents of one sphere. Embedded inside, coincidental with the geometric centre, was a dense object with just the kind of neutrino-absorption cross section that you'd expect from a rocky world. It wasn't any planet we recognised, based on its implied density and size.'

Floyd risked a contribution. 'A snapshot of another world?'

'Yes. Frozen inside the structure like a perfect three-dimensional photograph. Of course, if we scoured the galaxy thoroughly enough, we'd eventually find the original – the world from which the copy was made. Assuming we were able to recognise it when we found it.'

'Tell me how all this fits together. Why would anyone want to make copies of planets and put them inside giant eggshells? And what the hell does it have to do with me?'

'Haven't you figured it out yet?' she said, with a snarl of irritation. 'Floyd was copied: him and every living person on the planet. After the snapshot was taken, he went on to live whatever life it was he lived. History rolled on and the world ended in twenty seventy-seven. And that should have been the end of it. But now Floyd's copy has come back to life somehow, hundreds of years later, and I'm talking to it at this exact moment, trying to explain to it why it isn't who it thinks it is.' She said each and every 'it' with deliberate, wounding emphasis.

'I can't be a copy,' Floyd said. 'I remember everything. I remember what I did when I was a kid and everything I did afterwards, until now.'

'That doesn't prove anything. You were copied with all of Floyd's memories intact, down to the last detail.'

'Wait a minute. If the copy was made a few hundred years ago, why isn't the copy dead by now?'

'You should be dead,' Auger said. 'And you would be, if the copy had been allowed to live immediately after the snapshot was produced. But it wasn't. The copy – the complete three-dimensional image of the Earth and its inhabitants – appears to have remained frozen until about twenty-three years ago, held in some kind of suspended quantum state.' Floyd saw her close her eyes, as she groped for a simile. 'Like an undeveloped photograph,' she offered.

'But someone came along and developed it.'

'Yes. Quantum states like that are very fragile, and a copy of an entire planet must be *astonishingly* fragile: a house of cards just waiting to collapse at the merest sneeze. But somehow whoever created it was able to isolate it to a sufficient degree to preserve it for a while. The weak radiation signals that came through the shell – the gravitational and neutrino emissions – obviously weren't enough to upset the stasis, or whatever you want to call it. But still there was some kind of trigger. By your calendar it was nineteen fifty-nine when we met, agreed?'

'Yes.'

'We also know – from studying historical events in your timeline – that your world was on more or less the right track until at least the mid-thirties. By the end of nineteen forty it had changed – the German invasion in May of that year failed – which implies a build-up of small events over a period of years that eventually had a significant impact. Most likely, the snapshot took place somewhere around nineteen thirty-six, twenty-three years ago as far as you're concerned.'

'If you say so,' Floyd said grudgingly, conceding nothing.

'Now look at the same span of time in our chronology. We know that time passes at the same rate in your world as it does in mine. It's twenty-two sixty-six now. Subtract twenty-three years and we're back in twenty-two forty-three, which is more or less when the Slashers had control of Mars and its moons, including Phobos.'

'Where we're headed,' Floyd added, if only to show that he was paying attention.

'Yes. And I can't believe that's a coincidence. My guess is that the snapshot began to evolve forward in time from the moment the Slashers opened the portal on Phobos. A little bit of the external universe must have begun to leak into the ALS, collapsing the image into a normal state of matter. The snapshot came alive.'

In his mind's eye, Floyd had a sudden, horrible mental image. He pictured a kind of theatrical stage populated by stiff mechanical dancers, still as statues, coated in years' worth of dust. And then they began to move, slowly at first, choreographing their clockwork movements to music from a grindingly slow fairground organ. As the tortured, wheezing music gained speed, so did the dancers, whirling and gyrating in orbits and epicycles. He tried to shake the image, but the little figures danced on, gaining speed.

'But even if that were true,' Floyd said, 'even if I and everyone I know had been kept asleep for all those years – all those hundreds of years – shouldn't we remember it?'

'You wouldn't remember a damned thing,' Auger said. 'You skipped over three-hundred-odd years between heartbeats, Floyd – you and everyone else on the planet. Maybe you felt the tiniest moment of déjà vu, or some other thing the French have a word for, but that would have been it.'

'Everyone on the planet would have felt it?'

'Maybe. But how many of you would have even thought to remark on it?'

'You can't expect me just to accept this,' he said.

'Floyd, I'm not asking you to accept anything.' She sounded, for a moment, desperately sorry for him. Hearing that in her voice only made him more afraid that she was, indeed, telling the truth and nothing more.

'I'm not a copy of Wendell Floyd,' he said, panic rising in his voice despite his attempts to keep it under control. 'I *am* Wendell Floyd.'

'You're a perfect copy. That's precisely how you would feel.'

'Then what does that make me? Some kind of ghost, some kind of phoney imitation?'

'That's the way some people might see it.'

'And is that the way you see it?'

'No,' she said, after just too much hesitation. 'Not at all.'

'Now I know why you were so worried that I wouldn't be able to pass through that censor thing,' Floyd said.

'I couldn't know what would happen. No one had tried to bring anyone out of E2 before.'

'It treated me like any other human being. Isn't that good enough for you?'

'Yes,' she said. 'I suppose it is. But listen to me, Floyd: you will never belong in my world. Your world is back in Paris, as real or otherwise as it might be.'

'Don't worry,' he told her. 'I have every intention of returning.'

Something caught her eye again: some glint of meaning in the tumble of numbers racing across the display screens. She flipped banks of switches, peered at the numbers again. Her face was a mask of intense, troubled concentration.

'It's still getting closer?' Floyd asked.

'I'm worried about this. It almost looks as if . . .' But then she shook her head, as if trying to dislodge whatever upsetting thought had taken up residence. 'It can't be.'

'What can't be?'

'I might be making a mistake here,' she said.

'I'll take the risk. What's got you so rattled?'

'I think what I'm seeing is the end of the tunnel behind us. It's acting like a reflecting surface, bouncing signals back towards us.'

'But we left Paris behind hours ago.'

'I know. And I think something bad must have happened just as we left. The numbers make it look as if the tunnel's collapsing, folding shut just behind us.'

'Can that happen?'

'I guess so. Skellsgard always said there might be a problem if the throat contracted too quickly during an insertion. It looks as if the robot couldn't handle the injection procedure. Or else it was programmed to find the one solution that would get us out of Paris, even if that meant sacrificing the link, and itself . . .'

'What does that mean?'

'It means we're sliding down a pipe that's getting shorter all the while, with the closed end catching up with us.'

'That doesn't sound good to me.'

'It doesn't sound good to me, either.' Auger tapped a finger against another display. 'But these numbers back me up. They show our speed through the hyperweb, with our estimated ETA at Phobos. We're picking up momentum, shaving hours off our projected journey time.'

'Isn't that a good thing?'

'No. Because it's nothing that the transport is doing, and it can't be due to another ship or pile of debris behind us. It must be due to something pretty fundamental happening to the hyperweb. I think it's the field geometry in the walls, squeezing us forward like a pip. As the crimped end gets nearer and nearer, we're being pushed along faster and faster by the in-closing walls.' She turned to Floyd. 'But the ship isn't built to handle speeds much faster than this. And I don't know what will happen when the curvature becomes really severe, and we end up squeezed into the end of the tunnel.'

'Is there anything we can do about it?'

'Not much,' Auger said. 'I could fire the steering jets, try to push us away from whatever is following us. But the jets aren't designed for sustained use. We'd buy a few minutes, maybe half an hour.'

'We're in a heap of trouble, aren't we?'

'Yes,' Auger said. 'And I'm shot and not feeling at my sharpest. But we'll get out of this, don't you worry.'

'You sound rather sure of yourself.'

'I didn't come all this way for nothing,' she said, a frown of determination etched firmly into her forehead. 'I'm not going to let a little space-time difficulty spoil my day.'

'Why don't you get some rest,' Floyd said, 'see if you can catch some sleep before things get too bumpy? I think I can just about cope with the ship at the moment.'

'Are you a good driver, Floyd?'

'No,' he said. 'I'm a lousy driver. Custine always says I drive like a grandmother on Sunday.'

'Well, that fills me with confidence,' she said, reluctantly releasing control of the ship to Floyd and trying to relax.

Floyd took the joystick, feeling the slight lurch as the ship fell under his control. Perhaps it was his imagination, but the ride already felt rougher. It was as if they had left a smooth stretch of road and were now rumbling over a dirt track. Around the cabin, the fixed instruments and displays appeared slightly blurred. He squinted, but that did nothing to make the view clearer. Somewhere behind the metal panelling of the cabin, something made a shrill, tinny vibrating sound, as if it was about to work loose. Floyd tightened his grip on the joystick, wondering how bad things were going to get before they got better.

THIRTY

Auger woke to intense turbulence, the ship shaking and shimmying as if only an instant away from swift annihilation. Through blurred, gummed eyes, she glanced at the principal instruments, remembering as much as she could of Skellsgard's technical briefing. The situation was acute: far, far worse than when she had gone to sleep. According to the numbers – and again, a lot depended on her imperfect interpretation of those dancing, tumbling digits – the collapsing end of the tunnel had almost caught up with them. Simultaneously, it had accelerated them even faster. It was as if they were caught in the pressure wave in front of an avalanche: pushed ahead, but with an ever-dwindling lead that would soon see them engulfed.

The ship was showing signs of mortal damage. Many displays were simply dead or showing only static. Some dials were inactive, jammed against their limits. Others were wheeling around like dervishes, spinning like the altimeter in a dive-bomber. The guidance display on her side of the cabin revealed ragged blind spots in the flowing contours of its stress-energy grid. In her mind's eye, she visualised critical machinery – sensors and guidance mechanisms – ripped clean away from the hull, trailing sizzling hot electrical ganglia with them. Warning lights were flashing, and yet the klaxons were mysteriously silent.

'Floyd,' she said, her mouth sluggish and dry. 'How long was I under?'

'A few hours,' he said. He still had his hand on the joystick, and as she watched he made tiny, precise adjustments.

'A few? It feels like—'

'More than a few? It was probably more like six, or maybe even twelve. I don't know. I guess I lost count.' He looked at her, his face a study in exhaustion. 'How do you feel, kid?'

'Better,' she said, rubbing experimentally at the wound. 'Groggy . . . sore . . . but better. The UR must have eased the inflammation, taken care of the bleeding.'

'Does that mean you'll hold together until we reach the end of this funfair ride?'

'Should do,' she said.

'But you'll still need help when we arrive?'

'Yes, but don't worry about that. If we get there, they'll take care of me.'

The ship veered violently, then knocked hard against something and slid on a sideways trajectory with an ominous bone-crunching rumble. Floyd grimaced and pulled the joystick hard over. Auger heard the sequenced pop of the steering jets and wondered how much propellant Floyd had already consumed holding them together until now.

'I was out for twelve hours?' she said, his words just sinking in.

'Maybe thirteen. But don't worry about me. The time simply flew by.'

'You did good getting us this far, Floyd. Seriously, I'm impressed.'

He looked at her with a genuine and rather touching surprise, as if the last thing he had been expecting was praise.

'Really?'

'Yes. Really. Not bad for a man who shouldn't exist. I just hope the effort will turn out to have been worth it.'

'You're still worried about what will happen at the other end?'

'We're going to pop out of this tunnel much faster than the system was ever designed to deal with – like an express train hitting the buffers at full tilt.'

'You have a bunch of people at the other end, right? People like Skellsgard?'

'Yes,' she said, 'but I don't know how much good they're going to be able to do. Even if we could warn them . . . but we can't even get a message through to them. You can't bounce signals up the pipe while there's a ship in it. Not according to the book, anyway.'

'Won't they have any warning at all?'

'Maybe. Skellsgard has equipment to monitor the condition of the link – but I don't know if it's going to be able to tell her that the link itself is collapsing. But she also told me about something called bow-shock distortion. It's like a ripple we push ahead of ourselves, a change in the geometry of the tunnel propagating ahead of the transport. They have equipment to pick it up, so that they can tell when a ship is about to come through the portal. I think it gives them a few minutes' warning.' Auger scratched at a crusty residue that had collected in the corner of one eye. It felt dense and geologic, hard and compacted like some mother lode of granite. 'But that won't help us,' she said. 'They'll have even less warning than usual because we're going so much faster than we should be.'

'There must be something we can do,' Floyd said.

'Yes,' Auger said. 'We can pray, and hope that the tunnel doesn't speed us up any faster than we're already moving. Right now we might just walk out of this alive. Any faster, and I think we've had it.'

'If we get to that point, would you mind not telling me? The coward in me would rather not know.'

'The coward in both of us,' Auger said. 'If it's any consolation, Floyd, it'll be quick and spectacular.'

She checked out the numbers again. No act of denial could avoid the fact that they were now travelling thirty per cent faster than the ship she'd taken on the inbound leg of the journey. The ETA now had the total trip taking less than twenty-two hours. Of that time, about sixteen hours had already passed. And they were not getting any slower.

'Floyd,' she said, 'do you want to take a break? I can fly the ship for a while.'

'In your condition? Thanks, but I think I can keep my eyes open for a few hours more.'

'Trust me: it's going to take both of us to get this thing home.'

Floyd studied her for a moment and then nodded, relaxed his grip on the joystick and almost immediately slumped back into his couch and into a deep sleep. It was as if he had given himself permission to slip into unconsciousness, after holding it at bay for so long by a sheer act of will. Auger wondered how many hours at sea had honed that particular skill and wished him sweet dreams, assuming that he had the energy to dream. Perhaps unconsciousness would be the kindest state for both of them to be in, when the end approached.

'Find a way out of this,' she said aloud, as if that might help.

The four hours that followed were the longest she could remember. She had taken the last of the UR pills, hoping that this was the right thing to do. For the first hour, she felt a shrill, slightly unnerving clarity of mind. It was like the ringing caused by a finger circling the wet rim of a wine glass. It felt fragile and not quite trustworthy, making her wonder if she was, indeed, making the right decisions, even when they felt absolutely, unquestionably correct. When, at last, that bell-clear intensity began to dull and she started to feel foggy-headed, unable to focus on any particular problem for more than a few seconds, it came as a kind of relief. At least now she had objective evidence that her thought processes were likely to be impaired. She could factor that dullness into her activities, allowing for it wherever possible. It was, she supposed, a measure of her lessening hold on reality that she could even consider this a minor victory.

The ship was moving even faster now: fifty per cent above conventional tunnel speeds, and still accelerating. By now, Auger had enough of a grasp of the numbers to estimate their emergence speed, and the news was not cheering. They would hit the Phobos portal at twice the expected rate, and even that was likely to be an underestimate, since the rate of acceleration was itself beginning to quicken as the geometry of the pinched tunnel underwent convulsive readjustments. The apparatus in the recovery bubble would never be able to cope with that kind of momentum. The transport would smash through the arrestor cradle and the glass sphere of the bubble, then smear itself against the plasticised walls of the chamber a couple of kilometres inside Phobos. It would be a very lucky day if anyone made it out of that mess alive, let alone Auger and Floyd.

Spectacular? Hell, yes.

But the speed hurt them in other ways. The forward-looking sensors had already been damaged by tunnel collisions, but even in those areas that were not affected by blind spots, the sensors could not peer far enough ahead to give ample warning of micro-changes in the tunnel structure. Obstacles and wrinkles that the guidance system could normally have coped with – steering around them with finessed, calibrated, fuel-conserving bursts of steering thrust – now came upon the ship too quickly for it to respond in time. The ship was still managing to dodge the worst of them, but the effort was draining the steering jets at a worrying rate.

But even that was not the main thing on Auger's mind. For a while, she did not even think about the problem of slowing down, or the bullet in her shoulder, or the Slasher activity in Paris.

She thought about Floyd, and how she was going to explain things to him.

Because with the tunnel unzipping behind them, Floyd was going to find it very difficult to make his way home. There would no longer be a hyperweb connection between Phobos and Paris; no way for him to make that return trip. Even if the two of them somehow survived the next few hours (and she preferred not to think about the odds of that), Floyd would still find himself marooned countless light-years from E2 and – more importantly – three centuries upstream in a future that didn't even regard him as a genuine human being, rather a very detailed living and breathing copy of one . . . a copy of a man who had lived and died in a time when the world still had a chance to fix the mess it was in. A man so happily ordinary that he hadn't left the faintest trace of himself in history.

Around two hours after he had slipped into unconsciousness, Floyd stirred beside her. There was no telling what had woken him: it could have been the increasingly rough ride, or the emergency klaxon that had just come on, accompanied by a recorded female voice calmly informing them that they were about to lose steering control.

'Is that as bad as it sounds?' Floyd asked.

'No,' Auger said. 'It's worse. A lot worse.'

The guidance system had depleted most of the reaction mass in the steering jets. What was left would be good for about ten minutes . . . at most. Less if their speed kept increasing, which it showed every intention of doing. By Auger's reckoning, the pinch at the end of the tunnel had nearly caught up with them, and the pinch was still showing definite signs of acceleration. Maybe if she had Skellsgard's grasp of hyperweb theory, imperfect as it was, she might have been able to explain why that was happening and how it related to the underlying metric structure of the collapsing quasi-wormhole. Not that such knowledge would have been particularly useful in any practical sense, but . . .

'If we can't steer,' Floyd said, 'won't we crash into the walls? I mean, more than we've already been doing?'

'Yes,' Auger said. 'But the system reckons that we're only one hour from Phobos now – maybe less, depending on how much more we accelerate. There's a faint chance that the ship might hold together long enough to get us there, even with complete loss of guidance control. Emphasis on the "faint".'

'I won't pencil in anything for next week.'

'It's going to be bumpy – worse than anything we've experienced so far. And we'll still have the small problem of hitting the portal at two and a half times normal tunnel speed even if we make it that far.'

'Let's just deal with one thing at a time, shall we? That friend of yours – Skellsgard?'

'Yes,' Auger said.

'She sounded as if she knew what she was doing. She'll find a way out of this, if we can hold together until the end.'

Poor Floyd, she thought, *if only you knew what things are really like*. The future might have been crammed with miracles and wonders, but it also offered truly awesome opportunities for screwing up.

'I'm sure you're right,' she said, doing her best to sound reassuring. 'I'm sure they'll think of something.'

'That's the spirit.'

'Final warning,' the soothing feminine voice said. 'Attitude adjustment control will cease in ten . . . nine . . . eight . . .'

'Brace yourself, Floyd. And if you have any lucky charms, now might be the time to start sweet-talking them.'

'Attitude adjustment control is now off-line,' the voice said, with a kind of cheery resignation.

For a deceptive ten or twenty seconds, the ride became dreamily smooth again. It was as if they had tobogganed off the edge of a cliff into the absolute stillness of midair.

'Hey,' Floyd started to say, 'that's not too—'

Then they hit something, the side of the ship grazing hard against the tunnel wall. It was a bigger jolt than anything they had experienced so far. They felt and heard an awful wrench as something large and metallic was plucked from the hull. Floyd grabbed the joystick and tried to correct their trajectory, but nothing he did had any effect on the oozing contours of the stress-energy display.

'It's useless,' Auger said, with a stoic calm that even she found surprising. 'We're in uncontrolled flight now.' To emphasise this point, she released her own dead joystick and folded back the control console. 'Just sit back and enjoy the ride.'

'You're going to give up that easily? What if there's still some fuel left in the tanks?'

'This isn't a war film, Floyd. When the system says zero, it means it.'

After the first collision, there was another hiatus as the transport rebounded to the other side of the tunnel. Auger still kept an eye on the grid and the cascading numbers. The ship's nose was beginning to point away from the direction of forward motion. There was going to be another bad jolt when they—

The impact came sooner than she had anticipated. It slammed through her like an electrical shock, snapping her jaw shut. She bit her tongue, tasted blood in her mouth. Warning lights flashed all around the cockpit. One of the surviving klaxons came on, barking a two-tone scream into her skull. Another taped voice – it sounded suspiciously like the same woman – said, 'Caution. Safe design limits for outer-hull integrity have now been exceeded. Structural failure is now a high likelihood event.'

'Hey, lady!' Floyd said. 'Tell us something we don't know!'

But Auger had no idea how to turn off the automated voice messages. Almost as soon as the first one had ended, another chimed in, informing them that safe radiation limits for the crew had now been exceeded.

Then they hit again, and rebounded, and hit again, and then the nose of the transport came around through sixty degrees, so that the next kick imparted a sickening roll to their motion, which only became worse with the next collision. With each rotation, Auger was pushed into her seat and then dragged out of it, her entire body straining against the webbing. The wound in her shoulder, numb for hours, now began to reassert its presence.

The stress-energy contours were flowing too fast to read, the interpretive system just as confused as Auger. Not that it made a damned bit of difference. When you had lost all control, flying blind was almost a mercy.

Something else was ripped away from the hull with a squeal of tortured metal. She felt a pop in her skull as the air pressure suddenly notched down.

'We just lost—' She did not have time to complete her sentence. Air shrieked out of the cabin, becoming thinner with every breath. Through blurred eyes, she saw Floyd's panicked expression as his body was buffeted to and fro by the same cartwheeling motion that was shoving her in and out of her seat. She struggled to reach her good arm up, feeling as if she had to push a boulder out of the way. Her hand closed around the striped yellow toggle of the emergency mask hatch. She pulled it down, cursing the system that should have dropped the masks automatically. She pressed the hard plastic of the mask to her face and took a cold and instantly reinvigorating breath.

She motioned for Floyd to do the same and waited impatiently while he located his mask and slipped it on gratefully. 'Can you hear me?' she asked.

'Yes,' he said at last, but his voice sounded thin and distant.

'The blow-out's stabilised. I think we're down to about a third of normal operating pressure. We'll need to keep—'

The words were jolted away from her as the careering, tumbling ship smashed itself against the wall again. She heard more chunks of hull ripping away. Most of the displays were by now either dead or showing nothing comprehensible. Auger tried to focus on the ETA, but even that kept changing, varying by tens of minutes with each rotation as the ship reinterpreted its tunnel speed. Another jolt followed, sending a compression wave up her backbone that whiplashed her skull against the back of the seat.

She blacked out for an instant, drifting back to consciousness through a bloody haze of red-tinged tunnel vision. Her hands seemed impossibly distant and ineffectual, anchored to her body by the thinnest of threads. Her thoughts were foggy, unfocused. She was dreaming this, surely? No, she wasn't: she was in it. But even the prospect of imminent death had lost some of its edge now. Perhaps blacking out really wasn't such a bad option after all . . .

She looked at Floyd and saw his head lolling from one side of the chair to the other as the ship rotated. His mouth was open, as if in a gasp of ecstasy or dread. His eyes were narrow, pink-tinged slits and fresh blood seeped from beneath his bandage.

Floyd was out cold.

The ship kept tumbling; tumbling and crashing and slowly dying. Auger tried to press herself more tightly into her seat, clutching the armrests and stiffening her torso against the padded back. From a distance, as if from another room, a woman's voice said, 'Warning. Final approach to portal in progress. Final approach to portal in progress. Please ensure all systems are stowed and all crew members are braced for deceleration procedure. Failure to comply . . .'

'Please shut the fuck up,' Auger said, and then prayed for unconsciousness.

The jolting and buffeting reached a climax. There was an instant – it couldn't have lasted more than two or three seconds – when it seemed completely impossible that either the ship or its fragile human cargo would survive the next few heartbeats. The rapidity and severity of the collisions were just too severe.

But the end never came.

The tumbling continued, but – with the exception of the occasional thud or bump – the brutal collisions ceased. Even the tumbling settled down, becoming regular and almost tolerable. Once again, it was as if the transport had sailed off the edge of a precipice and was now in a deceptive free fall: a spiteful remission from the damaging impacts that were bound to resume at any moment.

But they didn't.

'Numbers,' Auger mumbled through a bloodied, swollen tongue.

But the numbers told her nothing. The ship had finally become blind and senseless, unable to assemble any coherent picture of its surroundings. A change in the tunnel geometry, Auger thought – that was the only thing that could explain what had just happened. The collapse process must have somehow caused the end of the tunnel near the throat they were approaching to swell wider, increasing the diameter of the tunnel so that the transport had much further to travel between impacts with the sides.

She could think of no other explanation. They had certainly not undergone the crushing deceleration that would have been necessary to halt them within the recovery bubble. And they were still tumbling. The ship hadn't been caught or snared or arrested by anything.

But the tunnel would have had to swell ludicrously wide. They hadn't suffered a serious impact for at least two minutes, just those minor knocks. Had the picture changed so dramatically that those were, in fact, the glancing impacts? Had the tunnel walls become softer somehow, better able to absorb the collisions?

Another thud, and then something even stranger: a drumlike pitter-patter of tinier thuds, like rain.

Then nothing.

Floyd made a groaning noise. 'I wish those elephants would stop sitting on my head,' he said.

'Are you all right? What do you remember?'

'I remember thinking I needed a new career.' He touched the side of his head, straining to hold up his hand against the centrifugal effect of their tumbling motion. 'Are we dead yet, or is it just me who feels that way?'

'We're not dead,' she answered. 'But I don't know why not. We haven't had a major collision for a few minutes, but we're still spinning.'

'I noticed. You have a theory for this state of affairs?'

'No,' she said. 'Nothing that makes any sense.'

It was, she realised, very quiet. The ship made little creaking and groaning sounds, but there were no klaxons blaring, no pre-recorded voices announcing impending disaster. It was exactly as if they were tumbling through . . .

'Can you make sense of those numbers?' Floyd asked, interrupting her train of thought.

'No,' she said. 'The ship hasn't got a clue where it is. What it's showing would only make sense if we'd left the portal behind. Which, obviously—'

'Maybe if we opened the window shields, we might have a better idea,' Floyd suggested.

'You open those windows in mid-tunnel, you'll be wearing dark glasses for the rest of your life.'

'I always thought they suited me. Can't you crank the blinds open just a crack? It might tell us something.'

She groped for an objection, but found none that she thought likely to convince him. Besides, he was right: at the very least it would tell them something, even if the information had no practical value. But she would still rather know where she was. It was, she supposed, a basic human need.

'I don't even know if they'll open,' she said, 'after the pounding we took back there.'

'Just try it, Auger.'

She folded down the control console and found the switch that operated the armoured window shutters. Just when she had convinced herself that nothing was going to happen – that the shutters must be buckled tight – a fan of hard light cleaved the cabin in two. One of the shutters was broken, but the other was still operational. She allowed it to open to the width of three fingers, then held it at that position.

She squinted, raising a hand to shield her eyes. After more than a day in the subdued lighting of the cabin, the glare was intensely bright. But it was not the murderous electric-blue radiance of the tunnel.

The light blinked out.

The light returned.

'It's timed with our rotation,' she said after a moment. 'It's as if there's a light source to one side of us, rather than all around us.'

'Does that make any sense?'

'No. But then neither does the fact that we're alive.'

Floyd's seat was positioned too far from the window to let him see through it. 'Can you see anything you recognise?' he asked.

'No,' Auger said. She allowed the shutter to open to its fullest extent, but she could still only tell that there was a light source somewhere outside. 'I'm going to leave my seat, see if I can get my head closer to—'

'Easy, soldier. That's not a job for someone in your condition.' Floyd was already trying to extricate himself from his seat harness, his fingers sliding over the complex plastic buckles.

'You can talk.'

The harness released him. The tumbling continued, but because it was now regular and confined to one axis of rotation, Floyd was able to push himself out of the seat without too much difficulty. He used one arm to brace himself against the cabin wall, and another to lever himself closer to the window, keeping one foot hooked around the rest at the base of the seat.

'Careful, Floyd,' Auger said, as he pressed his face to the glass. 'Do you see anything out there?'

'There's a bright light off to one side,' he said. 'I can't see it directly. But there is something else out there.'

'Describe it.'

'It comes into view once every rotation. It's like . . .' He adjusted his position, the effort etched in his face. 'A bright smudge. Like a cloud, with lights in it. Lights around it, as a matter of fact. Some of them moving, some of them flashing. There are dark things in front of the cloud, moving outwards.'

She tried to visualise whatever it was he was seeing, and drew a comprehensive blank. 'That's it? That's all you can see?'

'That's about the size of it.'

'Well, what colour is it?'

Floyd looked back at her. 'I don't know. I'm not exactly the guy to ask when it comes to colours.'

'You mean you're colour-blind?' Despite her fears, she couldn't help but laugh.

'Hey, isn't that a little rude?'

'I'm not laughing at you, Floyd. I'm laughing at us. We make quite a pair, don't we? The colour-blind detective and the tone-deaf spy.'

'Actually, I meant to ask you about . . .' But Floyd trailed off. 'Auger, you may not want to hear this, but damned if that thing doesn't seem to be getting smaller.'

Whatever Floyd was seeing, it bore no relationship to anything Auger had been told to expect during her mission briefing. It meant, surely, that something very odd and unanticipated had happened to them.

She felt a prickle of comprehension, like an itch at the back of her head. 'Floyd, I think I have an idea—'

'There's something else out there as well. It's very big. I can just see the edge of it.'

'Floyd, I think we've slipped into a different part of the hyperweb. Skellsgard said there was no way any other tunnel could intersect with the one we were in . . . but what if she was wrong?' Auger forced herself to calm down and speak more slowly. 'What if there was a junction, and we found it by accident when we were bouncing around back there? Or what if we hit the wall so hard we actually punctured it and slipped through into an adjacent part of the network?'

'Are you listening to me, Auger?' Floyd said, staring at her as if she'd gone completely insane. 'I'm telling you there's something really, really big out there.'

'The light source?'

'No. Not the light source. It's on the other side of the sky. It almost looks like . . .'

Auger reached out to the console panel again. 'Get back in your seat. I'm going to try something hopelessly optimistic.'

'My kind of girl. What are you going to do?'

'I'm going to see if there's any juice left in those steering jets.'

'We already tried that,' Floyd said, lowering himself back into his seat and pulling the harness tight. 'They died on us.'

'I know. But the system might have been reading empty even when there was a tiny amount of pressure left in the reservoir.'

Floyd gave her an odd look. 'You said it didn't work like that.'

'I lied. I swatted down your suggestion because I was feeling nasty and petulant. Not that it would have done us much good back then, anyway—'

'Of course not.' He sounded hurt.

'I'm sorry,' she said. 'I'm not dealing with this very well, OK? Believe it or not, this isn't a situation I find myself in every day.'

'Consider yourself forgiven,' Floyd said.

'Look,' Auger said, 'all I need is a couple of squirts of reaction mass, just enough to kill our spin, or even simply to alter it so that we have a different view.'

'You might make things worse.'

'I think we have to risk it.' Her hand closed on the joystick. She flipped up the trigger guard and readied her finger, trying to picture the orientation of the tumbling ship from the outside. Skellsgard had not told her how to recover from a spin of this kind – the briefing had never envisaged that things could go this splendidly, abjectly wrong – but all she had to do was change things slightly, just enough to bring something else into view. Then, in a sudden fit of misery, she wondered what the point of that would be, given that she had already failed to make any sense of Floyd's initial impressions . . .

She squeezed the trigger. Instead of the usual sequenced percussion of steering jets, all she heard was a low, dying hiss that faded as soon as it had begun. Earlier, with the emergency systems blaring and the impacts making an unholy din, she would never have heard that feeble whisper of last-ditch thrust.

Would it be enough? She had felt nothing that would indicate a change of course.

But the angle of the light source – the scything fan of light that touched the cabin interior with each rotation – had altered slightly.

'All right,' she said. 'My turn to look now.'

Auger released her seat harness, and with great effort and equal discomfort she managed to stand and brace herself so that she had a view through the window. The ship continued to tumble. The light source flared hard into view, making her squint and avert her eyes in reflex. It was an intense white disk with the faintest tinge of yellow. It looked, in fact, a lot like the Sun.

Then Floyd's smudge came into view. She had to hand it to him: his description was on the mark. It was a ruby-red nebula, like a blow-up from an astronomical photograph, flecked with spangles of light, smears of brighter red and clotted with very dark patches, like dust lanes. Even as she watched, even before the rotation had pulled it out of view, a hard pink light flared within the cloud and died.

'I don't know what it is,' she said. 'I've never seen anything like it before.'

Then the rotation brought something else into view. It was a gently curved arc of rust-orange, fringed by a pale wisp of atmosphere. Unlike the smudge, this was something she had definitely seen before. She could even pick out the white scratches of the tethered dirigible lines, and the ribbon-bright channels of the irrigation network.

This was the other thing Floyd had seen.

'It's Mars,' she said, hardly believing her own words. 'The big thing—'

'And the light?'

'The Sun,' she said. 'We've come out around Mars. We're in the solar system.'

'But you said . . .'

She looked at the light-pocked smudge again. Just as Floyd had described, it appeared slightly smaller than the last time she had seen it – even though the smudge itself seemed to be roiling and expanding, like the cloud from an explosion . . .

And then the brightest light she had ever imagined – brighter even than the radiance of the wormhole throat – rammed through the smudge, like sunlight piercing a stained-glass window, and reached a crescendo like a second sun. Then it faded, dying like the last chip of the setting sun, and when darkness had returned, the smudge was completely dark, undisturbed by any smaller flashes.

'Where's Phobos?' Auger asked.

THIRTY-ONE

There was nothing more that could be done to slow the ship's tumbling motion. Auger kept the shutter open, and periodically one of them would climb up and examine the view, but the safest and easiest thing was to stay strapped into their seats. Damaged as it was, the transport did not actually seem to be getting any worse: no more systems had broken down since their emergence around Mars, and the cabin pressure had stabilised at just under one-third of an atmosphere. It was too thin to sustain life, so they kept the masks on, but at least they did not have the chill of vacuum to contend with. With the battery-powered heaters still running, the ambient temperature was low, but not unbearably so.

'We're safe, for now,' Auger said. 'All we have to do is sit tight until someone figures out where we are.'

'And someone will manage that?'

'Count on it. They'll be scouring every centimetre of space looking for us right now. Even if there isn't a working transponder on this thing, they'll find us with their own sensors. It will only be a matter of time.'

Her confidence had a thin, brittle edge to it, like ice that might break at any moment.

'I take it from this that you have a theory about how we survived?' Floyd asked.

'Aveling's people must have taken the decision to destroy Phobos,' she said. 'That smudge of dust and gas is all that's left of the moon. We must have hit a little debris coming through it, but not enough to do us any harm.'

'They blew up a whole moon? Isn't that rather drastic?'

'It was the only way to save us,' she said. 'They must have picked up our bow-shock distortion and realised that we were coming in much too fast to

384

decelerate into the recovery bubble. But the bubble's only function was to maintain vacuum at the wormhole throat. If they got rid of the pressurised chamber – and Phobos with it – then they wouldn't need the bubble. We'd have been emerging into vacuum anyway.'

'But you said they wouldn't have much warning of our imminent arrival,' Floyd said.

'They must have had a procedure in place for just this contingency,' she said. 'Emergency evacuation measures to get everyone off the moon in a couple of minutes. Nuclear demolition charges sewn throughout the whole thing, ready to take it apart at the press of a button, giving us a clear route to space.'

'All that, in a couple of minutes?'

'There's no other explanation, Floyd.'

'Well, I can think of one off the top of my head: somebody else blew up that moon, and our arrival didn't have a damn thing to do with it.'

'No, Floyd,' she said patiently, as if lecturing a child on some arcane matter of the adult world. 'Nobody else blew up that moon. That's not the way we do things around here. We may be in a state of crisis, but no one in their right mind . . .' Then she froze, and made a small clicking noise in the back of her throat.

'Auger?'

'Fuck. I think you might actually be right.'

'And there was me kind of hoping I'd be wrong.'

'There were explosions in that debris cloud,' she said, remembering the staccato flashes of light, 'as if something was still going on there. As if they were still fighting.'

'Who could have blown up that moon?'

'If it wasn't deliberate, if it wasn't set off by demolition charges, then only the Slashers could have done it.' She followed the slow, fatigued churning of her exhausted mental processes. She was too tired to think clearly, or else she would never have considered the possibility that Phobos might have been blown up for her benefit. 'That last flash,' she said. 'The really bright one?'

'Yes?'

'I think that was the wormhole dying. We were surfing the collapsing end of it all the way home. We popped out, then the collapsing end of the pipe hit its own throat. It was like a stretched rubber band snapping back on itself. I think the blast took out all the combatants left near the debris cloud.'

'And my way back home?'

'It's gone. The link is finished.'

'I figured as much.'

'I'm sorry, Floyd,' she said.

'You don't have anything to apologise for. I got myself into this every step of the way.'

'No, that isn't true. I have to take some of the blame. I should never have let you cross the censor, and I definitely shouldn't have let you get aboard this ship.'

'Face it, kid: you'd never have got home without me.'

She had no answer for that. He was right: without Floyd's help, she would have died somewhere along the now-collapsed thread of the hyperweb, dashed to pieces in an unwitnessed fireworks display.

'That still doesn't make it right,' she said. 'I've ripped you away from everything and everyone you ever knew.'

'You had no choice.'

She touched her wound. It was hot and tender again, as if the inflammation had begun to return. The UR she had taken was not the kind that stayed inside the body for ever. The little machines had probably dismantled themselves by now, donating their essence into the chemical reservoir of her body. She had assumed that she would be getting expert medical attention as soon as the ship popped into the recovery bubble.

'Are you all right?' Floyd asked.

'Just a bit crisp around the edges. I'll handle it.'

'You need medical attention.'

'And I'll get it just as soon as they pull us out of this can.'

'If they're looking for us,' Floyd said.

'They will be. Skellsgard will have told Caliskan that we're on our way back and also that we have important information.'

'You ready to tell me a little more about why this matters so much? I mean, now that we're here . . .'

'Take a look out of the window again, Floyd. Take a look at Mars.'

Auger told him about Mars. She told him about Silver Rain, and what it had done to that world.

Silver Rain was a weapon, cultivated during the last conflict between the Slashers and the Threshers from samples of the original rogue nanotechnological spore that had ended life on Earth. With deft, snide brilliance, the military scientists of the USNE – aided by defectors from the Polities, who supplied the necessary expertise in nanotech manipulation – had taken the excessively crude bludgeon of the original spore and honed it into something sharp and rather lovely, like a Samurai sword. Then they had seeded it into the thickening atmosphere of the partially terraformed

Mars, the spore encased in myriad ceramic-jacketed ablative pellets, and it had sunk down to the surface, spreading across a vast footprint.

The Polities had never assumed that their enemy would use nanotechnology against them. It was the one thing that the Threshers abhorred above all else.

It therefore made an ideal weapon of surprise.

Silver Rain was very difficult to detect. The Polity specialists on Mars were expecting something much cruder, and consequently their nanotech filters were tuned to ignore something so fine, so cunning, so deadly. It infiltrated organisms quietly, initially doing no harm. Not just people and animals, but every living thing that the colonists had persuaded to survive on Mars. It slipped through seals and airlocks; through skin and cell membranes and the blood-brain barrier. Even the droves of nanotechnological mechanisms that the Slashers carried within their own bodies failed to recognise the intruder. It was that good; that precise.

And for days it did nothing except insinuate itself more thoroughly into the colonists' world. It seeped into the irrigation system and used the canals to travel beyond the original infection footprint. It transmitted itself by means of physical contact between people and animals. It used the weather, riding the winds. It replicated itself, efficiently and systematically, but never consuming resources that would have drawn it to anyone's attention. People began to report that they were feeling a little under the weather, as if about to come down with a mild cold.

But no one in the Polities had come down with a cold in living memory . . .

The USNE battle planners had programmed Silver Rain to trigger on 28 July 2243. It was a coincidence that the day and the month happened to be shared with the events of the Nanocaust: the timing of the Silver Rain deployment had been dictated by strategic considerations elsewhere in the war. But once that coincidence became apparent, the generals saw no need to alter their plans. It would send a signal – subtle or otherwise – to the Polities. This is payback, it said. This is the price you pay for the harm your ideological ancestors did to Earth.

When the trigger was operated, every infected organism died in the same convulsive instant as the machines erupted, little time bombs crammed inside every living cell. Recording systems showed people stopping in mid-stride, mid-sentence, mid-thought. They fell to the ground, every biological event in their bodies aborted like a rogue computer process. They didn't bleed. They didn't even undergo any of the medically recognised phases of putrefaction. They just became a kind of dust, loosely organised into the shapes of corpses. When the cities and settlements began to fail, pressure-containment systems breaking down through lack of human maintenance, the corpses simply blew away like so many piles of ash.

It had never been the intention of the USNE to destroy all life on the planet: they had too many Martian interests of their own to go that far. Had Silver Rain slipped from their control (it had never been tested on such a scale before, and its effects were not entirely predictable), they would have deployed a counter-spore designed to neutralise the original weapon before it did excessive harm. But there was no need for that. The Silver Rain had worked exactly as advertised.

In the aftermath, the Slasher forces were paralysed by the scale of the atrocity. Sixty thousand people had died on Mars – more than the total number of casualties sustained in the conflict up to that point. But just when the Slashers were ready to launch a devastating counter-offensive against Tanglewood, using weapons that they had kept in reserve until then, there was an equally shocking turn of events amongst the Threshers. Senior officials denounced the actions of the battle planners who had developed and deployed Silver Rain. A moderately bloody *coup* followed, and those responsible for the crime against Mars were tried and executed. The punishments seemed to sate the Slashers. Within weeks, ceasefire terms had been agreed, with hostilities ending by late August. Mars returned to nominal Thresher control in 2244, but with significant concessions to the Slashers. While it was not exactly true to say that Mars had recovered from its assault, it had begun the healing process. The terraforming programme soldiered on, never getting any closer to its goal, but it was something to live for, regardless. Ambitious new settlements appeared in the Solis Planum and Terra Cimmeria regions, and the refurbishment of the high-orbit port, abandoned and mothballed during the war, brought a healthy dose of commerce.

But even now, after twenty-three years, the Scoured Zone was still lifeless. By accident or design, the gene-tweaked crops never took root there again. None of the settlements inside the Silver Rain footprint were ever reinhabited. They stood there now, half-buried in Martian dust: bone-white ghost towns, left exactly as they had been at the time of the atrocity.

Auger remembered her dream of Paris: the drummer boy on the Champs-Elysées.

'That was twenty-three years ago,' she concluded. 'Officially, the weapon doesn't exist anymore. Even the blueprints were supposed to have been destroyed. But Susan White didn't write those words on a postcard for nothing. Someone's got hold of it again. Maybe even improved it. And the next target isn't a few tens of thousands of Martian colonists. It's three billion people – the entire population of your version of Earth.'

'But why?'

'To erase what should never have been. To wipe out those three billion lives as if they were rogue programs in some vast computer simulation. To turn back the clock to the moment of the quantum snapshot and obtain a pristine copy of the Earth, unencumbered by anything as messy as living, breathing inhabitants.'

'It's monstrous,' Floyd said, horrified.

'From one point of view. From another, it's simply a question of tidying up – like airbrushing a photograph. Remember what that war baby said in Berlin? All you really are to them is three billion dots.'

'We have to stop this.'

'And we're trying to. But we may be too late. If they already know the physical co-ordinates of the ALS, all they need to do now is to get there and deliver the Silver Rain—'

'Then we have to get there ahead of them.'

'Nice in theory, Floyd. But *we* don't know where the ALS is. There's an awful lot of galaxy out there.'

'Then we need to find out those co-ordinates as well. They must have smuggled them out, right?'

'Floyd, we're talking about three numbers. They don't even have to be big ones. No one needs to specify the position of the ALS to within a centimetre. It's like looking for an island in the Pacific Ocean. All you need is a grid reference accurate enough to rule out any other possibilities.'

'Then we look for a grid reference.'

'It could be anywhere, hidden in any form. It could be a telephone number, or something even less obvious.'

'But those numbers must be somewhere. Could they have been hidden in the things Susan White was sending back home?'

'She was on our side, Floyd.'

'I'm not saying that she knew what she was carrying, just that she might have been acting as a courier for the bad guys without ever realising it.'

'It's still hopeless. Even if we knew for a fact that the numbers were in those papers . . . where would we start? The co-ordinates could be stored in the tiniest microdot, or in one telephone number amongst the thousands in the classified adverts.'

'All I'm saying is that we have to do something.'

'I agree,' she said, 'but maybe our first priority ought to be getting rescued.'

Something distracted her: a slight change in the quality of light flooding the cabin. They were still tumbling, the Sun still flashing through the window once a rotation, but now there was a pinkish glow that stayed with them all the time, as if the transport was enveloped in its own little cloud of glowing light.

'You still think someone's going to pick us up?' Floyd asked.

'They're looking for us,' Auger said.

'Even if the blowing up of that moon wasn't part of the plan?'

'Someone will still want to know what happened to us.' But even as she said it, she felt her certainty draining away. By its nature, the hyperweb portal was ultra-secret. Most of the people who knew anything about it would have been inside Phobos when the attack took it apart.

'Auger?'

'I think we may be in more trouble than I first thought. Aveling and Barton are dead. Apart from Niagara and Caliskan, I don't know who's left out there to look for us.'

'Niagara and Caliskan?'

'Niagara's our Slasher mole, the man who fed us the know-how to make the Phobos link operational in the first place. Caliskan is the man who sent me to recover Susan's belongings. Niagara may have been inside Phobos when it was destroyed, but Caliskan's probably still in Tanglewood.'

'Then we'd better hope he hasn't forgotten about you.'

'Floyd, there's something not right about this.' She closed her eyes, silencing a moan as the discomfort in her shoulder took on a sharper, nastier edge. 'The more I think about it, the more I'm coming to believe that none of this was an accident.'

'None of what?'

'The collapse of the wormhole. Granted, the whole thing was becoming increasingly unstable, but the snake robot should have been able to compensate for that. It should have been able to manage a safe contraction of the throat.'

'So what are you saying?'

'I think the robot was sent there to destroy the link.'

'But the robot helped you.'

'Yes,' she said. 'And it probably meant to save my life. I don't think it had any idea that it had been tampered with. The sabotage order could have been buried deep beneath its surface programming.'

The pink glow had intensified: fingers of light now licked around the armoured aperture of the window. It still bothered Auger, but she wasn't sure why.

'Why would anyone want to sabotage the link, if that's the only way back to Paris?' Floyd asked.

'That's what worries me. Not just because it implies that someone within the organisation set out to collapse the link, but also because it must mean that the Slashers no longer need it themselves.'

'Why would they throw away something like that?'

'They wouldn't,' Auger said. 'Not unless they already had another way of reaching Paris.'

'You mean they already have the co-ordinates of the ALS?'

'Either that, or they're very close to finding them out.'

The thing that had been bothering Auger about that pink glow finally pushed its way to the front of her pain-fogged mind. She felt herself go quite cold, even the stab of the wound no longer her most immediate concern. 'Floyd, do something for me, will you? Climb up and take another look through the window.'

'Why? You think someone else is out there?'

'Just do it.' She watched him intently as he did as he was told.

'Now tell me what I'm supposed to be looking for.'

'Tell me if Mars looks any bigger than the last time you saw it.'

Floyd took a look and then stared back at her, light and shadow slipping over his face with clockwork regularity. His expression told her everything she needed to know. 'This isn't good, is it?' Floyd asked.

'Get back in your seat. Fast.'

'What's wrong?'

'What's wrong is that we're not in orbit around Mars. If that planet looks bigger, it's because it's closer. We're falling towards it. I think we're already skimming the upper atmosphere.'

Floyd returned to his seat and lost no time in buckling up. 'How do you know?'

'I didn't, for a while. I just had a bad feeling that it might turn out this way. Phobos was in orbit around Mars, moving at exactly the right speed for its altitude. But we came out of the portal with our own velocity relative to the moon – hundreds of metres per second, at least. Whatever trajectory that put us in, it wasn't going to be the same one as Phobos. There's a chance we might have lucked out and had a boost in the right direction, away from Mars—'

'But today isn't our day for lucking out.'

'No,' she said. 'Doesn't look as if it is. We came out at the wrong angle, at the wrong speed. We're hitting the atmosphere.'

'And that's as bad as it sounds, right?'

'Ever wish upon a falling star, Floyd? Well, now's your big chance. You'll even get to be the star.'

'What will happen?'

'What will happen is that we'll burn up and die. If we're lucky, we'll have been crushed unconscious by the G-force before that happens.'

'That's an interesting view of luck.'

'This thing isn't made for atmospheric re-entry,' Auger said. 'No matter what angle we come in at.'

'This isn't the way it's meant to happen, Auger. Not like this. Not after we made it all this way.'

'There's nothing we can do,' she said. 'We can't steer this thing. We can't slow it down or speed it up. We can't even stop it tumbling.' The glow, faint at first, had now intensified, flickering through shades of blue and pink like a quilt of pastel light wrapped around the ship. It was mesmerising and rather lovely. Under other circumstances, it might have been a thing of wonder. 'Maybe if the hull wasn't already shot to shit,' she said, leaving Floyd to draw his own conclusions.

'But it is.'

'I'm sorry,' she said. 'This is all my fault.'

The glow flared to a hard white light, and in the same instant the transport shuddered violently. The tumbling motion became haphazard and all around her, Auger heard shrieks and groans of protesting metal as the aerodynamic and thermal stresses of Mars's atmosphere began to toy with the fabric of the ship. G-force built up with surprising speed. It was nothing at all like the smooth insertions she remembered from her trips to Earth. One moment, all that was pushing her into her seat was the gentle and steady pressure of the unchecked rotation, and the next she was being pushed and pulled in random directions, yanked against the bruising restraints of the harness. She jammed her head into the shaped restraint at the back of the seat, trying to protect her neck from the whiplashing dead weight of her skull. The ride became even more turbulent, the noise deafening. She was beginning to find it difficult to breathe as the G-load worked against her lungs. She felt light-headed, consciousness beginning to break up into discrete, interrupted episodes.

'Floyd . . .' she managed to say. 'Floyd, can you hear me?'

When he answered, she could barely hear him over the scream of the dying transport.

'You did good, Auger.'

How he managed it, she would never know, but somehow Floyd found the strength to reach out and close his hand around hers. She felt his fingers tighten, anchoring her to this place in space and time, even as everything else in her universe came apart in light and fury.

THIRTY-TWO

When she awoke, it was to the shining cool whiteness she had always imagined Heaven would be like. She would have happily stayed in that serene white limbo for the rest of eternity, void of any care or anxiety. But the whiteness held nagging suggestions of structure: pale shadows and highlights that sharpened themselves into the details of a room and its white-clad occupants.

One of these occupants took on the form of a very beautiful girl, surrounded by a mirage of twinkling lights.

'One lying little shit to the rescue,' Cassandra said.

Auger forced her way through layers of groggy recall, pushing memories back into place as she surfaced. 'You,' was all she managed to say.

Cassandra nodded sagely. 'Yes. Me. I'm glad you remember. It would have made things a lot more difficult if there was deep amnesia.'

Auger became aware that she was lying on a bed, at a slight angle, with various twinkling machines hovering around her. Some were so tiny that at first glance they might have been mistaken for dust motes. Others were as large as dragonflies or hummingbirds, shimmering with the moiré patterns of intense microscopic detail. Dimly it occurred to her that – despite the absence of any lumbering items of bedside monitoring equipment – this was some kind of sick bay or recuperative ward.

'We were falling—'

'And we were tracking you, trying to intercept your transport before it hit the atmosphere. As you may have gathered, we only just got to you in time. Our medical science can work wonders, but it can't work miracles.'

Sweet relief that she had survived welled up inside her. Then she remembered that she had not been alone.

'Is Floyd all right?'

'The other occupant of the shuttle is fine. He's under observation in another room, but he didn't merit the immediate attention you did.'

'And the transport?'

'The transport is gone. We jettisoned its remains as a decoy. But don't worry: we emptied the cargo first.'

'Cargo?'

'The archival items. A most interesting collection, I must say.'

'I didn't load any cargo. It was the last thing on my mind before we left E2.' Then she remembered the snake robot. Even as part of it was busy sabotaging the link, another part would have been diligently loading the transport with Susan White's accumulated possessions.

It took a machine to be that stupid, Auger thought. 'OK. Now tell me what the hell you're doing here.'

'Other than saving your life? Oh, I thought *that* was obvious. I'm a spy, Auger. Ever since we picked up rumours and hints that you Threshers had reopened the Phobos portal, I've been trying to worm my way into Caliskan's confidence in order to find out what's going on. And it worked, too, didn't it? That little trip to Earth was most invigorating.'

'I always said you couldn't be trusted.'

'Ah, but the point is that you have no one else *to* trust. I'm your last, best hope.'

'I think I'll take my chances with Niagara,' Auger said.

'Oh, yes. Dear, dependable Niagara. Shall I break the bad news now or later? Niagara was also a spy. The difference is that he was working for the really nasty people.'

The white walls were curved, merging seamlessly with floor and ceiling. Fine gold threads wove themselves through the white in calligraphic swirls that oozed and flowed in a way that seemed to calm Auger on some utterly primal level.

'I don't believe you,' she said, snapping her attention back to Cassandra. 'Niagara showed us how to make the link work. Why would he have done that if he was working against us?'

'Because he needed the link up and running, you silly-billy.' Cassandra sighed, planting one hand on her hip. 'Look, I'll spell it out for you: you were all duped. Niagara was a plant, working for a particularly vicious splinter faction of the aggressors. He wasn't a moderate sympathiser at all, but your worst enemy.'

'Nice of you to let us know.'

'And nice of your government to let *us* know it had found the Phobos portal in the first place,' she countered. 'If your people hadn't been so keen to keep that from us, we might have learned about Niagara's activities sooner than we did.'

'Or you'd have made sure you controlled Niagara.'

'Are you going to keep this up for ever, Auger? Or would it kill you to trust me?'

'I can't trust you, Cassandra. You lied to me on Earth, posing as someone you weren't.'

'At the behest of your government, not mine. It wouldn't have bothered me in the slightest if you'd known I was a Polity citizen. It was Caliskan who insisted on that particular charade.'

'That still doesn't excuse the fact that you were prepared to testify against me in the tribunal.'

'Testify as in "tell the truth", you mean? Well, I can't argue with that.'

'They'd have hung me out to dry.'

'And you'd have deserved it. Nothing was worth risking a human life the way you did, Auger. Especially not some useless paper relic from two hundred years ago.'

'Is this the reason you rescued me? To rub my nose in it?'

'Do I detect a note of contrition?'

'Detect what you like. You still haven't explained what you were doing around Mars, if you're so friendly.'

'We were doing what we could to limit the damage,' Cassandra said. 'It can't have escaped your attention that there is civil war in the Federation of Polities. That disagreement has now spread to the inner system.'

'With Phobos one of the first casualties. I hope you're proud of that.'

'Oh, very proud. Especially as fifty-four of my moderate friends died trying to defend your precious little moon. You can't imagine how proud *that* makes me feel.'

'I'm sorry,' Auger said, chastened.

'It doesn't matter. They were just Slashers, after all,' she said bitterly.

'I never realised—'

'The aggressors had been taking a particular interest in Phobos for some time,' Cassandra said, ignoring her. 'We had been shadowing their movements, trying to infiltrate their circles, but we didn't know what it was about Phobos that had them so excited.'

'Now you do.'

'You were in hyperweb transit when the moon was destroyed, weren't you?'

'Is there anything about us you don't know?'

'A great deal,' Cassandra said. 'I haven't read your minds. We have no firm idea where the portal led to, or what you were doing at the other end. We don't know exactly what Niagara wanted with it, except that Silver Rain plays a role in his plans. But we *have* learned something puzzling about the man.'

'Floyd?'

'You shouldn't have brought him with you.'

'I had no damned choice.' Auger forced herself to sit higher in the bed. As she moved, the bed effortlessly readjusted itself to support her. Beneath the silky white sheet she was wearing some kind of hospital smock. She reached up and touched the area of her shoulder where she had been shot.

No pain. No inflammation. She pushed her hand under the collar of the smock and traced the region of skin where the wound had been. It was baby smooth, revealing its healed newness only with the faintest tingle.

'We dug out the bullet,' Cassandra said. 'You were very lucky.'

'Where are we?'

'Aboard our ship – the one that pulled your transport out of Mars's atmosphere. We call the ship—' And her syrinx played one of its little ditties, although Auger heard none of the music in it. 'I don't think there would be a lot of point in attempting a translation into flat language.'

'Where is the ship now? Are we still near Mars?'

'No. We're on our way to near-Earth space. There are, however, complications.'

'I need to talk to Caliskan.'

'He's expecting you. It was a message from Caliskan that warned us to keep an eye out for you. It was a moving transmission, probably sent from a ship. We're still tracking the message's point of origin. Once we're closer, we can open a tight-beam channel.'

'Can I see Floyd in the meantime?'

Cassandra made a precise mimelike gesture, signalling the machines hovering about her bed. A number of the smaller ones moved into Cassandra's own cloud, becoming part of its twinkling whole. She breathed in and the cloud contracted to about half its previous volume.

'I think you're allowed to move now,' Cassandra said, after digesting whatever information the machines had imparted. 'But do take things carefully.'

Auger started to force herself up from the bed. As soon as she moved, more hummingbirds and dragonflies appeared from nowhere and assisted her, exerting gentle pressure where she needed it. Her feet barely touched the floor. Once she was free of the bed, the sheet levitated, wrapped itself around her and formed a kind of loose, billowing gown.

'This way,' Cassandra said.

The golden threads running through the walls oozed to form the outline of a doorway, which had a slightly Persian look to it. The door puckered wide, admitting them into a throatlike corridor with no recognisable floor or ceiling. The corridor curved up and around, bringing them to a blank part of wall that obliged them with a doorway when they were close enough to touch it.

They stepped through. Inside was a smaller recovery room than the one Auger had been in containing a single bed with a single occupant. Floyd was asleep, lying flat on his back, a twinkle of machines around his head. The Slashers had dressed him in a similar smock to the one Auger was wearing. His face was completely blank and masklike, with no sign of his head injury.

'He looks dead,' Auger said.

'He isn't. Just unconscious. We're holding him that way for the time being.'

'Why?'

'We didn't want to alarm him.' Cassandra's cloud commingled with the machines around Floyd, some brief information exchange taking place. 'When we healed his head wound, we naturally examined his DNA. It turned out to be very peculiar. He doesn't have any of the chromosomal markers that would identify him as a descendent of someone who lived through the GM excursions of the early twenty-first century.'

'He wouldn't,' Auger said.

'It would take extensive rescripting to remove those markers. Why would anyone go to so much trouble?'

'They wouldn't.'

'That's what we thought.' Cassandra touched a finger to her lower lip. 'It's almost as if he's a man from the past, from before the twenty-first century.'

'Good guess. What else did you figure out?'

'He must have come through the hyperweb, from the other end of the link. What did you *find* there, Auger?'

'If I don't tell you, you'll just take it from my memory, won't you?'

'If I decided you were withholding something of strategic importance, I'm afraid I'd have little choice. Regrettably, this is war.'

He surfaced to the sound of Auger's voice. She came into focus, looking down on him against a background of spotless cinematic white.

'Floyd. Wake up. You're OK.'

His mind was as clean and clear as the dawn sky. He was vaguely affronted by this on some level, feeling that he should have been allowed a grace period of disorientation and grogginess. Even his memories felt bright and sparkling, as if they had been taken out for a quick spit and polish.

He ran his tongue around the inside surface of his teeth. None of them were broken. They felt like church gargoyles that had been taken down and sandblasted clean.

'What happened?' he asked.

'We were rescued,' Auger said. She was standing over his bed, wearing a kind of satin toga. It moved around her in strange, unsettling ways, flowing like one of those very flat fish that skim the seabed. 'We're all right, at least for now.'

He sat up and touched his scalp. There was no sign of the injury, although his hair had been shaved almost to his scalp where the cut had been. 'Where is this place?'

'We're aboard a ship.'

'A *space*ship?'

'Yes. You can cope with that, can't you? I mean, after what's happened to us, a spaceship is not the strangest thing imaginable, is it?'

'I'll cope,' Floyd said. 'Who's running this jalopy, and are they the good guys?'

'I know the woman who seems to be in charge. She's a moderate Slasher by the name of Cassandra. I've already had dealings with her on Earth. In theory that makes her more trustworthy than the aggressors.'

'You don't sound convinced.'

'They've taken care of us. It doesn't mean they have my automatic gratitude. Not until I know what's going on, and where exactly they're taking us.'

'Haven't they told you?'

'They're supposed to be homing in on the location of some kind of transmission from Caliskan. That's all I know.'

Floyd rubbed a hand across his face. They had even shaved him. It was, by some distance, the best shave he had ever had. 'You don't like them much, do you?'

'I like them even less after . . .' But she stopped and shook her head. 'If she wants to know everything, she can damn well work for it. The only person I want to talk to is Caliskan.'

Floyd pushed himself upright. He was on the point of asking Auger if she knew where he might get a drink when the dryness in his throat was suddenly gone, as if he had been imagining it all along.

'What did you tell Cassandra?' he asked.

'I told her everything. If she'd suspected I was holding anything back, she'd have read my mind anyway.'

'How'd she take . . . me?'

'I'm not sure she thought your being here was a great idea.'

'That makes two of us,' Floyd said. 'I also know there isn't much point in complaining about it.'

'I'm sorry about all this.'

'Auger – do me a favour and stop apologising, will you? No regrets. Never.'

She smiled. 'I don't believe you for a second. But I'm still glad you made it, Floyd.'

'I'm glad we both made it. Now how about a kiss, before they come to put me in the monkey house?'

At first, Auger thought that Cassandra had somehow lost her way and led them into the wrong part of the ship: some kind of waiting room or chill-out den, perhaps, but definitely not a tactical room. It was another white chamber, brightly lit where she had expected subdued, vision-enhancing reds. Instead of urgent, cycling displays, the walls were the usual gold-threaded white. There was a toadstool-shaped table in the middle of the room, rising seamlessly from the floor, and around this stood half a dozen toadstool-shaped chairs. The chairs had a spongy, haphazard look to them, like the furniture of a gingerbread house. Six Slashers occupied them, facing each other across the equally spongy table. None of them were in what Auger would have called a tense or particularly agitated posture. One of them rested an elbow on the table, hand supporting his chin. Another woman (although she could have passed for a child) pressed her steepled fingers to her brow, as if in meditation. The other four Slashers had their hands tucked limply in their laps, as if they were waiting their turns in a slow, dull parlour game. No one was saying anything and their eyes were either closed or heavy-lidded. There was, however, a dense cloud of twinkling machines hovering above the middle of the table, and the extremities of this cloud encompassed all six participants, its boundary shifting from moment to moment.

'Tunguska,' Cassandra said. 'Can you spare enough of yourself to talk to us?'

The one with his elbow on the table turned his head minutely in their direction. He was a large man, black-skinned and round of face, with sad, heavily lidded eyes and long silver-black hair tied back in a pony-tail.

'I can always make time for you, Cassie,' he said in a very slow, very deep voice.

'Tunguska is my battle manager,' Cassandra said. 'He's also my friend and ally. Tunguska and I go back a long way.'

'I didn't know an outmoded concept like friendship was tolerated in the Polities,' Auger said.

'Then you know even less about us than you think.' Cassandra nodded at Tunguska. 'Our guests are curious. Can you show them the state of play?'

'Let me see what I can do.'

Tunguska turned to the wall and with brisk hand gestures somehow made an area of it become black. Circles and spheres dropped into place: a view of the solar system, looking down on the plane of the ecliptic. The view zoomed in on the inner system, as far out as the orbit of Mars. Mars itself was indicated by a red sphere, very much out of scale, accompanied by one intact moon and the glowing smudge that had recently been Phobos.

'The collapse of the quasi-wormhole knocked out all forces within a few dozen kilometres of the moon,' Tunguska said, his voice as slow and measured as if he was reciting a sermon. 'But that still leaves a large concentration of ships within the immediate volume of space around Mars. We're tracking at least two hundred distinct thrust signatures.'

'Who do those ships belong to?' Auger asked.

'Everyone who has a stake in controlling the inner system. Various Polity factions account for about seventy per cent of active combatants. Twenty per cent are USNE, with the remainder made up of non-aligned parties: lunar breakaway groups and suchlike.' As Tunguska spoke, icons dropped into place, forming a bustling crowd of flags and emblems around Mars. It was quite impossible to make any sense of it.

'Did anyone make it out of Phobos alive?' Auger asked.

'We're tracking a number of slow-moving spacecraft that seem to have left Phobos before the main attack commenced.'

'Why?' asked Cassandra. 'Were you thinking of anyone in particular?'

'I had a friend . . .' Auger said, faltering. 'I didn't really know her very well, but I want to believe she got away in time.'

'I'm afraid I can't offer any guarantees,' Cassandra said. Perhaps reading something in her face, she continued, 'However, it seems at least plausible that some people—'

'There's a good chance she made it,' Tunguska said.

'Never mind,' Auger said. The last thing she needed right now was empty reassurance. She would just have to hope that Skellsgard had been on one of those early ships. 'Just give me a straight answer to my next question. Who's winning?'

'If you don't mind,' Tunguska said, addressing Cassandra, 'I really need to focus on the task in hand, or the answer to her question is not going to be one we'd all wish for.' He nodded at Floyd and Auger. 'It was nice to meet you. I hope you both make it home safely.'

He turned his head back to face the table and closed his eyes.

'I'll answer your question,' Cassandra said. 'There is no clear outcome in sight. If it was a straight contest between Polity and Thresher assets, there'd be little doubt of victory for the Polities, at least around Mars. But the moderates are siding with the Threshers. So far, that's evening things out.'

'Then let's hope things reach a stalemate,' Auger said.

Floyd, standing beside her, had said nothing so far. But he still nodded, evidently sharing her concern.

Cassandra shook her head. 'Wishful thinking, I'm afraid. The moderates have deployed all their assets into the inner system, but the aggressors still have forces in reserve. They're on high-burn approaches even as we speak.'

'But this is insane,' Auger said. 'They might have the military strength to take Mars from us, and they might even have the means to capture Tanglewood and the rest of the inner system. But the moderates won't let them do that without a fight, and they still have that little scorched-earth problem to worry about.'

'What scorched-earth problem?' Floyd asked.

'My side ringed Earth with bombs,' Auger said. 'Insurance against the Slashers trying to take it out of our hands again.'

'You mean you'd blow up the planet rather than let someone else have it?'

'In a nutshell, yes.'

'I hate to tell you this, Auger, but you're all as crazy as each other.'

'Bet you're sorry you signed up for this now, aren't you, Floyd?' Not waiting for his answer, Auger turned back to Cassandra. 'Where are we in this sorry little mess?'

'Oh, we're nowhere near Mars now,' the girl said. 'We've been on our own high-burn trajectory ever since we snatched you out of the atmosphere.'

Another icon dropped into the image, about halfway between Mars and Earth, which were both situated on the same side of the Sun.

'That's us?'

'That's us,' Cassandra confirmed. 'Maintaining a high-burn trajectory, with a second ship just behind us.'

'A high-burn trajectory?' Auger shook her head. 'It doesn't even feel as if we're moving.'

'Trust me, we're moving. We're also executing some rather violent evasive patterns.'

Something wasn't right. Auger had heard many things about the Slashers' advanced technology, but she had never heard that they had developed the means to nullify acceleration. Perhaps they were even further ahead of the USNE than intelligence had ever suggested.

'What do you know about this second ship?' she asked.

'We think it might be one of Niagara's allies, or possibly the man himself. It's a Polity design, part of the original concentration of aggressor elements. It may be responding to Caliskan's signal from Tanglewood.'

'We have to get to him first,' Auger said.

'That's more or less the idea,' Cassandra replied laconically. 'We'd be there in eight hours under optimum conditions. Unfortunately, the ship behind us is doing its best to make life difficult. These violent evasive manoeuvres are costing us time and engine fatigue.'

'Maybe I'm missing something,' Auger said, 'but I don't feel any violent evasive manoeuvres.'

'Mm.' Cassandra said thoughtfully. 'There's something you need to see, I think.'

'What?'

Cassandra led them across the chamber and opened a door into another corridor. A little way along, she stopped at a smooth expanse of convex walling and created an observation window. 'I may as well show you something else on the way. Apart from the two of you, there are eighteen other casualties on this ship.'

Auger brightened, remembering Skellsgard. Perhaps she was safe after all, despite Cassandra's doubts. 'Refugees from Phobos?'

'Not directly, no. I'm sorry – I know you want good news about your friend, and I would give it to you if I could.'

The observation window overlooked a large interior chamber. Cassandra made the lights come on, revealing the stubby, streamlined form of a Thresher-manufactured spacecraft: the kind that could skim in and out of an atmosphere and land on a planetary surface, such as Mars or Titan, or on one of the high-altitude landing towers on Venus. It was about twenty metres in length, just small enough to fit into the bay. The shuttle had bulky thrust nacelles and bulging insectile undercarriage pods; against the scorched white skin, Auger could make out a green flying horse logo near the black heat-absorbent panelling of the nose.

'That's a Pegasus Intersolar ship,' she said.

'Yes,' Cassandra said. 'As a matter of fact, it's a transatmospheric shuttle from the liner *Twentieth Century Limited*.'

The ship was braced into the chamber on enormous shock-absorbing pistons, gripping it from all angles. Even as Auger watched, the ship lurched one way and then another, as if subject to immense lateral forces. 'I took the *Twentieth* to Phobos,' she said, feeling slightly seasick. 'What's one of its shuttles doing here?'

'The liner was hijacked. Hostile ships made rendezvous and hard docking beyond reach of systemwide law enforcement.'

'Slasher forces?'

'Not obviously so. According to eyewitnesses, they behaved just like your run-of-the-mill extralegal agents. Pirates, in other words. Luckily, the liner was running at nowhere near maximum capacity. There was room for most of the passengers and crew to escape on shuttles.'

'And the pirates just let them go?' Auger asked incredulously.

'They had nothing to gain by butchering those on board. There wasn't enough room for everyone on the shuttles, and some of the crew elected to remain aboard. They were allowed into a secure compartment with life-support capability and provisions. That's where the ones who stayed aboard were all found, when the *Twentieth* drifted within reach of Thresher police.'

Auger thought she had misheard her. 'Drifted?'

'She had been gutted,' Cassandra said. 'Stripped of her entire drive assembly.'

'That's insane.'

'Oh, there was some attempt to dress up the piracy as being for the usual reasons,' she said, 'but it was all cover, really. The main thing they were after was the drive core.'

'But why would anyone want the drive core of an old junkheap like the *Twentieth*? The Slashers will happily sell anyone a more efficient engine, provided they stump up the costs.'

'That's precisely what bothered me,' Cassandra said. 'The entire operation to steal the *Twentieth*'s engine must have been quite expensive in its own right. Several ships had to make that rendezvous, including one large enough to contain the entire drive assembly. It's not the sort of thing you dismantle.'

'It doesn't make any sense,' Auger said.

'But you sense a connection none the less. Why steal an antimatter engine when we can offer something infinitely safer, and just as powerful? The only practical use for such a thing would be—'

'As a bomb,' Auger said.

'I'm sorry?'

'Think about it, Cassandra. It has to be a bomb. That's the only thing that drive can give the Slashers that you don't already have. Your bleed-drive engines suck energy from the vacuum in tiny, controlled doses. I know. I've seen the sales brochures.'

'They're very safe,' Cassandra said defensively. 'The vacuum potential reaction is self-limiting: if the energy density exceeds a critical limit, it shuts off.'

'In other words, very useful for making a safe drive, but not much use as a Molotov cocktail.'

Beside her, Floyd smiled. 'I almost thought I was going to get through a whole conversation without understanding a single word. Now you've gone and spoiled it.'

'I confess I have no idea what a Molotov cocktail is,' Cassandra said. 'Is it some kind of weapon system?'

'You could say that,' Floyd said.

'I still don't understand,' Cassandra said. 'You're implying that someone wanted the antimatter engine to use as a bomb. But what use is such a thing? A ship large enough to contain the stolen drive assembly could never approach close enough to a planet or habitat to do serious damage. It would be intercepted and destroyed in interplanetary space, light-seconds from any target. As soon as we issue a systemwide alert—'

'Go ahead and issue your alert,' Auger said, 'but I don't think it will make any difference. I think you'll find it a lot more difficult to track those ships than you're expecting. I also don't think they intend to use that antimatter against anything in this system.'

'You're making me most anxious to have a peek inside your skull,' Cassandra said ominously. 'I thought we had an agreement.'

'And you said you had something else to show me.'

'It concerns the evacuees,' she said. 'And, in a way, you.'

She made the window vanish, then led them a little further along the corridor and opened another gilded doorway.

The room beyond was a kind of dormitory. Inside, ranked against the two long, incurving walls, were twenty or so coffinlike containers. Again, they had the spongy, vegetative look of recently extruded hardware, their bases merging into the floor. Pulpy, rootlike tendrils connected the pods to each other and the walls.

'This is where we're keeping the eighteen passengers and crew from the shuttle,' Cassandra said, inviting Auger to take a closer look at one of the pods. The upper part of it consisted of a curved, glossy lid, veined like a leaf, through which the head and upper body of one of the evacuees could just be discerned. She was a tall, dark-skinned woman, encased in what looked like a thick turquoise-blue support matrix of some kind. Auger even thought she recognised her as one of the other passengers she'd seen on the *Twentieth*.

'Is she ill?' Auger asked.

'No,' Cassandra said. 'See that bluish gel she's floating in? Pure machinery. It's invaded her completely, right down to the cellular level.'

'Who gave you permission to do that?' Auger asked, outraged. 'These people are Threshers. Most of them would never consent to having machines pumped into their bodies.'

'I'm afraid they didn't have a lot of choice in the matter,' Cassandra said. 'It was either that or die. We can quibble over consent later.'

'Die of what? You just said that none of them were ill.'

'It's the evasive pattern, you see. We're sustaining ten gees, which would be bad enough in its own right, but our random manoeuvres superimpose one or two hundred gee transients on top of that background load. It's quite intolerable for an unmodified person. Without the buffering from those machines, they'd be dead.'

'Then why aren't we?' Auger asked.

'I'll show you.'

Cassandra waved them through to the back of the dormitory. 'I mentioned eighteen evacuees from the *Twentieth*,' she said, 'but you'll notice that there are twenty caskets in this room. We wouldn't have bothered creating the extras without good reason.' She gestured to the last two, set against the far wall. 'You and your companion are in those two.'

'Wait . . .' Auger began.

'There's no reason for alarm,' Cassandra said. 'Come closer and look inside. You'll see that you're perfectly unharmed.'

Auger looked through the transparent cover of the first casket. There, suspended in the same blue gel as the woman, lay the sleeping form of Floyd, his eyes closed, his face an unmoving mask of serenity. She stepped aside to let him see, then viewed her own body in the other casket.

'Why does this feel as if everything's just turned into a bad dream?' Floyd asked.

'It's all right,' Auger said, reaching out to squeeze his hand in an attempt to give reassurance that she didn't really feel herself. No matter how much this bothered her, she could not begin to imagine what Floyd was feeling. 'Isn't it, Cassandra?'

'I didn't want to alarm you immediately,' the Slasher said, 'knowing how Threshers tend to feel about our machines—'

'She's telling the truth,' Auger said to Floyd. 'We are on a spaceship and we were rescued from Mars. I'm pretty certain that much is true. But we still haven't been woken up.'

'I feel pretty awake for someone who hasn't been woken up.'

'You're fully conscious,' she said. 'It's just that the machines are fooling your brain into thinking that you're walking around. Everything that you see or feel is bogus. You're really still in that tank.'

'It's the only way we can keep you alive,' Cassandra said, with evident concern. 'The acceleration would have killed all of us by now.'

'So you're . . . ?' Floyd began, not really knowing how to frame the question.

'In another casket, as are all my colleagues, somewhere else in the ship. I'm sorry that a small white lie was necessary, but everything else I've told you was the truth.'

'Everything?' asked Auger.

Cassandra cleared a portion of the wall and created a three-dimensional grid, into which she dropped the tiny form of their ship. It veered and swerved, the ship's lithe, flexible hull bending and twisting with each change of direction. 'This is our real-time trajectory,' Cassandra said. 'You saw a hint of it when I showed you the captive shuttle. I could have doctored the view – it would have been trivial – but I chose not to. You'd have guessed sooner or later.'

'Are we really all right?' Auger said.

'Absolutely,' Cassandra said, 'although the healing processes are still taking place. You'll both be good as new by the time we arrive at Tanglewood.'

'If we ever get there,' she said.

Cassandra smiled. 'Let's err on the side of optimism, shall we? In my experience there's very little point worrying about something you can't control.'

'Even death?'

'Most especially death.'

THIRTY-THREE

Auger was picking her way through an orange when Cassandra reappeared, stepping through a curtained doorway that rippled in an imaginary breeze.

The girl-shaped Slasher made a chair appear from nowhere, then lowered herself into it. 'How are you feeling?'

'This is the best fruit I've ever tasted,' Auger replied.

'The best fruit you've *never* tasted,' Cassandra said, correcting her with an amused smile. 'It's rather unfair, of course: how could any real food compare with direct stimulation of the taste centre?'

Being reminded that the orange was a figment of her imagination was enough to kill what little of her appetite remained. 'Is this what it's like for you every day?' Auger asked. Beside her, Floyd continued to attack a bunch of grapes.

'More or less.'

'I suppose you get used to it, in the end. Being able to experience anything you want, when and wherever you want to . . .'

'It has its attractions,' Cassandra said. 'But so does unlimited access to candy, when you're a child. The simple fact of the matter is that we learn to live with what we have, and the novelty begins to wear off after a while. The machines in my environment can reshape any room – any space – according to my immediate needs. If the machines can't respond quickly enough, or there's a conflict with someone else's requirements, I can tell other machines in my head to achieve the same thing by manipulating my perceptions. If there's a memory that troubles me, I can erase or bury it, or programme it to surface only when I need some reminder of my shortcomings. If there's an emotion I find unpleasant, I can turn it off or lessen it.'

'Like anxiety about the future?'

'Anxiety is a useful tool: it forces us to make plans. But when too much anxiety freezes us into indecision, it needs checking.' Cassandra leaned back in her seat, making the wooden joints creak. She reached for an apple from a bowl on a nearby table and bit into it. 'It's a matter of balance, you see. These things may sound miraculous to you, but to me they're simply part of the texture of my life.'

Floyd pushed aside his plate. 'It sounds like Heaven to me. You can make anything happen, or at least make yourselves think it's happened. And you live for ever.'

'Cassandra's people have no past,' Auger said. 'We don't have much of one, but what we do have is sacrosanct.'

'I'm not sure I follow,' Floyd said.

'Everyone alive today is a descendent of someone who was living in space when the Nanocaust hit,' Auger elaborated. 'No one on the surface of the planet made it out alive, so we're all descended from the colonists who had already begun to settle the solar system.' She looked at the Slasher. 'True, Cassandra?'

'True enough.'

'But getting into space was difficult back then. Every gram had to be accounted for, argued over, justified at the expense of another gram. We didn't bring books when we could make do with digital scans of the texts, preserved in computer memory. We didn't bring films or photographs when we could more easily transport digital versions of them. We didn't even bring animals or flowers, making do with transcriptions of their DNA.'

'It went the same way for both of our ancestral peoples,' Cassandra added. 'The only difference being that Auger's grouping – the ancestors of the USNE – embraced the digital with slightly less gusto than we did. They were cautious – rightly so, as it happened.'

'We brought some physical artefacts into space,' Auger said. 'A few books, photographs. Even some animals. It cost us terribly, but we sensed that the storage of so much knowledge in the form of digital records – in the memories of machines – made us vulnerable. After the Nanocaust, when we'd seen machines go wrong on such a scale, we embarked on a crash programme to convert as much of that electronically stored information as possible back into solid, analogue format. We made printing presses to produce physical books. We burnt digital images back on to chemical plates. We had factories churning out paper as fast as our printers could swallow it. We even had armies of scribes copying texts back on to paper in longhand, in case the printers failed before the work was done. We did everything we could – everything we could think of doing – to make copies we could touch and smell, like in the old days. It almost worked, too. But we just weren't fast enough.'

'We call it the Forgetting,' Cassandra said. 'It happened about fifty years after the Nanocaust, when our respective societies had regained some measure of stability and self-sufficiency following the death of Earth. Even now, no one really knows what caused it. Sabotage is sometimes mentioned, but I'm inclined to think it was an accident – just one of those things waiting to happen.'

'The digital records crashed,' Auger said. 'Overnight, some kind of virus or worm spread through every linked archive in the system. Texts were turned into garbled junk. Pictures, movies – even music – were scrambled into senselessness.'

'Some archives survived,' Cassandra said. 'But after the Forgetting, we could never be certain of their reliability.'

'We lost almost everything,' Auger said. 'All we had left of the past was fragments. It was like trying to reconstruct the entirety of human knowledge from a few books saved from a burning library.'

'What about institutions?' Floyd asked. 'Didn't they keep the originals of all this stuff?'

'They'd been falling over themselves to shred and pulp their paper collections for years,' Auger said. 'They couldn't do it quickly enough once they'd been sold on the idea that they could reduce all this cumbersome *volume* to a single sheet of microfiche, or a single optical disk, or a single partition in a flash memory array, or whatever was being hailed as the latest and best storage medium that week.'

'Perfect sound for ever,' Cassandra said, in the manner of someone reciting an advertising slogan. 'That, at least, was the idea; it's just such a shame that it didn't actually *work*. You see now why our people have followed two paths. The Threshers believe that the Forgetting must never be allowed to happen again. To that end, they abstain from the very technologies that could offer them immortality.'

'No one's immortal,' Auger said sharply. 'You're just immortal until the next Nanocaust, or the next Forgetting, or until the Sun blows up. And any one of us is free to defect to the Polities, if we don't like living under the iron rule of the Threshold Committee.'

'A fair point,' Cassandra said. 'We, on the other hand, have decided not to worry about the past. We've lost it once, so why worry about losing it again? We live in the moment.'

She extended her hand and made the room change, expanding it massively, the white walls racing away in all directions. Suddenly they were in a space the size of a cathedral, and then a skyscraper. It kept on growing, the walls receding until they were kilometres or tens of kilometres away, the ceiling rocketing into the sky until it took on the blue of the atmosphere itself, with a layer of clouds suspended just below it. The room's open window now looked out into star-sprinkled night.

It was a bravura display of control, but Cassandra wasn't finished. She narrowed her eyes and the distant walls flickered with vast, sculptural detail: fluted columns and caryatids as tall as mountains, buttresses and arches leaning across absurd reaches of empty space. She made stained-glass windows open into the walls, shot through with light in a spectrum Auger had never imagined. Cassandra must have been tweaking her brain on a fundamental level, altering her very perceptual wiring. Not only were the colours unfamiliar (and heart-wrenchingly beautiful), but she could hear them, feel them, smell them.

She had never known anything so lovely, so sad, so wonderful.

'Please stop,' she said, overwhelmed.

Cassandra returned the room to its prior dimensions. 'I'm sorry,' she said to Auger and Floyd in turn, 'but I felt that some demonstration was necessary to illustrate what I understand as living in the moment. That's the kind of moment I mean.'

'I have just one question,' Floyd said. 'If you can do this, if you can have everything you want, whenever and wherever you want it – then why are some of you so keen on getting your hands on Earth?'

'That's a shrewd question,' Cassandra said.

'So answer it,' Auger said.

'We want Earth because it is the one thing we cannot have,' Cassandra said. 'And that, for some of us, is intolerable.'

Cassandra was waiting when the veined lid peeled aside. 'Well, Auger? Was the reintegration as painless as I predicted?'

'I'll cope. Can you help me out of this thing?'

'Certainly.'

Another Slasher was already helping Floyd out of his casket. Auger looked around with bleary eyes while the last remnants of the blue fluid gathered into larger blobs and flowed back into the open maw of the casket.

'Come,' Cassandra said. 'I'll bring you up to speed. We're very near Earth.'

They returned to the tactical room, which was almost as Auger remembered it except for the absence of any Slashers. 'They're still in their acceleration caskets,' Cassandra explained. 'If we need to make a sudden movement, they'll be better able to manage the tactical situation.'

'Are we still being chased by Niagara?'

'Niagara – or whoever was in that ship – isn't a problem anymore. It ran into one of our missiles just before we reached the outer cordon of Tanglewood defences.'

'You mean he's dead?'

'Someone's dead. It may or may not be Niagara. If it isn't, we'll find him sooner or later.'

'You better had.'

'Perhaps if you told me exactly why it was so important to reach Caliskan, I might be able to do a little more to help you.'

'I've told you as much as you need to know,' Auger said firmly.

'You only told me half of the story.'

'And I'm not quite ready to trust you with the rest of it. Maybe when I've spoken to Caliskan . . . Are you close enough to send a tight-beam message to him?'

'There'll always be a slight risk of interception . . . but yes, we're close enough now.' With a flourish of her fingers – a gesture that Auger suspected was as much theatrical as anything else – Cassandra assigned part of the wall as a flat screen. For a moment it was blank, awaiting a response. 'You may speak,' she said, prompting Auger with a nod of her head.

'What's my location?' she asked.

Cassandra told her.

'Caliskan,' she said. 'This is Verity Auger. I believe you wanted to hear from me. I'm alive and well, within half a light-second of Tanglewood. I'm aboard a Slasher spacecraft, so you'll have to pull some strings to let me get any closer without all hell breaking loose.'

A second or two later, the assigned panel lit up with swathes of blocky primary colours, which quickly sharpened into a flickering, low-time-resolution pixel image.

'That's Caliskan?' Floyd said, when the face of the white-haired man had assumed a recognisable shape.

'The man who sent me to Paris, and the only one who has a hope of sorting out this mess,' Auger said.

'Face looks familiar. It's almost as if I know him,' Floyd said, peering more closely at the image.

'You can't possibly know him,' she said. 'You've never met him.'

Floyd touched the side of his head, as if in salute. 'Whatever you say, Chief.'

Caliskan's glasses flared light back at the camera. 'Auger . . . you're alive. You can't imagine how much this pleases me. Please pass my thanks on to Cassandra. I didn't dare believe you'd made it out of the Phobos catastrophe.'

'We made it, sir. Both of us did.'

She waited for the response. The one-second delay was just long enough to impose a certain stiltedness on the conversation, as if both of them were speaking a language neither felt comfortable with.

'Both of you, Auger? But Skellsgard said that the war babies had killed Aveling and Barton before you helped her escape.'

'And so they did, sir. I'm with a man called Floyd, who was born on E2.'

Behind Caliskan, she could make out the ribs, spars and instruments of a spacecraft cabin interior: a modern Thresher ship, but something much less advanced than the Slasher vessel she had woken up inside.

'That's a serious development,' he said.

'There's more we need to talk about,' Auger said. 'Can you clear our approach with the Tanglewood authorities?'

'Check the news, Auger: there *are* no authorities. The Tanglewood administration's made a run for the hills. I'm already having a hard time evading the pirates and looters, and I have a fast shuttle.'

'My children are in Tanglewood.'

'No,' he said. 'Peter took them away a couple of days ago. As soon as Skellsgard came through, we began to fear that something bad was imminent. Your children are safe.'

'Where are they?'

'Peter thought it best not to tell anyone. He said he'd make contact with you as soon as the situation calms down.'

Auger closed her eyes and said a small, silent prayer of thanks.

'Sir,' Auger said after a moment, 'I have important news. There's something I really need to tell you. I know what Susan White was on to, and it's big. You have to act now . . . use all your contacts to pull in assistance before it's too late.'

'It's all right,' Caliskan said. 'We figured out most of the details from Skellsgard. It was remarkably brave of you to send her back the way you did.'

'Is she all right?'

'Yes, she's fine. Safe and sound.'

That was another debt to add to the pile. Her children were safe and so was her small, scowling friend from Phobos.

'I still need to talk to you,' she said. 'Can you suggest a suitable rendezvous point?'

'I already have a place in mind. It's somewhere the pirates and looters won't dare follow us. I suspect even the Slashers will have second thoughts.'

She knew exactly where he meant, and it scared her. 'You're not serious, Caliskan.'

'I'm more than serious. Does that ship you're in have transatmospheric capability?'

She turned to Cassandra. 'Well?'

'We can fly in. But there's more to a trip to Earth than just flying in. A Thresher ship may be sufficiently robust for the furies not to pose an immediate risk, but we are rather more . . . susceptible.'

'I thought the Slashers had protection against furies now. Isn't that why you're so keen to get your hands on Earth?'

'Experimental countermeasures,' Cassandra said. 'Which – I regret to inform you – this ship doesn't happen to be carrying.'

Auger turned back to Caliskan. 'No dice. She says the ship isn't equipped to fend off furies. We'll have to pick another RV point.'

'Tell her not to worry,' Caliskan said. 'The fury count near my designated RV is low. I know because I have direct feeds from Antiquities monitoring stations in the vicinity. Our enemies won't have this information, which is why they won't be so keen to come charging in.'

Auger glanced at Cassandra. 'Does that sound reasonable to you?'

'He spoke of a low count, not a zero one,' Cassandra said. 'I can't risk taking my ship deep into the atmosphere, especially with eighteen evacuees in my care.'

'This is very important.'

'In which case,' Cassandra said, 'we'll have to consider an alternative means of transportation.'

'You mean the *Twentieth*'s shuttle?'

'There isn't much fuel left aboard, but it should still be capable of making the round trip.'

'Can it fly itself?'

'It doesn't have to,' Cassandra said. 'I can take care of that.'

Auger returned her attention to the screen. 'We're following you in, but we'll need a few minutes to get our act together. Don't get too far ahead of us.'

'Make it as quick as you can,' Caliskan said. 'And if you have any cargo from Paris, now might not be a bad time to hand it over to me. Given what's happened around Mars, it may be the last consignment we ever see.'

'There isn't much,' Auger said. 'Just a few boxes that the snake robot put on the transport before it sabotaged the link.'

'You're still working for Antiquities. Bring what there is. Then follow my trajectory precisely, no matter how inefficient it looks.'

'Where are you taking us, sir?'

'For a dinner engagement,' Caliskan said. 'We're dining with the ghost of Guy de Maupassant. I just hope he doesn't mind the company.'

THIRTY-FOUR

They hit atmosphere. It was a rougher ride than Auger had been expecting – the Slasher ship's aerodynamic effectiveness had been badly compromised. By Cassandra's reckoning, the ship had lost thirty per cent of its mass during the chase, discarding parts of itself to act as chaff and decoys while the main section executed increasingly desperate hairpin reversals, sidesteps and swerves.

'Did Caliskan make it through?' Auger asked.

'We're still tracking his ship. He's about twenty kilometres ahead of us, slowing down to supersonic speed. He seems to be headed for the northern part of Europe, specifically—'

'Paris,' Auger said. 'It would have to be Paris.'

'You seem very certain of this.'

'I am.'

'What was that business about having dinner with Guy de Maupassant, anyway? Is he another colleague of yours?'

'Not exactly,' Auger said. 'But we'll worry about that when we get there.'

'Mind if I add a contribution?' Floyd asked.

'Go ahead.'

'I really do know Caliskan. I told you his face was familiar – I think I've placed him.'

'I know this is going to sound mean,' Auger said, trying to soften her words with a smile, 'but you're really not qualified to have an opinion on Caliskan.'

'Maybe not, but I still know that face. He's someone I've met, I'm pretty sure, someone I've had dealings with.'

'You can't have met him. He's been in E1 space the whole time. There's no way he could have slipped through the portal without everyone knowing about it.'

414

Cassandra leaned forward in her seat. 'Perhaps Floyd has a point, if he feels so certain of his observation.'

'Don't encourage him.'

'But if Caliskan had knowledge of the Phobos link, isn't it conceivable that he might have made a trip through it?'

'No,' she said firmly. 'Skellsgard would have told me, even if no one else did.'

'Unless Skellsgard was given specific orders not to tell you,' Cassandra said.

'I trusted her.'

'Perhaps she didn't know what was going on either.'

'But if that's the case, then we can't even be sure that we can trust Caliskan any more. In which case, who the hell *do* we trust?'

'I still trust Caliskan,' Cassandra said. 'My intelligence contacts have never pointed to him having an ulterior motive.'

'They could be wrong.'

'Or Floyd could be mistaken.' Cassandra consulted with her machines for a moment, then said, 'There is another possible explanation.'

They both looked at the dark-haired girl.

'Well?' Auger asked.

'According to the biographical file we have on Caliskan, he had a brother.'

'Yes,' Auger said slowly. 'He told me about him.'

'And?'

'Caliskan reckoned I had a grudge against Slashers. He didn't think it was justified. He said that if anyone had a right to hold a grudge it was him, because of what happened to his brother.'

'The biographical file says that his brother died in the final stages of the Phobos reoccupation, when the Slashers were ousted,' Cassandra said.

'Yes,' Auger confirmed. 'That's what he told me.'

'Maybe he believed it, too. But what if his brother didn't die?'

'She could be right,' Floyd said. 'You know the link was open just before the reoccupation. It's the only way those children could have come through.'

'But Caliskan's brother wasn't fighting on the side of the Slashers,' Auger said.

'Maybe they got to him,' Floyd said. 'Maybe they took him prisoner and got to him later. Maybe he sneaked through at the same time.'

'And you just happened to bump into this man in E2?'

'I'm just telling you what I've seen.'

'You told me nothing about any children,' Cassandra said.

'They weren't children,' Floyd said. 'They were like you . . .' He paused. 'Only uglier.'

Auger sighed. Now that Floyd had let the cat out of the bag, nothing would satisfy Cassandra until she had an explanation. 'Neotenic Infantry. War babies, we called them. They must have opened the link to the ALS during the Phobos occupation twenty-three years ago.'

'And they've been there ever since?'

'They're not exactly a pretty sight by now.'

'Most of them would have already died,' Cassandra said. 'Those first-line neotenics were never designed for longevity. Any survivors must be near the ends of their lives.'

'They look like it. They smell like it,' Augur said with disgust.

'Why don't you just tell me what they were doing there? As I said, I can always suck it out of your brain if you don't. I'd rather not, but—'

'All I have is guesswork,' Auger said. 'They were making something, some kind of machine – a gravity-wave sensor, I think – for establishing the physical location of the ALS. The trick was that they had to construct it using local technology.'

Cassandra mulled that over and nodded primly. 'And the purpose of this data, once they obtained it?'

'To enable them to reach the shell from the outside.'

The ship rocked, hitting turbulence. The floor quivered, as if about to spring up and around them in a protective embrace.

'What do they want with the ALS?' Cassandra wondered, frowning.

'They want to depopulate it. They want to seed the atmosphere of the duplicate Earth with Silver Rain.'

'That's monstrous.'

'Genocide generally is. Especially on this scale.'

'All right,' Cassandra said, still frowning as she assimilated the new information. 'Why not deliver Silver Rain via the link itself?'

'They can't. There's a barrier that prevents anything like that from entering Floyd's world. The only way in is to sneak around the back.'

'But there's still the small matter of breaking through the shell,' Cassandra said. 'Ah – wait a minute. We've covered that already, haven't we?'

'The theft of the antimatter drive from the *Twentieth*,' Auger said.

'That's their – what did you call it? Molotov device?'

'So it would seem.'

'The neotenics couldn't have put this together by themselves,' Cassandra said. 'They're resourceful and clever, but they were never engineered to think strategically, especially not for twenty-three years. There must have been others privy to the same plan.'

'We already know about Niagara.'

'But Niagara had no easy means of communicating with the neotenics. Those children needed leadership and co-ordination, someone to give them orders. Adult-phase Slashers, perhaps,' Cassandra suggested.

'No,' Auger said. 'Not unless they were prepared to live without their machines. It was all right for the war babies: they're purely biological, with no implants. But no one like you could have followed them through the censor device with all that nanotech running around inside them.'

'Then an unaugmented person: a normal human being – like Caliskan's brother.'

'Possibly, if he decided to turn traitor.'

'And if there was one such, there might well have been more,' Cassandra said. 'A lot of people died or went missing during the reoccupation.'

'They could all still be alive,' Auger said, 'living in the ALS, meddling with the course of history.'

'But why would they meddle?' Cassandra asked.

'To hold things back. To stop Floyd's people developing the technology and science that might actually have made them a threat to their grand plan, as soon as they realised their true situation.'

'Given time and the accumulation of random changes, the two timelines would be bound to diverge eventually,' Cassandra said. 'How can you be sure there was conscious intervention?'

'Because it's all too deliberate. In Floyd's timeline there was never a Second World War. Whoever went through the link twenty-three years ago knew just enough about the actual course of events in nineteen forty to change them. All they had to do was get the right intelligence to the right people. The fulcrum was the German invasion through the Ardennes. It came close to failure in our timeline, but the allies never knew how vulnerable the advancing forces were. No one acted. But in Floyd's timeline they did. They got bombers into the air and pounded those tanks into the mud. The German invasion of France collapsed.'

'So there was never a second global war. I presume millions of lives were spared because of that.'

'At the very least.'

'Doesn't that make it rather a good thing?'

'No,' Auger said, 'because those lives were only spared so that billions could be extinguished now. It was a purely clinical intervention. Saving lives had nothing to do with it. The only motivation was to keep those people in the dark.'

'Then a crime has already been committed. The children will soon be dead. But their leader – or leaders – must be found and brought to justice.'

'Then you need to find the ALS as well,' Auger said, 'before one crime becomes another.'

'Niagara's allies must indeed be close to acting,' Cassandra said. 'They wouldn't have moved on the liner unless they were ready to attack the ALS. This is very grave.'

'You said it, kid,' Floyd commented.

'The more I think about it,' Cassandra said, 'the more I wonder if this entire attack against Tanglewood and Earth isn't a diversionary tactic. They never really wanted our ruined Earth back, did they? They always had their sights set on a bigger prize.'

'We have to stop them,' Auger said.

'Agreed,' Cassandra said. 'But do you think Caliskan will be able to help? Do you think he can even be trusted, if his brother is indeed a traitor?'

'He thinks his brother died,' Auger said. 'I'm inclined to take him at his word. Anyway, we can't afford *not* to trust him. He has contacts, including allies in the Polities.'

'So do I,' Cassandra said.

'But Caliskan has political clout. At the very least he can publicise the Slasher plan and maybe shame them into not acting.'

'This could be a trap,' Floyd said.

'I'm trying very hard not to think about that possibility,' Auger replied.

Cassandra's face became glazed as she absorbed a welter of data concerning their approach to Paris. 'Trap or not, we're in the thick of the clouds now. Slowing to subsonic speed. I think this is about as low as I want to go in this ship. The particulate density is already rather on the high side for my liking.'

'Can we release the *Twentieth*'s shuttle?'

'Now is as good a time as ever,' Cassandra said. 'Follow me.'

They howled through clouds as thick as coal, bellowing with thunder and flickering with lightning in slow, pink-tinged bursts.

'Still tracking Caliskan?' Auger asked.

'With difficulty,' Cassandra said, turning briefly away from the antique control console. 'Did you have any more luck with figuring out who that de Maupassant fellow Caliskan mentioned is?'

'Yes,' she said. 'I think I know exactly what he meant. It doesn't matter if we lose his trace – we can still make the RV.'

'Couldn't he have just told you where to land?' Floyd asked.

'Caliskan likes his little games,' Auger said, smiling thinly. Around them, the hull creaked and groaned like a very old chair.

'Cloud density is lessening,' Cassandra said. 'I believe we're nearly through the worst of it.'

Through the cabin windows, the grey took on a rushing, streamlike quality, evoking great speed. The ship slammed through two or three final scarves of attenuated cloud before entering clear air above the city. This was a true Parisian night, as dark as it ever got except when there was some calamitous failure of ground-side power. The only sources of steady illumination were the artificial lights installed by Antiquities, mounted on buildings and towers or slung from hovering dirigibles and drone platforms. Now and then, lightning flickering above the clouds shone through the circuitlike patterns via which the clouds communicated, etching a negative ghost of those patterns on to the icebound streets and buildings laid out below.

They were about five kilometres up, a high enough elevation for a panoramic view of the entire city, right out to the artificial moat of the Périphérique defences.

'I don't know whether you're going to like this,' Auger said to Floyd, 'but welcome to Paris. You've never been here before.'

Floyd looked down through the small windows set into the lower part of the cabin. 'I guess this means you were telling me the truth all along,' he said, struggling to deal with the enormity of that final realisation.

'Did you still have doubts?'

'I still had hopes.'

She directed his attention to the edge of the city, where the tower-top beacons of the perimeter defences flashed red and green in sequence. 'That's the Périphérique,' she said, 'a ring of roads encircling Paris. It didn't exist in your version of the city.'

'What's the wall?'

'The ice cliff. It's armoured with metal and concrete, sensors and weapons, to keep the larger furies out, the ones that are big enough to see. Most of the time, it more or less works. But they still get through now and then, and when they do, they come in quickly.'

That was the problem with Paris: the spiderweb of Métro and road tunnels offered numerous swift routes in from the perimeter. It didn't matter that half of those tunnels were blocked by cave-ins: the hostile machines would always find an alternative route, or burrow their way into the older system of water and sewerage tunnels. The smallest of them could slip through telegraphic conduits, optical-fibre trunk lines and gas pipes. If push came to shove, they could even drill new tunnels of their own. They could be stopped – they could even be destroyed – but not without inflicting unacceptable damage on the very city that the researchers were trying to preserve and study.

'I don't recognise much,' Floyd said.

'You're looking at a city frozen more than a hundred years after your time,' Auger said. 'Even so, there are still some landmarks you should recognise. It's just a question of learning to see them, under all the ice.'

'It's like the face of a friend under a funeral shroud.'

'There's the curve of the Seine,' Auger said, pointing. 'The Pont Neuf. Notre Dame and Ile de la Cité. Do you see it now?'

'Yes,' Floyd said, with a sadness that ripped her open. 'Yes, I see it now.'

'Don't hate us too much for what we did,' she said. 'We tried our best.'

Above, the clouds rippled and surged with a strange, oblivious intelligence. The ship pitched and yawed, sinking lower. 'Might I trouble you for the landing site?' Cassandra asked.

'Take us south of the river,' Auger said. 'Do you see that rectangle of flat ice?'

'Yes.'

'That's the Champ de Mars. Line us up with it and hold altitude at three hundred metres.'

She felt the ship respond almost before she had finished speaking. Servomotors made a crunching, grinding sensation under her feet, as flight surfaces were redeployed.

'Is there something significant about this area?' Cassandra asked.

'Yes.'

A bolt of lightning chose that moment to punch through the clouds, landing very close to the mangled, attenuated stump of the Eiffel Tower, at the limit of the Champ de Mars.

'That's where we're headed,' Auger said.

'The metal structure?'

'Yes. Bring us down on the upper stage, as best as you can.'

'It's sloping. I'm not sure if I trust that metal?—'

'It'll hold,' Auger said. 'You're looking at seven thousand tons of Victorian pig iron. If it survived two hundred years under ice, I think it can take our weight.'

For two centuries, the ice had swallowed the lower third of the three-hundred-metre-high tower. Some forgotten, unwitnessed catastrophe had ripped the upper seventy-five metres into history, leaving no trace of the wreckage within the excavated bowl of Paris. The first two observation decks remained, plus most of the much smaller third stage, which was perched atop a slanted, corkscrewed stump of twisted metal leaning far out towards the frozen Seine.

'I can see a parked spacecraft on the third level,' Cassandra said. 'Thrusters are still hot. Size and function matches the type of shuttle Caliskan was using.'

'That's our meeting point. If he's being nice, he'll have left us enough space to park.'

'It'll be tight,' the Slasher said.

'Do your best. If necessary, you only have to hold station while we disembark, or bring Caliskan aboard.'

'And Mr de Maupassant?'

'He won't be joining us. He's been dead nearly four hundred years.'

'Then I confess—'

'Caliskan's little joke,' Auger said. 'He knew I'd get it. De Maupassant despised that tower. In fact, he hated it so much that he insisted on having lunch in it every day. Said it was the only place in Paris where it didn't spoil his view.'

The tower thrust up below them, its distorted lean even more apparent now that they were hovering directly above the third stage. From this perspective, the latticed metal shaft curved inward, like an eroded cliff, while the far side was bent so far from its intended angle that the ironwork had begun to curl away in buckled sections, like the hackles of a dog.

Lighting stabbed close again. The play of shadow and light made the entire structure appear to move, wobbling like jelly.

'Bring us in, Cassandra,' Auger said. 'The sooner we're down, the happier I'll be.'

The third-stage observation deck was an apron of square metal tilted at five or six degrees to the horizontal, pierced by the jagged uprights of severed girders and the shafts that had once carried the elevator cars to the top of the tower. Buckled metal railings were still in place around much of the perimeter. Caliskan's barb-shaped shuttle was parked in one corner, its tail jutting out into empty space.

'That's his ship,' Auger said. 'Can you land?'

'I can try.' Cassandra threw a bank of levers. 'Landing skids are down and locked. We'll burn fuel in VTOL mode, but there's nothing I can do about that.'

The ship hovered, sliding from side to side as Cassandra feathered the vectored thrust nozzles. They dropped a little, held station, then dropped again. Nearing the platform, the backwash from the thrusters sent loose metal scurrying across the deck, smashing through the railings and over the sides. Then they were down, the landing skids absorbing the impact with a bounce of pneumatics.

Cassandra powered down the engines, conserving every drop of fuel. 'We should be all right for the time being,' she said.

'Good job, that,' Auger said. 'For your next trick, can you re-open a channel to Caliskan?'

'Just a moment.'

One of the screens flickered, then filled with Caliskan's features. He pushed unkempt white hair back from a glistening brow. 'Are you secured?' he asked.

'Yes,' Auger said, 'but I'm not sure there's enough fuel left in the shuttle for us to make it back into orbit.' She glanced at Cassandra, who made an indecisive face and an equivocal hand gesture.

'How many of you are there aboard?' he asked.

'Three,' she said, 'plus the cargo. But Cassandra's hoping to fly the shuttle back on her own. Only Floyd and I need to come with you.'

'There should be enough room for all three of us, and the cargo. Do you think you can make the crossing?'

'Depends on the fury count,' Auger said.

He glanced away, consulting some concealed read-out. 'It's low enough not to be a problem, provided you wear normal environment gear. No special precautions necessary. Just watch your footing.'

'Why did you bring us here? I mean, I understand why orbit wasn't the safest place—'

'Precisely because of the fury count, Auger. The big machines never get this high. Monsieur Eiffel's monstrosity is the safest place in the city.'

THIRTY-FIVE

Floyd and Auger stepped on to the leaning floor of the third-stage observation deck. Above, the constant motion of the clouds created a dizzying sense that the entire structure had chosen that exact moment to topple over. Floyd had never been good with heights, and this predicament seemed to encapsulate every vertigo-tinged nightmare he'd ever had. They were walking on a slippery, sloping, rickety surface pocked with holes and weak spots, almost three hundred metres in the air . . . in a gale . . . in heavy suits that made vision limited, every gesture clumsy, every step perilous, and they were also carrying four heavy boxes between them loaded with paper, books and phonograph records.

'You all right, Floyd?' Auger asked. Her voice was shrill in the diving-helmet affair the Slasher had just bolted into place over his head.

'Put it this way, Auger: when I last got out of bed, staggering around on the mangled wreck of the Eiffel Tower wasn't exactly on my list of things to achieve by sunset.'

'But look on the bright side, Floyd. Think of the great stories you'll have to tell.'

'And think of the fun I'll have finding someone prepared to believe me.'

With an appalling and very audible groan of stressed iron, the deck suddenly lurched, its angle of tilt increasing. Loose debris came skidding towards them, squealing across the metal surfaces. Floyd dived to one side, dropping one of the boxes in the process. Before he could reach for it, a girder slid by and snagged on the side of the box, dragging it along for the ride. While he fumbled for a solid purchase – something to prevent him from sliding the same way as the box – he watched it cruise all the way to the edge of the deck and out into empty space. The box tilted, spilling books, magazines, newspapers and records into the air above Paris.

'Floyd! Are you all right?' shouted Auger.

'I'm fine – but I just lost one of the boxes.'

He heard her swear, then bite down on her anger. 'Can't be helped. But this whole structure feels as if it's about to give up the ghost. Must be the weight of the ships.'

Lightning strobed the horizon, brighter than before.

'That looks like a bad electrical storm,' Auger observed. 'I'd really like to get out of here before it arrives.'

'Me, too,' Floyd said with feeling, standing up. 'I've seen enough of the view for one lifetime. It gets old real quick.'

Caliskan's ship had slid a little closer to them before its movement had been arrested by the obstruction of the ruined elevator shaft, its truncated iron cage pushing up through the floor. From this angle, Floyd made out a stepped ramp folded down from the silver barb of the ship. A suited figure leaned out at the top of the ramp, beckoning them closer with a gloved hand. Then the figure started down the steps, meeting Auger halfway. She handed him the first of her two boxes, then waited while he loaded it into the ship and took the second from her. Then she crossed back to Floyd and helped him with his one remaining box. He joined her on the laddered ramp, recognising the face of the man in the spacesuit as the one he'd seen on various Slasher screens. It was Caliskan.

He directed them aboard into a small double-doored room the size of a pantry. The outer door closed, silencing the storm like the needle being pulled from a record. The boxes were piled up in one corner, like so much junk waiting to be thrown out.

When they had passed through the inner door, Caliskan removed his helmet, indicating that they should do likewise. 'You made it,' he said, palming his white hair back into some approximation of order. 'That was a little touch and go, wasn't it?'

'Can I speak to Cassandra?' Auger said. 'I want to tell her to get out of here.'

'Of course.' Caliskan ushered them into the narrow forward section of his little ship. It was all exposed metal, pipes and spars, about as warm and snug as the inside of a midget submarine. 'The link is still open. I'll see her actions receive appropriate recognition once this mess is sorted out.'

'Cassandra, can you hear me?' Auger said.

'Loud and clear.'

'Save yourself. We can take care of ourselves from now.'

'Can Caliskan get you out of there?' she asked.

Caliskan leaned into the field of view of the camera. 'I'll take care of them, don't worry.'

424

Now that he was seeing Caliskan in the flesh, Floyd felt more certain than ever that he had met him – or possibly his brother – before. Still wearing most of his spacesuit, Caliskan leaned down to peer through a circular porthole in the side of his ship. 'Why isn't she lifting off? Doesn't she know how unstable this structure is?'

Lightning flashed again, painting Caliskan's face with harsh highlights, like a retouched photograph.

'That storm's getting closer,' Floyd observed.

'Cassandra,' Auger said, assuming that the link was still open, 'is there a problem?'

There was not even a crackle of response. The screen was blank. With a worried look on his face, Caliskan settled into his flight position and started throwing controls, methodically at first but with increasing urgency. 'Something's wrong,' he said, after a minute of this.

'Fury infiltration?' Augur asked, alarm clear in her voice.

'No . . . the counts all looked low.'

'And now?'

'Everything's dead, including the monitors. The ship's switched to reserve power – basic functions only.' He nodded towards the porthole. 'Given the age of that ship you arrived in, Cassandra may be experiencing the same difficulties.'

'But if it's not furies . . .' Augur began.

There was another flicker of lightning, brighter and closer and more violent than before. A metallic rumble shook the observation deck, transmitting shockwaves through the parked ship. It felt like a passing freight train.

'I don't know what's happening out there,' Auger said, 'but we have to get out of here before that storm hits, or this tower collapses, or both.'

'We're not going anywhere for a while,' Caliskan said. 'I don't think those are lightning flashes.'

'If they're not lightning flashes . . .' Auger began, her mouth suddenly drying up with fear.

When Floyd caught a glimpse of her face, her expression was enough to put the fear of God into him. 'What is it?' he asked, reaching out to her.

'Scorched earth,' Auger said. 'It's begun. Missile bombardment from orbit.'

'I fear she's right,' Caliskan said. 'Those flashes look rather like nuclear strikes to me. Hundreds of kilometres away . . . but they seem to be coming closer. That may or may not be deliberate.'

Auger buried her face in her hands. 'As if we haven't screwed this planet up enough as it is.'

'Let's worry about the planet later,' Floyd said. 'Right now our necks have priority. How do we get off this thing? Why aren't the ships working?'

'Electromagnetic pulse damage,' Caliskan said. 'These ships are Thresher designed, with a heavy reliance on electrical subsystems. They're not built to tolerate that kind of thing.'

Floyd had no idea what Caliskan was talking about, but he assumed it was serious. 'Will they fly again?'

'I don't know,' Caliskan said, continuing to work the controls, as if they might come back to life at any moment. 'Some of the systems are trying to revive themselves, but they keep falling over because the other systems aren't awake. If I can juggle the reboot sequence . . .' His fingers danced with manic speed across a keyboard, while pale numbers and symbols marched in columns across a ceiling-suspended screen.

'Keep trying,' Auger said, jamming her helmet back on. 'I'm going to see if Cassandra's having any more luck.'

'No need,' Floyd said, looking back through the porthole at the other ship. 'She's on her way over.'

'Are you sure?'

'See for yourself. She must have decided it was too risky to stay aboard.'

Cassandra had donned one of the other standard-issue spacesuits from the shuttle's emergency inventory. Either the angle of the deck had worsened or the gale had intensified, because she was almost unable to walk, leaning like a bent-backed old woman, placing each footstep with aching deliberation. Every now and then, some jagged piece of metallic debris slid across the deck or sliced through the air, narrowly missing her.

'Careful . . .' Floyd breathed. He looked around the tight confines of Caliskan's ship, trying to imagine how they were all going to fit inside, in the unlikely event that the machine could be persuaded to fly.

'Looks as if the nuclear strikes have eased off a bit,' Auger said, watching proceedings from the other porthole. 'Maybe there's still somebody up there with an ounce of sense.'

'Don't count on it,' Caliskan said.

The observation deck lurched again, its angle becoming even steeper. Floyd felt the horrible beginnings of a slide as Caliskan's ship lost traction against the metal plating.

'We're going over,' he said, a sick feeling churning in his stomach.

But then suddenly they were still again, and the angle of the deck seemed to level out. He looked at Auger, and then at Caliskan, but saw nothing in their faces to indicate that they understood what was happening, either.

'Cassandra's nearly here,' Floyd said. 'Lower that ramp again, will you?'

But then Cassandra slowed her approach. With obvious effort, she stood up straight against the roar of the gale and looked at something to her left. Floyd followed her gaze as far as the restricted angle of the porthole allowed, and saw what had brought her to a halt.

'You really need to see this,' he said.

'What?' Auger replied, from the other side of the cabin.

'Come here and see for yourself.'

He waited until her face was jammed next to his, looking through the same porthole.

Beyond the edge of the observation deck, something enormous was rising ponderously into view. It was huge and bulbous and aglow with mysterious lights, arranged in curves and coils and cryptic symbols that suggested the luminous markings of some titanic, tentacled sea monster, rising from the deeps to tower over some hapless little ship. Cassandra stood silhouetted against this moving mountain of light, her arms slightly outspread as if in welcome – or prayer.

'Caliskan,' Auger said, 'I think help's just arrived.'

Caliskan looked back over his shoulder, while his hands continued to work the controls. 'What did you say?'

'There's a significant chunk of Slasher hardware hovering off the side of the tower.'

Caliskan left the control panel and took Floyd's place at the porthole.

'Damn thing must have followed us in,' Floyd said.

'Cassandra's walking towards it,' Auger said.

Caliskan returned to his controls, letting Floyd resume his position next to Auger. 'What's she doing?' he wondered.

'I don't know,' Auger replied. 'I suppose it's possible that she might be trying to communicate with—'

Multiple lines of light speared from a gunport in the swollen belly of the monstrous ship. They ripped through Cassandra like rays of sun through cloud, pinning her in place even as her tiny body danced like a flag. Then the beams of light were gone, and Cassandra was still there, but with ragged holes etched through her. She collapsed to the ground, and then the whipping force of the gale slid her crumpled form towards the edge of the deck. Her limp body tumbled limb over limb like a rag doll, then splayed itself across the remains of the railings, like washing hung out to dry.

Hard white flashes pocked the horizon.

The huge ship began to swivel, turning to bring some other part of its structure into line with the observation deck. It was as large as the Hindenberg, Floyd estimated, or an aircraft carrier. Larger, perhaps. A thing like that had no business just hanging in the sky.

Caliskan's face was grave. 'It looks as if they've come for one – or both – of you.'

'Did you bring them here?' Auger asked.

'No. I was trying to keep you from them. They must have the fury countermeasures. Or else they want something so badly that they'll risk anything to get it.'

The Slasher ship now presented its long side to the tower. Floyd was reminded of a museum piece he had once seen: a deep-sea squid preserved in formaldehyde, with its tentacles coiled into a single corkscrewing blade. The ship had something of the same daggerlike functionality. The lights and symbols on its sides seemed to lie beneath a layer of translucent jelly. The ship was creeping closer, like a bank of luminous fog.

'This doesn't make sense,' Auger said. 'I don't know anything about their plans that they don't already know for themselves. And yet if killing us was what they wanted, they could have done that already.'

'Then perhaps I was wrong,' Caliskan said with sudden urgency. 'Perhaps it isn't you they're interested in after all. Or Floyd, for that matter.'

'Then that only leaves one thing,' Floyd said. 'If it isn't us, and it isn't you, then it must be something we brought with us.'

'The cargo,' Auger said.

Caliskan played the controls one last time, then abandoned them with a dismissive sweep. 'Put your helmets back on and find somewhere to hide outside on the observation deck.'

'They'll find us,' Auger said.

'They'll certainly find you aboard this ship. Outside, with the storm and the electrical interference, you have a fighting chance of staying alive until reinforcements arrive.'

Auger weighed the options. 'I think he's right, Floyd,' she concluded, reluctantly.

'You don't have time to cycle through the airlock,' Caliskan said. 'I'll have to blow the outer door as soon as you're inside it.' He reached beneath his seat and produced a melted thing that looked like Salvador Dali's idea of an automatic pistol. 'Take this,' he said, handing it to Auger. 'I'm sure you can work out how to use it.'

'What about you?' she asked.

'I have a spare. I'll do my best to cover you until you can reach shelter.'

'Thanks.' Auger slipped the gun into the equipment belt of her spacesuit, then helped Floyd latch his helmet into place. Her voice came through to him again, rendered thin and buzzing by the helmet's internal microphone. 'There must be stairs down to the next level,' she said. 'We'll try to find them.'

'Go,' Caliskan said. 'Now.'

Floyd was first through the blown door. He hit the metal decking hard, nearly landing on his face. He looked back in time to see Auger emerging, lightning freezing the expression behind her helmet glass.

'We'd better keep radio silence from now on,' she said. 'Stick by me and we can shout if we need to make ourselves heard.'

The luminous wall of the Slasher ship nudged the observation deck, making it sway. It would have cost that behemoth nothing to plough through the tower, smashing it like a wooden jetty.

'Auger, have you any idea—'

'Floyd,' she hissed. 'Not now. They're almost certainly listening in for EM traffic.'

They walked in a crouched, crablike fashion, using the debris for cover as they scurried from shadow to shadow. When they had reached what appeared to be the upper entry point to a stairwell, Auger touched him on the shoulder and pointed through a mangled heap of girders and sheet metal to the enormous spectacle of the ship. She pressed a finger to the chin of her helmet, signalling him to silence.

A doorway had opened in the side, forming a drawbridge across the gap between the hovering ship and the edge of the observation deck. Figures were emerging from the bright aperture of the doorway, six of them in total. They walked slowly across the makeshift bridge. They wore suits of their own – seamless blobs of highly reflective armour that shifted constantly as if made of mercury. The squad reached the observation deck and stepped gingerly on to the tilted platform. They walked upright, the only sign of hesitation being the deliberate way in which they planted each footstep before proceeding with the next.

Auger pushed Floyd lower. He shifted his footing until he found one of the embossed metal steps that led below. He didn't want to think how far down those stairs went – or not, for that matter.

She touched her helmet against his. Her voice came through the glass: she had turned the radio off. 'We have to go lower.'

'I want to see what those guys want with Caliskan.'

'Leave it, Floyd. Can't you see that he didn't set us up?'

'Kid: someone set us up, and I've had doubts about Caliskan since the moment I saw him.'

'Well, maybe someone set Caliskan up,' Auger said. 'Is that such a leap?'

The silver-suited men fanned out, picking their way through the labyrinth of traps and pitfalls on the surface of the platform. They were linked together, bound by a network of very thin silver strands extruded from their armour. It formed a shifting cat's cradle, floating above the deck at head height, connected to each man by the crown of his helmet.

Caliskan appeared at the entrance to his ship, gun in hand. Using the rim of the door for cover, he took aim at the nearest trio of advancing men and zapped them with the gun. A line of bright light stabbed from the muzzle, connecting with the middle man. His silver armour evaporated in a flash, revealing a stooping human core. Caliskan ducked back, adjusted something on his gun and then fired off another shot, aiming at the unprotected man. The man's right arm puffed away at the elbow and he bent double in pain. But before Caliskan could fire again, the silver armour of the two uninjured men on either side of him became diffuse, expanding in size until it formed a protective cloak around their comrade.

Caliskan readied the gun again and delivered another lancing beam to the merged form of the silver figures. But now their armour resisted his attack: swelling in size, shimmering brightly, but not dissipating. Floyd wondered when they were going to retaliate, instead of just lapping it up. He had no sooner thought this than light scythed from the hovering ship, piercing Caliskan's head.

He slumped to the ground next to his ship, the gun slipping from his fingers.

Floyd guessed that answered his doubts about the man.

The six men had only sustained one injury. While the first party stepped over Caliskan's body and examined his ship, the other three worked their way along the side of the platform until they reached Cassandra, her body still draped limply over the railings.

Auger tapped Floyd's elbow and gestured 'down'. Floyd motioned for her to wait, torn between fear and an urgent need to know what the men were interested in. They knew Cassandra was dead. Why did her corpse concern them so much?

The brightest explosion yet tore the horizon open. Floyd jammed his eyes shut, but still saw everything in negative as the glare tore through the metalwork. A few seconds later, he felt that same freight-train shudder as the entire tower rattled.

'Getting closer,' Auger said. Her hand was on the melted form of the weapon Caliskan had given her, but she had not yet removed it from her belt.

He risked another glance across the observation deck. The three figures had convened around Cassandra's splayed form. Their silver armour had merged and was now pushing from its chest region a thick, splayed tentacle, as wide across as a thigh. With a vile questing motion, the tentacle touched Cassandra in different places, gently, methodically, as if trying to elicit some last twitch of life.

'What are they looking for?' he asked queasily.

'I don't know,' Auger replied.

The three figures stepped back as one. The silver tentacle suddenly gathered strength, whipping back before plunging into Cassandra's chest. The ensemble took a further step back, and as they did so they peeled the impaled body from the railings. Then the tentacle made a flicking motion too fast to follow and the speared body flew apart in five or six pieces.

The bloody tentacle crept back into the linked body. The three men remained merged together for a moment or two longer, and then the armour began to divide, separating them into individual entities once more. They looked around, stepped away from each other and once again began to search the deck.

'Whatever they're about, they're not done yet,' Auger said. She drew the melted gun and pressed it to her chest, ready for use.

Floyd looked down. She must have already realised that the stairwell offered no escape. It ended less than a dozen steps below them, hanging uselessly above empty space. It was at least thirty metres down to the second-stage observation deck, and the only possible routes to it were via the elevator shaft (assuming that wasn't severed as well) or the girders forming the legs of the tower itself.

They weren't going anywhere.

Floyd looked back to Caliskan's ship. Two of the figures had gone aboard while one waited outside. Floyd tapped Auger's shoulder, alerting her to what was happening just as one of the men emerged with a box. A moment later, the second man brought out the other two boxes of artefacts.

Floyd glanced back to the other three. They had left Cassandra's remains where they had fallen: whatever they were looking for, they had obviously not found it on or inside her body.

He returned his attention to the others, feeling Auger resettling herself, raising the silver gun a little higher. Two men stood outside with the three boxes, while the third had gone back in again.

'Careful,' he hissed to Auger.

Then he noticed something new nearby: a metallic smudge in the air, like a thousand twinkling bees, which somehow moved towards the tower against the force of the wind. He flinched, thinking it had to be something to do with the men who had killed Cassandra and Caliskan. But the smudge was approaching them in a series of furtive darts and feints, suggesting that it was just as eager as they were to avoid the attention of the search party. Close to Floyd and Auger now, it settled over them, concealing itself in the same hiding place. The twinkling mass flexed and flowed, forming brief patterns and shapes.

Floyd touched Auger gently on the shoulder and directed her attention to the dancing form. She flinched as well – she hadn't seen it until then – and snapped the gun towards it. The smudge pulled away nervously, but didn't retreat beyond the sanctuary of the stairwell. The gun trembled in Auger's hand, but she held back from firing. Then, very slowly, she let the barrel fall until it was no longer aimed at the smudge.

For four or five seconds, nothing happened.

Then the smudge darted for her, wrapping itself around her helmet. Auger thrashed at the halo of twinkling stars, trying to swat them away. She cried out in terror or pain, and was abruptly silenced. Horrified, Floyd watched the cloud of twinkling things shrink in size as one by one they found a way into her helmet.

Then Auger was suddenly very still.

The stairwell shook, loosening rusted bolts free into the endless space below them. Tons of metal went crashing down through rusted spots in the observation deck, tumbling down to dash against the lower limits of the tower. Squeals and groans of agonised metal bellowed through the night.

Something snapped inside Floyd. Before Auger could react, he pried open the stiff fingers of her hand and removed the gun. The gun seemed eager to oblige, squirming from her grip to his almost as if alive. In his own gloved hand, it felt as fragile as something made from aluminium foil.

Auger showed no reaction. She was perfectly still now, a constellation of twinkling lights swarming behind the glass of her helmet.

So they'd got her, after all. Soon, he presumed, they would do the same thing to him. There was no way off this tower, and the three searchers would soon be upon them. If he waited, there might be no time for even a gesture of defiance, however futile it might be.

Sometimes, a gesture was all you were allowed.

He pointed the gun at the nearest silver figure and squeezed the teatlike nub that he hoped was its trigger.

The gun quickened in his hand, writhing like an eel and spitting out a blast of *something*. The figure's strange armour came apart like ash on the wind. Floyd fired again, blowing a chunk out of the exposed Slasher. He fell to the deck, lost amidst the tangle of broken and buckled metal.

Now the other five were joining forces. The three near Caliskan's ship walked close enough to each other for their armour to merge, while the other pair combined their own armour and began to approach the trio. Floyd levelled the gun again, aiming it at the larger group. Again it shifted in his hands, and again the silver armour dissipated, blowing away in twinkling flurries. But this time the damage was much less significant, the combined armour having formed some kind of reinforcing shield.

Beside him, Auger finally moved. 'Give me the gun,' she said.

She took it from him before waiting for his answer. She made quick adjustments to the settings, then sprang out of their hiding place and fired the gun with inhuman speed and accuracy, squeezing off burst after burst until the barrel was as bright as molten iron. Her shots were only intermittently aimed at the advancing party. She had gone mostly for the ship itself, shooting at its gunports.

She fell back into shelter. 'I've bought us a little time. I hope it's enough.'

'Is is safe to talk?'

'For now. My reinforcements are jamming their communications and sensor activities.'

'*Your* reinforcements?'

'This will take a little explaining.'

Floyd looked down just in time to see a blur of light streak through the spread legs of the tower, between the second and third stages. He followed the motion as best he could, peering through a dark complexity of girderwork, and made out another moving clump of lights shadowing the first. Floyd tracked the sleek, flexing shapes as they arced higher, reaching an apex before hairpinning and diving back towards the base of the tower. They moved so fast that they cleaved rippling lines in the air, suction vortexes that pulled loose debris into them.

'Please, explain away,' he said.

'I'll try. You saw what just happened?'

'You dying, you mean?'

'No one died. Especially not Auger. But it's not Auger speaking right now.'

'You feeling all right, kid?'

'You're talking to Cassandra,' she said. 'The tiny machines you saw belong to me.'

'But we saw you die.'

'You saw my body die. But the machines got out in time. They fled my body at the moment of death, before Niagara's aggressors were able to subsume and interrogate them. Now they're using Auger as an emergency host.'

'You just . . . did that?'

'There's nothing trivial about it,' she said, with a touch of defensiveness. 'These machines can encode and transfer no more than a shadow of my personality and memories. Believe me, dying isn't something I take lightly, especially here.'

Floyd looked up again, certain that the silver men could have killed him by now if that was their intention. But they had stopped their slow advance. They were hesitating, pinned between their ship and the quarry they sought.

'Maybe we should talk about this later,' he said.

'I wanted you to know what was going on, Floyd. I'll continue to control Auger until we're out of this mess. Then she can decide what she wants to do with me.'

'What will her options be?'

'She can continue to harbour me until we find a suitable Polity host, or she can order me to leave and I'll die. Whatever happens, I assure you she will come to no harm.'

'Did she give her permission for this?'

'There wasn't time to ask. Matters, as you've doubtless noticed, are at something of a head.'

The huge Slasher ship was under attack. Smaller ships – two of them, at least – were strafing it with lines of slicing light. The light gouged painful hyphens into Floyd's eyes, as if someone was slicing them with razors. He forced himself to look away.

'Is this your cavalry?' he asked.

'Yes. I requested assistance as soon as we left Mars, but I didn't know how many ships would be able to respond.'

'Are we going to win this one?'

'It's going to be close.'

The larger vessel was fighting back. Through narrowed eyes, Floyd risked a glimpse, watching parallel lines of light surge from undamaged gunports along its flanks, connecting with the aerial attackers. All three ships in the engagement were protecting themselves with movable shields: curved sheets of translucent material that sped from one part of the hull to another, flexing and flowing to adjust to the changing shape beneath them. Wherever a beam touched, one of the shields would dart into place, absorbing the damage, glowing along its edges like paper about to burst into flame. After a few seconds of this, the shield would erupt with light and shatter into a million little sparks that rained down towards the Champ de Mars.

Gradually, though, it became clear that the big ship was taking the worst of the damage. Its shield movements were becoming increasingly frantic, yet still too sluggish to parry the darting assaults from the smaller craft. A third of the way along its length, an explosion ripped through the translucent blubber of its hull, puckering it out in petalled folds like an exit wound from a bullet. Bright grids of machinery shone through the gash. A smaller chain of explosions chased each other to the tail of the ship. The luminous symbols under the translucent layer began to warp and flow, losing sharpness.

'She's dying,' said Cassandra, speaking through Auger.

The quintet of silver men broke up into individuals, severing the connections between their armour. Three of them rushed to the cargo boxes, gathered them up and headed for the ramp leading back into the wounded ship. The other two resumed their unhurried stroll towards Floyd and Auger, unconcerned – it seemed – by whatever was happening to their compatriots or their one means of escape.

The access ramp was sliding back and forth as the ailing ship struggled to hold station next to the tower. For one moment, it looked as if the three silver men would miss their step and fall into the abyss, taking the cargo with them. Somehow they made it, dashing inside as the access ramp slowly hinged back into the ship, like the closing jaw of a sated whale.

More explosions peppered the length of the ship. The tail was now hanging lower than the nose, as if – absurdly – she was taking on water. One of the attacking ships had sustained a fatal strike and was slowly losing altitude, with ink-black smoke – or something that looked very like smoke, at least – billowing from a gash in its flank. Floyd followed its progress down as it gradually lost height in a gyring death-spiral, until it finally exploded somewhere near Montparnasse.

The two silver men had nearly reached the top of the stairwell. In a few seconds they would be within easy sight of Floyd and Auger.

'Listen to me now, Floyd.'

'I'm listening.'

'We need to leave. I've sent small clusters of machines into both shuttles, in an effort to regain some degree of control.'

'And?'

'Both ships are beginning to wake up from the EM pulse. Our best hope is Caliskan's shuttle: it's smaller, faster and less likely to be picked up by interdiction weapons.'

'Then what are we waiting for?'

Across the ruin of the observation deck, something pulled Floyd's attention to the embattled ship. A slot opened in its back and something jetted out, emerging quickly and gaining speed with every second. At first he assumed it was some new, last-ditch weapon. But the pip-shaped object continued to rise, squirting fire from one tapered end.

'What was that?'

'An emergency escape vehicle. But whoever's in it won't get far.'

The one small ship that remained peeled abruptly away from the larger vessel, making an obvious effort to intercept the other vehicle. There was a brief exchange of fire between the two vessels before the escape craft punched through the geometrically textured quilt of the clouds. The clouds lit up with a hard-edged flash, chased by a drawn-out peel of thunder.

Through a crack in the clouds, Floyd caught a momentary glimpse of the pip clawing its way back towards orbit, cutting across the night like a shooting star.

'You want to rethink that?'

'They won't get much further. The interceptors in near-Earth space will take care of them.'

The main ship could no longer maintain station or attitude. It had tilted to forty-five degrees, spewing smoke and fire, its hull feverish with a dance of scrambled symbols. It began to rotate, bringing its lower extremities into contact with one of the four main supports holding up the observation deck. The entire structure slid sideways a few metres, accompanied by a terrible metallic rending noise. Through the gap where the stairs ended, Floyd saw tons of metalwork hurtling down towards Paris. But the dying ship wasn't dead yet. It was still rotating, pushing against what remained of the tower's uprights. Another lurch ensued – almost enough to throw them from the narrow sanctuary of the stairwell.

'Look,' Floyd said, aghast.

Calsikan's little barbed vessel slid over the edge of the landing stage, dashing itself against the tower as it fell. It dwindled, tiny as an egg, tumbling end over end and occasionally bouncing against the latticed metal legs of the tower. Somewhere near the bottom it blew apart in a veined, brainlike fireball. Floyd felt the tower rock with greater force than ever before. The other parked ship – the one they had arrived in – had slid towards the middle of the deck as the angle of tilt altered, but it would only take another resettlement to send it toppling over the edge.

'Bang goes our preferred escape route,' Floyd said.

'Then we'll have to take the other ship. We'll only know if it's capable of flight when we get there. By then we won't have the option of returning to this hiding place.'

'I'm ready to take my chances.'

'Then let's go.'

Auger left the cover of the stairwell with Floyd hard on her heels. They crab-walked against the shifting force of the wind, ducking behind obstacles as often as they could. Auger used the gun again, firing it with the same inhuman precision she had shown before. Sometimes she didn't even look in the direction she was shooting, but she still managed to hit her targets unerringly. The weapon was inflicting only superficial damage on the two remaining members of the search party – either the gun was running out of juice, or the men had beefed up their armour – but at least they no longer had the hovering ship to assist them. Instead they were advancing on the *Twentieth*'s shuttle and extending a tentacle of silvery light from their merged armour to block access to the door. The tentacle flexed and undulated in the air, its tip widening to form a more efficient obstruction. At the same time, another pair of thinner tentacles was creeping through the air towards Auger and Floyd, lashing above them like two loose hawsers. Auger kept on shooting, targeting both the tentacles and the main body from which they'd emerged. Her accuracy was still spot-on, but even Floyd could tell that she was being more sparing with the shots. It was all she could do to ward off the two tentacles above them.

'They're definitely weakened,' she said, between breaths. 'They can't keep extending their armour indefinitely. Unfortunately, I'm running out of power.'

They were only a dozen paces from the shuttle, taking temporary shelter behind a mass of collapsed metal. The door was still blocked by the flexing form of the main tentacle. There was no way they'd get through that alive, not after what the armour had done to Cassandra.

'We can't give up,' Floyd said.

'We're not going to. But these controlled bursts aren't doing enough. I've got enough charge left in the weapon for six shots at normal discharge strength. I'm going to blow the whole lot in one go. It'll fuse the weapon, but that doesn't matter now.'

'Do whatever you must.'

'It won't kill them,' she said. 'It'll only take the wind out of their sails.'

She made the necessary adjustments to the weapon. 'No matter what happens,' she said, 'I want you to run like hell for that airlock. Get inside the ship and don't hang around if I'm not behind you.'

'I'm not going anywhere without you.'

'The machines will take care of you. Let's just hope it doesn't come to that.'

The tentacles lashed above them, and then began to extend themselves downwards, narrowing to sharp, rapierlike blades as they descended.

'Whatever you're going to do,' Floyd said, 'now would be a good time to do it.'

She levelled the gun, holding it at arm's length, and aimed at the merged body of the Slashers. The gun fired just as it had before, but with much greater intensity. The beam of light daggered into the conjoined figures, boiling off layers of armour in a flash of hot silver. Then the gun itself erupted with light, flaring in Auger's hand. She held on until the discharge ended and then flung the molten, spitting thing away with a howl of anger or pain.

'Run!' she shouted.

Before it died, the weapon had clearly inflicted grave harm on the two

Slashers. Their armour was wobbling, oscillating around them like jelly. The sharp-edged tentacles had pulled back into the main mass, while the tentacle guarding the door had been severed and was thrashing around like a decapitated snake. The shuttle door was now unguarded. Floyd dashed over to it and pulled down the chunky striped handle that was obviously meant to be used for opening the door from the outside. To his relief, the door slid up, recessing into the hull and admitting him into the small compartment where the air was exchanged. He looked over his shoulder, expecting Auger to press against him at any moment.

But she wasn't there. She had barely moved from the position where she had fired the gun. She lay on her side, one gloved hand a scorched black ruin where the gun had destroyed itself. She was crawling across the iron decking, one pained centimetre at a time.

'Floyd,' she said, with obvious difficulty. 'Leave now.'

'I'm not leaving you here.'

'I'll take care of Auger. Just get yourself out of here.'

He looked back at the remnants of the search party. One of them – the man Caliskan had injured earlier – now lay on the ground, devoid of armour. The remaining volume of armour had huddled around the other Slasher, but there was something nervous and imperfectly co-ordinated about the way it flowed and shaped itself, as if the armour, too, was hurt. But the severed piece was still writhing and whiplashing its way back towards the main mass. When it got there, the armour would probably become stronger again . . .

Floyd left the shuttle and ran across the observation deck to Auger.

'Get out of here,' she said.

He knelt down and picked her up. The effort was nearly too much for him – they were both wearing heavy suits and Floyd hadn't exactly been training for this kind of thing.

'No one's leaving anyone behind,' he said, trying to shift her weight in his arms so that they wouldn't both topple over when he stood. 'I noticed you weren't in a hurry to abandon Auger the way you did your own body.'

'My body was mine to throw away,' she said. 'You just don't do that with someone else's.'

Staggering as he stood, Floyd found his footing and started back towards the waiting ship. 'Even if it kills you?' he gasped, the exertion making his breathing ragged.

'Don't talk, Floyd. Just walk.'

He reached the door of the shuttle and lowered Auger into the internal chamber. He forced himself into the same tight space and found the counterpart to the striped handle he'd pulled on the outside. He yanked it down and waited for the door to lower itself.

Down below, at the base of the tower, the stricken Slasher ship had finally reached the ground. As the door slid down, Floyd watched it die, burying its nose in ice and fire. The carcass collapsed in on itself, blossoming with a thousand miniature explosions. Next to it, the tower rattled in sympathy, dislodging even more of its rickety superstructure.

'I think Guy de Maupassant's about to get his dying wish,' Floyd said.

He had one last view of the tower and the Champ de Mars as the shuttle hauled itself into the clouds. Enormous explosions ripped open what remained of the body of the crashed Polity ship. Perfectly circular shockwaves raced away from the scene, out towards the perimeter shield. Paris quivered. Slowly, like some great wounded giraffe, the tower began its terminal collapse. One of the legs supporting the third-stage deck buckled, splintering into a million iron shards. The other three legs could not support what remained of the structure, although for a few seconds it looked as if they might. But a process had now begun that could have only one outcome. After centuries of stalemate, gravity was winning over twisted iron girders and rusted iron bolts. The tower began to lean more acutely, and the remaining legs slowly began to bow under the conflicting stresses. Hundred-ton girders popped free, twanging into empty space like flicked playing cards. As thousands of tons of metal slammed into the ground, a veil of powdered ice rose hundreds of metres into the air. It served as a kind of screen, camouflaging the tower's final moments. Floyd saw the third observation deck tilting into that whiteness, caught in a stutter of jagged lightning, and then he looked away, some part of him unable to watch until the end.

He decided, for all its faults, that he preferred his own Paris.

It was such a shame that he would never see it again.

THIRTY-SIX

'I appreciate that circumstances might be better,' said the man in the white captain's uniform, resplendent with epaulettes and sleeve braids, 'but I still want you to feel at home on this ship.'

Tunguska offered Floyd a cigar from a little wooden humidor. Floyd declined the cigar, but accepted a shot of whisky. They sat in upholstered armchairs in the luxuriously appointed parlour room of what was either an ocean liner, airship or transatlantic flying boat. Through the square windows, only a rain-washed darkness was visible, and the droning hum of engines was sufficiently nondescript that any of the possibilities could have applied. Ceiling fans stirred the air above them, rotating with laboured slowness.

Floyd drank half his whiskey. It wasn't the best he'd ever tasted, but it still took the edge off his day. 'What's the news on Auger?' he asked.

'She's stable,' Tunguska said. 'The physical injury from the malfunctioning weapon was easily attended to, and ordinarily wouldn't have caused any difficulties.'

'But on this occasion?'

'She went into shock. It's quite possible that she would have died without intervention from Cassie's machines. As it is, the machines have consolidated their hold on her. It's like a coma.'

'How long is she going to be like that?'

'No telling, I'm afraid. Even when one of us willingly accepts to become the host to someone else's machines, it's still a process fraught with pitfalls. The kind of field transfer that Cassandra achieved down in Paris . . .' The captain jogged his cigar sideways, by way of illustration. 'It would have been difficult even if Auger had been another Slasher, with years of preparation and the requisite structures already present in her head, ready to accept the new patterns. But Auger is only human. To compound matters, she was injured shortly after the takeover.'

'If Cassandra hadn't taken her over, we'd both have died down there, wouldn't we?'

'More than likely.' Tunguska helped himself to another cigar, snipping off the end with a clever little silver guillotine. He hadn't smoked the first, or even appeared to grasp its basic function other than as a social accessory. 'By the same token, Cassandra would have died without Auger as a host.'

'I don't think she exactly volunteered for that job.'

'Trust me,' Tunguska said, 'there would have been a degree of negotiation, no matter how fleeting. It isn't etiquette to storm someone else's head, no matter what the crisis.'

'What are Cassandra's chances now?'

'Better than they would have been without a host. Her machines would have survived, but her personality would have begun to break up without the anchoring effect of a physical mind.'

'And now?'

'She has a fighting chance.' He stabbed the cigar forwards for emphasis. 'Thanks to Auger.'

'I think Auger misjudged you,' Floyd said.

'She misjudged some of us. Concerning the others, she was – I regret to say – entirely correct in her opinion.'

Floyd had already told Tunguska all he could of the Slasher conspiracy. Doubtless he had some of the details wrong, and was vague about other things that Auger would have understood better. But Tunguska had nodded encouragingly, and had asked what seemed like more or less the right questions in the right order.

'What will happen now?' Floyd asked.

'With Auger? We'll keep her under observation until we can identify a suitable new host for Cassandra's machines. It's not entirely clear what they're doing to Auger, but I think we'd best leave them to their own devices for the time being.'

'But will she be all right?'

'Yes. Whether she will ever be quite the same, however . . . well, that's a different question.'

Floyd cradled his drink and nodded. There was no point shooting the messenger, when Tunguska was doing the best he could. 'Before we left Paris,' he said, 'Cassandra said she'd given orders to intercept the escape vessel.'

'We received them,' Tunguska said.

'I was just wondering what the deal with that was. Did you boys make your kill?'

Tunguska glanced sideways, as if checking that no one else was in earshot. 'Not exactly. It would seem that one of the interceptor ships was compromised. The one that had the best chance of catching the escape craft just . . . let it slip through the net.' He spread his fingers wide. 'Unfortunate.'

'You can't let that thing escape.'

'We did what we could, but there was another, faster ship waiting in translunar space, within one of our temporary sensor shadows. *Very* clever.'

'And this faster ship – how big is she?'

'Big enough to carry the antimatter device from the *Twentieth Century Limited*, if that's what you're wondering,' he said. 'We can't be certain that it's the same craft that was involved in the hijacking, but given all the other factors . . . well, it seems more than likely. Incidentally, we've connected that ship to Niagara.'

'You have to stop him.'

'Tricky, unfortunately. His ship's already on a high-burn trajectory, heading towards the Sedna portal.'

'So shut it down,' Floyd said.

'We've already tried that. It would appear that Niagara's allies have control of the portal. We'll have a military presence there within the day – enough to oust the aggressors – but not before that ship makes it through to the hyperweb.'

'And then we'll have lost her,' Floyd said heavily.

Tunguska shifted in his seat, the leather groaning as he resettled himself. 'Not necessarily. We at least know that the ship's headed to the Sedna portal, and we know where that portal comes out. There's a triad of portals at the far end – Niagara will have to take one of them. If we can keep sufficiently hard on his tail, we may be able to read the signatures of portal activation and determine which rabbit hole he's bolted down. At that point we'll risk entering the hyperweb link while another ship is still in transit. This is an unorthodox procedure even for Polity ships, and we'll have to override safety controls on the portals to attempt it at all. But at the very least we'll be able to follow Niagara part of the way, if nothing else.'

'Much good that'll do.'

'It's better than turning away now. Niagara's craft is a big ship, fast in a straight-line dash, but it won't be able to make portal-to-portal transitions as fast as we can. That's about our only advantage.'

'And you've still no idea what corner of space Niagara's headed to?'

'None at all,' Tunguska said. 'That, unfortunately, is the bit we haven't figured out yet. I don't suppose you've had any bright ideas?'

'If you want bright ideas,' Floyd said, 'you've definitely come to the wrong guy.'

442

When they had finished their drinks, Tunguska led Floyd through a warren of panelled companionways to his quarters. 'It's not much,' the Slasher said, opening the door to a bedroom Howard Hughes could have used for landing practice.

'I'll manage,' Floyd said, fingering the teak inlay of the door. 'Is all of this real?'

'Perfectly so,' Tunguska said. 'Ours is a large ship and we can afford to reallocate some resources for your comfort. If we need those resources back again, I'll do my best to give you fair warning.'

'Thanks . . . I think,' Floyd said. 'About Auger?'

'You'll be notified as soon as anything happens.'

'I'd like to see her.'

'Now?'

'Perhaps in a little while.'

'She still won't be able to talk to you,' Tunguska warned.

'I know,' Floyd said, 'but I want her to know that someone cares.'

'I understand,' Tunguska replied, guiding him into the room. 'You've made quite some sacrifice by coming here, haven't you, Mister Floyd?'

'I've made worse.'

'But you must appreciate that there is no guarantee of your ever returning home.'

'I didn't know that when I helped Auger escape.'

'Perhaps not. But would that knowledge have made any difference to your actions?'

Floyd thought about that for a moment, trying to answer truthfully. 'Maybe not.'

'I doubt that it would have. I may not be an excellent judge of human character, but I suspect you would have made exactly the same choices even if you'd had full knowledge of the consequences.' Tunguska patted him gently on the back. 'And I find that rather admirable. You would have thrown away everything – the world and the people you love – for the sake of another human life.'

'Well, don't elevate me to sainthood just yet,' Floyd said. 'I had an idea that it was a good idea to help Auger get home. That was a kind of selfishness. And there's still a chance for me to make the return journey.'

Tunguska studied him intently for a few moments, one finger gently stroking the heavy undercurve of his chin. 'If we pinpoint the location of the ALS, you mean?'

'Yes.'

'Well, that's true enough. But there's still the small matter of breaking inside. The aggressors will attempt to deploy their antimatter device, which may or may not be sufficient to crack open the ALS. We, on the other hand, will do all we can to prevent them from doing that. If we can detonate the antimatter device prematurely, that is what we will do.'

Floyd hadn't thought things through to that level of detail. Tunguska didn't need to spell it out any more clearly that this could well turn into a suicide mission, if that was the only way to prevent Silver Rain from reaching E2.

'I'm sorry,' Tunguska added, when he saw Floyd's reaction.

'And there's no other way inside for me, is there?'

'None that we know of. Of course, if the ALS is ever in our possession, we'll have all the time in the world to find a way inside . . . but that's the one thing *you* don't have.'

'You must do whatever it takes to stop Silver Rain,' Floyd said. 'That's what Auger and I risked our necks for. It's what Susan White, Blanchard and Cassandra died for, and all the other innocent people that got involved in this.'

'We can still hope for a satisfactory outcome,' Tunguska said, forcing a strained note of optimism into his voice. 'I'm just saying that we ought to be prepared for the worst.'

Tunguska left Floyd alone in his quarters, while the ship raced across the system towards the compromised portal. Floyd roamed around the enormous room, exploring its parameters like a laboratory hamster. It was comfortable enough, and it was obvious that his hosts had gone to quite a lot of trouble to make him feel at home. But he had a nagging suspicion that he would have been happier with the naked reality of the ship, as it presented itself to its usual occupants. Up close, the décor and furnishings of the room had the same sketchy quality as the parlour room. It was like walking through someone else's vague daydream. Rather than relaxing him, it put him on edge.

There was a huge old upright wireless set by the writing desk, with a sunrise motif cut into the wood around the speaker grille. He turned it on, fiddled with the tuning dial. There was only ever one channel broadcasting. On it, a man delivered updates about the state of play in the system, with particular emphasis on the events in and around the portal towards which they were headed. The wireless announcer spoke with the speeded-up drawl of a horse-racing commentator, punctuating his monotone dialogue with little bells, whistles and xylophone jingles. It wasn't a real news report – Floyd figured that much out for himself in very short order. It would have sounded dated and phoney in 1939. It was a digest of the real situation, packaged in a way that was meant to be soothing and reassuring for him.

He listened to the wireless for an hour or so, which was about as much as he could take. Niagara's ship had reached the portal and made a successful insertion. Fears that the aggressors might attempt to collapse the portal after making their insertion turned out to be unfounded, at least for now. One theory was that the technical staff left behind had refused to follow the orders to collapse the throat. Another was that the throat collapse would be delayed until the last minute before moderates regained control of the portal, so that the collapse wave didn't have time to catch up with and damage Niagara's ship. A third possibility was that the aggressors had chosen to keep the portal open, despite the risk of pursuit. Closing it would have endangered the possibility of future access to the ALS, making their entire scheme senseless. They wanted to sterilise E2, and then bring everyone else around to the idea that this had been the right and proper thing to do. And then, presumably, they wanted to talk real estate.

Floyd turned off the wireless and thought about Auger again. It was less than a week since she had walked into his life. And yet he couldn't imagine spending one moment of the rest of his life without her. Every other concern seemed thin and trivial when set against the necessity of her survival.

Presently, Tunguska came back to see him. 'Good news, Floyd – Auger is making progress.'

'You've found another host?'

'Not yet, no. Cassandra's machines seem quite keen to entrench themselves, for now at least. It may be that they've decided to stay inside Auger until this crisis is resolved.'

Floyd stood up. 'Can I see her?'

'I said she was making progress,' Tunguska said, with a sympathetic smile. 'I didn't say she was lucid.'

'How long before she's properly conscious?' he asked, slumping down on the bed again.

'We'll be well inside the portal by the time she's ready for visitors.' Tunguska held a box in his hands, jammed full of what Floyd at first took to be papers. 'I'll have to ask for your patience until then.'

Floyd accepted this information with as much grace as he could muster. 'All right. I guess there's no point in arguing.'

'None at all, I'm afraid. We have Auger's best interests at heart, but we're just as concerned for Cassandra's wellbeing.' He walked over to the bed on which Floyd was sitting and placed the box at his feet. 'In the meantime, I thought this might make your stay here a little more tolerable.'

Floyd looked down. The box was full of records: labels and sleeves he half-recognised. 'Where did you get those from?' he asked incredulously.

'The cargo you brought back from E2,' Tunguska said, looking pleased with himself.

'But I thought we lost it.'

'We did. These are copies, reconstructed from scans of the original cargo. You can thank Cassandra for that particular piece of foresight.'

Floyd extracted one of the records. Seventy-eight r.p.m.: Louis Armstrong, with King Oliver's Creole Jazz Band, playing 'Chimes Blues'. The original, on the Gennett label, was worth a ton of money in mint condition. Floyd had a scratched copy that was worth a bit less. All the same, he'd still played it a thousand times, trying to get his head around Bill Johnson's bass moves.

This was a newer copy, on a reissue label, but still not one that Floyd had seen before. The sleeve was made of an odd, slippery material that felt like wet glass. 'You made these?' he asked, rubbing the strange paper between his fingers.

'It was simple enough, given the available information.'

Floyd tipped the sleeve, letting the disc roll out into his hands. It was very light, as if pressed from cuttlefish bone. It felt as if it ought to snap into a thousand pieces at the slightest touch.

'I wasn't even sure you people still listened to music. Auger didn't seem very keen on it. Nor did Susan White.'

'Did Auger talk about that at all?'

'I kept meaning to ask her, but events got in the way. What's the deal, Tunguska? Is music seen as a primitive art form here, like cave painting or bone carving?'

'Not exactly,' Tunguska said. 'We still listen to music in the Polities, although it's a rather different sort of music than any you're likely to have experienced. But Auger and her compatriots simply don't have the option of listening to music at all. It was all our fault, you see. We stole music from them.'

'How can you steal music, Tunguska?'

'You engineer a viral weapon. It can't have escaped your attention what a central role music plays in the morale of a nation at war. Now imagine taking that away, in a single stroke. We'd already designed a viral weapon that could have killed them all, had it been allowed to infect a sufficient number of hosts. But we didn't want to kill them: we wanted to turn them to our own ideology, so that our own numbers could be strengthened. Besides, a lethal virus is rather difficult to deploy across a wide sphere of battle. As soon as people start dying, quarantines are enforced. Brutal measures are taken to curtail its spread. So our thinkers went away and re-honed their weapon to attack the part of the mind associated with language, thinking that such a virus would have a better chance of spreading before its effects were noticed.'

'Nasty,' Floyd said.

'But still not satisfactory,' Tunguska continued, his voice as measured and untroubled as ever. 'Our forecasts showed that the end result would still be tens of millions of deaths, as their habitat-based society unravelled due to lack of communication between key workers. So again our thinkers reworked the weapon. What they came up with was *Amusica*: a virus keyed to certain areas of the right brain hemisphere, analogous to those left-brain foci associated with the perception and generation of language. It worked beautifully. Victims of *Amusica* lose all sense of music. They can't make it, can't sing it, can't whistle it, can't play it. They can't even listen to it, either. It means nothing to them any more: just a cacophony of sounds. To some it's actively painful.'

'Then Auger . . . and Susan White?'

'*Amusica* spread through Thresher society very rapidly. By the time anyone had noticed what was happening, it was far too late to do anything about it. Even now there are mutant strains of the virus in circulation. And because of the way the weapon was designed, once you have it, you pass it on to your children . . . and your children's children. That's the future, Floyd: a world without music, for most of them.'

'Most of them?'

'It didn't touch them all. One in a thousand escaped its effects, although we still don't know why. They consider themselves very fortunate. They're hated and envied in equal measure.'

'But if you can take music away . . . can't you put it back?'

Tunguska smiled tolerantly. 'We've tried, in a spirit of bridge-mending. But volunteers are naturally reluctant to submit to even more neural intervention. Most Threshers wouldn't trust us to set a broken leg, let alone rewire their minds. And the few that do volunteer . . . well, the results haven't been startlingly successful. If they remember what music once sounded like, they complain that it now sounds pale and unemotional. They might be right.'

'Or they might just be feeling the way we all do,' Floyd said. 'No one ever took music away from me, but I'm damned if it ever sounds quite as good as it used to when I was twenty.'

'I confess that was also my suspicion. But given the harm we've done, the least we can do is give these people the benefit of the doubt. Perhaps there is something missing after all.'

'What about your people? If this virus is everywhere, shouldn't you have caught it by now?'

'We would have, except the machines swarming through our bodies and minds keep the virus at bay.' Tunguska hesitated. 'Now that the subject has been broached, Floyd, I should warn you that, since you lack these machines yourself—'

'That virus could hop aboard any time it likes.'

'You're probably safe at the moment,' Tunguska said. 'You'd need to be exposed to more than one carrier before the virus has a chance of establishing itself. But if you were to remain in the system – moving freely in Thresher society – then the virus would eventually find you.'

Floyd looked at the disc, his own reflection gleaming back at him. 'Then I'd lose music, just the way Auger did?'

'Unless you had the good fortune to be the one in a thousand who can resist the virus . . . then yes, I'd say it was more or less guaranteed.'

'Thanks,' Floyd said. 'I'm glad you told me.'

Tunguska looked a little taken aback. 'Thanks wasn't exactly the reaction I was expecting. Hatred and condemnation, perhaps, but not gratitude.'

'Bit late for condemnation, wouldn't you say? What's done is done. I don't get the impression you're particularly proud of what you did.'

'No,' Tunguska said, sounding genuinely relieved. 'We're most certainly not proud. And if there was anything we could do to make amends—'

'Maybe once you get this small matter of a war out the way,' Floyd suggested, 'then you can think about rebuilding some of those bridges again. But first we have to stop Niagara.'

'There was something in the cargo he needed,' Tunguska said. 'But he knew what he was looking for. We don't. It would be difficult enough trying to find it even if we still had the cargo, or if Cassandra had had enough time to scan the contents at a higher level of resolution.'

'Wait,' Floyd said, turning the record over again. 'If she didn't have time to examine the cargo in detail, where did this copy come from?'

'Cassandra did the best she could, which means that the books and magazines and other journals haven't been subjected to the kind of scrutiny she might have wished. But the recordings? It was actually a rather simple matter to make a holographic scan of the groove. A lot easier than scanning a paper document at microscopic resolution, looking for some hidden message.'

Floyd tilted the sleeve this way and that. 'But if there was a hidden message here, you'd have missed it as well.'

'A hidden message like the co-ordinates of the ALS? Yes. But you already know that it would only take a tiny amount of data to specify that position. A few digits . . . easily hidden anywhere.'

'Then it's useless.'

'I just thought the recordings might help the time pass. Given how much you like music—'

'Yes,' Floyd said. 'Very much so. And the gesture's appreciated. But without something to play these on . . .'

'Come, now,' Tunguska said, with a playful gleam in his eye. 'You don't think I'd have forgotten *that*, do you?'

He was looking at something behind Floyd, on the bedside table next to the sunrise wireless. Floyd turned around. There stood a phonograph set, a good one, where there had definitely not been one a minute ago.

'That's a pretty good trick, Tunguska,' he said, smiling.

'Enjoy the music, Floyd. I'll return when I have some news.'

After he had gone, Floyd slipped the disc on to the phonograph turntable and lowered the diamond-tipped needle into the groove. It crunched on to its track and then became quiet, except for the occasional click of static. Then the music began, Armstrong's trumpet filling the room effortlessly, Lil Hardin's piano bright and clear and cool, like rain on a hot day. Floyd smiled – it was always good to hear Satchmo, no matter the time or place – but there was something about the music that couldn't rescue his spirits. Perhaps he was too worried about Auger and the rest of it to let the music have its intended effect. But even his scratched old Gennett copy had a life to it that was missing from this version. Somewhere between Paris and Cassandra's ship, some essential spark had been bled from the music. Floyd pulled the platter off the turntable and returned it to its sleeve. He leafed through the box, finding the other jazz recordings and trying some of them, before abandoning the exercise. Maybe it wasn't the recordings so much as the player, or the acoustics of the room, but something was wrong. It was like listening to someone almost whistle a tune.

Nice try, Tunguska, he thought.

Floyd leaned back on the bed, hands crossed behind his head. He turned on the wireless again, but the news was still the same.

'You can speak to her now,' Tunguska said. 'But please – take things easily. She's been through a great deal in the last couple of days.'

'I'll treat her with kid gloves.'

'Of course. By the way, Floyd – how are you getting on with those recordings?'

'They're a real nice thought,' Floyd said.

'As in – "it's the thought that counts"?'

'I'm sorry, Tunguska, but there's something off about them. Maybe that phonograph needs a new needle. Or maybe it's just me.'

'I just wanted you to feel at home.'

'And I appreciate the gesture. But don't worry about me, all right? I'll cope.'

'You put a brave face on things, Floyd. I admire that.'

Tunguska led him into the bright white chamber of the recovery room.

'I'll leave you alone with her,' Tunguska said. 'The machines will let me know if she experiences any difficulties.'

He stepped back through the white wall, which sealed itself tightly behind him, like blancmange.

Auger was in a state of drowsy wakefulness, sitting up in bed with a fog of silver machines twinkling around her head and upper body. She saw him walking towards the bed and – despite her evident weariness – managed a smile.

'Floyd! I thought they were never going to let you see me. I began to wonder if you were really all right.'

'I'm fine,' he said, sitting on a toadstool-shaped pedestal next to the bed. He took one of her hands and stroked the fingers. He expected her to pull away, but instead she tightened her grip on him, as if she needed this moment of human contact. 'Tunguska wanted you to have some peace and quiet while you got your head together.'

'It feels as if I've been here for a hundred years, with my head ringing all the while.'

'Is is better now?'

'A bit. It still feels as if there's a small debating society holding their annual meeting in my skull, though.'

'Cassandra's machines, I suppose. You remember what happened, don't you?'

'Not everything.' She pushed a strand of sweat-damp hair from her eyes. 'I remember Cassandra dying . . . but not much else.'

'Do you remember her machines asking permission to set up camp in your head?'

'I remember feeling very frightened about something, but knowing I had to say "yes", and that I didn't have long to think it over.'

'You did a very brave thing,' Floyd said. 'I'm proud of you.'

'I hope it was worth it.'

'It was. For the time being, anyway. Do you know where you are?'

'Yes,' she said. 'At least, as soon as I realise there's something I don't know, the information seems to pop into my head. We're back on Cassandra's ship, except that Tunguska's running the show now.'

'You think we can trust him?'

'Yes, absolutely,' she said firmly, as if that should have been obvious. Then she frowned, just as suddenly less sure of herself. 'No. Wait. How *could*

I know him that well? That must be one of Cassandra's memories . . .' Auger shook her head, as if she'd just taken a bite from a lemon. 'This is strange. I'm not sure I like it.'

'Tunguska said that Cassandra's machines seem to have taken a shine to you,' Floyd said.

'Don't tell me I'm stuck like this for ever.' She said it in an off-hand way, but not quite convincingly enough.

'Probably just until the crisis is over,' Floyd said, doing his best to sound reassuring. 'Do you remember that escape craft Cassandra was confident they were going to shoot down?'

'Yes,' Auger said, after a moment.

'Well, it got away. Made rendezvous with a bigger, faster ship. According to Tunguska, the evidence trail points to Niagara.'

This, at last, seemed to push Auger towards full alertness. She sat up straight in the bed, pushing her hair back. 'We have to stop that ship before it reaches a portal. Nothing else matters.'

'We tried,' Floyd said.

'And?'

'No one could catch up with Niagara. And he'd already taken control of the portal.'

'I thought you said we were still chasing him.'

'We are. Tunguska sent reinforcements to regain control of the portal. His boys kept it open for us. We're in the hyperweb at this very moment.'

She looked around, perhaps doubting his words. Floyd, too, had found it difficult to believe that a portal transition could be this smooth, this unexciting. It was like a ride in a well-oiled hearse.

'So where is Niagara right now?' she asked.

'Somewhere ahead of us, further along the pipe.'

'I didn't think they ever put two ships in at the same time,' Auger said, frowning.

'I don't think it's exactly routine.'

'Does Tunguska think we'll catch up with Niagara's ship, or maybe get close enough to shoot it down?'

'I don't know. I think he's more worried about what will happen when Niagara pops out the other end. There's a danger we'll lose the trail.'

'That can't be allowed to happen,' Auger said. 'If we lose the trail, then we lose everything. Your whole world, Floyd – everyone you know, everyone you ever loved – will die in an instant.'

'I'll tell Tunguska to throw a few more chairs in the furnace.'

'I'm sorry,' she said, sinking back into the hollow of her pillow, as if drained of energy. 'I don't know why I'm making this any more difficult for you than it already is. Tunguska's bound to be doing all he can.' Then she looked at Floyd sharply, some random dislodged memory slotting back into place. 'The ALS co-ordinates,' she said. 'Did you figure them out?'

'No. Tunguska's still chewing on that one. He says we may never find them.'

'We're missing something here, Floyd. Something so damned obvious it's staring us in the face.'

Tunguska came to see her a little later. He was a huge man, but he moved and spoke with such unhurried calm that Auger couldn't help but relax in his presence. His mere existence seemed to assure her that nothing bad would happen.

'Have you come to let me out of bed?' she asked. 'I feel as if I'm missing all the excitement.'

'In my experience,' Tunguska said, making himself a temporary seat, 'excitement is always better when it happens to other people. But that's not why I came. I have a message for you. We intercepted it shortly before entering the portal.'

'What kind of message?'

'It's from Peter Auger. Would you like to see it?'

'You really should have told me sooner.'

'Peter specifically asked that you not be disturbed until you were feeling better. Anyway, there was no possibility of replying. We told Peter that you would be unconscious until we were already in the hyperweb.'

'Then he knows I'm safe?'

'He does now. But why don't I just play the message?' Without waiting for an answer, Tunguska cast a hand towards one wall and conjured a screen into being. It filled with a flat, static image of Peter, looking a bit more harried and rough around the edges than usual.

'I'll leave you to view the message in private,' Tunguska said, standing and gesturing for his seat to dissolve into the floor.

The image came to life as soon as Tunguska left the room.

'Hello, Verity,' Peter said. 'I hope that this reaches you safe and sound. Before you start worrying, I want you to know that the kids are all right. We're in the protection of Polity moderates – friends of Cassandra's – and they're taking very good care of us. Tunguska will make sure we're all reunited once this madness is over.'

'Good,' Auger mouthed.

'Now let's talk about you,' Peter continued. 'I still don't have all the facts – and I don't expect to get them until we're face to face – but I've heard enough to know that you're basically intact and that you're in excellent hands. I'm sorry about what happened to Caliskan and Cassandra. I know you've been through quite an ordeal since you returned from E2, never mind what actually happened at the other end of the link. All I can say is – and I know this is going to sound strange coming from me – but I'm proud to know you. We would have been satisfied if all you'd done was complete the mission that was assigned to you. But you did so much more than that. You lived up to the memory of Susan White. You made sure her death was not in vain.' Peter paused and held up a flat display screen upon which a complex three-dimensional form – like a metallic snowflake or starfish – twisted and tumbled. 'You probably won't recognise this. It's a single replicating element of Silver Rain – the same strain that Cassandra's people think Niagara has got his hands on.'

He was right: she shouldn't have recognised it. But she had felt a glimmer of familiarity when she first saw the rotating form. Cassandra's machines recognised it, even if Auger didn't.

'Officially, it never should have been possible,' Peter went on. 'All stocks were supposed to have been incinerated twenty years ago. Unfortunately, that's not what happened. In blatant violation of the treaty, the Polities held on to a strategic reserve. They even dedicated a small team to making improvements in the weapon.'

'Bastards,' Auger said.

'But don't be too harsh on them,' Peter said with a glint in his eye, as always knowing exactly what her response would be. 'We did just the same. The only difference is that our research teams weren't quite so inventive. Or, perhaps, clever.' He tilted the display screen so that he was able to look at it for himself. 'Really, what the Polity scientists did was very simple. The original Silver Rain was a broad-spectrum anti-biological agent. It couldn't discriminate between people and plants, or any kind of micro-organism. It infiltrated itself into all living organisms and killed them all at the same pre-programmed moment: that's why we still have the Scoured Zone on Mars. Very good for destroying an entire ecology . . . not so good for surgically removing one element of it. But the new strain is able to do just that – it's human-specific. When it's done its work, there will be nobody left alive anywhere on E2. In a few weeks there won't even be corpses. Yet in every other respect the ecosystem will remain untouched. To the rest of nature, it will feel like a brief, bad fever has just ended. A million-year fever called *Homo sapiens*. The cities will crumble and decay. The dams will crack and collapse. The wilderness will reclaim what was rightfully its own. The animals probably won't even notice the difference, except that the air will taste a little cleaner to the birds, and the oceans will sound a little quieter to the whales. There won't even be any nuclear power stations or ships to run out of control, poisoning the world when their masters depart.'

Peter cleared the panel with a flex of his wrist and placed it aside. 'Why am I telling you all this, when Niagara already has the weapon? Simply because you are our only hope of stopping this from happening. If that weapon is released into the atmosphere of E2, understand that it *will* work. There is no realistic probability of failure. No antidote we can release later, and hope that it mops up the replicators before they trigger. The only way to stop this happening is to intercept Niagara before he reaches Earth. If he isn't intercepted, the murder of three billion souls in E2 will be bad enough. But that's not the end of it. If the aggressors fail, then I believe we have a hope of ending this insane war before it escalates any further. We may have lost the Earth, but we don't have to lose the entire system. But if Silver Rain reaches E2, the hardliners on our side will never consent to any ceasefire, even with the moderates. It will go all the way. It will be the end of everything.' He shrugged. 'We'll lose, of course. I just felt you needed to be absolutely clear about that, so that you know what's at stake.'

'I know,' Auger said. 'You didn't have—'

'I know, I know,' Peter said, nodding. 'After all that you've gone through, all that you've done for us, to have to ask this much more of you . . . it's neither fair nor reasonable. But we simply have no alternative. I know you have the strength, Verity. More than that, I know you have the courage. Just do what you can. And then come home to us. You have more friends than you know, and we're all waiting for you.'

Later, she had another visitor. The dark-haired girl walked into the room without invitation, then stood demurely at the foot of her bed with her hands clasped behind her back, as if awaiting some mild reprimand for late homework.

'I could make myself transparent, if you thought that might help,' Cassandra said.

'Don't bother. I know you're not real.'

'I felt it best to appear in person. You don't mind, do you? Compared to what I've already done to you, altering your perceptual feeds seems rather tame.'

'What is this about, Cassandra?'

'It's about you and me. It's about what happened to us, and what we do about it.'

'I'm under no illusions,' Auger said. 'You hijacked my body to save us in Paris.'

'I also saved myself in the process. I can't deny that there was a degree of

454

self-interest involved.'

'Why? I'm sure those machines of yours could have hidden themselves out of harm's way until the danger was over.'

'They could have, but I wouldn't have survived very long without a host mind. A personality is a fragile thing at the best of times.'

Auger felt some chill sense of what Cassandra had endured. 'How much of you . . .' But she couldn't find it in herself to finish the question.

'How much of me survived? More than I could have hoped for. A lot less than I would have liked. Mentally, I had time to write a message in a bottle. You're talking to that message.'

'And your memories?'

'In principle, the machines would only ever have been able to encode and transfer a tiny fraction. My memories feel complete . . . but thin, like a sketch for a life rather than the thing itself. There's no texture to them, no sense that I actually lived through those events. I feel as if my life is something that happened to someone else, something I only heard about at second-hand.' She composed herself, looking down at her shoes. 'But perhaps that's what life always feels like. The trouble is, I can't remember if there was a difference before I died.'

'I'm sorry, Cassandra.'

'Oh, don't get me wrong – it's better than being dead. And when we sort out this mess, there'll always be a chance that I can reintegrate backed-up memories from the Polity mnemonic archives. If they survive.'

'I hope they do.'

'We'll see. The main thing is that I've made it this far. I have you to thank for that, Auger. You could have refused me.'

'I don't remember a discussion taking place.'

Cassandra gave a half-smile. 'Well, it didn't take very long, I'll admit. And in the process of me storming your brain, you probably lost the last few seconds of your short-term memory. But I assure you I had your permission to do what needed to be done.'

'You saved us,' Auger said. 'And when I was injured, when Floyd came back to rescue me, you stayed with me.'

'What else was I supposed to do?'

'You could have fled my body . . . abandoned me in Paris. I'm sure your machines would have coped until they found another host. You could have made do with Floyd, after all.'

'You have the wrong idea about us,' Cassandra said. 'I would never have abandoned you. I would rather have died than live with that.'

'Then I'm grateful.'

'You saved me as well. After all that has gone between us, it was nothing

I counted on. You have my thanks, Auger. I just hope that in some way this has taught both of us a lesson.'

'I was the one who needed the lesson,' Auger said. 'I hated you because you told the truth about me.'

'Then I'll make a small confession. Even as I was preparing to testify against you, I admired your dedication. You had the fire in your belly.'

'It nearly burnt me.'

'But at least you cared. At least you were ready to do something.'

'This little mess,' Auger said, 'is all because of people who were ready to do something. People like me, who always know when they're right and everyone else is wrong. Maybe what we need is a few less of us.'

'Or the right kind,' Cassandra said, shrugging. She shifted awkwardly. 'Look, I'll come to the point. I meant everything that I just said, but the reason I came to talk to you is very simple: it's your choice now.'

'What's my choice?'

'What you do with me. You're healed. You no longer need me in your head to keep you alive.'

'Then you've identified a new host?'

'Not exactly. Tunguska would take me if he had spare capacity . . . which he doesn't, not with all the extra tactical processing he's having to do. The same goes for the rest of the crew. But there are techniques. They can hold my machines in suspension until we return to the Polities and find a host.'

'Answer me truthfully: how stable would that suspension be, compared to you remaining where you are?'

'The suspension procedure is more than capable—'

'Truthfully,' Auger said.

'There'd be some additional losses. Impossible to quantify, but almost inevitable.'

'Then you're staying put. No ifs, no buts.'

Cassandra flicked aside her lick of black hair. 'I don't know what to say. I never expected this kindness.'

'From me?'

'From any Thresher.'

'Then I suppose we both had things wrong. Let's just hope we aren't the only ones who can find some common ground.'

'There'll be others,' Cassandra said. 'But that doesn't mean we can't play our part. When we've dealt with Niagara, when we've returned to Sedna, there'll be some very raw wounds that need healing.'

'If anyone's left alive.'

'We'll just have to hope things haven't gone to the brink. If they haven't . . . if the progressive Threshers and the moderate Slashers can put their differences aside . . . then there may be hope for all of us. Whatever the case, an example of co-operation could make all the difference.'

'An example like us, you mean?'

The little girl with the dark hair nodded. 'I'm not saying I should stay in your head for ever. But when the peace is being negotiated, someone who could be trusted by both parties might be a very important player indeed.'

'Or they might choose not to trust us at all.'

'That's a risk,' Cassandra conceded. 'But one I'd be prepared to take.' Then something seemed to amuse her. 'And you never know, Auger.'

'Never know what?'

'This could be the beginning of a beautiful friendship.'

After much insistence, Tunguska finally caved in and permitted Auger to walk around the ship. She was washed and alert, the voices in her head no longer quite so insistent. A sheet of intelligent bedclothing hugged her every move, preserving her modesty and – whenever she caught a glimpse of herself in some polished surface or actual mirror – quietly flattering her as well, she noticed. A little while ago, she would have been appalled at the thought of allowing Slasher machinery to become so intimate with her. Now, whenever she tried to summon the appropriate reflex disgust, it just wasn't there. In spite of her little tête à tête with Cassandra, she wondered whether this was because the machines were surreptitiously doctoring her thoughts, or whether the events of the last few days had finally forced her to realise that not everything about the Slashers was automatically repugnant. At the same time, she wondered if she really needed an answer. The simple fact was that she no longer hated them as a matter of principle. It was also a source of shameful amazement that she could ever have wasted so much energy on groundless prejudice, when acceptance and tolerance would have been the easier, even the lazier, course.

Tunguska and Floyd sat on one side of an extruded table, watching patterns play across the wall opposite them. As Auger approached the table, a chair bulged up from the floor in anticipation.

'You're quite sure you feel well enough for this?' Tunguska asked.

'I'm fine. Cassandra and I have come to an . . . accommodation.'

Tunguska offered her the newly formed seat. She took it, sitting between the two men. Tunguska was dressed in a simple two-piece outfit of white flannel, slashed low across his broad, hairless chest, while Floyd wore a clean white shirt, with black trousers supported by striped elastic braces. Those were definitely not the clothes that Floyd had been wearing when they left Paris, so Tunguska must have conjured them up for him. She wondered if he had dug them out of some obscure memory, or followed

Floyd's specifications.

'We have an echo from Niagara's ship,' Tunguska said, gesturing towards one of the image panels on the wall. Gold-threaded lines formed a flowing contour map reminiscent of the navigational display in the transport, but with a great deal more complexity. Cryptic symbols hovered in boxes around the edge of the diagram, connected by thin lines back to knotty features in the contour plot. As the features shifted and merged, the symbols altered from one perplexing configuration to another.

'We're sending acoustic signals up the line,' Tunguska continued, 'using the same high-speed propagation layer you employ for your navigation and communications channel.'

'I thought you'd have come up with something more sophisticated than that by now,' Auger said.

'We've tried various things, but the acoustic technique is still the only reliable method open to us. As you probably know, it's difficult to push a signal through when a ship is in transit. The ship acts as a mirror, bouncing the signal back to us with a high reflection efficiency.'

'And you're getting a signal from Niagara?'

'A faint one,' Tunguska said, 'but definitely there. With a smaller craft, there'd be various things he could try to damp the return bounce. But that's a big, fat ship, and it doesn't leave him with a lot of scope for stealth.'

'All right,' Auger said. 'If you can bounce a signal off him, can you tell how far ahead he is?'

'Yes. Of course, spatial distance is a rather slippery concept in hyperweb transit—'

'Just give me your best guess.'

'His ship must be about two hundred kilometres ahead of us. Assuming the usual propagation speed, he'll exit about an hour before we do.'

'Two hundred kilometres,' Auger said. 'That doesn't sound all that far.'

'It isn't,' Tunguska agreed.

'Then haven't you got something you can fire ahead of us, something that will cover the distance before his ship exits the tunnel?'

'Yes,' Tunguska said, 'but I wanted to discuss it with you before I acted.'

'If you have something,' Auger said, 'then damn well use it.'

'I have beam weapons,' Tunguska told her. 'But they don't work well in the hyperweb for the same reason that EM pulses are ineffective – due to scattering off the tunnel lining. That leaves missiles. We have six warhead-tipped devices with bleed-drive propulsion.'

'So use them.'

'It's not that simple. Objects under thrust behave unpredictably in the hyperweb: that's why we surf the throat wave, rather than flying through

458

under our own power.'

'It's still worth a try.'

Tunguska kept his voice level, but his face was beginning to show concern. 'Understand the risk. With a beam weapon, we'd have a degree of surgical control if we could get close enough to avoid the scattering effect. We could disable his ship sufficiently to prevent him from making it to the next portal.'

'I'm not interested in disabling him. I'm not interested in interrogation, or whatever it is you'd do to Niagara if you got your hands on him. I want a clean kill.'

'Don't underestimate the value of interrogation,' Tunguska said quietly, with the gently reproving note of a kindly schoolmaster. 'This conspiracy is almost certainly wider than one man. If we lose Niagara, we lose any hope of catching his associates. And what they have attempted once, they may attempt again.'

'But you just said you can't disable him.'

'Not in the hyperweb,' he said, raising a finger. 'But if we can catch his ship in open space, between portals . . . then we might have a chance.'

Auger shook her head. 'Too much risk of him getting away.'

'We'll still have the missiles,' Tunguska said. 'But the one thing they're not is surgical.'

She imagined a school of swift, dolphinlike missiles skewering Niagara's ship, blowing it apart in a soundless orgy of light. 'I'm not going to shed any tears over that.'

'Or over your own death, which would doubtless ensue in the process? It would be suicide, Auger. His ship is carrying the Molotov device. That's enough antimatter to crack open a moon, and it's only two hundred kilometres away.'

Tunguska was right. It would have occurred to her sooner or later, but she was so fixated on killing Niagara that she had not really considered what his execution would actually entail.

'Even so,' she said, forcing out the words one by one, 'we still have to do it.'

Tunguska's expression was grave but approving. 'I thought you'd say that. I just had to be sure.'

'What about Floyd?' she asked, her voice quavering as the realisation of what she had just decided slowly sunk in.

'Floyd and I have discussed the matter already,' Tunguska said. 'For what it's worth, we arrived at the same conclusion.'

She turned to Floyd. 'Is that true?'

Floyd shrugged. 'If that's what it takes.'

Still looking into Floyd's eyes, she said, 'Then launch your missiles, Tunguska. And quickly, before any of us changes our minds.'

The faintest of shudders ran through the floor.

'It's done,' Tunguska said. 'They're launched and running.'

THIRTY-SEVEN

Two hundred kilometres up the pipe, she thought. It was nothing in spatial terms. The missiles should have leapt across that distance in an eyeblink. But the hyperweb appeared to actively stifle attempts to pass through it more rapidly than the normal speed of a collapse wave. The missiles – according to Tunguska's telemetry – were streaking ahead of his ship, following the expected acceleration curves for their mass and thrust, just as if they had been deployed in external space. For a little while it was even possible to bounce an electromagnetic pulse off them, or read the acoustic signal induced by their exhaust as it washed in a widening cone against the tunnel sides. But then something began to happen to them. They slowed, their acceleration curves levelling out, as if they had flown into spatial treacle. The faint, dwindling whisper of data from each missile reported no anomalies . . . but they were no longer travelling ahead with sufficient speed to intercept Niagara's ship.

Tunguska stared at the spread of tactical displays – which were more for their benefit than his, Auger suspected – with obvious dissatisfaction. 'This is what I feared,' he said. 'There's no telling whether any of them will reach Niagara in time.'

'Will we know when it happens?' she asked.

'Would you like to know?'

'I'd like to know that we'd succeeded, before . . .' Her voice trailed off. There was no need for her to state the obvious.

'I'm afraid you probably won't have that luxury. It's anyone's guess how the matter-antimatter fireball will travel back down the pipe, but it's likely to be swift. There'll be no time to reflect on victory. Equally, your deaths will be mercifully swift.'

Auger didn't need reminding that she had effectively signed her own

461

death warrant if one of the missiles got through. She was trying to push that knowledge to one side, but it kept squirming back to the forefront of her thoughts.

'Will you sense anything?' Floyd asked Tunguska.

'I'll have an inkling,' he said. 'When the fireball hits the skin of my ship, the information from the hull sensors should reach my skull an instant ahead of the destructive wave itself.'

'Giving you enough time to form a thought?' Auger asked, lacing her hand tightly with Floyd's. 'Enough time to extract a crumb of comfort that your sacrifice will have been worth it?'

'Perhaps.' Tunguska smiled at them. 'It doesn't have to be a very complicated thought, after all.'

'I'm not sure I envy you,' Auger said.

'And perhaps you're right not to, but there it is. I could disable the connection between my neural machines and the hull sensors, but I don't think I have the nerve.' He looked back at one of the wall images, studying it with suddenly alarmed eyes.

'What's wrong?' Auger asked.

'Nothing that I didn't expect, I suppose. The telemetry feeds from all the missiles are now silent.'

'Does that mean the missiles are dead?' Floyd asked.

'No – not necessarily, just that the data they're trying to send back to us can't find its way home. The missiles probably can't hear our signals to them, either. They'll have switched to autonomous flight mode.'

'Somehow I preferred it when we knew for certain that they were still out there,' Floyd said.

'Me, too,' Tunguska said. Then he reached out and placed his own hand over theirs, and the three of them sat in silence, waiting for something to happen, or for everything to stop happening.

Silence was the one thing Auger didn't want. It left a vacuum in her head into which certain thoughts were too easily able to slip. She wanted the easy cadences of normal human conversation, the gossip and the small talk. She wanted to be able to think about anything other than that killing wall of furious light, the explosion that might even now be rushing towards them, faster than any advance information of its arrival could possibly travel. Faster than any possible news of success. How long had it been since the missiles had streaked away? She had lost all sense of time; it could have been minutes or hours. But when she tried to say something, the words always seemed trite and inadequate. Nothing measured up. When any moment might be their last, there was nothing she could ever imagine saying that had the necessary dignity to fill that instant. Silence was better.

Silence had its own dignity.

She looked at the other two – Floyd and the Slasher both – and knew that in their own way they were working through exactly the same thought process. As if in some silent acknowledgement of this, all three of them chose that moment to tighten their hands together.

Suddenly, a convulsive change occurred in the displays on the wall. Auger had an instant to register this, and another instant to let the implications unravel in her head. One of the missiles must have found its mark, and now the ship had detected the approaching hellfire . . .

But the voices in her head, quiet of late, told her no, that was not what was happening.

It was bad, but it was some other slightly less piquant flavour of bad.

In another instant – another tick of the clockwork grind of consciousness – the ship began to execute some drastic evasive manoeuvre. Auger had just enough time to feel her weight shifting dangerously to one side when her gown stiffened into a protective cocoon and the furniture, floors and walls reshaped themselves into a protective matrix.

Then came the awful moment when the ship forced its breathing apparatus down her throat.

She experienced a momentary blissed-out sense that, in truth, being smothered into helplessness was actually quite pleasant . . .

Two or three missing frames of consciousness.

Information trickled into her skull, via Cassandra's machines. They were talking to Tunguska and the rest of the ship.

One of their own missiles had just locked on to them. The peculiar spatial properties of the hyperweb tunnel had confused its navigation system, while the echoing babble of chaotic EM signals had caused it to disregard the message that Tunguska's ship was friend, rather than foe. There was no time to aim and fire the beam weapons. The ship had flexed itself, bending its hull to let the missile slip by at the last instant, like a supple combatant avoiding a lethal stab. Once the missile had streaked past into the portion of the tunnel behind the ship, an emergency detonation command had gnawed into its tiny, murderous mind and made it self-trigger.

The explosion had caused a local alteration in the geometry of the tunnel cladding, sending propagation shocks haring away in all directions; meanwhile, re-radiated energies bounced around in a storm of short-wavelength photons, chewing through the protective armour of Tunguska's ship and into the soft living tissues of the passengers within.

Sensing further danger, the ship kept its occupants locked within the gee-load cushioning while it strained ahead with every sensor that could claw some scrap of information about the forward state of the tunnel. The reverberations from the missile blast had blinded the acoustics, for now at least. Frantically, the ship switched to backup systems it would never have relied upon during normal flight. Neutrino lasers and wide-spectrum EM pulses peered into the bright, swallowing mouth.

Another two missiles were haring back towards them, groping for a target.

Premature-detonation signals were transmitted at maximum signal strength. Beam weapons, deployed and ready now, locked on and prepared to fire if the missiles did not self-destruct.

One of the pair ripped apart in a controlled explosion, dampeners limiting the blast radius. The other missile shrugged off the kill order and increased its acceleration rate, sprinting for final interception. The ship swerved and contorted itself, pushing its structural limits beyond all conceivable safety margins. Shrill reports of irreparable damage hit Auger's brain. The ship could still tolerate more damage – but not much more.

The beam weapons swung hard and locked on to the third stray missile. They fired, impacting at a range of only two kilometres up the tunnel from the ship. With its dampening systems not engaged, this missile's explosion was the most violent of the three.

They raced into the fireball. The ship screamed, writhing in cybernetic agony.

Then it was through.

Faster than language, a thought made its way into Auger's head.

'We deployed six missiles,' Tunguska told her. 'Three have come back. Three more must still be out there.'

At lightning speed, the cloud of machines in her head wove a response. Had Auger answered, or was it Cassandra framing the question? She didn't know. 'How many more close hits can we take?'

'None,' Tunguska said.

Over the next five minutes, two more missiles came back. The first was limping, damaged by glancing encounters with the tunnel lining. The beam weapons engaged and killed it with swift efficiency, destroying it at a range of sixty-five kilometres, the very limit of detection.

The other missile surrendered itself to the kill-order, puffing apart in a damped blast that inflicted only minor damage.

'One's still out there,' Tunguska said.

'Perhaps this wasn't such a good idea after all, was it?' Auger observed wryly.

'It was the only one we had,' Tunguska replied phlegmatically.

During the next ten agonising minutes, a sixth missile did arrive, coasting on a high-speed intercept trajectory. It showed no inclination to obey the destruct commands, even when it was very close. Tunguska's beam weapons gored it open, but the warhead refused to detonate. The missile veered in a hairpin turn, then speared itself at a right angle into the tunnel cladding. Half-blind as they were, the acoustic sensors could still track its progress as it bored through the stressed laminate of artificial space-time. Somewhere deep inside the cladding it finally blew up, and the entire wall bulged outward.

'That was number six,' Auger said. 'All six are down. We're home and dry.'

'No,' Tunguska said. 'At least, we can't be sure. That last one . . . it wasn't one of ours.'

'But you sent six—'

'And five returned. That last one was a gift from Niagara. It means he knows we're here.'

By the time Tunguska's ship emerged from the portal, automatic damage repair had taken care of the worst of the wounds the ship had sustained in the tunnel. There were some things that could not be put right without specialist attention, but they would have to wait until the vessel returned to Polity space. For now, it was still capable of continuing the chase, albeit at reduced effectiveness, while the bleed-drive was nursed back to full health.

'If only we could be sure of the route Niagara took,' Tunguska said.

Auger leaned forward, resting her elbows on the soft padding of the extruded table. The ship had released its grip on its occupants. They had all been dosed with UR, the tiny machines now swimming through their bodies on a mad errand to correct the genetic damage caused by the radiation from the undamped missile blasts. 'I thought you were hoping to catch him between portals.'

'I was,' the Slasher said. 'And there was always a chance of that. Unfortunately, Niagara was just a little too fast. He may have cut some safety margins now that he knows we're chasing him.'

'That missile attack really backfired on us,' Floyd said.

'On the other hand, it may have helped us,' Tunguska said. 'Niagara may believe that his return strike destroyed us. With all the acoustic noise, there's no way he could have bounced an echo off us.'

'So it could go either way,' Auger said. 'That's the top and bottom of it, right?'

'I confess that there are a number of unknowns.'

'It would help if we knew which door he'd taken,' Auger observed.

The hyperweb transition had thrown them thousands of light-years across the galaxy. Auger didn't need to know the details. There was still at least one transition ahead of them; maybe several. Given the knotted topology of the hyperweb links, they could end up almost anywhere, if they ever succeeded in following Niagara's trail to the ALS.

'Even if Niagara made his next throat insertion before our emergence,' Tunguska said, 'I was still hoping for an unambiguous sign of which portal he used.'

'And?' Auger asked impatiently, tapping a fingernail against the table.

Tunguska had already called up a display of the immediate volume of space around the four neighbouring portals. They were all anchored to anonymous rocks orbiting a compact, dark binary where major planetary formation had never taken place. It was a bleak, hellish place, sizzling with high-energy particles chewed up and spat out again by the twisted Siamese magnetosphere of the binary stars.

'At maximum thrust, with all safety margins disengaged, he could have reached any one of the three outgoing portals a shade before our emergence,' Tunguska said. 'He must have been confident that the Molotov device could tolerate that kind of acceleration without its own containment mechanisms failing . . . but then again, perhaps that was a risk he was prepared to take.'

'Can you see a thrust trail?' Auger said.

'No. Too much ambient radiation around for us to be able to sniff out the ionisation products.'

'What about the portals?' she asked. 'Didn't the staff see which one he used?'

'There are no staff,' Tunguska said. 'Apart from routine visits for maintenance, these portals here take care of themselves.'

'Then the machines—'

'All three tell the same story,' Tunguska said, one step ahead of her questions. 'They were all activated, geared up for throat insertion and controlled collapse. Niagara sent activation signals to all three – like a man opening all the doors in the corridor in order to mask the one he really stepped through.'

'Clever guy,' Floyd said. 'You have to give him that.'

Auger buried her head in her hands. She felt a tremendous, welling frustration with Tunguska. Despite all his technology, all his cool, calm Slasher wisdom, he was still powerless against a single agile adversary. It was unfair, she knew, but she couldn't help herself. In the presence of a wizard, she wanted miracles, not excuses.

'This is not good,' she said. 'Don't you have any clues? He only had one ship. Only one of those portals was really used.'

'That's our only straw,' Tunguska said. 'As it is, one of the portals shows a slightly different collapse signature compared to the other two he might have used. If I had to put money on it, I'd say that's the one that really had a ship squeezed through it.'

'How much money?' she asked, smiling.

'You'd rather not know.'

'OK,' Auger said. 'If that's our only option . . . we have to take it. Once we're inside, will we be able to bounce an echo off him?'

'Perhaps,' Tunguska said, 'but the absence of an echo won't necessarily prove that we chose the wrong door. He could be just too far ahead of us for it to reach him.'

'Do we have any other options?'

'No. That's why I've already committed us to the portal with the odd signature. As soon as drive repair is complete, we'll ramp up to maximum pursuit thrust.'

'Good,' Auger said. 'I'd rather be chasing a shadow than sitting around here talking about it.'

'Unfortunately, chasing shadows may be all we end up doing. Even if that signature is real, it's at the limit of readability. If Niagara had shaved just an additional hour off his arrival time, we'd never have seen it.'

'Then we'd better not waste a minute.'

'That's the problem.' Tunguska replaced the schematic image of the quadruple-portal system with the fractured-glass map of the galactic hyperweb network. He zoomed in on one little area, highlighting a conjunction of four filaments. 'This is where we are now,' he said. 'And this – given our best guess – is where Niagara will emerge, after an eight-hour transit.'

He directed their attention to another part of the map, further around the great clockface of the galaxy.

'Another cluster of portals,' Auger said.

'Six, all told, including the one we'll enter through. There's no ALS there, so it can't be his final destination. He'll be taking another portal.'

'We'll just have to hope that the same trick works twice.'

'It won't, I'm afraid,' Tunguska said. 'The time differential between his departure and our arrival will be too great. There'll be no detectable difference between the portals, regardless of the fact that only one of them will have had a ship fly through it.'

'Meaning what?'

'Meaning that unless he has spectacular bad luck between here and there – we'll have lost him.'

'We can't lose him,' Auger said. 'That's simply not an acceptable outcome.'

'We may have to live with it. He knows the way to the ALS. We don't. It's that simple.'

'Cassandra should have looked at those documents in more detail,' Auger said, with an odd feeling of self-criticism, as if she was reproaching herself for some unacceptable omission or failing.

'She did the best she could,' Tunguska said. 'At the time, she had only a vague idea that they might be of strategic importance. It's lucky we got what we did.'

'Lucky?' Auger snapped. 'The cargo told us nothing.'

'I'm sorry,' Tunguska said. 'If there was anything I could do . . . We'll continue the chase, of course, and hope for good luck.'

'That's the best you can offer?'

'I'm afraid so.'

No one said anything, until Floyd raised his hand and spoke. 'Anyone mind if I make a small contribution?'

THIRTY-EIGHT

The bleed-drive was still not ready for maximum thrust. While they toiled at a leisurely one gee towards the suspect portal, Floyd led Auger and Tunguska back to his quarters.

'This had better be worth it,' Auger said.

'You got any viable alternatives?'

'I just mean . . . don't raise false expectations here, Floyd. I know you're trying to help, but really.'

He looked back at her, wounded pride on his face. '"But really" what?'

'This is a very technical matter,' she said.

'What she's saying,' Tunguska interjected, adopting a conciliatory tone, 'is that there are some things you might be reasonably expected to have a useful opinion on . . . and some things you might be reasonably expected not to have a useful opinion on.'

'I see,' Floyd said tersely.

'And I'm afraid the matter of hyperweb navigation falls resoundingly into the latter category,' he went on.

'At least hear me out, Jack.'

'Floyd, I know you mean well,' Auger said, 'but we really should be preparing for when the bleed-drive is back on-line.'

'Wouldn't you like to know that you're headed in the right direction, before you light that torch?'

He opened the door into the vast enclosure that served as his temporary quarters. The three of them walked towards the bed and its little entourage of attendant furniture.

'Floyd – give me a clue, will you?'

'It was something you said yourself, Auger: how the hell did they make sense of the numbers coming out of that antenna thing, if they had to do it in nineteen fifty-nine?'

'Enlighten me,' Auger said.

'And me, while you're at it,' Tunguska said.

'We were looking for a microdot, or something like it,' Floyd said, 'because we thought we were only looking for ten or twelve digits – the map reference of the ALS.'

'Go on,' Auger said, feeling a little shiver of excitement despite her misgivings.

'Well, we were dead wrong. I think.'

'Floyd – don't drag this out.'

Floyd sat down on the bed and offered Tunguska and Auger the two remaining chairs. 'Face it: it was always hopeless looking for something like that. You said it, Auger – the message could have been buried anywhere, in the tiniest smudge or the tiniest change in the position or weight of some printed characters. You'd have to know exactly what you were looking for in order to find it.'

'Floyd . . .' she said warningly.

'But that still leaves a big question unanswered: how did they come up with those numbers? It was one thing building that antenna, but making sense of what it was telling them – well, even you speculated that it would have been difficult, given the way things are in my nineteen fifty-nine.'

'Computers don't exist in Floyd's world,' Auger explained to Tunguska. 'They are even further behind than our fifty-nine, since they never had the Second World War as a spur to drive computing progress.'

'I see,' Tunguska said, stroking his chin. 'In which case, it's difficult to see how the data from the gravitational wave device could ever have been processed. It would be a tricky little exercise even now.'

'Not too tricky, I hope,' Floyd said, 'because I think you're going to have to do it.'

'What have you found?' Tunguska asked.

Floyd reached into the box at the foot of the bed and pulled out one of the records inside it. Auger saw the label: Louis Armstrong.

'This,' he said simply.

'I had the distinct impression that you were a little underwhelmed with those discs,' Tunguska said.

'You were damned right.'

'And now?'

'I'm wondering if that wasn't the clue we were looking for all along.' Floyd tipped the sleeve so that the grooved disc slid into his hand. 'I think the information you're looking for is here,' he said.

'In a microdot on the label?' Auger asked, still puzzled.

'No. Something more complex than that. I think it could be in the music itself. Not just ten or twelve digits, but the actual numbers from the antenna. You were right, Auger: there was no way to interpret the data in nineteen fifty-nine. So they didn't even try.'

That shiver of excitement had now become a full-blown tingle, lifting up every hair on the back of Auger's neck. 'So what *did* they do?' she asked impatiently.

'They shipped the information back through the portal. Niagara's boys got their hands on it and did all the clever stuff on the other side.'

'So there's something encoded in the music?' Auger asked.

'Someone's been flooding Paris with cheap bootlegs,' Floyd said. 'It's been going on for months. Now we know why.'

'You can't be sure there's a connection,' she said.

'Yes, I can. My old friend Maillol even pointed me to a link between the Blanchard case and his own anti-bootlegging operation. I just couldn't see how they could possibly be connected at the time.'

'And now you can,' Auger asked.

'Custine spoke to one of Blanchard's tenants – guy by the name of Rivaud – who'd seen one of your nasty little children hanging around the building. When I tried to talk to Rivaud myself, he'd put on a disappearing act. A few days later, Maillol tells me they found his body floating in the flooded cellar of a warehouse in Montrouge.'

'Nice,' Auger said, wrinkling her nose with distaste.

'It gets nicer. Guy had abrasions on his neck, as if one of those children had been encouraging him to keep his head below water.'

'And the significance of this warehouse?'

'It was the same place Maillol turned up that counterfeit pressing plant.'

'Do you think Rivaud was in on the bootlegging scheme?'

'He might have been,' Floyd said, 'but then we'd have to explain the coincidence of him living in the same building where Susan White ended up as a tenant.'

'Big coincidence.'

'Too big. More likely, Rivaud caught sight of one of those children again and decided to do some gumshoe work of his own. Tailed the child all the way back to the warehouse. Maybe he was even lured there, if the children thought he'd seen too much already.'

'Floyd may be on to something,' Tunguska said. 'Here. Let me examine that disc.'

'Is that an original?' Auger asked.

'No – it's a facsimile based on the surface scan of the original made by Cassandra,' Tunguska said. 'But it should be accurate enough for our needs, if there's genuinely latent information buried on it.'

'Take my word for it,' Floyd said, 'either that music-killing virus has already found its way into my head or there's something wrong with that recording.'

'There could be a high-frequency signal encoded in the groove,' Tunguska said. 'Enough to hold a significant chunk of that antenna data. I can verify this very quickly—'

'How quickly?' Auger asked, her impatience getting the better of her.

He blinked. '*That* quickly. It was just a question of examining Cassandra's holographic data and looking for something anomalous in the structure. It's always much easier to identify a pattern if you have some idea of what you're looking for.'

'And?' she persisted, barely able to keep still in her seat.

'Floyd is correct. There is an additional channel of information imprinted on to this recording. Not enough to render the original music unbearable, but enough to upset someone with Floyd's refined tastes.' He awarded Floyd a gentle, rather admiring smile. 'We'd never have noticed it otherwise.'

Tunguska turned the platter this way and that, admiring the play of light across its reflective black surface. 'A thing of beauty, really. But also something of a double-edged sword.'

'We helped them,' Auger said. 'We got that information out of Paris, thinking we were saving priceless artefacts.'

'They must have known all about your efforts to smuggle cultural data out of the city,' Tunguska said. 'Given that Niagara's agents needed to smuggle their own data out at the same time, your operation suited their purposes perfectly. All they had to do was bury the information in those recordings and make sure they fell into Susan's hands. Flooding the market with fakes was by far the simplest option.'

'You know what?' Floyd said. 'I wouldn't be too surprised if the Paris sphere was in that same warehouse complex. Even if Maillol had found it, he wouldn't have had any idea of its significance.'

'They tricked us,' Auger said, outraged and embarrassed at the same time.

'You mustn't blame yourself,' Tunguska said sternly. 'Thanks to Susan's efforts, a vast amount of priceless material was saved from Paris. It's neither your fault nor hers that some of those artefacts were deliberately tainted.'

'But that one disc can't possibly hold all the information,' Auger said.

'We have a box full of records,' Tunguska said. He blinked again: some part of his mind whisking away to sift through Cassandra's data and her report on it. 'It appears that a third of them have a similar microscopic structure. The rest, presumably, are genuine recordings.'

'But we've been extracting records ever since we opened the Phobos portal,' Auger said. 'That's hundreds of thousands of recordings.'

'It may not matter,' Tunguska said. 'You'll remember that Niagara was extremely keen to get his hands on the final shipment. It could be that the earlier shipments contained data that was in some way provisional or flawed. They may only just have got their antenna into a properly functioning state. Allowing time to combine the data strands from all three spheres . . . and to imprint the signals on to these recordings . . . and to distribute the recordings in such a way that they would fall plausibly into your hands . . . well, I have no difficulty believing that the final cargo was the most significant.'

'Then we have a chance,' Auger said. 'If you can decode that embedded signal, of course.'

'I don't anticipate huge difficulties,' Tunguska said. 'Remember, it would have taken significant computing power to effect a complex encryption, which would have been as problematic for them as interpreting the data on E2 in the first place. I don't believe the encoding will tax us.'

'I hope you're right.'

'I'm already merging and processing the data,' he said. 'I've assigned a significant portion of my ship's computing resources to the effort. Of course, we could still be chasing shadows—'

'We're not,' Floyd said firmly.

With a certain reverence, Tunguska slipped the Louis Armstrong record back into its sleeve. 'We're nearly ready for full bleed-drive thrust. We'll continue on our present heading, taking the most likely portal. Once in transit, we'll have eight hours to crack the numbers and determine the position of the ALS. It will be difficult – it may even be impossible – but at least it gives us the hope of one more lead against Niagara.'

'You have your uses after all, Floyd,' Auger said.

'Don't thank me,' Floyd said. 'Thank the music. I always said it would save the world.'

THIRTY-NINE

It was a little-travelled arm of the hyperweb, one that had seen only sporadic traffic since the Slashers had begun to map the network's further fringes. Five portals lay close together in a loose, drifting quincunx, separated by no more than a light-second of interstellar space. There were no suns here, no worlds, no rogue moons – not even the rocky fragments of them, unborn or shattered. Only the spired husks of five large comets, dry and dead for billions of years, each of which formed an anchor for a single unmanned portal.

But there was something else. Sensors groped for it in the darkness. It was unthinkably dark, illuminated only by starlight. It was also unthinkably huge: as wide across as the sun itself, with room to spare.

'Are we too late?' Auger said as Tunguska assembled a composite picture of the ALS on one of the walls.

'I don't know. If my timing's correct, Niagara should only have achieved portal egress . . . ninety minutes ago.'

'Then why don't we see him?'

'There's a faint thrust trail,' Tunguska said. 'It suggests that Niagara's already passed around the limb of the ALS. Again – assuming that the usual margins were ignored – he would have had just enough time to do that.'

'So follow him.'

'We are. Unfortunately, the bleed-drive needs further attention. This is the maximum acceleration we can sustain.'

The composite image of the ALS gained detail by the second, as Tunguska's sensors teased more structure out of the darkness. Complex statistical methods squeezed the maximum information from meagre data. Auger recalled the briefing she had been given aboard the *Twentieth Century Limited*. Peter's schematic representation had been tinted a dull blue-grey, but there was not enough light here to trigger the eye's colour receptors. Tunguska's schematic ignored the faint ambient illumination and painted the entire structure a flat grey, with no shadowing except that necessary to suggest the platelike surface texturing. In Peter's overview, that platelike structure had made her think of something viral or crystalline, but now the hide of the ALS reminded her of some magnified view of human or animal skin, with a rough hint of irregularity and – here and there – signs where healing processes had not quite erased the evidence of former injuries. It was as if the ALS had been grown, rather than constructed.

Perhaps it had. No one had the slightest idea where the raw materials had come from. Maybe there had once been an entire solar system in this pocket of space, which had then been efficiently strip-mined to create the hard, thin shell of the sphere. Or perhaps the necessary mass-energy had been conjured out of nothing, in some vastly more sophisticated version of the principle that underpinned the bleed-drive.

Auger looked at Floyd, wondering how he was taking all of this. 'Not many people get to see this,' she said. 'If that's any consolation.'

'I could have lived without it,' he said. 'Somehow I rather liked the idea that I could trust the night sky, or that the Sun was real.'

'Your world is real, Floyd, and so are you. Nothing else matters.'

'I'm picking something up,' Tunguska said with quiet urgency. 'It could be Niagara.'

'An echo from his ship?' Auger asked.

'Not close enough for that,' he said, 'but there's a moving patch of enhanced brightness on the skin of the ALS. It's probably the reflection from his drive. He's doing his best to hide it, but there's only so much he can do if he still wants to steer.'

'Remind me: do we have any more missiles in this thing?' Auger asked.

'None. I've instructed the factories to make more, but I can't afford to divert too much repair capacity away from the bleed-drive. I think we'll have to rely on beams, at least until later.'

'Are we in firing range?'

'Not yet. We'll have to close quite a bit of distance for that.'

'Can we get close enough?' Auger asked.

'Not if Niagara maintains his latest heading. But that reflection signature suggests that he's slowing down, relative to the ALS.'

'Why would he do that?' asked Floyd.

'Probably because he's ready to deploy the Molotov device,' Tunguska said.

'You have to hit him before he has a chance.'

'Are you sure you want that, Floyd? If that antimatter bomb doesn't blow a hole in the ALS, you won't be going home.'

'Just do it,' Floyd said. 'Worry about my return ticket later. A few hours ago I wasn't even expecting to live this long.'

'I don't think any of us were,' Tunguska replied. His forehead creased, revealing some glint of interest in the storm of numbers flooding his head. 'Ah. Now this may be significant.' He looked around at their expectant faces. 'I have some refined data on that reflection pattern. It looks as if there are two sources of light, rather than one.'

Auger wondered if she understood him. 'Two thrust beams?'

'Yes – but far enough apart that they can't be associated with the same craft. It looks as if Niagara's deployed a smaller ship from the larger one. We should have a hard echo any moment now . . .' He pressed a thick finger against one side of his temple.

'That makes sense,' Auger said. 'His main ship is just large enough to carry the Molotov device, right?'

'So it would seem.'

'He's probably going to plough it into the ALS like a battering ram. Too much trouble to extract the antimatter core, when he already has a ready-made delivery system.' She pushed forward in her seat, ignoring the tension in her back. 'The other ship must be a shuttle, something with enough range to make it to E2.'

'That would be the ship carrying Silver Rain,' Tunguska said.

'And Niagara,' Auger added.

Tunguska shut his eyes, blanking out the extraneous distraction of the real world. 'I see the shuttle, and the mother ship,' he said. 'The shuttle is on a high-gee burn trajectory away from the Molotov section.'

'Looks like it's trying to put as much distance between itself and the blast point as possible,' Auger speculated.

Tunguska nodded, his eyes still closed.

'Well, you would, wouldn't you?' Floyd commented.

'Any chance of a beam strike any time soon?' she asked.

'Not yet. Believe me, my trigger finger is itching.'

There was nothing to do but wait for the distance to be closed. Tunguska's long-range view gradually sharpened, confirming that the two ships had indeed separated, and that the heavier of the two – the main craft, the one that they had been following from Earth – was racing on an accelerating trajectory towards the surface of the ALS, gunning its bleed-drive to the wall. The excess radiation from the tortured drive made it an easy object to track, even across such a distance. An hour earlier it had been moving parallel to the surface of the sphere, but now it was daggering down on a course that would intersect the surface at a right angle.

476

'We can't stop this, can we?' Auger said, exasperated. 'That damned thing is going to hit the ALS no matter what we do.'

'But admit it,' Tunguska said, with more playfulness than she cared for. 'Aren't you just a little bit curious to see what will happen?'

'I could stand not knowing,' she said.

Tunguska opened his eyes. 'Report from the bleed-drive: we're ready to increase our thrust to five gees. Can't risk anything higher than that, for now at least. We won't need the acceleration caskets, although the ship will still have to immobilise us.'

'Whatever it takes,' Auger said.

The room quivered and swallowed them.

In the soft grip of the ship's protective systems, time surged and dragged in unpredictable, dreamlike waves. She wondered how it was for Floyd, whose head was free of twinkling machines. What was he thinking now that he was so close to home, and simultaneously so close to seeing everything he knew destroyed?

'By my estimation,' Tunguska said, 'the Molotov impact will happen in fifty seconds. I'm deploying expendable sensors, but closing off all our usual channels. No one's ever seen a big matter–antimatter explosion up close, and there's no telling what kind of reaction the blast will provoke from the ALS itself.'

'How close is that shuttle to the impact point?' Auger asked.

'About half our present distance,' Tunguska replied. 'His shielding had better be good if he wants to be alive at the end of this. Thirty seconds—'

'I can do without the countdown, Tunguska,' Auger said, bracing herself. 'Just tell us if we're still alive at the end of it.'

She felt, when it happened, some ghostly report of the blast, even though Tunguska assured her that no signals could possibly reach her through the barricades he had put in place. It was long and drawn out, like a distant peel of thunder.

'The Molotov device has detonated,' Tunguska said. 'And we, self-evidently, are still alive.'

'I was being sarcastic.'

'I wasn't. It's always good to confirm these things.'

When the expendable sensors deemed it safe, Tunguska unshuttered the ship's more delicate eyes and turned them on the scene of the crime. It took a little while for them to make sense of the data, for the view was obstructed by a slowly expanding debris plume, spreading away from the impact point like a cherry-red fountain. Auger grappled with the scale, but she still couldn't adjust to the mind-numbing size of the ALS object. The plume was huge – hundreds of thousands of kilometres across and still growing – but it was just a tiny detail on the surface of the sphere.

'Debris is clearing near the epicentre,' Tunguska said. 'The view is foreshortened, so it isn't easy to see exactly what damage has been done.'

'Just show us what you've got,' Auger said.

They had to wait twenty minutes until the plume had dissipated sufficiently, and their angle of observation improved enough, to allow a clearer view. By then, Tunguska's ship was following the same arcing trajectory as Niagara's, curving around for a hard interception with the ALS. They were still sustaining five gees, cocooned against harm.

'They've broken through,' Tunguska said.

He pushed an image into Auger's head. The Molotov device had punched a surprisingly neat little entry wound into the skin of the ALS. The hole was a hundred kilometres across and nearly circular. The kilometre-thick skin glowed painfully brightly around the edge of the hole, shading down through blue and yellow and charred red out to a distance of perhaps two or three hundred kilometres from the epicentre. There were hints of wild, lashing structures in the exposed cross section, flailing like severed nerve endings.

'Dear Christ,' Auger said. 'They did it. The damned thing didn't put up any kind of fight at all.'

'Did you expect it to?' Floyd asked.

'I expected *something*.'

'What about the other ship?'

'Still tracking it,' Tunguska said. 'She's under thrust and maintaining the course she was following before the blast. It will take her through the wound in under ten minutes.'

Maybe he shouldn't have been so concerned about the state of Niagara's shielding, she thought. 'I take it we're still not within beam range?'

'No.' Tunguska sounded genuinely embarrassed. 'We'll have to follow her in for that.'

'Through the wound?'

'Yes,' Tunguska said. 'Into the ALS. I'm afraid it's the only course available to us.'

FORTY

By the time they were about to pass through the hole that Niagara had punched into the ALS, the debris cloud had completely cleared. The wound remained raw and bright, spilling a faint shaft of re-radiated golden-white light back into space, twinkling off the few remaining shards of hot matter still hanging around the impact site.

'That light has the spectrum of solar radiation,' Tunguska said, when they were falling down the column of light. 'It's a perfect match for the Sun, at the limit of our instruments.'

The transition between outside and inside happened in an eyeblink. One kilometre of shell thickness was nothing compared to their speed. One moment the surface of the sphere was swelling larger, with the wound growing rapidly from a searing, white-rimmed eye to a swallowing mouth . . . and then they were through, falling towards the heart of the ALS.

Tunguska's sensors took immediate stock of the interior. Behind his ship, the receding wound embraced a circle of the perfect blackness of interstellar space. It was rimmed with bright, agonised matter on this side as well. But instead of the quilted blue-grey material of the outer skin, the inner surface of the ALS was made of something far stranger; something far less susceptible to easy interrogation by Tunguska's instruments.

They had always known that the inner surface of the shell had to function as a kind of near-perfect planetarium, projecting an image of the sky that would have been seen from the original Earth. There were false stars, their brightness and colours reproduced precisely, aligned into exactly the right constellations that the inhabitants of E2 had learned to expect. Some fraction of the stars must even have been programmed for variability – to dim and brighten according to intricate astrophysics-rich algorithms.

They were all required to move with respect to each other, following the slow, stately currents of proper motion, or the wheeling gyre of binary orbits.

Beyond the stars, there were galaxies, vast shoals of them in every direction. Each and every galaxy had to stand up to the same scrutiny as the stars. Novae and supernovae had to flare and die . . . whether they were noticed or not.

It was awesome and astonishing. It was also doomed to failure, for no such tapestry could ever have withstood arbitrarily close study using the kind of astronomical tools available in Auger's era. Even a simple interplanetary probe would have eventually sniffed out something odd about those stellar positions . . . just before it dashed itself to atoms by colliding with the inner surface of the shell. No: it wasn't perfectly foolproof, nor must that ever have been the intention of its builders. It was good enough to withstand examination using the crude science of Floyd's time, but it was never the intention that the shell should form an utterly convincing illusion. Sooner or later, it must have been assumed, the inhabitants of E2 were bound to discover the truth. The function of the ALS was to protect them from outside interference until precisely that moment. After that – at which point they would probably direct their energies into breaking through the shell – they were on their own.

But there was already something amiss with the view of the heavens around the inside edge of the open wound. For thousands of kilometres in all directions, the stars were distorted, elongated and spermlike, their stretched, tapering tails pointing like accusing fingers towards the hole Niagara had made.

'The zone of distortion is spreading,' Tunguska said. 'Frankly, they're going to have a hard time not noticing that on the Earth, even if they somehow missed the initial flash.'

'What will they make of it?' Auger wondered.

'I don't know. But if an inexplicable astronomical puzzle is all they have to worry about by the end of the day, they'll be doing rather well.'

'Can we shoot that shuttle down yet?' she asked.

'No,' he replied. 'But I'm ready to squeeze a little more out of the bleed-drive. If my estimates are good, we still have a chance of intercepting her before she hits the atmosphere.'

'Don't hesitate, Tunguska.'

'I won't. There is something I feel I should mention, though. It's just an observation, and it may be misleading.'

Auger didn't like the sound of that at all. 'Tell us anyway.'

'The wound appears to be healing itself. The aperture was more than a hundred kilometres across immediately after the detonation of the Molotov device.'

'And now?'

'A shade under a hundred. It may not mean anything – it's rather difficult to define the precise boundary – but I thought I should draw it to your attention.'

'Keep an eye on it,' she said. 'I don't want that damned thing closing on us while we're still inside.'

'I'll have a better idea of the closure rate in a little while,' Tunguska said.

'Squeeze as much speed out of this thing as you can. Then we can all go home.'

For the next hour, they pushed deeper into the ALS, following the lone echo of Niagara's shuttle. All attempts at communication were ignored, although that did not stop Tunguska from making repeated offers of negotiation. He was, he said, prepared to consider any proposal that would stop the deployment of Silver Rain. But no acknowledgement of his messages ever returned.

Despite the urgent need to intercept the shuttle before it reached Earth's atmosphere, Auger could not help marvelling at the experience of being inside the ALS sphere and seeing her world as it should have been. This was an Earth that had never known nuclear war, or runaway climatic catastrophe, or smart weather, or a Nanocaust. The sight of it made her want to weep. No image had ever come close to the heartbreaking beauty of this small blue world, a beauty all the more acute now that she knew how exquisitely fragile it was. It was the beauty of a butterfly's wing.

E2 hung at the exact geometric centre of the ALS. Orbiting it, or at least moving in a convincing simulacrum of Newtonian motion, was what appeared to be an identical copy of the Moon. Auger presumed it had been captured in the same quantum snapshot as E2, but it would take close-up investigation to verify this. The Moon could just as easily be a mocked-up representation, imbued with enough detail to fool surface observers and enough gravity to lift tides on the Earth. The remaining contribution to the tides – the solar component – must have been achieved through some deft trickery of gravitational manipulation – invisible small orbiting masses, perhaps – for there was no sun. Instead, there was a golden-yellow disc of exactly the right temperature and apparent brightness shining out from the inner surface of the sphere. But it was only designed to look convincing from the vantage point of the Earth's surface, and close to they saw how its shape was distorted by the sphere's concavity.

'There's your source of solar-spectrum radiation,' Auger said. 'From outside the sphere we were seeing its light, leaking through the hole. How long do you think it would have taken Floyd's people to figure that out?'

'Even without spaceflight, they'd have begun to notice some puzzling things about it within a few decades,' Tunguska said. 'In our timeline, a great deal of attention was focused on measuring the circularity of the solar disk, since it turned out to be a way of discriminating between competing cosmological models. With that kind of attention, the illusion probably couldn't have been sustained for long.'

'Or maybe they'd just pick another theory,' Auger said.

'Perhaps.'

'Anyway, Floyd's world hasn't achieved the science ours did even by nineteen fifty-nine.'

'They could quickly make up lost ground,' Tunguska said. 'And then they might put up too much of a fight if someone attempted to do what Niagara is attempting now.'

'Which means that whoever was working behind the scenes had serious co-ordination,' Auger said. 'Enough to change the outcome of the Second World War before it became truly global. And whoever did that is still down there.'

'You think they deserve retribution, don't you?' Tunguska asked.

'Of course. Don't you?'

'They stopped a war in which millions died in our timeline, Auger. No Final Solution, no Russian Front, no Hiroshima, Nagasaki.'

'They didn't stop that war out of the goodness of their hearts, Tunguska. They stopped it because it interfered with their plans for global genocide. And now I think they should pay for it.'

'Well, we're almost within attack range, if that's any consolation. That little shuttle is having to decelerate in preparation for atmospheric flight. If it released Silver Rain at this speed, even the ablative jackets wouldn't protect the nanomachinery at the heart of the weapon. There's some uncertainty, but I can begin attempting the strike within three minutes.'

'What about the missiles you promised us?' she asked.

'Nearly ready. Patience, please.' She heard a note of diffidence in his voice. 'Concerning the other matter . . .'

'What other matter?'

'The healing of the wound. I've been keeping a close eye on it and I can now state with some authority that—'

'Is there still time for us to get out?'

'Yes, allowing for—'

'I don't need anything *else* to worry about, Tunguska.'

'Good. In which case I won't mention the bleed-drive.'

Tunguska was as good as his word. Barely two minutes later, Auger felt the slight change in the ship's attack posture that indicated it was bringing its beam weapons to bear. When they powered up and fired, discharging in timed salvos, she felt the surging and ebbing of massive accumulators somewhere in the ship's gut.

'How long can we sustain this fire rate?' she asked.

'For as long as it takes. Energy isn't a problem.'

The shuttle had anticipated a beam-weapon strike – Tunguska said this was almost inevitable – but it was limited in its defensive options. It could drop reflective chaff by shedding discrete layers of its hull, but not indefinitely. It could change its course randomly, making it more difficult for the beams to lock on to the bright aura of its drive flame – which was pointed away from them now, but still visible against the background of E2 and the inner surface of the ALS sphere – but every course correction cost it some of its hard-won lead. For the pilot of the shuttle, it was the trickiest of trade-offs to balance.

'Whatever Niagara does,' Tunguska said, 'it will hurt him in the long run. All my simulations now point to a successful interception before he's within drop-range of the atmosphere.'

There was something about the cocksure confidence of that statement that gave Auger goose pimples. It was like an invitation to fate.

That was when the bleed-drive chose to fail again.

She felt the ship stall in its chase, suddenly losing ground on its victim. The drive stuttered, pushing hard and then cutting out. The cushioning embrace of the ship did its best to smooth over the sudden changes in acceleration, but Auger still felt several lapses in consciousness as the blood in her brain sloshed around like mud in a bucket.

'Tunguska . . .' she gasped, when she was able, 'maybe you want to rethink . . .'

The ship was in free fall. The drive had died completely, shut down by emergency control systems before instabilities opened a drooling mouth in the flesh of space itself.

Over the next several minutes, repair estimates began to trickle in. The drive was still fixable, but the patches put in place since the missile attack had now outlived their usefulness. It would take many hours before even a moderate push of one gee could be achieved.

Sensing that its charges no longer needed to be buffered against the jolts and swerves of combat, the ship relinquished its hold on Floyd, Auger and Tunguska, the white cocoons collapsing back into the familiar forms of table, chairs, floor, walls and ceiling.

'I hope,' Auger said, 'that you have a backup plan, Tunguska. Because otherwise we're screwed.'

Tunguska, to his credit, still managed to retain a credible gloss of authority. 'I've already reviewed the options,' he said. 'You'll be pleased to hear that there is still a way of intercepting that spacecraft.'

'The missiles?' Floyd asked.

'No.' He gave a self-critical grimace. 'Well, *yes*. But it's not quite that simple.'

Auger looked at Floyd and rolled her eyes. 'It never is. What's your plan?'

'The missiles don't have the range from here. My internal repair factories have license to manufacture almost anything except complete bleed-drive assemblies. I had to settle for small, crude fusion power plants. They're fast and agile enough for the task and they'll double as warheads, but only if they're given a helping hand.'

The tone of his voice said *beware*. Whatever he was offering them, it was not without its costs.

'Such as?' Auger asked.

'They'll need a delivery system. We can't get close enough at the moment, and by the time the ship's fixed it'll be too late. But we still have the shuttle from the *Twentieth*. I had it fuelled and repaired as a matter of insurance. It's a trivial matter to attach two missiles to it – they can grip the hull themselves, like parasites.'

'Can the shuttle make it in time?' Floyd asked.

'Just, although the margin for error is on the tight side. Someone will have to fly it.'

'Don't you have a snake robot that can do it?' Auger asked.

'Not one that I can spare from the repair work.'

Auger made to stand. 'Then what are we waiting for?'

Tunguska motioned for her to stay where she was. 'When I said someone has to fly it, I meant myself.'

'There's no reason why I can't fly it instead,' Auger said. 'Whatever knowledge you have, Cassandra can give to me.'

'That's not a good idea,' Tunguska said.

'Why not? The machines will show me what I have to do.'

'That's not the point. I have no doubt that they could give you the necessary competence, but it's much better if I take the shuttle, with Floyd as a passenger.'

'I don't follow,' Auger said.

He sighed, as if he'd been hoping that he would not have to explain. 'The problem is that whoever rides that shuttle may never make it home.' He made a steeple of his fingers, slowing his voice so that every word had the measured emphasis of some terrible pronouncement. 'Intercepting Niagara is still feasible, even now. But by the time the shuttle releases its missiles, it will barely have time to return to this point, let alone leave the ALS completely. The wound is closing. It will be a very, very close-run thing, even if the wound does not quicken its rate of closure. Which I cannot guarantee.' He took a deep breath and looked at Auger. 'Which is why you cannot be on that shuttle. You will remain here, ready to depart the ALS as soon as the bleed-drive can be restarted.'

'And you?'

'I will ensure that the missiles find their mark. When that is done, I will return Floyd to the surface of E2.'

'And then?' she said.

'I will evaluate the situation. If circumstances permit, I will attempt to return to this ship. If they don't . . . well, I can't leave the shuttle lying around in the ALS, where Floyd's people might find it. I'll arrange for its disposal. It shouldn't be difficult.'

Auger wanted to make sure that she understood exactly what he meant. 'Kill yourself, in other words.'

'If you must put it so bluntly.'

She shook her head. 'That's not how it's going to happen. You already said I could fly the ship as well as you.'

'What I said—' Tunguska began.

'I'm taking Floyd home,' she said. 'I dragged him into this, so I can damned well drag him out of it.'

Floyd reached out and took her arm. 'No. Listen to Tunguska. He's talking a lot of sense.'

'You'd condemn him, to save me?'

'No one's talking about condemning anyone. He doesn't have to commit suicide. He can always keep looking for another way out.'

'Then I can do the same,' Auger said. She snapped around to the Slasher. 'Get us on that ship.'

'"Us"?'

'Floyd and me.'

'And Cassie?' he asked slowly.

'We've discussed the matter,' Auger said. 'Cassandra wants to come along for the ride.'

Tunguska's face formed an expression of defeat, and he shook his head. 'You shouldn't make me do this.'

'But I am.'

'I still need another twenty minutes to finish the missiles and interface them with the shuttle's avionics. I've figured that time into my calculations, so use it wisely. There's still a chance to change your mind.'

'I don't need more time – my mind's made up,' Auger said.

Tunguska gave a weary smile, accepting that there was nothing to be gained from further debate. 'I always knew you'd want it this way,' he said. 'I just had to be certain.'

'May I ask one small favour, before we say goodbye?' Floyd asked.

'If I can help, I will.'

'I need something from you. Two things, really.'

Tunguska spread his hands wide in a gesture of reasonableness. 'What can I do?'

'You can make almost anything on this ship, can't you?'

'Within limits.'

'I'm not asking for the world. I just need you to conjure up some strawberries for me.'

One corner of Tunguska's mouth pulled up in a half-smile, as if he'd either misheard or was the victim of a joke he didn't get. 'Strawberries?'

'Can you do that?'

'Yes.' Tunguska mulled the point. 'Or at least something that looks and tastes like strawberries, even if it wouldn't be exactly the real article.'

'I'm not fussy. Can you do that in twenty minutes?'

'I can do that in five, if you want to eat them immediately.'

'They're not for me,' Floyd said. 'I don't even *like* strawberries. They're for a friend. So I'll need them in a bag.'

'In a bag.'

'That's right.'

Tunguska nodded, his expression grave. 'And the other thing?'

'I need some of that magic medicine of yours.'

'UR?'

'Someone I know is dying. It's the same lady who wants the strawberries.'

FORTY-ONE

Tunguska led them through winding white corridors where weightless conditions applied, until they reached a clean, vacuum-filled kernel somewhere near the stern of his ship. It was here that he had entombed the shuttle from the *Twentieth Century Limited* since he had rescued them from falling back on to the frozen Earth. The shuttle looked newer than when Auger had last seen it from the outside, its surfaces buffed and bright, dents and bumps repaired, scratches healed, scorch marks gone. Had it not been for the flying-horse logo of its owning company, she doubted that she would have recognised it as the same vessel.

'I'm amazed that you didn't throw it out as a piece of junk,' Auger said.

'I'd have been more likely to recycle it for raw matter,' Tunguska said. 'But, like I said, it's insurance.'

'Never hurts,' Floyd said.

The two missiles were in place now: sleek, smooth, sharklike forms hugging the hull and attached to it with extruded pads.

'They'll do the job? You're sure of that?' Auger asked.

'I'm a little wary of dogmatic assertions after the last little débâcle. But yes, I have a measure of confidence in them.'

'And the shuttle?'

'She'll hold.'

'Then let's go.'

Tunguska escorted them aboard. The ship was already humming, powered up for immediate flight. It smelled clean, like something that had just been unwrapped.

'Fuel tanks are full,' he said, indicating the control console. 'Had to siphon some hydrogen from our cooling system, but I don't think we'll miss it.'

'Thanks, Tunguska,' Auger said.

'If there was anything else I could do for you . . .'

'You've done more than enough. You and Cassandra both . . . all of you. I'm very grateful.'

'That goes double for me,' Floyd said.

'We all share a collective responsibility for Niagara's crime,' Tunguska said.

'Then let's hope he doesn't get a chance to commit it.'

'Can you forgive us, Auger?'

She thought about it for a moment. 'I think we all need a little forgiveness, don't we?'

'Some more than others.'

She took Tunguska's big hand in her own. 'I know what I'm doing here. So does Floyd. Don't wait around for us. The minute you get that bleed-drive back up and running, haul yourselves out of here.'

'I'll be waiting for you on the other side,' Tunguska said. He squeezed her hand. 'In the meantime, good luck. Give my regards to Niagara. I wish I could deliver my sentiments in person.'

'I'll make it count for both of us,' Auger said.

Departure was routine. When they were an hour into the flight, Auger turned to Floyd and said, 'There's something we need to talk about.'

'Can it wait until we've dealt with Niagara?'

'There might not be enough time then.' The script – the words she had prepared in her mind – dried up somewhere in her throat. All she could manage was, 'What are you going to do now?'

He looked at her as if it was silliest question anyone had ever asked. 'Now?'

'With the rest of your life, I mean. Now that you know . . . everything. Now that you won't be able to take a breath without remembering that nothing around you is really what it seems.'

'I guess I'll do what everyone else does: get on with my life and forget the big questions.'

'That's not much of an answer.'

'It's the truth. I still need shoes on my feet. I still need to feed myself and take care of the electricity bill. I still need to put a roof over my head, no matter what's above the sky. Anyway, that isn't to say I haven't got a few plans.'

'Plans you want to tell me about?'

'My first duty is to Custine,' Floyd said. 'I still have to get the police off his case. That means dealing with Maillol, and maybe finding some leverage over Inspector Belliard. There's at least one dead war baby in the tunnel at Cardinal Lemoine. Maillol may need a live one before he can do anything for me. But I won't know until I telephone him.'

'That won't take for ever.'

'That isn't everything I've got planned. After that, I'm going after the other fish – whoever they are.'

'Other fish like Caliskan's brother?'

'If he's there, I'll find him. And if I find him, I'll make him talk.'

'These are dangerous people,' Auger said.

'I know.'

'They're organised and willing to kill to protect their secrets. They have no qualms about attempting to murder three billion people. They're not going to lose any sleep over one little detective.'

'Then maybe they won't see me coming. And I won't be alone. I'll have Custine on my side. Maybe Maillol, if I can talk some sense into him. Between us, we might make a difference.'

'You've already made a difference,' she said. 'If you hadn't taken Blanchard seriously, everything that Susan did would have been lost. We'd never have known about Niagara's plan.'

'It was a case,' Floyd said, with an easy shrug. 'It needed closing.'

Floyd felt the shuttle shudder as the first missile unglued itself and sped away, riding a spike of flame like a splinter chipped from the sun. It was six hours since they had departed Tunguska's ship, but it had felt more like twenty. There had been nothing to do but wait as the shuttle positioned itself for the strike; nothing to do but worry that Niagara was going to pull some last-minute trick that would throw all of Tunguska's careful stratagems into disarray. But the chase had unfolded with meticulous obeisance to the attack simulations, right down to the last moment before missile release. Niagara had nothing else to offer; no alternative but continue his race towards E2's atmosphere and hope that he arrived there first. He must have known that it had become a suicide mission for him; that even if he succeeded in dropping the Silver Rain spore on to E2, he would never survive to see their murderous effect.

The two ships were now close enough to accommodate the limited range of the makeshift missiles. Niagara's shuttle was on a forced parabolic that had already carried it to within a thousand kilometres of E2's surface, while the *Twentieth's* shuttle lagged behind by less than half that distance.

They watched the thrust trail of the missile stab down towards the cloud-flecked hemisphere of the Pacific Ocean. None of the instruments aboard the shuttle were capable of displaying the disposition of the missile, but

Cassandra's machines ferried a constant commentary directly into Auger's head; a ceaseless babble of telemetry that occasionally made her wince in protest as the numbers overwhelmed her ability to process them.

Floyd looked at her, waiting for an update.

'Closing,' she said. 'Still looking good.'

Below, against the backdrop of the ocean, Floyd could just make out the glint of the ship they were chasing. It was still five hundred kilometres away, but – apart from the missile – it was the only thing moving against the face of E2, spitting a brilliant, quivering flame as it continued to make evasive course changes, still trying to dodge anything they might throw at it.

'Four hundred kilometres,' Auger said. 'Missile still looking good. Tunguska might have built it in a hurry, but he did a pretty good job.'

'I'm glad he's on our side.'

'Me, too. Floyd: this might not be the ideal time—'

'When is it ever?'

'Whatever happens from hereon in, I'm not sorry we met. I'm not sorry we had this adventure.'

'Really?'

'Never in a million years.' Then she frowned as the machines delivered another bulletin straight into her skull. 'Two hundred klicks and closing. Niagara knows there's a missile on his tail now.'

Floyd saw the little spark of Niagara's drive flame become even more agitated, lashing from side to side like a feather in the wind. He wondered what that kind of swerving meant for anyone still alive in that ship. Perhaps Niagara and his associates were all dead by now, mashed by the forces of the escape, sacrificing themselves so that their cargo might still find its way to E2.

Or maybe he was still alive, and in pain.

Floyd knew which option he preferred.

'Something's changing,' Auger said. 'The albedo of Niagara's ship . . .'

Floyd saw it too: that moving glint becoming a moving smudge of silver light, just for an instant.

It looked as if Niagara's ship had blown up. He dared to believe that might be the case, that the missile had somehow leapt across space faster than it was meant to. But the spike of the drive exhaust continued to burn, sharp and clean as a stiletto.

'What just happened? Did we—'

'No, we didn't. He just sloughed a large part of his hull, discarding it like an old skin. That can only mean one thing, Floyd: he's ready to drop the spore.'

The ship shuddered. The second and last missile was away.

'First missile closing . . . sixty klicks . . . forty . . . twenty . . .'

Floyd stared down, willing an outcome with all the strength he had. But the silver smudge kept moving.

'Zero,' Auger said. 'Zero. *Fuck*.'

The first missile cleaved into the atmosphere, pushing down into the skies above some spray of mid-Pacific islands Floyd didn't recognise. 'Can't turn it around in time,' Auger said.

'Try it.'

But the missile had already selected its own fate. A pinprick of light blossomed, rapidly becoming bright enough to hurt, and just as quickly faded.

'Warhead self-detonated. This isn't good.'

'Second fish?'

'Homing. Closing on three hundred klicks.'

The moving smudge of Niagara's ship suddenly reversed its direction of thrust. Even without magnification, Floyd saw the craft visibly alter its crawl across the backdrop of the ocean. The great sea was as bright and clear and smooth as a marble, clouds and islands dappled across its unblemished face with painterly precision, in broken lines and elegant curves. It was his world, as no one had ever seen it before, and it was enough to make him gasp.

He was sorry. It was a wonderful, glorious sight, but there just wasn't time to enjoy the view.

Maybe next time.

'Bastard's slowing,' Auger said.

'He's ready.'

'Two hundred and fifty klicks. Missile slowing.'

'Slowing?'

'The missile's learning from its mate, trying not to make the same mistake.'

'I really hope it knows what it's doing.'

'Two hundred klicks . . . still slowing. Maybe it's malfunctioned. Oh *shit* I hope it hasn't malfunctioned.'

'If it has, we need to think about ramming with this thing.'

Auger looked back at him. He couldn't tell whether her expression was impressed or horrified. 'Don't worry about that,' she said. 'I've already got the intercept programmed in.'

'Nice of you to tell me.'

'I'd have got round to it.' She blinked, started to say something. Floyd could almost feel the torrent of numbers sluicing through her head.

'The fish, Auger?'

'Slowing to one hundred kilometres . . . No, wait.' She hesitated. '*Wait.* It's sprinting again.'

'Keep talking.'

'It's too late. It's not going to . . .'

The second warhead detonated. The same pinprick of light, swelling in size and brightness . . . but this time it kept on swelling. Floyd jammed his eyes shut and still that did no good, the light pushing through his skin, through his bones, cleansing every thought in his head save the acknowledgement of its own intolerable luminosity, like a proclamation from God.

And then a slow, stately fade, and then nothing.

Just empty skies.

'There were no dampeners on that detonation,' Auger said, her voice distant and disconnected, like someone speaking in a dream. 'It made no effort to limit its blast. It must have been confident it could make the kill.'

'There's nothing out there.'

'I know.'

'That means we did it,' Floyd said. 'It means we saved the Earth.'

'One of them,' she corrected.

'One's enough for today. Let's not get greedy.'

FORTY-TWO

It was daylight over the Pacific, and therefore night over Paris. Clouds wrapped the city, fog choking its streets with cold, constricting coils. The shuttle dropped through the weather like a stone through smoke, conserving fuel, retarding its descent with the minimum expenditure of thrust. Closer to the ground, it reconfigured its flight surfaces and became passably aerodynamic. Hypersonic, then supersonic, then subsonic, until the shuttle lowered itself through the main swell of clouds into a gloomy window of clear air. Districts of the city, picked out in the lights of buildings, streetlamps and moving cars, poked through the low quilt of fog. Here the swell of Montmartre and the Sacré-Coeur; there the dark ribbon of the Seine; there the glowing carnival of the Champs-Elysées, like a river of light.

'Look,' Auger said, with a childlike glee. 'There's the Eiffel Tower. It's still here, still intact. It's still standing.'

'Everything's still here,' Floyd said.

'Isn't it wonderful?'

'It grows on you.'

'We never deserved this second chance,' she said.

'But sometimes you get what you don't deserve.'

The console chimed. Auger strained forward and answered the call.

'Tunguska here,' they heard. 'I must offer my congratulations. We saw the kill strike even at a distance of three light-seconds.'

Auger let him finish speaking before asking, 'The spore? Could Silver Rain have survived the blast?'

His reply crawled back six seconds later. 'Unlikely.'

'I hope you're right.'

'I hope I am, too.' He sounded more amused than alarmed, as if he had exhausted any final reserves of worry. 'I suppose at this point, all one can realistically do is hope for the best. Are you both intact?'

Auger flashed Floyd a glance. 'As intact as we'll ever be.'

'Good. You did well. I'm afraid, though, that there isn't much time to dwell on your success. The wound is closing fast. Our bleed-drive is a little unsteady, but we can begin to limp our way to the exit.'

'Go, then,' Auger said.

'The thing is,' Tunguska said, 'I was rather hoping you'd come with us. There's also the small matter of you now being Cassandra's custodian, and I would like nothing better than for her to return to Polity space.'

Floyd leaned over, straining against his harness. 'She's keeping that appointment, Tunguska.'

'Floyd . . .' Auger said.

'Start your limp home,' Floyd told Tunguska, 'but be prepared to pick up this shuttle at the last minute. As soon as Auger's dropped me off, she'll be on her way back to you immediately.'

'Telemetry suggests you have sufficient fuel,' Tunguska said guardedly. '*If* you begin your return journey practically as soon as you land. If you delay, there are no guarantees. I hope I make myself clear.'

'In Technicolor,' Floyd said.

It was a strip of vacant ground between two abandoned churches, somewhere south of the Longchamp Hippodrome. If anyone had seen the shuttle lower down through the fog, screaming out of the night on vertical thrust, they had elected not to stay around for the end of the performance. Perhaps a few vagrants, drunkards or gypsies had seen it arrive . . . before scratching their heads and deciding that this was really not the kind of thing they needed to be involved in, especially given the city authority's usual attitude to people poking their noses where they weren't welcome. Whatever it was, they would have concluded, it was very unlikely to be there in the morning.

Now the ship sat on its lowered undercarriage, gleaming in reflected lamplight like a chromed egg, the fog swirling around its hot exhaust ports in curious little eddies, while the ship ticked and cooled like an old oven. The flying-horse logo of Pegasus Intersolar seemed to strain towards the sky, anxious not to spend a minute longer on the ground than necessary.

Floyd and Auger stood under the ship, at the base of its lowered access ramp.

'Did you remember the strawberries?' Auger asked.

Floyd held up the little bag. 'As if I'd forget.'

'You never did tell me who they were for. Or the UR you persuaded

Tunguska to give you.'

Floyd fingered the little glass vial in his pocket. It contained a harmless-looking silvery-grey fluid, tasteless and odourless. But slipped into the right person's diet, it would infect their body with a billion tireless machines, which would identify and cure almost any illness known to Slasher science. It was bottled immortality.

Well, not quite. Tunguska had quailed at the thought of giving him the kind of full-strength UR that would keep someone alive for ever. At the time he had handed over the gift, they were, after all, still trying to prevent someone else from introducing a plague of tiny machines into E2. The UR would heal someone of any illnesses they had at the moment of ingestion, and the tiny machines would endure long enough to steer them to full health and through a period of grace thereafter. But then they would quietly disassemble, flushing themselves from the person's body as so much microscopic metallic dust. That person might go on to live for many more years, but by the same token they might fall ill of some other complaint a month later. If they did, the machines would not be around to save them a second time.

So it wasn't immortality. But from where he was standing, it was a lot better than nothing.

He took his hand out of his pocket, leaving the vial where it was. 'You have to go now, Auger.'

'What if I said I was staying?'

He smiled. She was putting on a brave face, but deep down he knew she had made her mind up. He just needed to make her feel better about it.

'You have a life back home.'

'This can be my home.'

'You know it can't. Not now; not ever. It's a nice dream, Auger. It was a nice vacation. But that's all it was.'

She pulled him closer and kissed him. Floyd kissed her back, not letting her pull away, embracing her there in the fog as if by force of will he could hold back time, as if time itself might make a compassionate exception in their case.

Then, gently, he pulled away from her. She was crying. He wiped her tears away with his sleeve. 'Don't cry.'

'I love you, Floyd.'

'I love you too, Auger. But that doesn't change anything.'

'I can't just leave you like this.'

'You have no choice.'

She looked back at the waiting ship. He knew what she was thinking – how every second now counted against her escaping from the ALS. 'You're a good man, Floyd. I will see you again. I promise you that. We'll find another way in, another way back to Paris.'

'Maybe there is no other way.'

'But I won't stop looking for one. Not just for you, but for the other agents stuck here – the people you and I have never even met. They're still out there, Floyd: still somewhere in the world, in America or Africa, unaware that there is no way home. Maybe some of them got enough of a warning to start their journeys back to Paris . . . but they won't have got here yet. Some of them won't arrive for weeks or months. When they do, they'll make their way to Cardinal Lemoine, or Susan's apartment . . . anywhere they think they might find an answer. They'll be confused and scared, Floyd. They'll need a friend, someone who can tell them what happened. They'll need someone who cares, someone who can give them hope. Someone who'll tell them we're coming back, no matter how difficult it is, no matter how long it takes.' She pulled him closer, but it was just a hug this time. It was past the time for kisses.

'You should go,' he said at last.

'I know.' She let go of him and took one step on to the ramp. 'I meant what I said, about not regretting a minute of this.'

'Not even the dirt, and the bruises, and the part where you got shot?'

'Not a damned minute.'

Floyd lifted a finger to his brow, in salute. 'Good. That's exactly how I feel. Now please – would you get the hell off my planet?'

She nodded, saying nothing more, and walked back up the ramp, keeping her face turned to him. Floyd took a step back, his eyes welling with tears now, not wanting her to see them. Not because of some stupid male pride in not crying, but because he didn't want to make this any harder on the two of them than it already was.

'Floyd?'

'Yes?'

'I want you to remember me. Whenever you walk these streets . . . know that I'll also be walking them. It may not be the same Paris, but—'

'It's still Paris.'

'And we'll always have it,' Auger said.

She stepped into the ship. He saw her face disappear, then her body, then her legs.

Then the ramp lifted up.

Floyd stepped back. The ship growled, spat fire and then slowly clawed its way back into the sky.

He stood there for many minutes, like a man who had lost his way in the fog. It was only when he heard a distant rumble of thunder that he turned around and began to make his way back to the city he knew; the city he felt some tenuous claim on.

Somewhere far above him, Auger was on her way home.

Tunguska had cleared a large area of wall and assigned it to display a visual feed – suitably doctored to bring out detail and colour – of the closing wound in the ALS. They were through it now and back into empty space, but the last hour of the escape had still been as anxious as any Auger could remember. The wound's rate of closure had surged and decelerated with savage unpredictability, mocking any attempts to predict its future progress.

'Things might actually have been worse than I feared,' Tunguska said, his voice as slow and unperturbed as ever. 'It might not just have been a question of our being trapped inside the sealed shell of the ALS. We don't know what will happen when that wound closes itself.'

'I don't follow,' Auger said. With Cassandra's guidance, she had fashioned a stool for herself, next to Tunguska's. 'We'd have been trapped inside. That would have been bad, but it's not the worst thing I could imagine happening. There'd have been people on the outside who knew we were there, trying to find a way to rescue us . . .'

They were free now and it was easy to talk of such things lightly, no matter how terrifying they had seemed at the time.

'There's more to it than that,' Tunguska said gently. 'The ALS is entering a new state we haven't seen before, or at least one we haven't witnessed directly.'

'Again,' she said, 'I don't—'

'For the last twenty-three years there's been a connection between the interior matter of the ALS and the flow of time in the outside universe. I'm talking about the hyperweb link, of course. We know that it was activated – or brought to full functionality after a period of dormancy – during the Phobos occupation. Until then, Floyd's world had been frozen at the instant of the quantum snapshot. Presumably, it was the establishment of the link that caused time to flow forwards at the normal rate. Twenty-three years in our world, twenty-three years in Floyd's.'

'Yes,' she said slowly. 'That much I get.'

'But now there is no hyperweb link. It hasn't just been put into a state of dormancy, as was the case after the Phobos re-occupation until the rediscovery of the portal two years ago. It's been completely destroyed. There is no longer any detectable portal machinery in Mars orbit.'

'But we've been inside the ALS since then,' Auger said. 'We saw E2. We saw that it wasn't frozen in time.'

Tunguska looked at her with infinite kindness and compassion in his heavily lidded eyes. 'But that was before the closing of the wound,' he said gently. 'Now we have no idea what will happen to E2. Events may continue to roll forward at the normal rate . . . or the matter inside the ALS may undergo a phase transition back to its frozen state, as it was for more than three hundred years.'

'No,' she said. 'That can't happen, because . . .' But even as she was speaking, she found herself unable to frame any plausible objection. Tunguska might be right, or Tunguska might be wrong. They simply didn't know enough about the ALS or its functioning to work it out.

'I'm sorry,' he said. 'I felt I needed to mention the possibility, no matter how remote.'

'But if that's the case,' she said, 'then I've condemned—'

He placed his huge hand on hers. 'You've condemned no one to anything. Even if the world freezes again, nothing inside it will have been lost. Three billion lives will just stall between one heartbeat and the next, as they did at the moment of the snapshot. They'll feel nothing. It will be kinder than sleep. And perhaps one day something will happen that will enable that next heartbeat. The world will wake again. We can only hope that when that happens, wiser minds than ours will intervene from outside to assist the world towards its destiny.' He patted her hand. 'But perhaps it won't happen like that anyway. Perhaps the world won't freeze. Perhaps, once awakened, it will always flow forward.'

'We'll know one day, won't we? Floyd's people won't take long to open their eyes. They must have seen what the wound did to their sky. If they puzzle over that long enough, sooner or later someone's going to make the right connections.'

'And then it'll be them knocking to be let out, rather than us knocking to be let in.'

'Or they won't knock at all,' Auger said. 'Do baby birds knock to get the mother bird to let them out of the egg?'

'I confess I've never seen one,' Tunguska said.

'An egg? Or a bird?'

'Either. But I take your point. The one thing we'd be very unwise to do is underestimate the capacity of Floyd's people. Something very like his culture did, after all, give rise to our own.'

'The poor fools,' Auger said.

A little while later, they reached the outgoing portal. A chirrup from the automated monitoring station informed them that a real-time communication relay had been established with Polity space.

'It's Maurya Skellsgard,' Tunguska said. 'Shall I put her on?'

'Please,' Auger said.

The transmission quality was poor: routing the signal through multiple portal connections was difficult at the best of times, and almost impossible given the chaos back around the Sun. Skellsgard's image kept flickering or going sound-only.

'I'll keep this brief,' she said. 'We're only holding things together with spit and prayers at this end. These Slasher technicians are good, but they can't work miracles. If the link fails, we'll just have to catch up with each other when you make it back home. In the meantime, everyone's very proud of you. I heard about Floyd, too. I'm sorry it had to end that way for you both.'

'I'm all right,' Auger said.

'You don't sound it.'

'OK, I'm a wreck. I was never fond of goodbyes, under any circumstances. Why the hell did I have to *like* him, Maurya? Why couldn't he have been a prick I couldn't wait to get rid of?'

'That's the way the universe works, honeybunch. Better get used to it, because it's going to be around for a good few Hubble times.'

Auger forced out a laugh. 'Just what I need – a sympathetic shoulder.'

Skellsgard's voice became serious. 'Look, the main thing is that the two of you are safe. Given the range of outcomes that were available to us a couple of days ago, I'd say that has to count as a result.'

'I suppose you're right.' Her thoughts kept returning to Tunguska's speculation about the quantum state of the ALS, but she didn't want to think about that now. 'Anyway, it's good to know you're OK as well. I'm glad you made it. How are things back home?'

'Dicey.'

'I'll need calibration on that. Is that better or worse than a day ago?'

'I guess you'd have to say it was better, by about the width of one of Planck's toenail clippings. The good guys on both sides have brokered some kind of . . . well, I hesitate to call it a ceasefire just yet. Call it a reduction in the scale of hostilities. That has to be something, right? And of course some of us have already managed to put aside our differences, or you and I wouldn't be having this long-distance chat.'

'What about the Earth?'

'Tanglewood reined in the nuclear strikes. The place is going to glow nicely in the dark for a few centuries, but there should still be some ruins worth poking around in.'

'I guess we have to take what we're given and be glad it's not worse. When all this is over, I'm still going to have to carry my begging bowl to the funding committees.'

'Actually, Auger, that's the reason I called.' Skellsgard's permanent scowl softened fractionally. 'I have some news for you. Not quite sure what to make of it yet, but I do have my suspicions. This is, needless to say, about as preliminary as it gets.'

'Tell me,' Auger said.

'You know what they say about an "ill wind"?' She waited a moment for Auger's reaction, but her face remained blank. 'Well, never mind. The point is, we're all upset because we lost the Phobos portal. I've looked at the numbers, too – beefed up with some hot new Slasher know-how – and it really does look as if we've blown that particular connection.'

'We shouldn't give up,' Auger said firmly. 'We should always keep trying to reinstate it. E2 is too valuable to give up on.'

'No one's going to give up on it, not while there are still so many loopholes in the theory. But for the time being it may not be our highest priority.'

The image fuzzed and gradually reassembled, block by block.

'What have you got?' Auger asked.

'When the Phobos portal blew,' Skellsgard said, 'something weird happened. We didn't notice it at the time – our monitoring equipment just wasn't sensitive enough. But the Slashers? Different story. They had the whole system laced with sensors tuned to pick up portal signatures. For years they hadn't detected a squeak; nothing to hint that there were any portals other than the one on Sedna and the one in Phobos.'

'And now?'

'When the Phobos link died, it must have given off some kind of death-scream vibration that drew a sympathetic resonance from other dormant links in the vicinity. The sensors picked up faint signals from fifteen different locations around the system.'

Auger wondered whether she'd heard Skellsgard correctly. *'Fifteen?'*

'That may not be the end of it. The weakest signals were at the limit of detection: could be there are other sources they missed entirely. The whole damn system could be riddled with portals we never even suspected were there. We'd never have found them by accident: they're all buried underground, on anonymous little iceballs no one ever paid much attention to before.'

'Jesus,' Auger said.

'Jesus squared. I hope you're impressed.'

'I am.'

Skellsgard smiled. 'I figured you needed cheering up. Like I said, it's preliminary. But as soon as things simmer down around here, we're going to put together a joint expedition and dig down until we find one of these things. Then we're going to switch it on and see where it takes us.'

'That's a big question.'

'I know. Out into the galaxy? But what would be the point of that? We already have the Sedna portal for that. Me, I think they'll take us somewhere else entirely.'

At first, Auger fought to keep the excitement from her voice. Then she decided she didn't care. What was the point? Skellsgard knew exactly how she'd be feeling.

'Inside another ALS?'

'That's my best guess. We know there are a lot of them out there. We know one of them contained a snapshot of Earth from the twentieth century. Why not other spheres containing other snapshots? There could be dozens of Earths out there, all frozen at different instants in history. One portal might be our ticket into the Middle Ages. Another might put us into the middle of the Triassic.'

'I need to be on that team,' Auger said.

'I wouldn't have it any other way. Just remember to bring your best digging clothes: we're not likely to come out so close to a tunnel the next time.'

'I hope you're right about this.'

'I do, too,' Skellsgard said, just before the communications link finally gave up the ghost. 'But even if I'm not, I don't think either of us will have to worry about funding committees for a little while.'

Floyd slowed his stroll, coming to a stop under a streetlamp. He reached out and took hold of the poster gummed to the lamp's fluted shaft and pulled it away, carefully this time, so as not to tear the thing in two. He held the sheet up to the light, peering at the printed image through a shifting veil of fog.

It was a picture of Chatelier. Except – now that he thought about it – the picture looked a lot like someone else he'd met recently. Not an exact likeness, but enough to raise the hackles of recognition. Not close enough to be the same man. But certainly close enough for them to be brothers.

Maybe it was just his imagination.

Maybe it wasn't.

He folded the poster and shoved it into his pocket. There was a telephone number at the foot of it for anyone who wanted to support Chatelier's political campaign. Floyd thought that maybe tomorrow he might think about paying Chatelier's people a visit. Just to ask a few questions. Just to make a nuisance of himself.

He carried on into the city, counting down the street numbers, looking for some essential landmark. Somewhere in the distance he heard a maritime foghorn blare into the night. A telephone kiosk loomed out of the void like a lighthouse. He stepped inside and closed the door, tried the money-return hatch and pulled out a single coin. His lucky day. Floyd fed the telephone and dialled a number in Montparnasse that he knew by memory.

Sophie answered.

'This is Floyd,' he said. 'I hope it's not too late. Is Greta there?'

'Just a moment.'

'Wait,' he said, before she stepped away to find Greta. 'Is Marguerite still . . . ?'

'She's still alive, yes.'

'Thank you.'

'I'll fetch Greta. She's upstairs.'

He waited, drumming his fingers on the glass door of the telephone box. They hadn't parted on the best of terms. How was she going to take his coming back now, after all the time he'd been away?

Someone picked up the receiver.

'Floyd?'

'Greta?'

'It's me. Where are you?'

'Somewhere in Paris. Not exactly sure where. I'm trying to find my way back to rue du Dragon.'

'We were worried, Floyd. Where have you been? We've had people out looking for you all day.'

She sounded concerned and confused, rather than angry. 'I've been away,' he said, wondering what she meant by 'all day'. He'd been away longer than that, surely? 'With Auger.'

'Where is she now?'

'Gone.'

'Gone as in . . . ?'

'Gone as in gone. I don't think I'll be seeing her again.'

She seemed to go and then come back. When she returned, something had changed in her voice. Some crack of forgiveness had opened up. 'I'm sorry, Floyd.'

'It's all right.' But it wasn't all right. Not at all.

'Floyd, where are you? I can send a taxi—'

'It's OK. I need the walk. Can I come around tomorrow?'

'Yes, of course. I'll be here all morning.'

'I'll be there first thing. I'd like to see Marguerite. I have something for her.'

'She still thinks you're going to show up with strawberries,' Greta said sadly.

'I'll see you in the morning.'

'Floyd . . . before you hang up. I'm still serious about America. You've had time now, haven't you? Time to think. And now that you don't have any other distractions—'

'You're right,' he said. 'I've had time to think. And I think you're right. America will be good for you.'

'Does that mean you've come to a decision?'

'Kind of,' he said.

He put down the receiver and stepped out of the kiosk. Suddenly, the fog cleared a little, enough to give him a better view of the street on which he stood. Some glimmer of recognition teased his memory. He knew where he was, more or less. He had been heading in the right direction all along.

Floyd reached into his pocket. The bag of strawberries was still there, like some token from a dream that had no business existing in the real world. The little vial of UR was there as well.

He thought of Greta getting on that seaplane to America, turning a new corner in her life. Something brighter and more wide open than he could ever offer her in Paris. Something brighter and more wide open than he could offer her if he went to America with her, too. And then he thought of her staying here, out of love, nursing Marguerite out of her illness, while that other life slipped further and further from her grasp.

He took out the vial and dropped it on to the cobbles.

He crunched it underfoot and lost himself in the fog.

Acknowledgements and
Further Reading

A number of books proved invaluable during the writing of this novel. In searching for a plausible 'counterfactual' scenario for the events of May 1940, I am indebted to Julian Jackson's excellent *The Fall of France* (Oxford University Press, 2003) for suggesting that the Ardennes offensive could so easily have failed had the Allies appreciated the vulnerability of the advancing forces and taken action at the decisive time.

For general information on Paris, Alistair Horne's *Seven Ages of Paris* (Macmillan, 2002) proved very useful, as did Edmund White's *The Flâneur* (Bloomsbury, 2001). The versions of the city presented in this book, however, are only loosely congruent with the real one. The Maigret novels of George Simenon also provided an obvious imaginative stimulus. Respect, Jules.

The search for gravitational radiation from cosmic sources continues to this day, with expectations of success at any time. For an outstanding and highly readable account of this fascinating and contentious story, from the late Joseph Weber's pioneering work in the 1960s (mentioned by Maurya Skellsgard) to the latest ultra-sensitive schemes – such as the Leiden-based GRAIL programme, which is currently taking place only a few miles from where these words are being written – I recommend *Einstein's Unfinished Symphony* by Marcia Bartusiak (National Academies Press, 2000). One of Weber's students, incidentally, was the late Robert Forward, who went on to make a name for himself as a science fiction writer, and whose books contain much mind-stretching speculation about gravity and exotic physics.

The artificially engineered *amusica* virus is speculative, but the condition 'amusica' is, unfortunately, a real one – the musical analogue to the language-impairing condition of aphasia. Subjects with amusica typically

505

lose the ability both to make and appreciate music. I read about this condition in Harold L. Klawans' fascinating book *Toscanini's Fumble* (Headline, 1990). Like the case studies presented by Oliver Sacks, Klawans' medical stories often seem more science fictional than any real SF, and are as addictive as any collection of short stories.

Simon Singh's very readable *The Code Book* (Fourth Estate, 2000) provided much useful background on the history and workings of the Enigma machine.

For general information on the music of Floyd's era (which isn't quite the same as the music of *our* 1950s) I relied on *Jazz: The Ultimate Guide* by Ronald Atkins (Carlton, 1996), and the splendid five-CD supplement to Ken Burns' *Jazz: The Story of America's Music* (Sony, 2000). The Gitanes series of 'Jazz in Paris' CDs also proved very useful.

For useful discussions, and general help with stupid questions, I am indebted to Tony Ballantyne, Barbara Bella, Bernd Hendel, Peter Hollo and Christopher Priest. Any mistakes, needless to say, are entirely my responsibility, not theirs.